Marilyn French received her doctorate from Harvard University in 1972. Her two novels, *The Women's Room* (1977) and *The Bleeding Heart* (1980), are both international bestsellers and feminist classics. She has also written *Beyond Power: On Women, Men and Morals* (1985), *The Book as Word: James Joyce's Ulysses* (1976) and *Shakespeare's Division of Experience* (1981). Born in New York City, she now divides her time between New York and Florida.

Marilyn French

Her Mother's Daughter

Pan Books
in association with Heinemann

First published in Great Britain 1987 by William Heinemann Ltd
This edition published 1988 by Pan Books Ltd, Cavaye Place,
London SW10 9PG
in association with Heinemann
9 8 7 6 5 4 3 2

© Marilyn French 1987

ISBN 0 330 30436 4

Phototypeset by Input Typesetting Ltd, London

PART I PHOTO CREDITS:
1. Photograph by Jacob A. Riis. Jacob A. Riis Collection. Museum of the City of New York.
2. From *Bricks & Brownstone* by Charles Lockwood. Used with permission.
3. Culver Pictures.
4. 5. Author's collection.
6. Photograph by Jacob A. Riis. Jacob A. Riis Collection. Museum of the City of New York.
7. International Museum of Photography at George Eastman House. Photograph by Lewis Hine.

PART II PHOTO CREDITS:
1. © Bob Adelman/Magnum Photos.
2. 3. 4. Author's collection.
5. © Wayne Miller/Magnum Photos.
6. Author's collection.

PART III PHOTO CREDITS:
1. © Bettye Lane.
2. James Whistler. *Arrangement in Black and Gray: The Artist's Mother*, 1871. The Louvre. Paris. Lauros-Giraudon/Art Resource.
3. © Irene Bayer/Monkmeyer Press.
4. © Bettye Lane.
5. Author's collection.

For my mother
Isabelle
1904–1986

ALL DRESSED UP AND NO PLACE TO GO

Part 1

The Children in the Mills

Chapter I

one

My mother lived to be old, although she always said she would die young. All through my childhood she warned me – threatened me? – that because of her defective heart, she would depart early from this vale of tears, whereas my sturdy peasant-like father would live forever, drowning the memory of her fastidiously prepared meals in canned pork and beans, which he would enjoy just as much. When I was fifteen and searching through her bureau drawers one afternoon – hoping, probably, to discover some clue as to how she felt about me – I found a sealed envelope marked 'To Be Opened After My Death'. In a rage I tore it open, pulled out a piece of stationery, and found that her Limoges china service for eight (with some missing), her five crystal water goblets (one had broken), and her silver service for eight were to be evenly divided between my sister and me. Still furious, I burned the thing, and as it went up, I panicked and threw it into the toilet. The paper kept burning, so I slammed down the lid, not realizing it was plastic and flammable. When the toilet seat began to burn, I called the fire department. The neighbors clucked their tongues for weeks afterward about young girls sneaking cigarettes when their mothers were away from home. My mother not only didn't get angry, but she invited me to sit in the backyard with her and smoke. She never wrote another will. I checked.

In any case, her flawed heart did not noticeably shorten her life. She lived long, only she shrank. Or maybe my body blew up over the years, so that when we appeared together in the full-length mirror in the bridal shop dressing room where we were trying on dresses for my daughter's wedding, we looked like creatures from two different species. I can remember when we looked alike, when strangers recognized us as mother and daughter. But now she is tiny and frail for all her middle bulk. Her bones, her very skull, are delicate, smaller than a child's, and the flesh has shriveled on her arms and knit itself so tight on her small face that her eyes have almost disappeared. Whereas I am tall and broad-shouldered and thick (I don't quite know when that happened) and my face shines like a swollen moon. It wasn't even that we looked like two versions of the same product, one designed for light home use and the other for heavy industry; we looked like two different kinds of creature, like a fat smooth rhino and a wrinkled impala. If you knew that we were mother and daughter, you would suspect some mysterious voodoo process whereby I grew by sucking in all her fluids. Like midges. Midge mothers do not lay eggs, they reproduce young from inside their bodies without benefit of clergy, state, or even any informal male assistance. And the baby develops inside the mother's body, not in a uterus, but in her tissues, and eventually, she fills her whole body, as she devours it from the inside. When she is ready to be born, she breaks out of her mother/prison, leaving behind only a chitinous shell. They never have mother-daughter squabbles: midge mothers may sacrifice themselves entirely for their young, but the young never have to hear about it. It is also true, of course, that young so produced begin within two days to reproduce themselves in the same way. They hardly have time to complain about the quality of their lives.

Women of the past had no time for that either, and my mother has little sympathy for those who complain about the quality of life, feeling, I suspect, somewhat like a midge mother. Still, as she stood there in the dressing room mirror, miserable at the poor fit of the dresses she was trying on, wanting to look splendid for Arden's wedding, she swung her head away from the mirror angrily. I looked down on that tiny head and I wanted to caress it, to console her as one does a child, by touching, affection. But my mother is not a woman to be consoled. Her head is stiff on her neck. She gazed in the mirror again, not seeing that her lined face was unblemished by age spots or that her fine soft hair was still blond, and made a foul face at the person in the mirror, and asked me if that was really how she looked.

When my mother was in the her heyday – her second heyday, but the only one I saw – that is, when my sister and I were grown and married and she had a little money and leisure, she had her hair cut in a soft short bob called a feather cut, and went to an expensive shop and bought beautiful clothes. I still remember them: she had a red wool suit with a short jacket collared in leopard, and a black wool suit with a high round neck trimmed with mink, a navy blue wool dress with a skirt cut on the bias so it whirled when she walked, and a short white wool knit jacket, double-breasted with gold buttons. She drove an old Cadillac, and announced her address proudly to sales-women in the good shops. Into these shops she carried a stiff smile, eyebrows that seemed permanently raised, and her fine clothes. These shops were the only place she could obtain the sense of having a public life. Sometimes she and my father went out to dinner, but in those years she was so loudly disapproving of restaurant food that my embarrassed father resisted going. They played bridge once a week with my aunt and uncle, but a formal suit was a bit too warm for such an occasion. She seemed relatively content in those years.

But when she aged, her body changed. She grew shorter, the skin on her arms and legs shriveled, and she expanded in the middle. Her middle got to be four sizes bigger than the rest of her. It was impossible to find fine clothes to fit this alien body, and she began to buy polyester pantsuits with expandable waistbands, or wraparound skirts. One day, during a winter when she and my father were visiting Palm Beach, they walked into a shop on Worth Avenue, and the owner blocked their passage, asking rudely what they wanted. 'A golf jacket,' my mother blurted angrily. He nodded his head brusquely to the left. 'Try down the block. We don't have them.' She never got over this incident. 'He wouldn't even let us in, Anastasia! How did he know we wouldn't buy anything? What was it, do you think? Was it because we're old? Because my clothes look cheap?' She told this story repeatedly, always ending it with the same questions: she must have forgotten she had asked them before. I was never able to find answers that satisfied her.

It tormented her so that she was still talking about it a decade later, and I got the sense that the incident had plugged into a recurrent nightmare. As if you suddenly found yourself in real life peeing in a toilet exposed to a room full of people, or saw your hair falling out in clumps, or whatever your recurrent nightmare is. The storekeeper had treated her with contempt. It occurred to me that she had arranged her life so that she would never be exposed to contempt. Certainly none of her family would think of treating her contemptuously. Her husband treats her like his sovereign; sometimes he even refers to her as 'my lady'. And my sister and I and our children also defer to her as if she were royalty. We placate her, fuss over her, wait on her. When we speak, we direct our faces toward her and enunciate very distinctly, so she can read our lips as we speak. When we cook for her, we avoid oil, onions, garlic, most spices. She is helped, by someone, in and out of cars, up and down stairs, and even through doorways, because she is feeble, arthritic, and subject to the dizziness caused by inner-ear disease. My daughter's husband, meeting her for the first time, found her a grande dame. I was surprised to hear him say that. I had never seen my mother that way.

Not at all. We didn't defer because we feared her, because she held power that could strip us of our estates or rank, or heap them on us if we pleased her. We did it because . . . we always had. Because Daddy did. Because she seemed to need us to do it. It didn't seem much to give her, making her the centre, deferring. Because somehow we understood that she had suffered more than anyone, more than any of us, and that in some sense we were responsible for her suffering. When I was a child I could

As I said, my life is fine. Couldn't be better. Oh, well, could be, I suppose, if we lived in a different world. It would be nice, I suppose, to be able to love someone who loved me. I've gone beyond love, romantic love, all that stuff. Need and power struggle, that's all it is, and I have no needs. Truly. That is, I have no needs I cannot satisfy by myself. I don't know any successful woman with love in her life. Men can manage it, but not women. Disproportion in numbers, and besides, men are too threatened by independent women. They can always find one who will build up their ego. And I, we, independent women, can't find a man who doesn't need continual bolstering. Enough already. I've had enough.

God knows I've known enough men, had enough lovers, friends, and acquaintances that the sex is not unfamiliar to me. I even have a son, rotter that he is. You think I shouldn't say that, shouldn't speak so about my own child. Blame it on my mother, she brought me up to be honest. He's a conniver, what can I say? I didn't raise him to be a conniver, but on the other hand, I can't blame him for being one. Unlike me, he sees surfaces, sees them and understands the power lines so visible to those who look carefully. Why not? you say. Character sets itself gradually, like gel. His gel isn't completely set yet, it can still be melted into another shape, but at the moment he does not make me proud, even if he's fulfilling mothers' dreams and going to medical school. I feel like my own mother when nice smiling ladies hear what my son is doing and turn on me in a gush of praise: 'Oh how wonderful! You must be so proud!' I want to bite their lips right off their mouths so that when they smile in the future they'll look like the sharks I feel they are. And to tell the truth, my daughters aren't any better. Everything seemed okay until they grew up. Now, everything seems wrong.

So when I'm not bursting into tears at the sight of a motherless child, a childless mother, or a dead father, I'm snapping around the house like a wet towel. I can't seem to find a quiet heart, except when I travel, and nowadays I don't get commissions that often. I can't even get any sympathy. Last time I visited my mother, I came to feel very low as we sat around talking, and I told her about a fight I'd had with Arden. She'd been awful for a long time, hanging around the house smoking, glaring at me; playing the piano at its loudest, banging her way through every book of music in the house without bothering to correct the mistakes in any one piece; and refusing to help clean up, even to clean her own room. Not that the house ever really looks cleaned up even when it is, but with Arden around, it was beginning to look like a bus terminal. Then one night she opened the door to my developing closet even though the red light was signaling I was working inside and needed dark – something she's known since she was an infant. She wanted the car keys, and for some reason I'd taken my handbag inside with me. But I screamed. She'd completely ruined a dozen negatives I couldn't replace. I was a wild woman, I shouted, I yelled, I tore my own hair. She shrugged. 'I needed the car keys. I couldn't wait for hours until you came out.' She was sullen, surly, and I felt as if all the blood in my body had mounted to my head, and I slapped her, hard, across the mouth.

That was unusual enough, since I was never given to physical punishment, but she took it as a declaration of war. She slapped me back, I slapped her, we hauled into each other, twisting arms, socking each other, slapping. I was quickly reduced to pinching and twisting, because my daughter, although shorter and lighter than I, had studied karate, and had twenty-five years less smoking to slow her down. She got me pinned: I couldn't move: she shoved me backward, onto the arm of a stuffed chair.

'I could kill you now!' she hissed.

'Go ahead!' I yelled. 'It would be a blessed release from living with you!'

She let me go then, grabbed my bag and took the car keys, and stormed out of the apartment, slamming the door behind her.

This was the story I told my parents, and as I finished, my mother began to cry. I was astonished.

'Why are you crying?'

My father looked at me as if I were stupid. 'She feels bad for you, Ana. Of course she'd cry.'

Nonsense, I thought. She's never cried for me in her life. I turned to my mother, and asked again, severely, 'Why are you crying?'

She was sobbing now. 'Oh, I wish I could have talked to *my* mother like that! I never talked to her, I never told her how I felt, I never knew how she felt, and now it's too late!'

Well, that rocked me. Because in all the years I'd listened to my mother's tales, there had been these two, my mother and her mother, two throbbing figures in a landscape of concrete, suffering suffering, separately yet linked, like wounded animals wandering through miles of silent tree trunks oblivious to their pain. Like a woman I saw once, walking down the street in Hempstead, with a man on one side of her and a woman on the other, holding her arms. She was youngish – in her early thirties, and pretty, a little plump – but there was something on her face that made my heart tremble for her . . . No one else seemed to notice anything odd, people walked past her, around her, and did not glance twice at her. But that night I saw her picture in the newspaper: she was the only survivor of a fire that had killed her husband and her four children.

That was my image of them, these two women, Mommy and Grandma. And I had never had any inkling that anything lay in the space between them except their shared knowledge of grief. It was blind of me, of course, it simply makes sense that there had to be more. All my life I had rejected prettied pictures of life, slamming shut the saccharin children's books I was given at school, pulling wry faces in movie houses, questioning angrily people's sweetened explanations for things. I was an offensive child, and perhaps am an offensive adult, responding indignantly to anything that seems facile, designed to conceal, smooth over, sweeten, a reality I know to be grim and terrible. I would insult my mother's friends, announcing in outrage, 'I don't believe that!' or making faces at their gushing, swooping voices as they insisted that people were good and life was nice. Or the reverse.

Yet here I had all these years simply accepted as truth my mother's relation to her mother as one of total, unswerving love and devotion. Certainly, that was all I had ever heard or seen. My mother said her mother was a saint, and a saint was what I saw too. Quiet, sad, Grandma would sit in a small corner of the couch when she visited and open her arms to me, and I'd sit beside her and she'd take my hands in hers – so soft, as if the wrinkles had changed the texture of the fabric of her skin – and smile with love, saying, 'My Anastasia, my little Anastasia'. She and my mother would talk together in the kitchen in Polish, and my grandmother would laugh and nod her head. No anger ever came out of her voice or showed on her face. I can't imagine her angry. She would just cry when her grandson, my cousin, kicked her when she tried to put him to bed. She never raised her voice. Once, when she was visiting us, she and my mother walked the two miles to the German pork butcher for chops for dinner, and the butcher's wife said something to her husband in German. When they left the shop, my grandmother giggled: she was pleased at being able to understand their language without their knowing. What the woman had said was 'What a gentle face that woman has!' She was talking about my grandmother.

And whenever my mother spoke of her late at night, her voice would grow foggy and her eyes teary: 'My mother was a saint.' Then her voice would thicken: 'Poor Momma'. And then she'd go off toward one part of it, some part of it, the incredibly cruel man, the submissive woman, the brutalized children; or the poverty or the ignorance. All of it hurt her, my mother, equally, although when she came to the ignorance, her voice grew an edge, a bitterness that sometimes seemed almost ready to spill over on to her mother. But if I probed that, she would shrug: 'What could she do? She knew nothing.' When she spoke of the other things, she spoke like a child: her voice was high and thin and her sentences simple. And through it all, the same shrug, the same sigh: 'I was such a stupid kid. I didn't know anything.'

This is a part of my mother no one but me has seen. I know her as the nine-year-old she had been and in some way remains. My father would not want to listen to such grief; he doesn't like problems unless they are solvable mechanically, like a broken clock or a stuck window. These he enjoys, and brings considerable ingenuity to solving. Nor does my sister enjoy harping on past sorrows. She likes to pull herself up and address the present, finding in present action the only solution to past loss. And I am like her in that – at least, I always used to be, or anyway, I thought I was. Yet what have I been doing all these years, sitting with mother in the dimly lighted room as the clock hand moves silently toward four, smoke clouding the air? (My father, who in the days when he worked had to get up early in the morning, was forced to go to bed by one at the latest, had gone sighing and grumbling upstairs. At two or so, he would get up noisily and go to the bathroom for a heavy towel, which he would insert in the crack between his bedroom door and the floor to keep the odor of cigarette smoke from rising into his sleep – his small protest and reproach to us.) My mother and I agree to have just one more drink, and I get them, although sometimes at that hour (this was long ago), my mother would insist on getting up herself and making our drinks. But I would always follow her out to the kitchen while she did it, and carry my own back to the little room she called the porch where we would sit and talk. What have I been doing, listening over and over, asking over and over, obsessed with something, unsure what? Listening, putting myself into her, becoming her, becoming my grandmother, losing myself, as if I could once and finally lose myself inside my mother, and in the process give her the strength and hope she needs. Return the liquids I drained from her, become a midge mother in return, mothering my own mother.

And she would never tell these things to anyone else. Not even her sister, who 'doesn't know, she wasn't there, she didn't see what I saw, she doesn't remember, she thinks Poppa was wonderful, she doesn't want to hear anything else'. No, only I know this part of my mother, but it is her deepest part, the truest, the core. So when other people say things about her, I just look at them. I don't know what they are talking about.

three

And other people do say things about her. She is a difficult woman. She is deaf or nearly deaf, and angry about that; she gets irritated with people who speak softly, and grimaces and turns her head away disdainfully. People who don't understand what is happening think she is bored and rude. It is risky to give her a gift. She receives gifts, as well as certain acts designed to please, as challenges to which she is more than equal: she will in some way make sure the giver knows they have not managed to please her.

She is worst of all in restaurants, especially if one of us, my sister or I, have taken her. The place is invariably too noisy: with her hearing aid, on, she cannot filter sounds, and the scrape of fork on plate, or chair on floor, are as importunate as the sound of voices on her receiver. Usually, the place is too cold as well. Beyond that, the food is never good. My sister strains her budget to take Mother to dinner for her birthday, and is – as always – gay and brittle over the clams casino, the mushroom soup, the *médaillons de veau*. 'Isn't this great?' she exhorts Mother. 'Isn't it delicious?' Mother's mouth twists into a stiff smile. 'Very good,' she obviously lies.

Later, to me, she almost spits her disgust: the clams were nothing but breadcrumbs in margarine, the soup flour and water, the veal frozen. Later, my sister will be snapping at her children – why is the house such a mess, why can't they ever pick up their shoes, throw away their soda cans, empty their ashtrays. Glancing at each other, the children will ask how dinner was. 'Great, really terrific!' Later, her husband will tell her she is chewing on the inside of her cheek. 'Your mother upset you,' he will suggest, laying a kind hand on her back. Joy will flare up. 'She didn't! It was a great dinner! If she didn't like it, that's her problem, I could care less! I can't worry about it. I could care less! I could really care less!'

Sometimes my mother whines, sometimes she sulks. She is enraged if my father is not at her side to help at all times, but often when he puts his hand gently under her elbow to help her over a threshold, she will snatch her arm away and snap at him: 'I'm all right, Ed!' as if he were coercing her into helplessness. She turns her cheek to the kiss he confers upon her before every meal, just after he has helped her into her chair. Often, she sits alone, idle and silent, on the porch of their house, a broad glassed-in room overlooking the lake. But she no longer cries, and she no longer locks herself for days in a darkened room claiming sinus headache, the way she did when I was a teenager.

For many years, she granted me a small power, one that bound me to her irrevocably: when I came to visit her, she would rouse herself, she would talk and laugh and sometimes even forget her sorrow. This power she granted also to my sister. But for my sister, the business of rousing Mother, entertaining her, trying to make her laugh, was hard work; whereas for me, it was in those days a pleasure. It made me feel strong and full of laughter to laugh with her. She does not laugh anymore now though.

She is very lonely but does not try to make friends, and if it is suggested, she snaps 'I don't feel like it!' Other times, when she is feeling better perhaps, she sits in her rocker gazing out at the lake and says, 'There's no lack of drama in my life.' Then she tells me the latest scandal, the latest violence – for among themselves, the cardinals, the big blue jay, the robins, sparrows, ducks, geese, swans, rabbits, chipmunks, possums, squirrels, the neighbor's cat, the tiny red snapper that inhabit the lake, the woods, and the lawn behind my parents' house maintain a steady drama enacted it seems for her alone. This drama is full of war and murder and mothering and anxiety. Father ducks – she is sure they are father ducks – squawk angrily at mother ducks anxiously trying to extract their babies from the wire mesh of the neighbor's fence. Male geese – she is sure they are males because they are more aggressive and larger than the others – intimidate the females, and push themselves forward to gobble up all the bread she and my father throw out to them. Her arm is not strong enough to hurl the light crumbs out to where the smaller geese hover hopefully, so she turns on her heel in outrage and refuses to feed them at all. On and on, day after day, contests and resolutions.

A family of birds settled in the birdhouse and made a nest, but were so stupid they filled the entire house with twigs, so they could no longer enter it. My mother directed my father as he climbed the ladder and removed some of the stuffing. 'But those birds were really stupid,' my mother announced in contempt. The eggs were all at the bottom of the nest, underneath the stuffing, and they were all cold. She shrugged: 'It was a stupid bird family; it didn't deserve to live.'

She watched the soap opera of nature, over and over again: death and continuation. She finds some rest in this, and occasionally will lift the binoculars to her eyes to observe more closely. But she doesn't hold them long: they are too heavy.

My European friend Bertram, who speaks like a popgun attached to a cartridge belt, and who prides himself on his nonidealistic, nonsentimental view of the world, laughs at his mother. 'I never took any shit from her,' he boasts: 'she's impossible.' 'It became clear to me at an early age,' he enunciates with only a trace of an accent, 'that she loved me more than I loved her. I could walk out and she couldn't.' He did walk out too – many times. He went to prep schools, college, and university, all with the approval of his formidable mother and his kindly physician father. He became a geologist and screwed his way around the world. He doesn't mention, but I know, that he always returns to Mother in between journeys. He did not marry until he was forty – and he married then in order to give his mother a grandson, a task he performed efficiently. His wife having walked out on *him*, he remains, as he did before his marriage, in his small apartment on New York's Riverside Drive, just ten blocks from Mother and use of her Mercedes. He and his son visit Grandma several times a week: their bond could hardly be tighter. He's proud of her too: since her husband's death, she has had two love affairs. Her hair is still black, although she's eighty years old.

Impossible, impossible. It is a refrain. Henri Laforgue overhears me talking about my mother and exclaims, 'God save me from my mother!' Everyone at the table laughs.

We are sitting in a restaurant in Paris, charming with dark wood paneling and the small high windows of a three-hundred-year-old building. The tables bear big bowls of flowers and superb food: the restaurant is unknown to tourists. Henri is tall and robust; his round face and its chins sit smugly on the immaculate collar of his custom-made shirt. He is, as always, surrounded by women – his wife, Adèle, her colleagues Marthe and Martine, and me. All of them dote on him: they laugh when he laughs, direct their glances at him, attend devotedly to his needs before he says a word. His wife runs her own very successful business, a public relations agency, an unusual thing in France, but she also tends to their showpiece of a house, their three children, and Henri. He is away all week selling industrial chemicals, and wants to relax on the weekend. Adèle sees to it that nothing upsets him, and she also manages to keep herself soignée. 'Save me from my mother!' he cries again, laughing, and the others laugh too.

Save him from what? Of course he doesn't need a mother, he has all sorts of women dancing attendance on him everywhere he goes. Maybe his mother is like Henri, but being a woman, can't get the same service. I ask what is so terrible about her, but no one will tell me. They only laugh harder. I hug a certain resentment to me, like a stuffed animal. I am a mother myself: what is it in these mothers one constantly hears about that is so 'impossible'?

Anyway, even if they told me, I probably wouldn't understand. They'd use some word that is meaningless to me. They might call her *proud*, or *overattentive*. They might say she was *cold*. Someone said that once, about my friend Lee. I knew this was a term of disapprobation, a judgment: *cold*. Yet I also knew Lee had depths of understanding and subtleties of perception far exceeding those of her critic. If her critic – a coarse but warm, outgoing woman named Aline – meant that my friend did not gush, and took her time about making new friends, why, I was the same way. Was I too cold? Was Aline really trying to convey disapproval of me? Or was she saying that my friend made her feel inferior? What was she saying? What was this coldness?

I encounter such problems regularly. The first time

someone said I was 'sensitive', I knew she meant that I was to be forgiven for some response, although I wasn't sure why. What did that mean? That I was acute to nuances? Or got my feelings hurt easily? A shrink I know told me that I felt more deeply than other people, and I asked him what kind of instrument he had for measuring such a thing. Because I suspect that people have great dark abysses in them, things they rarely show. No one knows what people feel when they are alone in dim rooms as the light just begins to come up, the greyest time of day. I was utterly shaken when a man once told me I was 'somethin' else'. I'm embarrassed to report that I replied, 'What else? Else than what?'

Some years ago I went to Poland, alone and without tour guides or acquaintances. It was a shattering experience, partly because of my inability to read anything or understand more than about fifteen spoken words. People helped me, but I felt like an infant; they led me about by the hand, refusing to allow me to go out by myself – it seemed to them too dangerous for someone who could not read or speak even the simplest things. But that was an alien tongue. I have this problem with my own.

I remember one of the first times I was aware of this confusion about ordinary language. I was about eight, and walking the long empty blocks home from school alone as always, in my high brown shoes and white socks that kept slipping down into the shoes and disappearing. I walked strangely too, toeing in so extremely that sometimes I tripped over my own foot. I used to make up stories as I trudged what seemed a long weary way every morning and afternoon, stories about my family being saved by a sudden inheritance, or a fairy godmother, or my father's getting a better job. I'd think about where we'd live and about the kind of person I'd be.

A bunch of the rougher girls from my class came running down the street behind me, and I shrank into myself, terrified. I thought they were chasing me, and they were much taller and heavier than I, being two years older and considerably more developed. As they came nearer, I tried to disguise my fear, both out of pride and out of some intuitive awareness that fear is provocative, and I held my neck taut, my chin high, and plastered my face with hauteur. But they were simply playing some – to me – rough game, and passed me laughing, until one turned around and pointed, crying in great gasps of laughter – 'Look at Dabrowski! Oh, conceited!' And the others turned then too, and laughed, brayed at me, 'Conceited! Conceited!'

I maintained my dignified pace and did not change my expression. They tore off down the block and through the empty lot, leaping over abandoned rusting gasoline drums, bedsprings, and other litter, laughing. And my heart squeezed itself together, wanting to force a tear into my eye, but I controlled it. I went into my house through the back door, as always. My mother was mopping the kitchen floor with an instrument I particularly disliked, a mop with long spaghetti-like strands that swished around uncontrollably as she pushed the handle. I did not tell my mother about the girls. I don't know why. Although I told her many things other children would conceal, I concealed much, very selectively. I would have been ashamed to tell her about the girls. I wanted to appear in control of my away-from-home life. I waited on the threshold as she finished the last swipes with the ugly mop. 'If you take off your shoes, Anastasia, you can walk over to the table and I'll give you some milk and cookies,' she said kindly. I set my books on the table, which was near the back door, and removed my hated shoes, and did as she said. She brought me a glass of milk and some Oreos, and then sank into the chair opposite me, sighing. She lit a cigarette and crossed her legs: she was in her stocking feet.

'How was school today?'

'Fine. I got one hundred in the spelling test, and ninety-nine in the math test. It wasn't my fault that I got ninety-nine. The teacher thought my seven was a one on one problem. I told her it wasn't, but she said it was okay.'

She smiled. 'That's very good, Anastasia.'

'And in recess, we danced in a circle and I got picked three times.' This was an utter lie. I was almost never picked when we danced in a circle, and I knew it was because of my ugly high shoes. But I also knew that those shoes cost my parents a great deal of money they couldn't afford, and that they sacrificed to buy them for me so my flat feet would grow straight. Or whatever they were supposed to do. But this was a lie I frequently used because it seemed to make her happy. She smiled very broadly: 'Oh, how nice, Anastasia! You're popular!' When she smiled like that, I could almost believe it had happened, that I had been chosen, that the children did like me.

We fell into silence then. I finished my cookies and swept the crumbs into a little pile. Mother rose and got a dishcloth and wiped them up.

'Is it okay if I walk on the floor now?'

'Yes.' She tamped her cigarette out and sighed again. 'I'm so tired.' I glanced at her sympathetically. She was always tired. I knew her life was very hard.

'Mommy?' I turned to get my books. 'What does conceited mean?'

She was standing at the sink, running hot water over the mophead. 'It means someone who thinks they're good. Better than other people.'

I stood still. 'Oh.'

She turned her head slightly. 'Why?'

'Oh, some girls were calling that name – at Rhoda Moore – today. At recess.' I had used the name of the only girl in the class I envied, a tall, beautiful girl with long blond hair and big blue eyes. 'They said she was conceited.'

'Is she?'

'I don't know,' I faltered. 'She's the pretty one.'

'She probably thinks she's prettier than the others, then,' Mother explained.

I left the room so she would not see my hot face, my anguish at slandering poor Rhoda Moore, and deceiving my mother, and even worse, concealing my own true nature. For the moment she said it, I knew it was true. I was conceited, I did think I was better than the others. I ran upstairs to my room and threw myself on my bed. I could feel my pulse throbbing in my head, as if I had a fever. I felt utterly alone, without virtue. I wished I could disappear, just die there on the spot, just blow away, like some crinkled dried-up brown leaf.

I *was* conceited, I did think I was better than the others. But I *was* better than the others. I was clean and they mostly were not; I was smarter than any of them, in all subjects. They were ignorant and ill-spoken and their manners were bad and they were loud. I felt they were another order of being from me, another species even. And this was true: this was objectively true, I felt: that I was better in these ways, and that my superiority was recognized by the teachers, even the principal. Why else had they skipped me so often? Why did the principal come into the room and always stand behind me, gazing down on my work? Why did the teachers so often send me to his office with a drawing or a poem I had made? They thought it was good that I was superior. My mother did too. But it was conceited to be superior, and to be conceited was bad. I lay there in an anguish that was to become familiar to me over the years. What I was was good, and made some people like me but others hate me. I did not enjoy my isolation from other children, but I did not want to stop being superior either. Doing things – the things I could do – doing them well was practically my only source of pleasure.

I don't know what words I used to think about this. I do know it ramified far beyond itself, into something so complicated and interrelated with other things that it felt overwhelming. There was no solution to it that I could see except to not-be, to stop being what I was, in short, to die. I half-believed that if I could lie still as if dead for long enough, death would eventually creep through my body. But I never could do it. My body would always assert itself. An arm would fall asleep, a leg would absolutely demand to be moved, and would poke its demand into the oblivion into which I felt my mind fading. And so, heaving and sad, I would sit up and return to the life I had already recognized was a dead end, a double bind. There was no way to be oneself and to be good and to be loved. Whatever one chose, one sacrificed the rest. 'For matter is never lacking privation . . .' It was too hard for me.

Of course I went on, as one does, and even managed sometimes to forget this old insight. But I continued to suspect words. So when a woman said to me that my mother was strong; when others said 'Your mother is a lovely woman,' I'd simply smile and nod. If you question such statements, people look at you as if they have suddenly discovered you are retarded. Years ago, I would go off by myself and ruminate on such statements: *Is* she strong? What does that mean? How does it show? *Is* she lovely?

I took such judgments as authoritative, and believed they were based on profound perception. I did not then understand that people were in the habit of running around in the world making judgments on all sides without really thinking about what they were saying. I was a very serious child, and believed the state of adulthood was blessed with knowledge and awareness from which I was cut off. I saw adulthood as a special state, people sitting in a brilliantly lit room laughing and talking and nodding their heads, while I stand in the shadows just outside the room unable to understand why they are talking so animatedly about the weather or the traffic, knowing from their vitality and amusement that beneath their ordinary words was a world of hidden meaning, that language was a code known only to the initiate — adults. Oh, in time I learned to read the silences and pauses, learned what the omissions in conversation meant — sex or shame, money or scandal. But I still have trouble with the words. The only word I could place on my mother, surely without question, is one I have never heard anyone use: in her heart, at her core, my mother is furious.

four

Still, she was like me too, hanging back in the shadows, timid and alien, knowing herself unwelcome in the adults' room, knowing herself ignorant of it. She wore high shoes too, even higher than mine, but they were in fashion then, and she had the same long spaghetti curls she later visited on me. She would make me sit on the step stool while she heated the curling iron in the gas flame, the same flame she used to singe a chicken, which created a smell similar to that of the singed newspaper she used to twist the iron in before applying it to my limp hair. She would comb off a section of hair, twist it in the evil-smelling iron, then flip it loose and continue around my head until I was judged 'done'. Like the chicken, all its feathers having curled into wisps at the touch of fire, ready to be cooked.

'Did your mommy curl your hair like this?'

'Oh, no, Anastasia.' She said this in what I privately called her 'mad' voice, a tone mingling tiredness and disgust. But then she added mournfully, 'My mother never combed my hair.'

But it was there, in the picture, I insisted: Mommy at seven, my age exactly, with the same spaghetti curls. And I ran upstairs to get it, to show her. Her shoulders slumped, she grimaced. She was disgusted with me. 'Oh, I don't know, Anastasia, maybe the maid curled it.'

'I don't remember, Anastasia!' She is getting irritated now, as she rolls up the crimped newspaper and stuffs it in the garbage, lays the curling iron on the gas stove to cool, and pours herself another cup of coffee from the dull aluminum drip pot. She sinks into a chair at the kitchen table and lights a cigarette. Clutching the photograph, I leave the room, run to the front room we call the 'porch' and squat on the floor. High black shoes with buttons. They come almost all the way up to her hem. And the shy eyes, the shy smile, the look of being not-quite-there. This is my mommy. With her is her brother, Eddie, who is nine. He is there, self-possessed, dark, a round mature face. I recognize him, my uncle Eddie whom I love. He is wearing a white suit with knickers and a shirt with a rounded collar. I never saw a white suit like the one in this photograph except when Louis Ferraro died. He had appendicitis, and the teacher made all of us go to his house to pay respects, she said. He was lying in a box in a white suit, with flowers all around him. He was just as fat and tan as ever, but he was dead. His mother and grandmother and all his aunts had black dresses covering their huge bodies, all sitting around the coffin crying. They hardly even looked up, they hardly even answered the teacher. I couldn't understand that: he was only a child, after all. If I had died and was in a box and the teacher came to our house, I knew my mother would be polite and pleasant to the teacher. I thought they were pretending. They couldn't have cared that much about just a child.

When I asked my mother about his white suit, she said it was a Communion suit. Communion suit. That was new. I had heard of union suits, but not *Comm*union suits. I wondered if Eddie's suit was a Communion suit too, and I wanted to ask Mommy, but I knew it would be better if I didn't. I sat on the porch floor, knees together, ankles out, considering. This was a decision I had often to make, but I had no way to predict consequences. I urgently wanted to know if Eddie's suit was a Communion suit too. Finally, I decided to risk it, and jumped up and returned to the kitchen. Mommy was still sitting at the kitchen table, smoking. She was staring at the window, but she didn't seem to be looking at anything. When I entered the room, she didn't move.

'Mommy?' I asked tentatively at the door. 'Is Eddie's suit a Communion suit?'

She looked at me.

I held the photograph out. 'It's white, like Louis Ferraro's.'

She leaned forward and reached out her hand. 'Let me see.' She examined the picture. 'Well, it might have been. But he probably made his First Communion when he was seven – that's what the picture is, it's me in my Communion dress. So his Communion suit was probably too small when he was nine. But maybe Momma made it bigger, Momma was wonderful at that. Or maybe he had a new suit.' The weariness returned to her voice. 'I don't remember.' She returned the picture to me.

I stood transfixed. 'There are Communion dresses too?' My next question would be a big one, and I hesitated. 'What's Communion?' I had been lucky so far, and I knew from experience that I always pushed my luck a little too far. I did this time too.

She burst out tiredly. 'Go and play, Anastasia! Stop bothering me!'

I disappeared.

I went upstairs and lay on my bed. Whenever my mother spoke to me that way, I felt cast into some whirling black place, I felt wrong, I felt all the things she said I was when she was angry with me – selfish, willful. I felt like a throbbing wart, and I wanted to disappear completely. I wanted to die, and I wondered if she would cry at all, if she would be sorry if I did. Sometimes I thought she would, other times I thought she wouldn't care at all. Yet someplace I knew she did care for me, and that I would understand that if I could only understand her. And so I would think about her, that little girl just my age, and what it was like to be her, and I would remember what she had told me about her life, and the next time I sensed she was in a good mood, I would ask her more about it. I sat up, and leaned back against my pillow. I could feel a certain expression coming on my face. It still does, but now I know what word to label it with: renunciation. I sat there and felt calm, feeling I had a purpose, a cause, an approach – although I did not know those words. I would enter into my mother, and in this way discover the springs of her love.

Chapter II

one

In July of 1907, they lived on Grand Street, Williamsburgh, in Brooklyn. It was a neighborhood in the old sense. The cobblestoned streets were lined with little shops; above them were two tiers of railroad flats, where the people lived. The street was always full of action: trolleys clanked by, and drays pulled by great full-buttocked horses. Sometimes a couple pushed a cart through on their way to sell their wares in what everyone here called 'Jewtown'. Sometimes a dray would stop, and its driver would jump down, speak to the horses, then heave a heavy keg from the back of the dray and roll it into a shop. Many things came in kegs — flour, butter, barley, nails, beer. Men would pass by carrying sloshing pails of beer home from the saloon. Children ran through traffic, darted in and out of doorways. And above it all, the women, leaning from the windowsills, maintained a running critique. Everything that happened on the street interested them, and on everything they had an opinion. They would carry on conversations with those on the street below; they would shriek at the children; and sometimes they would turn sideways and speak to each other, window to window, after one disappeared to return with a plump down pillow on which to rest her arms.

It was a lively, vivid, tough, loud street, a place some might remember fondly. But not the three-and-a-half-year-old girl standing at the second-floor window. Hidden from the room behind her by a lace curtain, she stands so still she seems dead, so pale and fragile she could be a china doll propped there. She is small for three. She knows she is sickly, but does not know what the word means. It is like a synonym for her name: Isabella is sickly.

For her, although she stands often at this window looking down, the street is frightening. It is so noisy, so rough. People bump into each other, sometimes they push. The men have thick arms, and some roll their shirtsleeves up so the dark hair shows. The women have loud voices and cackle in laughter. The trolleys glide by, huge and terrifying. One time when Eddie took Bella for candy, a trolley came right up to her and she didn't see it. Eddie pulled her back fast and yelled at her she should look where she was going. Then he hugged her and bought her two pieces of candy, but she was still crying. She hadn't seen the trolley.

In fact, she doesn't see well. The cornea of her left eye was scarred by measles, but no one knows that yet. She sees well enough to be aware of the street, and to know she hates and fears it. Sometimes, when the sunlight makes everything shimmer in front of her, she pretends she is on a different street, one she saw long ago.

Momma and Poppa took her and Eddie and the baby to visit Momma's sister Mamie, who lives far away — two trolley rides and a long walk. Momma was fat and she carried Wally so Poppa let Bella sit on his lap; she gazed with fascination through the trolley windows at streets that had no stores at all but only houses all in a row, brown houses with high stoops and trees shading quiet sidewalks. There was a place for the children to play in this neighborhood, although no children were playing. But on one stoop, Bella spied a little girl with long yellow curls and a pink dress, sitting neatly and prettily, her figure splotched by the dancing of the unfurling buds of the tree. And Bella's heart squeezed so hard, she almost cried out. She longed to be that little girl and live in that quiet dignified house. Her yearning was a band tying her to the little girl, stretching further and further as the trolley moved down the street.

When Bella stands at the window looking out, she does not always see the street before her. Sometimes she is on another street, sitting on stone steps under the tips of the branches of a tree, wearing a pink dress. Her hours pass in vacancy, the vacancy of unselfconsciousness. She is unaware of much around her. But some things she knows.

She knows she has a momma and a poppa who are always gone. Momma is already in the kitchen making oatmeal when Bella rises from her tousled bed and trots, silently and barefoot, into the dining room, and climbs on to the couch and curls up in its corner. She can see Momma in the kitchen they share with the next-door neighbors. She is holding the round fragrant loaf of Jewish rye bread in her arm, slicing it toward her breast. She cuts three slices for Poppa and one each for herself and the children. She spreads them thickly with creamy white butter and puts them on a plate. She carries the plate into the dining room and lays it on the table, but she is rushing, always rushing, and she does not see Bella curled up in the couch. Bella jumps up and runs to the table and snatches her bread and butter, then runs back to the couch, snuggles in its deep cushions, and eats. Eddie comes roaring in, pretending to be something that makes noise, and grabs his slice and jumps up on the couch next to Bella; and Wally follows, crawling. He reaches the table and whimpers. He can't reach the plate: he can't stand up yet. Eddie jumps up and gets Wally his slice of bread, then lifts him on to the couch. Eddie is strong. Wally tries to put the whole slice in his mouth at once, and smears butter all over his face.

Eddie takes the bread away from him, and Wally begins to wail. 'Bites, stupid, take bites. Like this.' Eddie holds the edge of the bread to the infant, and Wally grabs it and bites down. 'That's right,' Eddie says. He has finished his bread, and sits in the center of the couch, his legs dangling, swinging back and Bella doesn't notice him, doesn't notice any of this. She has finished her bread and butter and is watching Momma scramble Poppa's eggs. She wishes they were for her. Momma puts Poppa's plate on the table just as Poppa comes into the dining room. He is wearing his shirt and tie, but not his vest. He sits down at the head of the table, removes his heavy linen napkin from its ring, and tucks it into his belt. He does not begin to eat until Momma comes in with the coffeepot and pours a steaming cup of rich-smelling dark brew for him. Her shoulders are a little hunched in his presence, but she is smiling at him. Momma is small and nimble and amiable. She always laughs or smiles or nods when Poppa says something. Poppa begins to eat his eggs and his three slices of bread and butter. Momma has eaten her bread standing up in the kitchen.

Momma leaves first in the morning, running the three blocks to the tailor shop, which she opens up, so that when Poppa arrives, everything is in order. She gets her coat and tells the children to be good. She runs out the door. When Poppa is finished eating, he goes back to the bedroom. Then the servant girl clears the table and slams down the children's bowls of oatmeal. Bella slides down from the couch and darts into the hall. She flattens herself against the wall and watches Poppa, who is standing before the mahogany-framed cheval glass adjusting his gold watch and chain across the front of his beautiful striped-satin white vest. He brushes the shoulders of his dark jacket with a fine soft brush with a tortoiseshell handle. Bella does not know the words for these objects, but she perceives their quality. Then Poppa pulls out each side of his mustache, sets his hat just so over his brow. He straightens up in the mirror. He is very fine. As he starts to turn to leave the room, Bella scurries back to the dining room and climbs up on a chair at the table.

Her oatmeal is lumpy now. She eats around the lumps, pouring heavy cream over them until she has a kind of soup-cream with lumps – and the servant girl comes in and sees her and slaps her hand and scolds her. 'Stupid Bella!' She slides down from the chair and runs away. She goes to the front room, which is rarely used and is off-limits to the children. She knows this, but she also knows that if she slips behind the lace curtain and stands very still, the servant girl will not look for her until nearly midday, when Momma will come running back home to make lunch for Poppa. Bella can see Momma running when she is a block away, and she can slip out and go to the children's bedroom and put on her dress and shoes. The servant girl has to button them, and will slap her for dressing so late, but she is used to these slaps now.

Momma was fat and stayed home and one night she screamed and then she got thin but she still stayed home. Bella wanted to sit on her lap, but the ladies shooed her away. They had a funeral. They were crying. A funeral was a party where ladies cried. Then Momma went away again, back to the tailor shop.

Bella is only vaguely aware of her brothers. She does not know what Wally is doing. There are no toys in this house, no books, no paper or pencil or crayon or paints. The children's room holds the one big bed they all sleep in and a trunk for their clothes. Sometimes when she goes in to get dressed, Wally is lying on the floor with his thumb in his mouth. He is a baby. Eddie has gone out. He goes out every day to play ball with his friends. They throw a ball at the brick side of the stationery store on the corner until the owner chases them away. Every day he chases them away, and the boys call him names as they run. Then he goes inside and gets a broom which he brandishes like a bat as he chases them. But they are small and quick and dart behind wagons and into doorway. The boys cry out, 'Old man Meinie has pimples on his heinie,' and giggle hysterically. Mr Meineke gets red in the face and the red lines on his nose look as if they will burst.

Bella cannot understand why Eddie is willing to incur such a terrible punishment – as the scene with its noise and violence seems to her – for such a foolish pastime. She followed him out one morning and stood beside him while he threw his ball, but the act seemed pointless to her and she could not understand why he wanted to do it. Eddie just laughs, he says he isn't afraid of old man Meineke. But Bella doesn't really believe him, even though Eddie is big. He is five. He had a birthday and Poppa made a speech. He pulled Eddie up onto his lap at the dinner table and he held up his glass and everyone else at the table held up theirs and he talked about his five-year-old son, and cried out 'Na zdrowie!' and everyone else called it out too and they drank. And Momma gave candy to Bella who had been allowed to stay up and was sitting quietly on the couch.

Bella hears a sharp screech and knows the servant girl has done the wash in the two deep tubs in the kitchen, and is hanging it on the line that stretches outside the kitchen window to a pole at the end of the yard. The pulley is rusty and screeches with each tug. Bella goes to the kitchen to watch, silently. She peers down from the window into the yard below, which is cluttered with refuse from the China-man's rice-cake shop that borders the plot of vegetables planted by the Chinaman's silent wife. She is tending them, moving slowly, hunched over the plants; she never looks around her. At night Bella could smell vegetables cooking in the evil-smelling oil they used, the same oil in which the Chinaman cooked his rice cakes. When she went out, Bella would stand on the street watching him make his rice cakes in the window of his shop. Despite the oil, they smelled delicious, and he made them just like Momma made pancakes on Sundays when the tailor shop was closed. Bella would gaze enviously at the people who stood on line to buy the rice cakes. But she never dared to ask for one because every time Poppa saw him he would boom out laughing: 'Oh, that Chinaman! Don't you ever eat those rice cakes of his! You know what he makes them from?

He makes them from rats' tails and chopped-up mice and spiders.'

He spoke in Polish, of course, so the Chinaman did not realize what he was saying. Everyone spoke Polish in Bella's world, although she recognized that when the boys called out to Mr Meineke, they were speaking in a different language. She did not know that language, but understood what they cried to the storekeeper. Bella was embarrassed by her father's insults to the Chinaman, and was grateful that the rice-cake man did not understand. She would watch his face sometimes as he cooked, and she felt something strange, as if they were alike, as if they were tied together. He never looked directly at anyone, and his expression never changed. He looked down at his rice cakes, at the money he changed. His eyes had no light in them. His wife never appeared in the front of his shop. If Bella had not seen her in the garden, she would not have known the woman existed.

Bella never tasted a rice cake. They are one of the only two things she can remember wanting, many years later, in her seventies, sitting with me smoking in the darkened porch. Rice cakes and white bread. She discovered white bread when she was four and in the hospital.

She vaguely recalls being sick, lying in semidelirium, people hovering around her bed. Once she awoke, and heard her mother whispering to a neighbor, 'The boy next door had the same thing and he died.' She wondered if dying was different from living. She recalls shouting, too, from far away, and soon after that she was moved someplace.

When she was grown up, Momma told her what happened. Poppa did not believe in giving good money to doctors or insurance companies and he would not let Momma call the doctor for her. But Mamie came, and saw Bella, and she screamed at Poppa that Bella's death would be on his head, so he let Momma call the doctor, who transferred her to the hospital. She had a mastoid infection that left her deaf in one ear. (Poppa listened to Mamie, but he told Momma she was not permitted to enter his house again. But she did! Bella knew she did! She wasn't as stupid as Momma thought.)

One day she woke up in a strange bed with high sides. A woman in a white dress was putting breakfast on a tray in front of her. There was a glass of orange juice, an egg, and something she had never seen before – white bread and butter with salt in it. Isabella picked up the bread and tasted it: saliva gushed into her mouth and she had to restrain herself from gobbling it all up fast. Slowly, lovingly, she bit tiny pieces of it.

The little girl in the next bed dawdled over her food. She was playing with her egg, her bread pushed to one side. Bella's hand suddenly darted out and snatched up the little girl's bread. She stuffed the whole slice in her mouth at once as a piercing scream rose. People ran into the room, all kinds of people, some in white dresses, some in blue-and-white ones, some in suits with white jackets over them and odd things hanging from them that looked as if they could do horrible things to you if you were bad. Isabella's heart beat so hard she thought her ear would burst, and she leaned rigidly against her pillow, her face ashen.

The little girl was only crying now, pointing to Isabella. A woman in a white dress and a funny hat said something calmly, and the little girl's sobbing abated. Everyone left the room, and after a while, a woman in blue and white came into the room with a plate and another piece of bread and butter and gave it to the little girl. Isabella stared straight ahead of her. But she wished she knew how the girl had managed to get another slice, for she wanted one herself.

two

The scene with the white bread was Bella's first conscious experience of terror. She had another, not too long afterward. She was home, and she had a friend, a little girl her age who lived down the street over the vegetable market, Olga. One day, before she went out to find her friend, she saw the servant girl baking chruściki on the wood stove. She ran down and began to jump rope with Olga, but after a while she remembered the chruściki. She ran back upstairs, and while the servant girl was in the toilet, she snatched up two of the cookies and ran down and shared them with Olga. This made both of them extremely happy. But she felt prickles on the back of her head, and turned, and looked up. There in the window of the front room stood the servant girl, glowering at her, waggling her finger. That day Bella stayed out as long as she could. She did not want to go home at all. Nor did she enjoy jumping rope anymore. Her body was cold and prickly and her head felt thick. But if there were consequences to the theft of the chruściki she does not remember them.

Food, food: it is mostly what she remembers: Momma making doughnuts, laying them out to dry on thick brown paper, spread across all the surfaces in the kitchen and dining room; and babka; and mushroom soup made from dried brown flaky bits, and thickened with barley; and *gołabki*, stuffed cabbage. There were potato pancakes with apple sauce; and sometimes, on Sunday, a roast of pork with crackly skin. Isabella did not care about the meat, she wanted only the skin, which crunched and made delicious juices in her mouth. And chicken broth with tiny soft noodles made of egg and flour that Momma dropped in patiently, from the tip of a teaspoon. Food. Bella loved food.

Olga's family moved and Bella lost her friend, and moved back into her silence. Momma was very fat again and stayed home some days, and when she was home, she had visitors. Momma had many friends, everyone liked Momma, Bella could tell that by the way they smiled and bobbed their heads at her, and Momma did the same. Momma would set the table and put out babka and almond cakes and glasses of tea, and the ladies would sit around the table with their hats on, talking. Sometimes Bella listened. Momma did not shoo her away in the daytime when Poppa was not there. She would curl up on the couch in silence. Sometimes she would fall asleep.

One day she heard a great cry, and raised her head. Momma had tears in her eyes and was embracing Mamie. They were whispering together, and Momma's eyes darted to her, to Bella. Then Momma turned back to Mamie and said, 'Ah, she won't say anything to him, and if she did – she's stupid, he wouldn't believe it.' And Mamie swept into the room, drawing another woman behind her. Mamie and the other woman wore beautiful broad-brimmed hats with flowers on them. They sat at the table and Momma bustled about just like she did for Poppa except her shoulders weren't hunched, and she was laughing and talking and every once in a while she wiped a tear from her cheek, and Mamie reached out a graceful arm and patted Momma's belly, and the women laughed, and Mamie caressed Momma's cheek. And when Momma had everything on the table, she sat down and the ladies drank tea and ate cake, and Momma held out a piece to Bella, and she ran to get it, then returned to her spot on the couch. The cake woke her up, and she listened.

Mamie was asking Momma for a favor. She wanted Momma to write a letter for her friend. Mamie could not write English; her friend could not write at all. The letter had to go to Immigration. Momma found some paper and a pen, and sat at the table, writing as they told her what they needed to say. Bella began to drift off. After Momma finished the letter, the women continued to talk. Mamie's friend – Pane Sliwowska – had a rich sister whose husband sold fur coats to very rich women. This sister lived in a brownstone (Bella wondered if that was what the little girl's house was called) with ten rooms and three toilets. Imagine! And she had a daughter named Anastasia, who had embroidered sheets on her bed and a set of underwear for each day in the week. Imagine! Ah-nah-stah-zya. Bella heard the name over and over. That was the little girl's name. It was Anastasia she had seen on the steps of the quiet benign house. Bella wondered if she had a dress for each day also. Maybe each day had a different color: pink, blue, white, yellow, green: what else was there? Black. No. Red. She would have a red dress for Sundays. Bella had never seen a red dress.

Anastasia. Anastasia knew only beautiful things. She knew the turning of the leaves when the rain was coming, and the colors of the sky. In summers her parents took her to places where the sun went down. Bella knew about this because, once, in the summer, Momma and Poppa had taken the children to the country, to Uncle August's house in Rockaway. She did not remember Uncle Gus's house, or Aunt Sophie, or anything except standing on the beach watching the sun over the water. The sun was big and red and it hung just a few feet above the sea and Bella watched it with her mouth hanging open. And they had to catch the trolley and Poppa had scolded Momma because Bella would not come away from the beach. And Momma, who never scolded, had spoken to her almost sharply, but she would not, she could not come away. At the end, she had to be lifted up and carried away. And she wept, because she had not seen it, and now she would never see it. 'Just another minute, Momma, please!' she cried, but Momma held her tight, and Momma had lines in her forehead as she ran to where Poppa stood with the boys. And even now she wanted to weep thinking about it because she would never know: what happened when the sun sank into the sea? Did the sea boil? Did it turn red like the sun? Did the sun make a big lump in the ocean? Did the ocean put out the sun, the way water put out the candles?

Thinking about this, she felt sleepy again, and laid her head against the sofa arm. Anastasia saw the sun go down every day in the summer, and knew what happened. And someday she, Bella, would know too. Someday she would see it. Her arm fell limply against the chair back as she drifted into an Anastasia sleep. She sensed her aunt Mamie kissing her temple, and smelled her perfume. Then she slept deeply.

Sometimes, Momma took Bella to Poppa's shop with her. Bella loved to go there, although she had to be very quiet and stay out of the way. Poppa's shop was large and bright, with great crystal chandeliers hanging from the high ceiling. The floors were polished golden wood, and everyone in the shop wore beautiful clothes like Poppa. Momma didn't of course, but she stayed in the back. Momma told her Poppa's shop was very fine, and that the mayor of New York City came to Poppa to have his suits made. Many people came from all over the world to

Poppa's shop, Momma said, and Poppa could speak to them because he spoke seven languages. So Bella had to be very quiet here. And she was. She stayed in the back, only peeping out sometimes through the brocade curtain that separated the front from the back. Usually, she curled up in a corner with bits of silk Momma gave her, scraps from linings and from shirts, and tried to make herself a little pocketbook like one she had once seen, but she didn't know where. She had made seven of them, but they were no good because the string did not close them. She did not know how to make them work.

One day, after she had finished the eighth bag, only to find that it, like the others, did not close, she sat and stared at it hard, and thought what would make it close. And it came to her, like a flash of light inside her head, that the two strings had to run opposite to each other. Quickly, she snatched a new piece of silk, red, with satin stripes like Poppa's vest, and painstakingly stitched a new bag. She sewed in string, one going one way and the other going in the opposite direction. Then, with tiny neat stitches, she hemmed the top of the bag, leaving two little spaces for the string to emerge. It took her all afternoon, and she had to concentrate very hard because she was in a hurry. She wanted to finish it today because she did not know when Momma would bring her to the shop again. And she did finish, and the bag worked! It closed and opened, just like a real bag!

But her pleasure in this accomplishment was brief. She showed her bag to Momma, but Momma hardly looked. And then, the next time Momma took her to the shop, she had nothing to do. She no longer wanted to make string bags, for the one she had was enough. Anyway, she had nothing to put into it.

By now, the children were allowed to sit at the table with Momma and Poppa for dinner, all except Eugenia, Euga (which they pronounced Aow-ga), the baby who had just come. But something was wrong. Momma no longer bobbed her head and laughed at everything Poppa said. She looked away when he spoke, and he spoke very loudly now, and sometimes after he had drunk many glasses of wine, he talked funny too. Momma would mutter things about 'her', 'she'. Poppa would stand and yell, rip his napkin from his belt and storm from the table. Bella gaped with alarm. She froze in her chair and heard nothing, saw nothing.

One night Poppa was late for dinner. Momma had been to the shop but had come home early. She didn't run anymore, her body moved as if it was tired. She set the round table and lighted the gas in the fringed lamp hanging over it. She set out the two chickens she had roasted and rutabaga sprinkled with dill and mashed potatoes and creamed spinach. Everything was getting cold and Momma was fretting. She walked back and forth from the kitchen to the dining room, and when the servant girl said something to her, she retorted sharply. Then they heard his step on the stairs, but it sounded funny, draggy. And he threw open the apartment door and strode in and slid on the floor and cursed, and Momma put her hand to her mouth in alarm, and stood very straight in front of the table. And Poppa came into the dining room, and his face had slipped, he was sneering at them, and he glanced around the room and peered at the table. 'You know I hate creamed spinach!' he roared and strode over and picked up the bowl of creamed spinach and hurled it against the wall. Then he turned around and strode out, and lumbered down the hall and out the door and down the stairs. They heard him slip and curse; then he began to descend again. Momma told the children to sit at the table. She went into the kitchen and found a rag and came back in and got down on her hands and knees and wiped up the creamed spinach. Bella's mouth was watering in frustration: she loved creamed spinach. She concentrated on the dinner they would eat as soon as Momma finished. Every dish on the table made her mouth water: the crispy brown chickens, the soft luscious potatoes, the tangy rutabaga with its sprinkle of dill. She wondered what there was for dessert. Maybe it could make up for the loss of the creamed spinach. She tried not to watch Momma, but she couldn't help it. Momma was hunched over, wiping up the gooey mess, her shoulders slumped. The servant girl, wide-eyed, was bringing her clean cloths, and taking away the ugly gooey greenish ones. Momma sighed hard. Slowly, she bent to pick up the pieces of the china dish. Quietly, the servant girl picked up those that had flown across the room. When it was all over, Momma sat down at the table and carved the chickens. She told the children to eat. Bella gobbled her food; she was so hungry she could not get full. She tried to savor the delicious tastes, but somehow, she couldn't. Maybe the dinner was too cold. As she spooned the food into her mouth, she kept seeing Momma on her hands and knees, with her back bent, wiping up the mess.

three

When Bella was five and a half, Momma sent her to school. She had a new dress, and stiff new boots, and a pair of eyeglasses. Momma kept reminding her she was not to lose them or break them. Momma gave her directions, and kissed her, but only perfunctorily, for she worried about Euga, who had a cold. Momma was carrying her around, bouncing her, talking to her to keep her from crying, but she still cried.

Bella walked the streets very carefully, reaching up every few seconds to touch her eyeglasses, to make sure they were still on her head. She found the building, and went where Momma said, into the office. There a grey-haired woman looked up and spoke to her. Bella simply stood there. She could not understand what the woman was saying. It was some sound like 'o', but it meant nothing to Bella. Finally, the woman waved her hand at Bella, as if she wanted her to leave, and returned to her work. When Bella did not move, the woman came out from behind the high desk, and took Bella by the arm and thrust her out the door.

Bella sat on the curb and cried. She was afraid to go home, where the servant girl would mock her, or worse. She was afraid to go to Poppa's shop, because she was not allowed to go there unless Momma took her. She stayed on the curb, lifting one foot, then the other, for her feet hurt in the stiff new boots. She watched the trolleys, the great drays that sometimes passed, the iceman's wagon.

She was hungry. She stayed until the school doors burst open and the children sprang out like peas ejected from a BB gun, and ran in all directions shouting, teasing, laughing. She stood up and turned around and looked at them. Why were they better than she was? Why were they allowed in the school and she not? She felt near tears again, but did not want to cry in front of them. She waited until most of the children were gone, and then set off toward home.

Her body was stiff with terror. What would Momma and Poppa say about her when they found out the school didn't want her back, a school that took all the other children, even those from their block for she'd seen Jan Szcepanski and Myron Goldstein running past her on their way home. But if they didn't find out, what would she do then? Would she have to come here every day and sit on the curb? Suppose it rained? Or snowed?

She remained tense and stiff as she entered the house, but only the servant girl was there, and she said nothing. And when Momma came home early to nurse the baby, she was busy, and then she had to get dinner. Bella stayed out of the way, on the floor behind the bed, staring at the grain of the wood floor. And then, when Poppa came, Bella shuddered, but he said nothing either, not even when they all sat down to dinner. Maybe they would never find out.

But then, after dinner, it was Eddie who brought it up – oh, Eddie! her face pleaded with him, but he did not stop. He asked her who her teacher was and if she was in that ugly corner room that got so hot and had paint peeling from the ceiling in big flakes that drifted down and settled on your head making everybody laugh and point at you.

Bella couldn't speak, but Eddie kept it up. Finally, he pointed to her, laughing, 'Cat got your tongue? I bet you didn't even *go* to school, scaredy-cat! I bet you were too scared!'

'I did! I did!' she protested, her face hot in splotches.

'Then what's your teacher's name?'

Bella burst into tears.

By this time, Momma and Poppa were paying attention, and they listened when Bella, sobbing and sniffling, told how she'd been expelled from school before she even entered. Poppa was angry, but not with her. She would go again tomorrow, they decided, but Momma would go with her.

The next day, she put on her new dress, which was wrinkled and dirty from sitting on the curb, and the stiff new boots and the new eyeglasses, and went with Momma back to the office of the terrible woman. And Momma talked to the woman in the same kind of words the woman used, and the woman made a face at Bella and looked at Momma as if she were dirty – although Momma had worn her hat, her black hat with the veil, that Bella loved. The woman pushed a piece of paper at Momma and Momma wrote things on it. Then the woman took Bella into the hall and down a long corridor with doors in it, and opened one of the doors and said something incomprehensible to Bella and took her in and whispered to a lady who was standing in front of lots of other children Bella's size who were sitting at little desks.

Bella's heart leaped. Would *she* be allowed to sit at a little desk like that and write on paper with a pen, the way they were doing? Bella had never held a pen. The terrible woman went out and the lady – she must be the teacher, Bella wanted to know her name, suppose Eddie asked her! – said something to Bella. But Bella just stood there. So the lady came to Bella and took her hand and led her to a little desk. Bella slid into the seat and smiled a dazzled, grateful, happy smile at the lady. And the lady spoke to her, kindly, to her, Bella, right in front of all the children! Bella stopped smiling, and lines of anxiety formed on her forehead. Would it be like this all the time? The teacher had stopped speaking; she sighed and her shoulders drooped, and she went to the big desk in front of the room and came back to Bella and put a piece of paper and a pen on Bella's desk. Bella understood that she was supposed to have her own pen and paper, and was humiliated. She knew the other children thought she was so poor she could not afford pen and paper. The teacher poked open the lid of the inkwell and showed Bella how to dip a pen in it, and how to hold the pen to write. But when Bella tried it, she made a big blot. The teacher sighed again, marched to the desk, and slammed a blotter down. Then she returned to the front of the class and said something. Bella heard her own name – Isabella Brez. That was all she understood.

Her heart was squeezed tight. She could hear the word 'stupid, stupid' running through her brain, and knew that was what they all thought – the teacher and the terrible woman and all the children. And she *was* stupid. That was why she could not understand their words. They all understood each other, even Alicija from the next block, who was sitting in the first row giggling behind her hand and glancing at Bella. But she would not cry. She would try to conceal her stupidity, so that people would not laugh at her. She practiced with her pen.

She watched the other children following the teacher's directions, and she did whatever they did. Even in kindergarten, they taught words to this potpourri of children from different backgrounds. and Bella copied meaningless words from the blackboard: BOY GIRL DOG CAT. In time, she came to understand what these words meant, but she could not put them in a sentence.

She went home that day and sat quietly waiting until Momma arrived. Then Bella told her she had to have a pen, a tablet, and a blotter. Momma said she had no money. Bella threw a tantrum. So astonishing was this to Momma that she left the house and walked back to the shop and got a nickel from Poppa and returned and gave it to Bella. With a shaky pride – only partly believing she had accomplished this – Bella walked to the stationery store on the corner clutching her nickel, directed the purchase of the tools of her education, and with great dignity, returned home.

She did not do well in school, but somehow, she passed. She was impeded by the fact that she did not hear everything that was being said, and did not know she was not hearing everything. But she admired – oh, she admired! – the children who had 100 written on the top of their test papers, or even 85. She fell into her usual pattern of behavior: quiet, docile, obedient, and somewhat abstracted.

(Stupid, stupid!) She was promoted, from first to second, second to third. But by then everything had changed.

My sophisticated mother blows smoke across the room. 'Oh, I was so stupid. I was so stupid I was left back in the third grade.'

four

My mother's mother's name was Frances Byzchkowska. She was the daughter of a storekeeper in Zmegrud, a tiny village in the Carpathian Mountains. Her friend Dafna Pasek was a distant cousin – most people in this village were somehow related – who would be the mother of my father. Frances was not a peasant. It was important that Bella understand that neither of her parents was a peasant. Frances went to a church school, and was taught to read and write in Latin; she could speak German, the language of the invader, the only language permitted in public forums. At home, she spoke and learned to read and write in Polish.

Why did she leave? For it must have been a terrifying journey for a girl of thirteen who had never even been to Kraków – all the way to Bremen, alone; buying her passage with the money Aunt Sophie had sent her from America, traveling steerage in the immigrant ship, locked in the bottommost deck with hundreds of others, some sick, babies crying, no privacy. And then the horror of Ellis Island, being treated like some subhuman creature by self-satisfied grey men important over their pens, their ledgers, their stamp pads. Maybe Aunt Sophie met her. I am writing that Aunt Sophie met her, because I can't bear it to have been any other way.

So she went to Aunt Sophie's and slept on a cot near the wood stove in the kitchen, and got a job as a servant girl in a Jewish family. She was abused, overworked, and underpaid: she developed a strain of anti-Semitism. Perhaps she had brought it with her. But she never built upon it. She saved all her money and sent it back to Poland, for passage for her two younger sisters. Why did they want to come?

Because, by then, they all must have known what it was like here. Sophie first, then Frances: the hard conditions, the strangeness, the near slavery, the awful poverty — families of twelve living in two rooms. So, one can only conclude it was worse at home. The country was partitioned. Polish culture was proscribed. Did they come here to speak Polish freely? My mother says they came for work. Frances worked hard. She moved up, to work in a sweatshop over a sewing machine. She learned to speak English, to read it and even to write it. She learned her way through the maze of Brooklyn, the red tape of American institutions. I like the thought of her then, she isn't a weight on me. She was slight, slender, sprightly; she edged her way past obstacles, she used charm. Perhaps she had intimations of Poland's future, accurate ones, for she survived and those left behind did not.

I needed to know . . . something. So, in 1975 I went to Poland. I had only a little money, because I went without an assignment, hoping I'd find some pictures that would interest somebody. Poland was hardly in the news then. I thought my small budget would be enough, because Poland is poor; I thought I'd get by, as I had in Greece, on three dollars a day. But I was totally ignorant about socialist governments, who set a currency rate and force you to prove you've bought money legally. The exchange rate they gave Americans was fifteen złotys a dollar, while the black-market rate was ninety. My trip to Poland was the most expensive I'd ever taken, even though I did not stay in hotels. I came back dead broke and exhausted.

Because I also did not understand that there would not be little hostels, pensione, whatever, for someone like me, that you had to have a hotel reservation for the exact length of your stay in each place, arrive and depart on precisely the date you had stipulated on your visa application. And hotels were booked a year ahead, because there were so few of them. A charming little sandwich seller who spoke to me on the train from Paris to Warsaw hit his cheek with his hand when he heard me say I expected to move around with my backpack and cameras, finding beds, meals, camaraderie wherever I went. He was French, but his parents worked in the French embassy in Warsaw, so he spoke Polish, as well as English. He spent the next hours trying to do something for me. Within an hour, everyone on the train knew about me, and came into my compartment to speak to me. Many brought their children, who were learning English at school and who could, they thought, speak it. People offered me fruit they had stowed away in Paris against the coming dearth – although I didn't know that then, and took an orange. The sandwich seller gave me his entire leftover stock at the end of his tour – two sandwiches and a small bottle of wine. For I hadn't anticipated there being no food on a twenty-four-hour train ride. He also found someone who offered to take me home – a retired judge named Anna Kosakievitch, who was a little older than I, and as shocked as everyone else at my situation.

Anna did not speak English or French, nor did anyone else on the train. Polish, a little Russian, considerable German: the irony of invasion. The train moved forward very slowly, and for an hour or more, ran backwards. I couldn't help thinking of all the Polish jokes I'd bristled at in the past. There was no water on the train, which meant that the toilet, after twenty-six hours of travel, was stuffed with soda cans, fruit cores, chicken bones, kielbasa string, and human shit, much of it mine – I was still sick from some mussels I'd eaten in Normandy. Despite all this, the train was noisy and cheerful until we crossed the border into East Germany, when silence and mean-faced guards with huge dogs descended upon us. There was a sigh as we crossed the border into Poland – of sorrow or relief or both I couldn't tell. Then there was absolute silence. A woman sitting opposite me – the compartment had filled up over the hours – leaned forward, poked the book I was reading and pointed to my suitcase. It took me a few minutes to understand her. I was reading Shulamith Firestone's *The Dialectic of Sex*, and she had understood one word of the title. She waved her hand to let me know such a subject was forbidden in Poland. I buried the book among others and, laughing to myself, pulled out Henry Miller's *Tropic of Capricorn*. But I had no trouble with immigration, only with the moneyman who came with a black suitcase and refused to give me złotys because my visa said I would remain in Poland for three to four weeks. That, he said, was imprecise and therefore forbidden. I argued that the visa had been granted with that condition. He closed his mouth and his suitcase. I shouted. The people around me were hushed and terrified, and put gentle hands on my arm. I continued to shout: I had paid for that money, I said, and I wanted it! I had no Polish money even to pay for a cab from the train station! He owed me those złotys, having taken my dollars. I could feel the trembling of the bodies seated near me, but I knew my man. He gave me the money.

As it turned out, I didn't need it. Anna was met at the terminal by all her friends – Keren, Marie, Krystyna, and Marie's husband Stanislaw, who brought his car – and they gathered me up along with her and took me to her house. Stanislaw was yelling, arguing, but the women ignored him. They took me to Anna's nicely furnished two-room apartment; I was black from the soot of the journey: they undressed me, and drew a bath. They took my clothes and put them in a little hand-run washing machine, and hung them up neatly to dry. Stanislaw was still yelling, but when I was clean and dressed, I opened a liter of scotch and put it on the table. His roaring settled down to an amiable growl, and the women and he and I all sat around Anna's table drinking – none of us able to communicate easily in any language whatever.

I stayed with Anna for two weeks. I saw her many scars, and heard about her operations. We spoke with a combination of sign language and a French-Polish dictionary. She took me around Warsaw and she and her friends told me about the tragedies of their lives – and all had, indeed, been tragic. Then I went off on a train to Kraków, with their anxiety hovering around me. They had managed, by pulling strings, to get me a hotel in Kraków, but only for two nights. What would happen to me then? They insisted that I write, but how? I said I would write 'Je suis bien,' and they could look up the words in the French-Polish dictionary. But on the train I met another instant friend, a beautiful, elegant young man named Adam, who took me home to his parents' house. They were conveniently away on a trip. Then Adam and his friends set about trying to find the particular Zmegrud of my grandmothers. There are many Zmegruds in Poland, but I knew this one was near Kraków.

After some days, they found a map that showed it. We spent a day standing in line to buy railroad tickets for Zmegrud, and another standing in line at a bank, so I could buy money. Then we went, early in the morning, six o'clock, by trolley, trolley, and a train. Zmegrud is less than a hundred miles from Kraków, but it took nearly four hours, standing all the way, to reach it. We had a coffee in the train station, a filthy place with little to eat – like other shops in Poland – and wandered around the town. There were a couple of nearly empty shops and a church. We tried to find the priest, but the church was locked and no one answered at the parish house door. Adam asked around for the road to Zmegrud, and we set off.

It was a beautiful August day, the pale land flat and green around us, few houses and no people in sight. We walked along a broad dirt road at an easy pace, conversing in the stilted way people do when one of them has learned a language from text books and language classes. Adam spoke English but I was never sure he understood what I said. Still, I jabbered, happy to be able to speak after my long near-silence. We were lovers, at my initiation, and happy.

Then, from a side road hidden by high wheat fields, a man emerged. I was old enough to realize that he was very young, probably only in his early twenties. But I paused when I saw him, and he stopped dead and his mouth opened as he stared at me. He was very tan and as wrinkled as newly washed linen. He had few teeth. His eyes were pale blue and empty. And he looked at me as if I were of another species, the way we might look at a six-foot-five Sikh in Manhattan, complete with red fitted jacket, white sash, scimitar and turban. I was forty-five, and the best-looking I'd ever been; I was thin, too. I was wearing a pale blue soft safari suit that I often took on hard journeys, a cheap straw hat with a stylish brim, and sunglasses, and I carried my heavy bag of camera equipment over my shoulder. But his expression suggested I was a goddess offering him a visitation.

And I thought: so that is what a peasant is. Or anyway, what *peasant* meant to my grandmother. Subhuman. The man may have been intelligent enough – he certainly knew crops and weather, animal husbandry – things I didn't know. But intelligence didn't appear on his gaping face; I could not imagine him speaking. He was a creature immured in blue sky, the wind, wheat fields, shaky wood-fenced yards full of dung. Circumscribed within nature, and benighted, benighted. I was shocked by him. I was shocked that the word *subhuman* crossed my mind. So this is what they meant, the old ones, when they talked of peasants.

The moment passed. He crossed the road and we walked on ahead of him. We didn't look back. We arrived at Zmegrud and wandered its two streets, looked at the few houses, the one closed shop, the church, also locked. But by asking, Adam discovered a man who claimed Dafna Pasek was his mother's mother's cousin. He took us home, where his wife and sons welcomed us like visiting royalty. They gave us a meal I could barely eat because the parents stayed in the kitchen, and I knew Adam and I were eating their portion. The sons – four of them – had been educated under the socialist government and were all professional men. Only three were there: the fourth, the pride of his mother, was a papal functionary stationed in Rome. The centerpiece of her room was a gift from him, a small model of the Vatican that could be plugged into a wall socket, and lighted up. They listened to my tale, through Adam.

They told us we were not really in Zmegrud. The old Zmegrud had been several miles down the road. But we had no way to get there and there was no reason to go there, they said, for there was nothing there. Zmegrud had been a Jewish town. I don't know if it was a Jewish town when my grandmothers lived there, or if it was mixed then, or if it became a Jewish town in the decades after they left. But it was a Jewish town when the Nazis came. The Nazis collected all the people of Zmegrud from their houses and marched them to a valley deep in the mountains. Standing behind the two hundred or so people – children, women, men – the Nazis forced them to dig a hole. Then they shot them so they fell into the hole. It is said that some were not dead when the lower-ranking Nazi soldiers filled up the hole with dirt and poured lime over it – lime speeds decomposition. But no one knows for sure.

What everyone knows and still remembers is the explosion that occurred a few days later. The lime, they said: there was too much, or it bubbled too much. The explosion blew up the burial pit, sending bits of limbs across the countryside for miles around. Children wandering in the mountains would come across a hand or a bit of leg. One found half a head, with an ear. Pieces of human bodies littered the mountains and the villages. The old folks have returned to the main room, where we are eating, to tell this story. Their faces are white and drawn, even now, thirty years later. Their voices have the tense hush of people who speak the unspeakable.

I hold myself in restraint, knowing the continuing anti-Semitism of Poles. But the horror in the faces of the old folk is not moderated by relief at the fact that the feet and hands were Jewish feet and hands. The old folks are probably not much older than I, although they would not believe that. They were only children when the Nazis came. But their parents may not have opposed the Nazi plan to solve finally the problem presented to Christians by the existence of Jews. Still, a foot hurled miles, landing at your front door, with one toe missing, and the heel bashed in from the impact of landing at such velocity – well, that would be a joke if you did not have to think about the people who arranged the situation that caused this joke. The breathlessness, the pale drawn faces, the hushed voices arose from remembering that this thing was done by people, by humans. Of the same race as oneself: the human race.

The Nazis killed one third of the population of Poland and ninety-nine per cent of its livestock; they burned Warsaw to the ground, and destroyed other cities before they left. All that is left of them now is the prison they used to interrogate and hold people in the center of Warsaw. It has been left as it was: the Poles understand monuments. The Jewish ghetto has been covered over with grass and concrete, and holds a park in which parents wheel their infants in carriages, and children play. They are not Jewish children.

five

The people of Zmegrud were annihilated in the fall of 1943; in May of that year, my grandmother died. So it makes no sense to talk about survival. The others were dead long before that: Dafna Pasek in 1937; her husband, my father's father Stefan Dabrowski, in 1939, the year Hitler set out on his triumphal project designed to ensure the supremacy of the Third Reich for a thousand years. Michael Brez intended to return to Poland in 1914 and settle down to be a gentleman – his true profession. Unfortunately, he died the year before. Or perhaps that wasn't unfortunate, given what happened in 1914.

The only photograph of Frances as a young woman is her wedding picture. She has a round placid face; my own resembles it a little, except the placidity got lost over the generations. She is small and delicate and beautifully dressed, but she seems stiff beside her taller, thinner, arrogant young husband. He has something fierce in his aspect that reminds me of myself. And he loved to drink and laugh, to enjoy himself, something I also identify with.

But the next photograph is shocking. They are older: three of their children appear in it with them, so it must have been taken about 1907, perhaps just after Frances lost her fourth child, which was born dead. Wally looks to be near two. And that arrogant man has become pure tyrant: his chin and mouth are set and thick, his eyes glare outward as if what he saw before him day by day was outrageously unworthy of his glance. And Frances! How can it be I never saw this before? She is a little thicker, a little older, but only about twenty-six, after all. It is a side of my grandmother I never saw or imagined. For there are lines of anxiety in her forehead and her mouth has a hard set. She looks enraged, fixed in anger.

Still, I guess there are worse things than anger, because

the next pictures I have of her show her old, worn, defeated. She is only in her forties and fifties, but her body has become shapeless, her hair thin and grey and pulled back in a little bun at the nape of her neck. She wears cheap cotton housedresses and she smiles, but there is no life in her face. Whatever spirit she had is gone.

Not my mother's though. It is in the pictures of her as a child that defeat and terror dominate. Her old face is disappointed and angry, but not defeated, and in between, well, there she is, a young flapper, hamming it up for the camera, posed coyly with one well-shod foot on the running board of my father's first car, an Olds V-8 or, hair streaming, arm in arm with Miss Poland of 1927, in a bathing suit.

Perhaps it is in my genes, the way I feel now. My grandmother was a fucking saint, and I'm turning into one too. Renunciation: it's not a fate I admire. But it is inevitable when there is nothing you can have that can ease your pain, you stop wanting anything. For my mother, for my grandmother, the moment when wanting stopped was the same: May 26, 1913. On that day, my grandmother was widowed, and she and my mother began their sojourn in hell. My mother says, 'My father died when I was nine years old,' as if she had not told me that hundreds of times before. She utters the statement with a tragic import – like someone saying a loved one was living in Hiroshima in the summer of 1945 – as if she is saying the world ended then. As hers did.

Chapter III

one

When the kids and I first moved into Pane Nowak's house on Powell Avenue, my mother came to help me move in. She unwrapped dishes from newspaper and washed them, dried them, piled them on the counters until I had papered the shelves where they would stand; she hung clothes in closets. She was sponging off my few china knickknacks while Arden and I unpacked our bathroom supplies and tried to squeeze them in the medicine chest. Arden spotted a thing hanging from a hook beside the bathroom door.

'What's that, Mommy?'

I peered. It was leather, a strap of some sort, about two inches wide and fourteen or so inches long. 'I don't know. Maybe it's a razor strop. The former tenants must have left it behind. We can throw it out,' I suggested.

'Oh, no! It's beautiful!' Arden breathed. It was the carving she liked. The entire surface had been decorated.

'Okay,' I said absently, and forgot it.

It was hours later when my mother came staggering down the hall (I could hear she was upset by her walk) into the kitchen, where I was lining the shelves, sitting on a counter, contorted around a cabinet, trying to get the damned paper to fit.

'Anastasia!' she cried, and I turned and saw her white face. 'What is that thing in the bathroom?'

I stared at her. Then understood. 'It's a razor strop, I think, Mom.'

'Why do you have it!'

I shrugged. 'It was here. Left behind. Arden likes it. She thinks it's pretty.'

She stared at me, incredulous, angry, but said nothing. I imagined her refusing to use the bathroom, and considered throwing the thing away. But Arden liked it, and Arden had to come first for me, even though I understood.

Business was going well for Michael Brez and in the fall of 1910, soon after Isabella entered first grade, he moved his family a few blocks, to Nostrand Avenue in Brooklyn. The new apartment was also a railroad flat, but the living room was a little bigger and they had a kitchen all to themselves. There were some new pieces of furniture in the living room, carved wood with mother-of-pearl inlays. Bella would tiptoe into the room when the servant girl wasn't looking and run her fingers over the smooth cool nacre, tracing the patterns of its colors. There were new lace curtains at

59

the window, but Bella rarely stood inside their comforting obscurity. She was a big girl now, she went to school.

She went every day, and dutifully copied what the other children were doing, but when she left, she tried to push the thought of school out of her mind. She never did homework; she didn't know such a thing existed. But she did know that she was stupid, and that the teacher and the children knew she was stupid, and sometimes she thought they made fun of her. The thing was they didn't know *how* stupid she was, for she was able to copy them. They didn't know she had no understanding at all of what she was copying. She longed for a friend, and whenever Momma gave her a penny, she would buy candy and take it to school with her to share it with some girl or other, just so they would talk to her. Then they did, but only as long as the candy lasted. They didn't like her because she was stupid.

She wasn't good at anything. She couldn't even cry. Whenever one of the children cried, Poppa would laugh and hoot at them: 'Louder! Louder! Cry louder! What about the rest of you? Whoever cries the loudest will get a nickel.' And all the children would yell and screech, and Bella would too, but she only won once. Only one thing could she do, and that was to get to the couch before the others, and nestle in her corner. There wasn't room for all four of them, and the one who got there last had to sit on the floor. Usually Eddie was the one left out, but he didn't care. And he was hardly ever home anyway. After school, Eddie and Wally would go out and play, every day. Eddie went to the playground, and Wally played ball against the wall of the corner stationery store. She was glad they had moved, because the new stationery store was Pane Kowalski's and she had a boy of four, just like Wally, and she let them play there. Sometimes Bella could find a little girl to jump rope with, but most days, she just went home. The servant girl was always snapping at her for hanging around the kitchen, so Bella would go to her room and sit on the floor staring out the window at the sooty brick buildings, the fire escapes and laundry lines that faced it. She would think about Anastasia and where she was and what she was doing. She wondered what Anastasia got for Christmas, which Momma said was coming soon. Bella liked Christmas. There were always lots of people around, and they put a tree right in the living room, with little candles flickering on it. Momma would light the gas lamps and they would all sit in the living room and look at it. Last Christmas, Bella had received a present, no, three presents: a blue dress that Momma made with a beautiful dark blue satin sash; and hair ribbons to match it; and a new set of underwear. She wondered what she would get this Christmas.

It was nice when people came. Then Momma smiled, and laughed, and talked, going round to everyone with plates of hard-boiled eggs and chruściki and sliced kielbasa with beets and horseradish, and everyone smiled at Momma and told her how good she was and what a fine cook. And Poppa was happy, he was laughing and talking. Poppa was always talking. He talked about things Bella didn't understand, about President Taft and Theodore Roosevelt and Boss Murphy, who lived in Tammany Hall. She tried to picture what kind of house that must be, to be called a hall – could you have a long narrow house? And Poppa explained to his ignorant friends about the Right Brothers, and something called radio. Bella wondered dimly how Poppa knew so much. Momma didn't know about these things. Bella gazed at her father in awe.

Sometimes the grown-ups would sit at the big round table under the fringed gas lamp playing cards, pinochle, late into the night, and drinking and talking and laughing. And sometimes, when Poppa began to talk about things he knew about, he would pound the table with his fist so hard the glasses trembled. Then she trembled too, remembering something she had forgotten, but she knew the others knew it, because they would all nod their heads at Poppa and say, 'Yes, Michał, you are right, certainly. That is true.' Just the way Momma used to. Momma didn't do that anymore. Poppa was a big man, but Bella didn't like to think about him.

Momma didn't speak much, but she didn't care if they were in the room. Many times she would pick up little

Euga and sit her on her lap and say my dear, '*Moja kochany*,' and kiss her. And if Bella slipped onto the couch when there was company, and Poppa didn't notice, Momma would pretend she didn't see her either. And when she was walking around serving people, she would sometimes slip Bella a chruściki or a piece of strudel behind her back so Poppa wouldn't see. Sometimes, when Poppa wasn't around and Momma was baking and cooking, she would mutter to herself about his peasant friends.

Momma baked and cooked all the time even when they didn't have company, late into the night. When they didn't have company, Poppa didn't come home. Momma said he was bowling, and Bella's mind darted to a bowl she wanted to forget. She pushed away the pictures that invaded her mind, of Poppa hurling bowls of food at walls. She didn't understand why he wanted to do that. But she knew she was stupid. When Poppa didn't come home, Bella would sit in the kitchen watching Momma bake great roasts of meat, or stir a huge pot of soup. It smelled so good she wanted some, but Momma always said she had to wait until tomorrow. Sometimes Bella would wake in the night and smell the delicious aroma of babka or pie, and would hop up and creep down the hall to make sure Poppa wasn't there, and then run into the kitchen. Momma would give her a chruściki as soon as they were cool; or let her lick the custard left in the bowl after she'd made a lemon meringue pie.

But some nights, after she'd returned to bed, she was awakened by loud noises – a stumbling on the steps, a banging on a door, or a slam. Then she heard cursing, and sometimes Poppa and Momma would talk very loud, sometimes they'd even shout. After months of this, she came to recognize what was happening, and understood that when noises got softer it meant that Momma had closed the kitchen door. But she could still hear a low mumble, still recognize without acknowledging it, the anger. It terrified her, and she would lie rigid in her bed, waiting. She did not think about what she was waiting for.

Then, one night, it happened again. The noises, the curses, the shouting, and then a soft cry, then a louder one, then a great cry, then sobbing. Her heart stopped, she wanted to leap up and run to Momma, to help her, to tell her not to cry, to make her stop. But she was too frightened; she just went on lying there, her body stiff, her eyes wide and unblinking. And as she lay there, a hot fluid poured around her heart that made her want to leap up and scream, or maybe instead, to die, because that fluid was telling her that she was small and weak and sickly and stupid, and that there was nothing she could do about what was happening even if she did get up. Nothing. She was helpless, and she hated hated hated Momma for doing this to her, for humiliating her, forcing her to recognize that she was nothing.

Eventually, the kitchen door opened. Momma was crying softly now, and she could hear Poppa's heavy unsure step tramping down the hall past her room. She stiffened herself even more and squeezed her eyes shut, but he didn't open the door. She heard him go into his bedroom. After a long time, she heard Momma go past slowly, as if she was tired. Bella lifted her head then to peer at Euga, but the baby was still sound asleep. The next day, Bella was careful not to look at her mother's face.

Then something else began to happen, something worse, so bad she could not think about it all. The noise was terrible and she would lie there trembling and rigid at once. She would try to put the pillow over her right ear so she could not hear, but the noise came through anyway. She would always glance at Euga, but the child always slept. Bella wondered how Euga could sleep through such sounds. But this happened only once in a while. Still, she never knew which it would be that night, when Poppa was out late: the noise, the noise and the crying, or the other.

One night when Poppa was out late and Bella had fallen asleep, she was awakened by hearing Momma's light step running down the hall past her room. She got up and opened the door a crack, then wider. Momma was in the boys' room and she was screaming softly, almost crying, telling them to get up, get up, quickly. Bella peered toward the kitchen: the light was on, but there were no sounds from it. She stepped into the hall just as Wally, his hair all tousled, his eyes half-shut, stepped into the hall. Behind him Eddie stood, eyes wide and alarmed, as Momma pushed them from behind. She grabbed Wally by the arm and pulled him toward their one closet, which she opened. She pulled open the white laundry bag that lay on the floor, half-full of dirty clothes, and nodded to Wally to step inside it. She helped him, because he could barely see to do it himself. Then she pulled the string at the top and pushed him swiftly inside the closet, under the bottom shelf. Then she looked around wildly, and Bella drew back, expecting to be reprimanded for standing there. But Momma didn't even see her. She pushed Eddie toward the girls' room, and pointed to the corner, where their clothes were lying in a heap. He ran to the corner and crouched down, pulling the clothes over him. Momma arranged them so they covered him. Bella could hear her breathing loud and fast. Then Momma saw her and hissed, 'Get back in bed,' and ran out, closing the door. Already, before Eddie had been concealed, Bella had heard the stumbling step on the stairs. Poppa was at the door before Momma could get back in the kitchen, but she might have been there before he got it open.

Then the usual noises began, the shouting and cursing, and then he stormed down the hall, and Bella breathed a little, thinking this might be one of the nights he just went to sleep. But no: she heard him in the bathroom, and it was not for doing that (at night he forgot to close the bathroom door, something he'd never do in the daytime), it was the other, he went to get it, and then he slammed open the door to the boys' room, and a moment later yelled, 'Where are they? What have you done with them?' and tramped back to the kitchen and began yelling at Momma. And the kitchen door was open and Bella could hear Momma saying, 'Go to sleep, Michał, you're tired, you had too much to drink,' and Poppa roaring, 'The little bastards, I'll show them, where are they, what have you done with them?' and the slapping noise as he hit it against the door-frame, and Momma weeping, but still saying, 'Go to bed, Michał,' and the slapping noise again, and then silence, and then he staggered back down the hall and threw up in the bathroom and then the long stream while he did that with the door open, and then he staggered toward the bedroom.

It was quiet. Bella let her body go a little, still listening. She heard Momma's soft step in the kitchen, and pans rattling, as Momma put things away. She waited until Momma had passed her door, slowly, heavily for her, walking toward the bedroom. She waited and waited. Then, after everything had been quiet for a long time, the pile of rags in the corner moved, and noiselessly, Eddie pulled himself out from under them. He stood up and crept to the door and opened it. Everything was dark. Bella watched him, and after he had closed her door, she got up and ran to it silently, and opened it a little. He was at the closet, holding the laundry bag in his arms, pulling it from the cramped space under the shelves. He loosened the string, and whispered into it. Wally came out, slowly, and Eddie retied the bag and put it back in the closet. He put his hand on Wally's little shoulder and guided him toward their bedroom. She heard the door shut, very softly. She stood there. She stood for what felt like a long time. Then she crept across the hall toward the bathroom, and tried to see in the darkness. The only light came from a transom high up over the bathtub and that faced another building, so the light was faint. Still, she could make out Poppa's razor strop lying on the bathroom floor.

two

What am I to make of this Michael Brez?

Whenever she spoke of him, whenever she told me stories about when she was little ('and what was your mommy like? and your daddy?'), she depicted her father as a monster, a terrifying incomprehensible vehicle of violence and cruelty. But always, something else would slip in, and I would garner these other things, hoard them, amass them toward some final understanding. What slipped in was he spoke seven languages; sometimes, it was that he was big, important, successful. She sounded proud when she talked about his fine shop. She always said, 'Momma', and 'My father'. Her tales were always black and white – no, not exactly. 'Momma' was always a saint, the complete victim, and 'my father' was always cruel and violent, but the undertones held something red, something proud and fierce, like the line around the sun that seems sometimes to encompass it and sometimes to be something the blinding sun is blanking out. I was adult before I could understand it with my mind, although it was long since engraved on my psyche: he was admirable because he was intelligent and successful; he had power. Admirable evil, he represented, while poor 'Momma' was virtue unrewarded. I felt all that.

I was adult before I began to think of him as a person, rather than as an incarnation of evil. I had never seen a picture of him until I was adult, married myself, going through a yellowed box of even more yellowed photographs. And there he was, with her.

No one even knows his real name. He entered the United States on a Hungarian passport in the name of Michael Sczyunz, which seems to be neither Polish nor Hungarian. But there is no question that he was Polish by birth. Probably, he could not find work in partitioned Poland, and like thousands of others, emigrated to the Austro-Hungarian Empire, which owned one-third of his native state. But did he go alone? Where were his parents? Did he write to them? Where did they live? And when did he go? He was apprenticed as a tailor: who knows how, stranger that he was. Perhaps there were many Poles in Hungary, willing to work in their sweatshops for below-standard wages. His passport says he was born in 1875, and he arrived in America in 1900: so he was young when he went to Hungary and learned what he learned. Seven languages: Polish, German, Russian, Magyar, Lithuanian, Yiddish, English: did he learn them in Poland and Hungary? Because by the time he went to Germany, he spoke like a native, and when he came to America, he adopted a German-sounding name, Brez.

He married Frances in 1901 and their first child, Edmund, was born in 1902. By the time the next one, Isabella, arrived in 1904, he already had the fancy shop, the staff of employees, the swallow-tailed coat and striped trousers. How did he manage that, this twenty-nine-year-old immigrant?

His face in the wedding picture is fine and sensitive, even noble. He is handsome and proud, with a certain fierceness of eye that makes me think of the Polish cavaliers who charged Hitler's tanks on their horses. Crazy pride, the kind of self-image so consuming as to lead men – and nations – to suicidal acts of bravado. Still, I like his face. The fierceness in his eyes rests in the back of my mind along with the fierceness I feel: hidden, but hot. He has something of the same quality my mother's face shows in early pictures – otherworldly, romantic, ethereal. But where her face advertises an absence, expresses a removal caused by yearning, the yearning itself doesn't show – the eyes are blank, the expression nullified; his, on the other hand, shows all that romance in service to some drive, some ideal. It is present, and vital.

By the next picture, however, the ideal has blown up, and all that is left is an aimless fire. It was taken in his shop and shows him surrounded by his salesmen, who are attired almost as elegantly as he. But his clothes do not suit him now. Here he's a stereotype, an angry man, thick and cruel, a redneck sheriff, a sergeant in the army, any army, a tough, a bully. He radiates complacency, knowledge of rightness, the sense that one is part of an institution so powerful it can confer legitimacy on all one's deeds, no matter how despicable they are. My grandmother does not appear in this picture, although she worked hard in that shop throughout his life. Like the wife of the Chinese rice-cake maker, she was relegated to the back room, behind the curtain that separates the legitimate from the illegitimate, the user from the used.

This picture was probably taken around the time my mother was born, because the next one, in which the three older children appear, could not have been later than 1907, and in that one he is far fatter, and his face has undergone further change. It is the face of a tyrant, a bully, and the eyes stare out madly even as the chin juts over the full-fleshed neck and broad-fronted body. He is the full pater-familias, except he lacks a beard. He looks insane.

Yet he had accomplished what he wanted to accomplish: he had a successful business, his wife was a slave to him at home and at work, and did her slaving well. He had three utterly intimidated children and a set of friends who deferred to his every opinion. Isn't that what he wanted? Did he think, when he set out to gain these things, that they would make him invulnerable, secure, on top of the heap of seamy humanity?

That he would want to get involved with other women is – to me at least – understandable. My grandmother may well have been worn out by childbearing: after Edmund and Isabella, she had Wallace in 1906, a stillbirth in 1907, and Eugenia in 1908. But even if they had had birth control, even if Frances showed no reluctance to make love, when the juices are running strong, it seems sinful not to let them run their course. It seems a waste of youth and vigor, a damming up of what should run free. But why did he have to hurt Frances, to act so that she would know what he was doing, and to use her miserably at the same time? Wasn't her servility enough? Or was he driven not by admirable heats of lust but by a need to prove himself to be . . . something. There are lots of men like that, and I know a bit about that myself.

And what drove him to become a drunkard? Oh, well, wine, women, and song, I know about that too. I remember playing a Strauss waltz by that name on the piano when I was eight, and catching from its lilt the world it expressed. I wanted to be in that world, but the title informed me it was for men only. Until I saw a movie of an operetta called *The Merry Widow*, about a gorgeous woman with a high-piled white wig, wearing a strapless black lace gown and holding a black mask over her eyes as she whirled glori-ously, her hooped skirts swinging out, in a room full of men. And then I wanted to be her, too, but I didn't know how to go about it.

In time, of course, I found my way into that world – well, one of booze, people, and song, anyway. I am pleased that I did, and regret none of it. But an evening of drinking and singing is a prelude to a few days of abstinence, if you want to get any work done. And there is as much pleasure in the work as in the play, so one balances them. But not Michael. Why? What did he want from life that he could not then have achieved, if he had known what to want? By 1907, he was a tyrant. My mother would say, 'My father sat at the head of the table.' It was a long time before I realized that round tables have no head, that wherever he sat became the head. Maybe he hated what he had become and did not know what else he could have become. Maybe he felt isolated in his eminence, lonely, without any way to bridge his loneliness. I don't know. I'll never know.

But the question of Michael is not academic for me, for of all my forebears he is the one I feel closest to, most like: Michael, the proud mad one. Is it possible that what drove him drives me?

three

Bella was eight when her parents changed. They didn't entertain so often, although Michael still stayed out most nights, and there was a kind of weight and worry in the house, a brooding silence that pinched Momma's forehead and made Poppa's mouth tense and hard. They had moved again, to Myrtle Avenue, to an apartment with smaller rooms. Business was bad – there had been a depression – and everywhere there were strikes, especially in the textile industry. And then there had been a terrible fire that had killed many women, in a Triangle, Bella thought, unsure what a Triangle was. Little as she understood of the little that was spoken before the children, Bella knew business was bad. She had no idea what that meant, but it comforted her that there was some reason for the way her parents were acting, a reason unconnected to her or the other children, or to her parents themselves.

The way she spent her nights left Bella exhausted in the days, and often when she came home from school, she would fall on her bed and sleep. But she developed in this time a stiff manner: her hands were always clenched into fists; when she opened them for some reason, her fingers and part of her palm were white. And she jumped at any sudden noise. These were habits she would never lose.

If Poppa still stayed out late at nights, Momma baked and cooked less now that they entertained less. Still, she would sit in the kitchen at night watching from the window for the figure approaching on the sidewalk, trying to detect whether this was a night she should hide the boys. But there were few nights like that anymore. Poppa didn't even hit Momma much anymore. So sometimes, Bella would sit beside her mother in the kitchen, the gaslight turned down so only a dim glow softened the room. But whenever the swerving or staggering figure appeared, Bella would get up and go to bed, and lie there rigid for a time, until the banging and cursing were over. She could not forget those things even though they didn't seem to happen anymore. For her, they were an intrinsic part of the night.

Momma had fallen into a deep silence. She never spoke except to send her on errands. She didn't even seem angry with Poppa anymore, and Bella never heard Momma talk about 'his women', or say, 'I suppose you were with *her*,' in the way she used to. Poppa went out with men now, Bella knew, because often one of them accompanied him to the house, walking crooked, just like Poppa, on his way to his own house – for often the man was Pan Swinka, who lived three doors down. Other times it was Father Stefan, the parish priest, whose church was three blocks away.

One night – it was soon after Christmas, a few weeks before Bella's ninth birthday, she sat with her mother in the dim golden kitchen, staring at the window. They never spoke, the mother and the daughter, only sometimes the mother would sigh a little. The kitchen still smelled of the yeast cakes Momma had baked a little while ago, the cakes sitting on the cupboard shelf under a clean white dish towel, cooling. Bella's mouth watered at the smell and she wanted to ask Momma if she could have a piece of cake, but she didn't. She knew that if Momma wanted her to have a piece she would have given it to her. The spirit that had led her to the awful act of snatching someone else's piece of bread had long since faded: Bella never asked for anything now.

From a distance she spotted two drunken figures walking arm in arm, caroming together on the sidewalk. The cobblestoned street was shiny under the gaslights, then turned to black, then shiny again at the next light. Momma saw them too, Bella knew, because her body became alert as she studied the degree of drunkenness from their walk. When Poppa was very drunk, he was not able to beat Momma and the boys (why doesn't he beat me?): he threatened, but that was all. Tonight he was very drunk. Bella got up to go to bed and was almost to the kitchen door when she heard Momma gasp lightly, almost choke. She ran back and looked out the window where Momma was staring. Down below the house, right under a gaslight, Poppa was vomiting in the street. Father Stefan stood beside him holding his fat belly and laughing. Poppa vomited and vomited. Bella stared. She looked at Momma, whose face was horrified. Then Bella ran to her room and leaped in bed, covering her eyes with her hands as if she could thereby block out the sight.

Poppa vomiting in the street! Shaming himself, humiliating himself! Her proud, arrogant father, allowing himself to be so demeaned! And right under the light! And the priest laughing! Cruel as Michael was, Bella wanted him to remain proud and noble, a big man. That way his treatment of his family seemed somehow justified, or anyway, permitted. If he was better than they, he was allowed to act so. But here he was, vomiting in public! Bella knew Momma was deeply shocked and shamed, and when she heard Momma's step in the hall, she sat straight up. Momma was going to bed before Poppa returned! She had never done that before. Bella wondered if she had turned off the gas lamp and left the apartment dark, if Poppa would fall, if he would be angry and beat them all. She remained sitting, listening for his step.

Beside her, Euga slept peacefully as the stumbling steps broke the night silence. There was no tramping tonight, just a kind of slurred sound. Poppa was a long time at the door. Maybe he couldn't find his key, maybe he'd dropped it. Eventually – it seemed an hour to Bella – she heard the sound of the door creaking open, and a stumbling shuffling step inside. Then the door slammed hard. Then silence. Bella waited and waited, but there were no more sounds. What had happened to Poppa? She wanted to get up and see, but was too frightened. Suppose he was angry? She waited, and was still waiting when she fell asleep; she waited all through her dreams.

The next day, when she got up, Momma looked grim, and Poppa was not to be seen. The bedroom door was shut. Bella did not dare to ask Momma where Poppa was, and if he had gone to bed last night – but she noticed his collar and tie, vest and jacket lying on the couch in the dining room. Momma said nothing. When Bella went down to the street on her way to her third-grade class, she tried to see without turning her head. It was there: a big puddle of disgusting yellowish green. She held her head rigid and walked on to school.

Birthdays in the family were not really celebrated, but usually Momma would make a special cake or get some candy for the event. This year, she entirely forgot Bella's birthday in January. Bella forgot it too, so it didn't matter. The situation went on the same, although it seemed Momma dragged more and Poppa was more subdued and yet even angrier. And Bella too dragged more, because she couldn't seem to do her work properly at school and she was failing all her tests. She didn't tell Momma, but each morning when she went to school, her stomach ached.

One night Poppa came in very bad; Bella could hear Momma almost dragging him to bed. But the next morning he was up and dressed, prepared to leave the house at the usual time. Momma had put on a light coat, for it was May and the trees near the schoolyard had little green balls on them. She was almost at the door when Poppa came in from his bedroom with his face funny – very white – and his mouth open as if he were going to cry (impossible!) and he reached out a hand toward Momma, and then he bent over and in a great gasp vomited all over the floor. Momma cried out and ran to him; the children stood where they were, unmoving, staring. On the floor around Poppa was a pool of blood – everywhere – on the walls, on his lovely jacket and vest – oh! .

Momma screamed, she just screamed. She screamed at Bella, 'Go get the doctor!' and at Eddie, 'Help me get him to the couch!' But the children were paralyzed. Momma kept screaming at them, she looked crazy, she screeched, and finally Eddie moved to her side and grabbed Poppa's other arm. Poppa was limp, his head was hanging down and he was breathing heavily through his mouth. Momma still screamed at Bella. Bella remained where she was.

Always me, she thought. Whenever anything has to be done, it's me she calls. Why can't one of the others go? Why is she screaming? She moved forward a step, reluctantly, leaving her cocoa and rye bread untouched.

'I don't know where the doctor lives!' she cried.

Momma stood up straight and sighed, as if Bella were an idiot. 'You go down two blocks to the pork store, then turn left and go to the middle of the second block, Dr Dlugosz, you'll see the sign, tell him to come right away, right away, it's an emergency!'

Bella went, delivered her message, and returned. By that time, some of the neighbor women had arrived, and were standing with their arms around Momma looking down at Poppa who seemed to be sleeping. Bella went to her place at table and sat down and began to drink her cocoa, but it was cold. She ate her rye bread. The servant girl had removed their plates and cups, but they still sat there. They didn't seem to be going to school. Bella was not unhappy about that, and when she was finished with her bread, she too sat on.

The doctor arrived, and all the children, as if a signal had been given, slipped down from the table. Bella didn't know where they went. She also left the room, and looking around first, slipped into the living room and tiptoed over to the window and slipped behind the curtain. She stood there for a long time, barely seeing the people walking on the street below, the pushcarts going by, the horse-drawn drays and coaches. She had long blond curls and blue eyes and was standing in a beautiful house gazing out at the sea, waiting for the sun to go down. She was wearing a beautiful pink dress and had pink ribbons in her hair, and behind her was a happy silence, the quiet of order and peace.

After a long time, she returned to the dining room. Four or five women sat at the table with Momma drinking glasses of tea. Father was gone. Euga was sitting on Momma's lap, whimpering.

'Quiet!' Mother yelled. Then she said roughly to Bella, 'Take her away, take her!' Bella stared at Momma: Momma never talked like that. Momma's face went wild again, she screamed at Bella, 'Take her and go, get out, get out! Take care of her!'

She stood Euga on the floor roughly and Euga cried. Momma put her head in her hands and began to cry too. The women gathered around her, stroking her back, saying soothing words. Poor Pane Brez, there there. Bella took Euga's hand and pushed open the outside door. Euga wouldn't let go of her hand, even going down the stairs. They reached the sidewalk and Bella realized it was still a little chilly and they had no coats. But she was afraid to go back upstairs. Nor did she know where else to go. They could go to the stationery store for candy, but Bella had no money. They could go to the playground three blocks away, but Bella was frightened of the big boys who played there. At a diagonal, across the street, was a nickelodeon. Bella had never seen inside it – it cost a nickel – but there were always photographs outside showing the people who were inside. They were funny people – sometimes they wore strange clothes, and sometimes the women had hardly any clothes on, but they were very beautiful. She would take Euga to look at the pictures.

She grasped Euga's hand even more tightly and started across the street. The noise shocked her, it was all around her, a great clamor – screeches and screaming and Euga was crying and people all around were yelling at Bella. She looked around, but things were blurred and she felt dizzy. After a few minutes, things settled down into forms, and she gasped at the streetcar that was standing just beside them. If it had moved a few inches farther, it would have hit Euga, who was still holding Bella's hand as she sobbed.

The conductor's uniform had gold on it, and he had a

gold tooth in his mouth too. Bella shrank: what would he do to her? He was waving his arm round and yelling. What was he saying? 'Stupid kid! Stupid! Why don't you watch where you're going? You want to get your baby sister killed? Heh?' All around her people were murmuring: Bella's face was hot, she could hear the disapproval in their tone. She was bad, terrible. She tugged at Euga's arm and pulled her out of the street, they ran, almost dragging her, down the block past their house, away from all the people. She glanced back once and saw the trolley moving on, the crowd of people was smaller, although some still stood there, talking and gesticulating. She wondered if they would tell Momma on her. What would Momma say? Terror invaded her heart at this new Momma.

She sat Euga down on the curb, and sat uneasily beside her. They did not speak. Would Momma get like Poppa now, and Poppa get like Momma? Bella wondered. Would the people tell Momma? Bella felt she couldn't bear it if Momma spoke angrily to her about it; she felt she would have to die if that happened. Momma said to take care of her and I almost killed her, she kept saying to herself over and over, until her heart slowed again to its normal rhythm.

four

Two days later, on May 26, 1913, Michael Brez died in the hospital of uremic poisoning, his dream of returning to Poland unfulfilled, his business near bankruptcy, and leaving no life insurance. He didn't believe in it: he used to say over the dinner table to his fawning friends that he wasn't going to leave behind a rich widow who would turn over his hard-earned money to some new man.

In the weeks after his death, Frances, desperate for money to bury him, sold whatever she could for whatever price. The business, already in trouble, simply disappeared. The counters, the chandeliers, the bolts of serge and twill, fine cotton and silk shirtings, the ties, all of it went for whatever she could get. She sold even the furniture from the house – all that was salable. She kept the old couch, the round table and chairs, a sewing machine from the shop, and her marriage bed.

Time passed in a daze for Bella, who saw nothing, heard nothing, remembers nothing. Only a few pictures remain in her mind:

She is standing at the kitchen window in the almost empty apartment, looking down at the sidewalk where Momma is standing talking to the used-furniture man. His horse-drawn wagon is heaped high with carved-wood chairs inlaid with mother-of-pearl and cushioned in crimson brocade; a mahogany sideboard; a Persian carpet; a carved-wood brocade couch; two mattresses; and several boxes of dishes, silver serving pieces, flatware, and ornaments. Momma is arguing now; the used-furniture man has tried at the last minute to cheat the Polack widow out of a dollar. Momma is losing, and looks around her in despair. The neighbors gather round, and Frances explains the situation to them with charming helplessness. They crowd the man in a tight circle, angrily yelling, the men raising their fists. The man looks contemptuously at them, pulls a dollar off his roll of bills and thrusts the bill toward Momma. The crowd still mumbles, calling him names, and he gets up on his wagon and flips the reins. He pulls slowly away, but the crowd remains, smiling and patting poor Pane Brez.

She is sitting with Momma in an office in a big building, she doesn't know where. They are inside a small office that is inside a big office that has long wooden benches with people sitting dejectedly upon them. It reminds Bella of the office in the school, whe she was expelled before she even started, but Momma is different this time. She is still wearing the black hat and the same black coat, but they are old and shabby now, and Momma herself is slumped over in her chair. The woman sitting behind the desk is like the woman in the school: she has grey hair and eyeglasses and the same kind of mouth. Momma's mouth is twisted, and she is twisting her hands too. The woman is speaking very slowly, very distinctly and very loud, as if

Momma were deaf. She speaks so clearly and loudly that even Bella understands her.

'You cannot possibly earn enough to support them,' the woman says.

Momma is near tears. 'I can sew. I sew all my life.' Momma is speaking English. 'Since I am nine years old I sew. I work in my husband's shops, I make coats, trousers. The mayor of New York City come to my husband's shop.'

The woman smiles thinly. 'That's all very well, Mrs Brez, but wages paid to seamstresses cannot support four children. We will have to take them.'

Momma bursts into tears. 'No! No! My children, my babies! You cannot do, no!'

The woman purses her lips and looks over Momma's head. She is waiting. After Momma stops talking, and her sobs are a little softer, the woman says, 'It's for their own good. It's for your good too. Surely you must see that, Mrs Brez. How will you feed them, clothe them? Who will watch the little one when you are at work and the older children in school? At the orphanage they'll be properly fed and clothed, and they will be taught a trade. It will be better for all of you in the long run.'

Momma sobs louder, hitting her fist on the desk noiselessly, over and over. 'No, no!' she keeps crying.

The woman twists her lips again, gazing at Momma. She looks down at her hands. Momma is crying as if she would never stop. 'No, no,' she keeps repeating in a little soft voice from way down in her throat. The woman clears her throat.

'Well, perhaps . . . I guess it would be all right . . . maybe we could let you keep one of them.'

Momma stops crying. Bella is embarrassed that snot is running down from Momma's nose to her upper lips. Momma digs in her handbag for a handkerchief and wipes it away and blows her nose. She raises her head tiredly, her shoulders slumped. 'I keep Isabella,' she says.

The teacher is handing out the report cards. Bella tries not to think about it. She gazes around her, seeing nothing. The teacher comes to her and hands her the card. Bella doesn't look at it; she slips it swiftly into her writing tablet. The class is dismissed, and the children tear out with that special energy and joy that marks the last day of school. Isabella Brez rises slowly from her seat and trails behind them slowly. She doesn't want to speak to any of them, to have them ask her anything. She doesn't want to know herself.

She walks home slowly, but before she reaches home, she sits down on a curb and looks around her. No one is watching her, the streetlife goes on as always. She reaches into her tablet and slowly pulls out the card. She looks at the grades first. She has failed everything. At the bottom, where it says———IS PROMOTED TO———/MUST REPEAT———, she sees that she has been left back. Isabella MUST REPEAT third grade, it says. Her heart stops. They have found out.

She stands, slumping, and drags herself toward home. Momma will be there, her head in her hands, sitting at the table over a cup of coffee, crying. Stupid. Stupid. Useless. Everyone knew she was stupid. It is a terrible thing, to be stupid and know it. She climbs the stairs slowly, and pushes open the door. Momma is alone at the table, crying. Bella enters softly, and goes to her room. She does not tell Momma she has been left back. Nor will Momma ever ask.

The man and the woman come into the almost empty apartment. They are dressed like the people in the pictures outside the nickelodeon: the man is wearing a bowler hat and a blue suit, and the woman has a big-brimmed hat with flowers on it, and a brown wool jacket over her long tan skirt. Her boots are black. They talk to Momma the same way the woman in the office did – very clearly and loud. Edmund, who is now ten; Wallace, who is six, and Eugenia, who is four, are sitting in their best clothes, rigid on the edge of the couch seat. Beside them, on the floor, are three boxes tied with string, containing their clothes. Each holds a bag in their lap – food Momma prepared for them. The man and the woman do not look at the children, and they are annoyed with Momma, who won't stop crying. The children gaze with white faces at the strangers. Finally, the man says something sharp and fast to Momma, and Momma looks up at him. Bella gasps. She has never seen Momma's eyes look like that before. The woman hurriedly helps the children up, and puts her hand on their backs to usher them out the door. The man quickly picks up the boxes and follows. But the woman doesn't go down with them; the man runs down the steps after the children. The woman comes toward Momma, who is still looking like that.

'Mrs Brez . . . it isn't forever. As soon as you get settled, earn enough . . . you will get them back.' Swiftly, she turns and leaves, as Momma, in a great gasp puts her head in her hands again and cries as if her throat were a cave, as if the howling winds came from her belly, she cries like a storm that will never end.

Bella walks slowly to the kitchen window and looks down at the carriage. She cannot see her brothers and sister, only the man, who is fixing the boxes on the seat beside the driver. The woman comes out and quickly steps up into the carriage and disappears. Then the man gets in. A strange noise comes out of Bella's throat, and Momma leaps up and runs into the kitchen and stares down at the carriage, when it begins to move, and then she screams, 'Killers! Killers! Beasts! Bastards!' She is screaming in Polish, using words she never used before (*Chuje*, she cries, and *Niech ich szlak weźniel*), the kind of words Poppa would say when he came in late at night. Bella shrinks from this woman. She walks slowly into her bedroom. Except for a heap of her clothes on the floor, it is empty.

five

She remembers nothing else. There must have been activity, Frances must have been busy, but Bella, wherever she was, was absent. Frances found a job in a sweatshop, ten hours a day, six days a week, for five dollars a week. She found a new place to live – it was on Manhattan Avenue, on a street like that on which they had lived before, but shabbier. The rent was six dollars a month. The apartment was only a few blocks away from their old one;

there were stores on the bottom, and one or two stories of apartments above them. But this time, they would not live above a store, or even on the street, but in the back alley. The enterprising owner of the front building had put up a house in his yard. It had a one-room basement, in which an old Russian immigrant lived alone until one night, a year and a half after Momma and Bella moved in, he turned on the gas in his bedroom without lighting it, and died in his sleep. Momma and Bella would live on the first floor, in two rooms, and there was a family upstairs in another two-room apartment – a mother, father, two children, and two boarders newly arrived from Russia. These boarders had long stringy beards and spoke neither Polish nor English, and they frightened Bella.

To reach the house, you had to go through a door beside a millinery shop that fronted the street, pass the staircase leading to the apartments above, and through a long hall, and out the back. There was a small open space, and then the back building. The toilet was in the front building, though, and all three families had to go through the back door and halfway down the dark hall to use it. The millinery shop would lock up at night, but the two doors were always open.

Mr Ettinger, who owned the building, was wary of a widow with a child, but he felt sorry for Momma. So did his wife, who sent over a box of clothes her daughters had outgrown, for Bella.

Momma sat over that box, shaking her tearful head. Bella understood. Of all their many friends and relatives, only Pane Dabrowska had come to see them after Poppa died. All the people they had entertained, the two sisters whose passage money Momma had sent: everyone abandoned them in this time. And Pane Dabrowska came, Bella thought, only because she was old and lonely, and wanted some conversation and a glass of tea. Bella's heart hardened in a way that would never change: Polish people, she felt, were shallow and mercenary, concerned only with what they could get. The only people who helped Momma were the Ettingers, strangers, and Jewish. Bella never forgot this.

In time, though, she became somewhat cynical about the

Ettingers, too, because once Mrs Ettinger found out that Momma could sew, she would bring over a length of fabric and ask Momma to make a dress for her daughter Yetta. She never paid her, but she brought extra material, so Momma could make a dress for Bella too. After a year, Bella had thirteen dresses – almost as many as she had endowed Anastasia with. But she knew there were things she needed more than dresses. And she felt that Momma only made her the dresses so she could show them to Mrs Ettinger, to prove that she'd made them.

Their apartment was dark; light entered it only faintly for a few hours in the afternoon. The kitchen had a wood stove, a sink, and two deep tubs, with some shelves along one wall. Momma set the round table with its fringed brocade cloth in the center, and put a kerosene lamp on top. There was a gaslight on the wall behind the stove. Momma set the double bed and an old trunk in the other room. There was a wall gaslight in that room too. Along two walls of the kitchen, Momma put the old treadle sewing machine and the old couch.

Momma left the house very early each morning; somehow, she knew what time it was, and got herself out by seven to walk the three miles to the sweatshop and be there by eight. She worked from eight until one, then had a half hour for lunch, the black bread and butter she carried with her in a folded-up towel, then worked until six-thirty. Since, most nights, Momma stopped at a market on the way back for something for dinner, it was often eight o'clock at night before she returned home.

Bella was alone all day.

'I remember being, but I don't remember thinking or feeling,' my mother says, pulling one side of her velvet robe over her knees. 'I was numb.'

Numb, and lonely, she would wander out to the streets, always busy by day, but filled mainly with men walking by, older boys striding through. A few women in babushkas and shawls and long skirts hovered at the open front of the vegetable stall, feeling tomatoes. From upstairs, she could hear Yetta Ettinger playing the piano. She walked back into the dark hall and stood there listening. What she heard was only scales and exercises fumblingly played, but it sounded beautiful to her.

She decided that Anastasia would play the piano, beautifully, even better than Yetta Ettinger. And for some weeks, this gave her an occupation. She made up a life for Anastasia, starting right from the beginning. She saw the room Anastasia was laid in after her birth (she passed over that part, which was fuzzy in her mind) and how her momma and poppa acted toward her. She kept careful track of just where she had left off on an evening, so she could start again the next day. The first few weeks she and Momma lived on Manhattan Avenue, Bella spent mainly in the dark house, sitting at the kitchen table and making up Anastasia's life. She tried to go slowly, because she knew the summer was long, but within a short time, she already had Anastasia going to school.

When Anastasia came home from school, she went into a large room with shining wood floors and a beautiful rug on it, and a long piano, like the one in the store on Nostrand Avenue, and played. She had long thin fingers, and music simply poured out of them. When she was tired of that, Anastasia went up to her room, which was all pink and white eyelet, like the bedroom in Halper's Furniture Shop, with a pretty little vanity table. Bella could never quite envision what was on the vanity table, so she left that blank for the time being. There was also a fluffy white rug which Anastasia never got dirty, and a little crimson slipper chair, like the one in Schneider's Furnishings, three blocks away. And her sheets were embroidered with her name, and she had a real closet in her room with fourteen dresses and two pairs of boots, one for everyday and one for good.

When Bella would occasionally go out on the street, she would walk like Anastasia, stepping daintily over horse droppings and peering haughtily in the shop windows. Sometimes, Bella would ask her what she thought of something in a window, and Anastasia would wrinkle her nose and say it was cheap-looking. Then Bella would walk on, not wanting it either.

Darkness would grow on the little house without Bella noticing, and when the door opened, Momma would speak harshly: 'You stupid, sitting in the dark!' and Bella would jump up and turn on the gaslight, although it was hard for her to reach. She would light the kerosene lamp too, as Momma put down her bags, and stare at the grey-faced woman. Momma wouldn't speak. She'd go to the stove and put wood in it for a fire; then she'd measure coffee into the drip pot, and put a kettle of water on the hot part of the stove. then she'd sink into a chair and put her face in her hands. When the kettle was steaming, she'd get up wearily and pour water into the coffee, and sit down again. After a little while, she got up and poured some coffee into a cup, and sat with it, her hands around the cup as though they were cold – but it was very hot, it was July.

Momma would sip the coffee, but in a few minutes, she'd choke, and the sobs would come out of her mouth the same way they had the day the strange man and woman came, as if her throat were a cave, and wild winds were trapped inside. She said bad thing, awful things, and Bella stood transfixed. Sometimes, she would pull back to the couch, the old couch from the dining room, that Momma had put in the kitchen, and lean her leg against it.

'*Psia krew! Chuje!* Devils! Devils! What did they do to me, why, why? They take my children, who the hell are they to do such a thing! *Niech ich szlak weźnie!* My children, my babies, my little orphans! *Moje biedne sieroty, moje drodzy!* Hell, hell, hell, why did this happen to me?'

She would sob and scream, cursing and using words Poppa had used, but that Momma had never uttered before.

Bella approached her warily. She touched her sleeve. 'Momma *I'm* here,' she said in a small voice.

But Frances lifted her arm brusquely, loosing the small fingers. She went on crying and screaming.

'Please don't cry, Momma,' Bella begged.

Frances ignored her: she was inconsolable. She was pounding the table with her fist, soundlessly; then she pounded her own chest so hard Bella could hear the thump. Bella drew back slowly, slowly, until the back of her legs touched the couch. Her belly rumbled. She was hungry.

Now Momma had her hands over her belly and was moaning and rocking back and forth. Then tears burst forth again, and she slapped her own face, she tore at her cheeks with her nails, she pulled out strands of her hair.

Bella watched, listened, but Momma never looked at her. Bella wished that Momma would hit *her*, scream at *her*, but Momma acted as if she wasn't there. Bella felt that she was being torn to pieces. She wondered why Momma had kept her, why she hadn't let her go to the orphanage with the others. After a week of Momma's nightly crying, a thought pushed its way into Bella's mind: I'd be better off at the orphanage.

When Momma's sobs subsided a bit, sounding now like wind through the cracks in the windows, she would lay her head down on the table. Then Bella would approach her again, and pick up her cup.

'Would you like some hot coffee, Momma?'

Momma would answer – or she wouldn't. Bella would pour more coffee into the cup and slide it back on the table, and Momma would sit up a little, and, her chin near the table, pick up the cup and hold it to her lips.

'Do you want me to go to the store, Momma?'

Frances would look at her, wild-eyed.

'For dinner, Momma.'

Then Frances would sit up farther, and slump at the same time. She reached for her purse and took out some coins. She would tell Bella to get some chop meat, or some bologna. Then she would go into the bedroom and take off her dress and put on an older one and tie on an apron and come back and begin to peel some potaoes. When Bella returned, they would be boiling, and Momma would be peeling carrots, or halving a head of cabbage. They would eat very late, and Bella's stomach twisted all through the meal. Bella helped Momma clear.

'I'll wash the dishes tomorrow,' she'd say, and Momma would nod. They would go out to the toilet, and then into the bedroom. After Bella was undressed and in bed, Momma would turn off the gas lamp and undress in the dark, and lie down beside Bella in the big lumpy double bed. Exhausted, Momma would fall immediately asleep, breathing loudly with a liquid rasp from the tears in her throat. She never caressed the child beside her. She never even said good night.

Chapter IV

one

The strange thing about misery is how it expands to take up all available space. A toothache can make you want to die, and while you are suffering it, you have no patience with someone who tells you that things could be worse – that you could be in a concentration camp, say, watching your family die; or in a cell being tortured by one of the specialists so popular with governments these days. I have wished to die with stomach cramps, and seen my mother willing herself to die with sinus headaches. It is hard to measure pain, just as it is hard to measure happiness.

The only measure we have, I guess, is permanence. For it is true that the moment the sore tooth, the headache, the stomach, are relieved, they are also forgotten. Pain accompanied by fear – a heart attack, say – endures longer in the memory, and maybe the fear never fully vanishes. And there are pains that never end, that pounce brutally on the heart at each recall until one dies.

The shrinks believe that we can reanimate our times of severe pain and find comfort in the understanding sympathetic therapist. Perhaps. Priests also offer comfort of a sort; like therapy, religious relief is dependent upon faith. Yet those who suffer worst are usually faithless, for pain destroys faith. And hope.

My grandmother never fully recovered from her ordeal. And although her ordeal was utterly different, neither did my mother. And my sister and I spent most of our lives trying to escape or evade the consequences of those facts.

Occasionally I read novels written by women of my own age who were raised in comfort with some affection, yet suffered wretched childhoods, felt forced into conformity, or pushed into invisibility, or in some way unappreciated. And by now I know that love can be the cruelest oppression. Still, I snort in contempt at the self-indulgence of these writers. I snort just like my mother, who cannot understand how anyone who has enough money to live without worry could succumb to depression, or even be unhappy. She should know better, but she scorns such people. And so do I. I have accepted my mother's standard: no one ever suffered more than she did. There is just enough truth in this idea to give it weight.

You say – but suffering is also determined by how you react to things. You say you know people who had terrible calamities in their lives, yet maintained their courage and spirit. Admirable, yes, but tell me this: what is it that enables them to do that? A certain ambience in their childhoods, a genetic propensity, a gift of love made early enough to be engraved on the soul? Are we responsible if these things are absent in our lives? Can we be blamed, can we blame ourselves?

I remember, in my childhood, curling up in a tight knot on my bed, my whole body consumed in liquid fire of pain because I felt unloved. Yet in a way I was loved – love being another of those essential things that cannot be measured, another of the qualities discarded and dismissed by our age which trusts only that which can be measured. I *felt* unloved. How much more then did Bella feel unloved? And how much deeper the effects of lovelessness on her?

And how can I make sense of Frances, whom I remember as so gentle and loving, so entirely tender and giving? I feel I may not presume to judge my mother, but I have spent much of my life doing so. My mother could never even consider judging her own. How could she? given the facts. Yet toward Bella, Frances was not tender or even gentle, but harsh and critical. Why was that? Did she see Bella as her other self, expect her to be adult and dependable and resourceful in equal measure to herself? Frances had been adult early – by thirteen certainly: she might have wondered why Bella was not. But then, Frances had had a loving mother, attention, had heard laughter in her early years – things she was not able to give her daughter, reserving them for her granddaughter, me, Anastasia. She must have loved Bella – why else would she have chosen her? Perhaps she loved her most, loved her as she loved herself, and therefore was hardest on her, in the same way she would be hard on herself. I know she loved her, I saw them together. But Bella never knew it.

Maybe for Frances it was the cost: how could this timid weepy child ever be good enough, ever be enough to justify Frances's suffering? For during those terrible years, Bella's survival was the entire apparent purpose of Frances's life. If this was what Frances felt, it was inherited, because that is what my mother felt too, about us, during the terrible years of our childhood. And I?

Still, I understand Frances. One night, after my second husband had left me, I had a few drinks too many and was lying in my room crying and Franny came in. She approached the bed tentatively, and I tried to stop sniffling, I sat up a little and blew my nose, and she sat on the edge of the bed and put her hand on my back. She was little, she was six. She asked me why I was crying. Then the other kids came in too, and gathered around me on the bed. They wouldn't understand because I couldn't tell them the whole thing. So I said I was crying because I was angry with myself for fucking up my life, for marrying Toni, for getting myself stuck in poverty again.

And Franny, who didn't understand at all, just rubbed her little hand over mine, smoothing it as if that could smooth my spirit. Arden's eyes were bright: I knew that look: it meant she was trying to transfer some of her intense energy, her fervor, to me in my depression. I knew the look because I'd given it, often enough, to my own mother. She said, 'But Mom, if you hadn't married Toni, you wouldn't have Franny.'

I kept my mouth shut. What could I say? That's exactly the point? I mumbled something.

Billy was farthest from me, at the foot of the bed, looking

down at the floor. His new deep voice rumbled incoherently, and I had to ask him to repeat what he'd said.

'I asked you if you felt that way about Dad. Our father. Bradley.'

I was angry enough to feel it was essential to be honest. 'Well, yes, to tell the truth.'

'But if you hadn't married him, you wouldn't have had us,' he went on in a drone, raising his head to look at me.

I sat up, my head hot with fury. 'So what?' I cried. 'If I hadn't had you, if I'd married somebody else, I'd have had other children! I'd have loved them just as much!'

Their faces paled. They stared at me. Inconceivable, it was inconceivable that I could have said that, that I could even imagine loving some other hypothetical children as much as I loved them, that they were not loved because of their personal qualities, their specialness, their wonderfulness. I leaned back, a bit regretful. 'I wouldn't have known you, see?'

They saw. They nodded solemnly. They were even saintly, they didn't storm off to their rooms and sulk, but offered me tea and some music, both of which I swiftly accepted. they put on my music, not theirs – one of the late quartets, which did nothing for my mood. But I could only smile my appreciation, as radiantly as I could manage. After all, they were proving that I was wrong, weren't they? I had to be wrong.

Mother love. There is supposed to be no room in it for coldness of heart, for a private cell for oneself, with doors that sometimes clank shut. And the more you love your children, the more shocked they are to discover that you possess a single strand of ambivalent – or negative – feeling. Insatiable for this love we expect to be absolute, we cannot forgive its mere humanness. Well, I thought, that's one fault *I* don't have. I'd long accepted the limitations of my mother's feeling for me. I was adult.

Fathers aren't subject to such demands. They are allowed to be almost anything, and if they give any love at all, kids feel grateful. Goddamned unfair. Still, fathers are dismissed in a way mothers aren't: they aren't given the same importance. But they can do just as much harm. Look at Bella.

If Bella felt her mother did not care about her, what on earth did she feel about her father? It was probably fortunate in some ways for his children that he died as young as he did, before he could fuck them up even more. The damage he did was mainly to Bella and Wally – Eddie had a kind of imperviousness, and Euga was too young to see. Then too, it was Bella and Wally who resembled him – the thin face, the nervous gestures. For Bella, Michael Brez would stand forever as her image of what men were. Cruel and capricious and unpredictable and utterly selfish; yet brilliant, dashing, popular, charming, and able to make money, able to take care of a family in a way a mother could not, no woman could. Men could be dangerous, treacherous, and perhaps even brutal, but you needed a man absolutely. I remember when I was divorced and had the two kids – before Franny was born – and living from hand to mouth, which was the way I spent most of my life, and my mother would have nightmares every night. She told me she would dream that the kids and I were living in a Volkswagen bus. This terrified her, and she urged me to get married again. It wasn't that she thought much of the man I was seeing, only that he had a good job and was a man. You get one, you keep him, and you see to it that he stays in his place. For my mother, that was the only solution.

A man had nothing to give a woman except economic security. From a man you would not get friendship or understanding or sympathy. Sexual pleasure – well, that faded fast. You got support and legitimacy for your children, and you had to make sure your man didn't try to assert himself in other ways. If he did and you allowed it – you were finished, you'd be subject to a tyrannical brute for the rest of your life, and your children too. But you could not live without one.

My mother taught me these lessons early – she started when I was nine years old.

two

If my mother began to teach me about men when I was nine, she also taught me about the nature of women – but her lesson expurgated much. I knew nothing about Grandma's crying, about her treatment of my mother, until I was over forty, and she nearly seventy. We were sitting, as usual, in the little side room she called the porch, smoking and drinking, the street outside quiet and dark except for the streetlights, the towel already stuffed under my father's door. She had begun again the litany I had heard so often.

'My father died when I was nine years old. I have been cooking since I was nine, I had to go all the way into Jewtown – it was so terrifying . . .' She is still composed. Her voice has not broken with tears, she is still speaking in adult rhythms. I listen, as always, but tonight my own depression is severe, and I cannot tell her about it. This makes me edgy. I understand for the first time that in our relationship there is room only for one history, one truth – hers. I am permitted only to be Anastasia as she demands Anastasia be. So I challenge her a little.

'But how did you come to do it at all? I mean, what gave you the idea, and how did you do it? Where did you get the money for the market, how did you know how to cook?'

So she told me about the crying, and as she does, she cries herself, in great wrenching sobs, her fist at her forehead. 'Tearing me to pieces, to pieces, I wished she'd hit me!'

Bella sat in the apartment daydreaming about Anastasia, and it got dark, and Momma came in and growled at her, and she leapt up and turned up the lights, and ran to Momma and hugged her around her hips and said, 'Hello, Momma, I was waiting for you.'

And Frances patted her head gently, lifelessly, and went toward the stove.

But Bella ran ahead of her. 'Sit down, Momma, I'll make your coffee, you must be tired.'

And Frances sighed, and lowered herself into a chair. But Bella wasn't thinking about Momma's tiredness, she had no conception of what her mother felt. She was nine, and Momma was an absolute, like the North Pole, and whatever she was or did or said created the world Bella lived in, a world she couldn't attempt to explain or understand. But the thought had entered her mind that if when Momma came home at night, the lights were on and her coffee ready, she might be less unhappy. And then things might be a little better for her, Bella.

She piled wood in the box and lighted the thinner sticks. She filled the kettle and put it on the stove. She measured coffee into the old tin pot the way she'd seen Momma do it.

While they waited for the water to boil, Bella said shyly, 'Do you want me to go to the store, Momma?' She tried to keep any sound of reproach out of her voice, tried to keep Momma from knowing that every night when she came home, the first thing Bella looked for was whether she was carrying a little package from the butcher shop, and that, when she was not, Bella's heart sank.

Frances nodded and reached for her purse. 'Just get some baloney, I'm too tired to cook tonight.'

Bella poured the coffee for her mother before she left, then took her coat and stepped out into the cold dark night. She never told her mother how frightened she was to go to the market at night, even though she had to walk only a couple of blocks. If she could go in the daytime, it would be better. Gradually, a plan formulated in her mind, like a wave gathering height. For Bella had never before in her life thought about doing something to change something. But maybe . . .

Over their baloney and black bread, with some cucumbers Momma had prepared the night before, Bella launched her idea. 'Momma, why don't you give me the money for dinner at night. Then I could buy it in the daytime and we wouldn't have to eat so late.'

Her mother nodded wearily. She said nothing. She would cry, Bella knew, as soon as they had finished eating. She jumped up as soon as they were through.

'I'll wash the dishes, Momma. You rest,' she urged.

But Momma barely heard her. She was leaning forward, her elbows on the table; a line of tears ran from each eye down her cheeks. 'Oh, my babies, my little orphans,' she cried in a small thin voice.

Bella cleaned up and sat on the couch. She would have liked to go into the other room, maybe even get into bed, but she could not. She no longer reminded her mother that she was there, or tried to touch her, but she could not go away from Momma when she cried. She knew that in time, exhaustion would overwhelm sorrow, and she would stand up wearily and say, without expression, 'Bed, Bella,' and they would go together to the double bed in which they slept but never touched.

Tonight, though, Bella stopped her mother. 'Are you going to give me the money?'

Frances opened her purse and took out fifteen cents. 'Go to Jewtown,' she said in her drained voice. 'It's cheaper. Get half a pound of chop meat and some vegetable.'

Bella accepted the coins wide-eyed. She felt she was accepting a sacred trust. She must not lose them! Oh, don't even think about that!

The next day, Bella woke groggily, as usual, when the sun was already hot, the room steamy. But then she sat up with sudden energy: she had important work to do that day. She dressed and ran out to the toilet and came back and made herself some coffee. If she was an adult, she should drink coffee like an adult. She sat there, going over in her mind how to prepare the meal she planned. Then she took the coins Momma had left from the cupboard shelf, and set off.

The streets were filled with children playing, cursed at continually by the drivers of passing drays. There was no trolley line on this narrow street, and people swarmed across the cobblestones. Farther down the street, she saw some girls jumping rope: Yetta Ettinger and her friends. She slowed for a minute, watching them, wondering if she could still do that. Then she pulled herself up: I am a big girl now. Jumping rope is for children.

She walked steadily until she entered the Jewish quarter,

then slowed. Terror gripped her. So many people, so much noise! And no one was speaking Polish. The streets were massed with pushcarts, with large-armed women thrusting cabbages and turnips at customers who wrinkled their noses and pointed to others, vendors calling out to passersby to come and buy their fresh fruit, in loud voices, in words she could not translate. It was worse than school, for there she could understand some of the words.

So many men, in dark suits and bowler hats, men with beards, men with funny high hats, women in full long skirts and shawls over their heads, boys with long curls, new clothes pegged to lines hanging over counters full of more clothes, and the noise! Bella clutched her money tightly, and stepped into the street. She walked carefully, threading her way among the pushcarts. Her teeth were clenched. She did not look around her any more than she had to. Then, suddenly, she stopped again. On the step in front of a shabby door sat a girl about her age, holding a large baby on her lap. The baby was probably two, and, sitting down, was almost as big as the girl. Near them was a huge tin can full of refuse of spoiled vegetables and fruits. The smell was disgusting and flies surrounded it. The girl looked at Bella; Bella looked at her. The girl's eyes were large, and sad, and . . . something else, something hard. Bella shuddered, and walked on, shaking her head to get the image out of it. She found the stall Momma went to and got the meat, and two cents worth of carrots at a stall farther down. She still had six cents left, so she followed a trail toward a baker's, and took a long time choosing two things that looked like chruściki, but were different. She clutched the four pennies change. Momma would be glad. She turned back then, and faced the scene once more, but when she did, she felt faint, she thought she would fall down. She leaned against something – the end of a pushcart – to catch herself. Suppose she fell down here! So many people would trample her, run her down the way the streetcar almost ran down Euga. She felt she could not go back. But she had to.

She thought about Anastasia. Suppose something bad happened to Anastasia, suppose she lost her momma while they were shopping, and wandered into this maze? What would Anastasia do?

Bella pulled herself up and lifted her chin. Like a duchess in a throng, she picked her way through the massing people, the goods, the noise, the smells, without noticing any of it. Women yelled from windows, men chatted under the awnings of shops, men read newspapers with funny letters on them, standing right there on the street, but she barely noticed. Head high, lips firm, her face as close to a mask of hauteur as she could manage, she escaped from Jewtown into her own less crowded neighborhood. When she reached home, she fell on a chair. (Just like Momma.) It was some time before she felt she could move.

When the yard grew dim, Bella stirred. She stood and turned up the gas lamp, then went to the stove and piled the wood for a fire. Then she began to scrape the carrots, as she had seen Momma do it. She peeled an onion. It was hard, it took a long time, and her eyes streamed tears. Then she got the bacon fat from the shelf and melted it in a cast-iron skillet, and chopped the onion up. She put it in the pan and laid the pan over the fire before it was really hot, the way Momma did. Then she sliced the carrots and put them in a small pan, with a little sugar and some butter and a little water. She put the pot beside the warm grate. When the onions were glistening, she removed the skillet and tried to pour them in a bowl, but the pan was too heavy for her to lift that high. She put the bowl on the floor and tried again, holding the short handle of the skillet with a crumpled towel. This time she could do it, but some of the onions stuck.

Sighing, she pushed hair from her damp forehead. Why didn't Momma seem to have these problems? She rummaged in a drawer for a large spoon, returned to the pan which was now on the floor, and tried to lift it with one hand and scrape it with the other. She could not manage this: the pan was too heavy. So she set it down again, and spooned up the bits of onion slowly, painstakingly, and dropped them into the bowl. She returned the pan to the stove – in a cool place – and put the bowl on the table. Then she unfolded the orange paper and put the meat in the bowl too.

She sighed. She was already tired. She tried to think. Yes. She went to the cupboard where Momma put stale rolls when there were any. There was half a roll in a yellow bowl. She took it to the sink and with a knife, cut off the crust and all the poppy seeds. Then, over the bowl, she crumbled the roll between her palms, the way Momma did, and poured some milk in too. The mixture swam. Maybe it was too much. She could barely reach the second shelf of the cupboard, where Momma kept the small bowls, but she could get her hand around the stack and push it forward. Then by tilting them a bit, she could grab one with her other hand. She sighed again, but there was a certain satisfaction in these sighs.

She carried the small bowl to the table, knelt on a chair, and poured some of the milk from one bowl to the other. She would not waste it. She could use it another night. She found an egg in the larder and added it to the meat. Then salt, pepper, paprika. Then, carefully, she mushed the whole thing up with her hands, the way Momma did. When she had finished, she examined it. It didn't look just like Momma's. There were big white lumps from the roll. She worked on it again, and finally just gave up. Then she formed the mixture into four good-sized balls, and washed her hands. But the fattiness would not come off in the cold water. She wiped her hands on the towel, and put water in the kettle, and set it over the grate. The fire was hot now.

Then she set the table, trying to do it the way Momma used to in the old days. But the napkins and their rings were gone, and so was the white damask tablecloth. She found some old napkins in the back of a shelf, and placed them on the aged tapestry cloth that covered the table, set out plates and flatware. They had only the old stuff, but in the dim light it looked all right.

When it was really dark, she put the carrots on the part of the stove that was medium hot and peeled some potatoes. The water was boiling, but now she didn't need it: her hands weren't greasy anymore. So she put that aside for the coffee. She washed the potatoes and put them in a pot and covered them with water. She added salt and put them over the hot part of the grate. She was quite damp now, on her face and even a little bit under her arms. She considered the potatoes: she liked mashed potatoes, but she wasn't exactly sure how to prepare them. They would have to be boiled. She looked in the bin and found a scallion, and tried to peel it, but when she did, there was almost nothing left. So gathered up the peelings and sliced those. She found the small skillet and took a tiny slice of butter from the plate in the larder, and put it in the skillet, which she placed on the warm part of the stove.

The carrots were slowly cooking, the potatoes were boiling, and the butter was melting. It smelled very good, and her mouth got full of saliva. She wondered how she had known to do all this. She was nervous, but somehow she knew she did know how to do it. She tried the potatoes with a fork, the way Momma always did, and when they felt soft, she took them off the hot part of the stove and put the big skillet on. She added a teaspoon of bacon fat to it. Then she tried to pour the water off the potatoes. But the pot was so heavy with all that water, and so hot – she had to hold it with both hands as she tilted it over the sink, and . . . ! Bella's heart stopped. The potatoes had slipped out too and were lying, broken and crumbled in the bottom of the sink. She stood still, near tears. Then, with a towel, she gathered them up again and put them back in the pot – all of them, even the smallest crumb – and set it back on the warm part of the stove. She dropped the chopped scallions into the melted butter and picked up the meatballs gingerly and laid them in the big skillet. Immediately, they began to spatter and sizzle, and again her heart thumped. What did she do now? She moved them slightly away from the hot part but they still spattered. Her dress was getting grease spots on it. Momma would be mad. She was standing paralyzed when she noticed Momma coming through the door to the shop, her figure outlined by the lights from upstairs. Hurriedly, Bella put the carrots in a bowl, and found another large bowl for the potatoes. She tried to pour them in, but had the same trouble she had before, but this pot wasn't so heavy, so she just put her hand in it and scraped them out. She burned her fingers, but ignored that. She poured the buttered scallions over them, and had just got the two vegetables on the table when Momma opened the door.

'Hello, Momma,' she said shyly.

Momma looked at the table. She looked at the stove, where the meatballs were browning. She smelled the room. She looked at Bella. And Momma smiled.

three

Momma smiled. It was a weak smile, tired, wan, but there was something like gratitude in it, something like . . . it looked as if her eyes glistened. But that was probably only reflected light. Momma put her things on a chair and walked to the table with more energy than usual, and sat down less heavily than usual.

'Dinner's all ready, Momma. So I won't make coffee until later, all right?'

Momma nodded, and Bella set out the meatballs, and they ate. Momma said nothing. Bella recognized that the meatballs still had big lumps of bread in them, that they weren't exactly like Momma's, but she was hungry and ate with gusto. Also, the carrots had burned a little in the bottom of the pot, and the burned taste had seeped through to the others. But Momma didn't seem to notice, she was eating as if she were starved, and at the end she looked at Bella and said, 'Good.'

Bella sat up with pride. Her face shone. After that, Bella had dinner waiting for Momma every work night.

My mother always did the cooking for the family. I cannot recall a night she didn't even when she was sick and had spent the day in her darkened room with cloths on her head. Even when I was twelve and she went to work and had to stand all day in high heels, she would come home and cook. She never asked me to do it, although she allowed me to help. I watched her as she had watched her mother, learning without knowing I was. She'd have me string the beans or remove peas from their pods, or peel potatoes, making sure to get every tiny bit of skin and eye.

Putting dinner on the table was the high point of my mother's day. She didn't say or do anything in particular, but you could feel it. She was always hot and tired and her face was always pink, and she was a little cross from all the work, but she laid the bowls of food, the platters, on the table the same way the priest put the host in your mouth – as if she were laying out something sacred. It was her gift to us, her gift of love. The table was always nicely set, even if the napkins were paper and we ate with the everyday flatware and dishes. And the food always looked pretty in the bowls, arranged, somehow, not just thrown in.

Mother did the marketing too. She would put on a clean housedress and one of her old pairs of high heels, and put lipstick and powder on her face and walk to the markets, every Saturday afternoon. Often, she took me with her. She needed me to help carry the bags of groceries home. She was always long at the butcher counter, examining the meat the butcher showed her, and rejecting cuts she didn't like. For years I took her knowledge of meats and vegetables for granted, but then when I was a mother myself, I realized that in all the years of watching her, I hadn't learned anything, and couldn't tell a good cut from a bad one.

She could carry only so much, though, and the big box of Oxydol, the huge bottle of Clorox, were bulky and heavy; so were the potatoes. So often during the week she would have to market again, but this time she would send me. Three blocks away was the Italian grocer who sold vegetables and had a wall of glass cases, like bookcases, except each one held a different kind of pasta – a word I did not then know. I was fascinated by these. We never had any except the long skinny kind called spaghetti, which my little sister called seggid/eggi, and the small round macaroni. I'd have some coins in my hand, and strict orders: a bunch of carrots, or a pound of peas or lima beans, or some spinach. It was never much. And then, by Friday, my mother would be out of food and out of money, because my father got paid on Fridays. If she had any at all, she'd give me fifteen cents and send me to the local butcher, just a block and a half away, for a pound of chop meat. If she didn't, there would be a funny tension in the house, and she would peel potatoes and set them in a big pot of cold water, and start whatever vegetable she had on hand, and when my father came home with money, she'd send me out for some lamb chops – my favorite meal. She bought four loin chops, small ones, and we each had one. I always longed for more.

One Friday as I ran up to the butcher, I lost a nickel of the fifteen cents. I don't know how that could have happened: there must have been a hole in my coat pocket. When I went to pay the butcher, I blanched. He knew us and liked my mother, and said he would give the meat to me and we could pay him later, but I feared incurring a debt, and said I'd have to ask my mother. I ran home, my heart thumping, terrified of her reaction. But why? She never never struck us children, never even raised her voice. Still, I dreaded telling her. I pushed open the back door to the kitchen and my story tumbled out.

Mommy just looked at me. She said nothing. I was babbling now, I told her that Mr Schinkle was willing to let her pay another time, and I would go back if she wanted; I said over and again, 'I'm sorry.' But she just stood there, and when she moved, she said calmly, softly, 'It's all right, Anastasia. I have some canned beans on the shelf. We can have that.'

I kept looking at her.

'It's all right, Anastasia. I know you didn't mean to lose it,' she said, and turned and quietly, tensely, began to heat the beans. I sat there silently, my body thrilled with pain. My mother was so *good*, so *good*, and because of me we would have a horrible dinner tonight.

We had the horrible dinner: to me, any dinner without meat, even if we had fish, was horrible. But Mommy never said anything and neither did Daddy. My sister, of course, was too young to consider what she was eating beyond whether she liked it or not. And we children liked everything. Even things we didn't like, like turnips, what other people call rutabaga – we ate. We were hungry. Mommy never told Daddy about the lost nickel. He would have been angry, he would have gotten that look on his face that told me he wanted to hit me, but didn't dare. But shame and guilt about it stayed with me clear into my adult years. Although our poverty was never mentioned, and indeed, we were relatively well off for our neighborhood – we didn't have big bowls of potatoes for dinner, like other families – it permeated everything in our lives. The dread that comes with poverty is the awareness that one lives on the edge – that beyond it is starvation ahd homelessness. It doesn't need to be spoken or threatened: it seeps, like polluted air into the houses near the mills. It doesn't need even to be conscious. It is there, like the weather.

Years later, when I was thirteen and had finally found some girlfriends, my parents used to go out on Saturday nights, to my great pleasure. For years they had gone nowhere, but now things had eased up. The war was on and my father had a new job and earned forty dollars a week, double his earlier wages. So on Saturday nights, Daddy would go out and pull open the big fence that separated our yard from the one next door, and drive the old long 1925 Packard out backward through the Dentels' driveway. We didn't have a driveway, and Daddy had asked Mr Dentel's permission to use theirs. Since they didn't have a car, and we rarely used ours (and didn't always have one, either), they were agreeable. He would park the car in the front of the driveway, and come all the way around to our back door and come back in and help Mommy with her coat and they would go out through the front door, always reminding me to lock it after them, and down the steps and then Daddy would help Mommy into the car, and they would drive to the movies or to Aunt Jean's to play cards.

And then my girlfriends would come to my house. I never went to theirs: their parents would not have allowed them to have guests, but my mother was happy I had friends. And we would listen to WNEW, to Martin Block and the 'Make Believe Ballroom', and to other music programs, and dance, and eat pretzels and drink Coke and giggle and talk about hairstyles and boys and movie stars.

And we were in love with this one disc jockey, who sounded young, and we fantasized about him, until one night I suggested we call him up and talk to him. The girls were thrilled and terrified: what will your parents say! I assured them, with complacent superiority (their parents regularly beat them), that *my* parents wouldn't mind. So we called.

It was thrilling. The disc jockey got a kick out of us, and we talked for a long time; and the following Saturday, we called again.

Then, one afternoon when I came home from school, after I'd had my snack and finished practicing the piano, Mommy came to me and sat me down. She asked if I had made any telephone calls to Manhattan. I'd already forgotten about them: they were like forbidden joys that happen in the dark. Then I remembered, and told her what we'd done.

She said, 'Anastasia, we got a bill today with twenty dollars' worth of calls on it. You know that's nearly half of Daddy's salary.'

I turned white. I did know. But I hadn't imagined telephone calls could cost so much. In fact, I hadn't thought about them costing anything. We had been so long without a telephone, had got one only the year before, in fact, that I thought the expensive part was getting it, not using it.

I mumbled some apology, but it was my look, I'm sure, that conveyed my feelings. Mommy said, 'It will take us a long time to pay off this bill. You won't do it again, will you?'

I swore I wouldn't, and the next time the girls came over and wanted to call Tommy, or whatever his name was, I said we couldn't, that it had cost twenty dollars to call before, and that my mother wouldn't let us call again.

They paled too. 'Twenty dollars! Was she mad?'

'No.' I was uneasy. You couldn't call what she was, mad.

'Did you get a whipping?'

'No!'

But they kept asking, and no matter how I denied it, they never believed me.

I never forgot that either – my mother's understanding,

my guilt, and their disbelief. It told me everything about their homelife. Or so I thought.

So I know something of what Bella felt in those years after her father died, when the consequences of utter poverty fell like the darkness on the little house in the alley. She continued her forays into Jewtown, which never became less frightening for her, although no untoward event ever occurred to her there. And she expanded her repertoire. She began with simple things – eggs and baloney, meatballs, or kielbasa with boiled potatoes and buttered scallions and beets. She would buy ten cents' worth of meat and two cents' worth of soup greens. As her courage grew, she felt able to ask Momma what cut of meat she should buy for lamb stew, for she was sure she remembered how to make it, or how to tell when to take the chicken out of the soup pot and put it in the oven to brown – as Momma used to do.

She made many mistakes. A few nights after her first success, she made meatballs again, and thriftily used the milk she had saved from the bowl. But after she had poured it in with the crumbled roll and the meat, she noticed a funny smell. She put her nose close to the bowl. It smelled sour: the milk had soured! But what could she do? It was already half mixed in. So she went ahead, just as if the milk were fresh, and Momma never noticed a thing, although Bella had trouble eating her dinner that night. It tasted funny. She knew how fussy Momma used to be about food, and wondered why she didn't spit it out and say ugh! the way she had in the past when the servant girl did something wrong.

She burned herself; she sometimes burned food; and her gravy and mashed potatoes – after she'd learned how to make them – often had lumps. But now she felt she could ask Momma questions, and on weekends she helped Momma and learned more. Life settled into a routine.

Frances had been hired to work on a sewing machine for five dollars a week, but she was so swift and accurate that the boss asked her if she could do fine handwork. Momma smiled charmingly, told him about her work in her husband's tailoring establishment. She was promoted to do fine tailoring in the sweatshop and given a raise to six dollars a week. They also let her work only half a day on Saturday, so she was home by one-thirty, and she and Bella would eat their lunch of black bread and butter together. Then Momma would do the laundry. It was easier for her that way – now she could just do marketing on Sunday, and perhaps have time to cook up something special for the week.

First, she heated kettle after kettle of water on the wood stove, and poured it into one of the deep tubs where the white clothes were piled. After there was enough water, she scrubbed the clothes on a board with hard brown soap, and Bella filled the other tub with cold water. As she finished with each thing, Momma dropped it in the rinse water, and Bella, using both hands, would pull it up and down to get all the suds out of it. Then Bella would wring it and put it in an enameled basin. When Momma finished washing the sheets and underwear, Bella would put the kettle on the heat again, while Momma wrung out the clothes again: Bella's hands were not yet strong enough to do it well. Then the two of them went outdoors, where a line was strung in the yard. Bella helped Momma pin the clothes on the line, flapping the big sheets so they would dry faster.

Momma would leave the small things for Bella, although she had trouble reaching the line, and go back and pour hot water into the tub over the colored clothes, and start again. Bella returned to the house and repeated the same process with Momma. After Momma had washed, rinsed, and wrung the second load, she left it in the enameled basin until the first batch was dry. She would rest for a while drinking coffee, and when the sheets were dry, Bella would go with her and help her to take them down and fold them. Momma would take the sheets and pillowcases indoors while Bella felt the underwear. Usually, it was still damp, so she could hang up only some of the colored clothes. When she went back into the house, Momma had the ironing board out, and an old tablecloth on the floor, so the sheets would not get dirty as she ironed them. Bella sat watching Momma, and sometimes Momma would let her iron the easy things, like the pillowcases, while she sat at the table drinking coffee. Every half hour or so, one of them would run outside to test the clothes for dryness, bring in the dry, hanging up what remained. They did not have many clothes, so they finished in a few hours. Then Momma would return to the ironing. She pressed everything, the underwear, and even their cotton stockings.

On Sundays, they would walk together to Jewtown, and Momma would buy the makings for a pot of soup or stew, and their staples – bread, butter, bacon, eggs, flour, sugar, and coffee. Together they lugged home the heavy bags, and Bella watched carefully now, and even helped Momma when, once in a while, she baked a cake.

Every night after dinner, Momma sewed. Sometimes she opened the machine and ran up seams, but often she sat at the table and did handwork by the kerosene lamp. Sometimes she would give Bella scraps and Bella would sew too. She made napkins for the dinner table, but Momma said they were too little, good for nothing. And sometimes, while she was sitting there sewing, she would put her hands to her face and sob, suddenly, startling Bella. Inconsolable, she would cry for a long time, while Bella watched her, listened to the cursing, the violence that was in her mother, terrified.

One Thursday night at the end of July, Momma was very late coming home and Bella worried about the fried peppers and bacon she had prepared. But when Momma came in, she was laden with bags, and she was smiling and her eyes were bright. This Sunday, she said, they would be able to go to the orphanage and see the children. And she ate quickly that night, so she could bake a cake; and the next night, she baked another. And on Saturday, after washing, she took Bella over to the Christian shops, and bought two plump chickens, and white bread, and onions and celery and cucumbers and dill, and potatoes, and butter and oil and sour cream. She was in such a hurry that they left before the sheets had dried and the second load was hung out, and she almost ran home, puffing with the weight of the shopping bag.

Momma made Bella take the clothes off the line all by

herself, while she singed the chickens. It was hard to do, getting the big sheets off and folded without dragging them in the dirt of the yard, and Bella felt teary. Momma was excited because she was going to see the others, but here was Bella, doing all the work. After she had piled the wash in the basket, she wandered out through the long hall to the street. A little farther down, in the middle of the quiet Sabbath street, Margie Kowalski and the Hunrath girls were jumping rope. They were chanting a song, and laughing. They did not seem to see her, and she moved forward a little, away from the edge of the building. None of the Jewish girls were playing, because it was the Sabbath. But they never played with the Polish girls anyway. Bella wondered why. The small Jewish children spoke only Yiddish, and the small Polish ones only Polish. But most of the older children could speak English, so they could play together. The Hunrath girls were German, and Margie was Polish, so they were talking together in English. But Bella still couldn't speak English well. She moved forward a little more, and Gertrude Hunrath, taller and gawkier even than Bella, spotted her. She let the rope stop and called out, 'Hey, Bella, wanta play?'

Bella's heart leaped, and she ran toward them, taking one end of the rope from Gertrude, and chiming in on the chant, following their sounds – for she didn't understand the words, or if she did, they seemed to make no sense. After a while, Margie tripped, and took her end, and Bella jumped. She did it heavily, and tripped several times, but they didn't make her take an end, they said she could have another chance. Bella's heart was pumping, her face was pink, her hair flew. It was wonderful!

Then, suddenly, there was Momma, standing at the entrance to the hall, grey-faced. 'Bella! Bella!' Her voice was harsh and high. 'Stop that! You'll break your shoes!' And Bella paled, and looked down at her old boots, and understood there was no money for new ones, and reluctantly walked away from the girls, shyly turning to say (in English!), 'I have to go in now,' and the girls watched her go, silently, understanding. Their lives, after all, were not so different.

Sullenly, Bella helped Momma chop the celery and the onions and simmer them in butter, and crumble the white bread. She wanted to beg a slice or two for herself: white bread was still a treat for her. But something stopped her, and she saw it all go into the bowl of stuffing, and watched Momma stuff the chickens and put them in the oven. Then Momma made her peel the hot boiled potatoes while she peeled the cucumbers and·sliced them. It was easier to peel the potatoes hot, but they burned her fingers and she kept dropping them. She didn't care, even though Momma looked up each time she heard one fall into the bowl. Momma salted the cucumbers and put them on the cupboard shelf with a plate over the bowl. Then she took the potatoes from Bella, and swiftly, without minding the heat at all, sliced them into a clean bowl and poured in the celery she had chopped for the salad. Then she poured hot vinegar and oil over them, and salt and pepper, and mixed it well. Bella looked longingly at the salad, but Momma didn't offer her any. Then Momma ran the cucumbers underwater and squeezed them, and poured vinegar and sugar and water on them, and put them aside again. Tomorrow morning she would immerse them in sour cream with dill sprinkled over it.

When this was finished, Momma sighed and wiped her hands on her apron, and poured a hot cup of coffee for herself. Bella knew Momma still had the ironing to do, and that she had been up since six, walked to work and back, and sewed for five hours that morning. She was ashamed of her sullenness. She looked shyly at Momma: 'Are you tired, Momma?'

'No, no,' Momma said, then looked at Bella and smiled, 'Tonight I finish new dress for you, Bella.'

For *them*, Bella thought, then felt ungrateful and more ashamed. She went out to gather up the second load of wash, now dry, while Momma set up the ironing board. It occurred to her there was nothing for their dinner, and she ran inside, aghast.

'Momma! We forgot to get anything for *our* dinner!'

Her mother looked up wearily from the sheet she was ironing. 'Oh, Bella, it doesn't matter. We can just have some eggs. There are some boiled potatoes left over. Fry them in bacon fat.'

The next morning, Momma wakened her early and they dressed in their good clothes. Momma put on her old black straw hat. She wrapped the food in towels and laid it in a flat basket with two handles, and added plates and knives and forks and napkins. Bella crept up to examine them, and was relieved: there were five of each. Then they picked up the basket, each holding a handle, and walked to the trolley. They rode one trolley to the end of the line, got off and took another. Then they were in the middle of the city, in front of a huge brown building that frightened Bella. Men in straw boaters were walking around, even though it was a hot August Sunday, and a woman in a great broad-brimmed hat with flowers on it was running toward the building, laughing with a man in a straw hat, while behind them stood a little Polska carrying a great heavy bag. The woman turned. 'Come on, Marija!' she called impatiently, and the girl ran as best she could, red-faced, tugging the heavy bag.

Momma and Bella went inside the building. The ceiling was high, and there were wooden benches in a great open room. It was cooler there. They walked to the wall where a man stood behind a cage, and Momma said something to him and gave him money, and he gave her two pieces of cardboard, and Mommy turned swiftly and ran, and Bella ran after her, carrying the heavy basket alone now, until Momma realized, and stopped and took her end. They ran down some dark steps to a cavernous dark place with tracks running below a platform. Momma told her they were waiting for the train.

A train! Bella tried, but could not imagine what that could be, and when the thing came roaring toward them, she gasped and grabbed Momma and almost upset the basket, and Momma cried out, 'Bella!' and shook her head at Bella's stupidity. But the big light on the front, and the roar of noise terrified her and reminded her, as it plunged toward them, of the trolley that had almost killed Euga. They took seats and rode for a long time. Momma was fanning herself with her handkerchief, and breathing in quick little gasps. The city gave way to miles of green fields. Momma said they were potato farms.

Bella found she could read the sign where they got off: Farmingdale, it said. She didn't know what *dale* meant, but she understood that the place was a place for farming. There was a small white house near the tracks, that people were coming out of to get on the train, but beyond them, for miles around, there was nothing at all but fields. Bella looked at Momma, expecting her to burst into tears, but Momma seemed to know where she was going. She set off, and Bella followed, dragging a little on the basket. They walked for a long time, down a road surrounded on all sides by fields. Then they left the road and walked across the fields. The sun was directly overhead now, and very hot. Far off in the distance, Bella spied a small lump on the horizon. That must be where they were going. It was still miles away. Bella wondered how Momma knew to find it, but then, she thought, Momma always did know where things were and how to reach them.

Eventually, the building took shape: tall, gaunt, dark redbrick, sooty with age. The narrow windows had bars on them, and there were rusting black fire escapes on the sides. Bella shuddered. It looked like a prison. They had to walk around it to the front, because it was enclosed in a high fence of black metal poles. They had to stop at the gate and Momma had to talk to the policeman there, who sat in a little booth. But once inside . . . there they were! Eddie, Wally, and Euga! And they cried out, and Momma cried out and dropped her end of the basket and ran to them, and they all ran to her, and then they were all mixed together, the four of them, all their bodies intertwined, and Momma was crying, and Wally was whimpering, and Euga was staring wide-eyed, and Momma picked her up in her arms, and she kept saying, '*Moje drodzy, moje biedne sieroty*, my dears, my poor orphans,' and wiping her eyes, and hugging one of them, saying '*Moja najdrozsza, moja najdrozsza!* my dearest! Sweetheart! *Kochany!*'

Bella stood there with the basket, which was resting on the ground in front of her. Momma had completely forgotten her. She didn't matter. Then Eddie saw her, and

came over and smiled and said, 'You got something to eat?'
and she was shocked: it was the first time he had ever
spoken to her in English. She nodded, and he bent and
lifted the handles and started toward the building. Wally
was drawn toward the food, and he turned too, and
Momma followed them, with Euga in her arms. At the
door, she turned. Bella was standing by the gate. 'Come,
Bella!' Momma called gaily, and she ran to join them.

They were sent to the auditorium, a large dark room with
chairs fixed into the floor, and a stage in the front. There
was no one else there. They sat on the chairs in a back
row, Momma with Euga on one side and the basket on the
other, and Momma took out the food. She didn't know
where to put it, though, so Eddie got up and carried the
basket to the wide aisle, and sat down on the floor beside
it. They all followed, except Momma didn't sit on the floor,
and she wouldn't let Bella sit there either. 'You'll dirty
your dress.' So Momma crouched down and laid the plates
out in front of the three children, and put Bella's plate on
a seat. Then she cut up the chicken, and spooned out the
stuffing, and took the towels off the potato salad and the
cucumbers, and let the children help themselves. Momma
and Bella sat on the stiff seats, their plates in their laps.
The children ate greedily, cramming food into their mouths
with their hands. Momma said nothing. Momma hardly
ate anything, she watched them, and sometimes she'd grab
an arm or leg and cry out, 'Oh, so thin, so thin!' and begin
to weep. The children ignored her. They kept stuffing their
mouths. They ate the two chickens, all the stuffing, all the
potato salad, and most of the cucumbers. Then Momma
uncovered the cakes, and their eyes opened wide. But they
could not eat more than one big slice each, so Momma
wrapped the rest up in a towel, and gave it to Eddie. 'You
keep it. You give it to Wally and Euga.' Eddie tried to
explain that he never saw Euga, that she was in the girls'
section, and boys were not allowed there. But Eddie stumbled over this explanation – he had begun to forget his
Polish, although Frances, willfully perhaps, did not notice
this. Bella had to help him out. So then Momma took

another towel and cut off a big chunk of cake and gave it to Euga. Momma's eyes were still shining, and after she gave Euga the cake, she reached down from her seat and picked Euga up and rocked her against her body, saying, '*Moja droga, moja biedna sierota,*' over and over.

Then a door swung open and a grey-haired woman carrying a whole ring of keys came in. She nodded to the children, who looked up at her blankly. Eddie turned to Momma. 'We have to go now, Momma.'

'NO, NO, NO!' Momma cried, and began to sob again, as hard as she had the day they were taken away. The woman started to walk forward, her mouth a thin line, and Eddie glanced at her and got up. He wiped his mouth and hands on a napkin, and pulled Wally up by his arm. Eddie bent to kiss Momma, and Momma grabbed him and held on to him, crushing Euga on her lap. She was crying his name, crying out about her dears, her poor little orphans, and Wally came up and put his head on her lap, and she wailed louder, and the woman came near and said, 'Please, Mrs Brez,' but Momma didn't even hear her. The woman nodded her head at Eddie, and he walked toward her, pulling Wally behind him. Wally's mouth was smeared with grease and cake crumbs, but Momma didn't notice. Finally, the woman came and took Euga out of Momma's arms, and Momma's arms stayed extended long after they were empty, as she screamed in rage and sorrow. Euga was crying now too, peering over the shoulder of the woman and clutching her towel-wrapped cake. When they had all vanished behind the swinging door, Momma let her arms down, and her head fell, and she wrenched her throat with sobs, her whole body jolting with them.

Finally, she calmed down to sniffling, and bent wearily, the old Momma again, and cleaned up the plates, the forks, the unused knives, and stuffed everything back into the basket. She wiped her hands on one of the clean napkins, kept wiping them, over and over. She was still sniffling as they walked back across the fields, the sun halfway down now, but still hot, the grass whispering around their ankles. Bella noticed tiny spots of color among the green, and occasionally she would stop to examine them more closely.

They were tiny wildflowers. She began to pick them. Momma turned around. 'Hurry, or we'll miss the train,' she called. Bella ran, but she still stopped once in a while to grab a pretty blue, or yellow, or white blossom. Momma could carry the basket alone now. As they neared the station, Bella ran up to Momma and smiled, and held out her bouquet.

'Look, Momma, aren't they pretty? They're for you!'

'Oh, what do I want with a bunch of weeds!' Momma said in disgust, and taking them from Bella, threw them down on the tracks where the train would run over them.

After that, they went to the orphanage every two weeks. It was cooler in the fall, when the sky was a beautiful blue, and the clouds like white puffs. And one Sunday, Bella saw from the train, a line of trees with colored leaves – red, gold, orange – that made her gasp with their beauty. Aside from that, though, the journey was always the same.

four

The night before school reopened, Momma reminded Bella that she had to get up early the next morning. Bella looked at her blankly, not thinking to ask what time she should get up, or how she would know what time it was. Momma always seemed to know what time it was, Bella didn't know how. She had no sense that Frances had been raised in the country, and told time by the sun; nor did Frances perceive that Bella did not share this ability.

When Bella woke the next morning, after a whole summer of rising after the room was soaked with heat, the room was already hot. She leaped up. Momma had long since gone. She was probably already late for school. She dressed hurriedly, her haste keeping her from that dreadful thought of what awaited her: repeating third grade. She had been taller than many of the other children even last year, partly because her birthday was in January, and many of the others had been born six months later. But she was just tall, tall and gawky. This year she would feel like a giant among the smaller children, a year or more younger than she. Humiliation sheathed her in sweat, and she grabbed her tablet and pen and ran out without even stopping to drink the coffee Momma had left at the side of the stove.

She didn't know how long it took to get to school from their new house, so she ran all the way. But when she arrived, the schoolyard was empty, the doors of the school locked. She leaned against the fence and waited. She waited a long time, and her heart kept making little pings. Maybe Momma was wrong, maybe school didn't open until tomorrow. People would look at her and think how stupid she was, coming a day early. She stared firmly toward the yard, away from the street, so she would not see the people passing who might gaze at her as if she was an idiot.

She waited, it seemed, hours, and then children began to arrive and play in the schoolyard. Finally, a bell rang in the yard, and the teachers came out and lined the children up, preparing to march them into their classrooms. Bella dragged her body to search for the third-grade line. And when she found it, her heart stopped completely, for it was as she feared, she was the tallest in the class. She could not even conceal herself in the crowd. She stuck out like a spindly tree in an empty lot.

They reached the classroom and the teacher called the roll and assigned them seats by height, putting Bella in the back row, where she would not be able to hear. But Bella did not dare to say anything. Then, as she went through their names once more, she stopped at the name of Isabella Brez. She peered at Bella and said sharply, 'Isabella, it is expected that you will comb your hair before you come to school.' Bella's face burned, and the children looked around at her and tittered. She did not hear anything the teacher said the rest of that day.

After school, Bella dawdled, looking into shop windows in the new neighborhood, but not too long. She felt people were looking at her, that they could see she was gawky and stupid, and they would know from her manner that she had no friends. She would go home and drop off her books and take the money Momma had left for her and go right back out to buy food for dinner. Sometimes she passed girls playing ball or jumping rope in the street, and her heart yearned toward them a little, but she pulled herself up. 'I am a big girl,' she said to herself.

But then, there were hours to kill before it was time to make dinner, and she would sit at the round table drinking coffee and continuing the daydream she had been creating at school.

Bella/Anastasia had a clock to wake her up in the mornings, one with a bell that rang when it was eight o'clock. No. No. Anastasia/Bella's momma came in to wake her each morning, saying sweetly, 'It's time to get up, Anastasia, dear,' and when she got downstairs, Momma had cocoa with whipped cream on it, and French toast waiting for her. Yes. And Anastasia's poppa was there too, in a striped vest with a thick gold watch chain across it. He was eating his eggs and drinking his coffee, but he always looked up when Anastasia came in, and smiled, and said, 'Good morning.' And he would ask her how she slept, and whether she had pleasant dreams, and Anastasia/Bella would say yes, because she always had pleasant dreams.

And Poppa would kiss her forehead before he left for work, and then Momma would sit her on the high stool, and softly brush her long blond hair which, just like Bella's, was down to her waist. But Anastasia's hair made long spaghetti curls all by itself, and her momma would brush them into shape and put a pretty hair ribbon in her hair, one that matched her dress, like Margie Jasinski's. And Momma would kiss her goodbye, making sure she had her little bag of lunch. Anastasia's lunch was white bread and butter, with hard candies for dessert. And as she walked to school, people turned in the street and said, 'What a pretty little girl,' and Bella would always smile to herself with pleasure, but never let on that she heard. In the schoolyard, the girls her age were jumping rope, and when she entered, they would all turn and smile and cry, 'Here's Bella!' They would wait for her to join them, and she would run, dropping her books, and jump right in, she didn't even have to take an end, because they liked her so much. She jumped right in and never faltered, she jumped and jumped and her hair bounced, and after a while, she would stop and take an end just out of kindness, because it was only fair. It was fair to give the others a chance, because Bella never missed.

My mother always combed my hair. Every school morning, after breakfast, she would make me sit on the stepladder-stool that was painted the same color as the kitchen table and chairs, but had no decal on it, and would brush my long, thick, knotted hair with a hairbrush of pure pig bristle that she had bought from the Fuller Brush Man, and that, she told me many times, was a *very good* brush. She told me this in such tones of reverence, almost awe, that I thought it must be something extremely valuable and kept it for thirty years. I was shocked, when finally I was forced to replace it, to find that hairbrushes were not at all expensive.

As she stood behind me brushing, then combing, I would frequently cry out: 'Ouch!' Tears would stream down my face. I vowed that when I was grown up and had a little girl, I would not hurt her when I combed her hair. My mother hurt me every morning, and my scalp grew so tough that to this day I can pull out a single hair – the most painful way to pull hair – without feeling it. She brushed vigorously, combed straight down, and my eyes were ringed with red from tearing when she got through. She made two thick braids, and tied them with matching hair ribbons – if I had not lost one. If I had no hair ribbons, she just used the rubber bands.

On special days, when we were going out, she would curl my hair with the curling iron, making long spaghetti curls. I hated this even more than the brushing, mostly because of the awful smell of burning, and I vowed I would never inflict such a thing on any child of my own. Nor would I inflict upon them the morning dose of codliver oil my sister and I were fed, in a large tablespoon, before our orange juice. It tasted terrible, but Mommy said we had to have it, that it would keep us healthy. I hated the orange juice too, because it was cold and had little bits of orange in it – Mommy squeezed it fresh every morning – and it made my mouth burn. And then there was the oatmeal with cream. I hated that worse than anything except the codliver oil. Sometimes Mommy cooked Cream of Wheat, which was a little better. I would usually leave my glass of milk or drink only as much as Mommy demanded. I began to drink it only when she poured some coffee into it. Sometimes Mommy boiled an egg for me, but in those days, eggs were fresh and had been fertilized, so they had a strong taste which I now love but which in those days bothered my tender child's palate. All in all, I hated mornings. There wasn't much anyone could do to please me. The truth was, I didn't want to get up early, and wasn't hungry when I did: and this has remained true.

And every night, after the fight to get me to go to bed, my mother would kiss me good night, and send me to Daddy, who would also kiss me, and then Mommy would always say, 'Pleasant dreams,' and I'd say it too. I would go up and read by the dim light of my bed lamp until I heard Mommy and Daddy preparing to come upstairs. Then I'd switch off the light, and slide down under the covers and close my eyes and pretend to be asleep. But Mommy always came in to see that I was covered, and if I was awake, she would kiss me good night again.

When I had children of my own, I remembered my own prescriptions, and was very careful combing my little girl's hair into braids. Once in a great while, I'd pull by mistake, and she'd cry out grouchily, her eyes tearing, and glare at me as if I had committed this crime intentionally. I'd always say I was sorry, but inside I was smiling, thinking about how any misery expands to take up all one's space. And I never used a curling iron on her hair. But I did inflict braces on her.

And every night, I kissed my children good night and wished them pleasant dreams, and they returned the wish and went into their rooms. And before I went to bed, I would go in to check them, and they would be sound asleep, Arden with her eyes open just a crack, so you couldn't be sure she was sleeping, and Billy with his thumb in his mouth — clear through until he was ten years old. They would be pink and sweet-smelling from their baths and their sweat, and warm with sleep, and my heart would roll over as I looked at them, and often I'd kneel down by the side of the bed and lay my face on their cheeks and put my arms around them, and kiss their cheeks and just stay there for a while. They never woke, or knew I'd done this. And guessing from the way they act now, it seems they never knew, never felt my love.

And sometimes, as I knelt there beside them, my heart would ache about a cross word, or flash of irritation I'd tossed them that day. Not that they didn't deserve some reprimand once in a while, but on the whole, they were wonderful kids, and most of my crossness had to do with my own miseries. I felt sorry, I'd vow to be more careful the next day, and I would be, for a while. . . .

I must add that neither of them, or Franny either, has ever reproached me with the little acts of cruelty I visited upon them. There must have been some that I didn't notice at the time, so wouldn't remember. I guess if one has to put up with one's children not recalling the love, one is rewarded by them also forgetting the moments of hate. Or whatever it is. I remember one time, Arden was about thirteen. And she came in from school late, around five, very excited. Some friends were there, I was preparing dinner, Toni was helping me peel vegetables. And Arden was glowing, and cried out, 'Oh, Mommy! I've found the most wonderful book, it's like poetry it's so beautiful. Have you ever heard of it?' And she held up *The Prophet*, by Kahlil Gibran.

I groaned. 'Sentimental slop! I found it in the attic, it had been my mother's, she'd loved it, and at your age I thought it was wonderful too. But it's trash,' I informed her.

Her face fell. 'Well, I like it,' she mumbled. She left the room.

Toni turned to me. 'That was really cruel. She was all excited about that book. Why did you do that?'

I stopped. Why had I? Maintaining high literary standards, regardless of cost? How ridiculous! 'I don't know. You're right,' I said, puzzled at myself. But it was done, and could not now be remedied. Except that I never again doused her excitement like that. At least I don't think I did . . .

It was a Sunday in January, and I was eight. It was a grey day, cold and bleak, without snow, a depressing winter day. It was even more depressing because Mommy wasn't speaking to us. She often stopped speaking, and I never knew why; but this day was heavier somehow. She hardly spoke even to Joy, who went out early to play with a little girl from across the street. I stared out the kitchen window, and could see them toddling around in the yard, bundled up against the weather, trying to build a snowman out of the tarnished remains of last week's snowfall. The tension mounted in the house, and I spent most of the day in the front room Mommy called the porch, sitting on the floor and drawing. My father was working in the cellar. I never knew what he did down there. But he came upstairs for something, and I heard him ask my mother something in a pleasant voice. She barely answered him. I stood up, and when my father came through the living room, I went up close to him and whispered.

'What's the matter with Mommy today? She's so *mad.*'

Surprisingly, my father did not deny my charge. He whispered back, 'She's mad because we forgot her birthday.'

'When is her birthday?'

'Today.'

I was appalled. I went back to the porch and just stood there. My heart hurt. How terrible, to have your birthday forgotten! But then, I hadn't forgotten it, I had never known when it was. Mommy never had a birthday party – neither did Daddy. Well, neither did we for that matter, not at least that we could remember. But we got presents on our birthdays. I had not gotten a present for Mommy. And it was Sunday, and the stores were all closed, and anyway, I had no money.

I went up to the room Joy and I shared, and examined my few possessions: a scrapbook, a couple of games, and my small library, about eight books. There was nothing there Mommy would want. But I also had a few treasures.

I decided Mommy would understand that I didn't have money, and she might cheer up if someone remembered her, and if I gave her something pretty.

I worked for several hours, pasting cotton fabric into an old shoe box. The material was scraps from the slipcovers Mommy had made for the porch chairs. Then, I lay inside the few treasures I owned: a pretty pinecone I'd found in the fall; a picture of a beautiful lady I'd cut out from a magazine; and a necklace of unpolished stones that my uncle Eddie had made himself and sent me last year. The box looked terribly empty, so I took some hair ribbons whose mates had been lost, and made them into bows, and put them among the treasures. Then I closed the box and tied it up with another ribbon and, my heart beating with nervousness, ran down to give it to Mommy.

She was sitting at the kitchen table, smoking and drinking coffee. A roast was baking, and the kitchen smelled delicious. I ran up to her.

'Happy birthday, Mommy!'

She turned, surprised, and took the box I held out. Slowly, she untied the ribbon and removed the cover. She peered inside. She looked up at me angrily. 'What do I want this junk for?' she cried, thrusting the box back at me.

five

As I reconstruct it, Euga was not doing well in the orphanage. She was so young, only four and a half, to be separated from her mother; and I think they must not have had facilities for little girls. For whatever reason, the orphanage authorities told Frances that when Eugenia was five, ready to go to kindergarten, she would be released. The boys had to stay on. These priorities seem strange, but I think of the many photographs taken by Jacob Riis, a little earlier, of homeless boys sleeping in alleys. There were still thousands of them in the city.

Frances was overjoyed. Euga had her fifth birthday in August, and could start school in February of 1914. The authorities, though, let her go in January. The night they fetched her from the the orphanage, the boys watching them mournfully through the high fence (they had been allowed to walk that far with them), Momma didn't cry much at all – only when she said goodbye to her sons. She laughed and wiped tears from her cheeks that were a different kind of tears, and she carried Euga part of the long way back to the train, while Bella carried the empty food basket.

That night, they had strawberry jam with their black bread and butter, and Momma picked Euga up and sat her on her lap, and rocked back and forth. She almost crooned to her, 'My baby, my baby, my precious one, *moja droga* Genya.'

Bella was silent, watching from her seat at the table, as Momma sat on the couch with the baby, rocking for a long time, kissing her forehead, holding her close. If she wondered if Momma would love her more if she'd gone to the orphanage, she did not let the question enter her mind. She just sat and watched.

But next day Momma told her that she had to take care of Euga all day while Momma worked. So Bella didn't go to school for a while. She took Euga with her everywhere she went, and Euga would clutch her sister's hand, and hang on to her so beggingly that Bella's heart was touched. Euga was quiet and obedient, and she never cried.

One day Frances told Bella she had to take Euga to be vaccinated. Vaccinations were required for entering school-children. Bella paled.

'I don't know how,' she said tremulously.

'You take two trolleys, to the Board of Health,' Momma said impatiently. (How did she know? Did she take me? I don't remember.)

Bella just stared at her, and Momma grew more impatient. Bella was ten years old now, a big girl. She repeated the directions, and told Bella to ask someone if she was lost.

Bella set off the next morning, stiff with dread. Euga clutched her hand so tightly their hands got wet and slimy. But Euga would not let go, so every once in a while, they would change hands. They took the trolley, and got off at the end, then the second trolley. It was the same way they went to the orphanage, except you didn't take the train. Bella wandered around for a while among the big brown buildings, but finally saw a sign (she could read it!) that said Board of Health, and the two children climbed the steps and followed signs through the hall. They entered a large room that reminded Bella of the room with the lady who told Momma she could keep one. She began to tremble, and Euga trembled with her. Euga was a good kid. In a thin voice, Bella told the lady why they were there. The lady took a long sheet of paper with words and lines on it, and picked up a pen.

'What is the child's name?'

'Euga.'

'What is the child's name?'

'Euga.'

'What is it?'

'Euga. Euga Brez.'

'OLGA? Speak up, child.'

Bella shook her head. 'No, Euga, Euga,' she pronounced it carefully.

The woman sighed. 'How do you spell it?'

'I don't know.' Then, she had a moment of memory. 'Eugenia!' she said, pronouncing it Aow-gay-nya, as Momma did.

The woman grimaced. 'I'll put down Olga,' she said.

Bella protested, but the woman paid no attention. 'Address? Date of birth?'

Euga remained Olga for three years; when she entered third grade, Momma went down to the school herself and cleared the matter up. But Bella felt humiliated again, again a failure. My mother tells me this story along with the one about almost causing Euga's death, with the streetcar. She is morose, more depressed than usual.

'So they called her Olga for three years?' I laugh. She doesn't even smile. She is chewing on the inside of her lip, ruminating. The incident is one more black mark in the book of rage she is compiling against the gods she doesn't believe in.

Chapter V

one

A few years ago, I went to India to do a photographic essay on poor Indian women. The country provided me with spectacular material – the golden-skinned women in their brilliant saris, red, blue, yellow, against the sienna-colored sand, the pale green scrub tree, the sky that stretched unbroken blue for miles. I shot women carrying five shiny brass pots of water on their heads, walking barefoot along a dirt road; women at the communal pump, bending gracefully to fill their *matkas;* women so thin and brown they look like stick figures made of ebony, but wearing inch-wide ankle bracelets of heavy silver; women sitting vacantly holding their children, their eyes wide and dark and sad and angry, unlike the loving madonnas on all the posters, embracing bright smiling youngsters. The women and children I saw all looked hungry and tired.

Of course I talked with these women as I shot them, or before; I always try to form some kind of relationship with people before I take their pictures – that way it seems less like rape and more like encounter. I had translators with me wherever I went, and the women and the translator and I would sit on the bare floor of one house or another, and I'd ask them about their lives. The lives of poor Indian women are unspeakable: they have all the responsibility and no power. They are expected – and expect – to fetch all the water, fodder, and fuel the family uses, to give birth regularly, from the time they are married – at fourteen, fifteen, or sixteen – and raise the children, to do all the cooking, a time-consuming task, *and* to care for all animals and work in the fields for eight hours each day. They rise early and go to sleep late, and have no time during the day for anything but their work. And often, their wages are taken by their husbands, so they have nothing to say about how the money they earn is spent.

Whenever I asked them about how they felt about their

lives, they shrugged: there was no alternative, they said. A woman's life is what it is. They were convinced that if they were reborn in the future, if they had been reborn before, they would always be women, had always been women, and would always be married to the same man. Since I have always thought that of all the punishments in Dante's hell, the worst was the one he believed to be lightest – an eternal whirling in the same condition – I found their vision intolerable. The American in me insisted on change, and I asked them about schooling children, a different future, literacy classes – something, *anything*, to change their condition. They would smile their sweet smiles at me and nod their heads. 'Oh, we don't think about the future, about change,' one said, and the others would murmur in agreement and add, 'It's better not to.'

And even though my life has been as different from theirs as one woman's life can be different from another's, I understood profoundly what they meant. There are times when it is essential *not* to think about your life, and certainly not to think about changing it, times when no change for the better seems possible, and disappointment of any sort would be the true last straw, the blow that finally makes you stagger, fall and die. When you have to walk for miles bent under a load of faggots in the hot sun, and you know you will have to do this again three days later, and you still have to walk miles carrying water later the same day. . . . It is better not to think.

Bella spent years of her life not thinking. (So did I.)

By the time she reached fourth grade, Bella could read and write in English, and although she was still the tallest child in the class, she was no longer the oldest – other children too got left back – and she began to feel that perhaps she was not utterly stupid. Occasionally, when she read aloud, the teacher would praise her; and sometimes there was a note on her compositions complimenting her on how well she wrote. Then the teacher chose her for a good part in the school play, and the following term, she was given the lead.

She had a shoot growing in her – a fragile sense that she

was a person like other people, that she perhaps had some worth. She began to make friends at school, not with the gay well-dressed girls who always wore bows in their hair that matched their dresses, the popular ones, who giggled and whispered together; but with the quiet girls whose underwear sleeves sometime stuck out from under their puff-sleeved dresses, and whose hair was not done every day in long spaghetti curls and some days even looked uncombed. She still had to go to market most afternoons and cook every night; and now she had to take Euga with her everywhere she went. But Euga was sweet and appealing, and the older girls liked her, and she never caused trouble. And she never told Momma on the afternoons when she and Euga would go around the corner to jump rope with Margie Jasinski and her friends. Sometimes, if Bella had two cents, she and Euga would run to the corner two blocks down where the man sold hot sweet potatoes from his wheeled cart; or if Bella got out alone on a Saturday afternoon and had two cents, she would run to the bakery shop and buy herself a cupcake.

Momma was a little better, now that Euga was home. She was cheerful in the evenings, and after dinner, before she started to tire, she would take Euga on her lap and rock her and croon, '*Moja droga, moja biedna sierota*, My dear, my poor orphan,' over and over, and she would tuck Euga into their big bed every night. Bella would watch Momma hugging Euga and think, Well, I'm a big girl, now, I'm practically Euga's mother, and she would remember the girl she'd seen in Jewtown holding that huge baby on her lap, and try not to remember her eyes, try to blot them out.

But when Momma came out and saw Bella nearly invisible in the corner of the couch, sitting silently, she would speak sharply to her, say 'What the hell is the matter with you? What the devil are you doing there?' And after she began to sew, sometimes she would cry out as if a sudden pain had struck her, and bend over her work and sob. She would start tearing her hair, cursing, sobbing, slapping herself. She cried in soft wrenching noises that would not wake Euga, her sewing neglected in her lap.

Frances never stopped crying, not until the fall of 1916, when her sons were finally released. But she never did it in front of Euga, so none of the children except Bella ever knew the depths of rage and violence in their mother's heart.

The only time Momma ever got angry in front of Euga was when the two girls forgot, and slipped into English around the house. Euga had forgotten her Polish while she was at the orphanage, and although she picked it up again at home, English was now more natural to her, and the sisters spoke it at school and on the streets. But Momma, who had grown up in a country in which the Germans had forbidden the speaking of Polish even inside the home, went wild if they spoke English. She did not explain this; they only knew they were expected to speak Polish at home, and that Momma was unhappy when they did not. They were good girls, they tried to be obedient.

One day in the spring of 1916, when Bella was in sixth grade, the teacher made an announcement. She said that if the children wanted to learn a trade and get a good job after they finished school, they should sign up for P.S. 162 in the fall.

'What a fool I was,' my mother says, sipping the water she now drinks alternately with scotch, so she won't be sick the next day. 'I went running home and told Momma about it, and of course she trotted me right over there to sign up. Ugh. Those were the worst years of my life.'

I refrain from remarking that the worst years of her life are whatever years she is describing. I shun critical distance; yet at the same time I want it. If I were to be able to put my mother's life in perspective, maybe I'd be free of the burden of it; but if I do that, I will hurt her, I will in some way diminish what she has suffered. My stomach twists, but I remain silent.

So, in the fall of 1916, Bella went to P.S. 162 in Ridgewood. It was far from where they lived, so she had to get up very early in the morning. She would run out to the baker's for buns for breakfast; then walk in the windy fall days to the trolley stop. She had to take two trolleys to get to Ridgewood, to the dark soot-blackened brick school with its windows covered with mesh like the windows at the orphanage. There, from 8.30 to 11.45, she was taught history, geography, English, and arithmetic. But the teachers here were not as good as those in the old school, and she could not hear as well, and the work was too easy for her. One day she met a girl from her old school on the sidewalk, and they talked a little. The girl was excited, she was having trouble, she said, learning fractions. Bella could tell she was bragging even as she claimed stupidity; she thought it was very grown up to be studying fractions. They were not taught in Bella's school.

In the afternoons, after lunch, from 12.30 to 3.00, the children were supposed to be taught a trade. Bella was signed up to learn paper-box making. But the teacher almost never showed up. This was true, Bella discovered, of the teachers of dressmaking, millinery, and shop. The trade teachers rarely appeared, and the children would sit in the dreary cold rooms all afternoon until the bell released them. Four girls from Bella's school had transferred to P.S. 162 at the same time she did; within a few months, all of them had been removed from the school. Only Bella remained. She stayed for two years.

The dressmaking teacher came in more regularly in the second half of the eighth-grade term, and the girls all had to make a graduation dress for themselves. Bella made a beautiful middy, white, with ruffles, and Momma bought her a big white ribbon to wear with it in a bow in her hair. On graduation day, a teacher stopped Bella in the corridor.

'Oh, Isabella, how lovely you look!'

Bella, who had no thought that she looked in any way attractive, who was in fact feeling bowed down and hopeless, tried to smile. Some passing girls overheard and clustered around her.

'Oh, Bella how pretty! What are you going to do, Bella?'

She raised her head haughtily. 'I'm going to high school,' she announced airily.

'Ooooh! You're lucky! Which one?'

Bella named the most prestigious high school she knew, and the girls were impressed.

But Bella felt even more bowed down. The space around

her heart kept churning, and her heart felt as if something was hammering on it. She knew she had an enlarged heart and she thought perhaps she was about to die. She did not care. More than anything in the world she wanted to go to high school, but very few of the children did, and almost none of the girls. The Jewish boys were going, and a few Jewish girls. Bella remembered Yetta Ettinger playing the piano, and she wondered why Jewish people were kinder to their children than Christians.

The day after graduation in the June of 1918, when Bella was fourteen, Momma took her to Greenwich Village, to a loft on the third floor of an old dirty building, and Bella got a job working ten hours a day five days a week, and half a day Saturday, for twelve dollars a week. All day, every day, Bella made paper boxes.

But Momma grew happier in these years. Eddie's birthday was in October, and in 1916, when he was fourteen, he and Wally were to be released from the orphanage. Eddie could now get working papers and contribute to the maintenance of the family. All fall, while Bella was languishing in trade school, Momma hummed and bustled. She found a new apartment on Lorimer Street in Williamsburg for nine dollars a month – Momma now earned nine dollars a week. The apartment was over a candy store, but there were only two stores on the block – one on each corner; in between there were row houses with high stoops. And because it was on a corner, it had windows on three sides, so it was bright and airy, a release from the dark little slum they'd lived in for the past three years. And it had two bedrooms, and electric light! Momma bought two beds for the boys' room, although the three females still slept in the old double bed.

And the boys came home. There was crying and hugging and a great feast, but Bella remembers none of it. Her brothers were strangers to her, and a little frightening. They were good boys, but somehow they seemed noisy, chaotic, violent, and she shrank from them. Eddie was mature at fourteen; he looked like an adult, and acted like one too. He and Euga looked more like Momma; Bella and

Wally more like Poppa. Eddie and Euga had broader, squarer bodies, and Momma's warm eyes. But their hair and eyes were brown, unlike Momma's. But Momma's blond hair was almost completely grey now, and her blue eyes more watery and nearly colorless. Eddie combed his short hair neatly down either side of his head, and he was serious and steady. He had been trained in the orphanage, and he got a job right away, in a printing factory, for nine dollars a week. He was sober and polite and very kind to all of them, but he seemed often to be far away. And as soon as he could, he signed up for high-school night courses; and soon too, he began to bring things home – he brought a mandolin, a banjo, and a huge album of stamps. Bella never understood why her brother liked to do the things he did. But often, on Saturday afternoons after his half-day, when he got paid, as the children waited and watched, Eddie would walk home from work over the Brooklyn Bridge carrying six charlotte russes – one for each of them and three for himself!

Wally too had learned to play these instruments at the orphanage, and after Eddie bought them, the two boys would play together and they would all sing. At first it was fun. The boys knew many songs, but sometimes they would stumble over the words to a song and fall into fits of giggles. Wally laughed a lot. He was fun, he played, and when he got some cards, he showed his sisters card tricks. They had learned many things in the orphanage. But Wally was also – Bella did not know what to call it. When she was an adult, she thought of him as weak. Wally had been three months shy of seven when he was taken from his mother; and returned to her after he was ten. He was thin and nervous, like Bella, like their father; and pale with blond hair and blue eyes. His hair grew wildly, like a springing plant, and fell in his eyes; and his eyes were somehow vacant. (They would remain that way throughout his life.) He would laugh, he'd get almost hysterical, then fall into a fit of weeping. His gestures were quick and agitated, and he was always moving. He often threw tantrums over what seemed to Bella nothing at all. He was sent to the public school, but he did not do well, he was left back three times in the next years, and finally quit to go to work on his fourteenth birthday. In school too, he was unsteady: once, when a teacher criticized his work, he leaped up on the windowsill of the third-story classroom and threatened to jump. And every night after he returned from the orphanage, he would steal a roll or a bun or a piece of cake from the pantry and take it to bed with him. When Momma and Bella changed his sheets every Saturday, they would find crumbled, moldered bread under his pillow. He continued to do this for several years.

But Momma rarely cried anymore. The only thing that really upset her was the boys speaking English, and of course they did: they had forgotten all their Polish while they were away. Momma would cry and yell and weep, but they were funny, they weren't like Bella and Euga: they would laugh and kiss her, or make a joke and pat her shoulder, and go out with their friends. Then Momma would get hysterical and sit at the table with her head in her arms, crying the way she used to cry. And Bella would go to her and touch her sleeve and say, 'Momma, I'll speak Polish.' And she did, but it didn't seem to matter to Momma. For Bella, Momma always remained inconsolable. After a few months, Momma gave up: among themselves, the children spoke English. But Bella and Euga went on speaking Polish to Momma.

With the boys back, Bella became suddenly conscious that she was the servant in the house. She was alone: the boys had their friends, Euga had Momma. But it was Bella Momma yelled at when something went wrong, Bella who cooked dinner and did the marketing, Bella who was sent on errands. 'Bella do this, Bella do that,' my mother says in a high sharp voice, with an accent, remembering. To the others, Momma was kind, easygoing, even loving. To people outside the family, she was extremely courteous. She treated people as if they were special, and everyone liked her. She had a charming smile and manner, and acquaintances greeted her warmly on the street. Only to Bella was she different.

The boys brought the world into their house. Besides the

banjo and the mandolin and the stamp collection, they brought news of a different part of the world – the boys they met at work or at school. They made friends instantly, and there was much coming and going in the house. They taught their sisters to play cards and many nights the four of them would play pinochle or bridge while Momma sewed under the lamplight – not entirely content, because they were speaking English, but not weeping either. Then one night Eddie brought home a phonograph, and some records by a singer called Caruso, and made them all listen. Bella could not hear too well, but Euga was awed.

When Bella went to work, things changed again. Momma began to do the cooking again. Sometimes she cooked at night, after dinner, something big like soup or a stew that they could have for the next two nights. And she cooked on Sundays, baking cakes and pies and pastries for desserts for the whole week. And Momma did the laundry by herself now, and whatever cleaning got done. Bella was freed from one part of her servitude. She gave her wages to Momma, who gave her fifty cents a day for carfare and lunch. Since she usually took her lunch, she could save her pennies to buy something once in a while. But in fact she never bought more than hairpins. And at nights she and Momma would go to the movies together. The boys usually went out – alone – something the girls never dreamed of doing; and Euga went to bed early. Momma and Bella would go across the street to a movie and be home by nine or nine-thirty. It was only a nickel, and Momma always paid. Still, the next morning she would have to get up early and trudge with Momma to the trolley stop and ride into lower Manhattan and trudge up the three grimy flights of stairs to the dark crowded loft where for ten hours a day she pasted pretty fabrics to cardboard.

two

My mother had a fixation on education. She went back to work just before my twelfth birthday, standing all day in her bad feet in high heels selling high-fashion hats to middle-class women, to save money to send me to college. And she worked all the time I was in school, and Joy too: she wanted us to have what she hadn't. When my father was earning twenty dollars a week, she found one dollar a week for piano lessons for me, and another one later, for Joy. She squeezed out fifty cents a year for the WXQR Bulletin, and a dime for the WNYC Bulletin, so I could choose what classical music I wanted to hear on the radio. And at Christmas, she respected my wishes and never gave me a doll, but only books. Unfortunately, Joy and I let her down: neither of us finished college then; but her grandchildren have come through for her. She should, like the Jewish mothers of jokes, be sitting back, her girth uprearing itself, in great complacency, speaking of her grandson the doctor, her granddaughter the psychologist. But it all came too late, and her interest is distant and minimal, like someone checking in with an old friend, nodding approval at every success story about people she knew a hundred years ago. Like a person acting satisfied that the world works the way it should, knowing all the while that it doesn't really it doesn't it doesn't.

After about a year, Bella got up the nerve to tell Momma she hated her job, although in far milder terms than that, and Momma took her to the sweatshop where she worked, and Bella began to work on the sewing machine. This was a little better at first. She made more money and she was learning something. She was advanced quickly to the Merrow, a machine that does edging and buttonholes, a prestigious job in the shop. And she had even more prestige because she could fix the Merrow. But after a while, there was nothing more to learn.

'You know, they thought it was so great, but it was nothing at all. It was a simple process of elimination,' my mother explains. 'When the stitches were not right, either the belt was loose or worn, or one of the screws needed adjustment. An idiot could have fixed it.'

So that fall, she followed Eddie's example and began to take high-school courses at night. Because both her parents could speak German, she signed up for German, and also for English literature. The classes were held in a huge room with a high ceiling, and were filled with the children of immigrants – tired, hunched over in shabby coats, scrawling earnestly in notebooks. This wasn't Bella's idea of education. She saw the ads in the magazines: What the Harvard Man wears: with a handsome clean-shaven American-looking young man in a neat shirt and tie, with a beautiful jacket. Still, she tried. But she could not hear the teacher, and although she religiously did her homework and read the books, she felt very much as she had when she first started school, as if what she were hearing (when she heard anything) was a foreign language. She read *War and Peace*, *The Brothers Karamazov*, *Vanity Fair*, and *Zuleika Dobson*, but she did not feel she understood what she read, even though she understood the words. She did not do well on exams, and after a year, she gave up night school and signed up instead at Woods Business School. For what could she do with German and English literature anyway? The best she could hope for was to be a secretary. But although she applied herself assiduously to typing and stenography, she had the same problem: she could not hear.

And her days remained the same. She would get up around six-thirty – Euga now went for the morning buns – have coffee and a bun, dress, and walk to the trolley. It was always cold at that hour except in the hottest part of the summer; and the light was always pale, pearly, the air thin. It made Bella feel awful, as if she were part of a servile population that rose before the masters and went out to work in the world while others were still stretching, lingering over a fragrant cup of coffee. Momma and she took the trolley together, and walked together up the four flights to the sweatshop, where the other women greeted them (they always greeted Momma more warmly) and sat down at their machines.

All morning, the foreman watched, hovered, threatened: you could not stop for a minute and stretch without his noticing and scolding; you could not talk to the girl beside you. At noon he blew a whistle and you could stop and stretch a little. Your body felt permanently fixed in the posture you adopted for work, and you had to remind it that it was permitted to move in other ways. So you stretched and wriggled your fingers and moved your shoulders up and down, and smiled at the other girls who were doing the same, and then you'd stand up and walk out into the hall and down the stairs to wait on line outside the single stinking toilet, and back up a story, where you would pull your sandwich from your coat pocket and sit on the steps with the others and eat, the aroma of salami pungent throughout the stairwell. Most of the others were heavy-bodied, tired women who chatted to each other in Polish or Yiddish or Italian, eating their sandwiches and drinking the water they had carried from the sink tap in cracked old cups. Among them Momma bobbed and smiled, she was always in the centre of a group of women, and Bella would gaze off into space. Sometimes she would talk with some of the younger women – but they seemed to her older than herself – and hear them describe weekend outings to Luna Park. There were castles and ballrooms there, buildings with turrets and minarets; there were elephants and men in turbans and Vernon and Irene Castle danced there. Bella's mind would wander in this scene, imagining, and she would sit there longing, longing to go to Coney Island.

Then the bell would go and the women would rise, not eager, their bodies tired and unwilling, but nervous, because they could be reprimanded or docked for lateness, and return to the machines. All afternoon, as in the morning, the foreman watched them closely to see they did not talk to each other, or pause in the work, or stretch, or laugh: and he would shout if he saw anything like this, and often, a woman would be fired. Sometimes a woman would trap her finger under the needles, and scream, and the foreman would bustle over and release her, and if she were badly hurt she would be sent home. She would never return: they would replace her with another woman. Most of the women had families, many children to feed, and they wore shabby housedresses and old worn coats to work – like Momma. They had greyish hair pulled back in a bun, like Momma's, and they hunched their shoulders when the foreman spoke to them, and smiled, and said, 'Yes, Mr, No, Mr' Whenever the foreman came close to Bella her heart would beat very fast, and she would bend closer to the machine. But he always said, 'Good, Bella.' She hoped he would never yell at her, because she did not know what she would do if he did. Sometimes when a woman was fired, she would burst out crying, and would beg for another chance. She would explain she was only asking for advice about something, something wrong with this fabric, or a machine that didn't stitch evenly, but the foreman wouldn't listen. 'No excuses,' he'd say curtly, 'get your pay and go.' And the woman would leave, all bent over, weeping. It was horrible.

Every night the foreman blew his whistle at six-thirty. The women would stand, their pale faces drawn from the tension of not looking up, not pausing, for all those hours, from the bad air, bad light, the ache in the back. Then they all picked up their coats and handbags and trudged down to the toilet, quiet, subdued from weariness, and stood on line in front of the evil-smelling water closet, before going out into the dark winter night to stand on another line for the trolley or subway. Bella felt like one of a herd of cattle trudging down those stairs, just one more of an infinitely replaceable species seen by the bosses as so many head, treated that way.

Now Euga was working too, although no one called her Euga anymore, but rather Eugenia. She worked in a sweat-shop that made hats for famous Fifth Avenue designers, and she was very good at her work. Every morning the two sisters walked together to the trolley stop, and rode to downtown Manhattan; and every night they met at the Manhattan stop and rode home together. But they never spoke of anything serious or upsetting; they never discussed their family. They chatted about fashions and movie stars and gossip about some mutual acquaintances.

Two nights a week, Bella went to Woods. Hard as it was for her, and stupid as it made her feel, she was determined to learn to take dictation and to type, because she knew that she had to get out of the sweatshops. For Bella, the difference between working in a sweatshop and working in an office was huge. The young women she saw on the streets could easily be divided into two classes: there were the ones like her, with long hair, no makeup, wearing longish skirts, usually shabby – something Bella was not. The others had bobbed hair, shorter skirts, and lipstick, and they looked smart, modern. She felt people would think differently about one kind and the other. She was not aware of the word *class*, nor the social division of lower, middle, and upper, but she knew what she saw.

It was at Woods that she met Sue Corry. Sue was also working in a sweatshop, making knitted sweaters, and was trying to improve herself. She was exactly Bella's height, and she was also blond, but she had a smart bob and wore light lipstick. Bella was thrilled by her; she knew she could never invite her home – Momma would be shocked at the way she looked – but she never invited anyone home. Sue was eighteen, a year older than Bella, with freckles on her face and a wide easy smile. Bella did not understand why Sue liked her, but she did not question her good fortune in having found a friend. It was Sue who first asked Bella if she wanted to go shopping.

Shopping? What was that? But Bella did not want to betray her ignorance, so she did not ask. Sue said she loved to go shopping on Saturday afternoons, and would sometimes splurge and have lunch out. In a restaurant? Bella breathed agreement, her mind dazed with glamorous images, and they met the next Saturday after work. At first, they walked around Union Square and gazed in the store windows, S. Klein and Mays and smaller shops. They didn't go in until they reached Woolworth's, and it was there Sue suggested they have lunch.

They went in and sat at the counter, and a girl handed them two greasy cards listing dishes. Bella studied hers intently: few of the items listed there were familiar to her. But she covered her ignorance with an appearance of being discriminating, and only a few minutes after Sue announced that she would have a bacon, lettuce and tomato on white toast with coffee, did Bella say, 'That sounds good. I think I'll have that too.' Then the girl brought them their sandwiches and coffee and put the food right in front of them. Bella looked around her to see if other people were looking at them, thinking what smart young women they were. Her heart felt large and generous and she pitied the poor women bent over in their black coats, carrying heavy shopping bags. She was a modern young woman eating out in a restaurant!

She and Sue talked of many things. Sue was so interesting! She even had a boyfriend. And she knew about all the latest styles and hairstyles and what the movie stars were like in private. Bella wondered how she came to know so much. But she never asked: she listened and smiled and her eyes opened with wonder.

After lunch, which cost them each twenty-five cents, Bella noticed that Sue left some pennies on the counter, and she did the same. The girl behind the counter came over and pocketed them, and smiled at the two women. Bella felt like a great lady. The poor girl, working for pennies! Then she and Sue walked about the store, stopping at one counter or another. Bella was drawn to a big square of counters, that had a piano inside it, and a man playing popular hits. On all four sides the counter was heaped with sheet music. Bella stood and listened for a long time, her heart full of longing. Oh, if only she could play! The young man played wonderfully, she thought, and he just flowed from one song into another. After a long time, Sue bought, for fifteen cents, the sheet music to 'My Buddy'. Bella sensed Sue wanted to move on and dragged her body away from the counter. She was content that she could hear the music even from other counters. But she was also nervous: she felt she must buy something, but had little money and did not know what to buy. Finally, she found a paper of hairpins for seven cents and bought that.

Her mind whirled all the way home. She went home alone because Sue lived in the Bronx. She felt as if wires had been plugged into her head, her arms, her legs, and were sending impulses through her body. Everything was new, and interesting, and wonderful, and she was allowed to enter the new world. But she would not have dared to enter it alone: she needed a friend.

The Saturday-afternoon expeditions became a custom; the friends went at least twice a month. In time they gained courage and went inside some of the clothes shops and looked over the merchandise with slightly snooty looks on their faces, as if they could afford anything but found everything in some way wanting. In fact, Bella rarely saw anything she wanted. Momma made all Bella's beautiful clothes, which were far nicer than anything in the stores. She had matching dresses and coats in navy blue and beige; and she had two pleated skirts and one slimline skirt with a kick pleat with buttons above it.

Then they began to walk uptown along Fifth Avenue, or Madison, and gaze in the windows of the really expensive shops. They never found the courage to go inside these, but they oohed and aahed about the exquisite embroidered satin nightgowns and bed jackets and slips; the cashmere sweaters; and the beaded dresses that stopped above the knee. Some days they just walked. They passed great hotels, the Hotel McAlpin and the Waldorf. Sue had a friend who had been taken to tea at the Waldorf, and said it was really beautiful, with palm trees and everything, right in the room! A space formed in Bella's heart: tea at the Waldorf! Oh, what would that be like! But Sue said even if they had enough money they could not go there, because a man had to take you. Bella learned so much from Sue. They would walk arm in arm, and press themselves together, although Bella felt a little uncomfortable about this, and shifted herself slightly away each time. But Sue was very affectionate, she even used to touch Bella's arm when she spoke to her.

One Saturday during an uptown jaunt, Sue suggested they have lunch at Schrafft's. Schrafft's! With gold letters on its front window, and venetian curtains – so elegant – and real tables and chairs! Feeling daring, ready for anything, Bella clutched her handbag and agreed. They sat at a table and had chicken salad sandwiches and coffee and it wasn't so expensive, it was only thirty-five cents. Bella realized that Woolworth's wasn't so great after all – it was only a counter, a luncheonette. Schrafft's was a *real* restaurant, and now she was a young woman of the world.

One day as they sat over their coffee, Sue began to talk about religion. Her mother was very pious, she said, and went to church every day. Sue was religious, but she felt that was excessive. What did Bella think?

Bella didn't know.

'You're Catholic, aren't you?'

'Yes, I guess so.'

'You guess so! Did you receive?'

'Receive?'

'Holy Communion! You must have received!'

Bella had a dim memory of a white dress and white silk stockings, and a bouquet of flowers, back in the old life, before Poppa . . . 'Yes. And my father was close friends with our priest . . . ,' she began.

Sue warmed to that. She leaned forward, her face glowing. 'I *knew* you had to be Catholic. I told my mother you were. She doesn't like me to make friends with people who aren't Catholic.'

Bella just looked at her.

'And of course you must have been confirmed, too,' Sue went on.

Bella shook her head.

'But, Bella, you're seventeen! You should have been confirmed at twelve or thirteen!'

Bella's mouth opened. 'My father died,' she said finally.

That was something Sue could understand. 'Oh. Yes. But Bella, you must be confirmed.' She talked for a long time then, softly, persuasively, about the sacraments of the Church, and its Laws, and Salvation. If you weren't saved, she said, when you died you went to hell with all the non-Catholics and sinners, and burned forever in eternal fires.

Bella was appalled. How was it that Sue, who was only eighteen, knew all these things, and Momma, who was forty, did not? Why was it that everything she learned she had to learn from her friends? Why wasn't Momma concerned with the state of her soul? Did Momma want her to go to hell? Oh, what a home she had! A place to sleep, eat, and play cards, nothing more. She had never learned anything in her home, never. If not for her friends she would have gone on forever in ignorance and stupidity. Bella barely listened to Sue's description of hell: she felt she knew better than Sue what hell was like, and that she had spent several years there already. Maybe if she had been confirmed, and had experienced God's grace, as Sue said, all that wouldn't have happened.

Bella squeezed Sue's hand and promised she would go for instruction in the catechism. Sue smiled radiantly at her convert, lifted to another plane, she and her friend shining with God's light. She told Bella she would introduce her to a priest whose parish was near where they worked, downtown – she occasionally popped into his church for First Friday, she said. And he would teach Bella. And soon Bella went from work on Tuesday nights to the rectory where Father Ambrose tested her on the catechism questions she was supposed to learn that week. Bella learned it all, but for her it was just words. She felt stupid again: she simply didn't understand what the Holy Ghost was supposed to be, or what grace was, or sin, for that matter. How could a baby be born with sin on its soul?

Nevertheless, in the spring of 1922, after her eighteenth birthday, Bella went to church in a white dress and stood on line behind fifty twelve-year-old children (towering over them again, she thought grimly; then thanked Sue that she was saved at all), and felt the bishop put his hand on her head, and tried to feel the Holy Spirit descending upon her. And when she could feel nothing, she concluded she was just too stupid to recognize what was happening to her.

Sue came to her confirmation with her boyfriend, and afterward, he took the three of them out to a hotel and bought them a Communion breakfast – eggs and bacon and orange juice and champagne! Bella had never had champagne before, and she decided that making her Confirmation and having champagne meant that she was now, really and truly, grown up.

Sue's boyfriend, Andy, liked Bella, who was shy of him and simply smiled a lot. And Sue loved Bella, feeling responsible for the very state of her soul. The two of them invited Bella to go with them one Saturday night to the Cotton Club, the famous nightclub in Harlem. In great excitement, Bella told Momma she needed a new dress, a fancy one. Bella chose the fabric, a melon chiffon, and Momma made her a dress with little straps and a flat bodice, with a skirt that was many different lengths, all overlapping. And Bella used her last savings to buy herself a pair of silk shoes with high heels and a strap across the instep, and have them dyed to match the dress. As a surprise, Momma made her a silk coat just a few shades darker than the dress. And Bella went to the Cotton Club.

'Oh, I was such a stupid kid,' my mother says with disgust. 'I don't know where I was, I was always in a dream. Here I had all these chances – they took me to the Cotton Club many times, I heard all the great musicians, like Duke Ellington and Count Basie and . . . oh, all the great ones. And I didn't even know what I was listening to, I didn't realize!'

I have just put an Ellington record on the hi-fi. I always listen to music turned up loud when I clean, and it's time for the semi-annual straightening up. The kids' shoes and underwear are strewn around the living room, and my papers are heaped on every surface. There's no room to sit down, here or in the kitchen, so I think I'll have to do something. Then I hear this unsteady step on the walk outside and peer down from the front window, and there she is, tottering up the walk in her high heels. Saved from cleaning! I hastily pick up piles of things and stack them on other piles, so there will be someplace to sit down, and go into the kitchen and put on a kettle for tea. It takes her a long time to mount the stairs to my apartment, and I fidget, fighting the impulse to run out and help her. She arrives at the top breathless, annoyed, pink in the face: 'Those steps!' She comes in and gets settled. Unlike my ex-mother-in-law, she is not bothered by the messy way I live. But she complains about the music. I go to take the record off, commenting, 'I thought you liked Duke Ellington.' And she goes into her tale of the Cotton Club, which I have heard dozens of times before. The moral of her story is the same as ever: her ignorance of what she was hearing is one more source of grief; grief is the only residue of the experience. For the first time, I wonder why.

Bella finished her business course in the spring of 1923; she decided that armed with a certificate verifying that she had completed two years of study, she could risk looking for a job in an office. But she was very nervous about doing this. Momma had gotten her her other jobs, had introduced her to the foremen, who liked Momma and smiled and bobbed their heads, saying, 'Ah, your daughter, Mrs Brez, a good girl, I'm sure,' and Bella had smiled and almost curtseyed. To go alone into a world she had never entered before terrified her, and she kept putting it off. There was a late summer that year; the weather remained chilly right into June. Sue married Andy. They had a nice apartment in the Bronx with a living room and bedroom suite of new furniture. Bella visited them once, taking an embroidered bridge cloth and napkins, and Andy had served them champagne. But since then she had had no occasion for seeing Sue, who dropped out of Woods and was now pregnant.

Weekends were dull; and evenings too, now that she did not go to Woods anymore. The boys seemed to be at loose ends. Everyone in the family was working, and they were all doing well except Wally, who had trouble keeping jobs – he was an apprentice electrician – and they all gave most of their wages to Momma. Bella still got only fifty cents a day, as did Eugenia; but the boys, she knew, got more. And Eddie had insisted that Momma open a bank account and save money: every week he checked the balance and announced it with satisfaction. They now had $118.42 in the account.

One Friday night, Eddie came home late with a camera. It was a little rectangular box. When you opened it, a kind of nose came out, with accordion pleats on its sides. That Sunday, Eddie insisted that they all get dressed up in their best clothes so he could take their picture. Bella wore her black satin with the white satin lapels printed with roses; Eugenia wore a blue chiffon with accordion pleats; Wally wore knickers and a golfing cap (although he'd never even seen a golf course); and Eddie wore his new winter coat, a long dark brown full-skirted coat with a fur collar. Even Momma put on her best dress. He trooped them up to the roof of their building and lined them up against the brick chimney, and took a number of shots. Then he joined them in the line and asked his friend Oscar Ball, who was visiting that afternoon, to take their picture together. Of course, they couldn't see the pictures right away, and all of them were excited and nervous, waiting for the sight of this miracle. It took two weeks for them to come back from wherever Eddie had sent them, and he laid them before the family with pride. And indeed, there they all were: four young people and a mother, all of whom looked far older than they were, standing on the tar roof in front of the dark brick of the chimney, while behind them spread the roofs and walls of tenements, as far as you could see. Eddie laughed and laughed. Bella could not understand why he was laughing. Then he took a pen and wrote across the bottom: ALL DRESSED UP AND NO PLACE TO GO.

Bella was restless. Summer still didn't come. At least, in summer, the four of them and their friends could go to the Rockaways and spend the day on the beach. She knew she had to make her move soon, but felt paralyzed. One Saturday, missing Sue, it occurred to her to stop in at the church. Maybe God's grace would give her strength. She had not been in a church since her Confirmation.

She walked in timidly, not feeling at home in this place. The church was nearly empty at five o'clock on a Saturday afternoon. Only a few people sat in pews near the confessional booths at the sides of the nave, waiting their turn. A few stood on line near each booth. Bella went to the front of the church where the candles flickered, and looked up at the statue of the Virgin, and the great white skinny figure of crucified Christ on a cross near the altar. She knelt in a front pew and bowed her head. But she didn't know what to do then. As she sat there, something in front of her moved. A few rows closer to the altar, a woman was kneeling, with bowed head. She was so small and bent that Bella had not seen her before. As she finished praying, the woman straightened up a little more and Bella's heart stopped: Momma! It was Momma! Then the woman stood up and worked her way out of the pew, and turned to walk down the aisle. Her face was swollen and wet, and she kept her head down as she walked. It was not Momma, but the woman looked like Momma – the same weariness in the body and the walk, the same defeat on the face. And Bella was filled with outrage. Suppose it had been Momma?

She could not bear it that her mother should bend her knees to the powers that had wrecked her young life, blighted it irrevocably. It would outrage her if her mother were to enter a church, pray, ask forgiveness. Forgiveness for what? What sin had Momma ever committed? Oh, she was often angry with Bella, but that was because Bella was so stupid. Images crowded into her mind, of Momma retching with tears in the office of the woman who took the children away; or sitting under the lamp sewing, her head falling onto the table as a cry of pain engulfed her. Or the night she had crept out of bed and peered through the crack of light showing around the kitchen door and seen Poppa with the razor strop, raising it high and slamming it down on poor Wally's little behind. And Wally, only five then, a baby, screaming, while Eddie sobbed in a corner. And behind it all, herself, a statue, a stony paralyzed image, watching, watching. What had God, if there was a God, ever done for her family that was merciful, just, or good?

She raised her head and looked around her. The crowd had left. There were a couple of people on line at one confessional but none at the other. As she looked, the priest's door opened and he emerged, yawning and red-faced. His great belly was stiff under his cassock, and he trudged down the aisle toward the alter. As he approached, Bella noticed that he had the same little threads of red on his nose and cheeks that Father Stefan had had, and she recalled the sight of the priest laughing as Poppa vomited in the street.

She stood up unsteadily. How could these men, who were only men like Poppa, know what was good? Did Poppa know what was good? Did any man? Men, who did things like hit babies and hit Momma, who was a saint? She stiffened her lips and walked out of the church. For a few minutes, for the first time in her life, Bella felt furious. It passed quickly after she left the dark damp church and mixed with the people on the street. But it changed her somehow. It was that afternoon that she made up her mind to do what she had been wanting to do for a long time.

She waited until the following Saturday. Summer had finally arrived and the city air was soft and damp, and men walked carrying their jackets and hats, while women fanned themselves with handkerchiefs on the trolley. She had picked the place out long ago, wandering around with Sue, peering into windows and watching the way the operators worked. She considered the way the women looked when they were finished, and she had decided on Alicia's. It was only a few blocks from the shop, and she had told Eugenia she would be going out with a friend after work. She stood outside briefly, then straightened and boldly walked right in.

'I want a bob,' she said.

Bella's hair had never been cut. When it was down, she could sit on it. It was ash blond and very wavy, and every morning Bella had to brush it for a long time, then comb it, to get out the knots. Then she fastened it back with a clip to which she had attached a large bow. But it was a baby way to look, she felt. And she was grown up now. Sometimes she put it in a big bun with hairpins, but they loosened and fell out and her hair fell down; or if she put a lot in, they made her head ache during the day. And all the women in the magazines and the movies had short straight bobs and wore glittering headbands and black around their eyes. They were *chic*: Bella felt a surge of pride at knowing that word and even how to pronounce it properly. She had heard girls at the shop say 'chick'.

Her hair fell around her in long showers, and Bella's heart hurt a little. It was all over the floor and she looked down at it as if it were a limb she was having removed. But when Alicia was finished, Bella looked in the mirror enchanted. It was not Bella, it was a new person who stared back at her, someone modern and chic. Gone was the little Polska, the ignorant immigrant girl who worked in a sweatshop. She stood, dazed, and paid Alicia the money she had been saving for months. Then, still dazed, she wandered around the streets, and in some kind of mad daring, walked into a little hat shop and bought a cloche, black straw with a little bow on its side.

When she got home, the family was all there and Momma was placing the bowls of food on the table for dinner. She walked in, and Wally glanced up from his newspaper and gave a long wolf whistle. Then Eddie turned around from the table where he was working at his stamp collection. 'Wow!' he said, and Eugenia, standing behind Momma, holding a bowl of mashed potatoes, just stared looking terrified. Momma screamed: 'AAAAIIIEEEE! What have you done!'

Bella smiled uncertainly. Momma screamed again. Then she began to attack Bella in Polish. 'You are no daughter of mine, no daughter of mine cuts her hair, what nice girl does that, it is a scandal, a sin, a shame, shame on you, how can you come in my house looking like that, a woman of the street, she goes about like that, no daughter of mine . . .' Momma went on for a long time. Then she slammed down the plate of pot roast she was carrying and went back into the kitchen. Eugenia smiled furtively at Bella, dropped the bowl of potatoes lightly on the table, and followed Momma into the kitchen. Bella could hear Momma screaming and cursing in the kitchen. Wally got up and came over to Bella: 'You look terrific, kid,' he said in his slangy man-about-town way. But she knew he meant well, and she smiled at him gratefully. Eddie was still looking at her. 'Momma will get over it, Bella,' he said kindly.

But Momma did not come to the table at all that night, and the family, very subdued, ate without her. After dinner, they cleared the table and the girls washed the dishes and then they all sat around the table playing pinochle and still Momma did not come out of her room. Every once in a while Eugenia would go into the bedroom the three women shared and check on Momma, but said nothing when she came out except 'She's all right'.

So tense were they that they began to giggle at nonsense, and before long, they were really laughing, having a good time. And Bella, in the middle of this, looked at them and said, 'One more thing. I'm not Bella anymore. If anyone calls me Bella I won't answer. My name is Belle.'

three

Momma did not speak to Bella for two weeks, and when she did, her voice sounded wounded. Frances had won the battle and lost the war. She had regathered her children, had kept her family together after all, only to lose them to America. Confused, hurt, and helpless, she subsided still further into the old woman I knew when I was a child – she was only forty-seven when I was born, younger than I am now, and sixty-two when she died. Not very old, in our accounting. But she was bent and old by forty-five.

Belle, armed with her bob and her new name, got herself a job at Crowell Publishing Company as a file clerk. She had to accept less money – another source of outrage to Frances, but she fought less hard now – but she got to work in a beautiful building with a marble lobby and elevators, and she sat all day in a big room full of desks, well-lighted and far less noisy than the shop because there was only the clacking of typewriters, not the continual whir of sewing machines. Impaired as she was, noise bothered Belle because over it she could hear literally nothing. She looked around at other modern young women like herself, and sighed with satisfaction. She had made it into the middle class. She was saved.

These days, she had lunch out every day with the other girls in the office, at Rexall Drug Store. By now she knew whether she wanted a chicken salad or a grilled cheese and tomato, and didn't dally over the menu, but ordered with the rest and gossiped about the office, and clothes, and movie stars, just like the others. And after they had coffee, Lillian Gutman, who was the daring one who said daring things about the bosses and made them all laugh, brought out cigarettes and passed them around. Belle always took one, and smoked it right down, her eyes bright, glancing around to see if people were looking at these smart-looking young women having lunch out, laughing, and smoking. For a few months, she felt glorious: she was one of the girls she had envied back in grade school, gay and laughing, sophisticated, well-dressed. She knew how to belong.

But the job itself was horribly tedious. It was even worse than the sweatshop because you could not daydream as you filed or you would make a mistake; whereas you could work a sewing machine without thinking at all. And she earned less money and spent more, for the lunches every day ate up her entire allowance. She had no money to buy shoes, or anything else, no money to go out on Sundays. She always had to ask Momma. and although Momma always gave it to her, she also gave her a look of grim contempt. She could hear what Momma did not say: 'You see? You see?'

So when after six months she got a raise of a dollar and a half, she did not tell Momma. She worried about it all the way home. On the one hand, she would have liked to brag a little, to show Momma how well she was doing in this foreign world, to prove to Momma that she was still good. But she could not bear the looks Momma gave her. She reminded herself that the boys were allowed to keep far more of their wages than she and Eugenia. And besides, now she needed money for cigarettes. The others now all took turns buying them and passing them around – it wasn't fair that Lillian supply them all. So Belle had to, too. She argued with herself, and won. The dollar and a half was secreted each week in a special part of her purse.

And before long, Eugenia too came home with a bob. Momma cried again, but she was never as hard on Euga as on Bella, and the shock soon passed. And then Euga said she wanted to be modern too, and would henceforth be called Jean. The boys went along with all this cheerfully: they liked having modern, smart sisters. Only Momma stubbornly continued to refer to her daughters as Bella and Genya. And when both sisters worked on her, showing her pictures of the modern young women in the fashion magazines, she stopped protesting entirely, and even made them dresses with short hems.

'You girls are flappers!' Wally crowed.

On a Sunday near Easter in 1924, the family had a surprise visit. People in those days did not telephone, for few people had telephones; nor did they write. They simply came, taking one or two or three trolleys or trains, and descending upon you *en famille*. That was one reason why Sunday dinners were always so ample: you never knew if someone might stop in.

The visitors were Momma's sister Mamie, who had married only a few years before, her new baby and the older girl, and her husband, who was an *artist*! Belle had never met an artist and she looked with awe at this tall thin handsome face with the shapely mustache, who walked around as if he owned their house, and talked, like Poppa, as if he knew what he was talking about and others did not. He was a real artist, he had sculptures in the Metropolitan Museum, Mamie whispered to Momma.

Mamie's husband's name was Jan Sokolowski and he was a little like Poppa. He loved to drink wine, and had brought a bottle with him; and he loved company and talk. He liked Belle, who was so flattered her face felt hot the whole time he was there. And he treated her like a person – he asked her about her work, what she did and how she liked it. Belle answered shyly. She was proud of the place she worked in, grateful she did not have to say it was a factory. But she was not proud of the work she did.

'And you like it, Isabelle, eh?' he asked in Polish. The whole family spoke Polish.

Belle flushed and gazed at him. 'It's all right. I wish . . . I would love . . . I feel I would be happier doing something more artistic.'

One of Sokolowski's expressive eyebrows rose. 'Why don't you come to work in my shop? It's an interior decorating shop and full of artists.' At which he laughed hard and long.

A white glaze settled on Belle's mind. 'An interior decorator!' she breathed, remembering the shops she used to see on Madison Avenue. 'What would I do?'

'You would be creative, you would make lampshades. It's a good trade, and it requires someone artistic.'

Belle gave notice the following Monday, and two weeks later, she began work at Ostrovsky's. It was in midtown Manhattan, off Madison, and the front of the shop was glass, with beautiful things inside – furniture and lamps, pillows and comforters, little boxes and many paintings. There was a thick carpet on the floor and everything in the window looked expensive. But Sokolowski took Belle in through a side door that led straight to the back. This was a huge space divided into two sections. On one side five or six men stood before canvases, painting. Their pictures all looked vaguely the same, but to Belle they seemed extremely beautiful. They were landscapes and still lifes, and sometimes, beautiful rose-colored women with parasols, and children around them. It was here Sokolowski worked.

Sokolowski spread out his arm: 'It is a painting factory!' he said, and burst again into long loud laughter. Belle did not see any reason why there should not be a factory for painting as there was for everything else, and did not understand what he was laughing at. But she smiled. She did not feel frightened of Sokolowski whom she called, always, Pan Sokolowski even though he was her uncle by marriage, or cousin, or something – she was not sure. She looked up at him as she had to her father, but she felt sure he never hit his children or his wife, and she knew he would never hit her. Jan, still full of mirth, led her around the partition to another room where, at two long tables, girls sat on high stools making lampshades. Belle looked at the finished products: pale ecru silks, white organdies with pleats all around, slub silks with tiny pink roses as borders: they were beautiful! She would love to make such things, and besides that, think how it would sound to say you worked for an interior decorator!

Belle learned the craft quickly. First, she had to cover the metal spokes of the frame with soft padding, and sew it down securely with tiny even stitches. Then came the cover. If it was silk, it had to be spread around the shade so that no crease or ripple appeared; then a lining was spread around the inside, and the two had to be sewn together in such a way that no stitches showed. It was very delicate work, requiring patience and a talented sewing-hand. The final step was the trim, which might be a Greek key, or rosettes, or a simple gold line: this had to be attached with the tiniest stitches of all so it would be firmly and strongly, but invisibly, fixed. Organdy shades were pleated, and for this you needed long strong fingernails to press and fix the pleats. The organdy was then sewn on the padding, then lined and trimmed in the same way as the silk shades. Sometimes they used linen, too.

Belle found this work pleasant, and she did not feel oppressed sitting in the large room with the other girls. Mr Ostrovsky was not a tyrant: they could chat as they worked, only not too much. And it was with joy that Belle recognized, sitting at the table, her old friend Gertrude Hunrath, who still looked the same, and grinned at her, cocking an eyebrow when she saw her.

'You've changed, Bella,' Gertrude said.

'I had my hair cut,' Belle admitted shyly. 'And please call me Belle.'

Gertrude laughed. She had a long long face and a nose that matched it; a wide mouth and a tall lanky body. She was as out of style physically as a woman could be, and she wore nondescript clothes. But for some reason, Gertrude always seemed happy, just as she had on the block, years ago. She lived with her sister, who resembled her, and their short, fat, dumpy mother: the father had absconded many years before. And the three of them were always laughing together. 'So you're modern!' Gertrude cried, amused but without irony.

Gertrude and Belle immediately renewed their friendship, and soon they were going on Saturday-afternoon shopping expeditions. Some Sundays they went to Manhattan and visited the Metropolitan Museum. Belle could not really see any difference in the paintings hung there – except the really old ones, which she did not like – and the paintings done in the factory. She liked paintings of pretty things – vases of flowers, landscapes, and especially, women. She lingered over Renoir and Sargent, following every line of body and clothing in their women. But she revered even those paintings she did not like – those she said she did not 'understand'. She couldn't understand, for instance, why anyone wanted to paint bowls of fruit over and over; and she hated crucifixions. She read the cards on the wall, and soon she knew who the Impressionists were, and that they were her favorite painters.

Her little knowledge did not give her confidence, however; it only opened up another enormous area of ignorance. She was conscious of this because Sokolowski had begun to ask her to go with him to galleries and openings. Mamie was always surrounded with babies, and he did not like to go alone. She was presentable; she thought that was why he asked her. But she was honored, and trailed behind him as he greeted friends and drank champagne – always getting her a glass first – at openings in the Fifty-seventh Street galleries, or to parties at someone's studio. She was awed at such gatherings and would stand, trying to look poised, gazing around her at what she imagined was a room full of famous people. They all seemed to know each other, and they had so much to say. At first, her ignorance isolated her, like a black pall: she was too intimidated to say anything at all. But she soon realized that that was exactly what was expected of her: a shy, smiling silence along with a good appearance. She felt safe with her tall handsome relative, and he was invariably proper and courteous to her. And if she was bored at the gatherings, she banished the feeling: she knew it was an honor to be among such great people.

They were at a party at the studio of a friend of Sokolowski's drinking red wine and standing around, when Belle saw a beautiful young woman who seemed as silent and isolated as she. So alone did the woman appear that Belle was able to overcome her own shyness and approach her. She smiled radiantly at Belle and her words tumbled out of her mouth nervously. She was a newcomer, she knew no one but her brother, who was over there with the men surrounding the easel, commenting on a painting. Her name was Adele Kosciuszko and she had just emerged from a convent. Adele had large pale eyes, of a color between blue and violet, and long blond hair wavy in the way Belle's used to be. She gazed enviously at Belle's bob and said she wanted to cut her hair too, but her mother forbade it. Belle giggled, and described the scene in her house on the day of her haircut. She was amazed to hear herself talk in this way – it sounded almost as if she were making fun of Momma – and she quickly stopped, but Adele was laughing too, and Belle knew some bond had been established between them. Adele looked longingly around the room and asked who this one was or that one. Belle told her the few names she knew, and Adele gazed at Belle as if she were a sophisticate, at ease in this strange world. She said she wanted very much to get a job, but she didn't know what she could do. Belle asked her if she could sew, and when she said she could, Belle asked her if she would like to work with her, making lampshades at an interior decorating shop. Adele gasped, 'Oh, yes!'

Belle knew Mr Ostrovsky liked her. He often said she was

his best worker – her shades were the neatest and cleanest, and she was also the quickest of them all. In the six months she had been with him, he had given her two raises. She knew she could get him to hire Adele, and indeed, it was done. Now she had two friends at work, and felt herself the center of a circle. It was glorious. Gertrude asked them if they wanted to go to dances, and once or twice a week the three would meet and go to the dance hall. They each paid ten cents to enter, and spent the evening doing decorous dances with strange gentlemen. Belle loved it. Dancing was one thing she felt she could do well. And in the spring, Adele and Belle signed up for a tap-dancing course, which they attended twice a week.

Belle felt she was finally having the life she had yearned for, and her triumph overflowed when, in a contest two years later, Adele won the title of Miss Poland. She had let her hair down – it hung far below her waist – and put on one of the shocking new bathing suits, a one-piece knit with two-inch wide straps at the shoulder – very daring. And she won and there was applause and ginger beer, and they tied a ribbon across her front, and her picture was in the newspaper. Belle showed the picture to her brothers and Jean: 'This is my friend!' she announced.

Often, when she arrived a little early at the shop, Belle would stand in the doorway to the showroom and gaze in. The room was light and spacious, and carpeted with a beautiful Chinese rug, beige with a design in different shades of blue. On the walls, inside heavy gilt frames, arranged in pleasing groups, were the paintings of Sokolowski and the other men in the 'art factory'; and there were different pieces of furniture, also artfully arranged. Belle had learned to see the difference among styles and even some names – Chippendale and Louis XIV, Sheraton and her favorite, Queen Anne. There were occasional chairs, a sofa, a sideboard, and some small tables with drawers. And on the sideboard, the tables, the Regency desk, were lamps, some bearing shades she herself had made. And there were little boxes, and porcelain miniatures, and embroidered doilies. And in one corner of the shop, thrown gracefully on a brocade-covered chaise, were embroidered sheets made of silk and linen, and towels and even some nightgowns and bed jackets. Each time she stood there, Belle would study a few objects carefully, as if she could absorb them, take them into herself by osmosis. After months of observing, she found the courage to enter the shop – carefully, as if her presence might create such turbulence that everything would collapse. She listened to the clerks talking to Mrs Ostrovsky, who ran the shop, and learned their language – Regency, Louis Quatorze (which she thought was spelled Catoars, but memorized it anyway, wondering at the strangeness of things).

Mrs Ostrovsky insisted on being called Madame: she was Russian by birth, but had gone to France during the Revolution, whatever that was. Belle knew only that Madame frequently began her utterances with 'Before the Revolution, in Petersburg . . .' Madame was tall, with a hard face and coarse skin, heavily powdered. Her hair was blond and pulled away from her face severely into a bun in the back. Well, not quite a bun. It was nothing at all like Momma's, it had, Belle knew, style. Lydia, one of the girls who made lampshades, said it was called a French knot. Madame had a full body shaped rather like a bolster, firmly encased from top to bottom of her torso in what Belle imagined was a corset. She always wore a simple black silk crepe dress and black suede pumps (except in summer, when the pumps were patent leather, and the dress a lighter silk), with a diamond pin and diamond earrings and many rings on her fingers. Madame had a nasty tongue, and Belle feared her, but she respected her too: after all, Madame knew so much and had beautiful taste, and was able to run this fine shop. Belle hungered to learn, to know as much as Madame.

In 1926, on Belle's twenty-second birthday, when she had been working for a year and a half at Ostrovsky's, she was standing in the doorway absorbing the things in the showroom, when Mr Ostrovsky came and stood beside her.

'Beautiful, huh, Belle?' he smiled at her.

'Oh, yes,' she breathed, and without even thinking, added, 'It must be wonderful to work here.'

Mr Ostrovsky was startled. He didn't know she was simply uttering a daydream out loud, and had had no intention of making a request of him. 'You want to be an interior decorator, huh?' His immense forehead crinkled. 'I will have to speak to my wife.' He walked away heavily. Everyone knew that Mr was terrified of Madame.

All day Belle's stomach churned. She had not really meant to say that to Mr Ostrovsky, and she worried that he would think she was unhappy making lampshades. And she wasn't, she really wasn't, although it was no longer as much fun as it had been. It had become routine, too easy, and she could not be really original – she had to follow prescribed patterns. But could she do it, could she work in the salon? – as Madame called it. She thought of Paul, the salesman who knew the most, saying, 'Yes, aren't they charming? All eighteenth century, Madame found them in a collection of boxes squirreled away in a château in the Loire Valley . . .' Or, 'Indeed, madame, very fine work. Notice the grain of the inlay, and the burl! Gorgeous! We don't have workmanship like this today, madame.' Would she be able to sound like that?

All day she waited, her stomach churning, and all day nothing happened. Except one of the artists threw a tantrum and screamed at Mr Ostrovsky to take his schlock art and . . . do something with it, Belle didn't understand. And the telephone kept ringing in Madame's office that day. Eventually, Belle drifted into daydreams, and so was startled at hearing Madame's furious voice saying 'Stupid Polack!' and Mr O.'s quiet rumbling. Belle shivered and her finger trembled and she messed up the border she was sewing, and had to take out the stitches. This was bad because reworking something soiled it, and the lampshades had to be immaculate. She bent her head very close to the shade and took painstaking tiny stitches to repair the error. It was all right, she understood. Why would Madame want her, a stupid Polska, who knew nothing at all? She'd been a fool, and she bit down hard on her tongue to punish herself for having said anything at all to Mr O. She finished the shade and held it away from her, examining it. It was not as good as her shades usually were, but it would pass. She picked up a scrap of silk and wiped her cheek, which was wet. There was no dance tonight, nothing to look forward to. Maybe Momma would like to go to a movie.

She was clearing her part of the table, preparing to leave, when Mr Ostrovsky came out of the office. His face was pink, and sweaty, and she felt sorry for him and she tried to paste a smile on her face.

'So you want to be an interior decorator, Belle, huh? So okay, next Monday you start. My wife says okay.'

She arrived at her usual time – eight o'clock – on Monday morning, although the salon did not open until ten. She had decided to wear her old black satin. It was still good, because she had not worn it much in the six years she'd had it, and she wanted to look as much like Madame as she could. And she had applied – very delicately – eyebrow pencil and powder bought at Woolworth's on Saturday in excited adventurousness. She waited until she got to work to apply the makeup, so Momma wouldn't see it. She had also bought a pale pink lipstick, and she traced it lightly against her lips. She squeezed her lips together: the paint was hardly noticeable. Then she went to the door of the salon and stood there, waiting for Madame to arrive. Her friends were already at work on the lampshades, and kept smiling at her over their shoulders, and leaning over to whisper to each other. They all had told her she looked beautiful, and as she gazed at them, she felt sorry she was leaving them. She loved them.

Madame didn't arrive until close to nine, and didn't notice Belle, who was now standing inside the salon gazing at some lace-trimmed satin pillows Madame had recently bought. She came striding in and glared at Arthur, saying, 'Why wasn't that bench moved! I told you on Saturday to change that arrangement!'

Arthur jumped. 'Yes, madame, I was just wondering if you wanted the mirror on this wall or that . . .' he began apologetically.

'That wall, of course. No, no,' she said irritably as Arthur moved a low carved bench to one side, 'not like that.' She pointed: 'I want that chaise here, and the small table there, with the bench alongside the chaise.'

Belle saw immediately the effect Madame wanted, and stepped forward shyly. 'I could help,' she offered, starting to move the chaise.

Madame looked at her briefly, questioningly. 'Oh, yes, Isabelle, isn't it?' Then she turned back to Arthur. 'NO, you idiot! This way!' As Arthur moved the heavy piece, Madame gave each piece a twist, so that the arrangement had a certain flair. I knew that, Belle thought, her heart warming. Maybe I can do this. Then Madame tossed a paisley shawl over the back of the chaise. The effect was wonderful. Madame turned and started for her office, then looked back. 'Come with me, Isabelle.'

Belle followed Madame into the office, a place she had never entered. It had a Louis Quinze desk and chair, and ugly metal file cabinets all around the walls. The desk was heaped with papers and fabric samples. Madame went through the office into the stockroom and beckoned Belle. 'These packages have to be delivered this morning and when you are through, go over to Acme and pick up the fabric I've put a rush on. And take trolleys or subways, no taxis, you hear? I'm not paying for taxis! Get going!'

Belle stared at her. It took a few minutes before she comprehended what she was supposed to do. Then obediently she accepted the packages and checked the addresses, and found out where Acme was, and set off, the boxes stuffed in a shopping bag. And as she walked the many blocks to the first spot, something inside her was laughing and crying at the same time: a messenger girl! That's what she was to be! Interior decorator, hah!

There was much excitement at home these days. It was Eddie's idea, as usual. They had over $500 in the bank now, and he said that was enough to buy a house. They had lived long enough in apartments over stores, in slums. They would have a regular house with a garden, and Momma would stay home and take it easy, it was about time. And they would have a regular Momma to cook and do laundry and clean for them, and they could invite friends to the house.

Only Momma was less than enthusiastic about this plan, but she bowed to it as she bowed to everything her children did these days. So on Sundays, the brothers and sisters traveled by trolley out to Queens, where they looked at houses, and at last bought one, on Manse Street in Forest Hills. It had a living room, dining room, and a kitchen, with a pantry and a back door and a little deck outside, and a nice garden in back, and a garage. Upstairs there were three bedrooms and a bathroom.

It was just beginning to be summer when they moved in, and Momma seemed happy because she had a garden for the first time since she left Poland. If she missed going to work, or seeing her Polish friends, she said nothing. If she did not enjoy being the servant to her children, she said nothing about that either. But she subsided into an even deeper sadness, and became indifferent to her appearance. Not that Momma had ever dolled herself up. But now she let her hair hang in wisps when it slipped out of the bun; she wore the same housedress for days without washing it; and she wore always a long-sleeved ugly brown sweater with a great hole at the elbow. She walked many blocks to the markets in which no one spoke Polish; she cooked huge meals for her big family; she washed and starched and ironed and mended. Occasionally, she cleaned the house. Otherwise, she sat in the kitchen, drinking coffee.

Belle had savings of her own, and she immediately put a down payment on a piano, an old upright; and signed up to take piano lessons. She could bring her friends home now, although she was a little ashamed of Momma, with that big hole in her sweater, and her teeth gone, and her . . . well, she had a little odor. Still, it was the best time of Belle's life, and she lived in a constant state of excitement. All of the children had friends, and the house was crowded with visitors on weekends. Stanley Berger knew how to play piano, and the boys would bring out the mandolin and banjo and the whole crowd would sing. Now when Bella went into Woolworth's, she would buy a new folio of sheet music, the latest hit. Momma baked huge trays of chruściki for them, or coffee cakes, and they drank coffee, and they smoked cigarettes. Belle even smoked right in front of Momma.

Momma insisted that the girls take the big bright front bedroom, and the old double bed was moved in there. They bought Momma a used but still good mattress and springs, and Momma slept alone in the narrow dark middle bedroom. The boys' two beds were moved into the back bedroom, which was fair-sized and had light, if not as much as the front one. There were real closets in this house, and a gas stove, and a glass-fronted china cabinet built right into the dining room wall. At first the house looked sparsely furnished, but every week Eddie came home with something new – a rug he had bought at an auction (How did he do that? Belle wondered. How did he *know* to do that?), a lamp, a china tea set.

And in her new happiness, Belle had the confidence to leave Ostrovsky's and get another job. She found one with an architect, but there wasn't that much to do. There were just the two of them in the office, and Belle typed and answered the telephone, but the architect himself didn't seem to have much to do. And every time he passed her, he put his hand on her shoulder or arm, and she would pull away and look at him, but he'd turn his face away. After three months, he fired her.

So she went to Wall Street and got a job decoding secret messages sent from one bank to another. This job paid fairly well, and it was a respectable job, but it was horribly tedious, because even after Belle had decoded the messages she couldn't understand them. She remembered the beauty of the interior decorating shop with longing; and her treatment by Madame with bitterness, and as she thought about all of it, she realized what she wanted to be. In the fall of 1926, Belle enrolled in Pratt Institute to study art.

four

When I was little and asked my mother about her life, it was these years at Manse Street that she concentrated on: the time when she had many friends, when the house was filled with activity. She talked lovingly of her friends, who were unvaryingly beautiful, intelligent, and talented. Gertrude was somewhat stinted in these accounts – she was the loyal old friend. But Adele, Miss Poland of 1927, was the most beautiful girl in Brooklyn; and Mala Megerian, whom she met in art school, was her introduction to an exotic and rarefied world. Mala, a gorgeous Syrian, came from a wealthy family who lived in a house furnished with Middle Eastern antiques and art, and when Belle visited, 'everyone there was a doctor'. 'Everyone?' I asked, since for me everyone included women. 'Everyone,' she assured me. They were not all medical doctors, although there were a couple of those, but truly educated men, with Ph.D.s. 'Oh! The men!' I exclaimed. She didn't notice.

I even met these old friends, who visited my mother occasionally in my childhood, and they were indeed the rare creatures she had described. Even Gertrude, who was as horse-faced and homely as ever, having, when I met her, a bit of a mustache, and who still lived with her sister and mother in an ornately furnished apartment in Brooklyn, as spirited and jolly in her forties as she had been earlier.

It was not until, claiming illness so I could stay home from school, and burrowing around in her vanity, I found the wonderful boxes and jars of makeup that she told me she'd been a member of a drama group. I loved this stuff – greasy deep purple and grey and green eye shadows, pink and crimson rouges in little pots, a dried-up mascara, and heavy black eyebrow pencils – and would occasionally resort to it at times of boredom, making my face over into a new face, wishing I could make it over even more. Then she showed me the photographs of her drama group – a bunch of arty types posed in a wonderful room with beaded curtains and paisley throws, some holding cigarettes, their heads all pointed upward so the fine line of chin and neck would be captured in the picture. I could hardly recognize my mother, she looked so young and glamorous. I was deeply impressed, but my mother, oddly, made nothing of it. 'It was nothing really. I didn't act, I couldn't act. They were all actors, not me. I lost touch with them after I got married.'

It was hard for me to connect this mother I knew, with her three cotton housedresses and her one good dress, a rayon print, this mother I saw at the stove, at the washboard, hanging clothes on the line, with the glamorous scene of the picture. Then I began to rummage in the huge old trunk that was kept in the closet I shared with my sister – the only one big enough to hold it. And I found a violin ('Oh, yes, I wanted so badly to play the violin. I took lessons. I took piano lessons too. But I had no talent. All I had was dreams'), and a portfolio of her sketches from art school, and a stack of tiny postcards and some books of photographs. These fascinated me, because the photographs were all of naked women posing among trees and flowers; and the postcards were of paintings. There were several hundred of them, all, I knew only later, of Impressionists, except for a few Turners. I used to pore over these – the photographs and the postcards – for hours, and pinned several of the cards up on the walls of my room. My favorites were Corot and Turner, and I would study the pictures minutely. They were hard to see, since they were only about two-by-three-inch reproductions, but they were MINE, I insisted, from my first glimpse of them. I studied the sketches too; they were all life studies of nudes, and I thought they were wonderful. But my mother dismissed those too.

'They're not good. I should throw them away. I had no talent.'

I clutched them. 'Don't throw them away!' I cried.

She didn't, and forty years later, as my parents are about to move from their house to a new one on the water, she finds them in the attic. Joy and I and our children clamor to see them and reluctantly, but with a little pride, she brings them down. I examine them. They *are* good, I wasn't wrong. They are not anatomically perfect, she needed more training, but they have something – an almost magical quality, as if the bodies were not flesh and bone but light, spirit. I tell her so.

She shrugs. 'Well, I spent three years in art school, and not one teacher ever told me I was good.'

'You were a girl,' Arden pipes up. 'Art teachers never praise girls. Only boys.'

My mother gazes at her. 'Is that true?' she asks me.

I solemnly assure her it is, although in fact I have no idea. But Arden's best friend is a painter who has suffered through many art schools, and she begins to recount Irena's story.

My mother's attention drifts. This is all too late for her. She turns to Arden and Billy. 'I received my diploma from Pratt just before your mother was born. I walked up on the stage pregnant. I was sure she would be an artist,' she concludes regretfully.

'Well, she is!' Billy announces fiercely.

My mother shrugs. 'Oh, photography . . .'

But when Mommy was not talking about her wonderful friends and her fun-filled life, she was talking about the other part. It began, 'My father died when I was nine years old.' I could not connect these two parts, nor did I perceive the gap between them until I was older, an adolescent. By then, some of the gap had been filled in with 'I only went to the sixth grade,' 'I went to work in a factory when I was fourteen,' and 'I was sent home from school because I couldn't speak English.' There was a particularly cruel story that I mulled over night after night in bed, vowing to get revenge when I grew up. In it, my mother was assigned in fifth grade to copy some maps from her geography textbook. Unsure of herself, she made many trials, and did painstaking sketches and finally produced maps she thought might pass. She handed them in the next day, and when the teacher saw them, she cried out, 'You traced these!' and tore them into shreds. My timid mother was unable to protest, and was merely heartbroken. I pictured scene after scene: I would find this teacher, track her down, and walk into her classroom and slap her face and say 'That's for what you did to my mother!' Or I would humiliate her in front of her class. This story bothered me for more than a decade, and I was nearly grown when I finally discarded the hope of punishing the villain.

I never told my children the story about the maps: by the time they were born, it had faded from my mind. But when my first volume of photographs was published, some man gave it a brief and especially nasty review in a photographic magazine. Arden was about fourteen, and we were not getting along well. Yet without my knowing it, she wrote a letter to the editor complaining about the critic's blindness and stupidity, and for unnecessary viciousness. I never saw her letter and wouldn't have known about it had he not replied, rather sweetly, explaining to her that no one wanted to harm her mother, but that was the way things were in the public world. She wasn't satisfied, tossed the letter down in a huff, and cried out. I held her close to me, I tried to console her. I couldn't, any more than I could console my mother. Children do not understand that nothing they do can repair the past. Only my father knew how to do that: he could fix its broken clocks and necklace clasps, its collapsed furniture. He didn't deal with hearts, though.

Among the questions I asked my mother when I was four and five and six were how she met Daddy, and how they came to marry each other. There was more to these questions than interest in romance – something even a tiny child is exposed to in the world we live in. For my parents seemed to have nothing in common, no shared pleasure; and my mother invariably turned a cool cheek to my father's warm nightly kiss. It was obvious even to a small child that my father adored my mother, but my mother simply tolerated him. So what was it that led her to marry him?

Mommy was extremely evasive about such questions. Sometimes she said she didn't remember how they met, and that they just drifted into marriage – this was very unsatisfying. Sometimes she said they'd known each other since childhood, and just drifted into marriage, and when I asked how, she said they would take walks along the city streets, and when they gazed in at a furniture store, would stand there and talk about what kind of furniture they would buy after they were married. Given the rather ragtag furniture we had, I found this story unsatisfying as well. Sometimes she said they had mutual friends, and just naturally hung out together. Then I would ask what Daddy was like then, and she was evasive again: he was polite, she said. He had a car.

By the time I was an adult, and could study with a more informed eye the photographs of their youth, I had made up my own mind about why they married. Because there was something about my father in those pictures that set him off from the other men, from Wally and Eddie and Stanley Berger and Oscar Ball and all my parents' other friends. He was nice-looking, but not quite what you'd call handsome. He wore glasses and had a full head of dark hair. It was the way he lived inside his body. The other men wore their bodies like borrowed clothes. One sagged; another lifted his neck as if he wanted to disavow everything beneath it. Wally always looked as if he were about to fly out of his; my uncle Eddie looked sturdy but unconscious of his. The women in their dresses or bathing suits looked as if they were displaying whatever they wore, fashion models in front of a camera. But my father's body was a living thing, it was he, himself. He had a good, nicely formed body in a bathing suit, but even when he was in an overcoat standing proudly beside his gorgeous car, he looked like someone who would know how to give a good hug. I wouldn't let the word cross my mind, but I thought he was *sexy*.

I had not seen this when I was a child because he never gave us hugs at all. And it wasn't until I was in middle, my mother in old age, that she finally put words on it.

'What attracted you to Daddy?' I asked for the thousandth time:

'Well . . . sex, I guess,' she confessed reluctantly.

No one remembers when Stefan Dabrowski or Dafna Pasek came to America, or how they happened to do so. Stefan was born in 1873, and Dafna in 1885, but no one recalls their birthdays or when they were married. Stefan made custom shoes, and Dafna was a seamstress. They had five children in two sets: Edward, born in 1906, Krystyna born in 1908, and Daniel born in 1912. Then there were my aunts Maria and Eva who, born in 1921 and 1925, could have been my older sisters. My father has little memory of his parents. He remembers sitting in his high chair at the dinner table and waving a herring at his father, crying, 'You're afraid of the fish! You're afraid of the fish!' And he remembers that his father was very stern and used to beat him with a strap. He is sure, however, that he deserved such punishment.

'Yes,' my mother grimaces, 'you had done something awful, I suppose.'

'Yes, you know,' my father agrees mildly, 'I'd probably left a mess around or something.'

'Horrible,' my mother says. I'm not sure my father hears her sarcasm.

My mother remembers Stefan though. He was a grouch, she says. He spent most of his time at home in the cellar, and when he came upstairs to eat, the noisy children at the dinner table all simmered down into silence. He was always grumbling, complaining about something.

This triggers my father's memory. 'Yes, if we had lamb chops, he'd look at them and say, "What are these things with tails?" He hated meat with bones in it. He liked lots of potatoes and pot roast, things like that. My mother let his complaints roll off her back. Of course my mother wasn't a very good cook.'

'Your mother hated to cook. She would spend all day at her sister's; Josephine was a wonderful cook. Your mother would rush home, pushing some child or other in a baby carriage, carrying a big bowl of borscht from Josephine's.'

'My mother was always cheerful,' he recalls.

'She was social, cheerful – like Joy,' my mother says with a tinge of disdain. 'She loved to be out with people. She went to Josephine's every day and the two of them would walk over to the Hasidic section of Williamsburgh – Josephine lived near there then, remember? And they would stay there all day, chatting, laughing – they both spoke Yiddish – and buying a few things. Josephine was a brilliant cook. She made tripe – well, she wouldn't give anyone her recipe, but it was the most delicious thing I ever tasted. She made her own kielbasa. But your mother was a genius with a needle. She could make anything, and without a pattern.'

My mother turns to me. 'When I was in the hospital after you were born, she wanted to come to see me, but she had no money for a present. So she rummaged through her boxes of scraps and found a bunch of old ribbons – all different colors and widths. And she made me a bed jacket of those ribbons – it was exquisite! I've never seen anything like it, anywhere.'

My father is probing his memory. I wonder if he wonders

why it is he recalls so little. 'I remember the first penny I ever earned,' he announces with pleasure. 'It was during the Jewish holidays, and an old Jewish man beckoned to me in the street. I went to him and he asked me to turn on the gas lamp. I did it, of course. And then he said, "There's your penny". He didn't touch it, it was lying on the table, he must have laid it out the day before. And I took it. That was the first penny I ever earned.'

He cannot remember, but he must have had trouble in school, because he did not finish high school until he was nineteen. I ask if it is not possible that he had trouble because he could not speak English when he started. It could be, he shrugs. He doesn't remember. He too had no toys or books or pencil and paper.

'But it didn't matter, because I made my own toys!'

I am suddenly aware that while my mother fastens on whatever sorrow was inherent in a situation, my father fastens on triumphs, successes.

He made, first, a scooter, the kind I remember boys making in my own childhood – a crate on its side was nailed to a board, and wheels nailed to the bottom of the board. Somehow, the way the crate was attached permitted it to be used to steer the vehicle. 'Yes, one of those. I made it when I was thirteen. And then I made a high-speed scooter!' He laughs. 'I put a bar in front instead of the crate – less wind resistance, higher speed. And then all the kids on the block copied me! So then I added a sidecar!'

I have rarely seen my father enjoy himself this way.

'Yes, and then I made a model airplane. This was only about 1920, 1921, you know, people didn't make things like that then. We used to have egg crates made of wood, not plywood, we didn't have that yet, but very thin wood. And I cut it in eighth-inch strips and planed each strip down, and made the fuselage and the wings. I even made the propeller, and I attached it with long rubber bands. It had a thirty-six-inch wingspan. Everybody came to look, they all rubbed their chins, they couldn't figure it out.' He laughs again, then stops. 'But it hardly flew at all – just across the lawn. I would have had to tighten the rubber bands to make it fly better, and that would have made the whole thing collapse.'

He subsides inside himself, and I know he is wondering what else he could have done, how it could have been managed, making a plane that would fly.

My mother pulls him out. 'And you made a radio,' she urges.

'Oh, yes! I made a crystal set.' He explains in detail how this was done, and does not seem to realize that I can't understand what he is talking about: wires, circuits, crystals. 'Yes, and I needed to put up an antenna, and the way the distances were, it had to go on the second floor of the house across the street. So I went over and asked them if I could attach it, and they were terrified. They'd never heard of radio, they thought it would bring lightning and burn their house down. I can't remember how I convinced them, but I did and as I was putting it up, all the men in the neighborhood came around and asked what I was doing. And when I told them, they looked at each other. "Radio?" they said. But within three months, there were antennas all up and down the block! And I called my father when I first heard it and he came over and took the earphones. It was KDKA in Pittsburgh! Imagine! All the way from Pittsburgh! And my father said, "Pittsburgh!" '

I'm smiling, delighted with his delight. 'And what did you hear? What kind of broadcast came over on KDKA?'

'Oh, that I don't remember. Maybe music, some kind of music. Talking. I don't know. You know, it didn't matter. It was getting it that mattered.'

I mull that over, remembering when he built his first hi-fi set. He would listen intently, but I soon realized he did not *hear* the music at all: what he heard was sound – every distortion, scratch, imperfection, was a cry for his attention. Whereas I heard only the music, and filled in or ignored distortions. Are these things built into our genes?

'And THEN,' my father announces his masterwork, 'I bought a car!' He doesn't remember how he earned the money to buy it. It was an old one, it probably cost about a hundred dollars, an Olds V-8, a big one. 'And I knew nothing, absolutely nothing, about cars. The first day I had it, I picked it up someplace around Prospect Street, and I drove it down Bedford Avenue, and I realized I didn't know how to turn it, and I was so frightened I just kept going straight, and I drove it all the way to Sheepshead Bay!' He laughs, we all laugh. 'So there was the water, and I had to turn it around! And the next Sunday I took the family out for a drive to Asbury Park, and I stopped for gas, and the mechanic said, "Do you want me to check the oil?" And I said "Oil?" I didn't know there was oil in the engine!'

But there were still strange sounds in this car, and it smoked, and he felt something was wrong. So, knowing nothing about cars, he took apart the engine, replacing, refiling, cleaning various parts, and put it back together again. He did this in a garage around the corner from his family's house in Quincy Street in Bedford-Stuyvesant, a fine neighborhood then. And the men who patronized the garage came and watched him and asked what he was doing, and when, three months later, he put his car back together again and it ran perfectly, all of them asked him if he would take care of their cars. And so, he suddenly had his own business.

'That was after Columbia,' my mother says coolly.

'Ye-es.' He is confused again.

'You were a college boy when I met you,' she adds, and I hear something in her voice, and I know what it is.

Dafna Pasek had come from the same village as Frances; in later years, the two women knew about each other in the way members of an ethnic community know about each other even when they rarely meet. Stefan's mother, Pane Dabrowska, came over only many years later, and she used to visit Frances, was the only person who did, after Michael died and they were impoverished.

'She was a terror. She only came because she was lonely, she didn't know many people. She'd come into the house and yell at Momma, "Go get me some tea!" Dafna and Stefan paid her passage and she was supposed to live with them and help out around the house. But they had five children, and Josephine had none, so she soon moved over to Josephine's. Then Stefan was so angry he forbade his family ever to visit Josephine again. But they did anyway – every day,' my mother recounts mournfully.

And once, Belle and Ed played together in the front yard of Josephine's house on Ten Eyck Street. Although they were only six and four or thereabouts, they both remember that. They met again when the Brez family was settled in Manse Street, and Jean was learning to play tennis with a girl who played at the Forest Hills Tennis Club, and who knew Krystyna Dabrowski. The friends planned a tennis party – they would each bring some friends. Krystyna arrived in a lovely car driven by her brother Ed, and Jean brought Belle. Whatever it was on my mother's side, I know it was love at first sight for my father.

What did he see? There she is, in her bob, her flapper clothes, her coy poses with her girlfriends, copied from magazines. She is not conventionally pretty – her eyes are too small and deep-set (they are my eyes too), her face too long and narrow for the popular female look. But there is a fineness in her features and expression, and something I have to call character in her face, that set her off from those surrounding her. She would not have spoken of her past – besides, it is a past he shared, although his family never reached the depths of poverty. She lived in a nice house in Forest Hills and worked in Wall Street; she was a member of a drama club, and she took piano and violin lessons. She spoke well. She acted fine, a fine lady. She went to Pratt at night. And she was a great dancer. How accomplished she must have seemed to this boy from Brooklyn! But maybe it was less her accomplishments that drew him than something he probably had no words for then, and still does not, something fragile and tentative that matched the delicacy of her face, something tight and frightened that needed his strength.

And she saw a nice-looking young man with a splendid car, a college man! He was unlike her brothers, he had been to high school and was at Columbia, and he could play tennis, he ran in races, he had built his own radio! 'He was a man,' my old mother tries to explain, 'he did things men did, but had more in his life, a little more, he had some education.' And there was that chemistry. And the fact that she was not afraid of him. She knew from the first that he would accept anything she did. Belle was terribly afraid of most men.

'He was polite and deferential to his parents, and they lived in a lovely house then, a brownstone. And he was always polite to me, to Momma and my sister. Only he was a little quiet.'

A lover of mine, who'd been a street kid and had fought his way into adulthood, a beautiful boy who got caught by culture just as he was entering manhood, once told me I'd converted him. 'Where I grew up,' he said, 'they said men were either fighters or lovers. And I wasn't too good at this love business, so I became a fighter. But now I'm a lover.' He was, too. And so was my father – always. Violence dismays him inordinately, and so do depictions of sex. As his family raised themselves into the middle class, he raised himself as a gentleman. From my present perspective, I know my mother chose well. But it did not seem so when I was growing up.

five

Ed did well at school once he learned English; if he was not too good at reading, he excelled at math. On the strength of his math and science grades, he was accepted into an engineering program at Columbia. But Ed had a disability he didn't know about, and probably attributed to stupidity. Since he remembers nothing unpleasant, he remembers nothing of this and did not recognize it when it reappeared in his daughter Joy, who grew up thinking she was stupid despite much evidence to the contrary; it appeared again in her son, Jonathan, in whom it was finally diagnosed as dyslexia. It is hard for them to read – the letters jump around in front of their eyes, and some letters appear upside down or on their sides.

So Ed finished only one year at Columbia. He could not do the work, despite the brilliance attributed to him by his family, many of his teachers, and sometimes, by himself. For several years he had been working at the garage around the corner from his house, working at nights doing small mechanical jobs. After he rebuilt his Olds, though, and had car owners thronging to him, the garage owner was glad enough to let Ed have space in his shop in return for his servicing the forty-four cars that were kept there. They were grand cars, owned by prosperous professional men and one woman (who always puzzled Ed: she was single, lovely, and had no known source of income, but a grand Chrysler convertible). Ed began to take care of these cars mechanically and even did bodywork with a rubber hammer so well that people thought he had replaced the dented fender or door. And he bought himself a new car, a jade green Hupmobile convertible with a black top.

It was in this car that he came to pick Belle up for dates. He never honked, like some of the other fellows who came to their house. He always parked the car and got out and came to the door, and led Belle out holding her arm gently, seeing she did not trip on the steps, helped her into the car and shut her door firmly, but quietly. They went out together for three years, and Ed was always courteous and devoted.

She must have felt some relief, finding herself after all to be like other girls. For all the other girls she knew had dates, or were married, all except Gertrude, who in fact would never marry, and Adele and Mala, who had real careers. Girls talked about boys a great deal, she knew. But the few dates she had had were dismal evenings she preferred to forget. There was something about men that made her pull away, pull back: she sensed a violence in them, an aggressiveness that their easy camaraderie could not conceal. Even her brothers . . .

And if she had, on occasional nights, investigated her own body, and received some pleasure from that, she knew it was a dark and shameful thing, to be hidden. Ed did not attempt to do anything shameful whatever, although he was athletic and strong. And his nice open sensual face was warm, and when he looked at her his eyes glowed. She must have felt something for him, something romantic and melting, because this most unsentimental of women sent him a Valentine's Day card in February 1929, picturing a young girl in a ruffled dress and pantaloons sitting before an easel, painting. I know this because he still has it.

She knew Pane Dabrowska did not like her. Dafna saw her as a flapper, sophisticated, who would corrupt her son – even though Belle was very careful never to smoke in front of her. Mr Dabrowski though, always had a special smile for her. But really, none of that mattered because Belle was terrified of marriage, and they did not spend much time with Ed's family. Ed often came to Manse Street and sat watching Belle as she played a new song she had learned on the piano, or stood singing with the others around the piano. And he always smiled at her, and was gentle.

So when did it start, and how, his importuning, his warm body pressing against hers? And did she want it too, her young body clamoring for that kind of love? Was that what the Valentine meant?

'Only one time, Anastasia, that was all it was, just that once. And in a hallway! There wasn't even any penetration, I thought nothing could happen.'

Well, I can't quite picture this scene. What hallway? Because I remember the house on Manse Street, and its hallway was open to the living room where surely Wally would be sitting reading the newspaper, and beyond, to the dining room where surely Eddie would be sitting at the table working over his now extensive stamp collection. This was a family of night people. And if they were not there, why stand up, why not go sit on the couch? Standing up in a hallway with no penetration, with something cold and sticky running down her leg? Could my mother be lying to me?

Why not? She does not owe me the truth about this. I see it in the car, on the luxurious leather backseat of the gorgeous car that was soon to vanish. Backseats – the loci of so many of our beginnings. I like to picture it as having passion.

In any case, wherever and however it happened, there she was in March 1929 with her Wall Street job, her Pratt portfolio, and no period. She remembers nothing about the time that followed except walking onstage pregnant to receive her diploma, and crying. Crying, crying, unable to stop.

Finally, she told them, her family. Momma said nothing. Neither did anyone else. They looked at her: Jean shook her head and lamented, 'Oh, Belle!' Eddie made some joke about Ed Dabrowski. Only Wally seemed to understand what it meant to her, and he took her aside later and said he could arrange for an abortion for her if she wanted it. She cried on his shoulder.

She wanted the abortion. It was all too shameful. God was punishing her because of one time, one time! She would be so humiliated in front of her friends. But she sensed without knowing how it would be to have an abortion – a dark street, many stairs, a dirty room, filth and corruption and sin and shame and it was illegal besides. And expensive. And inside her was a living being.

She sat alone in her darkened room and cried, thinking about her life as a huge joke, all her attempts, her struggle to find a place where she could breathe, where she could be on the outside what she felt inside, and here she was trapped, forever, she would never escape now. And this had been her destiny all along. How could she have imagined anything else? The only thing she wanted to be was an artist, but she had no talent, her teachers never praised her, so what else was there? She was a woman, all women ended up like this. She had all these years been a worm wriggling and twisting on a hook that had held her all along, impaled on nature's decree, ignorant not just about life but about this too.

When she was exhausted with crying, when her nose was sore from being wiped and her eyes rimmed with red, she thought about what to do. She knew Ed was frightened but would leave the decision up to her. He was only twenty-three and just starting in life, and hardly knew if he could support a family. But if she wanted an abortion, he would find the money for her and go with her and hold her hand. And if she did not, he would marry her, grateful for her if not for the child.

In early June 1929, she and Ed drove to Washington. They found a little church and told the priest they wanted to be married. He told them they must confess first. Belle knelt in the confessional, dumb. She could not remember the prayer she was supposed to start with, 'Forgive me, Father . . .' or how long it had been since she had gone to Confession. She began to cry and told the priest she was pregnant. Curtly, he barked out a long penance and slammed down the shutter. Then he charged out of the box and grabbed Ed by the arm and cursed him, called him vile names. Grimly, in fury, he married them.

Oh, Ed, poor Ed. Standing there, the gentle boy who loved this woman, who had wanted her in the fullness of his devotion and desire, who had not meant harm, heard himself reviled and recoiled from it, yet at the same time accepted it. He knew the priest was right. He was a man and men were like that, yes, he had pressured her, he had not thought about the consequences. He did not think the word *evil*, but he felt it. He knew the Father was right: fathers were always right, no matter how harsh they might seem; boys had to submit to fathers. The entire question was too hard for him and he let it go. But neither Belle nor Ed ever entered a church again of their own volition, and all Ed retained of his Catholicism was a discomfort with eating meat on Fridays.

They left the church on a dismal grey day and wandered around Washington a little, then drove back to New York. Ed saw Belle into her house, then kissed her, and drove off to his. They did not tell their families they had been married, though Belle's family no doubt knew. Later they would tell everyone they had been secretly married a year. The lie enabled them to hold up their heads even though they knew no one would believe them. It gave everyone a story they could accept and treat as truth.

But shame crumpled Belle's stomach, and whenever she was alone, she cried. They both continued to work and save every penny. They went out, like any engaged couple, and Ed bought Belle an engagement ring with a real diamond in it. They looked at apartments, and in September, rented a nice three-room apartment in Kew Gardens, near enough to the subway, near to Belle's family. They looked at furniture, and Ed was impressed by Belle's knowledge, and by the Queen Anne sofa and chair she chose. They also bought a Tudor chair, with a high back and wooden arms, putting a deposit down and paying the furniture off on time. They bought an unpainted bedroom set, and painted it white and Ed put beautiful floral decals Belle had chosen on the fronts of the chests of drawers and the head of the bedstead.

They moved the furniture in, and began to live as a married pair in October. It was hard, because Ed was also giving money to his father to help the family out, and now Belle was no longer working. So Ed got a night job in a pharmacy. They worried, but they planned. And then, everything collapsed. The newspapers screamed in great black letters and rich men jumped out of office buildings. Ed's customers' cars simply vanished and their bills remained unpaid.

He still can't understand this. 'They were all rich, you know?' Nearly sixty years later, he sits scratching his still full head of white hair. 'They were doctors, stockbrokers. And not one of them paid me, not one!' He cannot comprehend this even now. They were respectable men, and respectable men pay their bills, especially if they have money and their creditor does not. This innocence of my father's, maintained all these years, seems sweet to me, and I reach out and touch his hand.

Overnight he lost his business. They could not pay the November rent on the apartment and Belle was shamed worse than ever before in her life. She went back to Momma's, and Ed went back to his family. At night, secretly in the dark, he and his brother loaded their furniture onto a rented truck and drove it away. And late in November, that month I always think of as bleak – the bare branches reaching desperately to a broad grey empty sky – I was born.

Part 2

*The Children
in the Garden*

Chapter VI

one

My mother cried. It must be my first memory. Alone in the dark narrow cold room, the two of us still bound together, she screamed and no one came and she cried. Once, the door opened and a sliver of light showed, but the nurse roughly asked her why she was making so much noise, she wasn't ready yet. She kept screaming, the pain was so terrible. She wept, and from her pain, I emerged, I Anastasia, her punishment, the midge daughter.

She kept crying after I was born, and the doctor gave her luminal. She swallowed it hungrily, day after day. But she still cried, and the crying was a scream against her life, like rain outside a window, concealing, distorting, dimming all else that occurred.

Ed came to take her home from the hospital, but she was not allowed to take her baby because they had not paid the hospital bill. She does not remember what trick they used, what ploy, but Ed got the baby out too. They carried her to the Dabrowskis where they were to live: it was a bigger house than the one in Manse Street. Dafna put her in an alcove off the kitchen, on a cot, with a box beside her for the baby. Ed slept in his old room, with Daniel. Belle cried. On the third day, in the afternoon while Dafna was at Josephine's, she got up and dressed and dressed the baby and went to the corner call box and called a taxi. She left no note. She went to Momma's house. Momma now slept in the big bed in the front room with Jean, and Belle refused to let her move. She took the dark narrow middle room. She gave the baby to Momma. She slept, and when she woke up, she cried.

Frances's arms reached out to the baby hungrily. She reached out and engulfed Anastasia, her first baby, the baby she had always wanted, the baby she had not been able to have when she had her own. She encompassed her and sang to her and talked to her and fed her endlessly. She bounced her and told her she was a hammer thrower, *moja kochany*, and she, Frances, was *Babcia*, Grandma. Frances was happy again.

Belle cried. She was only twenty-five and her life was over.

Her life had ended. Ed had no job, they had no money, she was no longer a carefree young flapper concerned about clothes and outings and piano lessons and violin lessons and art school and her wonderful friends. That was all over, over forever. She would never have it again, and in truth, she hadn't had much. Now it was done, and all she had was this creature, this clamorous thing that demanded to be fed from Belle's own body, when after all, how could there be anything in it? She nursed for a few weeks, then gave it up. Her milk was thin, sporadic, laced with luminal; the baby screamed and clutched its little fists, it was hopeless, Belle was a failure at this just as she had been a failure at everything else. Wally went out and bought some bottles for her.

Only once did she laugh, and that was at Thanksgiving dinner. Momma brought a roast chicken to the table – they were all in trouble, Wally too had lost his job, and Eddie and Jean had had to take cuts in pay. And Wally looked at Anastasia lying in her box on a dining room chair, and said they should have roasted and eaten her, she was bigger than the chicken. The laughter that followed required handkerchiefs to wipe away the tears, and Wally thought he had been really witty. He would repeat the joke to Anastasia many times as she grew up.

Then, one evening, Ed drove up and Wally let him in. Everyone looked up: but no one knew exactly what had happened. No one had asked any questions. He was stiff and tense, and so were they. He asked for Belle. She was in bed, crying. He went up.

Ed sat on the bed beside her. He took her hand and bent to kiss her, but she wrenched her head away violently. Tears sprang into his eyes and throat, but he remained beside her. He cleared his throat. He tried to stroke her brow, but she again turned her head swiftly, hard, away.

'I got a job, Belle,' he whispered.

She looked at him. Her head lay still. She waited.

'I'll be a tester and troubleshooter for Brooklyn Edison. It pays twenty dollars a week.' He was proud of himself. It was not negligible to get a job right after the Depression struck; he got it only because he had had a year of college. She saw this, and her mouth tightened. She knew it was a real accomplishment, that he must have tried hard for this job; but she had contempt for how easily he was satisfied. What did he think they could do with twenty dollars a week?

'We can't live on that,' she said.

He bowed his head. He did not dare to ask her to return to his father's house, nor to ask if he could come here. She watched him. She understood. There were no words.

'We can live in this room,' she said finally.

And he bent and kissed her forehead, and she let him. He sat there, stroking her hand for a long time. They did not speak. Then he said he had to go and would be back the next evening. The next night, he walked from the trolley stop with his suitcase. He had sold his car to pay the hospital bill. He moved into the dark little room where they would live for the next three and a half years.

Belle forced herself to get up each morning. Anastasia slept late and never woke her mother in the mornings, so Belle would rise and put on a robe and slippers and go downstairs and drink coffee while Momma cleaned up the dishes from the others' breakfasts. Ed Dabrowski rose first, at six, and prepared his own cereal and boiled egg and toast; but Momma still prepared breakfast for her children, for Eddie and Jean, who went out to their jobs at seven forty-five, and coffee and toast for Wally, who left at eight every morning just as if he had a job to go to. After several cups of coffee, the last shared with Momma who sat down with her, and two cigarettes, Belle would go upstairs and fetch the sleeping baby, who often did not want to be wakened, and was sullen and sleepy.

Belle heated a bottle and prepared Pablum for Anastasia. Then Frances would close all the kitchen doors and turn the gas jets of the stove up high and set an enamel basin in the sink and fill it with warm soapy water. When the room was warm enough to make most people faint, Belle would undress Anastasia, set aside her dirty diaper, and immerse her in the basin. Momma hovered holding a great towel. Belle rinsed the baby from the long arm of the tap and Momma grabbed her and covered her and dried her. Then Belle dressed her in fresh clothes, and laid her in a cushioned basket on the kitchen floor. Only then – neither woman noticed that they were staggering with the heat – did they turn off the gas jets. They did not reopen the kitchen doors for some time afterward, lest the baby catch a chill.

Belle would empty the diaper into the toilet off the kitchen, carry it down to the cellar to soak in the deep tub along with those from yesterday. Then she went back upstairs and scrubbed her hands, then toasted some bread and spread marmalade on it and ate, while Momma – who would *never* leave Anastasia in her basket – bounced and spoke to the baby, calling her '*moja kochanie*, my sweetheart, my little hammer thrower, Babcia's girl'. (Did the words pierce Belle's heart, still addressed to another?) Belle went back downstairs and scrubbed the soiled diapers on a board and rinsed and wrung them and carried them back upstairs in a basin. She pulled her coat on over her nightgown and robe, and went out to the tiny back porch and fixed them on the clothesline, which squeaked with each tug on the rusted pulley.

Then the two women straightened the house, made the beds, dressed. Around eleven, it was time to go out. Belle put on a dress and hose and high heels, and powdered her face and put on lipstick; Momma always wore her old cotton housedresses and the brown sweater with the hole in the sleeve and her shabby ancient black coat and a straw hat with a wilted brown rose on it. Anastasia was piled into layers of flannel and wool, every inch of her covered except her tiny face, and set into the carriage, a fine English pram that the brothers and sister had chipped in to buy. Momma was always very cheerful as they set out, whatever the weather: this was the high point of her day. They would walk to the Boulevard and stop at Momma's favorite markets. Momma knew all the shopkeepers – the German butcher, the German baker, the Italian vegetable man, the Scottish grocer. She always smiled and chatted with them, and they laughed and joked with her and made little lights go on in their eyes, and sometimes they even kissed her hand. This made Belle look at her mother in a new way. Momma, after all, was forty-eight years old now, an advanced age in Belle's eyes, and since she had stopped working, she had gained fifteen pounds – 120 was too heavy for her small frame. Her fine hair was still long and wound up into the same unfashionable bun, and the blond color had darkened into a mousy grey. She had a gentle face and a sweet smile but her face was etched with pain in hundreds of tiny fine lines. She walked a little too slowly, her legs swollen from years of hard work, her frame a bit bent from years of bending over sewing machines; and her clothes were shabby and shapeless. She looked like a worn-out peasant woman. Yet these men – could her mother possibly be thinking of . . . impossible! But there was no mistaking the way these men acted, the way Momma acted, almost fifty. Even the gaunt surly owner of the stationery store where Belle stopped every other day for a pack of Luckies smiled, showing his yellow teeth, and called Momma, 'Dear Mrs Brez'.

The women would buy only what they needed for the day. Although they had an icebox, they could not carry too much at one time even with the carriage, and besides, Momma loved the daily outing. And Momma loved being with Bella (she never adopted Belle's new name) and Anastasia, and Belle felt somehow calm being out with Momma, and all of them walked home looking forward to lunch. For lunch, Belle would scramble eggs or make grilled cheese sandwiches for her and Momma, while Momma fried bacon slowly until it was dark and crisp, then crumble it into bits and lay them on Anastasia's tongue. And Belle, eating slowly but with relish, would feel that this was the best time of the day, and would think – Grandma, mother, and baby, three-way, that's the way it should be. Then Momma would clean the kitchen while Belle changed Anastasia's diaper and gave her a bottle and set her in the basket for a nap. And Belle would look at the clock that hung on the kitchen wall over the stove and see that it was only two o'clock and her heart would sink. Anastasia would sleep for about two hours now; and Momma would go up to her room and sew. She was making a pink silk coat and hat, with embroidery, for Anastasia for the spring. She had lined the coat with white crepe de chine, and Belle had embroidered, in a paler pink, small flowers on the coat collar and the side of the hat. Belle was proud of the outfit, remembering the Ostrovkys' shop: no rich child had anything finer than this. But her part in making the outfit was done. She would pick up a book and go up to her room and lie on the bed and start to read. But soon she was crying again.

She did not understand why she cried so much. She tried to think, to cut through the tears with reason. But the back of her head was filled with a whirling fluid hot as tears, painful as cut flesh. And this hot crimson-purple fluid dyed everything it touched, heaved up like waves and drowned thought. It whirled her thoughts around too, so that she could not make them come out in neat lines, or squares, or sort out right from wrong. Was she wrong to be so miserable? Should she be happy? Was she neurotic, like Poppa, like Wally? How was it Ed was happy? Was he wrong to be happy, having so little to make him so?

She would think: I'm a miserable neurotic. I should be happy. After all I have a healthy baby, a nice place to live, we could be living in that slum, the old neighborhood! I have good food, and I don't have to go to work every day in a sweatshop. Ed is devoted to me. He has a job. Wally doesn't. Ed isn't standing on a street corner selling apples. She would think: it's nice here all day, just Momma and the baby and me, it's peaceful, and if I don't have a beautiful house and servants like rich ladies, I have clothes as good as theirs, and so does Anastasia; I eat as well, probably better, because rich ladies have things like one lamb chop and peas and a Waldorf salad for dinner, that's what their maids told Momma when they lived in the old neighborhood and Momma had lots of friends.

But as soon as she managed these thoughts, they would be overwhelmed with a horrid flaming rage: why wasn't Ed doing as well as her brother Eddie, or Eric Terschelling, Jean's boyfriend, who took her out to dinner in a restaurant every Saturday night and went to actuarial school nights to better himself? The fire would mount and transform itself into a great wave of grief that would knock her down. She would burst into full sobbing. It seemed to her that she was standing over her own coffin, seeing herself, her face primly made up with powder and lipstick and eyebrow pencil and set in the calm smile she tried to give it, lying there in her good navy silk dress with a flower at the bosom, and the thought would burst through that her life was over, over, that there was no longer anything for her.

Had she not watched her own mother grieve herself into old age in a few years? And now she was a mother too, no longer a person but someone who was supposed to care only for her child, a person permitted no other life, no other joy. All the past seemed futile beating against bars: the piano and violin lessons, the dreams of being a decorator, the years at art school. The truth was she had no abilities, none whatever, except maybe for the dancing, and what good was that? In her three years at Pratt she had learned nothing; Madame Ostrovsky had known what she was doing when she made Belle into a messenger girl. She couldn't even play parts well in her little drama group productions. She had no talent, no brain, she was good for nothing; all her longings had been stupid dreams, childish, infantile, ephemera that had not deserved to exist. What she had to do was set aside her dreams, grow up, accept what it meant to be an adult woman . . .

But this last thought rarely achieved full development before she was overwhelmed with a new burst of sobbing, which subsided very slowly, and left her weak with weariness. Then she would sink into sleep.

Momma would let her sleep as long as she needed to, going into the little dark room and softly picking up the basket that held the baby and carrying it downstairs. Then she would start dinner, talking all the while to the baby, feeding her bits of pie crust or chruściki or bakery cake, contented as she peeled vegetables and roasted meat, baked pies or bread, happy to be preparing dinner for her children, and for her little granddaughter. When Belle came down, newly powdered and lipsticked, her hair fixed in its marcel waves, and only her eyes dull with sleep and luminal, Momma would smile and bob her head and say, 'Have coffee, Bella, pour some for me too,' and sit down with her daughter and chat about the baby, the wonderful baby, the miraculous new being in her life.

Belle would gaze at the infant in the basket on the floor and think about how it came out of her. She would never be the same as she was before – her hips were even broader than they had been; there were stretch marks on her smooth pale belly and her buttocks; and her feet, already a source of embarrassment, had grown even larger, to an 8½. She had lost a tooth. And all of this came from a single moment, an act of darkness, a sin, the priest had said. Yet married people were supposed to do this. But not people who weren't married.

By now, Momma would have Anastasia on her lap. She'd bounce her and call her 'my little hammer thrower!' and hug her and cry out *moja kochanie!* and the words would pierce Belle's consciousness and she would look up and see her mother and the baby far away, like strangers seen through a window, when you pass by on a cold night shivering and look in and see them, mother and child, in warmth and the light shining on their hair, and you stand and watch for a moment, acutely aware of the freezing pane of glass that separates you from that scene . . .

Then thought would be swallowed up in activity. Wally would come home first, dejected from another futile day, or guilty because sometimes he did not hunt for a job but went instead to a chess club in Manhattan, a smoky smelly loft peopled with old Russian men with pipes, where he played for hours, beating most of them, forgetting his situation. Once he beat the world champion in this club – but as it was not an official match, it served only to bolster his image with his family. He sensed that all of them looked down on him, and he walked in always with a certain swagger, and talked tough, as if he knew the real world and they were mere innocents. But he forgot all that when he saw Anastasia. He reached for her with a great smile and lifted her up and bounced her and took her into the living room while the women got dinner ready and put her on his leg and played horsie.

The nights seemed long to Belle. Ed, her Ed, rarely came home for dinner. He went to his father's house, where he would eat and then go to work on the apartment he was putting into the basement. The Dabrowskis too were having hard times: people did not buy custom-made shoes these days, and Stefan worked only a couple of days each week. Daniel and Krystyna were working, but Maria and Eva were still in school, and Dafna was often ill. So Ed was building another apartment in the basement of the fine old brownstone on Quincy Street; its rent would supplement their income.

The others came home, though, and they would eat together, and after dinner, sometimes Jean and Belle would take a walk with Anastasia in her carriage. They never talked about anything serious. Some nights the four of them would play pinochle together or bridge or listen to the radio. Momma would sit beside them smiling, drinking coffee, sewing. They often played cards until midnight. By then Ed would have arrived and Belle would offer him some cake or pie and tea, and he would accept it, and they'd all have a second dessert with him, and go glutted to bed.

But some nights they were tired, or dejected: no explanations were ever made, no discussions occurred, but one or another would go up to bed early, and often, even when the others sat up, Belle went up alone. Sometimes, when Ed came home, the house was already dark except for the small lamp in the hall left on for him. He would sigh, carefully wiping his rubbers on the mat, and hanging up his coat. To be young, poor, and the parent of a baby is to be wretched, for sure. And Ed had enough reason for sadness. But he was less unhappy than he might have been. He had, has, a gift for contentment, maybe he even has a gene for it, inherited from his mother, inherited from him by Joy. He lives always in the moment; he does not think about the future, he has erased the past. He adored Belle, and there she was, in bed with him every night. He had good food and enough of it. And every day, when he went to work, an opportunity to use his brain. He was not humiliated by the job he had taken; on the contrary, he was proud of himself for having work and for doing it well. And best of all, his superiors always recognized his excellence.

'Yes, the other fellows all got two cents an hour – except Charlie Gundhauser, he got three cents, but I got ten cents! Mr Schumacher said my productivity was twenty-five per cent higher than anyone else's! He even patted me on the back!' Ed would tell Belle proudly, alone in their room at night.

And now his father too, that fearsome angry man who oppressed his childhood (but he has forgotten that) was pleased with him, patted him on the back and praised him. He was impressed with this son of his who could do carpentry, plumbing, and wiring, and do all of it so perfectly, so neatly, with solid excellence. He smiled and nodded at his son, he was even a bit awed by him. He listened to Ed's opinions and deferred to them. Ed glowed.

And then he went home to Belle. To lie beside her, even when she was sleeping, was for him like lying beside a movie star, someone great. Her pale skin gleamed in the dark, and she turned in the bed delicately, like a flower moving in a light wind. She was beyond him in some way, there were things about her he could not fathom. But he knew she needed him, was linked to him, hung on his unfailing arm, leaned against his sturdy body. Wherever she went, his glance followed; whatever she suggested, he agreed to. He was a strong machine designed to realize her desires; he was her axle, and she was his engine.

But he did not know what to do when she cried. He would sit on a chair beside the bed, watching her, listening, unable to console her. He'd press his hands together until the knuckles turned white. He belched frequently, quietly. She could not seem to tell him what was the matter. He watched her in wonder: she was so delicate, she felt things so deeply. As her crying began to abate a little, he would offer eagerly to fetch her a cup of tea, and sometimes she accepted, and he would run downstairs, and carry back two cups of hot liquid rocking on their saucers, and she would sip it a little and lean back on the pillow exhausted and stare into space. He was grateful when she finally subsided into sleep. He was willing to sit there forever, guarding her like a knight his princess. He didn't mind that her eyes were swollen, her breathing snuffly, her head averted, as long as she allowed him to be there with her.

He would undress in the dark and slip into the bed beside her, careful not to disturb her too much, and because he rose at six and walked all day, he would fall immediately into the deep sleep of the physically tired. And when he rose early the next morning, as Belle still slept, he rose energetic, eager. He wanted to be up and out, the fresh air was good, being outdoors was good, using his body was good. He walked quickly, aware of his limbs, his back, his stomach, feeling the goodness of using them. And although he never forgot Belle, not for a minute, for ten hours he was off on his own, doing, and he was happy.

Belle lay there pretending to sleep, feeling his warm body beside her, aware that he had put his arm around her waist and kissed her lightly on the cheek before he sank into the untroubled sleep of an animal, a mindless creature. She remembered how she had sketched nudes at art school, and how she began to sense something about the body – she wasn't sure, she had no words for it – as if the body glimmered with something, as if it was not just a thing identical with you that you need to sit or stand, a thing that had to be fed and purged, but something else . . . as if bodily expression was like facial expression, that gaunt man she'd drawn with the grim face, his body was a hungry thing, ready to spring . . . ah, she was too stupid to think it properly. But there was *that* body, and there was this body beside her, and her own body that had gotten her into this horrible mess, this shameful situation, because no matter how polite people were, they all knew and she felt it, the humiliation made her body feel hot, like her head, fluid, searing, wanting to disappear. And he had done this to her. Holding her, he was so warm, he clung, he loved her, yes she knew that, it felt all right when he pressed himself against her, it felt even a little bit nice, something in her own body answered him. But he had urged it on her, promising, begging, loving, and then he had done this to her, a thing that once done could not be undone. Her body had blown up, *her* body, not his, why couldn't it have been his? Where was the justice? He wanted it, he urged it, he was hot with eagerness and she, lukewarm, had allowed it, merely allowed it, and she was the one to bear the shame and punishment. She turned her body away from his in so strong a revulsion that he stirred, and her heart stopped for a moment, she did not want to wake him, she did not want him at her, clamorous, hot, drinking her in, up. She lay stiff and tense, barely breathing. But as she let herself gradually relax, his body heat began to permeate her side, and she turned, gently, toward him. His thick hair was spread on the pillow, and his fine sturdy body, in harmony with itself, raised and lowered itself gently with his breathing. She wanted to touch him, just to lay her fingertips on his back, to feel its warmth. Her toes and fingers were ice cold. She moved toward him a bit more, wanting, for a moment, to feel his arm around her, his chest pressed against hers, his body . . .

Then she thought about how cheerful he always was, how satisfied with how little. She thought about his preening satisfaction with his father's praise, that tyrant, a man she would in later years call a Hitler, how Ed bowed and bobbed, just like Momma, deferring, deferring, how he reported every instance of Mr Schumacher's praise. But could they live on what he earned? Was he a man to be respected? A hot milky liquid filled her brain, different from the one in her body but just as hot, full of contempt. He was unworthy. She turned her body away from his, and after a long time, fell asleep.

two

Since I knew her story I could understand Belle's horror when I, like her, found myself pregnant without benefit of clergy. She didn't consider my condition sinful, contrary to the laws of church and state; she didn't invoke God or society to pound guilt into me. She just sank, as if what I had done was to drown her. She had spent her entire adult life raising me and Joy for something better, for wider choices, a different kind of life, and here I was repeating her pattern. It was, for her, as if femaleness itself were cursed, as if there were no escape from body if you were a woman. With despair, she dismissed me. I ceased to be the daughter on whom she had lavished whatever kinds of care she could give. I had drowned her hope, the hope that had kept her going over all those dreary years; and with that I had drowned whatever special claim I had on her.

She didn't say any of this. After an initial gasp and slump when I told her my unwelcome news, a night of weeping, a deepening of the sag that had already set in on her chin and jowls, she was quiet, unreproachful. She went through the same motions: cooking dinner, marketing, cleaning the house, doing the laundry: but I knew I had broken her heart. After Arden was born, she helped me, like a proper mother. Once a week she would drive over to get me and take me to her house, and drive me home again. She'd watch as I did my laundry in her washer, and hold Arden when I went outdoors to hang the wash on the line. Occasionally, she would talk to the baby or even smile at her, but not often. Nor did she transplant her hopes to Joy: she expected little of Joy, who always had trouble in school, who showed no signs of my precocity. She just sagged.

I see now that my mother's withdrawal was based in anger, but at the time I would have denied it utterly, I did deny it, throwing in Brad's face the difference between my family's acceptance and the rejection of his. And although

Brad had some sense that the contrast I was drawing was somehow not so clear, he couldn't quite put his finger on what was wrong about it. We'd exchange some unkind words, then he'd say that of course my family accepted it, they were glad to get rid of me, as who wouldn't be, whereas his family wanted to hold on to him because he was so dear, and I'd pummel him, and he'd laugh and grab me and kiss me all over, telling me I was lucky he existed because there was at least one person in the world who found me adorable. In those days, we could never argue; all our conflicts ended with tickling and teasing, which inevitably led to the very act that had caused our conflicts in the first place.

I lied about my mother's reaction not because it hurt my feelings, nor because I was desperate for social acceptance, which had to start with her. No. I lied because I could not let myself know what she was feeling, because it would have destroyed me. I wasn't lying to anyone but myself. Because my deep involvement with my mother and her life had already inverted itself. I don't know when it happened exactly, only that by eighteen whenever I thought about her life, her grief, I would feel a wave of revulsion so extreme I felt my very body turning inside out. I was a swimmer with her teeth set, holding her head so high and stiff above the water that no drop could touch her face: I *would not, would not,* would *not* have a life like hers! I would not concentrate on the tears of things, the *lacrimae rerum* my Latin teacher mooned about, holding her Virgil against her large flattened bosom. I *would* be happy!

My passionate hunger for sex had begun when I was fifteen, and I'd done enough experimenting that my mother began to get the idea that I might be feeling something like desire. She sat me down one afternoon when Joy was at Scouts and my father at work, and explained that although sexual desire did not arise in a girl until she was eighteen, at the very youngest, a girl always had to be careful because boys were not responsible, and if I were not careful, I could end up with a life like hers. She didn't have to give any further explanation: if her mournful, grim face and tone were not enough, our silent tense family life was. But so contrary a girl was I that her warnings acted as spurs. In those years, whatever she was, I determined I wouldn't be; whatever she felt, I determined to feel the opposite. I was young enough to believe you could decide how you were going to be, to feel, especially if you were an artist, as I was, as I had determined I would be. I ran around like a gay girl, a gypsy; I had an image of myself as a great rebel against society – but my rebellion was really against my mother. I smeared on a purple Tabu lipstick and black eyebrow pencil and pulled my blond hair back so I looked older. I smoked with the boys in the high school parking lot, and was reprimanded for it by a teacher who spent her lunch hour staring out the window into the schoolyard. Many teachers looked at me askance – because my grades were good, they assumed I was one of the 'nice' girls, not the 'cheap' ones. I grinned, pleased at defying their categories, and continued to make all A's, even as I made out in the front seat of cars on Saturday-night dates.

By college, I was doing more than 'necking', as we called it in those days, but I *was* careful, Mother's warnings had had some effect. I made sure the guys had condoms, the only form of birth control available then. Typically, the guys could have birth control but the girls couldn't. You couldn't get a diaphragm unless you were married, and of course there was no pill then. The greatest risks I took were a flawed rubber, and a diminished reputation. I didn't care about the rep, I told myself. I was an artist, a bohemian, I wanted to *live*. I was so vocal about my sexual principles that I terrified lots of guys who might have tried to go further with a more silent girl, and yet who couldn't admit they hadn't succeeded with me because my reputation became awesome, so awesome that it toppled people's categories – it made *me* appear the sexual predator, and boys my victims. I laughed a lot at that. I loved it.

But all that ended when I met Brad. He was very tall and very skinny and he moved awkwardly, the way people do when they haven't quite occupied their new adolescent bodies. It was his awkwardness that touched me. Perhaps it would be truer to say, it made me feel safe. (I am trying to tell the truth. If you can't tell the truth at fifty, when can you tell it?) And I knew then, if I've managed to forget it since, that I was terrified of the male. Not boys, or not all boys, but a certain kind of man. I'm not sure how I came to feel this fear, it felt built-in. For instance, I had all women teachers in grade school, and the vice-principal was a woman, and all of these seemed accessible, they were people who smiled, who approved of me. But they all became tense when the small thin wiry man named Mr Fox (I had nightmares about foxes) walked past the class-room, or heaven forbid, into it. A man was the principal, and the women were all afraid of him, even Mrs McKinley, the vice-principal. But whenever Mr Fox came out of the cloud he usually walked inside long enough to notice a person, he too smiled, and patted one on the head, so why was I afraid of him?

And at Sunday school too, the nuns were all women, a fact it took me some time to understand. They were not like schoolteachers, though; they were forbidding, harsh and had thin grim mouths. But Sister John the Baptist liked me, I knew she did, although I was a little intimidated by her. But even she, the one nun with a man's name, bowed down all the way to the floor the day Father Burke opened our classroom door and came in. I was horrified. I wanted to leap out of my seat and pull her up from the ground and tell her she mustn't, mustn't ever bow to anyone. I didn't like bowing even to God, if he was really there inside the altar, another thing I had trouble compre-hending. But for Sister John the Baptist to bow to Father Burke! A contemptible little man who broke into Mass sometimes to announce in a thick brogue that unless people gave more in the collection, there would be no heat in the church that winter! When he drove around in a Cadillac, and most of the men in our neighborhood were out of work! He came into the classroom with a similar message, threatening that none of us would make our Communion if more money weren't given on Sundays.

And my own mother. Whenever Dr MacVeaney came to take care of us, she would be so deferential I couldn't recognize her, her submissive manner distorted her into a different person. And one day we were walking on the

Boulevard, my sister, Mommy, and I, in brand-new pinafores of flowered pink chintz, all the same, that Mommy had made us, and suddenly she grabbed us, one by each hand, and ran us across the Boulevard against the traffic, and I looked back, and there was a great gross man with a big belly and a red face stumbling along the sidewalk, and I knew my mother was frightened of encountering him.

And from the time I was about eleven, I had horrible nightmares in which I was chased by men, and I was humiliated because I had no clothes on, or no underpants, and the men were all around me, grabbing at me, and I tried to fly and did, but I'd have trouble getting enough altitude and one of them would grab my foot or ankle, and I'd be overcome by terror and wake up shaking, dripping wet.

So when I was being brazen, smoking with the boys, listening to their scatological jokes (which young boys' jokes tend to be), I was acting in the face of my fear, not trying to understand or overcome it, but to pretend I didn't feel it, to get rid of it by (I thought) confronting it. And what I learned to do was act as if I didn't feel it, but the fear didn't really go away.

When I went to college, the campus was filled with returned GIs, older, more poised and surer of themselves than the boys my age. And oh, how they appealed to me! They were trim, muscled, and they walked with a kind of quiet space around them, and looked around as if they could go click click with their minds and take in the entire scene, understand all the mysteries. Now I know that what I thought they understood was relations of power, and since I felt I didn't know anything about that, I felt terribly vulnerable to them. I wasn't drawn to all of them, of course, only the ones who seemed surest, the kind who were always surrounded by a couple of buddies who seemed lords-in-waiting to a king or prince, who hung on him, were ruled by him. And I thought if I went with one of those men I'd be like his men, only I'd be a lady-in-waiting, servant to a sovereign.

A number of these guys came on to me, and I was so drawn, oh, some of them were so beautiful, but I'd always be flip and wary with them. I wanted them, but I wanted to be equal to them, and I felt that I wasn't – being too young to be equal – and that if I were once drawn in, I'd fall into an utter subjection I could never escape from. They acted as if they knew exactly what women wanted and how to give it to them. I dated a few of them a few times. I remember one, Teddy Massa, whom I'd seen at the debating society and who had intense golden-brown eyes. My heart flipped when he asked me out, and then he took me on a real date, I mean, to dinner – something the younger boys couldn't afford – and I felt I was being treated as someone sophisticated, grown up. But then, afterward, necking in his car, he was insistent about going further and when I was equally insistent that we not go further, he looked at me lasciviously and said, 'I'll get you yet young lady.' He said that each time we went out – five or six times in all – until I told him I didn't want to see him anymore. Because each time he said it, my stomach would curl into a tight ball, and I felt that if I lost control, I'd scratch his eyes out. I couldn't stand the way he said that, as if I were a *thing* and he could *get* me, the way you get a puppy and domesticate it. Well, he never *got* me, and neither did any of the other knowing, sophisticated guys. And I had strangely mixed feelings about that. Because on the one hand, I felt I'd triumphed over them, I hadn't succumbed, been vanquished, been 'made' by them; but on the other hand, I felt diminished. I knew I was too cowardly to risk them, and had to settle for something less dangerous.

But I did have fun settling. I loved the awkward shy sweet boys who didn't pretend they knew all about sex, who were as fumbling and giggling as I was, and who, when things worked out, were as elated as I was. Brad was one of these boys, but he was special because he didn't fit into the world in any way at all. He wasn't good at studies, or at sports, although he liked to toss basketballs with the guys – or me, if there was no one else. But he was brilliant at the saxophone, and he was much loved. Because he'd retreated somehow. He didn't try to compete in most things, he just wouldn't. He'd turn serious discussions into silliness, and conflict into joke. He'd go off into his private space – you could see his eyes blank out whatever was around him and I knew he was hearing complicated progressions of music in his head. During a late-night Serious Discussion of Mahler with a bunch of our friends, he suddenly broke into song, offering, in a beautiful falsetto, '*Voi che sapete*'. He interrupted a political discussion around a cafeteria table by imitating Harry Truman chastising a reviewer for criticizing Margaret's singing – and then offered a sample of what he imagined Margaret's singing sounded like. Everything changed for me when I met Brad in the middle of my sophomore year at college. I entered what I thought of as his world, but he said it hadn't existed before he met me. Wherever we were in the evening, he'd grow restless and find or call someone with a car to come get us and drive us to one of the dinky roadhouses that used to dot Long Island, to listen to some jazz, and maybe he'd sit in, and we'd listen and smoke pot outside between sets with the guys in the band and feel like cynical worldly bohemians. We'd stay out all night, turning up after dawn at my house with a crowd of guys and make bacon and eggs and coffee, and then we'd play cards until we couldn't keep our eyes open. Naturally, we'd skip school that day, sleep the day away, and go out again at night, to another club. It felt enchanted to me, like life suspended on a high plane in which you did only what you wanted to do, and spent the weeks laughing, listening to music, and holding, oh closely holding, that dear body.

That body was tall and skinny, but with broad shoulders and chest, something that has always turned me on; and long slender fingers and feet. Brad had smoky eyes, sometimes blue, sometimes grey, and always a bit cloudy in color except when he was making music or making love: then they turned a dark grey-blue, clear and vivid. At first we had trouble finding a way to be together. He had no car, and of course neither did I and I felt uncomfortable at the thought of waiting until my mother went to bed – she went up late – then lying together on the living room floor (the couch was too short). But one day, when I went to finish painting the detail on a backdrop for *As You Like*

It, I realized there was a lock on the inside of the Green Room door, and also that there was rarely anyone in it until three in the afternoon. My eyes felt as if they were electric when I ran to find Brad to tell him this news, and his turned on the same way. We ran together, giggling like fools, and slammed in and fell back against the door and turned the lock and just slid into each other's arms, as if that were our natural state, and separateness a punishment.

I still believe it was.

After a while, when we could bear to pull our bodies apart, we searched for a place to lie down. The Green Room doubled as a storage room for props, and was cluttered with tables and chairs and couches and lamps, unpaired sneakers, old rags, a ratty fur coat used in the last production of *The Man Who Came to Dinner*, some cheap china and imitation silver pieces that looked fancy when seen from afar – all the odds and ends of real living, like a parodic inventory of The American Home. We found a couch heaped with dusty veiling – god knows what show that was used in – and sneezed as we lifted it and piled it on an overstuffed armchair with innards escaping from its side. We threw the rest of the junk that covered the couch on the floor, and brushed it off as best we could, and then we just stood there looking at each other. We couldn't, in those days, look at each other for very long without sliding into each other, and as soon as that happened, our bodies just as naturally slid onto the couch.

Oh how I loved him then. He was damp and smelled like dew and his thin arms felt strong around me, encompassed me, and mine encompassed him. His heart was beating even faster than mine, and when we'd taken off our tops and put our chests together, Brad began to hum and pop, making a complicated syncopated rhythmic progression out of our double heartbeats, and I piped in and then laughed and nuzzled him, god he was sweet.

After that, we appropriated the Green Room just about every other day, even on weekends. We tried to be careful – Brad brought condoms. But of course we hadn't had a condom that first luscious time, and that was all it took, although six weeks went by before we knew that. Still, I was never able to regret what we did, the wildness of our hunger for each other, the tenderness with which we felt it, the completeness, the insatiability of our passion. It felt like Truth, a thing I hadn't before believed in. I didn't know then that time can obliterate even the most ecstatic of experiences; and wouldn't have believed it. Neither would he, then. Then, I didn't feel cowardly anymore, or diminished, or afraid. I was blazing with pride and joy.

Even the discovery that I was pregnant didn't really penetrate the gorgeous world we had created. We talked, idly, about abortion, but neither of us really wanted to abort the baby. Not because we wanted the baby – we were babies ourselves, and had no idea what to do with another one – but because we couldn't bear the idea of something so beautiful ending in a dirty dark alley, a furtive visit, possibly filthy instruments, in squalid death. We talked, and we put off Decision. We continued to spend our time as we had, taking off from school on a weekday when Brad didn't have to prepare for an evening performance, and going into Manhattan and walking. We'd choose a particular area each time we went and walk in circles through and around it. We'd get tickets for Mozart operas and sit up high in the old Met, using opera glasses. Some Sundays we'd go to Nick's in the Village, where jazz musicians used to hang around in the afternoons. We'd drink Coke and listen to them play and I'd urge Brad to go ask them if he could sit in, but he was too intimidated by great names. He knew each one on sight. They were a grungy-looking lot, Brad's heroes, down and out, ravaged-looking, tired. They should have stood as a warning to me, but they didn't. Because when they picked up their instruments to play, their music was so sweet and poignant that it seemed then that whatever they had suffered had been worth it. Saturday nights I'd get a ride with somebody and go out to wherever Brad was playing and nurse a rye and soda and listen, surrounded by his friends – his and mine.

We stayed in our bubble, but my mind, at least, was working. Brad hated school and was there only because his father insisted he needed a degree. All he wanted in life was to play jazz. I was bored with school, even with the painting course: the teacher was rigid and expected his students to paint like him; I wouldn't so he snubbed me. In return I cut class. The only classes I would miss if I left were William Hull's, and that was because he was a poet and spoke and thought like a poet. I spent half my time in the cafeteria with my friends, and the other half backstage painting sets. I read a great deal – at least I had before I met Brad – but little of my reading concerned Modern European History, Biology 2, or Conversational French. Before I reached college, I had read my way through most of the great nineteenth-century English novelists and had begun on the twentieth century. Even my English classes were dull: we'd be assigned one Hawthorne story, but I'd read all of Hawthorne, and then sit utterly paralyzed with boredom as the professor explained in detail the symbolism of 'The Birthmark'. I was an arrogant kid, I always thought I knew more than my teachers, and they didn't help matters because they acted as if they thought the same thing. As I look back now, I think the truth was that I didn't know more than they but I knew things in a different way. For me, knowledge lay in the passions and any other sort was useless.

So why shouldn't we both quit school and go be artists together? I pictured some sort of life: I saw us married, living in a rented room in the Village under the eye of a benevolent landlady (Mother?) who would always be available for babysitting and who would take care of us too while she was at it. Brad would play in some club or other and every night I'd go to hear him and sketch the seamy side of New York à la Reginald Marsh, and then we'd have something to eat and go back together, arms around each other, to a room where we could lie in a proper bed and be together legally, and make love. Sometimes the baby made its way into my daydreams, as we mounted a bus, with assorted bags and baby, to Podunk, where Brad had a gig and where I would find new material for my art. I was sure we would be happy all the time. Why not? We didn't need much to make us happy in those days, Brad and I.

It didn't work out that way.

Brad's parents were horrified by the entire thing. He was only twenty-one and had a year of college still to complete. First they cast aspersions on my character. They didn't know my reputation, they would have done that to any girl. Brad, who *did* know my reputation, also knew the baby was his, and was noble through that phase – doing such heroic things as refusing to eat dinner, storming out of the house and disappearing for a few days (holed up at his friend Tim Derry's college apartment), then refusing to speak to his mother at all. Finally, they were forced to concede that my pregnancy could conceivably have been caused by their sweet boy. Then, they wanted me to have an abortion, and offered to pay for it. Under their pressure, my noble dingbat wavered, but I stood firm. So at last they were resigned to our getting married; their greatest problem at this point was how I was going to look in my wedding gown.

We solved this problem by getting married on a Saturday afternoon in a dingy office in Manhattan with Tim Derry and my friend Erma Greenspan as our witnesses; afterward we went to the Automat for coffee and dessert, laughing at our brass. For several years after that, Brad's parents were unable to look me straight in the eye; and they never recovered from the feeling that their poor naive sweet boy had been railroaded by a scheming desperate female. This attitude of theirs was subtle, but constant. It had no effect on Brad for the first few years.

What did have an effect was that they agreed to our marriage only on condition that Brad finish college, that he work weekends in his father's real-estate office, and go into his business after graduation. In return, Brad's father would pay him fifty dollars a week, so we could manage to live by ourselves.

It was useless for me to argue that he didn't have to do this. I protested, I kept summoning the pictures I'd invented in my daydreams, holding out an alternate path for us. He'd just shake his head. 'You don't know, honey, it would be really miserable. You don't really know the music world. It's no place for a baby, it's not even a place for a wife.' His father kept reminding him that society had decreed that a man take responsibility for his acts, and that responsibility lay in properly supporting his wife and offspring, and that to support them a man needed something reliable and steady (as if real estate were either!), he needed to provide a decent environment for a child to grow up in, etc., etc. The pressure never eased, because a life like theirs was what they wanted for Brad in any case, and Brad simply couldn't hold out against it.

My heart felt like a squeezed prune. Because what led him to give in to them was what I loved in him: his sweetness, his affection for his parents, his sense that people should do the Right Thing, his lack of aggressiveness. He would come to me at night after a session with his father, his shoulders curved, his neck pulled in. He looked shorter, older, smaller. He'd say, 'But they're right, sweets, you know they are. I mean, can you picture a kid growing up on Eighth Street?'

'They do!' I'd protest, and then immediately caress him, trying to restore his spirit.

'You didn't. I didn't. We don't know how to survive in that world.'

One night, when he sounded more determined than usual, I began to cry. I didn't want it, I said, I didn't want that kind of life. What was I supposed to be doing while he was out selling real estate? Taking care of the baby and cleaning the house? That was no life for a person! I didn't want to be married to a real-estate salesman, I wept, I wanted my off-in-the-clouds boy, with his silliness and joy, with his underwear shirt showing above the open neck of a frayed sports shirt he refused to throw away, his eyes dancing after ten minutes of Serious Talk, who would grab me and dance across the room to a polka that he managed to sing and whistle at (almost) the same time.

Through all this, Brad sat with tears in his eyes, aghast at the singular sight of me in tears, and when I calmed a bit, he held my head against his chest and patted my head. It was then I knew: he'd never patted my head before. And he said it then, in the Serious Voice I came to know so well in later years:

'Sweetheart, we have to grow up. We have to be mature. These dreams are just childish fancies. We have to put them aside. When you are a child, you speak as a child and understand as a child and think as a child; but when you become a man, you have to put away childish things.'

My head came straight up off his chest. That was not Brad talking, he'd never so much as opened the Bible. It was Brad imperfectly quoting his father, who was an elder or something at the Episcopal church they attended. Even his tone of voice was his father's. I'd lost him, I'd lost Brad.

'Well, I'm not a man!' I cried. 'And I don't want to put away childish things! If life has to be the way they live it, I don't even want to live.'

I rushed upstairs, leaving an embarrassed Brad sitting alone in the small side room my mother called the porch. But he was frightened, I guess he thought I planned to kill myself, and maybe I did at that moment. The bubble had completely blown away. All I could see was a life like my mother's, a life like those of the people all around us, and I could not bear it: in the car, out of the car, in the house, laundry, cooking, dinner, television, bed. Saturdays on Sunrise Highway shopping. Sunday dinner at a parents' house. NO.

Brad tiptoed upstairs. Although everyone knew I was pregnant, it still seemed forbidden for him to enter my room. But he did, and came to where I was lying with my hands over my eyes, not crying, just sunk in horror, and he touched me with the same light tender touch he'd always had, and sank down on his knees next to the bed and whispered. 'It can't be too bad, Stahz, can it, if we are together, if we have each other? We'll be able to be together all the time, we and the . . .' and he patted my still flat stomach. And of course I turned to him and put my arms around him and cried and held him and submitted, me the stiff-necked, the refuser, the proud fierce rebel, submitted to my fate.

three

We found a room with a kitchenette and bath on the second floor of a house in Lynbrook. We looked at it with my mother, who drove us – Brad still had no car – and took it because it was cheap, even though to reach the apartment you had to walk straight through the owner's living room. After we took it, my mother refused to visit me there because she was uncomfortable walking through the Charleses' part of the house. I stared at her.

'Why did you let me take it if you knew you'd never come there?' I asked in outrage.

She looked at me as if she didn't understand my words. 'What difference does that make?' She was bewildered.

And I, for once, was speechless. In our family, the word *love* was never mentioned, nor did anyone ever touch anyone else, except for my father's nightly peck on my mother's turned cheek. But, I thought, we felt it: *I* felt it, extraordinarily. All my sitting night after night with my mother, asking her about her life, my pain and rage at her life, my lying in bed night after night planning revenge on those who had hurt her, planning brilliant triumphs to lay at her feet, planning above all to buy her a mink coat as soon as I sold my first painting . . . And she did not know, she had no idea! How, how could she not have felt it!

It sank, this knowledge, into the dank place where I kept so much else. Because I could not bear to follow up this awareness with its corollary: that she could have been unaware of my deep feeling for her only if she did not love me back. I refused to think this, but thought it nevertheless, the way we do, as if we could stand on both sides of a door at once, the way we can do something and not let ourselves know we're doing it, something magical and strange about us, creatures for whom symbols are stronger than realities. I looked at her, her eyes pale and weary, her hair coiffed and blond, her clothes smart, her patent leather pumps matching her bag, and I wanted to get up from the lunchroom where we were sitting having roast beef sandwiches on white bread and coffee, and simply evaporate. Those days I often wanted to vacate my life. Maybe I would have if I'd been able to come up with any other life to enter.

Because underneath the wild foliage, the brilliant flowers of my behavior, there was a swamp of confusion. I claimed to be happy about being pregnant, about getting married, I assured everyone Brad and I would have an ecstatic life together, and for months I insisted we go to New York and take our chances living as artists. But my gaiety and laughter served as noise to drown out some other voice – just as, perhaps, my mother's crying had when she was pregnant with me. You need to drown out the voice because it possesses no language to express its knowledge.

It's easy now to say what I could not even let myself think then. I was not a foolish girl, not unrealistic or impractical, although I tried to be. I shrugged off reminders of practicality in the same way I cut classes, insulted teachers, ignored my art teachers' advice – out of terror of a fate that I felt hung over me, invisible but unavoidable. I could not bear constriction; yet I felt it was inevitably my lot. I felt it was *women's* lot.

You couldn't grow up during the Depression, with the double whammy of a depressed mother, and not know how vulnerable people were without money, without a place to live, decent clothes, decent food – especially if they had a baby. But I couldn't stand settling for those things. I knew I was an artist – I'd known that since I was a tiny child – and that I was learning, would learn, nothing in college; that there was no job on this earth that I could have that I wanted; that even male artists felt that the door to the future opened onto a concrete wall – but that a female had no chance at all. How many of the great painters were women? None, that's how many. The only woman painter I'd ever heard of was Mary Cassatt, and no one ever wrote about her, she wasn't respected. Besides, she always painted women and children, not important things like . . . well . . . it's true Degas painted a lot of ballet dancers, and Cézanne painted a lot of fruit, and Toulouse-Lautrec also painted dancers, and Renoir painted mainly women and children . . . but it was the way she did it, I guess, that made her insignificant . . .

Underneath everything else was my despair about myself. I could not envision a life for myself. What would I do, how would I live? Perhaps, if Brad had the courage to risk it, we could go out together into the big dirty dangerous world and try to survive on whatever he could earn playing the sax, while I painted. I could not imagine making money painting; nor could I imagine any work I could do that would satisfy me except painting. If I had been able to imagine either of those, I would have insisted we move to the city and try it; and I think that if I had insisted, Brad would have gone along with me.

But I was too frightened to try to live out my vision. And so I surrendered, became a passive person, leaving decision in god's hands just as if I believed in a god. Living like my parents, Brad's parents, the people around us, seemed to me like walking open-eyed into hell. But hell had a passageway leading to it: no other road was available. I surrendered to the fate that had always hung over me (didn't I know, when I watched my mother doing that fucking laundry, that someday I too would be doing it?). I surrendered to the ordinary in the same way my mother did.

And once I had, a possible future showed itself. Maybe, if Brad got a regular job, I could paint: if he sacrificed *his* art, I could pursue mine. It is a selfish thought, written out baldly like that. I guess it was selfish, even though it arose from despair. Because for some reason, Brad seemed *willing* to sacrifice his art. That might mean he was not as committed an artist as I. Or it might mean – but I didn't recognize this then – that as a man, he felt a terrible pressure to *be* a man as our society defines one – to produce money, to earn status, or, sentimentally rendered, to take care of his family – me and the thing growing inside me.

These confused feelings, thoughts, muddied my mind for the nine months of my pregnancy. I couldn't put them into words, I didn't dare. Had I dared, I would have revolted against everything – the way the world was set up, the way everyone I knew thought and felt, and even my own sex, my own body. I couldn't risk that, couldn't risk the rage, the hatred. So I took the coward's way out and buried it all. I said nothing, but expected my mother, at least, to know how I was feeling. And perhaps she did. But she treated me the way she had always treated herself when she was unhappy – she withdrew into vacancy, and went through motions. She was polite, even pleasant; but she treated me like an acquaintance, not like a daughter.

And something hard and cold entered my feelings for my mother for the first time. She had dismissed me; I dismissed her in return. I told myself I was damned if I would care so much what she thought, what she felt; she would no longer be the center of my sorrow, the spur of my ambition, the cause of my existence and its content.

Of course, telling yourself such things doesn't make them true, and I was deeply upset that she had allowed me to take an apartment she refused to enter. But Brad and I had signed the lease and paid a deposit and furnished the apartment with pieces from relatives' attics, so we had to move in or lose a year's rent – something we couldn't afford. I made jokes and pretended I was happy; I kept insisting we would have fun. I did what I could with the apartment.

There wasn't much daylight in the place, but I set up an easel in one corner of the small room and hung some powerful lamps above it. I put a small tottery table behind the easel for my paints. But in fact I painted only a few times. I blamed my neglect of 'my art' on Brad, who complained about sleeping in a small room pervaded by the odor of turpentine. The truth was that for a long time I had been unhappy with what I was doing. I knew I had a strong sense of composition, and a good sense of color, but I could not get my hand to realize what I saw in my head. Maybe the fault lay in my ignorance of technique, a quality I inclined to underrate in those days. All my art teachers had praised me so easily, for any effort; none of them knew much about technique. I had an easy schoolgirl fame, and a deep grating fear that it was unearned. I packed up the paints and brushes in a fury with Brad, but I knew, and maybe he knew too, that my fury was not with him. I walked around the town and on impulse walked into Jimmy Minetta's Camera Shop and asked for a job, and got one. In those days, all film was not sent to photo labs, and I was to help take orders and do developing. I'd always liked photography, I told myself. Besides, what else did I have to do, now that school was out and I was not in any case going back, now that summer had arrived and Brad was working six days a week at his father's agency, now that I was four, five, six months pregnant, waiting, waiting, waiting for whatever future would descend upon me? I left the easel up, with an old painting of mine standing on it, but after Arden was born, I packed it away too, to make room for her cradle.

Our bed – a daybed we pulled open at night – our licit, legitimate, legal bed, was never as much fun as the lumpy dusty Green Room couch. I don't know what happened. We didn't even reach for each other with the same absolute need, and we didn't seem to fit together as naturally and perfectly as we had. We didn't know if something had come between us, some shadow had fallen; or whether we had changed in the months since we'd last been together on the Green Room couch; or whether we misremembered the experience, endowed it with more radiance than it had actually had. We still loved each other then; it wasn't that. I felt it was that somehow the people we were now no longer satisfied the other's deepest dream; we had lost the enchanted realm. After a few months, after I'd been unable to reach orgasm dozens of times, after Brad had been unable to get erect a half-dozen times, we could no longer discuss it.

'It was the thrill of the forbidden,' he pronounced. 'Now it's legal, prosaic. That had to happen. We had to grow up. Besides, it's hard for me to make love to you with the baby there. I keep being afraid I'll hurt it.'

I acceded to this explanation, and we postponed sex for two months. But I saw Brad's face when he came home from the real-estate office every night – for it was summer, and he worked with his father six days a week now. He was drained and grey, and his mouth was set in lines that had never been there before. I'd make jokes and act silly, but he'd look at me with a new superior look and tell me to stop acting childish. Even his voice was different now:

louder, and somehow hollow, and he didn't talk so much as declaim. He was turning into his father, and if I complained, he said – naturally – that a man had to do what he had to do, that I was immature, oh, all the same things over and over, as if by diminishing in me the qualities we both possessed, he could destroy them in himself.

I was a lunatic that summer, because I was determined I would remain cheerful, happy, gay, when I had no reason at all for such feelings. I attached myself more to Jimmy Minetta, whose camera shop was the best for miles around, and attracted newspaper and magazine photographers who lived on the South Shore. They hung out there, in the back room, where Jimmy kept a bottle of bourbon and a coffeepot and plastic coffee cups, and they talked f-stops and light and wondered about all the new technology that had begun to appear on the camera market, and I listened and made coffee and helped out generally and was accepted as a servant-pal. There were no sexual innuendoes – how could there be when my belly was a foot out into space? But if Jimmy was busy in the front of the shop, the guys would launch into long laments about their relations with the women in their lives, and ask me why she was so . . . well, you can fill in the blank – angry, bitter, mean, helpless, weepy, unfaithful. . . . As if I knew, or could do more than murmur consolingly. But I liked these guys, and I felt sorry for them in their unhappy love lives, and each time I heard a new story about what Ellen or Mary or Doris or Betty had done, I'd determine, my teeth set, that I'd never do such a thing to Brad. Over the months, I determined not to do so many things that I could hardly act at all with Brad.

Not that he really noticed. He was so consumed with learning his new mature role, and with drowning his utter misery, that he no longer really saw me. His eyes were always opaque grey. It was hard for him. Selling real estate requires a certain kind of personality – a willingness to treat people as means, as walking money that you wanted to put into your pocket, and a habit of appraising everything – people's appearances, their clothes, their shoes, their cars, houses, furniture, everything – in terms of dollar value.

Brad, who if he had ten dollars in his pocket when he went out drinking, and the bill was four dollars, would simply leave the whole bill, had had no sense of money at all, and learning to see in this way required his killing some other part of himself. I watched it happening. And even then, young as I was, inexperienced, ignorant, I knew what it would do and I knew more than that, I knew I would have to leave him someday. That thought made my heart squeeze in pain like a mouth that has drunk straight vinegar; I pushed it away, stuffed it down into what I thought of as my basement, the room where I kept everything that was broken and dangerous, everything unusable, slimy, coated with dust and dirt.

How I lived in those days, it was really crazy. The thing is, I was trying to be *good*, I was doing, or not doing, things everyone said a woman should do or not do. I made Brad my center, I did everything around him, I didn't think about myself, or my 'career' or my art – I couldn't bear to think about that anyway. I thought about Brad's needs, his likes and dislikes, and I arranged myself as best I could within them. My old proud sense of myself as a bad girl had vanished – except in one area.

While Brad was trying to learn to be his father, his mother, Adeline, was trying to train me to be like her. Adeline stopped in regularly. She cleaned her house mornings, and made dinner for Brad Senior nights, but she went out every afternoon. I worked in the afternoons, and hung around the shop until around seven, when Brad would be getting home, and I'd throw something in a pan for dinner – hamburgers or hot dogs, usually, I didn't cook anything else except eggs. Adeline had wormed a key to our apartment from Brad, and she had no compunctions about crossing the Charleses' living room, so every few weeks or so, she would stop by to show one of her friends our 'darling little nest'.

Usually, Brad and I hung around the apartment in the mornings. We slept until nine or ten, had coffee leisurely and read the paper. Then Brad would go down to the agency in the car his father had lent him, and I'd make up the daybed and wash our coffee mugs and the pot, dress and walk down to Jimmy's. But after Adeline told him about her surprise visits, I began to leave everything as it was. The first time Adeline came in and found the daybed unmade and soiled mugs in the sink, she told me in horrified tones:

'Anastasia, I took Mrs Whitney by to see your darling little nest on Wednesday and my dear! The bed wasn't made and there were dishes in the sink! Were you ill, my dear?' she asked with mock concern across the Sunday dinner table. Brad – Junior and Senior – looked at me.

'Wednesday? Ill?' I thought about it. 'No, I can't recall feeling ill,' I answered innocently.

Brad Junior's mouth twitched: he was still on my side. But there was a ghastly silence from the elders, and it was some time before conversation could resume.

But even that didn't stop Adeline. She continued to take her friends in, and I, thinking I'd stopped her, had returned to cleaning the place up in the mornings. But now Adeline didn't tell me about her visits. I discovered them one evening when Brad and I drove over to his parents' house to drop off their vacuum cleaner – which I'd borrowed for my once a month sweep of the floor – and found a visitor, Adeline's friend Mrs Andretti. She was a warm little woman with bright red hair, and she engulfed me with affection, hugging me and announcing in an enthusiastic voice, 'And your place is so darling! Adeline took me around to see it last week, Anastasia, and you've just done wonders with it!'

I didn't look at Adeline. I smiled wanly. I couldn't imagine what wonders I'd done: what can you do with a daybed, a dresser, a night table and lamp, and a tottery kitchen table and chairs in one room?

'That easel looks so charming!' Mrs Andretti continued. 'And your painting! You really paint wonderful, Anastasia!'

I tried to be gracious, but I was plotting.

After that, I never cleaned up in the mornings – or evenings either, for that matter. I did dishes once in a while, when there were no more clean ones. When in later years Brad reproached me for my lousy housekeeping, I'd tell him to blame it on his mother. And if we made love –

when we still did that – I'd leave the stained sheet spread open on the bed. I did one more thing. Every morning before I left for the camera shop, I'd sprinkle a little talcum powder on the floor near the door. I'd watch, when I came home in the evening, being careful not to step in it, to see if it had been disturbed. Then I'd sponge it up before Brad came home. And one night when I came home, there was no talcum powder. Adeline had spotted it, attributed it to my sluttish housekeeping, and wiped it up herself. On that day, the sheet had been displayed in all its splendor. I continued to sprinkle powder, but Adeline never came again, nor did she ever mention my housekeeping again. I kept on sprinkling powder until the baby was born. After that, there was no need, I was always home.

The business of thwarting Adeline gave spice to my days. I loved being a bad girl, loved using insidious methods to fight back against Them, whoever they were. But it was a sad little affair, after all. It was a sign of my poverty of spirit that spiting Adeline gave me the most pleasure of anything in those months. Brad returned to school in September, taking classes in the mornings and afternoons, and working at the agency in the late afternoons and weekends. Nights he studied. His grades improved and his parents began to act as if maybe marriage had been exactly what their boy needed. But by now, Brad and I hardly spoke. It wasn't that we didn't care for each other, we still did. It was as if we had both been struck mute by what had happened to our lives. When I wasn't at Minetta's, I read. I read all of Proust, finished the works of Henry James, and read all of Faulkner. Time passed in a haze, I never knew what day it was, I thought about nothing, I was suspended, waiting for November, that sad month when my baby too would be born.

I had no one to talk to. I couldn't talk personally to Jimmy or the guys at the shop, and all my friends were in school, busy, and had different concerns. I couldn't talk to my mother. We saw my parents every other Sunday for dinner, and the chat was polite and social during dinner. We talked about the weather, food, and their upcoming/

past vacation; we talked about Joy the cheerleader, Joy's friends, Joy's new sweater, and I'd be silent with envious rage. And then we all trooped out to the porch and watched television, Sid Caesar and Imogene Coca. I felt dead.

Even after Arden was born, I couldn't tell my mother how I felt. I should have been able to – after all, she'd told me how *she* felt, giving birth. But I knew if I told her, I'd get a look that said, Didn't I tell you, didn't I warn you? But you, headstrong, willful, you had to go ahead and do it and now you have to make the best of it as I did, as I still do, your life a daily misery. I couldn't say anything about Brad since she'd disapproved of him from the first – not serious, not stable – and how could I complain that he was becoming serious and stable and I didn't like it? How could I complain to her about being poor and crowded and cramped and sitting there with him in silent misery?

How could I tell her that every morning I had to look at this grey-faced guy in a suit and bow tie, an aged boy who hardly ever laughed anymore, and whose sax was now neatly packed away at the top of his closet with his other childish things? And that every morning he had to look at me with my belly out to there, looking at him? What in my life had she not long ago warned me against?

Nevertheless, Arden's birth disturbed me. We'd decided on that name long before, talking about it lying in bed, playing with our fingers, twining and untwining them, and laughing lightly, a shadow of our former joy in each other, but the best times we had that summer and fall. Because *As You Like It* was being played that spring, and I was painting the backdrops and Brad was playing Jaques, and most of all because we felt we'd been living in an enchanted green place, we chose Arden as the name for our baby, whether girl or boy. Brad's parents were horrified to think we'd call a boy by that name, but my boy stood with me on that one. In any case, Arden turned out to be a girl.

In all those months of pregnancy, though, one major thing I never let myself think about was the moment itself, giving birth, and when it happened, I was shocked, incredibly shocked at myself, at the utter abject humiliation I felt with this thing coming out of my vagina, with my legs in those stirrups, with the nurses and aides and doctors milling around. Oh, I had determined not to act like my mother, and I didn't cry, I didn't utter a sound, and one nurse even patted my head and told me I was a good girl, and I was doubly humiliated at my craven cringing pleasure in her pinch of praise. And then she came, Arden, and I felt eradicated, I felt like an animal doing what nature decrees all female animals must do, I felt caught in a world scheme huger and more encompassing than anything I could comprehend, and helpless within it, squirming in my fate, but subject to it nevertheless.

I tried not to let any of this show, and I think I didn't, except that as I joked with the nurses afterward, and laughed with my friends at the ridiculous presents they brought me in the hospital – a bag of marbles, a bunch of bananas, a tiny slate with some chalk for drawing ('Just about my speed these days!' I laughed) – I could hear my voice starting to sound like Brad's, that hollow echo in it, as if it were a noise being made in a great cave, by a thin tinny string. I looked down at the baby in my arms and wondered what I was supposed to do with it, and looked up and made jokes: 'I never played with dolls, how do you get it to say MAMA?' 'Does it pee all by itself! What a miracle!' I compared the baby's face to the aspects of various animals, and generally mocked myself and it and entertained my friends. Later Erma told me I was the first new mother she knew who hadn't turned into a bore, but all the while I was making jokes I felt sick inside, as hollow as my voice sounded, as if I were a Henry Moore sculpture, all limbs with a hole in the center, knowing that somehow I was sinning, but not knowing against what.

What I wanted, I guess, was to be babied myself, but since I never had been, I didn't know how to ask, or even what exactly it was I'd wanted. Maybe if I had been able to, things would have been different with Brad. . . . One day the nurse was cleaning the stitches in my episiotomy, and she smiled at me, commenting that I was 'pretty down there', and I was so pleased, I wanted her to come and hold my head against her full stiffly bra'd breast, but of course she didn't. And I lay there wondering if there were differences 'down there', and what made one cunt 'pretty' and another not. I even asked Brad, but he didn't know either, not having had experience with women other than me.

Then, after five days, they sent me home. I stood up from the wheelchair they had pushed to the front door of the hospital, and they handed me this bundle wrapped in a blanket, and there I was. Brad held my arm as we walked to the car. I got in on the passenger side, not looking down at the bundle, and Brad started the motor, and we drove off and I sat there as stiff as a cardboard figure trying not to think, not to think: what do I do now?

For the first weeks, I treated the baby like some precious breakable possession – holding it gingerly as I fed it, changed it, bathed it. It cried often, usually at night, and it never took its whole bottle, and then it would wake up two hours later screaming, I thought from hunger, and I would have to warm up the bottle again, and it would take an ounce and fall asleep again. I had refused to nurse it: the humiliation in the hospital had been all I could handle, I couldn't go further in 'animal' ways. I got little sleep and never looked in the mirror, and walked around in a daze.

But after a month, I was more used to it, and it seemed to cry a little less, and I got more sleep and fell into a routine. Adeline had been stopping over with one of her friends two or three afternoons a week, always when I was napping with the baby, and I finally told her she had to stop. I think that was the final straw between me and her; she was never more than coldly polite to me again. But my life improved a little. And then my mother would come, once a week, on Thursdays. She'd drive up and I'd run down with Arden and the plastic bag stuffed with clean diapers, extra bottles of milk, water, and orange juice, a pacifier, a bib, an extra blanket, and dump them on her lap and run back up to get the great white laundry bag, the car seat, and a suit of Brad's to go to the dry cleaner, and put those in the back of the car, and then run back up again for Arden's little folding bed, a bag of soda bottles to be returned, and my purse. It was like going to Mass or something, every Thursday we went through this ritual.

Then Mom would drive me to the dry cleaner and the A & P, where I'd drop the bottles and buy stock items that were hard to carry, jars of baby food, canned vegetables (Mother would purse her lips at them), paper towels and toilet paper, and six-packs of beer and Coke for Brad. I no longer drank anything but coffee and tea, quarts of them every day.

Then she'd drive me back to her house and I'd feed Arden and lay her in the folding bed, and do the laundry in Mother's machine, and hang it out on the umbrella-shaped clothesline in her yard, and then we'd sit in the kitchen, looking out at the yard and the wash flapping, and gaze at the baby asleep by our feet, and drink coffee and eat grilled cheese sandwiches and talk. She'd ask how Brad was doing, if he'd sold any houses yet, and I'd ask how Joy was doing, and conceal my envy at her popular high-school-queen life, and then we'd talk about her, Mother, just as we always did, about her grief, her unhappiness, and her fears – she went through crisis after crisis thinking she had cancer in various forms – until I could get her laughing. Then we'd pull out the Chinese checker board and play ferociously for an hour until Arden woke up and it was time to put away childish things and change her and feed her and give her her bottle, and then we'd pack everything back in the car, the laundry neatly folded and back in its heavy white bag, the car bed folded up, Arden, head lolling with sleepiness, slumped in the car seat, and Mother would drive me back to Lynbrook, and I'd repeat the process of running up– and downstairs, and then I'd kiss her goodbye and she'd drive off, and I'd slowly climb the stairs one last time, carrying Arden close to my body and feeling utterly desolate.

four

Belle changed as Anastasia grew. From a clamorous lump needing feeding, changing, and bathing, the baby had become a personality, a being, herself, someone to be reckoned with. She watched people around her, she smiled, she pouted, and she cried, but now her crying seemed human, as if there was a reason for it, not being any longer sheer animal expression. So Belle felt. Now – at three months, four – Anastasia seemed a small creature who was in some way independent. She had a strong will of her own and no inhibitions to expressing it. Belle thought about going back to work.

But she decided that she did not want to do to Anastasia what had been done to her; she would not let her child spend her childhood in a house empty except for a servant girl who hit and yelled and did not ever smile. Oh, that terrible empty house, no books or paper or crayons, no music, no toys, nothing: no. She set her face firmly in its fine lines and smiled, and decided to remain with her child and bring her up herself.

She knew that Momma would be thrilled to have Anastasia to herself, and would care for her as she had never been able to care for her own children. But at this thought, her mind clanged shut like a metal door on a vault. Something rose inside her, hot, liquid, furious, adamant: Momma and a baby, *her* baby: no. She thought about the baby, who was changing every day. She was learning, Anastasia, she was quick. Belle would help her, teach her, provide her with culture, scrape every penny to make sure her childhood was richer than Belle's.

Anastasia was so grown up. She looked at the people around her almost as if she could understand what they were saying, what they were feeling. She was five months old and already sitting up. Evenings, Eddie and Wally would sit her in the middle of the living room floor and talk to her and tease her, tease and taunt, and she would glare at them until suddenly she would roll over on her side, and they would all howl. For she was already so fat from Momma's constant feeding that she could not sit without support. Jean thought she was adorable, and Momma adored her, but Belle knew she was a fierce baby, there was something hard and wary in her, she held herself to herself. And Belle was awed. She had been so vague, timid, terrified really, as a child, that she was awed to see this tiny infant hold her own as she did. She looked at all of them straight, without wavering, as if she were judging them. She rarely smiled. No cooing or cuddling pleased her, and she would wriggle and squirm to escape from embraces, from wrapped arms. She watched the adults as they jumped around trying to please her as if they were monkeys in a zoo and she a calm observer. Belle frequently at such moments repeated the story of the day she was wheeling Anastasia in her carriage and two shabby middle-aged women stopped and peered at the baby and chucked her under the chin and cooed at her and Anastasia glared at them as if she scorned such childish acts. Belle knew Anastasia did not like them because they were shabby. She explained this to her sister and brothers, who would gaze at Anastasia as if she were a miracle. She was their entertainment, their toy, and all of them were pleased with her contempt, her scorn, her outrageousness.

Only Ed disapproved of her, but he was rarely home. He disliked her for crying, for needing to be fed, changed, bathed. He resented Belle's attention to her. He wanted to see his beloved on an ivory throne edged with gold, himself on his knee before her, offering chocolate, and her hand on his head, accepting it, appreciating it. It was how he saw her, how he treated her, his beloved, and he was deeply hurt when she pulled sharply away from his touch and said the baby needed . . . whatever the baby needed. Still, on Easter Sunday, Belle and Ed dressed in their best clothes, and Belle dressed Anastasia in her new pink silk coat and hat, and Ed took his camera out and they sat on the front stoop of the Manse Street house and took pictures of each other with the baby, a fat disagreeable face done up in fancy clothes. And Jean's boyfriend, who was sometimes in the house on Sunday nights, thought Anastasia was spoiled and sullen, and said so, or when he didn't, simmered with anger toward her.

By now, Belle slept only an hour or two in the afternoon, and woke up when Anastasia did, and changed her and carried her downstairs and gave her a bottle, and Momma put crumbs of pie or chruściki in her mouth. Then Belle carried the baby out to the front room which they called the porch. It was narrow, the width of the old couch that spanned the side wall; and had windows all around. It was connected to the living room by glass-paned doors, and had a window seat in the front. Belle always sat on the window seat and laid Anastasia on the cushion beside her. Then she would look at her and talk to her. She would tell her that she, Belle, was Mommy, and that Grandma (whom Anastasia seemed to search for with her eyes) was in the kitchen baking good things for Anastasia's dinner. She would tell Anastasia about the life she would have: she would wear pink dresses and live in a beautiful house and sit under the trees. She would play the piano beautifully and draw beautifully and be very smart in school. The baby would listen, rapt, and follow her mother's face as it moved minutely with her speech. Belle felt Anastasia could understand her.

Belle began Anastasia's education when she was six months old. She would prop her on her lap at the piano and open the illustrated book of nursery rhymes that Wally had bought, and begin to play and sing. Anastasia never squirmed. Her eyes followed the marks on the page as if she could understand them. Sometimes she would bounce in Belle's lap and grunt, and Belle would stop and hand her the book and she would turn the pages until she found 'The Owl and the Pussycat', then return it to her mother to play.

In late spring, a new family moved in across the street – a young couple with two daughters and a baby just about Anastasia's age. The young woman, Elvira, was very tall and voluptuous. She was just Belle's age, but had married when she was sixteen, and had a nine-year-old daughter and one six. The baby was called Terry. Belle and Elvira made friends, and every afternoon the two young women would go for a long walk together, each wheeling a carriage, and they would talk, talk, talk. Elvira thought Belle was very well-dressed, and admired her for that, and Belle admired Elvira's way with makeup. Like girls, they sometimes suggested new hairdos for each other. They told each other their life stories. Like Belle, Elvira had gone to work at fourteen in a sweatshop. She liked it, and planned someday to leave her husband and support herself again in the corset factory. Unlike Belle, Elvira had had a wonderful rough-and-tumble childhood. She had adored her father and had always been crazy about boys. 'Oh I always loved the men!' she'd announce in a joyous booming voice, and laugh her deep rich chuckle.

She'd married Rollo, an intense and passionate man some years older than she, an electrician. But once she was pregnant, he left her alone all the time and threw tantrums if she saw anyone – even her family. So she left him, left her baby with her sister Bridget, and went back to work. Rollo followed, blustered, pleaded. She liked his passion if not his jealousy, and they reached an agreement. She would return to him on the condition that she could see other men. But within a few months of their reconciliation, she was pregnant again.

'What good is an agreement once you're pregnant?' Elvira complained. 'They've got you where they want you then.'

As soon as the second daughter was walking, Elvira left again and descended on Bridget – who had three children of her own, but was always willing to take her sister's as well. Again, Rollo pursued.

'He wants me when he hasn't got me, but when I'm there, he's out all the time. He just wants me there, in the house.'

This time she refused to return and Rollo went quite mad. He sat on the front porch of Bridget's house – Elvira wouldn't let him in – and beat his head against the uprights and moaned. Finally, Elvira wrested from him an agreement to which he had to testify in front of Bridget and her husband Chick, that she would return to him but each of them would live their own life with no questions asked.

'He agreed, but he didn't keep his word,' Elvira confided to Belle. 'He was always wanting to know where I'd been, and whether I had a boyfriend. But I didn't care, as long as I could get out. I can't stand being stuck in the house. And then – ' she pointed to the carriage – 'guess what! Oh, I cried and cried when I found out I was pregnant again. And Rollo wanted it, when he can't even support us as it is.'

By now, Bridget had six kids of her own, and Elvira's

girls were in school. 'I just can't pick up and go, and I have no one to leave Terry with. I can't stand it, Isabel, I really can't.' It wasn't the work that bothered her: for all her weight, she had great energy, and kept an immaculate house and was a superb cook. She couldn't stand the confinement. But she had plans. One of these days . . .

Elvira was wondrous in Belle's eyes because she said whatever she thought. Belle had never met anyone like her before. And her honesty allowed Belle to be honest too – as honest as she could be. Elvira knew exactly what was wrong with her own life: too much confinement and not enough sex. Everything else was fine. She loved her daughters and adored Terry. But she wanted to roam the world in search of fun. She had a rich hearty full-throated laugh, and she laughed often. 'Oh, I always liked a good time!' she'd explode, laughing, concluding the story of one of her adventures, and wipe tears from her cheeks. Belle laughed with her, a thinner, more refined, politer laugh. She felt almost happy with Elvira and if she would not choose to be like her, she felt very grown up and sophisticated to have such a friend.

The two young women would walk into Forest Hills Gardens, where the lovely houses were, and Belle would imagine what it would be like to live in one of them. When she was with Elvira, she felt almost as if there were something ahead of her, as if she had not already died. She would imagine living in a lovely stone house in Forest Hills Gardens with a man something like the men Elvira told her about – dark, mysterious, sexual. She knew it was only a daydream, and she never connected the mystery man with her own dark, sexual husband; she didn't want any of it to come true. She just wanted to imagine it. She could imagine herself different too, when she was with Elvira – sophisticated, experienced, free. Her mind danced with Elvira, and she felt she was getting better. She hardly ever cried anymore. And that December, after Anastasia's first birthday party, as the two women pushed their babies together through the little parks that dotted the neighborhood, Belle saw a pale pink rose blooming, right in the dead of winter.

*

How I clutched at the idea of that rose, the one bright thing in the sad season of my birth! My mother told me about it often, always in the same awed voice, with wonder, and as if she had not told me before. The memory of it consoled me: every fall as my birthday approached and the leaves fell and the branches turned grey and the air too, as the very earth seemed to turn to ash, I reminded myself that sometimes roses bloom even in November. I didn't feel responsible for the dying time of year, feel that I had caused the sad season, but that my coming had somehow brought mourning, grief, grey, bleak days, and that every year my birth was symbolized by such a season.

How would a person know such things, remember the season of their birth, the crying mother, the sorrow that was mostly masked when she was awake? Yet my daughter Franny feels like an intruder, feels unwanted, like an insistent monster who plunged through a wall of objections – and her feelings are accurate to what I felt, *but before she was born.* How could she know? Does emotion substantiate instantly into a child's bloodstream, like the nourishment they absorb in the womb?

My friend Barbara Greenberg tells me I should think about this differently, should fasten on the fact that an infant born in November sits up alert and awake in May, their first awareness green and budding; whereas an infant born in May sits up to see the death of nature. But it isn't *my* awareness that I feel this grief about, but theirs, the ones I came to, the ones to whom my coming meant sorrow: *A cold coming they had of it, at this time of the yeare; just the worst time of the yeare, to take a journey, and specially a long journey, in. The waies deep, the weather sharp, the daies short, the sun furthest off in solstitio brumali, the very dead of winter.* Yes, that was in December, and a very different birth, but it felt familiar to me as I read Launcelot Andrewes, as if my mother and father had to travail in an extraordinary way because of me.

I don't remember the sullen baby I was, although I know the sullen child; I recall the sense of being unwanted and unloved, and always, always unsafe. All I wanted, when I was a child, was not to be a child, to be grown up so I wouldn't be dependent upon those who didn't want me dependent upon them, to be free and out and away. This would surprise my mother, I imagine. She was so careful to give me those things she had painfully lacked in her own childhood that she can't imagine that the thing she really lacked wasn't attention or education, but that lap, that 'moja kochanie', that close embrace. Never having had it, how could she give it? For a baby rat taken from its mother at the moment of birth, before the mother has time to lick it clean, will in her turn, not lick her infant clean when she gives birth. And so on, down the generations. Even to the edge of doom, he wrote, and this is doom: unless there is some way to break it. The truth is it is not the sins of the fathers that descend unto the third generation, but the sorrows of the mothers. But when I was a young woman, I believed that I could break this chain by sheer will.

Time passed. Belle was more cheerful now she had Elvira, and Anastasia was growing every day. But she still did not speak, although by eleven months she was walking and by twelve was toilet trained (a great day for my mother). She was very fat, with plump dimpled arms and legs and a fierce determination. She liked to pound on tables and hum at the same time, as if she were drumming the rhythm to a song only she could hear; and she loved Grandma and bacon. By late summer and early fall, she was sturdy enough that Wally could put her on his shoulders on days when he came home early from job hunting, and carry her off to the ice-cream store on the Boulevard. He never complained if drops of melted ice cream fell from her cone on to his head.

Soon after Anastasia's first birthday, Belle and Jean planned a bridge party at the Manse Street house. Belle and Frances spent all day preparing thickly piled sandwiches and pastries filled with fruit and cheese for the party, Belle with pin curlers in her hair. She begged Momma to wear a new sweater she had bought to give her for Christmas, but gave her now, and Frances reluctantly agreed, a little surprised. Belle was excited. She had never done anything so elaborate before. And no doubt Anastasia felt that excitement and wanted to be part of it, because, although she was put to bed early so her mother could dress and do her hair, she lay there humming and hitting the side of her crib – she was too big for the basket now – watching her mother with wide wary eyes. Belle bent to kiss her, saying she should sleep now, and went down to greet her guests.

From downstairs the sounds of busy chatter and laughter rose, and with it rose Anastasia's rage at being left out. She climbed out of her crib and made her way to the top of the stairs, where she stopped, baffled. She could not yet climb stairs. She stood there and roared: 'I want to come down!' There was an aghast silence from below, then her mother appeared, white-faced. 'Is that you, Anastasia!' But she did not go up for the baby. She turned back to her friends. 'She's never uttered even a word before and suddenly she speaks a full sentence!' The women raved, what a smart child, what an amazing event, but still Belle did not come to get Anastasia. The baby stamped her bare foot on the floor. '*Now*! I want to come down *now*!' Belle went up then, and carried her down, where much fuss was made of her. Belle sat her on the couch beside Grandma and gave her a bit of a chicken salad sandwich and she watched the women play. So that was how you got what you wanted! You spoke!

This event convinced Belle that she had mothered a genius, and she set about educating Anastasia with determination. She read to her daily, and played songs on the piano. She even began to play her own songs, the pieces she had studied when she took piano lessons – 'Remember', 'Always', and 'My Buddy'. And Anastasia would sing along with her, stumbling over only a few of the words. By the time she was two, she knew all the nursery rhymes as well, and knew which ones were on which pages. When she was three, having used crayons and pencils for some time, she drew a perfect banana. Belle was deeply impressed, and saved the picture. For years after that she told Anastasia that she had known she would be an artist because she had drawn a perfect banana when she was only three.

*

Wally had found a job, finally, and was rarely home these days, spending his evenings at the chess club or, it was suspected, with a woman. Eddie spent most of his evenings in the old neighborhood at the Becks', visiting Martha, who had lived next door to them in Brooklyn. Martha was small, dark, and pretty with huge eyes, but Belle and Jean did not like her. They said nothing. Ed finished the apartment for his father and immediately found himself a second job working nights at a pharmacy. Because of this, Belle was able to buy some clothes for him and herself, and to put a few dollars in a bank account.

Then one Sunday, Wally, who had not been home since Friday morning, appeared with a tall blonde on his arm, and announced they were married. He and Jill wanted to live at home, he said; she was famous, a chorus girl for Billy Rose, a long-stemmed beauty. There they were. Eddie moved his clothes down to the little front porch and began to sleep on the old couch. Jill spent the morning in bed and expected Momma to bring her breakfast in bed. Momma did. No one said anything. Jill would descend around two, her hair in curlers, wearing a crimson silk robe over her nightgown, and sit on the front porch sullenly filing her nails. At four, she dressed in very high heels and a clinging frock, her hair piled high on her head, and went to work. She'd come home with Wally around three in the morning. One night, after about three months, she did not come home with him and indeed, the family never saw her again. No one ever asked Wally what happened, and afterward, no one ever referred to his divorce – something they only assumed he had done. The entire incident was treated as something so scandalous it could not be mentioned. Eddie went back to his bed upstairs, and soon afterward, Wally lost his job, and in disgust, signed up to go to CCC camp, a welfare project for young men unable to find work. He was gone for a year, and one summer Sunday, Belle and Ed and Anastasia drove up the Adirondack Mountains to see him, and although Wally seemed glad to see them, he paid little attention to them, and none at all to Anastasia. He stopped working, his shirtsleeves rolled up, his uniform smelling of wood chips, and stood beside their borrowed car for ten minutes. Then he went back to wood-chopping, and they drove back to Queens. Although Anastasia was only three and a half, she thought it was strange. But she found much of grown-up behavior strange. The house was very quiet now, with both sons away evenings, and even Eric Terschelling came no longer, because he was in a TB sanitarium. He had to give up actuarial school, he was overworked, and he had to use all his savings to pay for the hospitalization. Jean and Belle and Momma spent evenings in the dining room, sitting at the round table listening to the radio, sewing, or crocheting, or knitting. At eleven, Belle always rose and made tea and toast, which was ready just as Ed came in from his night job, and the four of them would sit there drinking in silence broken only by desultory talk.

Then, suddenly, everything seemed to happen at once. Wally came back from CCC camp tan and more muscular than he had been, his frail pale body looking almost healthy. He found a job and moved back into his old bedroom. Eddie became engaged to Martha and they planned an October wedding. Eric was released from the sanitarium cured, and now devoted himself totally to his job with the insurance company. He and Jean became engaged, and would marry as soon as Eric could restore his savings. All of this passed around Belle in a haze of luminal and indifference. Except for Elvira, and the education of Anastasia, nothing touched her, nothing mattered. And then, one night in August, Elvira pounded on the front door of the Manse Street house. She had a black eye and bruises on her arms.

'Rollo went berserk,' she explained. 'He followed me yesterday and saw me meet Al and get in his car, and when I came home last night, he gave me a present.' She presented her bruises for examination, satisfied by Belle's dead-white horrified face.

'Come in, sit down, let me get you some coffee,' Belle urged.

'No, Isabel, I just came to say goodbye. I'm leaving him, for good this time. I'll be at Bridget's for a while until I can get my own place. But I'll call you.'

Her face a mask, Belle clasped her friend's hand and watched her recross the street and get into Bridget's crowded car. Then she went upstairs to her bedroom and closed the door and sat on the bed and was startled when the wrenching noise emerged from her throat. And once it started, she could not stop. She cried the rest of the day and into the night. She did not go downstairs or tend to Anastasia. The only bright spot in my life, she kept thinking, My only pleasure, gone!

Several times Anastasia crept into the room and approached her mother, begging her to come downstairs and play with her, but Belle either ignored her or told her sharply to go away. Anastasia left and stormed downstairs the third time this happened. She decided she would play the piano herself, since her mother refused. Actually, she wasn't sure she couldn't already play, because she put her fingers on the keys along with her mother's when Belle played to her. She climbed up on the stool to get it higher. It spun around and around; she was delighted by it and was smiling broadly when suddenly the seat flew off the screw into the middle of the room, landing with a loud clank. Frances came running from the kitchen, cuddled her, comforted her, replaced the seat. But Anastasia did not want to be cuddled.

'Why is Mommy crying?' she asked Grandma.

'Not crying, no, Momma is tired, resting,' Frances assured her.

Anastasia gazed at her. Why was Grandma lying? Why did people always lie to children?

'I want to get up,' she said, and Grandma lifted her onto the stool. She put her hands on the keys, and brought out noises, but they didn't sound anything like what Mommy played. Maybe it was because she wasn't looking at the book. She reached up to the music stand and opened the *Mother Goose Song Book*. She recognized the songs, and turned to 'The Owl and the Pussycat', her favorite. She didn't know why she liked it: it didn't make any sense. Many of the rhymes didn't make sense, but this one made the least sense of all of them. And when she tried to get Mommy to explain it to her, Mommy wouldn't. Anastasia was sure her mommy, who was so smart, who could sing and play the piano and teach Anastasia to count and read the clock, knew what the song meant, but just wouldn't tell her.

Scrutinizing the notes on the page, Anastasia put her hands on the keys. But what came out was still not 'The Owl and the Pussycat'. A hot pulse of fury coursed through her body: she wanted to cry out in frustration. But she slid down from the stool and trudged out to the porch and climbed up on the daybed, where her coloring book and crayons lay. She opened the book quickly so she wouldn't cry, and riffled the pages seeking a nice picture. There were no nice pictures in the book. They were all gross and ugly, simple big stupid things. She hated them. She hated her crayons, too: red, yellow, orange, green, blue, black, white, purple: bright ugly colors. She had seen a box of crayons that had many shades, soft shades, and it was a big box. But Mommy said it was too expensive. These crayons were for little girls, she said. Anastasia hated being little. She scrawled wildly across one page, then another. The crying feeling was coming up in her throat again.

Grown-ups treated children as if they were stupid, and Anastasia was not stupid: she knew she could understand if they would just explain things. But they treated children as if they had to stay behind a veil watching, while the grown-ups spoke a secret language, or whispered, or lied. Anastasia sat on the couch, her small fists clenched. Frances, taking a pile of ironed clothes upstairs, noticed the child, and put the clothes down on a chair and came over to her and sat beside her. She stroked Anastasia's hand and spoke softly to her. She held out her arms. But Anastasia refused to enter them. Her babcia was just like the others: she lied to Anastasia. Frances said, 'Sweet baby, *moja kochanie*,' but Anastasia would not be consoled.

Would not be consoled, could not be consoled, Ed thought, sitting beside the bed on which Belle lay sobbing, her face and shoulders turned away from him. Never been right since . . . He took off his glasses and put his head on his hands. He was belching continually, but very softly. He pulled his head up suddenly, startled to realize that his hands were wet. He pulled his clean handkerchief from his pocket and wiped his glasses thoroughly; then he wiped his face and hands and put his glasses back on. Belle's sobs were coming at longer intervals now. He continued to sit there, his body bowed forward, his hands loosely clasped between his knees, waiting.

Belle tried weakly to sit up and Ed moved swiftly to help her. He pulled her up and put the pillows behind her.

'Cigarette,' she said in a small voice.

He glanced around, looking for the Luckies, and pulled one out and put it between her lips. Then he lighted it for her. She inhaled deeply, her body still shuddering with unvoiced sobs.

'Did you go to the doctor?'

She nodded.

'What did he say?'

'There's nothing more he can do for me!' she said in a tragic rush, as if she were announcing her death.

Ed put his fingers in his thick hair and began to shake it. He watched the white flakes of dandruff flurry through the air and sink to the floor.

'He can't give you a stronger dose of luminal?' he ventured after a time.

'No!' She turned on him in a rage, as if his attempt to find a solution made everything worse. 'It's as strong as he can make it,' she added, her throat thick with tears, her tone injured. 'The only thing left is morphine. But he says that if I take that I'll become an addict.'

He sat. It was impossible to know if he had heard her or understood her. He waited.

'Would you like a cup of tea, Belle?' he asked solicitously.

She smiled a little. 'That would be nice, Eddy.'

He rose heavily and left the room. Belle glanced over at the crib: empty. Anastasia was probably with Momma. Morphine. She imagined spinning rainbow colors, sleep, rest, the end of pain. It drew her, but – to become a drug addict! If she were going to do that, to blot everything out, she might as well kill herself.

She heard Ed's step on the wooden stairs, heavy, tired. Worked two jobs every day and every night came home to her like this. He handed her the cup and saucer, and she smiled at him. 'Thank you, Eddy.'

His voice was rich with gratitude. 'Sure, Belle.' He wanted to reach out and touch her head, caress her, just lightly, but he did not dare.

'You should go to bed, Eddy, you're tired.'

'Yes,' he sighed. He stood up and began to undress, and as he did so, she rose from the bed and put her wrapper on. For the first time, exasperation crept into his voice. 'What are you doing now?'

'I have to check on Anastasia.'

'She's all right! She's in bed with your mother!'

'I'll just see that she's all right. And I have to go to the bathroom. I'll be right back.'

He sighed in protest, and got into bed sulkily, but in seconds sleep like an undertow had pulled him into blackness.

The house was dark, everyone was sleeping. Belle carried her teacup into the kitchen, then walked through the dark rooms to the little front porch, and sat on the window seat. She lighted a cigarette.

Eddy was good, she knew he was good. Only he was not enough, somehow . . .

She smoked.

Besides, all he cared about was sex. He didn't even care what he ate as long as his belly was full. He couldn't talk. He didn't like Anastasia, he paid no attention to her at all. But at least he wasn't like Poppa.

Sex. She hated sex!

Nothing left but morphine. No pleasure in her life now that Elvira was gone. Nothing but day-by-day tedium. But other women didn't seem to mind it. What was the matter with her, that she was so dissatisfied? She was useless, even to herself, worthless, stupid, always had been. She was a nothing, and she had so wanted to be something. Now never. All her dreams.

Her eyes filled with tears again, and as the feeling of pain began to creep around from her heart into her limbs, she wondered how anyone could cry so much, how it was physically possible to have that many tears inside you.

Better to die than become a drug addict. But what else was there? Only this intolerable unending pain. Maybe she could start over: get pregnant again, have another baby, accept it this time, welcome it, accept her life. Maybe she could get strong that way.

Tears were streaming down her cheeks, and she was sobbing again. It surprised her, took her, as if she stood outside watching herself dissolve. Through her mind ran the few jewels she had culled from her twenty-nine years: the teacher saying she was lovely, Adele telling her she had artistic hands, the architect telling her she had real class, Elvira praising her clothes. Countered with these was a running voice, stupid, useless, you can't come to school you don't speak English you can't come to school like that you go home now and have your mother comb your hair comb my flaxen locks my hair my hair my mother never combed my hair

Ed stood beside her.

She looked up at him apologetically. 'I can't help it, Eddy, I can't help it!' she sobbed.

'Come to bed, Belle,' he said kindly, tiredly.

She allowed him to help her up. She blew her nose and stuffed the handkerchief in the pocket of her wrapper. She held up her head.

'I'm not going to take morphine. I'm going to have another baby. It isn't good for Anastasia to be an only child.'

'Sure, Belle,' he said. 'Whatever you want.'

At least one of her children was wanted. None of mine was, really; the first two were accidents. I was just beginning to think that Arden was old enough at nine months to sit in a playpen in the crowded backroom of Minetta's shop so I could work with him a few afternoons a week, when I discovered I was pregnant again. Brad was still using condoms because I was so ill at ease with the diaphragm I'd gotten after Arden was born, and god knows we had sex infrequently enough, but it happened just the same. The thing is that although Brad fully accepted the first pregnancy, knowing how rapaciously we'd reached for each other in those days, this time he felt suspicious and tricked as if I'd either put something over on him or the baby wasn't his at all. This difference was indicative of what had happened to us in less than a year of marriage.

Brad rarely sold a piece of property and if the agency had not belonged to his father, he would have been fired long ago. 'Well, of course,' I'd say to him when he came home depressed and grey-faced. 'You weren't cut out to be a salesman, you were supposed to be a musician.'

He'd just look out the window. 'Cut it out, will you Stahz?' He'd fiddle with his spoon, stirring and restirring the sugar he'd begun to take in coffee.

I knew he felt like a failure, and I knew my proper wifely office was to support and encourage him. But how can you encourage someone you love to go on doing something that makes them miserable and is all wrong for them? I couldn't bring myself to suggest that in time, if he watched his father, he'd learn the skill of selling. So I'd go maundering on about music and painting and our old dreams and how we could still do it, how all we had to do was pick up the phone, the guys still remembered him, he could pick up a few gigs, I'd get a part-time job, we'd get by. He'd sit there at the table in our one room staring at the coffee cup and acting as if I were not there until finally he'd get up in a rush and sweep out – where? There was nowhere for him to go. After a while, I'd go downstairs and peer out of the Charleses' front windows and see him sitting on the steps of their front porch, his head in his hands. And my heart would feel as if it were breaking. At first I'd go out and sit beside him, put my arm around him. Just sit there, say nothing. And after a while we'd both get up and go back upstairs to Arden's wailing – she was not used to being left alone in a playpen. But at some point, he'd pull away from me when I went out and embraced him, and sit inches away, miles away it might as well have been. So I stopped going out.

And then he sold a big parcel, an estate with tennis courts and swimming pool and a solarium, and made enough on it to keep us for a year. That was the turning point, because that sale raised his confidence and made him beam and shake hands and announce his name with the same hearty vapidity as his father. Success made him a success. And just in time, he announced to me cheerily, because the second baby was due soon and we had to get out of this dump. I hadn't much liked the apartment until he started to call it a dump, and then I found myself defending it rather fiercely – it was homey and cute, and we'd . . . well I couldn't bring myself to say we'd been happy in it, but it had been our first home. We found another apartment in East Rockaway, with two bedrooms, and rented it for a sum we could afford – sixty dollars a month, I think. Hard to remember things like that, although my mother remembers every dollar of rent, electricity, coal, and food that she spent in her early married life. We collected furniture from more attics, and moved a month before Billy was born. But now I was really stuck, because it was miles to the nearest store, and I couldn't go anywhere without a car. And of course Brad took the car his father had finally given him, writing it off on his taxes, took it every day, because now he never took a day off even though he was allowed to. And he began to take law courses at night at a local college, because he wanted, he said, to become a tycoon. A tycoon! My flaky lover? Ah well, he wasn't that anymore. Before we moved, I wheeled Arden over to Jimmy Minetta's to say goodbye, my stomach making it hard for me to reach the handle of the carriage. As we hugged and Jimmy wished me all kinds of happiness – he thought having babies made women happy – I suddenly found myself crying, sobbing right out loud, scaring poor Jimmy out of his wits. He sat me down and hauled out the dust-covered bottle of bourbon that he had stashed away in the cabinet where he kept developing fluid, and poured me a glass. I couldn't drink it, though, nor could I explain why I was crying, me the cheerful joker, the good pal, the girl who was one of the boys. I finally blurted out something about missing him and the shop and all the guys which Jimmy could accept, although he looked puzzled by it. And he told me I could come back to work for him anytime, just as soon as my kids were on their feet – literally, I guess.

But I knew I'd never go back there. I couldn't see much,

but I could see far enough ahead to know that having one kid is one thing and having two is three other things. I could foresee grey years of piles of laundry and dirty dishes, crying squabbling kids, hours in the supermarket, my cart piled high with magnum boxes of detergents, railroad-car-sized loaves of the gluey white bread Brad and the kids liked, and half-gallon bottles of milk. And it occurred to me that this must be how Brad had felt, a couple of years back, when the iron doors started to swing shut on him, and life constricted to a dreary pattern of the known, the preordained. And my heart ached, for him and for me, two children, I still felt – we were still only twenty and twenty-one – caught in a cosmic plan – that's how it seemed then – from which thought of escape was only a delusion.

I sniffled all the way home, but after that I never cried again. Not, anyway, until years later, when there didn't seem to be much reason for crying. Who knew then that you store up tears you fail to shed? I went home, and two days later we moved, and a month later Billy was born, and then it all came true, the nightmare I had foreseen, the dreary round of days. I sank so far in it that I forgot even the notion of escape, forgot that I had any existence other than mother, cook, and bottlewasher, or that life lived according to a different plan was even possible.

For Belle, having another child was to be the escape from her round of tears and luminal; she vowed to give up the drug the day she knew she was pregnant – but perhaps because of the luminal, she didn't get pregnant, and continued to take the drug. So the events of the household those turbulent years of 1932–33 happened far away from her, out there in the grey whirl of other people's lives. Eddie married Martha – Belle does not recall the wedding – and they moved into the house on Manse Street. Momma insisted on giving them the bright big front bedroom. Jean was sent to share Wally's room, which embarrassed her, and Momma herself would sleep downstairs on the old lumpy couch that had seen so much of this family's life. This event pierced Belle's consciousness and outraged her. She took all the money she had managed to save and went out and bought a new firm daybed for Momma to sleep on. Eddie and Martha hardly noticed. Martha, like Jill before her, treated Momma as a servant, a role Momma was always willing to fill, but bitterness rose in Belle and she glared at Martha with hatred. The anger felt good, pumping through the veins and arteries, creating energy, and she gave up the luminal; a few months later she was pregnant, and her biggest worry was how four of them would manage in the narrow little room they occupied.

As it turned out, that was an unnecessary worry. Jean and Eric married in the spring of 1933, Eric having in so short a time restored his savings, and they moved to a fine apartment they had furnished with all new things. Belle does not remember their wedding or the apartment, although Anastasia recalls a chaise longue, a thing she had never seen before, that stood in Jean's new bedroom. It was covered in mauve satin, and had a matching satin cushion against its one arm, with a white angora cat sitting against it. Anastasia thought it the most beautiful piece of furniture she had ever seen although she did not understand why the cat was there. Belle began a new plan: she wanted to ask Wally to take the dark middle room and to move with Ed to his room, the one with two beds and room for a chest of drawers. She knew Wally would agree. But in June, Eddie Brez announced his printing company was moving to Massachusetts, and that he, promoted to manager, would have to move. The dinner table fell silent at the news: no one said anything, but they all knew that Eddie really maintained the house, that what Wally and Ed Dabrowski earned could not support it. But once informed, Eric stepped in as rescuer. He would take on the mortgage payments, he would take over the house – and Momma. But Wally, Belle, Ed, and Anastasia would have to move out. Again there was silence. They were too embarrassed even to look at each other, sitting in the familiar living room with its shabby furniture, the home they had all worked for, the house that was their visible proof of escape from the slums.

Soon, Wally moved his two suitcases of worldly possessions to a rooming house in Trenton, where the job he was working on then was located. In the coming years, he would move from one to another of such houses, as new plants needing wiring were erected in Newark and the Bronx. He followed his work and never had a home. Belle and Ed found a small apartment in Jamaica, near Jamaica Avenue with its noisy elevated trains, its trolleys, its many small stores, but off it, across the street from a park. They collected their few pieces of furniture from the attics and basements where it had been stored, and in August, just a few months before the new baby was to be born, they moved.

five

Silence. No one spoke. Even footsteps were inaudible as Belle moved zombielike through the small rooms. Anastasia sat splaylegged on the floor over a coloring book, her eyes alarmed, her face pale, her fat vanished overnight. She grew thinner and thinner and paler and paler, listening to the silence. Grandma had gone away, Eddie had gone away, Wally had gone away, Jean had gone away, everyone was gone except Mommy, and Mommy was silent.

Mommy did not act as if anything were wrong, she did not cry. She did not yell. She was just far away. Anastasia knew that if she hadn't been so sullen and defiant, so insistent and willful, they would not all have gone away and left her alone in this silent place. In the first months after the move, she would lie in bed unsleeping, willing with all her strength that things would go back to the way they had been so that she, Anastasia, could have another chance, could show that she appreciated them all. But no matter how hard she wished, or willed, it did not happen, and she sank more deeply into the lethargy that had followed the first shock.

It was also dark. The living room, kitchen, and tiny bath of the apartment faced the side courtyard of the building, and because they were on the first floor, Mommy had hung curtains and drapes over the windows, so people outside could not see in. Only the front room faced the street and the park and was brilliant with sunshine every morning.

But it was so crowded with Mommy and Daddy's big bed, two chests, and Mommy's vanity and Anastasia's crib, that there was no place to sit in there, no clear spot of floor for her to color on, no chair for her to sit comfortably upon. She stayed in the living room and occupied herself with drawing and coloring. She had a whole stack of funny pads that Uncle Eddie had given her before he and Martha went away, long narrow white pads of thick paper with edges so sharp that she often cut her finger when she tore off a sheet. Daddy kept the pads and gave her one when she needed it. But she did not like her drawing very much. It wasn't the way it should be, the things she made were big and gross and ugly, when she wanted to make things delicate and subtle and balanced. So she would stop drawing after a while and lie down on the new rug Mommy had bought. It was red and had funny designs in it, nothing in it looked like anything real. Mommy was very proud of it, Anastasia knew, but she, Anastasia, thought the rug was ugly. Still, it fascinated her and she would lie on it for hours tracing with her tongue on the roof of her mouth the funny squiggles and shapes, things that were almost trees and flowers but were not trees and flowers, and she wondered why the people who had made it had not made it with trees and flowers that looked like themselves.

One thing she loved: the glass-paned double doors that separated the bedroom from the living room. She loved them because they let light stream through even when Joy was asleep in the bedroom and Mommy closed them; and because they were beautiful. She continued to love them long after the memory of their counterparts in the Manse Street house had faded. And one morning when she got up and walked into the kitchen, she saw that the chairs and table, which had been plain wood, were now a beautiful new color.

'What color is that, Mommy?'

'Aqua,' Belle said.

Aqua, Anastasia breathed to herself. Aqua. A beautiful color, a beautiful word. She hummed the word to herself all day, through the silence.

The living room was almost empty. There was the big

brown ugly piano that had stood in Manse Street, and a couch and two chairs and two standing lamps and the ugly rug. And over the couch, in a wide gilt frame, was a painting of a woman holding a baby, with another woman standing behind her and both of them looking at the child. But you could not see the baby's face, only the blanket it was wrapped in. The painting had a yellowish patina that Anastasia knew meant it was old, but it wasn't old, it wasn't what it pretended to be. Mommy loved the painting, and talked about her cousin Sokolowski the artist in awed hushed tones. Anastasia studied the painting for hours, tracing with her tongue on the roof of her mouth the shape of the mother's face, the dim shapes of furniture behind her, the window in the room she stood in, but she could not find anything beautiful in it. Anastasia decided she did not know what beauty was.

Every morning when she woke up and climbed down from her crib, she would pad into the kitchen where Mommy sat drinking coffee and smoking cigarettes, and Mommy would say 'Good morning, Anastasia', and get up and start to make oatmeal for her breakfast. But Anastasia hated oatmeal, so this did not make her happy. Then she would go into the living room and sit on the floor and color while Mommy cleaned up the apartment. Then, after lunch, Mommy would put on a fresh dress and put powder on her face and lipstick; and put Anastasia in a freshly ironed smocked cotton dress and shoes with little straps on them and white socks and her good coat and hat, and take Anastasia's hand as they crossed the street and entered the park. After a while there was Joy, and then Mommy did not take her hand anymore, but told her to hold on to the handle of the carriage. Anastasia resented this, and would bristle and say she didn't need to hold on, she was a big girl.

Anastasia hated the park. Mommy would sit on a bench, looking very elegant in her nice coat and the felt hat with the long feather pointing forward, and the other ladies would come too, with their children, and they would sit together, three or four of them, Mrs Wallis, Mrs Gold-thorpe, Mrs Thacker (who was old and had no children), and they would talk and tell the children to play. But Anastasia did not know how to play, and she would watch Lily Wallis and Eleanor Goldthorpe doing silly things and she would go off by herself and sprawl on the grass and make chains out of the little flowers of clover. She would slip them on her wrist as bracelets, but they always broke. She would gaze around her at the great vacant park, the trees, the grass, the sidewalked paths, and it yawned at her hostile and empty. There were people in it; children's voices floated in the air like the sounds of little animals, and people walked. But everyone seemed tired and stiff and old; or young and silly and noisy; and Anastasia could not find what she was supposed to do in a place like this.

But after that was over came the one time of day Anastasia loved. She and Mommy – and then Joy was there too, in her carriage – would walk to Jamaica Avenue to do the marketing. First they went to the butcher shop, which always smelled of blood mixed with sawdust but had lots of meat with different colors – pale pink, almost white, deep red – and lots of bologna and liverwurst, which Anastasia loved, and sometimes Mommy bought some. Then they went to the vegetable store, which was even better – beautiful things piled up in pretty heaps, all shiny purple and red and pale green and orange and yellow. All shapes, the tomatoes and the little green squash, and the shiny pods of peas and lima beans, and wonderful satiny eggplants and apples and lemons. She knew she was not supposed to touch, but it was hard to keep her hands down. She just wanted to stroke the things to see what they felt like, but she couldn't do it, Mommy said, until they got home. But Mommy never bought most of those things – it was always peas or green beans or carrots or cabbage – Anastasia hated cabbage – and so she never got to feel the others. But she could look at them and smell them, and that was something.

Then came her favorite, Moe's Butter and Eggs. Moe kept his eggs heaped in a big basket with a handle, and when Mommy bought some, he lifted them one by one with great care and put them into a grey cardboard box. Anastasia loved the way the eggs looked, and the butter too, in huge wooden casks set on their side. When anyone ordered butter, Moe would take a big knife and stab it into one of the casks – the pale yellow or the darker yellow – and cut out a chunk, swish, just like that, and keeping it on the knife, lift it to the scale, where, with his other hand, he had placed a sheet of heavy waxed paper. And he would say, a little less, missus? Or, a little more? but mostly the chunks were just what the ladies had said, a half pound. Anastasia was awed by Moe's skill.

The store smelled wonderful, of fresh butter and pumpernickel bread and crispy seeded rolls. But the most wonderful thing in the store, one of the most wonderful things in the world, Anastasia thought, was the beautiful deep pink fish that always sat on a marble block on Moe's counter. Sometimes a lady would order some – Anastasia never found out its name – and Moe would take a special knife, very long and thin, and slice, swiftly but carefully, ever so thin slices of this fish, and lay them gently on the heavy white paper. Anastasia pressed up against the glass to watch this. Once she asked Mommy if they could have some, and Mommy gave her an angry look. Outside the store, Mommy whispered that it was too expensive, so Anastasia never asked again. But she continued to wonder what the fish tasted like, so brilliant and vivid a pink. Would it taste pink?

Sometimes, after Moe's, they would go to Anastasia's other favorite, Fiedler's Bakery. Fiedler's was very beautiful: it had a broad glass front window with its name in fancy old-fashioned gold lettering across it, and inside, on shelves of different levels, were trays and stemmed plates, all with pretty paper doilies on them, and on top of the doilies . . . ! Well, everything! Linzer tortes, black-and-whites, Metropolitans with their tiny dollop of jelly inside the cream. And great big layer cakes creamed in white or tan or dark chocolate, and sometimes with pink or green decorations on them. But Mommy never bought layer cakes, she bought long stollens, which perturbed Anastasia because she could not understand why Fiedler's would sell or Mommy would buy a stolen cake. But stollens were boring, they just had sugar and nuts on them. Or Mommy would buy a crumb square, or a butter cake: Anastasia liked these better, and she always thought of Wally, who would ask Anastasia if she wanted a piece of crumb cake, and would cut a square for her, and then lift the whole rest of the cake onto his plate and look at her and laugh. She laughed too, because she knew it was a joke. Wally never ate the whole cake at once. And once in a great while, Mommy would ask Anastasia what she would like, and then she would panic, moving from one foot to another, incapable of deciding which treat she wanted most. She knew it did no good to point to the layer cakes: Mommy would not buy those. But a Metropolitan? Or a Linzer torte? Or a black-and-white? Or cupcakes? Or brownies? Oh, it was agony, and finally (she knew Mommy was impatient for her to choose) she would just say something, blurt it out, and Mommy would buy it and then she would forget the rest and walk home happily looking forward to her dessert after dinner.

But once that part of the day was over, Anastasia's spirits flagged again. They would walk home in silence and Mommy would take off her hat and coat and hang them up and put on an apron and tell Anastasia to go play in the living room because the kitchen was small and she'd be in the way, and she would sit on the floor coloring or drawing and she could hear the tinkle of fork on metal, the scrape of the spoon in a pot and smell frying onions, and her mouth would water. But everything was so still. She would look up from the page and feel the dimness of the room, the silence of the house, into which only this smell entered, offering tantalizing promises of something different – a warm house with the lights turned on, a good dinner, talk and laughter, a grandma who took you on her lap, an uncle who pulled you over for a hug. But then, she had already forgotten these things, the warmth of bodily contact or a sweet voice saying 'moja kochany', people talking and laughing around her; they were buried in a realm so deep she would never again have access to them, and with them went all hope for life lived among folk, rather than isolated, silent, still, empty. She felt she lived alone in a great void which, if it were to contain anything, she herself would have to fill. She would have to make it up. She would lie back across the rug she hated – it smelled dusty, and it was rough against her skin – and daydream.

Then she would hear the front door open and Daddy's step in the hall, stopping at the closet to hang up his coat or put his hat on the shelf, and then down the hall and into the kitchen, and she would hear his sweet 'Hello, Belle', but Mommy would say nothing, and then she would turn on the radio and call Anastasia, saying dinner was ready, and Anastasia would get up and go in and say 'Hello, Daddy', and kiss his cheek the way he kissed Mommy's, and get up on her chair at the aqua table and begin to trace with her tongue on the roof of her mouth, the designs Daddy had put on its edges, *decals*, Mommy called them, of peach-colored roses and little pink buds. And no matter how good the dinner had smelled, when she sat at the table Anastasia was not hungry, and would poke at it and pick around and ask to be excused, and would go back into the living room and lie on the awful rug and daydream some more until Mommy called her and asked if she didn't want some dessert. And if they had gone to Fiedler's that day, and her Metropolitan was waiting for her, she would go back and eat a piece of it that Mommy had cut for her. But if they hadn't, if the Metropolitan was left over from the day before, she didn't want it, it didn't taste good.

Lying on the floor, she could hear the radio, the Evening News with H. V. Kaltenborn, who had a funny high voice and made everything sound as if the world were ending that night. Then there were other programs that Mommy and Daddy listened to, and she could hear the program and the click of their forks and knives on their plates, and sometimes during dinner Mommy would ask Daddy how his day was, and he might say, 'Fine, fine,' or he might tell her what the big boss said to him, and then they fell silent again and she could hear the chairs scraping on the linoleum and the plates being stacked in the sink and the radio, and water running as Daddy washed the dishes and Mommy opening the cabinet to put away those she had dried, and then the kitchen light would go off and they would come into the living room and Daddy would sit in the high-backed chair with the wooden arms, the uncomfortable one, and open his paper and Mommy would sit in the corner of the couch, and they turned the lights on, so the room was no longer so dark, but it was still silent as Daddy read and Mommy darned her stockings with a funny needle with a little hook in it, and then after a while Mommy would say it was bedtime, and Anastasia would go into the bedroom and undress in the dark, by the light that filtered through the glass-paned doors, and get into her crib and lie there listening.

And sometimes Daddy would bring the radio into the living room and turn it on there, and they would sit listening. But other times they just sat, silent, for hours, so that Anastasia fell asleep, knowing that she'd been asleep only when she awoke at the smell of tea and toast being prepared, and knew that it was eleven o'clock, and her parents were having their bedtime snack. But she always fell asleep before they actually came into the bedroom and undressed and got into the double bed. She never saw or heard that.

Chapter VII

one

Belle moved like a person who has been very ill and is just beginning to walk independently again – as if every gesture had to be planned and executed with deliberation. In her youth, she had been quick of gesture, but now her movements were slow. Only when she was cooking did her hands work swiftly. And sometimes, as she bent for some task, she would raise her head in confusion, unsure where she was. She glanced at her hand: she held a man's white shirt, damp. What was it and where was she? Her glance fell on a porcelain basin on the tarpaper roof of an apartment building, rose to the scene around her – a sky dotted with dirty clouds, apartments, an elevated-train track. She turned slowly, like an arthritic. In one hand she held this wet shirt, in the other a clothespin. Well, she knew what she was supposed to do with those, and she did it, not bothering, for the moment, to decipher the clues around her. She knew everything would come back. She would bend again: another white shirt, and then some tiny underclothes, a child's. Anastasia's. Yes.

She could remember Anastasia, and even Ed, whose white shirt that was, but sometimes she could not recall how she had got from there to here, how her old life, so many years of it, had led her to *this* rooftop, *this* clothesline. Dispersed. Everything she had known was gone, dispersed. That was a real word, wasn't it? How had she learned such an elegant word, being as stupid as she was? It was a fine word. Dispersed. Dispersed. She believed she even knew how to spell it: d-i-s-p-e-r-s-e-d. Brooklyn and the rooftops there, not very different from this one, yet different; Momma, Poppa, Euga, Eddie, Wally; the school where the teacher spoke a foreign language and she was stupid; the streets, the peddlers, the pushcarts, the horse-drawn drays; the sweatshops, the machines, whirrrrrrrr. All day.

They had had their photograph taken on the roof of the house on . . . which one was it? Lorimer Street, maybe. So many streets, so many railroad flats, one worse than the other, the worst of all that terrible one behind the other building, always dark, you had to go outside and into another building to go to the toilet. Momma crying. . . . Dispersed. Yet things were not that different . . .

No, this thing she had in her hand now, it was a tiny bib, a baby's. Anastasia was four and a half, it wasn't hers. It was Joy's! Yes, the new one, the one who laughed and gurgled and reached out her arms to her mommy. Belle wouldn't have them say Momma the way she had, Americans didn't say that. She was American now. Americans lived in this place where she was now, Jamaica. They wore neat hats and high heels and dark wool coats and spoke very precisely without the slightest accent. And the only way they knew she, Belle, was different from them was from her name, Dabrowski, that was a foreign name, Polish.

They all had neat American names, Wallis, Goldthorpe, Thacker, Jones. Maybe Goldthorpe was Jewish, but Mrs Goldthorpe didn't look Jewish, and neither did Eleanor, her little girl. Belle thought she was American. Jews were like Poles, foreign, they ate black bread with sweet butter and spoke with accents and wore brown sweaters with big holes in the sleeves.

These diapers now, they were Joy's too. When had she washed them? She must have done it, they were clean. She couldn't remember. Joy. She wondered what joy felt like. She felt she knew what the word meant even though she also knew she had never felt anything like it: joy. But how could you understand a word denoting an emotion if you have never felt it? Maybe she had. Maybe the day she stole the chruściki and gave one to her little friend she had felt joy. What was her name, that little girl? Dispersed. No, that wasn't the right word.

Joy felt joy: she was a baby who smiled, not like Anastasia. But Anastasia was a genius, come out of her, Bella, a stupid kid who couldn't even manage to comb her hair, who couldn't understand what the teacher was saying, who almost killed her baby sister leading her across a street. How could that happen, a being like Anastasia, who looked at you as if she knew everything you knew and more and yet she was only a child. But she was cruel too. 'You don't love me,' she'd said to Belle, just the other day. When Belle had sacrificed everything, her entire life, for Anastasia; when she had given up all her ambitions, her dreams, her hopes, in order to have this child. Belle had felt unable to speak when Anastasia said that. She had turned away so Anastasia wouldn't see the lump in her throat. Love? Anastasia would never understand.

Joy would never say a thing like that to her mother, Belle knew it. Joy would grow up the way she was now, smiling and happy, her plump little cheeks pink, her eyes full of laughter. Everyone loved Joy, all the ladies loved her. Belle was lucky. She had had two daughters, just as she would have chosen. She never wanted a son. And here they were, so different, yet both came out of her. That was lucky. Yes, things were a little better.

She bent for the last pieces of laundry. She remembered now. She'd washed it in the deep tub in her apartment, scrubbed it on the board, rinsed it, starched those pieces that needed starch, blued the white things, wrung it out well. It was hard to wring with your hands. It hurt. But she wrung it out well and shook it before she pinned it to the clothesline here on the roof. She had done it well. She always tried to do things well. She wanted to be a proper lady. She didn't want to lie around crying all day, to cry all the time like Momma. And this afternoon, she would put on her hat and coat and stockings and heels and take the girls to the park, her girls, and say good afternoon to the other ladies and maybe even sit on a bench with them and chat for a while. That was what proper ladies did.

Her feet hurt. They had grown again during her pregnancy with Joy, and she had been able to buy only one new pair of shoes in a larger size, and she kept those for good, she wouldn't wear them to do the laundry in. These were her good shoes from before, black suede with a bow, but they were too small and crunched her toes. All her other shoes were far too small now, and had to be given away. It wasn't fair, really, that she had such big feet. She wasn't tall. Size 8 had been bad, but then she went to an 8½ with Anastasia, and now she needed a 9! Such big feet and hands, and thick legs too. Tears began to well in her throat and she stopped and stood very still and erect and breathed deeply.

She . . . had . . . to . . . Have to. Must. What? Hurry. Yes, hurry. Because downstairs. She had to go downstairs. Yes, because the children were alone, alone. Anastasia was grown up, she would know enough not to play with matches or climb up on anything but still . . . She had reached the bottom of the enamel basin and saw some water lying in it. If she tried to carry it back downstairs, it would swish and spill. But what would happen if she poured it out here, on the roof? Would it leak into someone's apartment? If they saw a puddle there, would they reprimand her? The superintendent might scold her. That would be devastating.

She picked up the wide basin, big enough to bathe a baby in (and often used for that purpose), and some of the water spilled over the side onto her old good black suede shoes. She walked carefully, carrying it toward the door of the staircase. Then she glanced around. There were many posts with clotheslines strung on them on the roof, and two other women had laundry hanging out. She glanced around, and tiptoed toward another woman's laundry, and poured the water out on the roof under her wash.

Thinking about her feet and legs had upset her, and she knew she must calm down. She tried not to count as she descended the stairs to her floor, to her apartment 1A, Dabrowski. Counting made her cry. Think about good things, the doctor had said: When you feel you're going to cry, think about good things. Well, it was a good thing the weather was fair and she could hang the wash outside. Otherwise she had to hang it in the apartment, and duck under it all day long, and the place smelled of clorox and dampness. And the laundry dripped and she had to put newspapers down under it. It was awful. It was good that the weather was good.

Yes, and when the weather was bad it was uncomfortable to take the girls for their walk in the afternoon. She wouldn't do it in bad weather if she could think of anything else to do with them. She would bundle Joy under many little woolen blankets and the leather protector that covered the top of the carriage, and put up an umbrella and try to get Anastasia to stay under it, and they would go out whatever the weather. But it was hard to hold an umbrella and push the carriage at the same time, although Anastasia loved to push the carriage, but she couldn't get it up and down the curbs . . . So it was good the weather was good.

What else was good? Joy was a good baby, she rarely cried. And Anastasia was good too, she had stopped asking questions all the time, driving Belle crazy. And she, Belle, had a nice hat and coat and good new black suede shoes and when she went to the park, she looked as neat and nice as any of the other ladies, and they could not tell she was poor, poorer than they, poorer than anyone else she knew. No, she could conceal that. That was good.

By this time she had reached her apartment, and unlocked the door. She walked down the short dark hall to the kitchen and put the basin on the dish drain and wiped it dry with a dishcloth. She took off the old suede jacket she had worn to hang clothes in, and shook her head a little because her hair felt damp. Then she went to check on the children. Anastasia was lying on the living room floor as she often did. 'Hello, Mommy,' she said, and sat up.

'Hello, Anastasia,' Belle said, on her way to the bedroom to check on Joy. Joy was still asleep in her little crib. Belle left the bedroom and went back to the kitchen, passing Anastasia without speaking. She was tired. She turned up the gas flame under the old aluminum drip coffeepot. There was some coffee left from breakfast. She would have a cup, and smoke a cigarette and relax a little. She let herself down in a chair and sighed. That would be good.

The silent months in Jamaica were broken by a few events so striking that they pierced the curtain of ice Anastasia felt had dropped around her. Sometimes, in the morning, when Mommy was washing or cleaning the house or taking care of Joy, Anastasia would put on her hat and coat and run outside with a ball and bounce it in the courtyard. Occasionally, she would venture to the sidewalk and gaze across the street at the park. The park was big and green, and it had a fence around it made of tall iron spears. Anastasia thought it looked like the fences around castles, although she had never seen a castle, and wondered how she knew that. Probably she had seen a picture, she thought. In the middle of the park was a bandstand, white wooden trelliswork with a peaked roof, and sometimes there were musicians sitting inside it playing band music, which was different from other music.

One day something was happening in the park, and Anastasia abandoned her ball bouncing and walked to the very edge of the sidewalk, as far as she dared go. There was band music and many people in the park, some carrying flags. She wanted to run inside and ask Mommy why all the people were in the park, but she knew Mommy would be tired. So she remained where she was and tried to answer her question for herself. She moved from foot to foot as she stood there, because her Mary Janes were too small for her and they hurt her feet. She had a new pair Mommy had bought her for Easter, but they were for good. She tried to stand on tiptoe to see farther into the park, but that hurt her feet even more.

Then a very fat man with a bulbous red nose came out of the wide park gate and started to cross the street. There were cars parked all along the curb, and as the fat man stepped into the street, one of them backed up and squeezed him flat against the car on his other side. Anastasia cried 'oh' and put her hands up in front of her eyes. There was blood in her eyes, blood on her hands. Blood. She tore back into the house, to Mommy.

'Mommy, Mommy! Come and see! A fat man got scrunched into a thin man between two cars. There is blood, Mommy!' she cried. She tugged at her mother's hand. But Mommy was tired. She was sitting at the table feeding Joy cereal.

'I can't come now, Anastasia,' she said in her tired voice.

Anastasia jumped up and down. 'Please, Mommy, please come! There's blood! (Would the fat man's fat all come out in one lump like from a lamb chop?) Mommy, a man got squeezed!'

'I'm busy now, Anastasia,' Mommy said. 'I'll come later.'

But Anastasia knew that later the man would be gone. She whimpered a bit, and stood there like a reproachful presence, but Mommy went on feeding Joy. Anastasia knew that if she cried or yelled, Mommy would talk to her in the very tired voice that sounded angry. She hung around the kitchen. She wanted to go back and see, but she wanted to go holding Mommy's hand, she didn't want to go out there again alone. But Mommy wasn't coming. She trudged back out, tentatively, and went slowly toward the edge of the sidewalk.

There was a big crowd of people around the place now. She could not see the man anymore. She couldn't see over the heads of the people. She couldn't see the blood. Maybe it hadn't happened. She slumped back into the house, and went into the living room and lay on the floor. She lay on her back so she wouldn't have to smell the horrible dusty smell of the carpet. She stared at the ceiling. What if the man had cried out asking for help when the car hit him? He was dead, he must be dead, and he wouldn't know that people had come and tried to help him. He would cry out and believe that no one came to help him.

Anastasia knew how that felt. She could remember the night she woke up and Mommy and Daddy were not home. She could not see Joy's cradle, either. The apartment was dark except for the light in the front hall. She called out, but no one answered. With the thought that she was alone, came terror. She was paralyzed, too frightened even to get out of the crib and go into the next room and find them. She was too frightened even to get out of the crib and walk across the room to see if Joy's cradle was there on the other side of Mommy and Daddy's bed.

She knew where they were. They had gone upstairs to Mrs Thacker's house to play bridge. Mrs Thacker was a retired schoolteacher, and Mommy respected her very much, Anastasia knew from the way she talked to her and about her, with reverence. Mrs Thacker was an educated person; she had white hair that was sort of blue, and she was very nice, but she didn't like Anastasia, she liked Joy. Joy always smiled and Anastasia always frowned, that was why Mrs Thacker didn't like her. But Anastasia couldn't help frowning, because . . . she didn't know why. Mrs Thacker always smiled and held her arms out to Joy and took her from Mommy and said 'goo' and 'coo' and the other silly things people said to babies. That made Anastasia frown more. But she didn't really understand why, because Anastasia didn't want those things said to her.

Mrs Thacker had a gentleman friend called Mr Howells, and they sometimes played bridge with Mommy and Daddy. And that's where they were. They'd gone up there without her, leaving her alone, but they'd taken Joy with them in her cradle. That's what had happened.

Thinking about this made Anastasia cry. She called out Mommy's name, called and called, cried it as loud as she could, shrieked it. But no one came. Mrs Thacker lived upstairs, directly above their apartment but on the third floor, and Anastasia was sure she could hear them all up there talking and laughing. They would have something good to eat. She could hear their forks scraping the china plates as they finished their pie. She could smell the coffee. She could hear the ice clinking in glasses of ginger ale. She screamed and screamed. She worked the crib as close to the window as it would go, and pushed her head back against the bars and screamed. Although at other times she could easily stand and get out of the crib – she was four and a half years old, after all – this night she could not find the courage to do what she knew she could do: get up, leave the apartment, climb the stairs to the third floor, knock on the door and insist on being taken in.

She knew she could do this, but somehow she could not. Her fury mounted, with herself, with them, and she screamed without end for ten minutes or more, until her throat was sore. No one came. No one heard. Mommy loved Joy more than she loved Anastasia, because Joy smiled and giggled and was ticklish, and Anastasia frowned. Anastasia knew that her frowning made people dislike her. But she could not stop it, she would not stop it. To stop frowning, to smile as Joy did, she felt, would be some terrible act, an interior collapse. She kept screaming, until, exhausted, she fell asleep. But she heard Mommy and Daddy come in. Suddenly unafraid to sit up, she did, as she heard them talking in the living room and saw the lights come on again. When Mommy opened the glass door to the bedroom, Anastasia cried out reproachfully:

'You went out without me!'

'Oh, Anastasia,' her mother said in her tired voice, 'we only went out for a little while. You're a big girl now, big enough to stay alone for a little while.'

Anastasia lay down again and mulled that over. She was a big girl, practically grown up. She couldn't tell Mommy she was frightened, that she didn't want to stay alone, that she wanted some pie, that she was hurt that they took Joy and left her. She didn't know how to say any of those things, and if she said them, Mommy would think she was just a baby. And Mommy didn't have respect for babies, Anastasia knew that. She knew it from how Mommy said,

'Oh, Joy is just a baby,' when Anastasia complained about Joy. To be a baby was contemptible. To be a big girl was good, deserving of respect.

Still, Anastasia didn't like being left like that, and she didn't know how to work that out. If you were a big girl, you didn't mind being left. She *could* have got out of the crib and gone upstairs. That was something a big girl would do, wasn't it? But she was too scared. Why was that? She was a scaredy-cat, Anastasia, a baby. She closed her eyes, her thin arms stiff along her sides, and fell into a dark haunted sleep.

When Anastasia was almost five, Mommy told her that Dr MacVeaney had said she had to have her tonsils removed. To do this, she had to go to the hospital, to Mary Immaculate, the big hospital up there at the top of the hill behind the park. It wasn't far away, Mommy said, and Mommy would go with her.

Anastasia said no.

Mommy said that tonsils were things that grew in the throats of little children and had to be removed before they grew up. Had Mommy's tonsils been removed? Oh yes, but not until Mommy was a big girl, much older than Anastasia, and then it was terrible, it hurt so, and it left Mommy weak and sick for days. It would not be bad if Anastasia would go now, while she was still little.

Less forcefully, Anastasia said no.

Mommy said the doctor said she had to go. And it would be nice there in the hospital. There were lots of big ladies in white dresses called nurses who did nothing all day but take care of little girls like Anastasia. And afterward, when her tonsils were out, Anastasia would have ice cream.

'Could I have peach?' Peach was her favorite flavor, but she rarely had it because Dixie cups came in vanilla and chocolate, and pops were vanilla with hard chocolate outside, and even Mello rolls only came in vanilla, chocolate, and strawberry. To have peach you had to buy a carton of ice cream, the expensive kind where the man took a silver scoop and dug into a big tub and scraped the ice cream into a container and it smelled so delicious, and you took it home and scooped it into bowls. She had hardly ever had peach.

Mommy promised her she could have peach, but even then Anastasia was not convinced.

'Would I sleep in a big bed?' That she, at nearly five, was still forced to sleep in a crib was humiliating to her. They could not fit a bed into the bedroom, Mommy said. She had to sleep in a crib until they moved to a bigger house. But someday Anastasia would sleep in a bed, Mommy had promised.

Mommy said, 'Yes, you will have a big bed.'

So Anastasia agreed to go to the hospital. They packed a little valise and Daddy walked her up the hill to Mary Immaculate while Mommy stayed with Joy. And then Anastasia found herself on a hard funny bed on wheels, and the room was cold, and they wheeled her into another room that was even colder and all white and it had big lights on the ceiling and Anastasia didn't like it. And they lifted her from the bed on wheels to another bed just like it, but without wheels. And then Dr MacVeaney was standing over her, smiling and saying her name. There were ladies there too, in white dresses, but they didn't like little girls at all, Anastasia could tell. Mommy was wrong. But how could Mommy be wrong? She knew everything. She must have lied. The ladies wanted to put something over her face and she tossed her head so they couldn't, and Dr MacVeaney stopped them. She loved Dr MacVeaney then, and she thought she would ask him to take the straps off her wrists and ankles so she could move. But he said, 'Anastasia, I want you to count to a hundred.'

'No!'

'Oh, go on. Do it for me.'

'No!'

'Oho!' he smiled. 'I'll bet you don't know how!'

'I do so! I do know how!'

'Well, you're going to have to prove it to me.'

So, Anastasia, all against her will, had to start to count. But, you know, he was lying! He didn't care if she knew how to count to a hundred or not, because before she could get past ten the nurse had put the mask over her nose and mouth and she had to stop because she couldn't think anymore. And she wondered why he had challenged her if he didn't really want to know if she could count to a hundred or not.

When she woke up, Mommy and Daddy were sitting in chairs and she was lying IN A CRIB! She felt too sick to raise her head. There was a kidney-shaped metal dish beside her face full of blood, and her throat hurt. And she felt awful, but still, she raised her head and yelled, she screamed as loud as she could with her throat so sore, 'You promised me they'd put me in a bed!'

And even though she was yelling, Mommy didn't get mad, she only smiled and said they'd move Anastasia to a bed the next day. But Anastasia didn't believe her, or only half believed her, and her head fell back against the mattress. Her throat hurt too much or she would have cried. She wanted to cry: she hated being little, why did people treat children the way they did, she wanted to be grown up, but she was helpless, sick, and her throat hurt and Mommy was laughing at her.

They never moved her to a big bed, but before she could protest she came home. She was lying on the couch in the living room, and Mommy was bringing her a bowl of ice cream, peach ice cream, and Anastasia's heart leaped, that part was true, anyway. She sat up when Mommy handed her the bowl, and lovingly spooned some ice cream into her mouth. But her throat screamed at the coldness, it hurt so much she couldn't even taste the delicious flavor. She tried again, and then put the bowl on the floor beside her.

'I'll eat it later,' she said to Mommy. 'My throat hurts.'

And Mommy took the bowl and put it on top of the piano and said Anastasia could have it later. Anastasia slid down on the couch and fell asleep. She knew she would never have the ice cream. By the time she was feeling better, Daddy had eaten it. He had to or it would have melted, Mommy said. Anastasia could have ice cream some other time. Peach. But she never did, not until much later, when she had almost forgotten the tonsillectomy. And she already knew all this when she slid down on the couch and went to sleep; she was thinking that it was so and that she had always known it was so: that grown-ups lied to children, that you could not trust them, that they all lied all the time. She hated that, and she hated them, and she hated being little, a child, a person who could be lied to. She would never forgive them, any of them who lied to her. And when she was grown up and had children, she would never never never lie to them, never.

A psychological theory published long after Anastasia had become an adult asserted that trust must be developed early in life or it never would. By the time she read this, Anastasia had forgotten all about tonsillectomies and cribs versus big beds; even her own children were past such concerns. She decided, as she read Erikson, that all the qualities necessary to a full rich adult life existed in her. It was true, she recalled, that she had had moments of distrust; but she had just as many, far more, even, of trust. After all, every afternoon when she came home from school, wasn't her mother there? (Except one terrible time during a hurricane, and then she was out searching for Anastasia.) Wasn't there always food, wasn't there always a warm house, didn't Daddy fix things that got broken? She knew she had hated her parents at some time, but that was merely adolescent rebelliousness, they were good people and had given her all they had to give. It wasn't their fault if they could not give more, was it? And anyway, all children had complaints about their parents.

It was Easter Sunday, 1964, and Anastasia had prepared a big dinner for her parents, her children, Toni, Pane Nowak, and some friends, in her small apartment. They had had to eat in the kitchen, but thank heavens, Toni and Arden and Billy had helped with the cooking, and her friends said the meal was wonderful. Mother rarely praised a meal. After dinner, they had embarked on a series of games.

It was Ellie who led this. He knew all the games there were, and some no one else had ever heard of, and he had Lee and Drew and Courtney and Toni and Arden and

Billy and Arden's friend Kai, and even little Franny totally involved. Dad never got involved in games, he just sat on the sidelines listening. He'd participate only if they needed a timekeeper or a referee. Mom wanted to play, but she couldn't hear, so she would wave them away with her mouth pressed together tightly, but her eyes looking superior and aloof. By the time Anastasia had got the kitchen in some kind of order, and dried her hands and come into the living room with a fresh drink, Mom was yawning and Dad was looking at her to see if she was ready to leave. But she didn't look at him, and she hadn't yet stood up.

Ellie was talking about trust games that they played in his psychodrama classes – where you lean back and hope someone catches you, or jump up into their arms. And there was Drew, all four feet nine of her, standing with clenched teeth ready to catch Courtney, whose six-foot-two frame was slowly bending backward dangerously. Everyone was howling already, even though it hadn't yet happened, and when it did, when Courtney reached the point of falling, Drew managed to push herself up against his back and hold him there, her shoulder against his spine, her arm thrown over his stomach. And everyone clapped except Mom and Dad, who gazed on this the way nursemaids might gaze at their small charges playing in mud, with glazed eyes expressing amazement at the things people will do.

Then Mom yawned, and Dad stood up immediately. 'Ready to leave, Belle?' he inquired solicitously, and she nodded without looking at him, and he went into the bedroom for her coat and hat. No one else noticed, they were still playing the trust game. Now Arden was falling back against Billy, but she couldn't let herself do it, and the friends were making catcalls and urging her on and laughing, and only Anastasia saw her mother frown with anxiety and speak to Ed, and notice him leave the room. She followed. 'Mother's glasses,' he said.

'Which ones?'

'The reading glasses – you asked her to look at some pictures,' he said with an edge of reproach.

They found the glasses and he carried them to Belle as if he were making a votive offering, bending as he handed them to her, expecting, wanting, praise and thanks. Got none. She put them into her bag and stood up so he could help her with her coat.

Heads rose.' Leaving already?'

'The fun's just started.'

'Aw, don't go yet,' Ellie begged.

Belle offered him a purse-lipped smile, murmured something about 'the old folks' needing their sleep, and tottered toward the door.

Arden was sitting cross-legged on the floor. 'You haven't even played the game, Grampa,' she argued sweetly.

'Oh, that's for you young ones,' he echoed Belle. He tried to offer her a hearty laugh.

'Well, he can play it now,' Anastasia cried out, and put her arm around his neck and jumped in the air, all five feet seven and a half inches of her, all one hundred and thirty pounds. 'Catch me!' she cried.

And he did – he put his arms out, one under her waist, and one under her knees, and then he staggered, and both of them went down in a heap together. The room splintered into a chaos of hysterical laughter; everyone was laughing except Belle, who smiled a little through her shock. Ed laughed, but quickly extricated himself and ran to her side as if she were the one who had fallen and needed help. He put an arm around her waist.

'Are you all right, Belle?'

Anastasia was laughing too hard to get up, and Toni came over and reached for her hand. There were tears running down her cheeks as she turned to Ellie: 'You see? The story of my life!' No one else heard her. They were all laughing too hard.

When the landlord of the Jamaica apartment announced he was raising their rent, a new knowledge pierced the cold wall of order Belle had built around herself. She recognized she had possessed this knowledge for a long time; but she had not known she had it. It was the understanding that whatever happened, she would have to do all the thinking for them, all the planning. She knew Ed had simply placed himself in her hands, and would do whatever she decided. And she knew that he knew that she would never do anything foolish or extreme, that he could trust her to be practical, to live within his earnings, and not to ask him to do anything he would hate. But she was not pleased with his trust. When this knowledge poked itself at her, she felt pity for herself – so alone she was – and outraged at Ed's dependency.

She began to scour the newspapers for houses for rent. There were many in those days, and often you did not have to look in the newspapers – everyone knew someone with a house for rent. But the Dabrowskis could afford very little rent, and Belle knew they had to have two bedrooms. They could not go on sleeping four to a room, although Ed would never complain or even suggest that they move. But Anastasia was getting big now and it was humiliating to Belle to think she might wake up some night when . . . Besides, soon Joy too would outgrow her crib. They would have had to move even if the rent hadn't been raised.

One Saturday in August, they took the children on the trolley back to Manse Street and left them with Momma. Wally was there on a visit, and had a car there, which they borrowed. Ed drove to the places listed in the ads Belle had cut out of the newspaper. They found a house in South Ozone Park. It was a little house in a neighborhood like the one in Forest Hills, much poorer – small one-family houses, a few with garages. There were trees in front and yards in back. The house for rent had a yard bordered with poplar trees, although the grass was overgrown; it had five rooms – three down, two bedrooms up, with a bathroom. The downstairs was supposed to be, Belle knew, living room, dining room, kitchen; but she had no dining room furniture, so she could call the front room the porch, the central room the living room. It was terribly important to Belle to have a porch. And the front room was bright and light, with five windows, as bright as a porch should be.

The problem was the house rented for $35 a month, and they would have to pay for heat. The apartment had been $35 a month, but the heat was supplied. After the raise, of course, it would be $40 – but Belle wasn't sure coal would cost only $5 a month, $60 a year. Still, she felt they had no choice. Maybe Ed would get another raise. He was earning $33 a week now; with a few more dollars, they'd probably get by. Anyway, she wanted this house. She loved it. It was little, and the neighborhood was poor, but there was something about it that charmed her – the trees in front, the front steps, the way people sat out on them that August evening. The small grass patch in front was bordered with a privet hedge, and had a big hydrangea bush in its center.

They moved on the first of September. Anastasia was to start first grade in September; and Joy was nearly two. They borrowed a truck from Martha's brother, Henry Beck, and he and Ed moved the furniture. Belle felt almost happy. The apartment had been small, cramped, and dark. The house was light, and bigger – their sparse furniture did not fill it. And she'd have a garden! All her life, Belle had wanted to be like the ladies who sat in their gardens in the afternoon, and now she would be able to do that.

The yard would have to be worked on, of course. It had been allowed to grow wild; the grass was waist-high, and as thick as reeds. Beyond the yard was a huge open field; far behind their back fence was a cleared space where boys played baseball. After the furniture was moved in, and Henry Beck had been given a couple of beers – Ed had one with him – and left, the small family went out on to the tiny back porch that overlooked the yard. Belle and Ed were both almost smiling. She said she'd plant a garden; Ed chuckled and said he saw he had his work cut out for him. Joy, in a sunsuit, let go of Belle's hand when she saw the reeds like a field of wheat. She toddled down the three steps to the concrete patch behind the house, and through the opening in the low hedge, and out into the overgrown yard. She cried out with delight, entered the reeds, and disappeared. All they could see, the three of them, was the rustling of stalks as Joy went exploring. And Mommy and Daddy began to laugh. They laughed and laughed as the reeds shook around invisible Joy. Anastasia stared at them, let her ears fill with the sound: laughter! Then she began to laugh too. The three of them stood together, watching the reeds move, laughing, and for the first time, Anastasia became aware of Joy, her cute little sister, with chubby arms and legs and hair so blond it was almost white, and immense blue eyes that begged you to look into them, to smile, to take her in your arms. And Anastasia *saw* her, invisible as she was, and her heart overflowed with love for this little creature who could make them all laugh together.

two

Things were hard in the new house because they needed furniture now. The children's bedroom held only the two cribs; and the front downstairs room was empty. Out of Ed's $33 a week, Belle had to set aside $10 for the rent and electric bill; Ed needed $3 a week for carfare, the newspaper, and coffee to go with the sandwich Belle fixed for him each night. She put aside another $4 a week to cover the coal bills and to pay for insurance – a policy for $2,500 on Ed and two she had taken out for the children's college. She paid $2 a month, and when they were eighteen, they would get $1,000 each – a huge sum, Belle felt, one that would see them through four years. That left her with $16 a week for food and clothes and other things – doctor's bills (please let them stay healthy!) and any furniture they might buy.

Ed would not let her buy anything that was poorly made, and she had high standards of taste, so they shopped long and hard to find two suites of furniture, both solid maple. She found a maple couch and two chairs with detached cushions for the 'porch', for $50; and a maple bedroom set – two bedsteads, two mattresses and inner springs, two chests of drawers and a mirror – for $75. Both sets cost $1 down, $1 a week, which meant $2 less a week for food. But if they stayed healthy, they could manage. Belle bought remnants at Montgomery Ward's fabric department, and made curtains for the kitchen, the bathroom, and the back door. She waited until Montgomery Ward had a sale on ninon curtains, and bought sheer white panels for all the other windows and the front door, which had glass panes.

These were a huge expense – $10 all at once – but she had saved for ten weeks. The saving and the worry made her brow furrow. Each week, she tried to slip a dollar bill underneath her bureau drawer, where Ed had suggested they hide their savings.

Ed set to work too. First he cleared the yard and planted grass and dug beds for Belle where she wanted them. She brought clippings from Momma and planted perennials along the outside rim of the yard, in a border. Then Ed brought his tools from the house on Quincy Street and began to clean and arrange the cellar of the new house.

Anastasia started school. Belle did her hair in braids and dressed her up on the first day of school, and pushing Joy in the kiddie car, walked with Anastasia to the dark redbrick building with cement courtyards and a high wire fence around it. P.S. 45, Queens: it was old; it had been built for the children of the poor, and looked it. But to Anastasia, it was a brave new world.

Shy and friendless as she had been, she was surprised to feel herself confident and happy in this new world where there were people, noise, talking, and things – books, papers, blackboards. She charged in with a big grin and devoured the reader the teacher had just handed out as their term text. She raised her hand and went up to speak to the teacher.

'May I have another book?'

The teacher glanced at her with irritation. 'Didn't you get your book?'

'Yes. But I've finished it.'

The teacher looked at her for a moment. Then she took her to the side wall of the classroom, where a shelf lay under the big windows. On the shelf were twenty or so books. 'Anastasia, take as many of these as you want. Be sure to bring them back, though. Then you can take more.'

Anastasia's eyes lighted. Books! At home there were only two books, both of which she had been able to read for a long time – the Mother Goose, and Robert Louis Stevenson's *A Child's Garden of Verses*, which she had been given last Christmas. She loved these books, but she had read them so many times she felt a little bored with them. Besides that, there were only the funnies. Daddy used to read her the funnies every Sunday morning: Mommy told him to. But one Sunday, after they moved into the new house, Daddy wouldn't read her the comics. He just said No. He was busy. He said Wait. She waited, but still he said no. Anastasia was near tears, but angry, and she picked up the paper and thought, I'll show him, I'll read them myself! She was looking at Tiny Tim: and suddenly, she realized, she *could* read them without him. But there were only a few comics each night when Daddy brought home the *Daily News*, and the books on Mommy's bureau were too hard for her. Now she had many many books to read. She took six home with her the first night, and returned them to school the next day. In the first week, she had exhausted the little shelf. She settled back into boredom until the teacher led her – only her – to the little library in the end room. After that, she always had books.

And the children were fun, and she loved recess. They played and danced, and Anastasia knew the boys all liked her, and she liked them too. And after a couple of weeks, four or five of them began to follow her home in the afternoons, and sometimes, after she'd had her milk and cookies, she'd go out and play with them, but sometimes she wouldn't. It depended on what she felt like doing. Sometimes she felt like staying in the house and drawing. Mommy always teased her about the boys, as if she, Anastasia, had done something flirty to make them follow her home, as if Anastasia were somehow . . . she did not know the right word, but as if she should feel ashamed or something. Still, she loved to go to school every morning. She would reach the schoolyard and run in and lots of children from her class would turn and cry out 'Here's Anastasia!' and her heart would fill up and she knew her smile was plastered clear across her face, and she would jump in their midst and start to play. She was always the leader, but the others didn't seem to mind that.

Belle too felt happier. She created a new daily order, as peaceful and quiet as her life in the apartment. She took some pride in this, for she had no real experience of family life. She didn't even know what a peaceful family life would be; she had to invent it, with some help from the radio. The families she had known were all ripped apart by raging fathers and weeping mothers; of all her childhood friends, only Gertrude Hunrath had not been reluctant to go home after school or work, and Gertrude had only a mother and sister.

Belle was determined to create another kind of home. She saw the look in Ed's eye when he happened to glance at Joy or Anastasia, especially if they were making any noise, or sitting on the floor in the middle of the room. She knew how he felt, and she had made up her mind that he would not be like her own father. One night when he came home from work, Anastasia was sitting on the piano bench sounding out 'Twinkle, Twinkle' with one finger, and he stormed into the porch with raised hand and shouted at her to stop. Belle called him into the kitchen and closed the kitchen door. She told him then: he would not raise his voice to the children, he would not raise his hand to them. The children were good children, and were allowed to talk, or play the piano, or sit on the floor. And if he abused them, she would leave him. She said it just like that. And he looked away as if he were ashamed, or embarrassed, but he never yelled or raised his hand again. She saw his face darken when he looked at them, and she heard him grumble at them, imagining she could not hear him with her deaf ear. But she heard. She shrugged. As long as he leaves them alone, it's all right. What can you expect of a man? Men hate children, that's the way they are. Ed was just normal. Only she would not permit him to be like her father.

Her new aspiration was a washing machine. They had quite good ones now, with a centerpost that rubbed the clothes as you would on a washboard, and a wringer that you could put the clothes through – so much easier than wringing them by hand. But she could not afford one. Maybe next year, when the porch furniture was paid off. Meantime, she scrubbed the clothes every Monday in the deep tub beside the sink, on a washboard with heavy yellow soap. Then she'd transfer each load into the sink itself, let the wash water out, and pour in fresh cool water to rinse them. Each Sunday evening Ed strung a long line from one tree to another in the yard, so it was there waiting for her in the good weather. If the weather was bad, he strung lines in the basement, but it was too small to hold all the wash at once.

The first things she washed were Ed's shirts; then the bed sheets and pillowcases; the white bath towels; the kitchen towels. Sometimes there was a white tablecloth as well. After washing these, rinsing them and wringing them, she heated starch in a pot over the gas flame. While it was thickening, she let hot water run into the shallow sink. She took the square of bluing from its package and inserted it, holding it in a net bag, in the water. When the water was sufficiently blue, and the starch sufficiently thick, she poured the starch into the sink as well. Then she put in the white clothes to soak while she filled the deep tub with hot water and soap and put in the colored clothes, underwear, and the printed tablecloth to soak. Then she wrung out the whites as hard as she could, straining her hands, and carried them outside in the enamel basin and hung them on the line. She loved the clean smell of them and the sound of the sheets flapping in the wind. Then she went back into the kitchen and scrubbed the colored clothes, rinsed them, and thinned the starch for Anastasia's blouse, Ed's underwear shorts, and Joy's dress, and her housedress. Each of them had three changes of clothing: Ed wore his white shirts for two days. On the rare occasions when they went to visit Jean and Eric over the weekend, he would have to wear a shirt three times, because he had only three of them and needed one for Monday morning. Around the house he wore old mended shirts. Belle had three cotton housedresses and one good dress. All her beautiful clothes were gone now – they no longer fit her since she had had the children, and besides, they were out of style. Some she had given away, some were packed away in the big trunk she kept in the children's closet.

After the colored clothes were starched, she hung them on the line too. Then it was time to make lunch for Anastasia and Joy. She would open a can of Campbell's soup and make a sandwich of bologna or peanut butter and jelly, or Velveeta cheese grilled in butter in a frying pan. She herself would have toast and tea, but the girls always had a big glass of milk. Anastasia hated milk, so Belle put Hershey's chocolate syrup in it from a can.

It was fun to call Joy in from play, to wash her little face and hands. Joy was always chirping about something, something silly of course, she was only a baby, but she made Belle smile. Anastasia was another matter: often she came in scowling and said little. She was so serious, so grown up. She never talked about silly things. But Joy adored her older sister, gazed at her as if she were from a higher world, and Belle saw that Anastasia often treated Joy with disdain. Sometimes Belle would reproach Anastasia for this:

'Joy is your little sister, and she adores you. She follows you around like a little puppy. She looks up to you. You shouldn't treat her that way.'

'I hate her!' Anastasia would flash back. 'She crayoned all over my new book, the one I got for Christmas. She ruined it!'

'She's only a baby, Anastasia, and you're a big girl. You have to overlook things like that, she can't help them, she's just a baby.'

But Anastasia only sulked and frowned and said nothing. Belle knew that Anastasia was a special person, and lived in her own world, and she did not try to intrude upon it. Whereas Joy, cute and funny as she was, seemed to be happy by nature, like Dafna Dabrowski. Bell believed Joy was a Dabrowski and Anastasia was a Brez, brilliant like Michael, and difficult. Whereas Joy, like Ed, could be happy with so little, with nothing at all, really. They, the Dabrowskis, really had no standards.

After Anastasia had gone back to school, and she had led Joy upstairs to her new big bed for a nap, Belle finished the laundry. The last batch was the dark things – Ed's socks, a dark skirt of Anastasia's, and a dark print house-dress of her own. The line was full now, so she had to wait until something dried before she could hang these things, but she was relieved when she finished with the washing, rinsing, and wringing, and starching. Then she could scrub the deep tub with Bon Ami, and replace the metal dish-drain that covered it. She sighed and sat down with a cigarette before starting the next step. She looked out at the yard and thought with pride that it looked neat and pretty – it was the prettiest yard on the block. She had dreams for it – maybe Ed could build some Adirondack chairs and she could sit out there next summer. Sit out in her own yard, just like a lady! In the air, in the sun, smelling the flowers! And maybe someday he'd build a table and benches for the children, so they could sit there in the summer and play, or have a little picnic lunch with fresh lemonade with mint in it – she had already planted some mint she got from Momma. They would have a child-hood, they would not be like her. The thought of the children sitting out under the trees on a summer afternoon, drinking lemonade and playing – maybe they would do a puzzle, maybe she'd buy Anastasia a jigsaw puzzle for her birthday – made a picture that moved her heart, that ached it almost, like a long-forgotten wound she had suddenly, accidentally, touched.

She began to bring in the dry things – the sheets and pillowcases, Ed's shirts and shorts. She let down the ironing board from the side cupboard where it was normally con-cealed, and got the high stool and the iron. Today she would iron only a clean shirt for Ed, for tomorrow. She was tired. She chose one, sprinkled it, and rolled it neatly into a loaf. Then she hung the rest of the wash on the line, put the starch pot in the sink and ran cold water into it, and wiped down the stove and sink with a damp dishcloth. She sighed. She was very tired, and she still had to cook dinner. Maybe tonight she'd make frankfurters and beans: everyone liked that, and it wasn't much work. She'd peel and boil some potatoes and pour butter over them. She'd send Anastasia up to the butcher for some frankfurters. She was just finishing ironing the shirt when Anastasia came in from school, and minutes later, Joy woke up from her nap. Anastasia seemed cheerful about something, but Belle was too tired to really listen. Her back ached when she bent to put on Joy's shoes and socks, and she did not speak, because she didn't want to scream at the baby. She never raised her voice to her children: she never had and she never would. Their lives would not be like hers.

three

Oh, I remember those years, the total immersion in babies, the isolation and confinement. After Billy – Wilton Bradley Carpenter, Jr – was born, almost all activities were too hard. Arden was only a year and a half old, and couldn't walk far or long. I had a seat that attached to the big carriage, so I could lay Billy inside it and sit Arden on top, but this made the carriage very heavy, and left little room for packages. Since I couldn't push it and pull a shopping cart at the same time, it was almost impossible for me to do much marketing at any one time. I complained about this to Brad, asking if I couldn't have the car one afternoon a week, but he said, with considerable self-righteousness, that I didn't have a license, was a terrible driver, and besides, he needed it. My mother would help me.

Before the children were born, we had been two kids in love with each other; even after I got pregnant, we'd been together, equally responsible for the pregnancy. But once Arden was born, and even after that, the children were mine – my responsibility entirely. Brad didn't want to hear that things were hard for me, and if they were, that was my problem. He had his own problems, and although he never explicitly said this, he conveyed it – I was on my own. His responsibility to me ended when he handed me thirty-five dollars a week to pay our bills with.

I didn't question this, I accepted it. I didn't question the thirty-five dollars either. I knew he'd made a lot of money with the one sale, but he hadn't had a big one since, and I assumed he had put the money in the bank to draw on in leaner times. I was unhappily surprised to discover later that he'd used the money to buy an empty lot just off Merrick Road as an investment. In truth, that land helped to make him a rich man years later, but in the meantime, we were often hard pressed. Brad did a number of things in those early years, following his father's advice, that would make him wealthy later on, but being a first wife, I never saw any of the fruits of our early hardship. And it is true to my character, I guess, that I never managed to be anybody's second wife – I did everything the hard way. I was too vague about such things even to teach my daughters to be only second wives, never first ones. So now Arden is living in a farmhouse that doesn't even have a toilet. I tell her it's bad enough to repeat one's mother's mistakes, but unforgivable to regress. She only laughs. She knows I can't get serious about money.

I wasn't then either. Maybe that came from watching my mother's face harden into lines of worry and disappointment, watching, all those years, as penny added to penny eventually purchased a washing machine or got paid to the doctor. Part of the problem was real enough – she sometimes lacked money for food. If Joy was sick, and she often was, or if the winter was especially cold and we needed more coal than usual, or if a large purchase like a warm coat for my father was utterly necessary, why then she tightened her mouth and made stew from the neck and breast of lamb (the best kind, in my opinion) and gave us Jell-O for dessert; or maybe just soup and bologna sandwiches and canned peaches. We were never so poor we were *without* food. We were without a telephone, a car, warm winter clothing, luxuries of any sort. But my mother's anxiety was not about survival; it was about something else, and I didn't realize what until I saw that will of hers I burned.

Because all the things she had listed in her will were expensive – dishes, glassware, sterling silver flatware – things that people had if they were members of the middle class. We were not in the middle class, but we had them just the same. They were wedding gifts. She also had a silverplated coffeepot and a tray for it; she had bought these herself before her marriage and planned then to fill out the set with cream pitchers and a sugar bowl, but she was never able to do that. Jean had a full set like this, only in a fancier pattern, on her dining room buffet, and when I grew up, I saw them in other people's houses: coffeepots with pitchers and sugar bowls, like emblems of class or money. They were always hideously ugly, and a pain in the neck because they had to be polished regularly. And our set was really silly, because it had only a coffeepot and a tray and Mother could never set it out anywhere – it looked naked. Anyway, we didn't in those years have a dining room buffet; we didn't even have a dining room. The Haviland Limoges, the crystal goblets, the silver service for eight, sat in their boxes and were brought out only two or three times a year, or maybe only once – around Christmas, when visitors came.

But that was what my mother's worry and her anger were all about: entering into the middle class. That was why the lace-edged tablecloth came out when a neighbor came in for coffee; and why we had piano lessons; and why she worked so hard to dress us with taste. What I thought and felt to be a struggle for survival was really a struggle for status. And status was beyond my father's ken, beyond or rather outside his aspirations. He probably had almost no sense of class except for manners: he was concerned always to behave like a gentleman, and he always did. But he could be happy with franks and beans, with work and dinner and bed and work and dinner and bed because he didn't imagine a whole entrancing life beyond those, a world in which the basic terms of existence were different. And my mother's rage against my father, which grew and grew during those years of my childhood, was rooted in this difference between them. She wanted something *more*, imagining that it would be different. He only wanted a car.

I don't know why, because I suffered from not having middle-class appurtenances, but when I was a young woman, these things meant nothing to me. Status be damned! I was a bohemian, an artist, I didn't care about middle-class values. And money – well, I refused to worry about it as long as we had food and a roof and a bed to sleep in. And in a weird reversal, Brad felt the same kind of contempt for me that my mother had felt for my father because of my indifference to dining room sets and even dining rooms.

If I was unhappy when the kids were little, it wasn't because we had little money, but because I hated my life.

I hated my life even though I had a washer-dryer in the corner of the kitchen, and we, if not I, owned a car and sometimes went out on Saturday night. I hated my daily life, day by day by day. Sitting alone over a cup of coffee, feeling very grown up (what else did mommies do?), I decided I had to change it. But I didn't know how: I hadn't a cent left over, ever, of the money Brad gave me. All my underpants were torn, and I kept mending them and putting in new elastics, but I couldn't even afford to buy a new pair of underpants. (That was all right. I knew Brad's mother would give me three new pair of Lollipops – pink, blue, and yellow – for Christmas. She gave us both underwear, and she bought Brad a new suit: every year.)

I discovered the public library. And what I found I was drawn to, after I had exhausted its collection of the novelists I wanted to read, and its few art books, was books on photography. The library hadn't many in those years, but I studied those it had. I'd had a camera, and taken pictures since my ninth birthday. I picked up the first photography book accidentally but found myself fascinated by the difference among photographers. After I'd examined, over and over, the books in the library I'd squeak out seventy-five cents every once in a while to buy a photography magazine. I discovered Man Ray and Cecil Beaton and George Rodger; Cartier-Bresson, and Eliot Porter, and Walker Evans. And then, oh heavens! I'd known about Margaret Bourke-White, but now I discovered Imogen Cunningham and Berenice Abbott, and Eve Arnold! WOMEN! Lots of them, not just one Cécile Chaminade, the way there was in music, a fact that so disheartened me when I was eleven that I abandoned (wisely) my ambition to become a composer. I became very friendly with the librarian at the little local library, and convinced her I was writing a book on photographers, so she got me books on photography from all over Nassau County, and sometimes even from larger New York State libraries.

There was frustration in all this, because I was not at the time *taking* photographs: I couldn't afford film. But one night I told Brad, sort of casually, that I wished I could take pictures of the kids – they were so cute, this age passed so quickly, every argument I could come up with. I was hoping only for a couple of extra dollars for film. But he got excited by the idea. He had little to do with the kids, he wasn't interested in them, but the notion of taking pictures of the kids appealed to him. A few nights later, he came home with a new camera for me ('All you have is that ridiculous Brownie, can't take decent pictures with that'), a big Kodak that made me almost cry because if I'd picked it out, I'd have bought a used Rollei, which would have cost only a little more. But I wasn't carping then, I took what I could get however I got it. And he bought me three rolls of film: color film. I knew of course that great artists with the camera used only black and white. But I didn't complain. I did wonder how he could afford these things. A new idea entered my mind: Brad had more money than I did. We weren't sharing, I was getting an allowance.

By then, our relationship had deteriorated to the point that I dared not mention my new awareness. Brad and I hardly ever saw each other. He worked every day, even though he didn't have to. He was trying, he told me, to 'take some of the load off the old man'. But I knew what he was doing was trying to prove something to the old man. On slow days, he did reams of paperwork for the agency. His father now had to come in only on weekends and maybe one or two days a week. The rest of the time, he played golf, 'making contacts', he claimed.

The truth was Brad didn't want to be home. Home meant a four-room apartment, two screaming kids, and me, wearing my old jeans and one of his discarded shirts, trying to think up a game that would occupy the kids until bedtime. Nights we sat, he with his newspaper, me with my photography book or a novel, at least until television became cheap enough for him to come home triumphant one night with a twelve-inch set, crowing as if he'd bought it for me. I hated the thing, but after that I couldn't escape it unless I went to bed early to read while he watched the roller derby or Milton Berle or wrestling or whatever other garbage was on it, anything rather than come to bed with me. I couldn't blame him. I wouldn't have wanted to go to bed with me either. When you have no self-esteem, you have no desire, and you can't imagine anyone else could desire you. Whatever sexuality I'd possessed had vanished, and I thought I finally understood Hamlet's outrage with his mother for wanting to fuck even though she was thirty-five or forty. Here I was, twenty-one and a half, and I'd already outgrown desire. Brad didn't have much either, so we rarely screwed. I noticed he was horny mostly after we'd been to the movies and seen something with almost-naked women in it, or with extreme violence. Then he'd be insistent about sex, and screw with his eyes closed as if he couldn't bear to look at me. And he'd ram himself into me as if sex were a kind of self-assertion, and he was proving he'd learned enough of it to be a good salesman.

Anyway, I acted thrilled with the camera and the film, and the very next day, I started to take pictures of the kids. But that's not a simple matter. All those adorable things kids do, they utterly refuse to do when there's a camera aimed at them. The first time I tried it, I had an odd kind of success.

I was feeding Billy, who was about six months old and able to slump in a padded high chair. Arden was hovering around us angrily, and I knew she was jealous, so I talked to her and tried to caress her as she passed me. But she darted away from my hand. There was a toy in the tray of the high chair – a suction cup with a rattle affixed to it. If you pushed the thing, it rattled, but didn't fall off the tray. It was intended to save mothers forty-four bends a day. Arden very suddenly went up to the high chair and looked at Billy and pushed the rattle. Billy grinned with delight, and Arden did it again. Although the expression on her face was not sweet, I thought she was being sweet almost against her will, and I was enchanted. It was the first time she had paid any attention to him at all, except to demand a bottle every time he had one – although she'd been weaned before he was born.

So up I got, excited. It was November, and grey. First I pulled Billy up out of the high chair right in the middle of his lunch, and set him on the floor and carried the high chair out to a little wooden porch at the back of our apartment. It had a roof, but more light than the kitchen.

I bundled both kids up in snowsuits, put on my own coat and hat, got the camera and some cookies, and went outside with them.

The light was pale and pearly, and I opened the shutter wide and held the camera to my eye.

'Push Billy's toy, sweetheart,' I urged Arden. She glared at me. 'Go on, do what you did before, honey. Then you and Billy can both have cookies.' 'Cookie' would be Billy's first word; Arden's first word had been 'no'. It was 'no' now, too. She was just about to be two, and had a head full of blond curls and big blue eyes with rage in them. Wherefore, I wondered. Whenever my mother was disgusted with me, she would announce, 'I hope when you have a daughter, she is just like you, stubborn and willful and impossible!' I thought my mother's curse had come true, because Arden had always been those things.

I sat down on an old wicker chair with a broken arm, and prepared for a long wait. While I waited, I played with them, pushing the rattle for Billy and telling Arden to look at the bird settling out on a bare branch, asking her if she wanted to play patty-cake, whatever. But she watched me as warily as any Eve a snake, and Billy drooled, oblivious to all of it. I kept this up for ten or fifteen minutes. My feet were getting cold. Then I urged her again. 'Come on, honey, show me you know how to push the rattle.' Saying this, I recalled Dr MacVeaney, and hated myself. But Arden was smarter than I had been. She headed for the back door, pulled the storm door open, turned to me and, setting her teeth in a wide grimace, she screeched long and loud.

I got a great picture, if not the one I'd intended.

Still, it wasn't the sort of picture other mothers would want, I knew that. I had to wait until the following summer to get that kind, wait for a time when I could be outdoors with the children, lying on the grass in the park with my camera ready at all times. I couldn't pose them. But eventually I did come up with a set of snapshots that would make every mother on my block jealous.

I caught Arden with a butterfly. I'd dressed her up in a little smocked dress my mother had made for her. I didn't normally put such things on her, because I hated to wash and hated even more to iron, but I bethought myself of my grand plan and put first things first. I'd taken the kids to my mother's that day. She had a nice garden, with three big beds of flowers, and a lot of green, and the old Adirondack chairs my father had made years before that were still as strong as new, and which he repainted so they still looked new. My mother and I were sitting outside drinking iced tea and the kids were running around in the garden and I kept putting the camera up to my eye and dropping it, so they'd lost any self-consciousness, and then it happened. A butterfly landed on a zinnia. And Arden was standing right there: her little arms were held out stiffly like wings, and her whole body leaned toward, yearned toward the butterfly, and her face was awed and open and I got it, I caught her.

In another one, Billy had toppled on his backside, as he often did, and he looked plain startled, and I caught that. And then, suddenly, Arden ran over to him and reached out her hand to help him up, and said 'Don't cry, Billy,' although he wasn't crying, but almost did, and I caught that too. A moment of sibling affection! I knew every mother on the block would drool for such a picture.

When my set was complete, I began to show them around. I knew most of the young women in the neighborhood – we all met each other pushing carriages in one direction or another. And sometimes I'd have coffee with one or another. We were all poor, we didn't have to be ashamed in front of each other. The distinctions were there – one's husband was going to law school, another was doing his medical residency: we knew who was upwardly mobile and who was not – at least we thought we did. Actuality often confounds stereotypes. Every degree of education mattered: the women who had one year of college felt a superiority over those who had only finished high school, and the one who had been a second-grade teacher tended to behave as if all of us were in the second grade.

I, of course, paid no attention to such snobberies. I was 'above' them. I was simply disguised by my lifestyle, but I knew that one of these days, I'd haul the easel back out and get some new paints and start again. Meanwhile, I was entertaining myself with photography.

As I had expected, all of them envied my wonderful shots, and wanted some of their children. No one had much money, though, and for a while, there was only the envy and the admiration poised over the coffee cup. But one day, Milly Cooper, the most good-hearted and open of the women on the block, burst out in her Nova Scotia accent: 'Oh, I wish you would take some pictures of *my* children!'

That was all I needed. I paused, considered, offered hesitantly: 'Well, I could, I guess . . .'

'Oh, could you, Stahz? I'd be ever so grateful!'

I acted as if I were only then figuring it out. 'Well, if you could pay for the film and the developing . . .'

'Oh, of course!'

'We'll have to have two rolls, to make sure we get a good set . . .'

'Oh. Well, sure, whatever you say.'

'And I'd just charge the price of an extra two rolls for my time. How's that?'

She was thrilled, and planned to go immediately to Modell's, which sold a cheap brand of film. I had to derail that, but I was able to soften the blow by saying my fee would be for the price of black-and-white, which was cheaper than color. I don't remember what the whole thing cost, maybe ten dollars or so, much less than a professional photographer would have charged. After Milly, the others, as I'd expected, soon came to strike the same deal. I had enough work to occupy me for months, because of course, the women on the block all had friends, sisters, sisters-in-law, and cousins who lived elsewhere, and who also talked, and who in turn had friends, sisters, cousins and so forth.

I had no idea at the time that my 'hobby' was the beginning of a career. I was doing it for pin money – well, film money. It took enormous amounts of time. We'd get together – the woman and her children and me with mine – at her house or the park. I preferred outdoor settings, but good weather would last only another few months. I didn't like using flashes on babies, and couldn't afford to buy regular studio lights. So I photographed almost every day, and sometimes twice a day, trying to garner as much film as I could for the winter, when, I thought, I'd work on my own.

We'd sit around – I told the mothers this was the only way – with coffee or a thermos of lemonade, with blankets and toys, and we'd wait. I'd take two rolls of thirty-six shots in the course of the afternoon, and since I was very patient there were always at least twenty-four wonderful ones. There would be shots of babies falling asleep; or their first sight of their mother on waking up; or rubbing their eyes, or crying – all cute as they could be, enough to make every mother melt.

I felt a bit squeamish about what I was doing, as if it were – unworthy. Well, I'd had a male education. I mean, I'd learned to respect what the philosophers, novelists, historians I'd read respected. I had been Very Serious as a young person, and I knew that the whole business of women and babies and housework was frivolous and mindless and even contemptible. No philosopher I had ever read had taken women seriously. What women felt about life in general, or their own lives in particular, didn't seem to interest anyone.

But here I was, listening to these women for hours every day, and I couldn't avoid seeing their unspoken anguish, their fears, their rage. Nothing around us in those days suggested that a woman had any such feelings, or any concerns beyond her children, her husband, her house, and her neighbors; and the women I knew felt illegitimate in expressing them. Still, they seeped out, steamed out, came out willy-nilly, and what I didn't hear, I saw.

Because often enough as I was aiming the camera at what promised to be an adorable shot of Johnny eating a cookie, what I caught was Johnny socking Mommy in the eye, and the rage that crossed her face in that instant. Or, as Mommy was arranging baby on a pretty pink blanket she'd washed and dried for the occasion, baby, naked as she was, decided to shit: the picture showed baby's pink straining face, a mustard-color stain on the blanket and Mommy's frustration. What I ended up with was a complete record of the emotional interactions of mothers and young children, with the anger and despair and frustration and weariness as well as the delight and affection. Whatever appears on film is in some way exaggerated: any instant, caught and frozen out of the flux of expression, seems stronger, more permanent, than it actually is. So when Baby comes over and wipes his hands on Mommy's fresh white blouse, laundered expressly for the picture-taking, and leaves behind a trail of chocolate from his Oreo, and she sees the mess, she will register dismay, anger, amusement, and forgiveness, all within the span of a minute. But if I am sitting there with my camera, I will catch only one or two of those expressions – the anger, say, and the sad tail end of the forgiveness.

I never showed the women the 'negative' pictures. They were not wanted. Still, I kept them myself. I don't know why. I could never use them for anything. Who wanted pictures of angry mothers? And besides the pictures were in color. Who knew then that it was precisely this kind of thing that would embark me on my later career? Whenever I get a commission these days, it's for some series of pictures of women and children – even though I first established myself as an action photographer, and did good work in war zones. Nowadays I often get in touch with the local UNICEF agency, for contacts and assistance, and every time I enter a UNICEF headquarters, there they are, huge blowups of Indian or Tunisian or Malaysian women looking adoringly at their babies, holding them, caressing them. I just shake my head, because you hardly ever see a poor mother treating her child like that. You see worn young mothers, cadaverous themselves, with babies lying on their laps in a stillness close to death; you see mothers watching their children with empty eyes, the little ones in rags, with sores on their bodies, as skinny as their mothers. The gaze of people long hungry or extremely tired and with little hope is not focused on this world; and they have no energy for gestures of love. The love is there: the women will give the children whatever food they have, denying themselves. But it does not advertise itself.

And it seems to me now – and I must have had an inkling about this back then in 1951 – that the relation of mothers and children is maybe more profound and important than anything else in life. If it is omitted from consideration by philosophy, philosophy is the less. In 1951, lots of psychologists were considering the relations between mothers and children, but mainly in order to indict mothers for everything that goes wrong with their kids. No one that I knew of then – or now, for that matter – really examined what it means to a woman to have a child, and to devote herself to raising it; or the real nature of that most profound bond of child and mother. When people write about bonds, they're telling people to break them. Yet in simple societies, mothers raise their children gently and lovingly, and the daughters often stay on with their mothers and have children of their own, and there is little conflict, and no one charges the daughters with failure to separate, to mature. In our world, we're all supposed to break all bonds, to be independent.

I don't mean to make great claims for myself. I wasn't thinking, when I took those photographs, in exalted theoretical terms. I wasn't thinking at all. I took them because I couldn't help myself. I used to wonder, when I saw all these pictures of rage and teary frustration piling up in my bureau drawer, that perhaps I was trying to console myself. Because of course I never felt rage at my children. No steam emerged from my voice, seeped from my eyeballs. Like my mother, I never raised my voice. But maybe underneath that 'insistent cheerfulness' that Brad later told me drove him crazy, there were other, negative feelings that I concealed from myself. Maybe photographing other women expressing emotions they were not expected or supposed to feel was a way for me to deal with what I did not let myself know I felt.

In any case, I was obsessed with doing this work, and I got better and better at it, coming after a while to know what kinds of situations led babies to relax – when a baby was simply too tired to continue, and should just be allowed to nap for a while. I derived considerable pleasure from these afternoons, far more than the few dollars I earned from them. I knew, I knew that kaffeeklatsching was a waste of time, a foolish occupation, and our conversation mainly trivial, but those trivialities came to seem very important, as if each little concern was really an emblem for a larger context of concerns. Mostly, we told stories, made comic fictions of our lives. What we enjoyed most were stories of meddling mothers-in-law (mine, about the semen-stained sheet, aroused no laughter at all, only hushed shock), overflowing washing machines, rice blowing up to fill the entire kitchen sink, pressure-cooker explosions, leaking basements. They were centered on things that spilled over boundaries, like mothers-in-law (in those days), like children themselves, like household appliances, like us, whose bodies had overflowed themselves to produce these angel-demons who tyrannized and controlled our lives.

I'd go home more cheerful than ever after these afternoons. I quickly earned enough money to buy the equipment I needed for developing, and all I could think of after a session was to develop the film and see what I had. I'd push, tease, kid, and laugh the children home, into baths, through dinner (as often as not, hot dogs, I'm ashamed to say), and put a couple of frozen dinners in the oven for Brad and me, but I was thinking, thinking, thinking. I'd blow up one print, crop another, my mind was almost entirely on the other prints I'd developed that week, and on waiting for everyone to go to bed so I could lock myself in the bathroom and set up my equipment.

Sometimes there was trouble. One night Billy started to cry when I was at a crucial point in the work and couldn't open the bathroom door. It was late, after midnight, and I knew Billy would wake Brad, but I thought, the hell with it, let him get up for once. Brad was not thrilled when he realized I was not answering Billy's cries, and a little later he began to pound on the bathroom door.

'Open up! Billy's been sick!' he yelled angrily.

'I can't open the door now, Brad,' I called out apologetically. 'Can't you clean him up? Use the kitchen sink.'

'SHIT!' was his response. I heard his bare feet stalk off down the hall.

It was another fifteen minutes before I could open the door and see how things were. I peeked in our bedroom: Brad was in bed, snoring. I looked into the kids' room.

Billy was lying in the middle of his crib, on a clean part of the vomity sheet. Brad had wiped his face – that was it. I picked him up, he was whimpery and needed cuddling. I took him into the kitchen – I had prints hanging over the bathtub – and sat him on the edge of the sink, pushing aside the dinner dishes I'd left to dry after washing them, and undressed him. His little pajamas were stinky and hard with vomit, and there was vomit caked in his hair. I talked to him gently, wiping him with warm water and soap, and he leaned against me, calmed.

After I'd cleaned him up, I carried him back to his room. I had to turn on the light to find a clean pair of pajamas and a clean sheet, although I knew that would waken Arden, and I'd get little sleep tonight. I remade Billy's crib, all the while talking to him, trying to find out if his tummy was still upset or if he was better – difficult because he couldn't talk yet. But he seemed okay, so I put him back in his bed, gathered up the soiled sheet and blanket, and covered him with one of my jackets because I had no other blanket. By this time, Arden was sitting up in bed asking what was the matter and why had Daddy yelled and why was Mommy locked in the bathroom. No way she was going back to bed. So I let her get up, turned out the light so Billy could sleep, and took her into the kitchen with me and fed her cookies and milk while I waited for my prints to dry. We discussed photography and its effect upon daddies. Arden informed me that Daddy didn't like my taking pictures. I don't know how she had gleaned this, because *I* hadn't. But it turned out she was right.

I thought Brad was pleased with what he called my 'hobby'. He'd taken some prints, blown up and framed and hung them in his office – the one of Arden with the butterfly, and the one where she is holding out her hand to help Billy up, and another, a close-up of Arden with the sun shining through her hair. He didn't seem to be interested in photographs of Billy. He complained about my housekeeping and the meals I served, but that had been the case before I began taking pictures. So I wasn't prepared for the explosion that occurred the next day.

I started it, at breakfast, the one meal I cooked. He was

eating eggs and sausages and English muffins with cream cheese and I was drinking coffee. The kids had had their breakfasts and were playing in the living room, still in pajamas. I closed the kitchen door. I said, in a low voice so the children wouldn't hear, 'Brad, what you did last night was really rotten – to leave that kid in vomity pajamas on a vomity sheet!'

He threw down his fork. 'What *I* did was rotten! What about you? What kind of mother doesn't go to her kid when he cries in the night? Won't come out of the fucking bathroom even though he's sick? You and your goddamned photography! Who do you think you are, Margaret Bourke-White? You're a stupid housewife earning some pin money by taking stupid pictures of stupid babies and their stupid mothers! And *that* is more important to you than your own child! What kind of mother are you, anyway! I'll tell you! No mother at all! You're still a spoiled brat kid who refuses to grow up and accept her responsibilities! Giving the kids hot dogs for dinner practically every night! And if I see another TV dinner, I think I'll puke! I want that photography equipment, that fucking developing equipment, your camera, all of it, out of this house when I come home tonight! I don't want to see it again, I don't want to bump into another clothesline full of prints, I don't want to hear the word photography again! Is that clear?'

My face felt as if it were 110 degrees and my heart was pumping too hard. If he'd stopped short of the final command, I would have been in trouble. I wouldn't have known what to answer. I knew it was my job to clean the house and provide decent meals, I just couldn't stand doing it. But I felt guilty about that. But his order to remove my photography equipment had carried him over the line from being right, or anyway justified, to being dictatorial. I stood up.

'How dare you!' I whispered, in a whisper that I could see penetrated his marrow. 'How in hell dare you talk to me that way? Who do you think *you* are? If you want to spend your entire stupid life in a stupid job like selling real estate, and immerse yourself in numbers and dollars for twenty-four hours a day, you are free to do so. But don't for a minute think you can dictate what my life will be!'

He had stood up too by this time. 'Who I think I am is the breadwinner of this family! I earn the money that supports your stupid hobby, and I have the right to order you to stop it!'

'You may earn the money, but I do everything else,' I countered, undaunted. 'I wash and iron your fucking shirts, just like my fucking mother. I scrub the floors and cook the food and raise *your* children. . . .'

I knew the minute it was out of my mouth that that was a tactical error.

'*My* children! So you say! Who the hell ordered them from the stork, I'd like to know. It certainly wasn't me. You ruined my life, you forced me into marriage and this career, and if you don't like it, lady, lie in the bed you made! *I* have to!'

He shouted this, and I was only grateful the kids could not possibly understand that he was denying his parentage of them, if they heard him, which they could not have avoided doing. Then he slammed open the kitchen door, stormed down the hall for his coat, and slammed out of the apartment.

I sank down in a chair again. My hands were shaking so hard I needed two to pick up my mug of coffee, and even so I spilled it on my leg and it was hot and I cried out, it burned so terribly, everything hurt so terribly. And the kids heard my cry and came running in to see what was wrong. I explained I had spilled my coffee, but Arden looked at me with a wizened little face, as if she were fifty instead of two and a half, and contradicted me: I was being punished, she said, because Daddy didn't like the way I made the bed.

I had an appointment to photograph that day, but I called and canceled it, saying I had the flu. The way my voice sounded after my crying backed up my lie, and we made another date a week off. After that, I just collapsed. I couldn't move. I let the kids play in the living room; they knew they were being given some sort of license, and were running up and down the narrow hall to the bedrooms, shrieking and laughing hysterically, still in their pajamas.

I sat at the kitchen table drinking coffee and smoking. I was trying to think, but it was difficult, because I had to work so hard at not crying. I didn't want the kids to see me crying, I didn't want to cry, I didn't want to be so vulnerable that I needed to cry. But I was. Suddenly, my old feelings for the old Brad washed over me like a huge wave that surprises you, coming from behind as you stand in knee-deep surf, and knocking you down. I remembered, oh I remembered. And I didn't want to remember. I didn't want to hold up our past against our present. I above all didn't want to *think* about what our lives had become.

The overriding priority was not thinking about what we had just said. Because I didn't see how, having said such things to each other, we could ever live together again. And I didn't know how I could manage to separate from him. I wanted to: I wanted to pack up our things and march us out of there and never go back. But how? I had – I checked – $11.38 in my wallet, and there was $145.68 in our checking account. (Brad had another checking account for business dealings – something I didn't know then.) Even if I drew all of that out, it wouldn't get me far. And how would I go? By baby carriage? I didn't have a car.

All I had was a mother.

I picked up the phone, and tried to sound casual. Mom was pleased: since I'd been doing photography, she hadn't seen much of me. She'd be glad to drive over and pick me and the kids up and take us back to her house for the day. That was fine.

I jumped up then, to prepare us, and was ready when she arrived. At first I didn't tell her anything about what had happened. We went back to her house and had lunch, and the kids went in for naps, and we played Chinese checkers and talked idly, and then we had a drink, and the kids woke up and I put them out in the yard to play. And then I told her, my voice shaking, that Brad and I were not getting along, that he had said unforgivable things, that he had suggested the kids weren't his, and that I didn't see how I could go on living with him.

We were sitting on the porch, both smoking and sipping scotch and water.

After I told her how things were with Brad and me, she was silent for a while. Then she said, 'I never thought he was stable.'

'You never said anything about it.'

She shrugged. 'When you set your mind on something, Anastasia . . . Besides, what else could you do but marry him?'

I was silent then too, remembering the other Brad.

'What will you do?' she asked at last.

'I thought I could go back to Jimmy Minetta's . . . he'd let me set up a counter of my own, I'm sure he would. I'd work part-time for him and part of the time I'd take photographs of children, the way I do now. But I'd charge a little more.'

'How much could you earn?' Her tone was discouraging. 'You couldn't earn enough to support yourself and the kids.'

'Maybe not.' I let my voice trail off, waiting.

She heard what I was not saying. 'I suppose you'd like to come back here to live.'

I didn't take heart from this. Her tone was too negative.

She sipped her scotch. 'But you know, I feel that I raised my children, I've done my duty. I'm tired.'

I felt utterly shut out, felt the breeze as the door slammed in my face; but I also felt the justice of her feelings. She'd done it once, and once is enough.

'Well, it could be just for a year or two, until I can get on my feet,' I said casually, trying not to sound as if I were begging.

'But it's Dad,' she went on as if I hadn't spoken, 'I really can't ask Dad to accept it. You know how he feels about children, you know how he was with you. I can't ask him to live in a house with little children again.'

And that was that. I knew my father would not be happy having small kids in the house again; their noise and chaos seemed to frighten him, he became grouchy and ill at ease when my kids were around. He was anxious every minute as if they would, in the next second, unleash violence upon furniture, rugs, walls, and windows. But I also knew that my father would accept whatever my mother asked him to accept – that if she wanted to take me in and urged it, that he would accept it completely. But I knew too that if I moved in with them, Mother would end up baby-sitting part of every day. I couldn't work and take the kids with me. Her new freedom and ease would vanish. I couldn't blame her for not wanting that. I could see things from her perspective, and as in the past, seeing things from her perspective made it impossible to see them from my own. So I had no way at all to respond. I just sat there, numb. Finally, I found a voice that wouldn't squeak:

'Would you mind if we stayed overnight?'

'Of course not. Did you bring pajamas for the children?'

I had. I had brought enough clothes to stay a week, but I didn't tell her that.

I didn't need them. We had dinner together, and I put the kids to bed upstairs in my old room, and we were sitting on the porch, my parents and I, watching television when Brad showed up, late, near ten. No surprise. He knew I had nowhere else to go. He sat with us through the eleven o'clock news, after which my parents politely, almost ceremoniously excused themselves.

When the noises of doors opening and closing had ended, and the bathroom light was turned off for the last time, Brad turned to me and spoke in a very low voice. It reminded me of how we had acted years before, before we were married.

'Are you planning to stay here?'

It came to me that he needn't know how desperate I was. 'Yes.'

'Look, I'm sorry I was so high-handed this morning. I was really upset.'

'Really?' I was cold. It surprised me to hear the coldness in my voice, I hadn't known I could sound so icy. 'I was thinking about the afternoon Billy hit Arden over the head with the carpenter's plane and cut her skull open and I had to get her to a doctor and didn't have a car, and I called your office and you were out showing a house. Do you consider that a flaw in your fatherhood?'

'Stahz, I couldn't help that. I didn't know about it. I was working!'

'And I was working last night. It may seem like nothing to you, but it's important to me. And what happened last night was nowhere near as serious. And you were there to take care of it, and, you shit, you left that baby lying in vomit!'

He chewed on the inside of his lower lip. He was drinking beer, and he held up the bottle and let half of it pour down his open throat. I never knew how he could do that, and I hated it. It seemed obscene to me, especially at that moment. I was so cold and angry, I was even armed against comments about my cooking – or rather, my noncooking. But he didn't make any.

'The place seemed so empty tonight when I got home.'

'And when was that? At nine-thirty? It took you long enough to notice we were gone.'

'No.' Shamefaced. 'I went out for dinner with Len Watkins. To talk over a deal.'

I made a face. I knew him too well. 'I see. And you did that without calling, so I'd be sure to worry, right?'

He didn't answer.

'Where'd you get the money to go out for dinner anyway? We can never go out for dinner.'

He squirmed in his chair, lighted a cigarette.

I decided to pursue my advantage. 'You may not like the way we live, but I'm not crazy about it either. I'm stuck in a place miles from any stores, without a car, with two babies. I have barely enough money to get by each week, yet you made a couple of hundred thousand dollars on that real-estate deal. . . .'

'No, no, I didn't. The agency got most of it.'

'So how much did you get?' I was relentless now. I'd never questioned him about money, I had wanted him to feel free, a big man, a big deal.

'Sixty.'

'Sixty dollars?'

He made a face at my stupidity.

'Sixty thou, Stahz,' he corrected impatiently. He was torn, I could see it. On the one hand, he didn't want to tell me how much he'd made because then I might ask for some of it; on the other, he wanted to seem a big deal in my eyes.

'Sixty thousand dollars!'

He wiped his hand across his face and mouth. 'Look, I know. But I spent most of it buying a parcel of land off Merrick Road. Dad says it's a sure thing. I'll triple or quadruple my money in a few years.'

'That's nice,' I said in a dead voice.

We sat in silence. He got up to get himself another beer and asked if I wanted another drink. I did, but I wouldn't let him get it for me. I waited until he came back and sat down, then I got up and got one for myself. I felt stupid and childish, but I couldn't help myself. Letting him get me a drink would somehow be giving in; it would be accepting his gift of a service, and I wanted him to think I wanted nothing from him.

'Stahz, come back,' he urged, finally.

'To what? A man who's never home, who refuses to have anything to do with his own children, who even suggests they're not his. . . .'

'I'm sorry. Really. I was crazy, I didn't mean it. I love you.'

'Well, I don't love you very much anymore.' I'd said it in pique, but was astonished, as I did, to realize it was true.

'Stahz, I'll make things better. I'll get you a car, and I'll give you more money. We'll go out for dinner. I promise.'

'You don't love me.' I was mortified to hear my voice sound thick the way it does when your nose clogs up with tears. I didn't want to betray the least degree of feeling. 'You hate that I can't cook.'

'Ah, Stahz.' He'd heard the nasal thickness, he knew he was safe. Damn it. He reached out his arms to me, and when I didn't move, he came and sat on the floor beside me and put his arms around my waist. 'I didn't marry a cook, I married a skinny long-legged kook, an artist, a bohemian, a crazy photographer.'

Now I was really crying. 'You didn't marry a photographer. I was a painter in those days, and would be one still if . . .'

Just as well I didn't finish that statement, lying through my teeth as I was. He kissed me, and I found myself kissing him back.

That was the way it went. I stayed overnight that night because I didn't want to waken the kids, but Brad came early the next morning to fetch us. I went back, or he brought me back: that was the truth of it. We never talked about what we felt, about our bad feelings for each other, our bad feelings about our lives. He offered me a bigger allowance, a car, and dinner out every two weeks, and he delivered all but the car. I had to wait for that. My allowance was raised by ten dollars. In return, I got out the cookbook my mother had given me when I got married, and tried to prepare real food. Dinnertime became tense, as everyone came to the table warily, examining what monstrosity I had managed to produce that night, and the kids said, often enough, that they wished I'd go back to hot dogs and hamburgers. The lima bean casserole was incredibly dry, and Brad had to go out and buy us a pizza; and the chicken orientale was swimming in pineapple juice. Arden suggested we drink it instead of eating it. In time, I was given permission by the entire family to abstain from an occupation I clearly had no talent for. But by that time I was determined to continue to try.

Nothing else changed in our marriage. I went on developing film at night, and when one night Billy woke up again, and Brad again pounded on the bathroom door, I told him to have Billy pee in the kitchen sink.

His response to that was a silence whose shock I could sense clear through the door. But somehow, Billy did pee that night, and was sleeping soundly in a dry crib when I checked him later.

I went on as before, taking pictures, charging a little more for them. I was able to buy developing equipment, a used Rollei, and a telephoto lens. My next goal was a Leica, for close-up portrait work. Photography consumed me, and if I never said anything like 'I am a photographer,' I knew myself to be one.

But something bad happened to me through this quarrel and its seeming resolution. I felt it happening at the time, but I didn't then think of it as bad. I thought it was natural, mature, that I was finally putting away childish things and becoming a man, I mean a woman, well, a grown-up. It had to do with the way I saw love and the relations between husbands and wives. I recognized that in our quarrel, I had essentially made a power play, had pretended strength I didn't have, had accepted material things as an emblem of victory. Something hardened in me. I began to see Brad the way he saw himself, as our breadwinner. Or to put it crassly, our meal ticket, our necessary evil. Only now – god knows it's more than twenty-five years later – do I really understand what happened that night. I lost my virginity.

four

Monday was washday, whether it shone or rained. When it rained, Belle hung the laundry in the basement, thanking heaven for the basement, remembering having to hang it in the apartment. It was harder to hang it in the basement than in the yard because she had only three lines there, and the basement was damp except near the furnace, and things dried more slowly and she had to keep running up-and downstairs. But at least it wasn't in the house itself. (She wasn't fanatic about the laundry, like some women – like Adeline Carpenter – who had to have their wash on the line before nine in the morning. Adeline considered women who didn't get their wash out that early sluts; she viewed them with the horrified contempt most people reserve for prostitutes. They were scandalous. So were women who served dinner in the kitchen. 'Shanty Irish,' Brad's father would pronounce when he looked across from their dining room windows to the family next door sitting around the kitchen table at dinner hour. Adeline simply went 'Tsk, tsk,' but her judgment of such people was harsher than his.)

Tuesday, Belle ironed. She had a system for this too. First, she sprinkled all the starched clothes and rolled them tightly together, and wrapped them in a dampened sheet.

She felt she was liberal, modern, about ironing. Unlike her mother, she did not iron socks, or the girls' underpants, or undershirts, although she ran a warm iron over her own rayon step-ins, and her brassiere, and starched *and* pressed Ed's undershorts.

First, she ironed things that required only a warm iron: her underwear and nightgown. As the iron got hotter she did Ed's shorts and pajamas; then blouses, dresses and handkerchiefs; then the kitchen towels, the sheets and pillowcases; and finally Ed's white shirts and the tablecloths. It took many hours, because she ironed carefully, every surface smoothed down, ironed inside and out. Her work was beautiful, and seeing it stacked on the kitchen table gave her pleasure.

Wednesday was relatively free. She did some mending, or if she were making clothes for the children, she did the bulk of it on Wednesday. On Thursday, and again on Saturday, she went to the market. This was the high point of her week. She would dress neatly, not in her good clothes, but in a neat housedress and heels and her old coat, but no hat. She would powder her face, fill in her eyebrows with the eyebrow pencil, and apply lipstick. Then she would walk the three long blocks to Sutphin Boulevard, and four more long windy blocks to the A & P, six to Big Ben.

These marketing expeditions were always efficiently planned. Belle always carefully examined the circulars sent out Wednesdays by the supermarkets, and knew in advance which sale items she would buy at which store. Her second consideration was weight: she tried to buy heavy items last, so she would not have to carry them as far. And because she had to carry the packages home those long blocks, she could never buy more than would fill three or at most four paper sacks. The third consideration was need and what is now called cash flow. She would walk the extra two blocks to Big Ben to get lima beans if they were two cents a pound cheaper there than in the A & P. The entire affair required painstaking management.

On Thursdays, they were often out of food, but she had to be extremely careful because she was at the end of her housekeeping money. Ed got paid on Fridays. Thursdays, she bought only food for that night and Friday. Things like toilet paper, soap, paper napkins and paper towels (used sparingly), and staples she would buy on Saturdays, along with roasts for the weekend, which she hoped would last until Wednesday. In bad weeks, when there was some unexpected expense (Joy was ill and she had to pay the doctor, the weather was extremely cold and they ran out of coal) she had only a few cents left on Thursday and would just send Anastasia up to the local butcher for fifteen cents' worth of chop meat or bologna.

Although she felt a certain anxiety about how much she was spending, she enjoyed marketing. It gave her pleasure to stretch her tiny store of money, and to produce the wonderful meals she gave her family. Friday-night dinner was the worst problem, because she had really run out of money by then. But since it was Friday, she had a good excuse for not serving meat, and that helped. Every other night, they had meat for dinner. Their portions were often small, and Belle adamantly shared what there was equally among the four of them: in her house, the poppa did not get the lion's share with the children watching hungrily, the way she'd seen meals in other families. No. They each got one meatball, or one lamb chop or pork chop. Only when there was a roast could they each have as much as they really wanted, but Ed was so mean, he tried to deny the children a second helping of meat. 'Have more vegetables!' he'd bark at them. And she would always have to say, 'Oh, Ed, give them another slice.' And he'd reluctantly carve another, so thin you could almost see through it, and she'd have to watch, and often to say, 'Give her a decent piece, Ed.' Then he'd be annoyed, and would not have seconds of meat himself, but would pile his plate with all the vegetables and potatoes that were left in the serving bowls. So she'd have to say, 'Oh, Ed, why don't you have some more meat,' before he would take another slice for himself, and he wouldn't take it even then unless he said first, in a loving voice, 'But how about you, Belle? A little of the outside?' If she wanted it, he'd heap her plate.

*

On Friday, Belle cleaned the house thoroughly. She didn't do the heavy work. That was done only twice a year, and Ed and the children helped. In spring and fall, she would take down all the curtains and wash them by hand and dry them on great wooden stretchers that filled the living room and porch. All the dishes came out of all closets and were washed, and replaced on cleaned shelves. All the books were taken from their shelves and dusted, and the shelves wiped down with a damp cloth. She and Ed together lifted the rugs and carried them outside, and hung them on the clothesline, and Ed would hit them with the carpet beater. And she and Ed together washed all the windows, inside and out, with ammonia in water and polished them with newspaper that she had saved up for a few weeks.

But every Friday, she tied an old cloth around the dry mop and mopped the woodwork around the ceiling, and the walls; then she used the dry mop itself on the wood floors. She vacuumed; and then she dusted. It was important to do the dusting last, or you would have to do it again. The bathroom was completely washed-down – tiles, the fixtures cleaned with Bon Ami or Old Dutch cleanser, and the inside of the toilet bowl cleaned with a hard brush. Later was the kitchen. The side cabinet was wiped down, and the glass doors of the dish shelves washed. You had to do this often in a kitchen because of the grease. She cleaned the top and front of the stove, and washed the kitchen floor with a wet mop. When that was done, she was finished – except for cleaning the mop – and she would treat herself to a cup of coffee and a cigarette, and put her feet up on another kitchen chair.

Other tasks were sprinkled in among these standing chores. She would bake a pie or an apple bar sometimes; and most days she made some kind of dessert early in the day. And she still had to dress Joy and bathe both girls, and sometimes she took Joy with her to the grocery store, if Anastasia was not at home to watch her. And in the evenings she would darn her rayon hose with a special needle she had discovered, that filled up ladders; and turn the collars of Ed's old shirts; and she always made each of the girls a sunsuit for the summer and a dress for Easter Sunday.

She was not altogether isolated. The Italian vegetable man came through with his wagon once a week, and she usually bought something from him and chatted a little about the weather. The iceman, also Italian, came by every few days in the summer, and every week in winter, often accompanied by his little son, who helped him carry in the big block of ice with a set of giant tongs. The iceman spoke very little English, but he was very sweet, and always smiled and nodded his head. The little boy was so shy he would hardly look up at Belle. He worked hard for a five-year-old, and she felt sorry for him. He made her remember. . . .

And sometimes the knife grinder came by too, but she never hired him. Ed kept her knives and scissors sharp. It was an unnecessary expense, and they had no unnecessary expenses. Belle never bought soft drinks or pretzels or candy. The only reason she bought canned goods was in case of a crisis; they almost never ate anything from a can except peaches out of season and Boston brown bread, which Belle loved when they had frankfurters and beans. She would steam it hot in the can, and breathe in the aroma as she opened it.

And in a very short time, she had come to know most of her neighbors. They were nice people, although Belle never allowed herself to get too close to them. There was Mrs Carle. She lived next door, and her husband owned the house Belle and Ed rented. He was tall and thin and very somber, and Minnie had already confessed to Belle that he beat her. It was terrible, especially since Minnie, who wore a lot of makeup and dyed her hair blond and had once been (she said) a chorus girl, was tiny, less than five feet tall, and had a humpback. Minnie went out every morning and cleaned the house of some wealthy people in Richmond Hill, and whenever she came over to have coffee with Belle, she would tell her about this rich family. Belle learned a lot from her about the way rich people do things. These rich people had a son in college, and they were worried about him. He was unstable.

The McClintocks lived across the street. Mrs McClintock worked as a telephone operator, and she told Belle how she had to hide her purse, because her husband would take all the money she had and lose it at the races. Belle thought privately that Mr McClintock, who was rarely seen by daylight, also drank, but Mrs McClintock never mentioned that. She idolized her daughter Dorothy, a nice-looking girl, sober and sensible, just starting high school. Her mother thought she was very smart. Belle thought that Dorothy at thirteen was not as smart as Anastasia at six, but of course she said nothing of the sort. Minnie Carle only worked until two each day, and so she came over for coffee often, pushing the buzzer of the side door and entering through the cellar steps into the kitchen. Mrs McClintock worked longer hours, and came over only when she had a day off, which wasn't often. Even when she had spare time, she had to take care of her house and do the laundry and the marketing.

There were others, too. In the afternoons, when her work was finished, Belle would go upstairs and wash herself and put on a fresh housedress and makeup, and fix her hair, and on nice days, sit out on the front stoop. People would pass by and stop and chat: Mrs Murphy, who was the organist at St Mary's and who lived up the block and had to pass Belle's house when she went to the church; and Mrs Callahan, whose husband, Belle soon discovered, was a thief and a drug addict. Mrs Callahan was very skinny and harried-looking, and she often had bruises on her face and arms, but she never confided in Belle. There were the Schinkels, and two families of Costellos who lived side by side and were neat and quiet and did not mix with the others in the neighborhood. Across the street were two more German families; Mr Bock was a butcher in Jamaica, and Mrs McClintock told Belle he used to chain his teen-aged daughter to her bed when he went out at night – and he went out every night. From his color, Belle sensed he drank considerably too. His daughter was never seen by the neighbors, and it was unknown whether she went to school. It was strange, in such a little neighborhood, such a nosey block, how many people were never seen. The

DiNapolis lived in the end house, directly across the street from Mr DiNapolis's parents. The older Mrs DiNapoli could sometimes be seen in their backyard, which bordered the sidewalk, sitting near a fig tree and bushes espaliered in the ancient way, in a black dress, huge, on a folding chair. But the younger Mrs DiNapoli never showed herself at all, and had it not been for the children who regularly appeared every couple of years, Belle would have doubted her existence.

Belle did not know why she felt superior to these people, only that she did. She had no concept of cultural class, and would never have said or even thought that none of these people knew who Mozart was, or had read books, or gone to art school. But this was the difference she felt. She did not find an Elvira in South Ozone Park, and she never confided any problems to the women who came for coffee. She listened, she did not gossip, she never told tales, she treated them with respect. They liked her, she could tell. She felt at peace. She was almost happy.

Anastasia was skipped past 1B, and again, and again, and soon she was miserable. She was as bored as ever in school; no matter how fast they skipped her, she could learn everything they had to learn in that grade in the first week, and after that, she sat daydreaming. The teachers sent her to the back of the room to teach slow students, or asked her to write the school play; or sent her to the small room that served as the school library, to catalog its holdings; or sent her to the principal's office to run errands. But she remained bored. In addition, she was no longer popular. Two years younger than her classmates, tiny in stature, and raised smooth in a rough neighborhood, she was overwhelmed socially, and crawled more and more into a dream life. She suffered frequently from stomachache, and Mommy would usually let her stay home. Then she could read and draw and play with her paper dolls and listen to the soap operas on the radio, and she was, if not happy, less unhappy than she was in school. She had no friends and her timidity was so extreme she could barely speak to another child. Surrounded by yelling roughhousing kids, she felt threatened, and cultivated a superior disdainful manner to protect herself. When she asked Mommy why the other kids didn't like her, Mommy always said they were jealous. Anastasia suspected this was not the case, but she gave her soul a hard shrug and told herself she didn't care about them anyway, they were all stupid.

She was just as frightened of the kids on the block, most of them either considerably older or younger than she, but she wondered at herself, because Joy, at three and four, ran outdoors first thing in the morning and played happily with the other children all day long. She didn't understand why she should be frightened of the children little Joy played with, but she was. She explained to herself that they were stupid and Joy was a baby and that was why they could play with each other. For she already knew, Mommy had told her many times, that Joy was just a baby, that she wasn't as smart as Anastasia, and that Anastasia had to be forbearing, like an adult, with her younger sister. Most of the time that was not hard, because Joy was sweet and always looked up at Anastasia with a sweet trusting smile; but sometimes, when Joy messed up something that belonged to Anastasia, it was impossible, and Anastasia would burst out 'I hate her!' and then Mommy would refuse to speak to her.

The best time of day was dinner. Mommy made such good dinners. One time, Anastasia had to go to fetch Joy from the Costellos, where she had been playing with Dolores, who was Joy's best friend, and she went into the kitchen and they were eating dinner, and they each had a big plate of potatoes in front of them. Just potatoes, imagine! Another time she went for Joy, they were eating cabbage. But Mommy told Joy it was rude to stay while the Costellos ate and she had to come home then. So Anastasia never saw if they had anything else for dinner.

In their house, they had something different for dinner every night. Mommy made meatballs; she mixed up chop meat (which Anastasia loved raw, but it was bad for you, so she would sneak a fingerful when Mommy wasn't looking) with bread and milk and onions cooked in bacon fat until they were yellow, and they were delicious. With the meatballs, they had mashed potatoes and peas, or peas and carrots, or string beans. They had lamb chops, but she always wished she could have two, but no one had two, even Mommy and Daddy only had one little loin chop. Sometimes they had pork chops, which were a little bigger than lamb chops and almost as good. Most of all, Anastasia loved the fat Mommy cut off pork chops before she fried them. She'd cut it into little pieces, and melt it in the frying pan, and take out the pieces when she put the chops in the pan. And Anastasia was allowed to eat some of the little pieces that were drying on a paper towel. Sometimes they had frankfurters and beans and brown bread, but Anastasia didn't like brown bread. She ate it because she was hungry. And Mommy made spaghetti with Mueller's spaghetti and a can of Campbell's tomato soup, and that was good too.

On Sundays, they had a big dinner: pot roast with gravy; or roasted chicken; or roast pork with crackling brown skin with applesauce; or roast lamb; or baked Virginia ham. Even when she didn't like something, like ham, she ate it because she was hungry. There were vegetables she didn't like, for instance: turnips, and brussels sprouts, and cabbage. Even with the butter melting on it, cabbage didn't taste good. But Mommy always said just take a little, and then you can have dessert. And Anastasia would, because she loved dessert.

Anastasia knew when Mommy didn't have money because of what they had for dinner, but she felt it didn't matter, because she liked the things they had to eat then just as well as the others. Mommy made lamb stew and put carrots and onions and potatoes in it and it was delicious. And sometimes they only had canned soup and bologna sandwiches, but Anastasia loved that. They had scalloped potatoes and baked potatoes and boiled potatoes with scallions and butter on them, but Anastasia's favorite was mashed. Spinach burned her tongue, but Mommy said it was good for her. And she didn't like cauliflower, but when Mommy put cream sauce and paprika on it, it tasted okay. Or sometimes, she would put little browned bread crumbs on it. She put them on asparagus too.

Only on Fridays, when she came downstairs from

reading in her room and smelled the dinner, many times her heart sank. On Fridays they didn't have meat, and Anastasia loved meat. But she didn't mind if they had macaroni and cheese with spinach; or french fried eggplant with tomatoes and scalloped potatoes; or creamed spinach with poached eggs and potatoes fried with onions. But sometimes they had vegetables she didn't like; and sometimes they had fish. Mommy would bake a mackerel in the oven, and as soon as she smelled it, Anastasia wanted to cry.

It was terrible, she knew it was terrible and babyish to be that way, but she so much looked forward to dinner, and when it was something she really hated, she couldn't help crying inside her heart. She never cried outside. She hated the smell of the fish and the taste, it was dry and tasted bad like liver, which they also sometimes had for dinner. But she wouldn't cry, she'd just play with her food and Mommy would say just eat a little Anastasia, and you can have dessert, and Anastasia would eat a few mouthfuls and Daddy would finish her dinner.

On Friday, Mommy would usually make a good dessert. Chocolate or vanilla pudding from a My-T-Fine package, with whipped cream on top; or Jell-O with whipped cream and fruit. Mommy made her own puddings too, but Anastasia didn't like them as much as My-T-Fine. Mommy made bread pudding, which Anastasia hated, but she would put a lot of the lemony hard sauce on it, and then it was good. And she made rice pudding with raisins, and tapioca. Daddy loved Mommy's puddings. Sometimes she made pie for Sunday dinner, and lemon meringue pie was Anastasia's favorite thing in the world except for lamb chops and icebox cake. When Mommy made icebox cake, she let Anastasia lick the whipped cream bowl. And sometimes she made crepes, little French pancakes. She'd fill half of them with jelly and the other half with cottage cheese mixed with sugar and cinnamon. Anastasia could never decide which ones she liked better. And in the summer, Mommy would make strawberry shortcake or banana shortcake, which Anastasia loved even though she didn't like bananas. In the fall, Mommy made baked apples with cream. That was bad, and Anastasia often didn't finish hers, which made Daddy happy because he could have two. But sad as it made her to have a dessert she didn't like, it didn't make her want to cry, the way fish and liver did. Sometimes for dessert they only had canned peaches, but that was all right, Anastasia loved them; she liked them better than canned pears. And *sometimes:* she didn't know why it happened: but *sometimes* they would have a big gooey chocolate layer cake from a bakery. And then Anastasia's mouth would water even before dinner, just looking at it. Her eyes would widen and she wanted to put her finger in the icing and lick it, but Mommy said she should wait, so she did.

If dinner was the best thing in the day, dinner*time* was not. If Anastasia's mouth watered when she smelled the lamb chops or the meat loaf cooking, she always tensed up as she approached the dinner table. They ate in the kitchen, because they didn't have a dining room, but Mommy always set the table nicely, with the silver laid out properly and the napkins on the right side and the salt and pepper and butter on the edges of the table with the bowls of steaming food in the center. They all would help themselves, except when there was a roast and Daddy carved it. But Mommy always got funny just at the time for dinner, strange, almost annoyed. She always was, putting the dinner on the table exactly as Daddy walked in the back door at 5:15. She had already called them: 'Children! Dinner's ready! Wash your hands!' And sometimes Anastasia looked at her hands and they weren't dirty, so she didn't wash them, and when she entered the kitchen, Mommy would always say, in her annoyed-before-dinner voice, 'Did you wash your hands?' and Anastasia would say 'Yes,' even if it was a lie. But sometimes Mommy would call her over and look at her hands, turn them over in *her* hands, and once they were dirty. Anastasia saw it before Mommy did: there was black from her pencil all over one finger. And Mommy said,

'Anastasia, your hands are filthy! You couldn't have washed them! Go and wash them!'

Anastasia walked toward the kitchen sink, which was

hard for her to reach, but Mommy insisted she go upstairs to the bathroom to do it.

She sounded really mad, so Anastasia ran back up to the bathroom, but she muttered 'Why do I have to go upstairs,' and she felt Mommy was being mean and petty for no reason (she didn't know the word capricious), was acting mad at Anastasia just because she was mad at something. Still, angry as she was, her throat had a lump in it and she wanted to cry because Mommy talked to her that way. She didn't understand herself. Because she heard other children's mothers talking to them, and they yelled and screeched and called them names and were horrible, and other children didn't cry. Sometimes they turned around and muttered something nasty like, 'Yeah, ya old man's mustache' (a phrase she did not comprehend, but knew to be insulting). And children talked about their parents in insulting ways, calling them 'my old lady' and 'my old man'. Anastasia would never describe her parents that way. But the other children didn't cry. Why did Anastasia always feel like crying? She couldn't understand it. The least thing made her teary. She was a baby. She knew it and she tried not to be, but she still was. She went back downstairs with pink scrubbed hands and a frown. But Mommy didn't even look at her hands, she was talking in her annoyed-before-dinner voice to Joy and then Daddy came in.

They always said 'Hello, Daddy,' whenever he came home and sometimes he would say 'Hello, Anastasia, hello, Joy,' in a friendly voice, and sometimes his voice wasn't friendly. But he was always nice to Mommy. He would come in and say 'Hello, Belle,' in a special voice, as if he loved her. Then he would carry his hat to the cellar door, where he'd put up hooks, and put his hat on one hook and take off his coat and hang it on a hanger and put that on another hook. And then he'd walk over to Mommy as if he were dancing, as if he were sliding across the floor, and he'd put out his arms to embrace her and bend his face to kiss her. And Mommy would turn her face quickly so her cheek was toward him and he'd kiss her cheek and sometimes he'd try to hug her. Anastasia would turn her head when he did this because she couldn't stand it. Because he wanted to hug Mommy and she wouldn't let him; and Anastasia felt terrible for her father because she knew that it must feel bad if you wanted to kiss someone and they wouldn't kiss you back.

Then Mommy would say 'Dinner is ready'. Mommy never asked if Daddy had washed his hands, but Daddy's hands were always clean. And then they could sit, and Mommy would pass the bowls around, helping Joy because Joy was just a baby. Mommy would cut up Joy's meat. Daddy used to cut up Anastasia's but now she was a big girl and could cut it herself. And each one would get some of everything, and then they would eat. It was very quiet. Sometimes Daddy would say something about the big boss, or Mommy would say 'Anastasia got a hundred per cent in an arithmetic test today', and Daddy would turn to her and say 'Good, Anastasia'. But that was all.

Once in a great while, Daddy would have steam coming out of him: once he told a story about niggers who had ripped out the stairs in a building to make a fire in their stove: he was appalled at that. Anastasia asked 'What are niggers?' and Mommy glared at Daddy and said it was a bad word she wasn't to use and Anastasia said 'Daddy said it', and Mommy said grown-ups could say it but not children and all it meant was people with brown skins. But Anastasia was still horrified by people who would tear out steps to make a fire, and she wondered why people with brown skins would do that. She decided they must have been cold, and if they were, then maybe it was all right, but Daddy seemed to think it was the worst thing he had ever seen. But mostly he said nothing and Mommy said nothing. Anastasia could hear Daddy chewing. He chewed carefully, he chewed each mouthful forty times, the way they did at West Point. He said they should do that too, Anastasia and Joy. But Mommy didn't have to do it. But Anastasia set her teeth and wouldn't do it. Neither did Joy. Anastasia hated Daddy's chewing, it made her feel enraged, crazy, she wanted to scream at him, to pound on the table. But of course she didn't.

And then, if they had a roast, Daddy never wanted to

let them have seconds and Mommy would always make him give it to them and he would carve a tiny piece and practically throw it on her plate and she could feel how he hated her. And she wanted to go to sleep, because she would feel very tired. Her dinner was gone, the best time of day was over, and she hated them, she hated Mommy who turned her cheek from Daddy and Daddy, who hated her and Joy, and yet she knew that Daddy would be happy if only Mommy would let him hug her and Mommy would be happy if Daddy made more money and she knew above all that the love her mother felt for her was there, in the dinner, in the food Mommy gave her, and somehow, although she loved the food, it wasn't enough.

five

Ah, it is impossible to make judgments. People do, of course: we make them all the time, running around in the world saying this is good and that is bad, and I suppose, believing what we say. But it's just so much nonsense. Even the shrinks, who, you'd imagine, would be beyond such things, insist on judgments. My friend Clara wants me to go to a shrink. She took me in hand one soggy night and led me to the only door left for me, she said. She said I was severely depressed. That surprised me: Cheerful Nellie, depressed? Of course, I'd spent the entire evening in her apartment crying. I took the hint. She didn't want to listen to *that* anymore: who could blame her? And who knows, maybe she's right. But I don't want to go to a shrink and be urged to make judgments. Because if you stand somewhere and call it yourself, and judge others according to what they do or don't do to you or for you, then you can never be better than biased and personal and *small*. Yes, *small*. You can't get the 'big picture', you have no perspective wider than your personal trivialities. And I have spent years of my life trying to get beyond the personal and trivial, to find the universal.

When I stand here looking down the long corridor of my memory to that Depression kitchen, the old gas stove on legs, with a tiny sharp ledge running around it on which I never failed to hit my temple when I went to kiss Mommy good night; the old sinks, also on legs, with an enameled metal drainboard covering the deep tub; the cabinet with its glass doors behind which were all our dishes, and the two deep drawers that held flatware and utensils, and the double-doored cupboard beneath that held all our pots, and the door to the pantry, where the icebox was; when I see that wooden table and chairs painted aqua and decorated with floral decals; and the four people sitting on those chairs: she powdered and lipsticked with bobbed marcel-waved hair, in a fresh housedress, a little prim around the mouth, a little tentative around the eyes; he in his white shirt that he wore carefully so it would be clean for a second wearing, and his muscular body and full head of black hair, his innocent boy's face that rarely smiled; they, the children, thin and gawky, the one all legs, the other a halo of blond hair, restless and uncomfortable, being scolded for putting their elbows on the table: when I see them sitting there in silence, all I want to do is cry. Cry for them all. Cry, cry, cry: I could die crying and still not cry enough to let out all my grief, their grief. For to perceive justly leads only to sorrow.

When you look at them all sitting there, whom will you blame? Her, with her vacant dreams, her artistic aspir-ations, her energy and hope and her sheer blind trying, years of it, directionless, without help from anyone or anything, narrowed into this, this marcelled hair and powdered face, this neat table with its good food, this small scene, the clean ironed tablecloth, the string beans on which she saved two cents a pound, this sullen pale child in her shabby after-school clothes, this round-faced baby in whose longing face there is already a kind of despair: her entire universe shrunk to this, to providing this meal in the house to these people? Go ahead, blame her. Blame her for her coldness, for her turning away from desire, for her inability to hold, to embrace even the children of her own body: cold bitch. Yes, blame her if you dare, you son of a prick! Who lived out her childhood in emptiness that was the eye of a violent storm, who was never held, never mothered, never once wrapped in warm strong arms so that she felt safe.

Maybe you'd prefer to blame him, the silent expressionless man who hated his children. He was not a terrible father; he never raised his hand to them, not even his voice. He merely walked around in a grumbling fury that was like a storm always raging just beyond them, from which they shrank in fear and forgot even that they longed for him. Blame him, the bastard. A simple man whose emotions had been beaten out of him by a tyrant, who wanted love and closeness and cared about nothing else, and who hated his children because he imagined that the goddess he adored was giving them the affection she denied him. Who loved to use his body and his mind in the ways he could use it, who had highly developed senses and remained open to travel and discovery all his life, who was miraculously capable of happiness, but who narrowed, narrowed, narrowed over the years into a rigid timid automaton. Be careful where you walk, the world is full of banana peels, and no one will pay your hospital bill, and while you are on your back, you will lose your job and your house and of course if you lose those you will also lose your wife. . . .

Perhaps we should blame the children, who are already as limited as their parents – the one a sullen unforgiving furious timid prodigy, the other a sweet, too sweet smiling sickly dependent dependent dependent.

The narrowing lives, the loss of dreams, are staple enough items in the cupboard of literature. But it is essential to remember what that shrinking feels like. Do you know? Can you imagine? Can you recall the day they first bound your feet? When they were still tiny? And afterward, how you could take only tottering little steps, and every step sent shocks of pain all the way up your leg? And how, certain days, the bones, which were being bent back in on themselves, cried out so fiercely that your mouth uttered it, and others turned to gaze on you with contempt, another ill-tempered female, just like the others. But it happens to all of us, female and male. Our bindings feel intolerable on certain days, when the weather is damp, when the bone is having a spurt of growth, when an image triggers the memory of whole feet. . . .

I try to not-feel. I try to think. About them, us. But I am overwhelmed with feeling – with hopelessness. It doesn't matter what you do or how you try: the same things happen, over and over and over and over. There is no escape.

Chapter VIII

one

The slow quiet years of the Depression flowed past; the children grew. Sometimes Belle feared they would not: Joy was often sick, and the only medication for most illnesses was merely aspirin. To these Belle added homemade chicken soup, hot tea with sugar and lemon, Jell-O, soft-boiled eggs, orange juice. Anastasia also came down with the usual childhood diseases, but she bounced back quickly. Joy did not, and lay in bed, eyes glazed with fever, round cheeks flushed, day upon day.

Added to her worry about Joy was her worry about paying the doctor's bills. Belle would tell Anastasia to watch over Joy and walk up to the corner near the gas station where there was a public telephone, and call kind Dr MacVeaney who would drive all the way from Forest Hills to South Ozone Park and charge one dollar, which sometimes Belle did not have. Still, he would nod and smile at her understandingly, and say 'That's all right, Mrs Dabrowski. Next time.' But sometimes she did not have the money next time either. He never pressed her, he never even handed her a bill. She kept track of what she owed him, and always paid it, although it sometimes took her six months.

When she was four, Joy had a terrible ear infection that reminded Belle of her own mastoid infection, and made her fear for Joy's hearing. Dr MacVeaney had to lance the infection without anesthetic; Belle stood watching him. Anastasia, also sick, watched from the next bed: the baby did not utter a sound, and when it was over, he stroked her face and she smiled radiantly at her torturer, who told her what a brave and good girl she was. Anastasia saw the expression around her mother's eyes, and knew Joy was very sick, but Mommy did not hug Joy. She went downstairs with the doctor. Later she brought up a dish of raspberry Jell-O, but Joy was asleep.

Aside from illness, there were few breaks in their routine. Every morning, Belle woke Anastasia for school, and when she had dressed and gone downstairs, there was always the fresh-squeezed orange juice, or half a grapefruit, and, in the winter, hot oatmeal or farina with cream; in the summer, corn flakes with milk and bananas. Anastasia hated all cereals. Sometimes Belle would soft-boil an egg for her, but she didn't like that either. She only liked pancakes, waffles, and French toast, but they had those only on weekends. She had to eat her breakfast, though, that was a rule. And drink a whole glass of milk, which she hated most of all. She would often persuade Belle to add a little hot coffee to her milk; then she could drink it. But after breakfast was the worst time, because then she had to take her cod-liver oil. Every morning, Mommy made her and Joy swallow a big tablespoon of it. She knew Mommy meant well, that it was good for her, but it tasted horrible. And then she would sit on the high stool while Mommy combed her hair, tears streaming down her face from the hurt of it, and then Mommy made long neat braids and fastened them with a rubber band and matching ribbons. Then Anastasia had a long walk to school. She hated to get up in the morning.

There were small pleasures in their life. In their first spring in the new house, Anastasia watched her mother plant seeds from packets in the flower beds that bordered the yard, and asked if she could have a garden of her own.

Belle gave her a long bed, three feet deep, just behind the hedge that separated the yard from the concrete court behind the house. Several boughs of a peach tree in the next yard overhung this bed, and Anastasia studied it as she planted her handful of seeds – marigolds, zinnias, cosmos, cornflower – and weeded them, and watched them grow. In summer little hard green balls appeared on the branches of the tree. Anastasia plucked one and bit into it: it was sour and hard. But the balls grew larger, and changed color, and she kept watching and asking Belle if the peaches were ready yet, and Belle said no. Then, just as fall arrived, and it was time to go back to school, there they were large and golden-red and fuzzy, and heavy, weighing down the branch. Anastasia felt the peach tree belonged to her, and wrote a poem about it in class, which the teacher inserted in the school magazine, *The Baisley Inkpot.*

Mrs Carle, who actually owned the peach tree, brought big bags of peaches to the side door and gave them to Belle, who made jam from them, and put it in big glass jars with rubber rings on top, which she stored in the basement. Anastasia liked the peaches, and she liked the jam, but neither quite lived up to her sense of the beauty of those branches, thick with leaves and hanging low, weighed down by golden-red fruit. Nor did her poem express her feelings about this tree. Nothing did, until many years later, when she took a photograph of fig trees on a wild Macedonian plain, and caught something of how she felt about the miraculous beauty of growing food.

When Anastasia's flowers grew, she picked the best ones, just the blossoms, and went into the kitchen and asked her mother for a jelly glass. They used jelly glasses to drink from, but Anastasia knew they were dispensable.

'I'm going to put some flowers and some sugar in this glass with water, and·make perfume,' she announced.

'That isn't the way you make perfume, Anastasia,' Belle said idly, looking up from the apples she was peeling to make a pie.

Anastasia stiffened. 'How *do* you make it, then?'

'I don't know. But not that way.'

'Well, if you don't know, how do you know this isn't the way?'

Belle put down her paring knife. She sighed. 'Anastasia, when you grow up and have a daughter, I hope she is just as willful and stubborn and fresh as you are!'

Anastasia left the room haughtily, and continued with her experiment. She slid the flower-sugar-water solution under the back porch, where it was dark and damp, she decided four days would do it. But she forgot about it and a week passed before she took it out, put her face close to the glass, and inhaled deeply. The stench was so terrible she almost vomited. She poured out the solution, and carried the glass back into the house. Her mother was peeling carrots for vegetable soup.

'I just wanted to tell you you were right about the perfume,' Anastasia announced and left the room.

Belle shook her head and grimaced. She did not understand how she could have given birth to so proud and headstrong a daughter. Only six, and so willful. Just last week, when Belle was making a lemon meringue pie, had finished piling the white froth on the custard, the pie was in the oven, and Anastasia came into the kitchen. She saw the eggbeater in the bowl, traces of the white froth in it.

'Oh, Mommy, can I lick the bowl?' she cried.

'No, Anastasia.'

'Why not!' Such dismay! About such a thing!

'It isn't whipped cream. You wouldn't like it.'

Oh, those eyes. She examines my face as if she thinks she will find some answer there. She acts as if I am lying to her. What is the matter with this child? I would never think of questioning my mother. If she said something, that was it. But Anastasia! She clamors, she insists, she says it is too whipped cream, if it isn't, what is it? So, finally, to show her, I say 'All right, Anastasia, go ahead.' Sighing.

And she gleams at me as if she's won something, what goes on in her head? The look on her face at her first taste of that egg white! Hah. She learned her lesson.

What did I do to deserve a child like that?

Belle's long days of labor required little of her mind except finding efficient ways of doing her work, and while she ironed, or peeled vegetables, or cleaned the house, her mind had little to work on. She listened to the radio. Ed had hooked up a speaker from the radio in the living room so she could hear it in the kitchen. He had even put a switch in the wall so she could turn it on or off from the kitchen. She listened to Arthur Godfrey – she loved him – and Mary Margaret McBride, who was her favorite, and to a few soap operas. But they often seemed stupid to her, and she would turn them off and daydream.

She thought about what it would be like if Ed got another job and made more money. The other men she knew were prospering. Jean's husband, Eric, was head of a department in his insurance company now, and made so much money he was able to help some of his friends. And of course, Jean still worked too, because she had Momma to help in the house and take care of the children. She now made high-fashion hats for Lily Daché, and once in a while she would make one for herself, a really smart little hat. And occasionally, when they played bridge together, Jean would whisper to Belle that Eric had had another raise, but Belle could see without being told that they were comfortable. They had all new furniture, and Jean had nice clothes, and they had a telephone and a new car every few years and their children's shoes were never too small for them. At Christmas, Jean and Eric's children got so many presents you would think you were in a store.

And her brother Eddie was doing nicely too. He and Martha would drive down from Boston each Christmas in a nice car, and Eddie and Eric would sit together discussing cars while Ed sat listening in silence. Once in a while, Eric would ask Ed's opinion of a certain model of car, but Ed couldn't say much because he wasn't informed about new cars. She knew Ed would love to have a car again. She decided that would be the first thing they would get if he got a raise – not a new car, but a used one. After a washing machine.

Even Wally made good money when he worked. God knows what he did with it, he spent little. He lived in boardinghouses near whatever job he was working on, and when the wiring for that building was finished, he'd get another job elsewhere, through the union. He often came to visit Jean or Belle, sleeping on their living room couches, and spending his days reading the *Daily News*. There was something sad about Wally, Belle felt; something homeless and yearning. But she had no patience with that: why didn't he make himself a home somehow? He had enough money, didn't he? Still, he was good: whenever he came, he gave her a few dollars toward food, and he always went up to the bakery and bought a crumb cake and some rolls. And he loved Anastasia.

Oh, Ed was doing all right. But he inched along, getting two- and three-dollar raises a year, not enough to keep up with the growing demands of growing children. But whenever Belle brought up the subject of looking for another job, he looked so pained and if she kept talking after a while he would start to belch. She knew he felt he was lucky to have a job at all. Of all the families on their block, only a few of the men had jobs. Mr Carle was superintendent of an apartment building; there was the German butcher; Mr Schinkel, Mr Leifels, and Mr Costello had jobs: the rest were unemployed as far as she knew.

And she was managing. She hit the table with her knuckles, thinking, Knock wood Joy doesn't get sick again, and recalled her plan. As soon as the porch furniture was paid off, in three months, she would invest in a washing machine. The next thing was a car for Ed. And then . . . well, her plans were mainly for the children. She wanted them to have a rounded education, to have a chance to know what they wanted to do and be in life. She wanted them not to be like her. She wanted them to have a chance to accomplish something.

She had already begun this program, but it hadn't worked out too successfully. She had enrolled Anastasia in a dancing class while they were living in Jamaica. Anastasia loved it, and was quite good at it, liked to show off her Russian kick and her tap steps and somersaults. But then it was announced that the dancing class was having a show for the first-year pupils. To be in the show, Anastasia needed a new pair of tap shoes – her old ones had become too short – and a costume. Belle couldn't afford the shoes or even fabric, and had to remove Anastasia from the class. Anastasia hadn't understood why she wasn't going anymore, and had been unhappy. Belle didn't want that to happen again.

But Anastasia was playing the piano a lot these days. She would just climb up on the stool and sound out the songs she knew. Belle wanted her to have piano lessons. She knew Anastasia wanted them. The thing was to squeeze the money out of her budget. Now, if she made cheaper desserts, could she save a dollar a week? And then, how to find a teacher?

Anastasia's first piano teacher was Mr Califano, who lived a few blocks away and had a sign in his front window. He was sort of fat and getting bald and Anastasia hated him. She hated him because he gave her ugly music to play: her pieces were all by Verdi, from *Il Trovatore* or *La Traviata*, and they all had a left hand that went ump-pa-pa and sounded cheap. She complained that she didn't like these pieces, but he said they were great music. She didn't believe him, but she was only a child, and couldn't argue. Also, when she made a mistake, he slapped her hand. No one ever slapped Anastasia, and she did not know how to handle this. She felt insulted. Still she liked being able to play.

One afternoon when Mommy said, 'Wash your hands and go through your lesson, Anastasia, because Mr Califano is coming this afternoon,' Anastasia made a face.

Mommy stiffened. 'What's the matter? If you don't want to take lessons, you don't have to. I told you that. It's up to you.'

'I know,' Anastasia said meekly. She gazed at her mother. 'But I don't like Mr Califano.'

But Mommy didn't get mad. She said 'Why?' and Anastasia told her.

'He hits your hand?' Mommy repeated. Then she said, 'You don't have to take a lesson today, Anastasia.'

And when Mr Califano came to the door, Anastasia hid in the kitchen, she didn't hear what Mommy said, or what he said. He never came back again, and Mommy found a new teacher for her. But Anastasia felt embarrassed for telling on Mr Califano. He wasn't mean or anything; he was just used to hitting children. Her next teacher was Angelo LaMatta, but he said to call him Angie. He had a disposition like his name, angelic, and he was a much better teacher than Mr Califano. Mommy said he went to Juilliard. He was young and had a sweet face and he gave Anastasia beautiful music to play, Mozart and Beethoven and Bach, not the real Bach, but his son, C.P.E. And that Christmas, Angie gave Anastasia a Christmas present – a year's subscription to *Etude* magazine! It was all about music. It was as big as a newspaper, like the *Daily News* that Daddy brought home every night, but it was bound and had thicker paper. Every month when it arrived, Anastasia would sprawl on the floor, knees in, legs out, and read it carefully. She was often puzzled by what she read, but she persevered. Particularly she did not understand the name of one regular column: 'Hemidemisemiquaver.' She tried the dictionary in vain, but deduced after a while that it was a made-up word meaning tiny little notes. Still, she failed to see why anyone would give that name to a column.

Joy started kindergarten. Once she started school, Joy was almost always sick, picking up, as children do, every communicable disease. She came home with measles, chicken pox, and mumps; soon Anastasia caught them too, all except mumps. Belle spent her days tending two sick children and worrying about them and the doctor bills. Joy missed most – five months – of her first-grade year and should have been left back. But her teacher, Mrs Hoffman, a young woman with dark curls, loved Joy. And, she told Belle, she was being promoted herself, and was to teach second grade the next year, and could not bear to lose Joy, so she promoted Joy too. Also, she added, any child Joy's age who could crochet was smart enough to be promoted even if she had not done the first-grade work.

Belle had sat with Joy crocheting when the child was recovering, and had patiently taught her how. She was proud of Joy for being promoted after such a year. But in later years, Joy was sorry about it: she never did learn the fundamental work she missed in first grade, and the lack impeded her throughout school.

One evening, when both girls were sick, Daddy and Mommy came upstairs, and Daddy looked very proud of himself. He was carrying a big box full of books. Someone in his company, hearing he had a daughter who liked to read, had given him the contents of a deceased relative's attic. Many of the books were for children. Anastasia grabbed the box greedily. These books were not as beautiful as those she had, but she had read her own books many times. The most beautiful of her books was *A Child's Garden of Verses* by Robert Louis Stevenson, which had many pictures in color: there was a little girl on a swing, looking out at a patchwork quilt of fields; and a little boy looking at his shadow; and children sitting in a slice of moon as if it were a boat. Also very beautiful was *Pinocchio*, but it had only a few pictures, and her first real books, *Grimm's Fairy Tales* and *Andersen's Fairy Tales*. She had *Snow White and the Seven Dwarfs;* that was all pictures. Mommy's friend Adele had brought it when she visited Mommy one afternoon last year when Joy and Anastasia were sick in bed; but she didn't like the story, it was fake. She didn't really like the pictures either.

But this box held treasures: *Hurlbut's Story of the Bible*; *Greek Myths* (for children); *Norse Myths* (for children); Charles and Mary Lamb's *Tales from Shakespeare*; *Little Lord Fauntleroy*; and *The Secret Garden*. For a month, she immersed herself in these new worlds, and every year afterward she reread them. She was often puzzled by what she read, and would lie in bed mulling it over. She never had problems with the books they were given in school. Those books either taught you something – geography or history or spelling – or they told stories that were intended to teach children to be good, obedient, respectful of their elders, honest, or clean, or fair. These stories were usually silly and fake and Anastasia's heart dismissed them. She knew children would not behave the way they did in those books. And no one she knew had a governess or lived in a mansion. And all the daddies in the book were so sweet and wonderful, although they might not be around much. But they weren't anything like the fathers she saw around her. She knew the German butcher across the street beat his daughter, and chained her to the bed at night when he went out; and she could hear the beatings of children in the DiNapoli house on the corner, often, when she walked past. Even Uncle Eric beat Errie with a belt, and so did Lily Wallis's father, he'd done it once when she was staying with Lily. And fathers who didn't beat their children, like her own, didn't have anything to do with them, but just grumbled and grouched at them all the time. There were no mean or violent fathers in the books she read, nor in the fairy tales, either, although there were giants and ogres, and just plain indifferent fathers, like Cinderella's. The mothers were always cruel jealous stepmothers. They weren't like the sweet mothers she knew, mothers who protected their children and took care of them.

Fairy tales, myths, and the tales from Shakespeare were not simple and transparent, like the schoolbooks. They bothered her, they kept her awake at night. She could not understand who the Ice Queen was, or why she wanted to kidnap the little boy; or why Daphne was happy to be changed into a laurel; or why King Lear was so blind about Cordelia. She realized that these stories had been left out of them. Reading them was somewhat like listening to grown-ups talk: there was something missing, something essential, that would make all the rest make sense. Like grown-ups, these stories lied to children. She determined that when she was grown up, she would discover the missing part, and go back and read these stories again.

Then there were Mommy's stories, but they were true. They were all very sad because Mommy's life had been very sad. The books she liked had that sadness in them too. *Little Lord Fauntleroy* and *The Secret Garden* were about children who felt sad in the ways she, Anastasia, also felt sad, and they were her favorite books. She wondered if her life, like theirs, would move into happiness, but when she thought about it, she couldn't quite see how. Sometimes, thinking about this late at night lying in her bed by the window staring out at the clouds and the moon, her mind would slide into the world of fairy tales, and she would imagine a fairy appearing in her room and offering her three wishes.

She spent considerable time pondering these wishes, but each time she imagined this fantasy, she came up with the same ones. Actually there was only one wish: that Daddy would make more money. If Daddy made more money, Mommy would be happier and she would love Daddy; and if Mommy loved Daddy, then both of them would love the children, Anastasia and Joy, and then they would be happy too. That's what Anastasia believed. So sometimes she would nobly tell the fairy she needed only one wish, and that she should give the other two to another child who needed wishes. But other times she felt she should not leave anything to chance, and would take all three: for Daddy to make more money; for Mommy to love Daddy; for Mommy and Daddy to love Anastasia and Joy. She wondered whether, if she could really believe in this fantasy, wish it hard enough, it could come true even without the intervention of a good fairy. But she never could have enough faith to find out. She would give it up, lying there humming a Christmas song popular in the Depression years: 'All I really want is this,/Daddy's smile and Mommy's kiss;/Let our lives be filled with bliss!/That's what I want for Christmas.'

Belle worked, watched her children, and planned. It took longer than she had hoped to buy the washing machine – all the doctor's bills, and a cold winter requiring more coal than she had expected – but eventually she got one. Ed went with her to pick it out. They chose a sturdy round Maytag that stood on four legs and had a green metal body. When it was delivered, Belle stood alone in the kitchen gazing at it, clasping and unclasping her hands. She kept remembering a phrase from a psalm: my cup runneth over.

Now washing was much easier. Now, on Monday mornings, she would gather together all the dirty laundry and sort it into three piles, and then pull the washing machine – it was very heavy, but it had rollers on its legs – from its corner to a spot beside the sink. She removed a wide black hose from inside the machine, attached one end to the sink faucet, and left the other end dangling in the machine. She piled the white things inside the tub, and turned on the hot water, which flowed directly into the machine. She added Oxydol, and when the water was high, Clorox. She removed the hose, put on the lid, and started the motor. While the clothes were washing, she prepared the starch. Then she could sit down and have a cup of coffee and a cigarette.

When the washing was complete, she pulled another hose up from the underside of the machine, and let it dangle in the deep tub of the sink. She drained off the dirty water. The next step was to replace the first hose and pour in clean water to rinse the clothes. She would prepare bluing and pour that in at the same time. When the clothes were rinsed, she repeated the draining process. Now she removed the soggy clothes and put them through the wringer. This was the delicate step. Sometimes Anastasia would help her with the washing, and always Belle would remind her: don't get your fingers too near the wringer. The wringer consisted of two rubber cylinders and a lever that brought them close together. You would put the piece of laundry in between the cylinders, then turn on the motor, and the cylinders would turn, squeezing most of the water out of the fabric. Each piece of laundry had to be carefully guided through.

When this was done, Belle put the items that had to be starched in the shallow sink, with warm water and starch. Then she began the washing process over again, with the colored things. While they were washing, she took the nonstarched things outside and hing them on the line – undershirts and the girls' underpants, and white socks. She drained, added rinse water, drained again, and wrung out the colored items. She put those that required starch in the starchy water with the others, and started to wash the dark pieces. But she rarely got this far without stopping to make lunch for Joy and Anastasia, who had to come home at lunchtime except on rainy days, when the school allowed them to bring a sandwich and provided containers of milk.

She would open a can of soup and make a bologna

sandwich for them; or scrambled eggs with toast; or a grilled cheese sandwich; or a tuna fish salad. While they ate, she sat beside them, drinking tea, eating toast, and smoking. She would listen to their chatter, but it seemed far away. She was thinking about what she wanted to do for them. She had so many plans. After they left, she finished the dark laundry, and then put all the starched things through the wringer again. At last, she had it all on the line. She always sighed and slumped down in a chair when she had gotten that far. There were still things to do: the washing machine to be wiped down, the sinks to be scrubbed, the starch pot to be scoured: but the worst was done. Thank heavens for her washing machine.

When Belle saw how much Anastasia loved music, she decided to take her to the opera. Belle had never been to the opera herself; neither had Ed. She wanted Anastasia to have that experience. She looked in the newspaper, and found out what tickets cost, figured the price of going into Manhattan, and began to save. She would take the four of them for Anastasia's ninth birthday, in November. She started saving for it in May.

It also occurred to her that her children had had no exposure to religion, and one day in September, before Anastasia's ninth birthday, she spoke to her.

Mommy was ironing when I came home and she said, in a formal kind of voice, 'Anastasia, sit down, I want to talk to you.'

The way she said it, I knew she wasn't mad, and that we were going to have a grown-up conversation. I felt honored, and I sat down very correctly, my back straight, not slumped.

'I am not a religious person. That means I don't believe in God. If you don't believe in God, you're called an agnostic. That's what I am. But many people do believe in God. And I was wondering if you would like to learn about God.'

Learn about God! What else did I think about night after night, lying up there in my bed beside the windows,

315

looking out at the stars and moon, and thinking about how wrong everything was on earth, and wondering how it could be made right!

'Oh, I would!' I breathed.

'Well. There are many different religions. Different people have different ways of thinking about God, and talking about God. These ways are called religions. Your father and I were raised in the Catholic religion. So I thought maybe it would be best if you went for religious instruction to the Catholic Church. Would you like that?'

My heart leaped.

So intense was my longing for understanding, that even after weeks of studying the catechism I knew to be mindless, to offer euphemism instead of knowledge, to pretend that saying something made it true, I was still entranced. My devotion was of the furious bloody sort: I believed none of the crap in the lessons I had to memorize but memorized them nevertheless; but I did believe there was a God and that he carried justice within him, and that if I persevered, I would discover that justice. I knew, though, that I would never find it, or God, through the ways urged by the nuns. Even as I followed the rules, learned the venial and mortal sins, learned what the sacraments were, even as I half-accepted these as part of the road to what I was seeking, I knew the rules were too silly to be God's. And I was fiercely determined to find the place where truth and justice resided. That – truth and justice – was what the word *God* meant to me. *God* did not mean love. Indeed, I didn't really know what the word *love* meant. Because I knew my mother and father loved me, but I felt they didn't. And I knew I loved them, but I hated them too, I mistrusted them and I saw their failings. No one else my age thought their parents had failings. Little communication as I had with children my age, I did know that. Parents might be cruel or violent, but they were always Right. I did not believe my parents were always right; I thought *I* was.

Still, I wanted at least to understand what I was learning, to the degree it was possible for it to be understood. Much of what I was learning was, I knew, purposeful mystification. But some things should have been clear. For instance, the Hail Mary. The night before religious instruction, Tuesday night, I had to recite my catechism lesson for my mother. I recited every Thursday night too, before the Friday tests with school lessons – I would give her my book, and she would ask me the spelling words or the multiplication tables, and I would spill them out. This evening, I had to recite certain prayers by memory, and when I finished, I said,

'Mommy, you know that prayer, the Hail Mary?'

She nodded.

I recited the first stanza: 'Hail, Mary! full of grace,/the Lord is with thee,/blessed art thou amongst women;/and blessed is the fruit of they womb, Jesus,' I recited, using the rhythms we'd been taught. 'Well, what does that mean? "Fruit of thy womb, Jesus?" What's *womb*?'

'Oh, Anastasia, I don't know,' she said.

'Mommy!' I protested.

'Look it up in the dictionary,' she said, as she always did when I asked her the meaning of a word.

'I did. It said *uterus*. I don't know what *uterus* is. I looked up *uterus*. It says *womb*.'

My mother seemed to me to be slightly smiling. She shrugged. 'Ask the sister.'

So next time we said the Hail Mary in catechism class, Wednesday afternoon (you were let out of school half an hour early for it), I raised my hand, Sister John the Baptist raised her eyebrows, and when we had finished the prayer, she said, 'Yes, Anastasia?'

She liked me, I knew that. That was because I always knew my catechism perfectly and the other girls didn't. In Catholic school, the girls were separated from the boys, you had different classes. But the other children were all much younger than I; it was normal to make your First Communion at seven, after a year of instruction, so they were probably around six. I was almost nine. I recognized that I was older than the others and didn't feel superior to them. But I didn't have anything to do with them, either.

'What does it mean, *fruit of thy womb, Jesus*? What is a *womb*?'

Sister John the Baptist stood stock-still. She gazed upon

us with a quiet expressionless face. 'Excuse me, class,' she said, and left the room abruptly.

The girls moved around in their seats, and a few of them whispered to each other, but that was all. We were public-school kids, far more unruly in our own school than here: maybe, as in the old joke, we were intimidated by the guy nailed to a cross up at the front of the room. Eventually Sister returned, and she went on with the class just as if nothing had happened. She never answered my question. By now I was doggedly determined to get a response.

I went home and told my mother what happened. Again, I had the strange sensation that she was smiling, but she said, again, 'I really don't know, Anastasia. Maybe you should ask the sister *after* class.'

So I did, I grabbed Sister after everyone had gone, and spoke to her in the hall. I explained that I had asked my mother this question and that she didn't know and had told me to ask Sister, that I asked Sister, but she'd forgotten to answer me. Would she please answer me now?

She looked at me meditatively, kindly. 'Do you come from a religious family, Anastasia?'

I gazed at her. 'I don't know, Sister.'

'Do you have holy pictures in your house? Holy water?'

'No, Sister.'

She patted me on the shoulder. 'I'll bring you some,' she said, as if she were offering a starving person food. And the next time the class met, she asked me to stay late, and gave me a shoe box full of holy pictures, a holy water dispenser, and a beautiful gold filigree cross with an ivory Jesus on it (at least it *looked* like gold and ivory). I accepted the box in utter bewilderment. I was pleased with the gift, but I didn't understand why I was being given this instead of an answer.

I carried it home reverently, and unpacked it carefully, holding up each picture to gaze at it. The holy pictures, which were reproductions of masterpieces of Italian art, were very beautiful in my eyes, except for the ones by someone called Murillo, which were full of pretty little boys that reminded me of the children in children's books. I tacked my favorite pictures to the wall beside my bed, and packed the rest away in the box. I carried the cross upstairs, and nailed a tack in the wall over my bed, and hung it there alongside the photographs of Margaret Bourke-White and Wendell Willkie that I had cut out of the newspaper. (They were my heroes at the time; Willkie would be my candidate for president the following year.) I didn't know what to do with the holy water dispenser. I took it downstairs and asked Mommy if she wanted to hang it on the wall, and she made a face, so I carried it back upstairs and laid it back in the shoebox, with the pictures. I placed them neatly on the bottom shelf of the rickety bookcase my father had built for Joy and me.

I continued to ponder this event. This was the first, and probably the only, time in my life I was rewarded for asking a question, but I had difficulty weighing the reward against the answer I still wanted. Obviously, the word 'womb' referred to something 'dirty' – why else would no one tell me what it meant? But if it was a dirty word, why was it in a prayer? And why did people who didn't let you use dirty words say this prayer and teach it to children?

All this not-knowing cast me into despair, and into fury. I would lie in bed at night so angry I wanted to scream, to bang against the bureau alongside my bed, to break something. WHY would people not tell children the truth? WHY was it necessary to conceal, to lie, to evade? What in life was so terrible that a child could not know it? Didn't children know terrible things even without being told them? What about those children whose parents beat them? What about me, when my mother turned her face away from me? Didn't that knowledge encompass everything that was terrible? The knowledge that one was alone, unloved, helpless, unable to control her own life, what could be worse than that?

But I had learned my lesson. I never asked another question at Religious Instruction. When I found something unjust or doubtful, I simply laid it aside. I refused to believe, for example, that my hardworking, suffering parents, would be damned to hell for not going to Mass on Easter Sunday. On the other hand, I worked as hard as I could to get them there that Easter, and I succeeded. It didn't matter, though: they never went again. And the Church got to me more than I now want to acknowledge. For I'll never forget my First Communion. It wasn't my new white dress and veil, the new white Mary Janes and long white stockings, the bouquet I carried, the gifts I received: no: it was taking that wafer on my tongue and believing it was the body and blood of Jesus, of God. My entire body felt suffused with radiance; I knew I was carrying something sacred within me. Of all children, I would understand that love was food. I believed I had ingested Jesus, and was filled with his love, which was holiness. At the same time, I didn't know exactly what holiness was. I knew it had nothing to do with being good, in the way children were supposed to be good. I think I felt it was power. So did that mean love was power?

two

I've often wondered about that dollar a week for the piano lesson: how did she scrape it together? When my father was earning only about thirty-five of them, how could she spare one thirty-fifth of their income? I've never done anything like that for my children. Oh, for doctor bills, yes. But for piano lessons?

What sacrifices she – they – made! – he because he just went along with anything she decided. But he never complained, he never impeded. He never said, listen, if you didn't insist on that kid having piano lessons, we could go to a movie once in a while. They never did. They never went anywhere and they never got anything new.

Yet even as everything they did was turned into nourishment for us, the children, they themselves turned away from us, into their own dim corners. To complain was to be ungrateful, and Joy never complained. She spent all her time outdoors, playing with other children, finding fun somewhere, somehow. Mother would criticize her:

'Joy, I don't see how you can bear to play with that Concetta. Her nose is always running, and she doesn't even know enough to wipe it. She's a disgusting little thing.'

Joy was wounded, and carried the wound into adulthood.

At fifty, she lamented, 'She used to criticize my friends, all the time. I had a little friend, Concetta, I loved her, and Mother tried to get me to stop playing with her because she had a runny nose.'

The wound, I deduce, came from Mother's giving Joy a new perspective on people, one she did not especially want. Runny noses were improper. Where did that leave love? Mother complained to me as well.

'Joy has no standards. She'll play with anyone. She even plays with that Concetta. The child is filthy and her nose is always running.' She shook her head, grimacing. I understood that Joy had fallen in Mother's estimation because she accepted so déclassé a playmate. I fervently assured her that *I* would never do such a thing: *I* was *her* girl.

She took the family to the opera. She chose *Carmen* as a good introduction (how could she know?), and we went to the City Center one November evening, and sat together in a box. Beforehand, Belle took Anastasia to the big library in Jamaica, to get the libretto so she would know what she was hearing. (How did she know about libretti?) Anastasia carried the volume to the performance, but didn't need it, because she had memorized it.

And what a spectacle! Way down there on the little stage were people, scenery, an orchestra below. Costumes, color, soaring voices, wonderful songs a child can remember! It was the grandest event of Anastasia's young life, and remained vivid to her for years afterward. Her intention to become a composer was strengthened: maybe someday she could write music as wonderful as Bizet's!

Wally brought them a gift during one of his visits – a small radio-phonograph, one that could stand on a table. Lacking a table, they stood it on the floor of the porch, where Anastasia lay sprawled beside it, listening to the three record albums that had accompanied the gift – Gounod's *Faust*, Bizet's *Carmen*, and Tschaikowsky's *First Piano Concerto*. Wally had asked Belle what he should buy, and these were the albums she chose. (How did she know?) In time, Anastasia, who had memorized the words and music to the operas, and the music to the concerto, came to listen only to the Tschaikowsky. This choice was not based entirely on musical values. Rather, it was because she was puzzled and perturbed by the role of the women in the operas. At first, she tried to imagine if she wanted to be any of them. She would rather be Carmen than Micaela, but she didn't want to die. And why shouldn't Carmen be able to love whoever she wanted to love without being killed for it? And the role of the woman in *Faust* didn't appeal to her at all. Better to stick to things without characters, without words.

Anastasia was always lying on the porch floor listening to music, when she wasn't writing music herself. Angie had had a concert at his house, and all his pupils played. Anastasia played a sonata she had written herself, and Angie was so proud of her, he made a record of it and gave it to her to keep. Anastasia intended to grow up and write symphonies, and make a lot of money. When she did, she would buy Mommy a fuhcoat. She didn't know what a fuhcoat was, but all the ladies talked about them, and when they said someone had one, even Mommy said 'Oh . . . !' Maria and Eva, Daddy's sisters, had come to visit, and they told Mommy that someone they knew had bought a fuhcoat, and all the women had sounded envious. There were different kinds of fuhcoats – mink-dyed muskrat and squirrel and Persian lamb. Anastasia decided that Persian lamb sounded the most elegant.

Sometimes they had a car. It was good when they had a car, because then Daddy would drive Mommy to the supermarket on Saturday, and she wouldn't have to carry home the heavy brown bags of groceries by herself. It was hard for Mommy to carry the groceries. One time when Anastasia went with her to the A & P and Big Ben's, they bought a lot of canned goods and potatoes and onions, and they had too many bags to carry. They walked the long way along the Boulevard, but when they reached 123rd Avenue, Mommy couldn't go any further. She stopped and looked at Anastasia, and her voice sounded as if she were going to cry and her face looked like that too. And she said, 'Anastasia, I can't go any further.' So she put a bag down right on the sidewalk, and told Anastasia to stay with it and guard it, and she walked home carrying one heavy bag and one light one that she took from Anastasia. Then she came back and picked up the other one and they walked home together. But one time this happened to Mommy when she was alone, and when she told Anastasia about it, she was almost crying again. She had had to leave a package under someone's hedge, and walk the long three blocks down to their house, and go back. She was terrified it wouldn't be there any longer, but it was.

(When Belle was eighty, she would remember vividly her terror and anxiety about this sack of groceries.)

And when they had a car, they would sometimes drive to Aunt Kris and Uncle Joe's. Anastasia liked Aunt Kris but in her house you had to be very careful not to put your hands on the walls or woodwork, not even when you were coming downstairs. And sometimes they went to Aunt Jean and Uncle Eric's for Sunday dinner, and they could play with little Ingrid and Errie. They would run in the front door of the house and out the back, chasing each other, and yell and scream and laugh, until Uncle Eric or Mommy said they had to stop. Then they would have a big dinner just like Mommy's big dinners. Aunt Jean, everyone said, was a wonderful cook, just like Mommy.

The first time they got a car, it was a long flat brown one. Their house had no driveway, but the house next door did, and the Dentels, who lived there, didn't have a car. So Daddy asked Mr Dentel if he could use their driveway. And then Daddy cut the back fence apart. Anastasia was fascinated. He took off a whole section of pickets, and put hinges on one side and a hook and eye on the other. Then Daddy would drive the car up the Dentels' driveway, get out, open the fence to his own yard, and drive the car right into the backyard! Daddy was very smart.

And if they had a car and it was summertime, Mommy would persuade Daddy to take them to Jones Beach once or twice during the summer. Mommy would start mentioning it on Friday, because if they were to go, she had to start cooking on Saturday; but then there was always a terrible tension inside Anastasia because she was afraid it would rain on Sunday and they wouldn't go after all.

Sometimes this happened, and then they would eat their Sunday dinner in the kitchen, like always, but out of the Everhot. But sometimes, the sun shone, and they went.

Mommy brought them all bathing suits, and herself a beach coat. Anastasia had never heard of such a thing, and she had never seen Mommy have anything new before, so she watched in wonder as Mommy put on her beach coat. It was long, all the way to the floor, and it had a double row of buttons in the front. It was striped in many colors, but the part that was striped was raised in little ridges in the cloth. Anastasia felt the ridges, and stroked the coat: she thought it was very beautiful.

Daddy would start loading the car early in the morning. First he put in Mommy's beach chair, and a blanket, and the umbrella: these were old, Mommy and Daddy had had them years before. Then there were towels and thermoses and pails and shovels for Joy and Anastasia, and a rubber ring for the children, and then he put in the Everhot. It was very heavy and even Daddy couldn't lift it; he had to sort of wheel it around turning it to move it. Mommy put dishes and napkins and knives and forks in a valise. Most things fit in the trunk, but the Everhot was set on the floor of the back seat, and all the way to the beach Mommy kept saying. 'Watch out for the Everhot, children, don't burn yourselves.' And a couple of times, Anastasia's leg grazed it by accident, and it burned her.

Then came one of the best parts. They would gather together the things from the car. Even the children had to carry something, because Daddy had the Everhot, the beach chair, the thermoses, and the umbrella, and Mommy was carrying the blanket and the valise. So they carried their pails and the rubber tube and towels. And then there was a long walk, down under a tunnel where you could yell and your voice would echo: Daddy would never let them yell, but bigger kids did. Then, after they came out of the tunnel, there were banks of flowers on either side of the walk, and they smelled so beautiful that Anastasia thought that was what the Elysian fields in her Greek myth book must be like. There were petunias and portulacas: Mommy told her the names, and she never forgot them and said them over in her head every time they walked past them.

They always went to Zach's Bay. Anastasia wanted to go where the waves were, but Mommy said it was too dangerous, so they went to the bay and Anastasia was always happy anyway. She would run off into the water even before Daddy had set up the umbrella and Mommy's beach chair and laid down the blanket. Joy would stay with Mommy, until Mommy took her hand and led her to the water's edge, but Anastasia wanted to stay in the water the whole time. She sat in her tube, and in the beginning, Daddy and Mommy stood with her while Daddy showed her how to swim. But soon she could swim without the tube, and she loved to jump up and down and hold her nose and go under the water, and float and splash. Mommy always made her come out of the water when her lips turned blue and her fingers were all wrinkled, so she would sit on the beach sullen and petulant, until her fingers came out again, and she could ask Mommy if she could go back in. If it wasn't late – Mommy wanted them to be dry before they got back in the car – Mommy would let her.

She had to come out, though, for dinner. Mommy had started dinner the night before. She put a roast in the bottom of the Everhot. This was a circular pot about two feet high and a foot and a half in diameter with thick inner walls that held electric coils. Daddy would plug the Everhot into a wall outlet in the kitchen. Mommy put the roast in and covered the Everhot with its heavy metal cover. It would cook all night. Then, early in the morning, Mommy would put the vegetables and potatoes into two pots shaped like half-moons, with hooks on them, that fit in over the roast, and hooked to the lip. There was room on top for rolls or bread, but they never had those.

When it was time to leave the house, Daddy would unplug the Everhot, but it would stay hot right up until they ate dinner. Mommy would put plates and knives and forks and napkins on the blanket. Daddy would carve the roast on a plate set on top of the Everhot, and Mommy would serve the vegetables. Then she would pour coffee from the gallon thermos they had brought with them, and milk from the smaller one. And they would have a regular Sunday dinner, almost as if they were home. Mommy would bring tomatoes, too, and slice them on a plate, or applesauce if they were having roast pork. But they didn't have a fancy dessert at the beach – only cookies. Anastasia didn't care. The food always got sand in it anyway, and she only wanted to be in the water.

She dreaded going home. Everyone seemed grouchy as they walked the whole long way back carrying all their equipment. She was tired and dragged along the sidewalk. Even the flowers didn't smell as good. Then Daddy would say, 'You wait here, Belle, and I'll bring the car around,' and they would slump down on a bench in the hot sun waiting a long time until Daddy got out of the parking lot and drove to where they were sitting with the Everhot and the umbrella and the beach chair and the two thermoses and the valise and the blanket and the towels and the tube and the pails and shovels and bathing caps full of sand. Everything was full of sand, and Anastasia's bottom hurt from sitting in it, and she knew there was a lot of sand inside her bathing suit and she wanted to reach in and scoop it out but she couldn't because that wasn't nice to do in public.

Of course, we'd always have to sell our cars eventually. Ed was awfully good about that, he never complained or protested. If I told him I owed Dr MacVeaney thirty dollars, or that I had no money for the next coal delivery, or when they turned the gas and electric off because we hadn't paid the bill – it was lucky Ed knew how to turn it back on or we would have been cold and hungry often in those years – he would just say 'I'd better sell the car', and he would. There was never a lack of buyers. All the men who worked with Ed knew how good his cars were. Whenever he bought one, he would take it completely apart and put it back together again with all its parts cleaned and honed, running beautifully. Ed is fussy about cars. So all the men wanted his old cars. He'd sell them for what he paid for them. It never occurred to him to charge more. It never occurred to me either.

But I liked having a car, it made my life easier. And then, there were things I wanted the girls to see. I'd ask Ed to drive us into Brooklyn and to the Lower East Side of Manhattan. I'd point out to the girls the neighborhoods I used to live in. Even in those days the houses had already been razed. They were such slums, so awful. And I'd show them what the streets were like, dirty, filled with people, so terrifying. And I'd remind them how lucky they were to have a nice little house to live in, with their own yard. Then we'd drive to the Lower East Side, where it was even worse. The girls would fall very silent, especially Anastasia. I could hear her thinking. There were people and laundry hanging from the fire escapes, and so much noise, and soot . . . oh, god, I can hardly bear even thinking about it.

And then, if no one had been sick, if I could afford it, we would drive into Jamaica on a Friday night after Ed got paid, and see a movie. I took them to movies they would like – Nelson Eddy and Jeanette MacDonald, or Deanna Durbin. It was a treat for all of us. But then my heart would wrench to see Anastasia afterward, when other people were going into Jahn's for ice cream, and we couldn't, and she wouldn't ask, she'd just look, and my heart would break.

Such an odd child to have come from me. The way she makes her own places. In the summers, she carts out piles of old bedspreads and drapes I store in the big trunk in the girls' closet – you never know when they might be useful – and makes herself a tent in the backyard. She drapes one end of things over the porch railing, and the other over the hedge – the shape *is* rather like a tent, actually. And she drags my beach chair in there and carries out the piano stool – it's heavy – for a table, and lolls on the beach chair reading, books and lemonade on the piano stool beside her. She tells me she's a Persian princess. I can never figure out what's going on inside her. But I love fixing her a glass of lemonade or iced tea. I chip bits of ice from the block in the icebox, and I send her out to pick some mint from the garden, and I squeeze the lemons, and make a big pitcher of tea or lemonade. I like it myself.

I like the summer. I sit outside on the back steps shelling

peas or stringing beans. Sometimes Anastasia helps me. It's so peaceful sitting there, quiet, the air so soft, still light even though it's nearing dinnertime. And Joy is out playing, and I know she's all right, she's such a happy kid, not like Anastasia. She's at the Callahans' this afternoon, I can see her over there in their yard. Mr Callahan loves her. He's supposed to be a drug addict, but he's certainly very nice to Joy. He bought her a cowboy suit – chaps, shirt, hat, everything. His own children have nothing like that. He loves Joy.

Sitting with Mommy shelling peas or stringing beans, I love that, we sit in the quiet afternoon together and I can feel that Mommy likes me, likes sitting together working. I don't even mind shelling the peas or stringing the beans because I can feel Mommy is almost happy. One night after dinner, it was very hot, and all of us sat out here on the back steps together, and it felt like a family, it was happy. And Mr Dentel called over from their back steps, where he and his wife were sitting too, and said he was making ice cream and would we like some. He has a machine that you churn and it makes ice cream that's better than what you can buy in the store. And Daddy asked Mommy, and Mommy said that would be lovely, and Daddy went to their yard and scooped some out into dishes for us, and it was peach, and it was delicious. We sat there until it got dark, the fireflies sparking, the crickets chirping, and all the birds fell silent.

Sometimes in summer when the Bungalow Bar truck drives round, I get a dime and buy two orange ice pops with vanilla ice cream inside for Joy and me. But that ice cream isn't as good as Mr Dentel's. I wish we had an ice-cream maker. I like the summer better than the winter, but in the winter sometimes I build an igloo. Joy helps me if she isn't sick: we pile snow in a circle, and keep piling it up and up to make walls. The hard part is to curve it in and make a roof. Lots of times after you get the snow packed down and curving, it just breaks off and falls, and you have to start over again. Joy giggles when that happens, but I don't see anything funny about it. Joy always gets bored and runs off, but I keep trying, and eventually it works. Then I like to build a fire inside the igloo. I'd like to sit inside it and read by the firelight. I tried it once. Mommy let me have newspaper and some kindling from the basement, and matches, and Joy was so excited she called all her friends, and they all tried to crowd into the igloo, but it was too small, so most of them had to stand outside. And I built the fire and Joy and I sat down next to it. But it was really cold, even with the fire, and my behind got freezing. It was too cold to read. I wonder what the Eskimos do. Maybe they sit on skins. Are there whaleskins? Or maybe, seal. But maybe the Eskimos don't read books.

I don't like it when it's cold. And in winter I have to go to school. I hate school, It's boring, and none of the children like me. Mommy says they're all jealous because I'm so smart, but I don't think that's it. I think it's because I'm so much younger than they are. They think I'm conceited. Conceited. I guess I am, but I can't help it. Some days I just can't bear to go to school and I tell Mommy I have a stomachache, and she lets me stay in bed all day. I don't even have to get dressed. I go down and get the little radio and fetch the chair from Mommy and Daddy's room and put it beside my bed, and put the radio on it, and listen to 'Our Gal Sunday' and Mary Noble, 'Backstage Wife' and Mrs Goldberg, and cut out paper dolls if I have new ones, or make them. I have lots and lots of nice pads Uncle Eddie brings down from Boston every Christmas. Only the paper is so heavy that the doll clothes I draw on them fall off the paper dolls I make, no matter how long I make the tabs. I wish I had a nice paint set, or those colored pencils that you can wet and make the color look all smooth.

But I love the paper dolls I buy in the five-and-ten. I have a set that look like Rita Hayworth, and a set that look like Ginger Rogers, and some of them don't look like anybody, just very pretty ladies. But all of them have gorgeous clothes, suits with fur collars, and dresses draped and pleated, and evening gowns. Joy says 'evening gownds', no matter how often I correct her. She says 'nightgownd', too. And 'seggideggi' for spaghetti. She's funny. She can't say 'doorknob'. She says 'nordob'. She's cute. When we're both sick, we play store. She sits in her bed and I sit in mine, and I get all my paper dolls. She always argues, but I always win, because it's only fair, they're my paper dolls. So she gets the hats and pocketbooks and shoes and I get the dresses and suits and coats and evening gownds. And we each get half of the dolls, and the dolls go shopping, and we're the salesladies, and we help them to pick out nice outfits. Of course, it isn't really that good because only the clothes that came with them fit any of the dolls, but we pretend they can wear any of them, and sometimes, if Joy likes a dress a lot, she'll buy it for her doll even though it doesn't fit her. We use Monopoly money. But after a while, that game gets boring.

And at night, Joy always wants to play radio, but that isn't really a game because I have to do everything. I tell her I get tired, and she promises she'll do things, but then she doesn't, the only thing she does is sing the jingle that opens the show, but even then she can't sing it without me because she can't remember how the song goes. So we sing the jingle together, and then I'm the announcer. Sometimes I do a singing show and sometimes I make up a story. But I have to do all the parts and I have to sing all the songs, and my throat gets tired. So lots of times, I won't play radio. Sometimes I teach her to sing in harmony – she sings the melody and I harmonize. But I only know a few songs: 'Joy to the World', 'Now Is the Hour', and 'America the Beautiful'. It's hard to harmonize. 'America the Beautiful', but I love it: 'For purple mountain majesties/Above the fruited plain.' It's pretty, not like 'Oh, say can you see'. That's all about war. Joy always giggles when we sing 'Joy to the World', because she thinks they wrote it about her. She doesn't really understand, she's only five. I was nine on my last birthday, and next month, in May, I'll make my First Holy Communion. But that doesn't make you grown up, because all the other girls in my religious instruction classes are little.

The other thing I like to do is swing on my swing. Daddy put it up and it's very strong and secure. Mommy came out to look at it when he hung it up and she said so. I can swing very high on it. I recite Robert Louis Stevenson's poem 'The Swing' while I'm swinging, and try to pretend I can see far off into the horizon, a patchwork of little square farms like the ones in the picture. But all there really is is an empty lot with a dusty square in the middle where the boys play baseball; beyond that is a high school, I don't know its name. Sometimes when I'm swinging, the DiNapoli boys go up on top of the roof of their garage, where they have a pigeon coop, and play with their pigeons. They send them out to fly, and I try to fly as high as they do. Only in imagination, of course. I wish I could fly. I fly in my dreams all the time, but there it isn't fun, because I'm trying to escape from bad people who are chasing me, and I can't ever get high enough to escape. Those are nightmares, I wake up shivering. Sometimes I run into Mommy's room, but she doesn't like me to wake her up. She's tired. She's tired a lot, because her life is hard. That's why she's always in a bad mood.

One afternoon when Mommy was in an especially bad mood, Anastasia had her cookies and milk, and went right upstairs to change her clothes, and lay down on the bed to read a new book from the school library. She was deeply immersed when Mommy called her. Anastasia raised her head reluctantly, a little dizzy. She read so much, so fast, that often she would feel a little sick when she put her book aside. And these days, she wanted to do nothing else but read. She would go down for dinner and leave the table as quickly as she could, to run back upstairs and read some more. She would have liked to read during dinner, but Mommy wouldn't permit that.

She went to the head of the stairs. 'What?'

'Don't say *what* that way, Anastasia. Come downstairs.'

She went down lingeringly. 'What?' she asked again, and her mother grimaced.

'I want you to run to the bus stop and meet Daddy. Ask him to give you a quarter. Then run to the grocer and get a package of Mueller's spaghetti, number eight, and then go next door to the butcher and get fifteen cents' worth of chop meat.'

Spaghetti and meatballs: ummm. Anastasia's mouth watered. But she didn't want to go the store. She wanted to read.

'Why can't you just wait until he gets home, and I'll go to the store then?' she complained.

'Because Daddy likes to have dinner ready as soon as he gets home.'

'Well, it won't be anyway,' Anastasia pointed out, and Belle raised her eyebrows and turned away. Anastasia knew that despite her mother's grimace, she, Anastasia, was right; on the other hand, she also knew that if she argued any further, Mommy would put on her jacket and go up and meet Daddy herself and go to the store herself and then come home and make dinner and be grouchy and not speak to Anastasia for the next few days. So she got her jacket sulkily and left the house.

It was a wonderfully fresh spring evening, and she had been inside the house all afternoon. She breathed in the air deeply, and was delighted at the tiny balls of green dotting all the spare branches. Like embroidery, she thought, little knots of green stitched on the brown. And in a few of the front yards, she saw shoots of green poking through the earth.

She trudged up the three long blocks that she hated. She didn't know why she hated them. She hated to walk. She would have liked to skate, or jump rope down the street. She arrived at the corner of 123rd Avenue and Sutphin Boulevard, but the bus wasn't there. She stood uneasily in front of O'Malley's Bar and Grill: Saloon, pondering those words. What was a bar? a grill? a saloon? She had peered inside the place and knew it smelled awful. It had little swinging doors, and sawdust on a wood floor and it smelled sour. Often, shabby men came out of there carrying big pails of sloshy foamy beer.

Finally, a bus drew up to the corner across the street, and people got off, but Daddy wasn't there. She hopped up and down, impatient. After a while, another bus came, and Daddy got off. She was happy to see him. She liked the way he looked. He was neat and nice-looking, not like the other men. And when Daddy saw her, he smiled! He looked happy to see her!

She waited for him to cross the street to her, and then ran up to him and told him her errand. He smiled again, and gave her the quarter. But instead of running directly to the store, as Mommy wanted, she walked along with him, skipping, talking, looking up in his face. He seemed glad that she was there!

She walked down two blocks with him, then cut up to the left and ran up the hill toward Rockaway Boulevard, where the stores were. And after that, she decided she would meet him every night. It was spring, then summer; the days were long, and it was light and the air was soft at 5:10, when his bus arrived. She would watch the clock so as to leave around 5:05, and she never had to wait more than two buses. Then they would walk back together, and sometimes they would hold hands. He always seemed happy to see her, and her heart felt good.

When summer came, often Mommy would be sitting on the front steps waiting for them when they reached the house, and she would smile and get up – she would never let Daddy kiss her on the street – and go inside and serve the dinner. Daddy didn't seem so grouchy anymore, and one day she went out to the yard while he was fixing the car, and asked him to explain the engine to her, and he did. But she couldn't understand the words he used: she didn't understand *generator* and *distributor* and *battery*. But she pretended she did, so he wouldn't become impatient with her.

It was vacation now, and Anastasia was happy. Then one day, when Joy was out playing, as she was about to go out and make her Persian tent, Mommy sat down at the table and lighted a cigarette, and asked her to sit down. She did so with a sense of the portentousness of her mother's request.

'You're really getting grown up, Anastasia,' Mommy said.

Anastasia was very pleased.

'You've made your Communion, you're finishing fifth

grade and going into sixth. I never went beyond the sixth grade in school. You're fortunate.'

'Why, Mommy?'

'I had to go to work.' Mommy's voice sounded sad and thick, as if she were going to cry. Anastasia looked sadly at her mother. 'When I was nine years old – just your age – my father died . . .'

She began to talk to Anastasia then, seriously. Over the years, Anastasia had often asked her about her mother and father, about how she met Daddy and why they got married (this especially puzzled her), and Belle had told her bits and pieces. She had said good things about Daddy: he was a tennis player and was so good he played at Forest Hills; he was a track star; he'd gone to college but had to leave before he finished because his mommy got sick and he had to take care of her. But he was very smart – he'd made a radio crystal set when he was only a boy, and he knew everything about cars. And he had manners: he came up to the door and rang the bell, he didn't honk his horn for her the way the other boys had. He was a gentleman. But Anastasia still couldn't discover how they had decided to get married, or what kind of wedding they had. She didn't understand why Mommy wouldn't tell her.

But this afternoon, Belle began telling her different things. And she continued, for months, to talk to the child in the late afternoon. She told about having to go marketing every day when other children were playing outdoors, and having to walk far to a terrifying place clutching a few coins, and buying food and coming home and cooking dinner for her mother on a wood stove. Every night. And she was only nine. Anastasia's heart ached, listening. And how poor they were and how no one would help them except a Jewish family they didn't even know. All the people in their family abandoned them. And Mommy couldn't speak English and was sent home from school, and later she was sent home from school because her hair wasn't combed.

'My mother never combed my hair,' Belle mourned.

And Belle told her how she had to take care of baby Jean, and how she yearned, craved, education but could never have it because they were too poor, and how lucky Anastasia was. And then when Belle was older, she still couldn't get education because she was blind in one eye from measles and deaf in one ear from a mastoid infection and couldn't hear the teacher or see the blackboard. And how she had dreamed and longed to play the piano and that's why she was making sure Anastasia had piano lessons. And Joy would have them too, in a couple of years, when she was old enough. And how she knew nothing, nothing whatever about religion, and hadn't made her Confirmation until she was eighteen, and she was tall and gawky and felt stupid with all the twelve-year-olds. Her life was very sad.

And it was still hard, because she had to scrape and worry because Daddy didn't earn enough money to support them. He had no ambition, he had no drive, he never planned a thing, she had to do everything for the children, all the hopes and plans came from her, not him. Everything came from her. Daddy didn't care about anything except a hot meal and a night's sleep and . . . He didn't care at all about the children.

'He loves you, though,' Anastasia interjected.

Belle snorted. 'He doesn't love anyone! Look at the way he treats his family! He marries me, he doesn't think about them, or call them, or go to see them. He would never have gone to see them once we were married, if I hadn't said, "Ed, we ought to visit your mother," and now that his mother is dead, I have to remind him we should visit his father. It's all been up to me, and they don't even like me.'

'Why don't they like you?' the child asked, pained.

'Oh, I don't know. I'm not a good enough Catholic, I guess. Or because I smoke.'

'We used to visit Aunt Kris. Why don't we go there anymore?'

'I don't know, Anastasia.' Belle was beginning to sound impatient. 'She got mad at Daddy for something. I don't know what. She won't say. And you don't see him trying to make up with her. Does he ever even mention her and Joe? Never. He doesn't care. It would be the same with us. If I were to die, he'd be married again in a month. And he'd marry someone who gave him nothing but frankfurters and beans to eat and he'd be just as happy, he wouldn't even notice the difference.'

Belle was going to die soon. She had a bad heart, had always had it, and she knew she would not live long. It made her so furious when the neighbor ladies praised Daddy. 'They all say the same thing – oh, how sweet Mr Dabrowski is, how lucky you are!' She mocked their voices, making them sound silly and feminine. ' "So nice, so polite. You're so lucky!" They don't know what he's really like, how he grumbles and grouches and has no ambition. They have no idea. They don't say he's lucky to have me.'

'You could tell them,' Anastasia said, keening on injustice.

'No. I'd never do that. They all gossip. They tell everybody everything. That's why I talk to you, Anastasia. I have to talk to somebody, but I can't talk to these women. But you mustn't ever tell anyone the things I tell you. They're confidences. I tell you because you're so grown up.'

Her mother's confidences struck deep inside Anastasia's heart, and lay there piercing her. She would lie in bed at night imagining her mother's life, trying to make it all happen over again, but with her present to save her mother from the sorrow and injustice she had suffered. If only she had been there! She would have helped her mother and made her feel better. And she would think about her father and her heart would harden. He made Mommy unhappy, he didn't care about them, all he cared about was himself.

Over the months this new relation with her mother came to obsess Anastasia. She realized quickly that she could not initiate these intimate conversations. She would come into the kitchen, and wait; she would show herself to be available. But if Mommy didn't feel like talking to her, she would be annoyed, and if Anastasia asked her a question, she would sigh and say, 'Go and play. Anastasia, I'm tired.'

It was Daddy's fault that Mommy was so unhappy, so tired all the time, in such a bad mood. Anastasia's stomach always knotted as she approached her home. She was unhappy enough at school, and glad when the schoolday was over, but then she would see her house and her stomach got tight. But sometimes when she walked in the back door, Mommy would smile and be glad to see her. Sometimes she was not. She was always in a bad mood on washdays, and Anastasia came to associate the smell of laundry soap and bleach with tight silent withdrawal, with greyness, bleakness, and isolation. She thought she had done something wrong, and would ask her mother what was the matter, but Belle always said, 'Nothing'. And if she pushed it, if she asked if her mother were angry with her, Belle would *get* angry: 'Why do you think you're so important?'

But it was Daddy's fault. She would be careful not to get angry with Mommy anymore when Mommy was in a bad mood, because now she understood that Mommy was angry with Daddy. She felt worry for Mommy, whose life had been so sad and was still so hard. She completely stopped running up to meet her father after work. Instead, she stayed with Mommy in the kitchen, or out on the front stoop. She understood that to meet Daddy was in some way to fail Mommy, to betray her. Anastasia pulled close to her mother and began to look at her father with bruised eyes.

three

As soon as he could afford it, Brad decided to move us to a house. Not just any house – it had to be elaborate, not to say pretentious. He wanted one with white columns and a portico on a main street in Rockville Centre. The point of the house was not comfort, but the degree of success it announced. I was able to block the pretentious one by insisting that it was too dangerous a place for small children; there was really no yard, it was all lawn, and at the intersection of two streets with heavy traffic. But Brad kept looking, and as a real-estate agent, he had an insider's view, and eventually he found one he believed I'd approve of: a big old Victorian house with a gallery all around the front and one side, a big yard with old trees, and on a prime location in Rockville Centre, the town where my parents lived, the most expensive town along the South

Shore of Long Island in Nassau County. The only town more expensive (in that area) was Garden City, and I could see Brad had his eye on that for the future.

I have to admit I loved that house. It was old and a little shabby, but it looked like a house a family could be happy in. There was a huge yard with big trees, and I pictured a swing for the kids, and a little wading pool. They'd been deprived of outdoor life in the years we'd lived in the apartment, but now they'd have it. They were the right age for it, too, four and five. And there was now room for me to have a darkroom in the basement.

But the move to the house didn't make Brad happy. He was a little anxious about money, because he paid a lot for it, and besides that, it had all those empty rooms we couldn't afford to furnish. Adeline found a hideous used dining room set for us for twenty-five dollars. Brad gave her the money but the furniture was so awful he wouldn't have it in the house and it stood in our basement waiting for him to refinish it, until the house was sold, years later. When I realized that Brad was never going to put up a swing, I asked my father to do it, so at least the kids had that, and the wading pool I bought them out of my housekeeping money. I had money of my own now, enough to put in the darkroom and even to buy a metal photograph file – a purchase that made me feel like a professional for the first time.

I had to start all over again, of course, in the new neighborhood, and it was harder here because not many people had children, and those who did had enough money to have professional photographs taken. It is a phenomenon I have often noticed – that when a husband does well, wives somehow do worse. I still had contacts with people who'd heard of me in the old neighborhood, and so still got some commissions, but they dwindled with time until I was doing only one or two a week.

One of my conditions for moving to a house with three bathrooms (all of which I'd have to clean) miles away from stores or public transportation was a car, and with much grumbling, Brad bought me a small used Rambler that wouldn't go over sixty. Brad had no patience with my complaints: 'You never clean anyway, so what difference does it make how big the house is?' he said. My other condition was a piano. I was starved for music and I wanted the children to study it. Brad was nice about that, and I found an old upright with decent tone. Only he didn't want it in the living room – he said it was an eyesore.

We moved in the late spring, just as things were springing into bloom, and I stayed outside with the kids and played much of the day. I was happy in the beginning. I felt rejuvenated, somehow. We'd play tag, and hide-and-seek, and sardines – joined by the few other children in the neighborhood or one of my friends from the old neighborhood with her kids.

I kept on photographing them, under the trees, in the garden: beautiful pictures, shimmering with summer and childhood and golden-haired cherubs. And every night I'd bathe them in the nice big tub in the upstairs bathroom (Brad and I had our own bathroom! What a luxury!) and play ice-cream cones with them the way my mother used to with us: making a great lather of the shampoo, and holding it in my hand and offering them a bite of my ice-cream cone. It set them giggling as hard as Joy and I used to; and I wondered in passing how my mother ever came up with that game. For surely no one had ever played it with her.

When fall came, I piled the kids and my cameras in the car and drove off to some exotic place to take pictures – the back of movie houses (wonderful dark red fire escape against the blank grey wall), the railroad tracks (old railroad cars rusting on sidings, the parallels of track taken from oblique angles, the wheel of an idle train taken up close, a deserted old railroad station), lots full of pipe waiting to be laid for sewers, crates piled up behind supermarkets: now, I thought, I would create art.

Oddly, Brad was often impressed with these efforts. He'd always been patronizing about my photography. He saw it as a hobby, too expensive for me; he liked some of my pictures of Arden, but he thought anyone could have taken them. Yet without my knowledge, he took a shot of mine, of a derelict car abandoned along the Southern State

Parkway (in the years before such things were common), and sent it into the local newspaper, the *Long Island Herald*. And they printed it! They sent me a check for fifty dollars, and asked for more of my work.

I was happy with that, of course, but even more I was touched by what Brad had done. I met him at the door the night the paper called to ask permission to print it, with a big smile and a hug. I was affectionate – the truth is, I climbed all over him. His act had renewed my old feeling for him, I felt (for a moment) we were buddies, companions, *together*, rather than opponents linked in a power struggle. I jabbered, I crowed, I spent the fifty dollars forty ways, and I gave him real meat loaf and mashed potatoes to eat. (The kids were always in bed before Brad got home at night. Just as well. He was always impatient with them. Like my mother, I shrugged and decided that was the nature of the male.)

He accepted my affection, although I sensed a kind of wariness in him. He accepted it through dinner, and into bed. After we had made love (I, disappointed, as had become usual with us), and were sitting up smoking, I said, 'Brad, what's the matter? You seem – I don't know – withdrawn.'

He turned on me then with an expression I'll never forget. It was tight, his teeth were a bit bared, and his eyes held utter hatred. It would have shocked me at any time, but just after we had made love, it made my heart really bang, as if someone had hit me hard in the chest with an oar.

'I notice that the only time I get affection from you is when you have success in your career.'

'Then why did you let me make love to you!' I cried out, and leaped out of the bed naked. 'If that's how you feel, why did you send the picture in? Why do you stay with me? What is this? What is going on? Let's just call it a day, Brad, there's no point! I feel violated, I feel raped! To make love at a moment when you are hating me! Horrible!'

I pulled on an old shirt of his that I used as a bathrobe, and stormed out of the room and went downstairs, thinking how convenient it was to have a downstairs to go to when you're having a fight. It was dark down there, and silent, the proper place to sit out a drama: And think how foolish I was, how even when my heart felt broken, I was thinking about how I appeared, how my actions would seem from the outside, about how much more of a statement I was making by going down into the dark living room than I ever could have made when we had only four rooms on one floor.

But my appearance didn't matter, because Brad never came down. I sat there in the dark smoking away (just like my mother) and staring out the window, and he simply turned out the light and went to sleep. At some point, I realized he wasn't coming, and then I had to stop in my tracks. I'd been feeling wronged and hurt and angry; now I had to recognize that what was happening was serious. It wasn't a momentary act of rage. Brad hated me.

The tone in which he said 'career' was one of utter contempt. And I couldn't see why, if he held my activity in such contempt, he had helped me in it; or why, if it was so contemptible, he was threatened by it. The whole thing mystified me, but I couldn't even think it through because I was so absorbed in feeling. And what I was feeling was overwhelmed with self-pity.

All kinds of things rose into my chest, as if my innards detached themselves from their proper places and floated upward, about to drown me. I felt willing to die, but they floated up up up and never did drown me. I couldn't even cry and let them out. Why? Why? What did I do that was so bad as to make him hate me?

But I knew. I had to hold it back, to keep it from coming into my mind, because it was too terrible. I knew why he hated me and I knew he was justified. I couldn't go further that night. I knew I'd have to do something, but I was too tired. . . .

I went to bed. I slept beside him, stiff, not letting my body touch his. That was the first time. I was to do that many nights afterward, sit up late smoking, thinking, planning, then go up sorrowfully, like an old woman burdened with eons of sorrow, and lay my ancient body coldly beside his in the lumpy bed. It was hard to lie on that old mattress and keep my body away from his, because it sagged in the middle, and I kept rolling down toward him. So for months, I slept poorly in a rigid posture on a narrow strip of the bed, as far from him as I could get.

I usually woke up with the kids around six, gave them some milk and dry cereal, and went back to bed again until nine, when Brad got up. I'd fix breakfast for him and sit with him, drinking coffee, until he left. Then I'd begin the business of the day. The morning after our fight – although you can hardly call it a fight, since he said nothing whatever to me after I yelled at him – I didn't get up for him. I stayed in bed until after he left. That night, when he came home around nine, as usual, I was working in my dark-room. I'd left him a plate covered with the lid of a pot, in the oven. It held dried-out chicken, vegetables, and rice. I guess he ate it, because the plate was in the sink the next morning, but I didn't check the garbage pail. After I'd finished my darkroom work, I sat in the living room until around two, smoking, thinking, planning, and then went to bed.

We went on living like that for weeks; he never took a day off, and I never waited to have dinner with him, as I used to. He'd write me notes: take grey suit to cleaner; have brown shoes resoled; shaving cream; club soda. Little affectionate things like that. I did whatever he ordered: that's what I was being given room and board for, wasn't it?

But meantime, I was struggling with myself. Because I knew what I was doing was dishonest, and therefore demoralizing; but I couldn't figure out a way to do anything else.

Brad hated me because I had lost respect for him. And I had, I couldn't deny it. It wasn't just because he had become a real-estate salesman instead of a sax player. Or, maybe that was the start of it, but he could have been a real-estate salesman and still been a person, a whole human being, couldn't he? Even if he adopted that pompous voice his father used, and the manners of a 'successful' man who belongs to the right clubs and was jovial and hearty, whose manner says 'I'm one of the crowd, boys, and used to being treated like one,' he could still be a tender person, he could caress one of his kids once in a while, couldn't he? Or couldn't he? Maybe when money and prestige become your goals, you lose touch with everything else.

I would sit in the living room watching the kids play together. They got along pretty well now, and Arden would make up games and Billy would join in. They walked around, two little self-important people with their little sweet voices, discussing the best way to set up a toy store – they were in the process of selling off all their toys – and I'd hear echoes of Brad and me in their remarks, and look at the sweet curve of their cheeks and the soft sweet hair that framed their faces, and their little chubby legs, and I wanted to embrace them and weep, to hold them close to me and cry for all I knew they would never have, any more than I had had it.

I had no business living with Brad if I didn't respect him. It was wrong, for him, for me. It was what my mother had done, staying with my father. It demoralized us all. I remembered how I felt, watching my parents together. But the truth was even worse. I didn't just not respect him, I didn't even like him. I didn't want to create the kind of home I'd been raised in. I should leave: that was clear. But how?

This was 1954. People didn't just walk out on each other in those days. How could I justify leaving him? 'I don't like him?' Hah! And then how would I live? Since installing the darkroom, I had in my sugarbowl a total of $69.80, if I included the $50 check from the *Herald* – which I had not yet received. The picture editor had said they'd like to see more photographs by me, but I knew enough not to inundate them with pictures, and even if they took one every week – which was improbable – I couldn't live on that. I could go back to Jimmy Minetta's, maybe, or find a job. But who would look after the children?

After several weeks of holding my head, staying up late, and walking around all day with a headache, I decided on a course of action. I would present the whole thing to Brad – tell him the truth of how I felt, of how I understood what he felt, and ask him to join with me in a separation in which he would help support the kids. It was a shocking business, but I was determined. I'd never known a divorced person, except Uncle Wally, and his divorce was never discussed. When my mother admitted it to me, she had whispered, even though we were alone in the room.

While I was mulling all this over, Brad had been following his own course. And it happened that the night that I decided to have dinner with him and tell him everything was the night he closed a major deal that had been in the offing for several years – a shopping mall parcel in Garden City, worth hundreds of thousands of dollars in commissions to the agency. So there I was, severe and grim and sad, sitting in the kitchen watching the roast dry out because he was late, and he came in pink and tipsy and smiling broadly.

'Hey, sweetie!' He embraced me as if we had never quarrelled. He ate the overdone meat without complaint; he kept drinking vodka and tonics while he was eating. He urged me to drink a few, too. 'It's a sale-a-bration!' he kept crowing, not noticing my shudders. He talked about the deal, or rather, about his foresight, persistence, brilliance, indefatigability, slyness, manliness, vigor, cleverness, and general all-around heroism. He was affectionate when he was finished eating, but I told him to go ahead up and I'd come up in a moment, after I'd finished cleaning up the kitchen. I knew he'd pass out the minute his head hit the pillow.

I did go up later, just to make sure he wasn't choking on his own vomit, and to make sure he'd been able to get his shoes off and his feet under the covers. He had. So I went back downstairs, and sat in the dark living room, smoking. And I thought that I had been wrong, that Brad was even more out of touch with me than I'd thought. He thought I felt good about him when he felt good about himself; when *he* had a success, he assumed my affection; when he was doing poorly, he assumed I was ashamed of him as he was of himself. In other words, he no longer saw *me* at all, only himself reflected over and over in the faces of others.

And he had treated me and my affection viciously that night three weeks or so ago because at that time he'd been worried the deal would not go through – this had filtered through the long narrative he'd offered – and since he was feeling bad himself, he couldn't conceive of my feeling good about him. So the only reason I would make love to him would be to get something out of him. His entire world had turned into a scheme of rewards and punishments, bribes and penalties, and he no longer saw that there was any other way to be with people. That was why he was so terrible with the children. When they were lively and making noise and bothering him, he thought they were doing something *to* him, that they were challenging him or trying to annoy him. He couldn't see that noise was an accidental by-product of young high spirits. So he shouted at them as if they were willful destroyers of his peace.

We began to live normally again, having breakfast and dinner together, and he took Mondays and Tuesdays off, as he had before. Now all he wanted to do on his days off was go shopping for furniture and rugs and lamps, something the kids really hated, and I too. But he felt he couldn't go without me. I don't know why, because we agreed about nothing. I don't like new furniture; it's ugly. I like old things, handmade, human-sized; but he liked huge heavy pretentious machine-made, 'perfect' pieces. He bought a ponderous 'suite' for the dining room, and another for the living room. Eventually I just stopped going with him; he found an 'interior decorator' – a friend of a friend of a friend – who went with him and supervised his purchases. She and he had similar taste, and so our nice old house was turned into a furniture store.

I guess I should have fought harder, should have tried to inject my own taste into it. But it would have been a bloody battle and he wouldn't have been satisfied, and after all, as he said, it was 'his' money. I drifted through the 'decorating' only half-conscious of what was going on, as if I knew I would not be there long.

I tried, a few days after Brad's drunken evening, to talk to him about separation, but he wouldn't hear me. 'Honey, of course I don't hate you, I love you, look, I was just in a low mood that night, you have to accept that once in a while, you know.'

I couldn't make him see. 'Absolutely not, I don't want a separation! No! I won't allow it!'

In those days you couldn't get a divorce in New York State unless you proved adultery – or had it set up – or got a power of attorney from your spouse, and flew to Mexico for a quickie divorce. In either case, you had to have your partner's consent. *One* unhappy spouse did not count. And, as I've said, I had nothing to go *to* – no better life, no happier house. So I went on as I was, we all did, in a strange marriage that was pure surface with nothing underneath. I was careful not ever again to initiate lovemaking with Brad, and he initiated it himself rarely enough that I could not refuse him, but just closed my eyes and got it over with as fast as I could. I felt dishonorable; lacking integrity. But integrity, I realized, was a luxury few women could afford.

Brad began to stay out late fairly often. His real-estate success had allowed him to enter the political circles of Nassau County, and he had dinners with minor figures in the political clique, talked 'deals', and gave big contributions to Republican candidates. (The 1952 election was the first presidential election I could vote in, and Brad's family was outraged at hearing that I voted for Stevenson: no Carpenter had ever voted Democratic before. After that, I kept my vote secret.)

We had one major fight in those last years we were together. Brad wanted to show off his fancy house, and decided we should give a big dinner party. I nearly collapsed. It wasn't just that I was a lousy cook, and didn't want to have to cook a big dinner for a lot of people, but I knew we didn't have the equipment, the stuff my mother had – silverware, crystal, good dishes, candlesticks, whatever. The way we'd married had assured our receiving few wedding gifts, and we hadn't bought such things since. Brad said we'd buy them. I sat down on the bottom step of the big (now carpeted) staircase that wound through the center hall of our (now fancy) house, and howled.

'I can't! I can't! Don't you see, Brad, that you're trying

to force me to be someone I can't be and don't want to be!'

'Yes,' he said thin-lipped. 'I see you're still a child and refuse to grow up. You think if you wear shorts and my old shirts and no makeup and go around looking thirteen, no one will expect anything of you.' He started to walk away, then whirled around. 'Even pigtails, for godsakes! Last night when I came home, you had your hair in a pigtail!'

'A braid,' I said with dignity.

'I don't have a wife, I have an overgrown child! Forget it, forget it! I'll take care of it myself!'

He did too. He borrowed everything we needed from his mother, who was thrilled to see things she'd had stuffing the closets all these years getting some use. She gave us one of her many sets of dishes, half her crystal, half her yellowed table linens, and the antique silver-plated flatware that had belonged to her great-aunt Florence. He hired a cook and planned the menu with her. He browbeat me and dragged me to Lord & Taylor's in Garden City and bought me a long tubular gown in a deep purple, and gold shoes, and gold earrings.

I looked at myself in the mirror the night of the dinner party, and it occurred to me that I looked nice – my skinny small-breasted body looked glamorous in that kind of dress. But I didn't know who I was. I looked like one of my paper dolls from childhood – I'd even put on eye makeup and lipstick for the occasion. Still, I didn't know how a person who looked like that would act, and I was terrified.

I think I did not acquit myself too well, but Brad made up for it in a heartiness and heavy drinking that astonished me. The men he'd invited acted the same way, and they at least liked me, kept calling me 'little honey' and one of them even patted my behind. I almost slugged him, but Brad caught my arm. I did less well with the women, who were a tough breed, heavy drinkers like their men, tanned, slim, soignée (except for a couple of motherly ones), who talked about tennis and servants and vacations at Biscayne Bay. I sat back, giggling from my two glasses of wine, thinking, 'Well, my dear, we have servants too,' because we did – that night.

Brad never proposed a dinner party again, though, in the years we had left to us. He stayed out more and more, and at some point I realized there was another woman, and I let that be, figuring that was my solution. As it was.

In 1940, Ed was promoted. He was called 'Special Tester', and concentrated on movie houses and theaters which were beginning to install air conditioning. Brooklyn Edison did not know how to bill for its huge usages of electricity, and it was Ed's job to work out a system. He got a raise to forty-five dollars a week. Part of the reason he was given this promotion was that he had taken a correspondence course in 1938–39, from an air-conditioning school in Chicago. Ed told Belle someday air-conditioning would be a big thing and that the course was worth the expense. In 1941, he was raised to forty-eight dollars a week. And then, war broke out.

It was easy to be cynical about the causes of war in those days, for war was the solution to the Depression: two years before there had been no money, men were out of work, or worked for the WPA, or were, they say, selling apples on the street. I never saw that myself. Then, suddenly, money is pumped into the economy, disposable money, for weapons are a unique commodity – they are made to be destroyed without any intervening usefulness. I mean, a car or a washing machine also breaks down and has to be discarded after some years, but in the meantime, it has provided some service. Weapons don't. Their use *is* their destruction.

Anyway, suddenly men and even women were in demand, and earning good wages. Ed went to the Stevens War Industries School for six months, finishing in the spring of 1942, and under Belle's continual prodding, found a new job with Control Instruments as an inspector of electrical and mechanical elements. He was hired at $56 a week, a huge raise for him, but because he also often worked overtime, he started to bring home almost $100 some weeks. Belle put the money in the bank. The only thing she bought was a refrigerator, because she reasoned that if the war lasted a long time, she might not be able to get one. And Ed bought a car for $50, a long low 1928 Graham-Paige, once a luxury car but long out of date. Under his hands, it ran like a sleek new limousine.

With the birth of her third child, Jean stopped working, and now that Jean was home, Frances could come to visit Belle. She would stay for four or five days, and although Anastasia fervently wished to give her her bed, she insisted on sleeping on the couch. While she was there, she would bake: she made peach cake and apple cake, and 'snails' made of raisins, cinnamon, and nuts. She made doughnuts, laying them out on brown paper that covered every surface in the house. She made babka and chruściki and poppyseed cake. She made only yeast cakes and would not use baking powder.

Sometimes she would make clothes for Anastasia and Joy – suits or coats. Anastasia hated that because she had to stand still for such a long time while Grandma fitted and pinned. Everything was made of fine wools that Mommy bought as remnants and everything was lined in rayon. Every buttonhole and lapel was carefully done by hand.

Anastasia loved Grandma and was happy when she came, but she also felt guilty during these visits. Because she could not talk with Grandma. Grandma spoke Polish to Mommy, but English to the children. But she didn't understand anything about a child's life, and Anastasia didn't understand anything about hers. She would sit beside her grandmother, very close, and Grandma would caress her and say *moja kochany*, but after a while, Anastasia would feel restless and want to go and read or draw or play the piano. She would force herself to remain for a while, but it was boring. And Grandma had a funny smell, musty: as if when people grew old they, like houses, corroded and smelled of damp rot.

One time when Grandma was visiting, Mommy grew worried about her. She told Frances that she had to take Joy to the doctor, and asked her to go along. They had a new doctor now. Anastasia did not know what had happened to Dr MacVeany, but the new doctor lived only eight blocks away. So Frances went with them, and when they arrived at his office, Belle went in and asked him to examine her mother. Then she went to Frances and asked her to come in.

Frances wouldn't move. She was shocked. 'What, Bella!' she exclaimed. She had never been to a doctor in her life. But Belle insisted, and the old woman – she was sixty-one – went in. The doctor examined her and pronounced her old and rheumatic. Belle gave him two dollars: she had a little money now, and could spare it. That was all.

But Belle felt her mother was dying. And whenever she came after that, Belle would take her by bus to Jamaica, to wander through the stores, ending at Woolworth's lunch counter. There she would buy Frances a pastrami or corned beef sandwich. Such days were a dazzling treat for Frances, who smiled broadly with happiness. She had never eaten out before. A sandwich at the counter of Woolworth's with her daughter was the greatest luxury she ever experienced.

When my mother was seventy-seven, I took a trip with her and my father to Florida. They had often driven down; I had not been there. But I had some money that year from a commission and I flew them down and rented a car, and took rooms in a hotel in Palm Beach. It was an old shabby place, but very expensive: I thought they might enjoy it because they always stayed in motels. But one evening, the elevator was out of order, and we had to walk the two flights up to our rooms. When we reached the landing, I looked at my mother. She was wheezing and lowing, like a pigeon. I said,

'Mom, you aren't feeling well.'

She gave me a long meaningful look.

'Have you seen a doctor?'

She shook her head.

'You have to see a doctor.'

'No, Anastasia,' she said, with tears rising in her throat.

'Why?' I was surprised. Mother haunted doctors' offices; she went at the slightest symptom, and was well-known to the friendly family physician who lived around the corner from their house.

She just shook her head, hard. My father was still parking the car. I gazed at her, thinking.

'You think you have cancer,' I concluded.

Her face scrunched up with tears.

'You don't,' I pronounced. I don't know where I get my gall. 'You have emphysema.'

She raised her head haughtily. I knew she would fight my diagnosis. It was cancer. She'd decided she had cancer several times before.

'Will you go? Emphysema is incurable, but it doesn't kill you right away. If you stop smoking, you can live many more years.'

She turned her head away from me.

'If I make the appointment, will you go?'

She bit her lip, tears in her eyes. She nodded. Then she turned back to me. 'But I don't want to know. . . .'

'You mean, if it's cancer, you don't want to know.'

She nodded.

'All right, I promise. If it's cancer, you won't be told. But you will go?'

She nodded. I laid my hand on her arm. She pulled away from me and fled – as fast as her tottering uncertain walk could take her – down the hall to her room. 'Now just leave me alone, will you! Just leave me alone!' She disappeared into their room as my father appeared. He raised his eyebrows. 'The lady went to bed?'

'Yes. Do you want to go for a walk?' My father and I were always tired at night from our days of physical restraint – we mostly sat, and when we walked, we had to walk very slowly with my mother, so we took brisk walks in the evenings, after she was in bed.

'Yes,' he smiled. 'But first I have to see that my lady is all right.'

I followed him into their room. Mother was sitting in a chair by the window, smoking. 'Would you like a drink, Belle?' my father asked solicitously. She nodded.

He went into the bathroom for a glass, and poured her

some scotch from the bottle they carried with them. Then he added water.

'Dad and I are going for a walk,' I said.

She nodded. She wouldn't look at me.

On our walk, I told my father what I thought, and that I would make an appointment with an excellent doctor in the city. He listened, sighed, said nothing. Then, 'Oh, I hope not,' he moaned, and began to belch.

'Well, I think it's only emphysema, Dad, which is serious, but not immediately life-threatening. Haven't you noticed how she sounds when she walks? That cooing noise.'

Well, he hadn't. Or had blotted it out. Who knows? We kept walking in silence punctuated by his belches, frequent and deep, the only sign my father ever gave of emotional upset.

four

I watched my children playing, saw how they ran up to Brad when they saw him, welcoming him like puppies, no matter how he treated them. He wasn't cruel; he'd smile and tousle Billy's hair and pick Arden up and kiss her. He wouldn't kiss Billy, and I'd get tears in my eyes watching his face as he watched his father kiss Arden, hold her in his arms. And I'd go out and pick Billy up and hold him, and kiss his cheek. But his head would turn away from me, yearning toward his father.

Sometimes I talked to Brad about them, asking him to be more affectionate, but he always said he didn't want to make a sissy out of Billy, and he had to counter me, since I was doing a good job of turning him into a pansy. I've never understood this logic – that affection turns a man, but not a woman, into a sexual deviant; and that lack of it assures his manliness. I couldn't penetrate Brad's prejudices, though.

And then I'd think about my own father, and how I yearned for his affection, and later, how I yearned for him to be something he was not. He has always tried, he still tries, to be *good;* but his idea of goodness is a child's. He tries to be complaisant with my mother – with Joy and me, too, now. And he was taught, in his childhood – he had to have been taught – that badness lay in developing an independent mind, in thinking and feeling and seeing for oneself. This had a profound effect on him.

He could *do* things by himself. He could fix anything, build anything. When I was about eleven, he built a collapsible Ping-Pong table that we could carry up from the basement and set up in the yard on fine days. But when we played, Joy or Mother and I, our balls would fly over or through the picket fence into neighboring yards, and Mother was perturbed. She thought the neighbors would object to our entering their yards to retrieve our balls. So she spoke to Ed, and he devised a retriever. It was a long broom handle with a tin can on its end, and a lever. We would stick the pole through the space between two pickets, lower the can on the ball, work the lever, and the ball would be captured, so it could be carried back to our own yard. We all thought he was a genius for inventing that, and showed it off proudly to our friends.

And once, on his own, without Mother's asking him, he did something for me myself. It was at Christmas, the year I was twelve.

Christmas was an important time in the family. Every year the weeks before Christmas were filled with whispering, concealment, and excitement. Joy was gay, excited with anticipation: Anastasia was not: she knew there would be no surprises for her. All she would get for Christmas was a book. If she was lucky, two or three books. So she felt the whispering and concealment were on Joy's behalf.

On Christmas Eve afternoon, Belle would roll up the children's hair in paper and send them up to bed for a nap at four o'clock in the afternoon. They could never sleep. They would lie there talking about what Joy would get and what there would be to eat. And for years Joy asked a lot of questions about Santa Claus. Anastasia had discovered the true identity of Santa Claus the first time she laid eyes on him, when she was two. She pointed to the familiar face under the red cheeks, the beard and mustache, and said 'That's Uncle Eddie!' But she had been asked to keep the secret from the younger children, and she did. Joy continued to believe there was a real Santa Claus until she was six or seven, and now Ingrid and Errie had to be protected from the truth.

At seven o'clock, Mommy would get them up and they would put on their best clothes, and she would comb their hair in spaghetti curls, and they would all go out when it was dark and get in their car (if they had one) or Uncle Eddie's and drive to Aunt Jean and Uncle Eric's house. Their tree would always be bigger than Belle and Ed's: their house was bigger too. Ingrid and Errie and now the new baby, Dorothea, would be dressed up too, their eyes wide and sparkling, waiting. They had to wait a long time, while the grown-ups talked and sipped drinks; the children would play a little, but not much, because they were too nervous. At the stroke of midnight, one of the grown-ups – it was usually Uncle Wally – would look out the window and cry out – 'Look who's here! I just saw him flying over the roofs across the street!' and all the little children would scream and run to the windows, Anastasia following them for the appearance. And then the doorbell would ring and in he would come. Santa Claus! The children would shriek, and he would say, 'Ho, ho, ho,' and Anastasia would look to see which one it was this year – Uncle Eddie, Uncle Eric, or Daddy – and he'd be carrying a huge white bag full of toys. Anastasia knew that none of the toys was for her.

Santa would come into the living room and sit down, and the grown-ups would be giggling and offer Santa something to drink, or something to eat and this was funny because whoever it was couldn't eat or drink with that white mustache and beard pasted on his face, and he'd laugh too. And then he'd give out the presents. Joy always got a doll; and maybe a little carriage and blanket, and sometimes a dress from Eddie and Martha. Ingrid usually got three dolls plus lots of other things. Errie would get erector sets, and trains, and all kinds of mechanical toys, and the living room floor would slowly fill up with piles of presents, all toys. When it was her turn, Anastasia would shyly accept her present. She always got a book from Mommy and Daddy: sometimes she got one from Jean and Eric, and one from Eddie and Martha, too. But sometimes Anastasia got a blouse or a dress from Jean and Eric, and then she nearly cried. She would gaze over at the huge mound of toys her cousins had received and wonder why she couldn't have the little she wanted: books. One year, Eddie surprised her and gave her a whole stamp collection – two almanacs, stamps, a magnifying glass, and pasters. And he showed her how to use it: Eddie had a very fine stamp collection, Mommy told her. And once Eddie gave Joy and Anastasia necklaces he had made himself of stone he had found in the mountains, and polished, and strung together. Anastasia wished it had been a book.

The Christmas of 1941 when Anastasia was twelve, she asked for two things. She knew she wouldn't get both, but she couldn't decide which she wanted more. One was, surprisingly, a doll. She had seen it in a store in Jamaica when they were shopping before Christmas. It was a child, not a baby doll, and it came in a trunk with hangers, and you could buy clothes for it. She explained to her mother: 'I know I've never liked dolls, but I like this one. I love the little trunk and hangers. Maybe I could sew clothes for it if you helped me. It's probably my last chance to have a doll, because I'm almost grown up now. This would be the only doll I'd ever have.' The other thing she wanted was a printing press.

In the weeks preceding Christmas, Anastasia sensed an excited tension in the house in the evenings. Daddy was always down in the cellar – well, he usually was when he was home – but Mommy did not usually worry that she might go down there. She only went down to sharpen her pencils on the sharpener Daddy had hung above the second step down, anyway. But there was rustling and putting things away if she came downstairs at night. Still she never expected what she got. That was the most wonderful Christmas Anastasia ever had, and the first one she didn't feel envious of her cousins.

She got the doll: it was about a foot tall, and made to look about nine years old. She was wearing a brown-and-white check dress with a white pinafore, and a bonnet to match. But in the trunk, hanging on the hangers, were a little pale pink chiffon dress with embroidery roses at the neck, and a grey velvet coat with real fur on the collar, and a hat to match, a beret with a fur pom-pom. Anastasia turned these clothes over in her hands. She recognized the fabrics – they were from old clothes of Mommy's that had been put away in the trunk. The clothes were beautiful; as she examined them, she saw the many tiny stitches Mommy had made so that the clothes were exquisite, like real clothes, with tiny little seams and edges. They had tiny white pearl buttons and minuscule buttonholes, all beautifully stitched. And she knew it had taken Mommy many many hours to make this for her. And besides that, Mommy had made an identical set for Joy, who had the same doll, except hers was wearing a pink dress.

But then, she got *another* package, and as she opened it, she felt something excited come up in her heart. For there was the press, and ink and a stack of paper in it, and a flat wooden box that might have been a cigar box, with a hinged lid with a screw fastener. And inside that box were forty compartments, each one holding a different character. And she understood that her father had made this for her, and that his making it had been his own idea. For she could envision how it happened.

Mommy would have bought the printing press and shown it to him in the evening, after the children were in bed. And he would have examined it carefully, the way he always did, picking up pieces and parts and seeing how they worked, and deciding whether it was well-made or not. And all the type probably came in a single little bag, all tossed together. And he would exclaim, 'Terrible! She'll never be able to use this. It will take her hours to find each character, whatever one she's looking for.' And he would sigh heavily. And Mommy would look at him questioningly. And he would mutter and carry the whole thing down to the cellar, and look around for something to use as a container. And then he inset, into the wooden box, all these tiny compartments, and did it so well that the inserts were solid and secure. Then he had separated all the characters and put them in their compartments, and that too had taken hours, and he had made this for Anastasia, without Belle saying anything. Anastasia never forgot it.

With the self-engrossment of a child, I never thought about the fact that during these Christmas Eve celebrations, grown-ups did not receive presents. One year, I recall, as I was in the kitchen helping Grandma and Mother and Jean set out the feast that followed the departure of Santa Claus, Jean held out her arm to Mother and said, 'Look what Eric gave me.' She was wearing a beautiful silver bracelet with gems studded in it, amethysts, probably. And Mother breathed out, 'Oh, how beautiful, Jean.' And it occurred to me that I had never noticed my father or mother giving each other presents at Christmas. They didn't give each other birthday presents either. They never got anything at all, at any time.

Only one summer – I was probably ten or eleven – an itinerant salesman drove onto our block in a car whose back seat was piled high with dresses. He went round ringing doorbells, and Mother went outside to look at what he had. When she returned, she showed me, proudly, two dresses. They were rayon prints, one with lilacs, the other a brown-and-orange paisley. Mother seemed so proud of them that I admired them inordinately, thinking all the while that they were nowhere near as pretty as the clothes belonging to my paper dolls. They had cost three dollars and two dollars, and they were the first new things my mother had ever bought in my memory, except her beach coat.

I had almost destitute years in my own marriage, but they didn't seem so bad. Maybe because the whole world wasn't depressed, as it was in the thirties; maybe because they didn't last as long. But above all, because I wasn't like my mother (*wouldn't* be like my mother), and refused to allow myself to care about things like clothes and food and cars and furniture. I cared only about having fun and taking pictures. Nothing else.

So I told myself. So I believed. It is amazing how completely one can fool oneself without ever fooling anyone else. I entertained myself and the children, daily, cheerful Nellie, Pollyanna, laughing, cracking jokes. But my kids remember quite another side of things.

'You weren't there,' Arden hisses at me. 'Except when you were playing with us, you were somewhere else! You didn't want to be with us, you didn't want to have us!'

'I tried,' I say shortly. 'If you can do better yourself, be my guest.' I leave the room.

'That's right, run away!' she calls after me in her vengeful voice. 'That's your solution to everything. COWARD!'

The coward cowers in her room with the door locked. It isn't true, I argue silently. I did want her, I wanted to have her. I just wasn't ready. It would have been different if Brad had taken some of the responsibility. If he'd felt any pleasure. It was his fault.

Sometimes, weighed down by the sorrow in her mother's stories, Anastasia would ask Belle if she had ever been happy. Then Belle's voice would lighten and she would talk about the wonderful beautiful girlfriends she had, about the wonderful times, visits to museums, the drama club, going to Pratt . . .

But there was always a cutoff point, and the more Anastasia questioned it, the more Belle evaded it, until Anastasia came to realize that what had cut off the good times was her birth, herself, Anastasia. And when she probed that, Belle was even more mysterious, so that when the truth finally emerged it was unclear whether Belle had finally revealed it, or Anastasia had deduced it and told her mother she knew. Anastasia doesn't know when that happened, how old she was when she sat listening to her mother's description of her shame, her thought of abortion, her decision to sacrifice herself to her, to Anastasia. And to the tearful shame that followed her birth, the interminable depression, the decision to have another child. Through all of it, Anastasia carefully avoided thinking that her mother had not wanted her. She thought about things as if she herself were Belle, as if Belle's perspective on the events were the only one possible. That her mother had not wanted her, that she had sacrificed herself mournfully to this duty and had conveyed considerable resentment to the object of her sacrifice, was outweighed by the enormity of the sacrifice itself, its completeness, and the intelligence with which it was carried through.

'I'd never say such a thing to my mother,' I said to Arden. But I had, many times, said, 'You don't love me.' Just never: you didn't want me.

Sitting there in the bedroom, wiping my eyes, thinking it was good Arden could say such things to me, a good sign, the girl was growing up. And wondering: does any woman want a child? Does anyone on earth want to have to give up everything else in life to tend a squawling baby, stinky with shit, hungry all the time, noisy, demanding? Who would choose it? And do those who do choose it know what they're getting themselves into?

But is there any difference between that, having children whether by choice or not, and marrying? Caring about someone? Because why should we? Isn't there as much pain in that as in anything else? All those years with Brad, telling myself I was cheerful, having fun, when in the back of my mind I felt like a half-dead person, a person not walking on earth but floating somewhere above it in a gray haze of years in which nothing significantly changed, in the dull pain that comes from not letting yourself feel sharp pain. A numb suspension, a sense you aren't real. Going through motions. Long empty years, the emptiness in my eyes infecting my children. And now? The children are grown. It's years since I've cared about anyone except them, yet they're worse now than they ever were. Arden hits against me as if she wants to kill me: trying to pierce my armor. I can't blame her. I can't blame my mother either. Except once after a year of great change.

Anastasia had started high school in the fall of 1942, and had made some friends. She had started to go for religious instruction to make her Confirmation, and she had joined the church choir. Belle was glad she no longer went to Girl Scouts: buying all that equipment was too expensive, and Anastasia didn't seem to get that much out of it. Belle had taken a job herself, because it was clear that she would have to start to save now for college for Anastasia. It was only four years away. She couldn't do much, but she felt she could look presentable, so she applied for a job as a saleslady, and got one in the finest store in Jamaica, B. Gertz. She worked in its loveliest department, selling hats. But it was hard. She had to wear a dark dress and high heels and stand on her feet all day. Salesladies could not sit down, and even when there was nothing to do, they had to look busy. When Ed came home early, he would pick her up with the car, but many nights she had to take the bus. When she got home, her legs and ankles were swollen from all the standing, but she still had to cook the dinner. She did the laundry on her day off. She put every penny she earned in the bank. But she was very tired.

It was very depressing at home. Anastasia didn't know why she was so unhappy. Of course, high school was frightening, it was so big and crowded and the other kids were so much more grown up than she was. But she had joined the high-school orchestra, and played the piano during rehearsals. During performances, though, she played the cello, because Mr Piatti, the conductor, needed a teacher to play the piano then. He lent her a cello and was giving her lessons free. She liked the cello, but didn't practice enough. She had lost some of her feeling about music. It had happened one day when she was sitting on the porch floor reading the latest *Etude*. And suddenly her head popped up, all by itself. It came to her like a punch, that all composers were men. She laid aside the magazine and sat, her shoulders slumped, pondering. She knew that there were things men did and things women did, and that some things were exclusive. For instance, a woman couldn't be a priest. But a man could be, well, not a nun, but a brother, which was just like a nun. Women and men were teachers, but men were principals. Women were nurses, men were doctors.

Did that mean she could not be a composer? No one had told her that. Angie had been proud when she played her sonata at his party. Now Angie was gone, though, into the army, and she had a new teacher, Harold Grunbacker. He wasn't as sweet as Angie, but he was a good teacher too.

All her piano teachers had been men. But Mommy had taken her to a concert, just last fall, played by a girl a little older than she, Ruth Sczlenzinska. But Anastasia didn't want to be a pianist. She knew she wasn't good enough. She wanted to be a composer. But maybe that would be impossible.

She would have to be something else. She joined the Latin Club, and the school magazine, and she had made three friends – Kathy McGowen, Teresa Kelly, and Carmela diFalco – and the four of them spent afternoons and weekends together. They had no money, and no place to go. They mostly walked. Sometimes Anastasia would take them home to her house, but she was never invited into their houses except once when Teresa's parents were out on a Saturday afternoon. And then it was obvious Teresa was nervous; she kept them in the kitchen, and after they had drunk their Cokes, she washed and dried their glasses. Teresa was adopted. Her parents had died. Kathy was crazy about Frank Sinatra, and they often talked about getting enough money together to go to New York and see him when he performed. They could stand outside the theater where 'Your Hit Parade' was produced, and see him get out of his limousine. All they needed was bus and subway fare. Finally, they went one Saturday night, and stood in a huge crowd of girls like themselves, all of whom screamed when Frankie appeared, embarrassed-looking and shy, and worked his way through the crowd. All the girls tried to touch him, and sometimes, Kathy said, they even ripped his jacket. But there were some men around him to protect him, and Anastasia and her friends were far back in the crowd, and saw no one touch him. But at least they saw him.

The girls would sit in the park, talking. Or they would go to Woolworth's, and once they stole things, just for a lark – hairpins and lipsticks and nail polish. Afterward, Anastasia felt so guilty, she gave her cache to Carmela. She didn't want to be found with stolen goods, even though they were far from the store by then, having gotten away clean.

And once in a while, if they had money, they would go

to the movies together. Only Carmela could never come, she always had to stay with her baby sister at night. Anastasia thought that her friends' parents hit them. They never said anything, and neither did she, but she knew they feared their parents.

When she was home, Anastasia read. She rarely raised her head from her book. She didn't want to be in that house, and was in it with her spirit as little as possible. She examined all the books in the bookcase, and tried to read most of them. But they were mostly boring: *The Meditations of Marcus Aurelius*, *Two Years Before the Mast*, the *Iliad*, by Homer. The Harvard Classics. Daddy had bought them from a man he worked with. Mommy was very angry about it, she said they couldn't afford it. Daddy said the man was down on his luck, and he thought Belle would be pleased: she was so devoted to education. But she shook her head and said she couldn't believe how stupid he could be, to buy expensive books when they barely had money to live. Still there they were, purchased for $1 down, $1 a week, for a year. Anastasia was glad they were there, but she wished they weren't all so boring.

Some of the books on the shelves were all right, though. They had come from the same attic as the children's books Anastasia had inherited: Radclyffe Hall, *The Well of Loneliness;* Thomas Hardy, *The Return of the Native;* Thomas Paine, *The Age of Reason;* George Eliot, *The Mill on the Floss;* and *The Constant Nymph*. Anastasia could never remember who wrote that one. But she read these books through, and read Paine several times. There was also Schopenhauer, *The World as Will and Idea*, but she got only to page 30 in that. And best of all was Friedrich Nietzsche, *The Case Against Wagner*, which she could not understand completely, but returned to over and over.

Every Wednesday night since she had been confirmed last June, she had gone to choir practice with Mrs Murphy. Mrs Murphy had stopped one day to chat with Mommy, on a pale soft evening when Belle was sitting on the front stoop. Mrs Murphy asked about the child who played the piano: 'So talented,' she said. She asked if Anastasia would like to sing in the choir. Anastasia would. So each Wednesday evening, Mrs Murphy stopped for her after dinner, and brought her back after practice.

Mrs Murphy was the organist for the church. She was large of body, with thick upper arms, and tiny red veins on her nose and cheeks. She was jolly, and she really talked to Anastasia, as if she were interested. She had seven children of her own, she said, and she would tell Anastasia about them. Choir practice was strange, and Anastasia sat on the fringe. There was a tiny little man with funny hair who acted very fussy about what he would sing, because he liked to do solos. And there was a grown-up girl, in her twenties, who did all the soprano solos. The rest of the people were old, like Mrs Murphy, and shabby and gossipy.

But Anastasia loved the music. It was wonderful what happened when all of these unprepossessing people opened their mouths together. Mrs Murphy would coach them, but mostly she just let them sing. The melodies were wonderful, and so were the chords. *Kyrie Eleison; Agnus Dei; Gloria.* It came from another world, and on Sunday, when they all stood upstairs in the choir stall and followed the Mass and sang, Anastasia could picture a different place from the one she was in, a church sparer and purer, without the hideous garish stained-glass windows of St Mary's, without awful Monsignor Burke saying Mass, but just white walls and slits of windows and voices and this music soaring. And it was especially wonderful at Easter, when there were banks of lilies in the church and the priests wore beautiful white and gold and purple robes and the music rose into the dank space and lighted it.

Then on Columbus Day, there was a great banquet given by the Knights of Columbus, and Mrs Murphy asked Mommy if Anastasia could go, and Mommy asked her if she wanted to. She didn't really want to go, but she was embarrassed to be asked right in front of Mrs Murphy so she said yes. Mrs Murphy said she had two tickets and Mr Murphy . . . well, he was indisposed or something. Anastasia never saw Mr Murphy. And although Anastasia wondered why Mrs Murphy hadn't taken one of her own children, she felt honored to have been asked.

Mommy told her what to wear – her good dress from

Easter – and helped her fix her hair. Mommy said this was Anastasia's first grown-up evening. Mommy even let Anastasia use some of the brilliantine she put on her own hair, and it looked really shiny. Then Mrs Murphy rang the doorbell, and together they walked up to the Knights of Columbus headquarters on Rockaway Boulevard. It was a big room over some stores, and when they walked in, Anastasia was terrified. There were hundreds of people, mostly men, all grown-ups. She was the only child. Some of the grown-ups were young, in their twenties, but most of them were as old as Mrs Murphy. But everyone was very friendly even to her, and didn't seem to mind that she was a child. They sat at a table and a waiter came and brought her ginger ale and Mrs Murphy had a drink, the kind Uncle Eric sometimes served to Mommy and Daddy, and there was a dinner and ice cream and speeches and singing and a little band. Anastasia remained at the table the whole night, even when Mrs Murphy got up to chat with someone across the room. She watched and listened.

Everyone was so *jolly*. Anastasia had never seen such an event. As the evening wore on, they got jollier. Everyone seemed to like everyone else, everyone talked and smiled and laughed a lot. And everyone knew Mrs Murphy and stopped at their table and spared a few words for the little girl. The didn't even treat her like a little girl: well, of course she was a high-school freshman, even if she was only twelve. And Mrs Murphy introduced her: 'This is Anastasia Dabrowski, and she is a fine musician and she sings in the choir every Sunday.' And the ladies smiled at her and said, 'How nice,' and asked her how old she was and what grade she was in and raised their eyebrows when she said she was in high school. But the men gave her funny kinds of looks she'd never seen before, and said things like 'Look at that hair!' and 'A real heartbreaker,' to Mrs Murphy. 'A lovely girl,' some of them said, always to Mrs Murphy never to her.

Anastasia let herself down into it. The big plain spare room was bright and noisy and filled with people laughing, and all of them were nice to each other and to her, and she felt herself slipping into the comfort of it, the sense that they were all together, all friends. 'A lovely Catholic girl,' several men said approvingly to Mrs Murphy who beamed and nodded. And Anastasia lowered her eyes, because she did not think she was so good a Catholic. She had felt nothing at all when the bishop tapped her at Confirmation, and she had no idea whatever what Confirmation was supposed to mean: what does it mean that the Holy Spirit descends into you? It wasn't like making Communion at all: then she had felt infused with passion, a vitality, a kind of glow. And besides, Thomas Paine said different things about God from what she learned in Religious Instruction, and Nietzsche hated Christianity.

Still, it was seductive, a spell, and as she sat there in what felt like a communal embrace, she could feel an ache in her heart that she was aware was constant, and she knew that these people were offering to heal that ache. If she just continued to come, if she let herself be one of them, they would surround her with this kind of affection, they would make her feel accepted. But what did they want for it?

She remembered vividly the night she had had a fight with Mommy, when she was ten. She had said something fresh, and Mommy had scolded her. But what she said was right, and Mommy refused to consider that, and scolded her just because she didn't feel like arguing or explaining or talking. And Anastasia went into the porch and sat down on the floor feeling very sorry for herself, and when Mommy called her to dinner, she didn't go. She sat there in the dark room while the others sat at the table eating, and she saw the light and heard the clicks of forks and smelled the warm food. Mommy called her again, but she wouldn't go.

Then Mommy came into the room where Anastasia was sitting and reached out her hand to Anastasia.

'Come on, Anastasia, come to dinner,' she urged.

Anastasia was shocked. Mommy had never done anything like that before. Whenever she got angry with Anastasia, it was Anastasia who had to apologize. Mommy would stop speaking to her, and she could go for days without talking, whereas Anastasia could not, so she would have to apologize. Still, she wouldn't rise.

'No,' she said, shaking her head, refusing to speak to

Mommy. Mommy knew she was wrong, that was why she did that. It was her way of apologizing. But Anastasia wanted her to say she was sorry, the way Anastasia always had to say she was sorry. And Mommy wouldn't. Mommy went back into the kitchen. And Anastasia sat there, her stomach churning with hunger, thinking that she could go with Mommy, she should have gone with Mommy, she could do what Mommy wanted and then maybe Mommy would love her, but she didn't want to.

She longed for Mommy to return, but she didn't. You can get love but you have to do something they want, Anastasia thought. You have to be exactly the way they want you to be. And if you're not, they don't love you. And it isn't worth it.

Eventually, she got up and went into the kitchen and ate her dinner, which was no longer hot. She sat silent at the table and did not look at Mommy. It wasn't fair, she thought.

So here were these people offering to love her, saying she was a lovely girl, a good Catholic girl. But that was only because they didn't really know her. She was nicely dressed, her hair was neat, they thought she was a nice girl. They didn't know that she doubted the existence of God, that she was stubborn and fresh and willful and selfish. And if they did know these things, they wouldn't like her. They would turn away from her the way Mommy turned away from her. They wanted her to be just the way they were, and they would love her only if she was.

The evening went on for a long time, but luckily, someone gave them a ride home in a car, so all Anastasia had to say was 'Thank you'. Mommy was waiting up and wanted to hear about it, but Anastasia could see that she was tired, and felt satisfied by the little she was told. Then Anastasia could go up to bed and lie there in the dark thinking about all of it, her heart a great gaping ache because she felt she was giving up something she treasured, felt she would never have it, would never let herself have it.

It was so depressing in the house. Mother refused to wake

her up in the mornings, because Anastasia was so hard to waken, and always went back to sleep after Mother called her. She stopped making breakfast, too, but there was always some coffee cake if Anastasia wanted it. Usually she was so late, she just ran out of the house without eating, and even so, she often missed her bus and was late for school. That wasn't so serious a matter in high school, though. But the allowance she was given hardly paid for lunch every day in the cafeteria; if she bought something to eat, she would have no money for movies on the weekends. So often, she just had a Coke at lunchtime. And then, when she came home from school, Joy's and Mother's breakfast dishes were still in the sink and the kitchen smelled from being closed up all day. She was supposed to wash the dishes and practice, but instead she sat and ate, one after another, slices of bread with peanut butter and jelly, or if there was some left over, chocolate layer cake. She would read while she ate, devouring food and huge Victorian novels. She read all the school library owned of Galsworthy, Dickens and Trollope. Mother came home, when she came by bus, about six; when Daddy picked her up, they were home by quarter of six. So a little after five, Anastasia would hurriedly rinse the dirty dishes, and run out to the porch and begin practice. She always told Mother she was nearly finished with her hour and a half of practicing, even if she'd practiced only half an hour. But some days she felt like playing the piano and would play for three hours.

When Mother came home, she spoke little. Sometimes she talked about the ladies she sold hats to, and what they wore. Or about the buyer, or the assistant manager. She took some of Anastasia's sketches to show the assistant manager: Belle thought Anastasia could be a fashion designer. But he said she had to learn fashion perspective: in fashion illustration, the body was far longer than the head, and not in realistic proportion. Also, he said to be a fashion designer, you had to know how to sew. Since Anastasia's two efforts at sewing dresses, in the seventh and eighth grades, had to be ripped apart and completely resewn by Mother the night before they were to be handed in, Anastasia thought that there was another career that was not for her.

Mother would ask how school was, and listen as Joy and she gave their tiny bits of news, but her mind was elsewhere and they could feel that. The dinner table was silent. Even on the nights when Daddy was home, as he sometimes was on weekends, there was no talking. And on the nights when he worked late, Mother would go out to the porch after Joy and Anastasia were in bed, and sit in the dark smoking. Anastasia knew this. She lay in bed, her stomach churning. There was nothing she could do any longer to please her mother, no way to make her smile, or even talk. Anastasia began to feel her mother had betrayed the intimacy she had initiated. Belle had abandoned her.

This recent depression of Belle's felt hard, angry, unyielding, like a door shut in the face of the whole world. Anastasia's stomach twisted, and her throat constricted; she felt as if there were lumps in her that had to come out or she would die: in her throat, in her stomach, under her armpits. She was weary, yet could not sleep; she read in bed, not caring if her mother discovered her. But she could not get far enough away to forget.

One night, lying there like that, she thought she had to speak or explode. She leaped up from her bed, and without thinking, ran barefoot down the uncarpeted stairs and into the porch. Her mother did not hear her. She was outlined against the window, the tip of her cigarette red in the dark room, but only for a second. Anastasia could hear her mother exhale the smoke.

'Mommy,' she began, and Belle turned, startled.

'Oh, Anastasia, you startled me! What's the matter?' Irritable.

'What's the matter with you? You never talk anymore, you're always angry, you're always in a bad mood, you sit here night after night in the dark smoking. What is it? What is the matter?' Anastasia herself could hear there was no warmth in her voice, no love: only anger.

Belle turned her head away from Anastasia. 'Go to bed,' she said in a cold voice.

'I won't! I won't! Not until you tell me what's the matter!

It's not fair! You act as if you were dying, you treat us horribly, and you won't say why!'

Belle stood then and walked toward Anastasia. In the dark, she was a darker form, outlined against the window. 'I told you to go to bed.' Icy.

'No!!' There were tears in Anastasia's voice now. 'You're horrible! You're mean! You don't love us!'

Then Belle raised her arm and struck Anastasia, struck her over and over. Belle knocked Anastasia to the floor. She lay there sobbing. Part of her wanted to get up and sock her mother back, hard. But she didn't. 'I hate you! I hate you!' she sobbed.

Belle returned to her chair and lighted another cigarette. After a few minutes, Anastasia picked herself up and went back to bed.

In the spring of 1943, Daddy's company had a day's outing for its employees: a boat trip up the Hudson, and a picnic at Bear Mountain. Belle bought flowered pink chintz and made the girls identical pinafores, and a sundress for herself. All the big bosses were going to be there, she said. It was an important occasion.

They drove to Manhattan, to a pier on the West Side, where the Day Liner was berthed. There were hundreds of people circulating around the boat, and some of the men came up and spoke to Daddy and called him Mr Dabrowski. Anastasia deduced he was their boss, and she felt proud. Then Daddy said, 'Belle, there's a very nice woman I think you might like, somebody to talk to, she works in my department. I'll introduce her to you.' And Anastasia felt something. Something felt bad, something was going wrong. And Daddy led them up the gangway, and up to the higher deck, and straight toward a group of women who were sitting together, just as if he knew where they'd be. And Daddy seemed nervous and excited, but he would be, because he never did anything like this for Mommy. But Mommy was like ice, and Anastasia was annoyed with her.

And Daddy said, 'Oh, there she is,' in his happy voice, and he started to say, 'Belle this is . . .' when Mommy turned on her heel and walked the other way. And Anastasia was shocked into stillness. She looked at Daddy: he was running after Mommy, calling her. Joy was looking at Anastasia, who took her hand; they walked after their parents. And Mommy stopped and Daddy spoke to her, but whatever she said was as if she had hit him and he reeled backward, and she looked over to them and said, 'Come, girls,' and Joy dropped Anastasia's hand and ran to her mother, and Daddy just stood there, and Anastasia walked slowly up to him and stood with him.

And all the rest of the trip, Mommy stood with Joy at the railing of the lower deck, and Daddy stood by a column, seventy feet away, staring at her. Anastasia stayed with her father. He hardly noticed it. Several times he said to her, 'Why don't you go with Mommy, she feels bad that you're not with her.'

'No, I want to stay with you,' she said.

He was not consoled by her presence. He looked intently, unwavering, at Belle, gazing at her standing seventy feet away as if she were behind glass in a museum, untouchable, unattainable, the object of his intensest desire.

That moment – it may have lasted an hour or two – is engraved on my memory. I don't recall how the day ended – obviously, it did. There must have been hamburgers and hot dogs and orange soda and trips to the toilet. There must have been walking together to the car and getting in it together and driving home together. I remember none of that. And in fact that day did not end for us. We returned to a gray tension in which a dropped fork could startle the whole room of us. We went back to live for months, perhaps, in a silent house in which no one ever raised their voice and no one ever smiled.

That was the one occasion in my life when I took my father's part against my mother. It was the first time in my life I ever openly blamed my mother for anything. And there is no question that this seriously disturbed me: I must have felt terribly guilty, because during that summer, on a horribly hot night when I slept with my head at the foot of my bed so as to get whatever breeze there was on my face, I dreamed a dream so vivid and clear that it remains with me still. I was lying there, with my head at the foot of my bed, when the curtains that shielded our room from the little landing were pulled open. A figure stood there in a long white nightdress, outlined against the light on the landing. It approached me, a pale faceless form in the moonlight, a woman carrying a knife. She came to stand just beside me, and then raised her arm and prepared to plunge it into my heart. I screamed. I kept screaming. I woke my mother, who came in.

'What's the matter, Anastasia?' Annoyed, angry voice.

'I had a bad dream, a nightmare,' I whimpered. 'A woman was going to kill me.'

'Oh, for heaven's sake,' she exclaimed. 'Did you wake me up for something that stupid? Go to sleep!'

But I couldn't go back to sleep, I was too terrified. I knew the figure had been my mother, but I couldn't accept it. Why should I dream so about my mother, my good mother who gave me everything, the mother who had bound me to her by sacrifice, whose wish was my wish, whose will my will?

Yet another strand of thought lived in my head, out of touch with this one, like two different people inhabiting the same space but never touching. For I knew why I had stood with my father. It wasn't even really that I was standing with him, because part of me knew he'd prefer to have me go to her: he didn't want her to be any more angry with him than she already was, and he knew, he utterly knew her jealousy, her possessiveness. (How? This man so emotionally dead?) I stood with him for myself. I stood with him because I had somehow understood that he loved the lady on the boat, and Mother was angry about that.

It was stupid for him to introduce her to the woman; he humiliated her. But she humiliated him in return by walking away so abruptly, by making him beg, by forcing him to recognize who was primary in his life. All that – his gaucherie, her revenge – seemed secondary, even unimportant. What mattered was that Belle did not love Ed and turned a cold cheek to him every night of his life. Every night of my life since I was a small child I watched her do this; and every night in all those years, my stomach had churned at the sight. I knew how he felt. (How?)

So he had found someone else who would love him: why not? Mother couldn't help it if she didn't love him, but she didn't have the right to keep him from finding love with another lady. And that lady's face had lighted up when she saw Daddy, she was smiling with her eyes as well as her mouth. Mother didn't have to love him herself, but then she had to let him love somebody else. That was the way it seemed to Anastasia.

All so long ago, yet it feels almost as if time were suspended there interminably, as if that moment had never passed. In a sense, perhaps it hasn't, for me. It passed for them long ago. They have forgotten or forgiven, whichever it is one does. But I have not. I have to laugh at myself, standing there courageously, standing opposed to my mother, standing for body and hugs and warm closeness, standing for sex. For I no longer stand for those things. I have become my mother. I am just like her now: I pull away from embraces, I offer quiet smiles and coldness emanates from my body. I am the ice queen of my fairy tale book. I am stiff and yield to no hugs. I do not want it anymore, closeness of any kind.

Oh, I tried it. But I gave it up. My mother just gave it up earlier in life than I did. I know all about love and I don't want it. It hurts too much.

five

It was when he didn't eat his dinner that she knew. All those nights he ate his dinner when he came home, no matter how late it was. She had never known Ed to pass up a meal. Even if he'd had a sandwich at five-thirty, he was happy to see a plate piled high with steaming food when he came home at midnight. So it was ridiculous of him to claim that the reason he wasn't hungry was because he'd had a sandwich at six. He knew that she knew he often had a sandwich and still ate his dinner. The only explanation had to be that he had already eaten a full dinner, and how did that come about?

She'd had suspicions. He wasn't as . . . importunate. Of course, he was tired, working these long hours, but that hadn't made much difference in the beginning. He was still always at her. Until recently. And a couple of times, she had tried to figure out his pay envelope: fifty-six dollars a week, with time and a half for overtime. It didn't work out right, and when she asked him, he just shrugged. He said maybe they didn't pay him for all his overtime, and she started to get indignant, to tell him to complain, but then she stopped. She fell silent.

She began to sit in the porch in the dark, smoking, waiting for him. All these years. Anastasia was twelve. Scraping and scrimping, pinching pennies to put a good meal on the table, to give them decent clothes, to keep the house looking good. All up to her, all of it. He handed her his pay, that was the end of his responsibility. In all those years, he'd never once taken her out to dinner, or even to lunch, but now he could afford to take someone else out. . . .

All this shabbiness all these years. Oh, how I hate it! How I have tried to ram him full of my dreams, my energy, so he'd get out there and make something of himself, always your humble servant, no get-up-and-go. And I haven't complained, I just went on stretching every dollar to hold a palmful of rain. I slave and he hums and goes outside and works on his car, tinkers from dawn to dusk, he doesn't care, he's happy. He gets what he wants.

All of what he wants. What's the matter with him that he doesn't know I know? Five nights a week he 'works late', and three of those nights he comes home and eats the dinner I keep warm for him, and twice a week he doesn't. So he's taking her out to dinner twice a week. How could I not know? WHAT IS THE MATTER WITH HIM?

So what I am now is a maid in a housedress who cooks for him, keeps his house clean, irons his shirts and under-wear shorts and pajamas and handkerchiefs, irons them beautifully and lays them carefully in his drawers like precious things. And watches him and worries and tells him when he needs a new suit, and goes with him to pick it out because he has no taste.

No taste, only appetite.

Maybe I could even understand that, forgive that. I know I don't feel the same way he does. It's one thing for him, he's always so full of it, but it's another thing for me, look where it gets you, I can't do it without remembering, without feeling it all again, the shame, the awfulness of having your body blow up like that, then the baby, crying, crying . . . and who had to take care of it? Not him. And no matter how many there were, it would be my job to find a way to feed them while he went on happily doing his little job, bringing home his little pay, handing it to me as if it were the crown jewels . . .

And anyway, how can you do it, let yourself feel it, when you're sick with worry about the bills; they turn off the gas and the electricity. And poor little Joy, so sick, so sick, her face flushed with fever, smiling up at me. 'Hi, Mommy,' and so weak I'd have to hold the bowl of chicken soup myself and feed it to her by spoonfuls. I thought she'd die. The good die young. But that can't be true because my father died young.

He doesn't care about the girls, like all men, only interested in his own fun. Grumbling at them, their little faces turned up to him so hurt, so pale. He'd be just like my father if I'd let him. They mean nothing to him. If I died, he'd probably abandon them, mistreat them. He'd find another woman, that would be all that would matter and she'd abuse them, use my good dishes and my crystal goblets and my silverware, not caring. He wouldn't even notice, and if they were unhappy, he wouldn't care. Only for a hot meal and a woman in his bed.

I bet he took her to a real restaurant, with white cloths on the table and a rose in a little vase and a waiter with a napkin over his arm. Picking up the menu. What would it say? You could choose whatever you wanted, a long list probably. Maybe they even have a glass of wine. I'll bet he was charming, he can be charming to women, he loves women. Maybe they even had dancing there, the way they used to years ago. Supper clubs. Tea dances. We went dancing once or twice, years ago. I used to love to dance.

But I'm old now. He's still young, he's not like me, things

don't weigh on him. Why couldn't he do that with me? Maybe I'd feel different. Give me his pay and say, 'Belle buy yourself a new dress and let's go out to dinner on Saturday night.' Oh God, if he ever said such a thing! But I'm just his mother, his servant, his maid. I can't blame him for wanting some fun. I'd like some fun too.

What I can't forgive is his assuming I don't know, his not realizing that I'd have to know. I wonder who she is. Young. She works in his department, I think. A secretary. Probably pretty, spends all she earns on clothes. The way I did. How would she like to take care of this house and market and sweep the floors and mop and dust and vacuum and scrub that old linoleum in the kitchen and do the laundry and cook the meals? How would she like to spend her days that way, watching over two children, one sick all the time, well she can have it, I'd change places with her, let her be me and I'll take her job and spend my money on clothes and go out to dinner with married men . . .

Belle dragged deeply on her cigarette, and tamped it out in the ashtray, then jumped, startled by a voice. She turned quickly to see a pale figure in a white nightdress standing a few feet away from her. A pale faceless form in the moonlight. Anastasia, calling her, calling her, demanding, always demanding. . . .

Anastasia was talking. She was attacking her, her, Belle, her mother! She was saying cold cruel things! Blood pulsed in Belle's temples, Anastasia looked red, blood mounted around Belle's heart, she wanted to kill. With all she suffered, with all her sacrifice, with everything she did for those children, her whole life given up to them, here was this spoiled selfish child criticizing her! She tried to hold herself back. She turned away.

'Go to bed,' she said as calmly as she could.

Cruel selfish brat: screaming now, protesting! How could she! When as it was, Belle barely managed to go from day to day . . . She would never have dreamed of speaking to her mother like that, how dare she how dare she. . . .

Belle stood and walked to the child and slapped her. She was hysterical, that was the trouble. Anastasia stopped speaking. Belle returned to her chair and lighted a cigarette.

Alone. Alone in gloomy isolation, a dark pit of suffering, in agony. She had never had anyone, and she never would. All of them out there with their puny desires, their selfish wishes, incapable of understanding. And she was here, in the darkness, her whole body torn by claws of wild animals, and all they could do, those who claimed to love her, those who were supposed to help, all they could do was add their clawings to her scars, scrape and shriek against her skin, oh what had she done to deserve such pain, and how could she go on living?

In the spring of 1943, Frances died. She was ill only briefly, and the doctor ordered an autopsy to determine the cause of death. When it was over, he came out wiping his hands, and spoke to Eric.

'The old lady was a real tippler, eh?' he laughed.

Eric was startled. 'She never had a drink in her life!'

The doctor shrugged. Frances had died of cirrhosis of the liver. That's what he said.

Belle said something else, but only to herself. She said nothing to Ed, or Jean. Belle said she had died of grief.

Perhaps. For when had she had a life of her own? Her children 'bettered' her by moving her to the house on Manse Street, which was a nice enough house, but far from any neighborhood where she might have heard Polish spoken, or made a friend. There was no old neighborhood for her: they had moved too often, and she had worked too hard to make enduring friendships. Her family, which had abandoned her when Michael died, was also dead or distant now. She devoted herself to her children as she had to him, became their slave, servant, caretaker. She knew no other way of life.

Then all the children had left and she was there in a house full of strangers, except Jean. She was a maid, an affectionately treated servant in her son-in-law's house. She was not paid for her labors; she was given room and board with a few pennies spending money. She raised the grand-children as she had her own children, never raising her voice or protesting. She worked, she served. And she was rewarded: they moved to a huge house in Locust Valley, a place with no sidewalks, no trolleys, no buses, and no Polish people. She worked, she slept in her room, the little maid's room beside the kitchen. She smiled, she nodded agreeably, she knew her place.

She said nothing when she read in the newspaper that Poland had again been invaded by the Germans, but a part of her heart died: she had been raised under the partition, and forced to speak German in the schools, in the street. Did she know what happened to her village, that the people who lived there were shot, thrown in a pit, and covered with lime? They were not 'her' people, they were Jews and Frances was raised Catholic, but were they not her people? She died in the same year the village of Zmegrud was destroyed.

Was it very different for her that she was saved? Living in a fine house in a neighborhood without sidewalks, with a country club, unable to drive, miles from the nearest public transportation, living on her son-in-law's charity. No one spoke Polish anymore. The old ways had vanished. She hardly knew her grandchildren, they were a strange breed in this country, a foreign land, she spoke its language but she did not understand it.

Not one of them knew her. No one, except maybe Bella, had ever understood her. For them, for their friends, for the people she entertained, she was just an old woman, a servant, a foreigner in an old brown sweater with a hole in the sleeve. It had been long, and hard, and what had it given her after all? Tired. It was time to die.

Chapter IX

one

Divorce can strip you down to your essentials faster than any other loss. When someone you love dies or falls sick, there is always something besides yourself you can blame. But when you divorce, you have to blame yourself. You don't need society to tell you you are a failure, as it assuredly did tell women who divorced during the fifties; you know you are a failure because after all, you wouldn't have gotten married if you didn't want to. So if you wanted the marriage to be a joy, and it wasn't, and it grew so bad you had to end it, you failed at an enterprise you once wanted to succeed. And then when it's over, you're not dead, you go on living, and living alone.

I used to feel so sorry for my children because of the way their father treated them, that I overlooked all kinds of bad behavior, and just hushed them up and cuddled them and told them they were good. And sometimes they weren't so good; and – although I didn't discover this until years later – they always thought they were bad when their father scolded them. So they came to think of me as either a fool or a liar, indifferent to their behavior. I used to think that if Brad and I could just separate, the children would be calmer, more contented: with just me around and no one to throw them into hysterical crying all the time, they would settle into the peace and love I could provide. Well, the opposite happened. They became moody and irritable. Billy spent hours in his room devising mazes and Arden became savage, storming in from school every afternoon and glaring at me as if I had somehow ruined her life; and then storming out again to play with one or another friend. Since she was stormy with her friends too, she often had no one to play with; and that was worst of all.

And I, who had been telling myself for years that I would paint if only Brad weren't around, had to admit to myself that I was never going back to painting, that I was not an artist after all. The best I could be was a photographer. It took me a few late nights sitting up in the dark to admit that to myself, and the pangs I felt brought tears to my eyes. But maybe photography could be an art too, I thought, trying to cheer myself up. People were beginning to write about it as if it were.

The worst thing I had to admit was that Brad had been right about me. I had tried to remain an eternal child. Now that I had to pay for everything, and wasn't given a weekly allowance anymore, I had to figure out amounts for rent and telephone and car insurance and electricity, and just starting to do that made me want to scream, all I could think of was my mother and her painstaking allotments of dollars and fifty-cent pieces to budgetary categories. Horrible! Not the way I wanted to live! But there I was. I never told Brad he'd been right, though. By the time our divorce was final, we were barely speaking.

Brad introduced the subject of divorce in May of 1958. He was almost thirty, I was twenty-eight. Arden was nine and a half and Billy had just had his eighth birthday. We'd been married just ten years. Brad had been staying out nights, and for several months he hadn't attempted to make love to me, so of course I knew. We still appeared in public as a couple – we went to dinner with friends, to movies and an occasional play, but our conversation was completely superficial. But that was no clue, since that was the only way Brad ever talked. He liked to talk about people's new houses; or their new boats; or their taking a trip to Europe. He'd remark that this one said that restaurant was good, and we should try it. He'd suggest I buy myself something decent to wear, and toss me a fifty-dollar bill. I'd tell him about the things that went wrong in the house (more appliances, more trouble), or cute things the kids had done, or their marks on tests, or what one of my friends or her husband had done: but that was all. I was just waiting, biding my time. There was no way I was going to get out of this marriage if *I* wanted to: I'd have to wait until *he* did.

And so the night he came home and acted serious over dinner and asked me to sit in the living room with him afterward and have a drink, I made him wait until the kitchen was cleaned up and I'd taken a shower and washed my hair. Let him sweat, I thought. I wanted him to be eager and unwavering. Then I joined him, carrying a rye and ginger ale. I'd recently been forced – given our social life – to take up drinking, but I still wasn't used to it.

He began by saying he'd been thinking about what I'd said the night soon after his great coup with the shopping mall, that we didn't have much in common anymore. And that I'd seemed to suggest I didn't care very much about him anymore. But I wasn't about to let him take the offensive, so I interrupted:

'Cut the shit, Brad, you're fucking around, right?'

He stopped, he stammered, he flushed. He said, 'Jesus!' and got up and left the room, and I was afraid I'd gone too far. But I could hear the ice clinking in the kitchen and knew he was just pouring himself another drink and getting time to compose himself.

I felt like a hypocrite, though, cheap and small. Because if there was one thing I *didn't* blame him for, it was fucking around. I'd have been fucking around myself if I had felt any desire whatever. I sat there sipping my disgusting watery drink, shaking my head at myself.

Because I had always tried to live with what I privately called integrity – I'd tried to be honest with myself and in my life. And sometimes I'd even feel a little self-righteous in the face of other women. I knew that Brad had loved me once, genuinely; and that what had changed was that he had adopted a role for himself, and wanted me to adopt the complementary role, and I wouldn't. I *was* being stubborn and rebellious and intractable; and even though I told myself regularly that I had the right to be the person and live the life I wanted, I only occasionally believed it. After all, no other woman I knew felt they had such a right. Whatever they'd been, or their husbands had been when they first married, all their husbands had adopted the role Brad had chosen, too; and their wives had gone along and been complements. Who was I to stand out against the whole world? Or what seemed like the whole world.

Brad didn't want a divorce because he no longer loved or liked me; he couldn't even see me, so how could he know who I was? He wanted a divorce because I was not playing the role he wanted his wife to play. He wanted a wife who cared about the same things he did. His friends' wives all acted as if they cared about the same things their men did, whether or not they felt that way. And none of those men really saw their wives as people, any more than the wives saw the husbands as people. They each saw each other as roles.

I didn't hang out with Brad's friends' wives, but when

we all went out to dinner together, I couldn't avoid hearing the things they said in undertones to each other, or reserved for the Ladies' Lounge while combing their hair or powdering their faces or washing their hands. I would stand there in the pink wallpapered, perfumed, mirrored, satin-chaired Ladies' Lounge, while they examined their parts to see if it was time for freshening of the dye, or lamented the appearance of a blackhead, or nearly wept, because they were developing enlarged pores, and listen to them slam Harry and Al and Doug and Len and the rest. And sometimes you could figure out that in fact Lydia must have been getting it on with Eileen's husband, because whenever Eileen said something nasty about Harry, Lydia would look away. Most of the women sympathized with each other and laughed about the men, and said things like 'It won't matter in a hundred years,' or 'What are you gonna do?' and went on jovially as ever.

They simply took their lives for granted. I mean, if they were unhappy, they thought it was because they'd married the wrong man, and that if they had just married a different one, life would be beautiful. They complained about their own men and flirted with all the others, and over the next ten years, many of this group exchanged mates. I wasn't able to feel that way. No one else's husband appealed to me that much, to begin with. But for me, it was clear that it was the life itself we all led that made me unhappy. I certainly didn't want to exchange being one man's wife just to become another's. I didn't want to be a wife at all. But I couldn't articulate that. In the first place, it was insulting to the other women; and in the second, what the hell else was I going to do, what else could I be? People have to, *somebody* has to do the laundry and the cooking and the cleaning of the house, and in our world it was decreed that somebody was women. Even if I weren't married, I'd still have to do those things. There was no escape. So to protest about it seemed ridiculous, futile.

Yet I did blame Brad for my unhappiness, I did! And I wasn't acting with integrity and walking out on him the way I should. The bar to honesty was – the children. And wherever I went or whatever I did, I'd still have those children. I wanted them, I loved them, they were mine, and I adored them. So what was I blaming Brad for? So now here I was playing the conventional game: outraged wife, unfaithful husband: not because I was outraged at Brad's infidelity but because I knew that that was the only flaw he was conscious of, the only sin he acknowledged, the only act he felt enough guilt about to force him to treat me and the kids decently after the divorce, i.e., to *pay*. He had to pay for us. Just as the world had decreed that women had to do the housework, it had made it impossible for women to do the paying.

So there I was despite all my self-righteousness, acting a part when Brad came back from the kitchen with a drink that looked like straight scotch, and sat down across the room glaring at me. He tried once more to get me on the defensive. I hadn't been all that interested in sex for a long time, he said. . . .

That one I didn't even let him get out. Me, with my old reputation, my old (oh Brad!) ardor? I was the one who had a complaint about sex, I insisted, sounding angry. And he should remember how he'd treated me the last time I initiated sex. He fell silent again.

Well, okay, he said finally, but I didn't want to be a wife.

'I *am* a wife. What the hell are you talking about?'

All of this was in fact making me irritable. Because I hated what I was doing. The truth was, we spoke two different languages, Brad and I, but I understood his and he didn't understand mine. And while his language had no validity whatever for me, I knew how to use it to his disadvantage. So throughout this scene, I felt I had the upper hand, even though I knew that by now he was fairly well off, and that he wasn't going to want to share his wealth with me, and that I wasn't going to try to force him to do that. I had such a sense of superiority, of greater power, in this discussion, that I let everything go afterward, maybe out of guilt.

'Well, you're not the kind of wife I wanted,' he said with some heat.

'I am the kind of wife you wanted,' I corrected him. 'I'm

not the kind you want now. But you're not the husband now that I want either.'

He pounced. 'So you want a divorce, too!'

'No,' I countered swiftly, 'I want you to change.'

This was the hollowest thing I said that night. Not because it wasn't true, because if only I could have had my old Brad back, I would have been in joy; but because I knew the old Brad was as dead as if what was sitting there in the room with me were a corpse electronically controlled to appear alive. Because I knew there was utterly no chance of Brad changing, except to become more of what he had already become.

He let himself be caught up in argument, fatal in a real power-struggle. 'Well, I want *you* to change.'

I stood up. 'I guess we're at an impasse, then,' I said and yawned. 'I'm going to bed.'

He panicked. 'Anastasia! I want a divorce!'

'You want to marry . . . what is her name?'

'Fern,' he mumbled. The one who helped him buy all the furniture. Well, *that* was neatly done at least. I looked around the room meaningfully, and Brad blushed.

'We weren't . . . this happened later.'

'You mean you weren't fucking around when she helped you pick out the furniture for her future home?'

'Will you stop using that word?' He was furious. He hated me to say *fuck*.

'You can have your divorce,' I said, and the lower part of his face relaxed. His eyes remained wary as he waited to hear how much he was going to be 'taken' for. 'I want the kids and enough money to take proper care of them. I want a car that is safe on the parkways. You can have everything else.'

His eyes remained wary, as they would until our separation agreement was signed. He knew a good lawyer could make me up the ante.

'You'll have to have a lawyer. Call Len Watkins, he's good.'

'Are you kidding?' Len Watkins was a golf buddy of Brad's. (Yes, he'd taken up golf too. He'd even joined the Rockville Country Club, and he was getting a paunch from drinking so much. He had everything his father ever wanted for him except the right wife, and now he was getting that as well. I'd met Fern, who was a sweet pretty woman with no moral force, no values of her own, and an ordinary mind. She'd go along with Brad on anything he wanted.)

'I'll get my own lawyer,' I announced with bravado, my mind flicking through everyone we knew. There were lots of lawyers among his friends, but when I thought about mine – well, Mary Sindona's husband drove a truck, Aline Golder's made sweaters, and Delilah Abramowitz's was an insurance salesman. Still, my refusal of his choice made Brad very anxious. He was sure I was going to soak him. He eyed me. He spoke through his teeth. I wondered if that was how he looked across the table when he made real-estate deals with people. God! Frightening!

'I'm going to pack a bag tonight,' he said. 'I'll be living over in Garden City until the thing is finished. I'll write the address and phone number on the pad in the kitchen. But it will be easier if you want to reach me to call the agency during the day.'

That stopped me. I gaped at him. 'You're going off, just like that?'

'Don't tell me you want me to stay. I noticed how you begged and wept.'

'What about the kids?'

He shrugged. 'Tell them whatever you want. I'm sure you'll make sure they hate me, just the way your mother made sure you hated your father. You have plenty of time to do it. So what does it matter what you tell them now?'

'You mean you want custody?' I was astonished.

'No judge would give me custody,' he said bitterly.

I sat down again. I thought. Maybe the reason he was the way he was with them was because he felt they were *mine;* maybe if he felt he could have them to himself once in a while, he'd be loving.

'Maybe we could share them,' I began.

'You mean you don't want to be a mother either?' he burst out. 'How the hell can I take care of them? You know I work, I don't have time to play tag and blindman's bluff all day!' He made those games sound like the occupations of an idiot. Maybe they are.

I backtracked fast. I hadn't really wanted to share them with him. I'd offered because I knew *they* longed to share *him* with whatever else mattered to him. But he must have thought I didn't really want the kids, would welcome some respite from them, and thought his new wife should provide it, because he added, very defensively,

'And Fern already has a child of her own, a little girl. She's a widow,' he added hastily, lest I think her fallen, like me. 'And we . . . we thought we'd like to have one together.'

He stood up then, having delivered the *coup de grâce*. He left the room and was very busy writing me notes, packing some clothes, finding papers he wanted to take with him. I was still sitting in the same spot, in the same position, when he stood in the archway of our fancy wall-to-wall-carpeted living room and said, 'Well, I'll be seeing you.'

I didn't answer him. I hated to let him see he'd gotten to me, but so deeply had he that I couldn't conceal it. He turned to leave, and my bitterness burst out.

'Leave your car. I'm going to have to be doing a lot of driving in the next few weeks, and although you clearly don't care about your children, I presume you don't hate them enough to want them dead. You can take mine.'

He was horrified. Drive my Rambler! But if he had the emotional last word, I had the economic one: he was too full of guilt to argue. He took the Rambler. I'm sure he traded it in the next day, but at least I didn't have to drive it anymore. I could ruin his Caddy with the things I transported: kids with muddy shoes, groceries that occasionally seeped and leaked, seedlings from my mother's garden, sharp-edged equipment like my tripod, and whatever else I could think of. Dirtying up that car was the only satisfaction I derived from the entire process of getting divorced. I didn't keep that car, I didn't want it. He got it back and bought me a used Chevy two-door. But he was brokenhearted when he saw it. He cared more about that car than he did about . . .

That was what had silenced me, and continued to silence

me. That was what made me cry when I told the children about our getting divorced. They deduced that Daddy didn't like us anymore, even though I tried to make it sound like a mutual decision. Billy wasn't surprised: he knew Daddy had *never* liked him. But Arden, who had felt moments of affection from her father, concluded that it was me whom Daddy didn't like anymore, and therefore it was my fault he was leaving. This didn't show right away, not at all. It took years for her to say it. I don't know what Brad's abandonment of them meant to the children, really. I only know what it meant to me.

That's what broke my heart. Not his leaving me – we'd left each other long ago, and who knows who took the first step? I had no right to feel sorry for myself about that, and anyway that kind of damage is reparable, or at least it can heal. But his not caring about them, his dismissing them the way he did, his easy talk about starting another family (whom he would probably treat the same way) as if families were like houses you can discard, replace, sell, buy, live in, and leave: well, that about finished me.

I sat there late into the night, that night, after turning off the lights and making sure the doors were locked, and turning down the thermostat. I pulled an old torn blanket around my knees and sat in a chair by a window in the room I called the porch, and I smoked. And through the darkness an image kept appearing to me – Brad, years ago, before we were married. He was standing in light, in the circle of light that illuminated the group he was playing with, and he was doing a solo. I had lost sight, over the years, of that side of Brad, the way he looked when he played, the way he was when I fell in love with him. Brad played the sax as if he were having a dialogue with it. His face was always screwed up in pain, in anguish, and as he played the notes, he seemed to be listening to what the instrument was telling him, as if he were *its* instrument for the expression of pain translated into beauty. He had more anguish in his face when he played the saxophone than he had had just now when he discarded his children – and me.

When I saw that image, I was able to squeeze out a tear

or two. My heart generally felt frozen. I told myself I was crying for my children, or maybe for the child I had been. For me, now, there was no need for tears. After all, I had what I wanted, didn't I?

It turned out that Mary Sindona's brother-in-law Steve was a lawyer; it also turned out that I liked him and felt I could trust him. Which should automatically have kept me from hiring him. He was too sweet to be a lawyer. But the way things worked out was partly my fault. I didn't, I really didn't, want any part of Brad's wealth. I wanted a decent percentage of his income until the kids were finished with college, and a car. I didn't want the house in Rockville Centre. It was too big, somehow, for the kids and me. Funny how the existence of one other person makes a big house justifiable. It was expensive to keep up, and it was old and in constant need of repair. And besides, I didn't like it so much since it had been fancied up. And I didn't especially want my kids growing up in that town where I had suffered so much as an adolescent; I didn't want them to be snobs, money snobs, spoiled suburban brats. Better to grow up on the Lower East Side, I thought. Of course, I'd never lived on the Lower East Side.

But I thought that would be where I'd move. To Manhattan, anyway. Brad hit several ceilings when he heard that. He yammered and yelled, he said he'd remove them from my custody, he threatened everything he could imagine, using every legal term he knew. In the end, I didn't do it, because after seeing the places I could afford on the settlement he'd given me, I decided it would be nothing short of a criminal act to take my children to such neighborhoods. But I mourned that: why wasn't there someplace decent for poor people to live in cities?

For I was now a poor person. Brad had agreed to give me $7,500 a year. That sounded like a fair amount to me. Steve said it wasn't enough. But I was still feeling guilty about how I'd maneuvered Brad into the divorce; and I have to confess now that I was very busy at the time proving to him my contempt for his materialistic values. So I insisted on taking it.

So if I was poor, it was my own fault. For years afterward, I heard that it was my own fault, from one person or another. And then, when women started demanding divorces and getting them, I heard about the typical female divorce role, in which women allowed themselves to be dictated to by their men, and acted passive, guilt-ridden, unworthy: oh, all that. All of us ended up poor, anyway, and everyone agreed it was our own fault.

But what I want to know is, how come no one said it was Brad's fault? He knew what things cost far better than I did. He'd kept me ignorant of all financial affairs. I didn't even know what our electric bill amounted to. So he knew what he was offering was shit, not enough to support two kids. How come he wasn't concerned about their welfare? Maybe he expected me to come back with some outrageous demand, and was prepared to come up, but when I didn't, how come he didn't say, Stahz, you really can't live on that. I'll give you . . . whatever. Even if he felt some bitterness toward me, as was likely, how come he wasn't worried about how the children, his children, would eat and be housed and clothed and educated?

I suppose I could have sued for more, but I *was* passive, just as I'd been when I let Fern decorate our house. I can't explain why. I just wanted to get shut of all of it, of Brad and money, money, money, of that whole world. I found us an apartment in Lynbrook. It was the top floor of a big old house, and had two small bedrooms for the kids, a medium-sized one for me, a living room, kitchen, and a tiny closet of a room that I could use for a darkroom. I loved it, it was just my size, our size, I felt. And Mrs Nowak, the widow who owned the house, lived downstairs; she loved children and wanted them to use the yard and offered to baby-sit for me. What more could I ask? I didn't have to walk through her place to reach my own: the front door opened onto a center hall, where the stairs were, and Mrs Nowak's apartment was closed off from it. She had a washer and dryer in her basement, and said I could use them. And she was Polish, and reminded me of my grandmother. I moved happily, except I had no furniture, since obviously I left Fern's Furnishings behind. It was back to the relatives' attics, and to old pieces that had remained in the upstairs rooms of Brad's and my house. That was okay. At least now I wouldn't have to be anxious all the time, reminding the kids not to scratch Brad's tables, tear the upholstery on his chairs, or bang their toys into the wooden fronts of his imitation Sheraton.

The first thing I did after returning was march down to Jimmy Minetta's: but he was gone. His shop had been replaced by a photo shop that sent its prints out for development, and offered a twenty-four-hour service. Jimmy? They didn't know. They thought he might have gone into Manhattan. So I went to the *Long Island Herald*, and offered myself as a staff photographer. They were sorry, they couldn't afford such a thing, they had a guy who could take pictures in a pinch, but who doubled as their police reporter. They used pictures from stringers, or from AP or UPI. I went home.

I sat there chewing my lip. The place was still a mess, full of cartons of books and pots and pans that I hadn't gotten around to unpacking. The kids were whiny and irritable. I tried to be cheerful with them, but it didn't help. And it was those years that Arden brought up, years later, describing me as tense and anxious, but concealing it. She said my concealment brought out their tension and anxiety, as they acted out what I felt. Maybe. What in hell was I supposed to do, I ask you?

Some nights, as I sat there after they'd gone to bed, I'd start to feel sorry for myself, finding myself so low through what felt like no real fault of my own. Then my mind would slide to Frances's tragedy and my mother's depression, and its effect on us; and I'd pull back hard. I would *not* be like Frances or Belle. Would not.

two

It was the totality with which she gave herself to her martyrdom that I resented. That my father had wronged her was for me a matter of debate, but I didn't question that her life was wretched. She was artistic and intelligent, but forced to spend all her capital of talent on things like

389

mashed potatoes and blued starched sheets. Not that there was anything contemptible about mashed potatoes and blued starched sheets, only that they were not a sufficient expression for what she possessed. But like the middle-class wives of Brad's friends, she found her husband, not her role, responsible for her misery. I'm not blaming her for not being political: I wasn't either, and I was twenty-five years younger, part of another generation. But her unspoken anger hung over the entire house like the smell of bacon cooked days earlier: cold, greasy, and thick. And it fell, naturally, mostly on the children.

Gradually, it abated somewhat. Just as we hadn't known why or when it began, we didn't know why or when it began to end. That's what it means to be a child in a so-called civilized society. Your life is hedged and protected, you are kept in a warm padded dark place from which you cannot see the forces that are jostling you, toppling you, pressing against you on one side or another, and sometimes lifting you clear off the ground. Whereas in so-called primitive societies, everyone knows everything about everybody, because there is so little privacy. So if one couple in the compound are quarreling, everyone knows about it and can follow the quarrel point by point, and even take sides. Such a context makes quarreling *normal*, part of everyday life. And when the quarrel ends, life goes on, and that's normal too. But for us, who put on happy faces, who act in public as if cross words never crossed our lips, quarrels are private and dark and fierce, and seem disruptions of the 'civilized' flow. They are aberrations, even though in fact they happen every day to everybody.

Years later, when I was nearly an adult, I asked my mother what had happened, and she said grimly that my father had promised to give up his lover, and that he seemed to have done so. He worked overtime less often, and his salary checks balanced. So she, slowly, forgave him, or anyway, let up a little of her heavy oppressive moodiness. No, she never really forgave him. Years after that, eons, she could still say bitterly, 'What I couldn't forgive was that he had no mind. What did he think he was doing? And then . . . oh, all of it – he – forced me to realize I *had* to stay with him no matter what he did. That was terrible for me. Terrible.'

She didn't forgive, but slowly, she buried it. Since we didn't know when or why or how about any of it, we remained tense for a long time. Joy remembers little of all this – well, she was only nine and ten. But she remembers the tension, the silence, and staying away from the house as much as she could. She was wary of her parents, and became a contained, distant child. Under the ready smile, the charming little anecdote, the quick laugh, she kept herself to herself. She remained that way all her life; she suffered, when she suffered, alone. The only hint that she was distraught was a higher edge of hysteria in her voice and laugh, and when she was little, bouts of vomiting, especially on Friday mornings, when exams were given. Belle understood the meaning of the vomiting, but not of the hysteria, for which she criticized Joy all her life.

Joy kept her own counsel, even when Mr Callahan, her friend, the man who had bought (or stolen?) that fantastic cowboy outfit for her – hat, chaps, boots, shirt, vest, the works – attempted to rape her. She was nine, and playing with his children in their yard. She went indoors to use the toilet, and he came out of his bedroom – his wife was working then – and grabbed her. He pulled her into the bedroom, panting, and saying things to her she didn't understand about her eyes and her cute ways, and he started to open the zipper on her pants. She did not scream or cry out. She pushed him, and he was physically unstable enough to feel the push a little and stagger enough for her to pull away, and redoing her zipper, run from the house. She left the yard and never went back. She would play with the Callahan children, but only in her yard. She never wore the cowboy outfit again, and when Belle asked her why, just shrugged and said it was too hot. She told no one until she was past forty, and Anastasia was asking her about when they were children. Belle never knew. Anastasia was, at that time, far more vocal. She came running home in a fury and in terror one February Sunday afternoon, after she had taken Joy to the playground, and met a young man with big pimples on his cheeks who kept wanting her to go on the monkey climb. He was so insistent that she became suspicious, and refused to go. She said she was going on the slide with Joy, and he shrugged and said, well, if she wanted to do that, he could show her a new game to play on the slide. Anastasia was still suspicious: why should a big boy like him want to play with two little girls? But he was so persistent she did not know how to shake him off. The new game, he said, consisted of his sitting behind her at the foot of the slide, while Joy climbed up and slid down.

'She'll hit us,' Anastasia objected.

'But just wait, you'll see, it will be terrific fun,' the boy-man urged.

Reluctantly, she agreed, and sat in front of him at the foot of the slide, while Joy ran around and climbed up. But before Joy even got going down the slide, Anastasia had jumped up and turned and was yelling at the man. 'What are you doing! Get away from me!' When Joy came down, Anastasia grabbed her and together they ran all the way home, and burst breathless into the house.

'A man put his hands in my pants!' Anastasia announced, and Belle sent Ed out to find him.

'But I should go with him,' Anastasia argued. 'He won't know who he is.'

'You said he was about eighteen and had pimples on his face. If he's there, Daddy will find him,' Mommy said.

Anastasia sat on the porch near the window, anxiously watching for her father. What was the point of this? she wondered. What will Daddy do if he does find him? And how could he be sure it was the same one? And besides, that guy wouldn't hang around the playground after we'd left. He'd be afraid to.

Ed returned after about an hour, full of his wanderings, his sightings, and reports of the utter vacancy of the playground, high-school grounds, and all areas surrounding them. Belle nodded. She seemed pleased with him, and he seemed pleased with himself. He's glad he didn't find him, Anastasia thought, because he wouldn't have known what to do if he had. What would he do, hit him? The boy was as tall as her father, as thick in the body, and younger.

Suppose the boy hit back? But he's pleased to have made the effort, and Mommy is pleased he did, too. Why is that? She knew she was supposed to feel protected and cared for, but she didn't. They couldn't protect her: they couldn't be with her every minute. And they couldn't protect her from the fact that she would in future see every approach by a strange man as a potential assault on her body. What was it about girls' bodies that men wanted to put their hands inside them? It made her sick. She decided she would grow up without sex. Everything she read in Nietzsche and Schopenhauer – and they were the men she most respected, of all the people she had read – talked only about men, not women. Except once in a while and then . . . ! What they said about women was horrible! But men were pretty terrible too, she thought. She would be neither. She would grow as spirit and mind, with a sexless body.

Even Uncle Wally. Whenever he came to stay and her friends were around, he always made them sit on his lap. And one day she saw that his arm was embracing Terry underneath her dress, as she sat there. And she said later, 'Were you embarrassed that my uncle was holding you that way?' And Terry got red in her face, and said, 'Yeah, but I dint wanna say nothing, because he was your uncle.' Anastasia said, 'I think that's terrible, and I'm going to tell my mother.' Terry's eyes widened. 'You are! I'd never tell mine, I'd be too scared.'

'Why?'

But Terry wouldn't answer. She blushed and turned away. Anastasia loved her friends, but she knew they came from different kinds of homes than hers. She had walked over to Terry's one night to pick her up for the movies, and her father was sitting in the living room listening to a ball game on the radio. He was huge, with a red face, and he looked at her suspiciously, and asked Terry a lot of questions about where she was going and what they were going to do. When Terry answered him, her voice sounded frightened.

Anastasia told Mommy about Uncle Wally. Mommy said, 'Don't worry, Anastasia, he won't do it again.' And Anastasia believed her, and in fact, he never did. He left their house the next day and it seemed it was a long time before he came to visit them again. She didn't mind. She felt uneasy around him. He was a strange man. He always tried to get her to cook for him, he insisted on it.

'I don't know how to cook!' she'd protest. 'And I don't want to!'

But he'd keep asking her, keep insisting, until finally, once, she tried. He wanted fried eggs, so she cracked an egg and held it over the frying pan and as it hit the pan, it broke. And he laughed at her, mocking her: 'You don't hold an egg a foot over the pan, dummy! Of course it'll break if you do. You hold it just a few inches over the pan.'

She glared at him. 'Well, if you know how to do it, do it yourself!' and stalked off.

But next time he came, he asked her again. 'Women are supposed to cook,' he wheedled.

She really turned on him then. 'Well, I'm not a woman, I'm a girl!'

She *would not* be a woman, she *would not*.

She couldn't forget the things Nietzsche and Schopenhauer said about women. Her mother wasn't the way they said women were. So maybe they were smart and knew about many things, but they didn't know about women. But when Nietzsche wrote about Christianity, she attended: for what he wrote sounded true. And what he said about the misery of most lives, their pointlessness, about people doing things they didn't want to do because they thought they were supposed to: well, that she understood perfectly.

She confided her doubts to her mother. 'You know, Mommy, all these men have different ideas about God. And some of them don't even believe in God. What do you think?'

Belle raised her hand. 'I don't know, Anastasia. I can't argue with you. Why don't you go see a priest?'

'He'd get mad at me.'

'No, he wouldn't. He'd probably be glad to discuss religion with you.'

Anastasia had her doubts, but the next time she went to Confession, she decided to try her mother's advice. She repeated the Act of Contrition, then said, 'Father, I have been reading some books that make me wonder about religion, about God. I wondered if I could talk about it to you.'

The priest, his face shadowed and crossed with the grill-work of the opening, drew back from her. She didn't know who he was: she didn't know any of the priests except Monsignor Burke. But the voice that emerged from the confessional box was more strongly Irish even than his, and not at all glad.

'Ya either take it on faith or ya get out of the Church!' it thundered.

Anastasia's heart thumped, and tears filled her eyes. The voice that emerged from her then came from somewhere outside herself, for she was surprised to hear herself saying, 'In that case, I'll get out of the Church,' and once having said it, she had to stand up and leave the confessional. As she trudged back home, she felt teary and forlorn, but she did not see what else she could have done. Her greatest sorrow was that she could no longer, in good conscience, sing in the choir – not that the priest would have known, or anyone at all.

In fact, it was not a painful separation. Religion as it had been presented to her was not satisfying intellectually, whatever it was sensuously, with the music, the flowers, the priests' gorgeous costumes. She continued to think about divine purpose, but if there were a deity, she was sure it had no special relation with Catholicism, or any other church. And by the time she was eighteen, she had discarded any notion of a Supreme Being. If she had a religion after that, it was centered on humans. But she never claimed to have a religion at all, and when she entered a Catholic hospital to give birth to Arden, and the clerk insisted on knowing her religion, Anastasia told her she was a Hindu. The clerk asked her how to spell it.

Belle saw that her children were becoming more independent, and was pleased by that. At last, Anastasia had some friends; at last, Joy seemed to be over her bouts of sickness, and was doing well in school. She had made the Honor Roll last quarter. But Belle was facing a serious problem.

The Carles wanted to sell both houses and retire to a small apartment in Jamaica. Minnie's back was bothering her greatly as she aged, and she felt she had to give up house-cleaning. With so much money around because of the war, Mr Carle felt he could get $9,000 for the house. Belle did not want to leave the little house; she was fond of the quiet neighborhood, the yard. But she knew that was too much money for this house; anyway, they couldn't afford it.

So began six months of househunting. They drove out in the shiny sleek old car, every Sunday, to different towns on Long Island. They looked at houses in Huntington, Douglaston, Hempstead, Freeport, and Rockville Centre. And each Sunday they had dinner out in a nice restaurant. Anastasia did not understand how they could suddenly afford this, or why it happened, but she enjoyed it. So did Belle, who oversaw the children's dress with great care each Sunday.

And while they were looking, Belle made the decision to change their name. They had often discussed it, she and Ed. It was déclassé to be Polish, and especially to have such a foreign name. But Ed had feared upsetting his father. But Dafna had died some years ago, after a long undiagnosed illness; and Stefan, despondent after her death, had followed her two years later. So there was nothing to stop them now. And Belle did not want to enter the new neighborhood with their present name.

'Poor Daddy suffers so,' she explained to Anastasia. 'In his plant, they call the men over the loudspeaker, and they always mispronounce his name. He gets called Dabooski and Dalouski and things like that. It upsets him.' Belle and Ed spent many evenings considering new names, and finally decided on Stevens, after Stefan. It sounded English, which was what Belle wanted to be.

The truth was, she was more English than Polish. She liked subdued simple clothes, in browns and blacks and tans; and bland boiled food; and the English style of home decoration. The women she would most admire in her life, except for Gertrude Grunbacher, were all of English extraction – Ann Gwyn, Mildred Bradshaw, and Martha Thacker. She liked their understated speech and manners, their avoidance of the emotional, their personal reticence. If she had met any Englishy people when she was young, you might have thought she modeled herself on them. When Anastasia pointed out that name was Englishy, and so was her mother, Belle was pleased.

But English name or not, soon after they moved into their new house in Rockville Centre, at the end of August 1944, Anastasia knew that they would not pass muster. Even the neat white frame colonial house could not disguise them. Disguise took money. Nothing could disguise their ridiculous-looking old car. In South Ozone Park, they had been viewed as rich because they had a car at all; but in Rockville Centre, the 1928 Graham-Paige was laughable among all the prewar but still snappy Cadillacs, Oldsmobiles, and Buicks. And while Belle rarely went anywhere except to the market or the dry cleaner, Anastasia was almost immediately invited into the houses of her new girl-friends. The difference was striking. For her friends' houses had maids in them, and gardeners taking care of the lawns. Inside there were wall-to-wall carpeting and lush couches, with ornate little side chairs, knickknacks everywhere, formal dining rooms furnished in imitation Sheraton. Some of the houses had little rooms just for the telephone; her friends had bedrooms furnished in antiqued white, with canopies over their beds, and matching vanity table skirts. The wealthiest threw their clothes in a heap after wearing for the maid to pick up. Many had collections of stuffed animals in the corners of their rooms.

Anastasia would sniff with contempt: I wouldn't want such things, she'd decide, then catch herself. You can't be sure you wouldn't want a thing until you have the chance to have it. Only then do you really know. And anyway, not all the girls were so rich, although all of those who weren't envied those who were. All except the 'tramps'. There were a number of these in the school, and Anastasia made friends with several of them. The school was divided into groups: there were two cliques, the Christian one and the Jewish one; then there were the drips; and the tramps. Anastasia knew she was destined to be a drip. The new school was dismaying.

In John Adams, she had studied musical technique and harmony; this school had no such courses. In John Adams, she had been a member of a group that went to Saturday-morning rehearsals of the symphony, and to plays. In her sophomore year there, she had seen Katharine Cornell in *Antony and Cleopatra*, Paul Robeson in *Othello*, and Maurice Evans in *Hamlet*. In this school, the rich boys owned cars and the clique (the Christian clique) went out on Friday and Saturday nights to roadhouses and bars, and got drunk, and trashed the bars or cracked up their cars. The girls owned cashmere sweaters, and were rated according to how many they possessed. And worst of all, *all* the kids acted as if they and their school were superior to all others.

All the wealthy girls belonged to one clique or another. The Jewish girls wore soberer clothes than the Christian ones, and they were allowed to be smart and get good grades. If you were a Christian and got good grades, you were a little suspect, and likely to be classified as a drip. But both cliques contained some girls who were not wealthy, but who had some special trait – charm, lovableness, or very good looks. Any girl who was popular with boys could be in a clique except the tramps; you *knew* (how?) that the boys took the tramps out, but they never spoke to them openly or took them to school functions. But when Anastasia came to know the tramps, she found them the sweetest of any of the girls. They were invariably poor, and came often from homes where they were abused. They were in some way more grown up than the other girls. They seemed a little sad, but very kind, generous. One of the tramps, a girl named Sally, would ask Anastasia to come home with her almost every afternoon. She seemed very sophisticated to Anastasia. She lived on the wrong side of town, in a tiny house. There was never anyone home, and Sally seemed to tiptoe through the small shabby rooms. She'd get two Cokes from the fridge, then take Anastasia up to her room, and they would sit beside the dormer window that lighted it, and talk. But Anastasia never had anything to say, she would mainly listen, and Sally just talked desultorily. She didn't say much, but she hinted at things. Anastasia was silenced by what she felt as something tragic in Sally or her life. After a few weeks, she stopped going. Sally didn't reproach her, and always smiled when she saw her afterward.

In her two years at the high school, Anastasia became friendly with a few members of each group, but she was never an insider, and always felt that. At the time, and even later, she did not comprehend what made one an insider. Wherever she was, whatever she did – whether she was going to the movies and out for a Coke with a group of the 'drips', or sitting in her own backyard with one of the 'tramps', or providing company for one of the Christian clique as she baby-sat, or working on the school newspaper with one of the Jewish clique – she felt she was wrong, outside, and must tread with care.

It was in the two years she spent in this unhappy environment that Anastasia formed, not her character, but her persona. She determined not to be trapped by their categories, and violated them all. She had no money for clothes, so dressed simply, like the 'drips'; but she wore her hair wild, and smoked with the boys in the parking lot at lunch hour. Even the 'tramps' didn't do that. She got good enough grades to be respected by the Jewish clique, but argued and contested with her teachers in class. She told everyone she was going to be an artist, and treated the shabby art classes with contempt. She wrote a term paper arguing that 'miscegenation' was perfectly all right, and paraded the *B* her shocked and horrified teacher had been forced to award her. She joined a campaign started by a boy in her class, to survey the black – then called colored – part of town and find out why there was only one black child in the high school, Alice Boston, who was wary and timid, and spoke to no one. Where were all the others? Rockville Centre had a large black neighborhood, drawn there by their work as servants in the richer houses. She wrote a little story about her childhood that was published in the school newspaper (this high school had no magazine). She described a black family moving into their block in South Ozone Park. They were apparently placed there by the Welfare Department – the house had been empty for a long time. The family had two children, and Belle had insisted that Anastasia and Joy go down to their house and knock on the door and ask if the children could come out to play. Joy was perfectly willing, but shy Anastasia had to be prodded. Belle explained that because they were black, many people disliked them, and none of the other children would play with them. This persuaded Anastasia, and down the two sisters went. A worn, thin, still-young light brown woman came to the door and opened it a crack. The children, together, piped their request. The woman said abruptly that her children could not come out. She closed the door.

A month later, the family disappeared.

This seemingly pointless story – for Anastasia had not made any point, had not felt up to writing about black fear of whites – won her no friends in her new school, except for one teacher, Mrs Sherman, who taught English and was, Anastasia thought, the most intelligent of the teachers. The story accomplished one thing: it consolidated Anastasia's position as an outsider.

Belle did not notice Anastasia reeling from the shock of this new environment. The child was out all the time, she had friends, her grades were all right, if not superb, as they had been before. And Joy seemed truly happy, having to walk only a few blocks to the pretty Hewlett school, and having almost immediately been embraced by its sixth-grade clique. Belle herself was consumed with worry and plans.

To buy the house, they had had to sell both Ed's small insurance policies, and the policies she'd taken for the girls' education. She asked Anastasia's permission to sell hers, which was fervently granted. Anastasia had always hated the neighborhood they lived in; she was eager to move. They were fortunate that the builder of the house, a man who appeared as solid and honest as the houses he built, had agreed to hold the mortgage on it. This meant they could pay only the interest, which came to about as much as they had paid in rent in the old house. But now Belle could not work in Gertz anymore. Travel there and back would be so expensive and time-consuming as to devour most of her wages. And she could not work on Long Island unless she could drive.

She asked Ed to give her driving lessons, and she got her license, but she never felt safe driving a car, and she drove slowly and uncertainly. She tried to drive only locally: like all the other ladies in the neighborhood, she went with her husband to the station every morning and drove the car back, then drove to the station in the evening to meet him. She drove to the supermarkets, the dry cleaners, and occasionally, dared the longer drive to Hempstead or Garden City, where the department stores were. She remained terrified to drive on the parkway, and for several years did not try.

She knew she should get another job. She was thrilled with her nice house, but it needed furniture badly. She couldn't even afford to buy curtains for all the windows. She had made the small side room off the living room her 'porch'. It had five windows, so was bright, and was too small for most uses. It was the room in which – after the kitchen – she spent most of her time. The people who had lived in the house before them had left a nice little breakfast set in the breakfast nook, and someday when Ed had time, she would have him repaint it. But that allowed her to put their old kitchen table and chairs in the dining room. Ed had already painted them grey, and she had bought a cheap blue-grey rug for the room, but it still looked empty. So she had him paint Momma's old sewing machine cabinet grey, and she set it against the wall like a buffet.

But the living room was her pride. It was true, she had no end tables, no tables of any sort, but there were the fine Queen Anne couch and chair, and the high-backed chair with the wooden arms; there was the old imitation Persian rug; and there was her new piano, a Baldwin baby grand. When Hal Grunbacher was drafted, he urged her to buy a new piano. They were on sale, he said, and were no longer being made since the war. He would help her pick one out. It was a beautiful piano, and everyone said it had wonderful tone. And Hal's mother Gertrude, who had taught him to play, was now giving the girls their lessons. She drove all the way from Forest Hills to Rockville Centre, and charged only a dollar and a half for the lessons. Belle knew Mrs Grunbacher thought Anastasia could be a professional pianist, if only she applied herself more. Still, where would they find the money to back such a career? She knew it took money. Hal had told them Anastasia could be a concert pianist, but that she had to have a special kind of education, spending five hours a day on music. Anastasia had said she didn't want to. That was all right. A career as a concert pianist was so hard. She played beautifully, which would help her find a man to marry, a big lawyer or a big doctor, someone who could give her a decent life.

The living room also held Sokolowski's painting in its broad gilt frame, in its place of honor over the couch, where it had hung in every house Belle had ever occupied. Belle knew that many of the houses in this neighborhood were very grand. But she loved this house. She was proud of it. She wished, oh how she wished that Momma could have seen it, that Momma could have seen her in it: My house, Momma. And Momma would have had to say, 'Good, Bella'.

But upstairs, there were no rugs, and the furniture was sparse. There was no way they could buy more furniture unless Belle worked. It took everything Ed earned even when he worked overtime just to pay the bills. Still, she did not want to get in the car and drive over to Hempstead to the Franklin Shops and apply for a job as a saleslady. She was forty years old; she had worked all her life; she was tired. She wanted to sit in her lovely home and gaze out at the quiet streets and the trees, and not have to work. She wanted to welcome Gertrude Grunbacher every Thursday, and serve her coffee and cake while they waited for the girls to get home from school. She lòved sitting in the garden, such a lovely garden, in the old Adirondack chair, for an hour in the afternoon, sipping iced coffee and smoking. Here she had finally got the house she dreamed of, her, a stupid Polska from the slums. She wanted to be in it.

They had been in the house only two months when the letter came. The kindhearted builder, who had lowered the price of the house so they could manage the down payment, was now demanding the mortgage be paid up completely. They would have to get an ordinary mortgage from a bank. That would mean they would have to amortize the loan in addition to paying interest. They could not do that. They would lose the house.

A new darkness descended on the household. Joy felt helpless in the face of her mother's depression, and simply restored her habit of staying out as much as possible. But Anastasia was old enough to be told what the problem was. She too was aghast, not because she loved the house so much or the neighborhood or the school, but because she knew what losing the house would mean to her mother. She offered to do what she could: she took a job at the five-and-ten afternoons and Saturdays, and she told her friends she was available for baby-sitting in the evenings. She began to work steadily, but she knew her working was little help to her mother, for all Belle had been able to give her before was seventy-five cents a week allowance. Still, she could buy Christmas presents for everyone, and maybe some clothes for herself, and she would not have to beg fifty-cent pieces from her mother for the Saturday night movie. Belle did not seem to notice Anastasia's efforts; nor did she remember her birthday that year. Not until it was Thanksgiving did she realize that Anastasia's fifteenth birthday had come and gone. She couldn't worry about that; she had too much else to worry about.

They obtained a mortgage from Eric's insurance company, but making the payments was impossible. Belle juggled bills, paying only small sums on the telephone, electric, and oil bills. Dunning notices arrived almost every day from one company or another. Belle was forced to serve paltry meals, which the family ate in a deeper silence even than usual.

Every morning, as she raised the shade in the dining room, and glanced at the house next door, Belle saw a heap of white things through the window. She saw the heaps increase and diminish, disappear and reappear. With her background, she had some idea what they were.

She had met the woman who lived next door, a lovely woman, Ann Gwyn. She and her husband and their twin sons had also moved in recently, and their house was almost identical to the Stevenses', having been built by the same man. Belle kept an eye out for Mrs Gwyn, and the next time they were both outside hanging clothes on the line – in this neighborhood, one did not have pulley lines; one had an umbrella-shaped dryer on which the clothes did not dry as quickly, but which looked neater – she called hello, and walked over, showing herself ready for a chat.

Ann Gwyn was a tall, gaunt, patient-faced woman of great dignity. She had a grave manner, but a deep sweet smile. The two women struck sympathetic chords in each other, recognizing without being told the other's pride and suffering. Over coffee and a bakery yeast cake, they spoke decorously, softly, intelligently, sympathetically to each other.

After a time, Belle ventured, 'Ann . . . sometimes I've noticed white . . . are they caps? . . . in your porch. Do you make them?'

Ann blushed. Her husband was an accountant, and made a good salary, but he was close with money. She did not say this. She said her husband's father owned a million-dollar business selling medical supplies – nurse's outfits, doctor's coats, wheelchairs, that sort of thing. And she was permitted to share his wealth. She sewed nurse's caps and he paid her 10 cents for each one. Of course, he sold them for $1.25. But they didn't take too long to make. She could earn a few extra dollars every week, and sit at home.

'It gives me a little money of my own,' she explained. 'I can buy a few things for the boys. Charles,' she laughed a little, 'you know how men are. He doesn't understand how important the right sweater or a little spending money is to boys their age. High school is such a hard time for children, don't you think?'

'Of course,' Belle said sympathetically. Then, nervously, 'Could I see them?'

'Certainly!' Ann gleamed with pleasure. She had been anxious that Belle might look down on her for this work, for not having money. But then, she had never seen the inside of the Stevenses' house. She led the way to her porch, through a living room very much like Belle's. There were four stacks of twenty-five caps each: high puffed organdy with a ruching border. A sewing machine was open, and there were big brown boxes filled with ruching standing on the floor.

'How do you make them?'

Ann was happy to show her. 'Well, Dad brings me bolts of organdy and tells me the size he needs. I cut out circles of fabric, using this cardboard as a guide.' She pointed to a stack of cardboard circles labeled with sizes. 'Then I cut the ruching to fit the cap, and I sew it, by machine, to the edge of the cap. Then I flute the organdy. You have to do that by hand, it's a little hard on the fingers because organdy is so stiff. It helps to have long nails, but mine are so soft they break.' She held out her hand. The pad and thumb of her right hand were covered with tiny cuts. 'The organdy has sizing in it, and that irritates my fingers. I've ruined some caps by getting blood on them. Now I put band aids on my fingers when I do it. That helps. It's really not hard,' she finished cheerily.

Belle examined a cap, and laid it down slowly. Ann looked at her carefully. 'Would you like to do some?' she asked softly.

'Oh, I'd *love* to!'

'I'm sure Dad would be glad to have you do it. He sells hundreds of these caps every week, and is always looking for women to make them.'

Belle went home elated. She began to plan. She could surely do twenty a day; that was $2. Maybe she could do thirty, or even forty. If she worked every day, that would be $15–$28 a week. She'd been earning only $18 a week at Gertz, and had had expenses – carfare, stockings – a real problem during the war – and she'd had to buy two good black dresses. Doing this, she'd have no expenses at all.

A few days later, old Mr Gwyn drove up in his Cadillac and rang her bell. He carried two large boxes, one of organdy, the other of ruching. He accepted Belle's offer of a cup of coffee and some bakery cakes. He was a man in his seventies, portly but manicured, with fine white hair and a satisfied face. He was on his third wife, and lived in a great house on the water in Long Beach. He liked Mrs Stevens, and was sure she would do good work. Some of the women he'd hired had not. There was a Polack, for instance, who'd lived in Freeport, who had ruined an entire bolt of organdy by cutting it sloppily. Mrs Stevens was an intelligent lady, he could see that, and would do fine.

Belle did not want her work to be apparent. Anastasia and Joy often brought their friends home, and she did not want them to be embarrassed. So she moved the sewing machine up to her bedroom, and set up shop there. She cut the organdy on the carpeted floor, being very careful not to allow it to get dusty. She would cut a hundred caps at a time. Then she would sew the ruching on. These two steps took her several days. Then she did the fluting. That was the most time-consuming task.

She would get up at seven to drive Ed to the station, return and have coffee and toast and call the girls, who no longer ate breakfast. She would finish her housework by ten, except on washdays. She had the small radio in the bedroom, and every morning except Monday, she would go up there and sit and work. It was a light bright room, and she could see out to the street, noting when Mrs Brand went out in her car, which was almost as old as Ed's; noting that Mrs O'Neill's sister was visiting her; and watching Ann Gwyn drive slowly past on her way to market, almost as nervous behind the wheel as Belle herself.

Joy came home for lunch every day, and at quarter of twelve Belle went downstairs to prepare a little meal for her. She would have a scrambled egg and some toast while Joy ate, and listen to the child jabber happily about her little schoolmates. Such a gay little kid she was, so unconscious of Belle's problems, so happy in her own world. It refreshed Belle to listen to her for twenty minutes. Then she went off again and Belle washed the dishes and returned to her bedroom, her workroom. Once in a while, every couple of weeks, she would call Ann Gwyn and ask her to come over for a cup of coffee, or Ann would call her. They'd sit for an hour in the afternoon talking, always decorous, always polite. Belle thought Ann was a very intelligent woman. And in the spring, she came to know her neighbor on the other side, a little. Mildred Bradshaw was much older than Belle, and had been a principal of a school in the Bronx. She had married after her retirement, a man older than she, and lived very comfortably. Mildred too was very intelligent. Belle felt honored by the friendship of these two women.

Still, her life was an unceasing round of labor. Ed's was too, but at least he worked among other men, had coffee in company, listened to gossip and griping. She had to keep pushing herself to make two hundred caps a week, along with taking care of the house, marketing, cooking, washing, ironing, all of which had to be done over and over, every day, every week. She noticed Ed grumbling about dust on the piano – but he grumbled at the girls. Of course, they were supposed to do it, but she didn't like to keep after them. They were young and wanted to be with their friends. She didn't want them to have a childhood like hers, who had to cook and take care of a young child before she was ten years old. Let them be free for a while. It would all happen to them soon enough.

The twenty dollars a week she earned helped to pay the bills. She tried, too, each week, to slip one or two dollars into an envelope she kept beneath the small side glove drawer of the low chest, an envelope she had labeled 'College, Anastasia'. But last week, when she went to add a dollar bill to her cache, her heart stopped. There had been sixty dollars in it. There were thirty now. Ed had taken it. He had not even asked her. He hadn't even mentioned it afterward. But she understood. She would not humiliate him by saying anything. She knew he'd needed it, because he paid the bills now, not she. She felt a rush of sorrow for the shame he must have felt, taking it that way.

Belle did not think about buying furniture. She did not even think about buying one of those new washing machines you did not have to fill and drain with a hose. Even Anastasia's college seemed a luxury now. All she concentrated on was keeping the house. They *would* keep the house.

three

Day after day she sits there. I pass her on my way up- and downstairs after school. The five-and-ten laid all of us off after Christmas. She's been worse lately. She's a dark shadow against the bleak grey light of February, already darkening at four. She's bent over the work in her hands, a small lamp illuminating it, shadowing her. Around her rise mounds and mounds of billowy white caps.

On the vanity beside her is a small pad and a pencil, and the other day I glanced at it and saw columns of figures written on it in a hasty scrawl. I knew instantly how she occupies herself over this solitary slave-labor of hers: she plans and plots and daydreams. She pays bills, she buys a washing machine, she sends me to college. She buys herself a nice outfit and sends herself out into the world where people turn and look at her – what a lovely-looking woman! Is there a man in her daydreams? close, or distant? Does she dream of affairs, or only admiration?

Sorrow at her life rose in my throat like a peach pit, hard and painful, I couldn't swallow. She did not know she was sorrowful though, she remembers only gratitude at finding a way to keep the house. So I felt her sorrow for her. And for me too, because what else did I do with my life but daydream, like her? All night, until dawn rose, I lay in my solitary bed daydreaming. Boys adored me, girls loved me, I was popular and accomplished, editor of the school paper, star of the school play, I was pretty and well-dressed and girls came up to me to ask where I bought my skirts. In my daydreams. A wave of nausea followed the lump, and I went into my room and sat on the window seat. I lighted the cigarette I had filched from Mother's pack in the kitchen. I stared out at February dusk, the empty street, the bare trees, a landscape of vacancy. I wanted, I yearned, to do something in life besides daydream, but how? When no satisfactions were to be had, when I was not popular or accomplished, when my clothes were shabby, the same three skirts, day in, day out . . .

No prospects. For me, for her, for any of us. Just survival, when the world beyond this house, beyond this street, seemed lighted up, carpeted with happy things happening behind the storm-windowed panes. I imagined scenes as I walked the long mile and a half home from school, I pictured the dimly lit houses brilliant with light, parties, mouths behind the glass uttering witty speeches, laughter, gay banter from which I was shut out. I never saw anything like that, but it must happen, perhaps late at night, when I am home in my room, lying on the bed reading one huge book after another, then closing them, lying back, closing my eyes, daydreaming. . . .

Like her. She's been worse lately. If you can chart her ups and downs. It's hard. She's always down. But sometimes, she's further down. She's suffering terribly, you can see it. As if she will not die but cannot live and exists suspended in a state outside desire, outside self even. *Why is she like this?*

Why wonder? Look at her life.

Still, why does she have to take it this way? These days, she hardly even gets dressed, she walks around in an old cotton wrapper and slippers all day long until it's time to pick him up at the station, and even then she just puts on shoes and a coat. And most nights, he works late, and she doesn't pick him up at all. She's afraid to drive at night, in the dark. He takes the bus from the station and walks the long dark cold blocks from the bus stop. No other men do that in this neighborhood. Only kids and domestics take the bus here. No man walks home from the bus stop. He doesn't seem to mind. He probably doesn't realize he's the only one, maybe he wouldn't care if he did. Doesn't notice things, doesn't notice anything: what saves him. Blindness.

But the way she talks to him! And he takes it. Contempt, spat-out remarks, as few as possible. Does he not notice that either? He solicitous, ingratiating. It makes me crazy, I want to scream, I lie in bed and kick the blankets up to the ceiling, over and over, crying lightly in my throat so no one will hear. I want him to *be*, I want him to stand up and *be*! Maybe if he were more of a person, she'd be different. . . . I know her life is hard, but is it tragic? It's the waste that's tragic, it's spending your life in daydreams, the way I do. . . .

Christ, why doesn't she get a job someplace out of the house! She'd earn more – well, she says she'd have to spend more, on gas and clothes and stuff – but at least she'd get out of the house, meet people, maybe make a friend or two. Although she never made a friend at Gertz. Or in South Ozone Park. Elvira, still her only real friend, comes for lunch once every three or four months; Mother goes there. Elmhurst. By train. Afraid to drive. Sitting hunched over, acting like an invalid, a person dying. Lying in her room with the shades drawn, a cloth over her eyes, sinus head-ache, she says. Day upon day. Then at night, working up there until bedtime to make up for the lost hours. Joy in her room, me baby-sitting. No one speaks.

How I wish I could get away from this house.

Belle felt better now that Christmas was over – such a paltry Christmas for the girls. Something would have to happen, they had to get more money, but Ed's boss had high regard for him, and maybe he'd get a good raise one of these days. What worried her most was getting money for Anastasia to go to college. Something would have to happen. Ed was still working overtime almost every night, but he seemed to think that things were winding down somewhat, that the war would end, and they wouldn't make gyroscopes anymore, he wouldn't work overtime anymore. What will we do then? He has to get a raise.

She liked her mornings. Ed got up early, at 6:00, and made his own breakfast and coffee for both of them. He would waken her at 6:30, and she would put on a wrapper and shoes and stockings and go with him to the station where he caught the 6.54 train to Long Island City. When she came back, she would sit with a cup of coffee, then squeeze some orange for herself and the girls. She woke them at 7:30, but Anastasia never got up. They didn't eat breakfast anymore, just maybe a piece of coffee cake. Anastasia was always late, she never ate anything. But Belle insisted they drink orange juice at least.

After they'd left, she cleaned up the kitchen and went

upstairs and made the beds. She didn't make the girls' beds, they were supposed to do that themselves, but of course they rarely did. She'd get after them when she was expecting a guest. Otherwise their rooms were a mess, clothes thrown everywhere, unmade beds. Anastasia needed a desk. The fold-out shelf in the high chest of drawers was not big enough for all her books and papers. Maybe next Christmas. But probably not. This past Christmas had been so puny for them. It couldn't be helped.

When the house was straightened, she went back downstairs and started a fresh pot of coffee and stretched herself in the silent house and looked out the windows at the front yards, the wide street. Even now, at the end of January, there were green things to see, pines and fir trees out back where their property line ended. All light. The houses on either side were rather close, but in front and in back, she had space to stretch her mind in. She loved her house. When the coffee was done, she poured a cup and carried it, with her cigarettes, out to the porch, her favorite room.

This house, this neighborhood, they were better even than the brownstone house she had seen so many years ago from a trolley window. She gazed out the front window. Such neat nice houses lining the street, and the O'Neills owned a plot next door to their house, so it remained open and empty, and green all spring and summer and fall. It was strange that all their many children never played there, and they didn't plant a garden there either. They just left it. Well, of course, Mrs O'Neill had her hands full with so many children, and Mr . . . well, he liked a good time, you could see that. She peered through the curtain at Mrs Brand's car pulling out of the driveway. Going to the market. She gets out early. Belle herself preferred to go to the market in the late afternoon, when she needed a break from the hats. Yes, no one would ever sit on the front steps of the houses here the way that little girl in the pink dress sat on hers. Not even the children. And no one walks on the sidewalks either, except an occasional child after school let out. Even the maids who worked in the big houses up the block were picked up and driven home by car or cab. When she thought about the streets of her childhood! . . .

A dark figure carrying a heavy leather bag over his back appeared on the sidewalk, and Belle's heart warmed. The postman, always on time, nine o'clock, such a nice man. He slid the mail through a slot in the door, so she didn't even have to open it and get a chill. And there was a little vestibule so they could close the door to the living room, and keep out all the drafts from the front door. It was a very well made house. Belle stood up. She always looked forward to the mail.

Usually there were only circulars and bills, but she read everything with interest. She bent to pick up a circular from Goodyear, one from the A & P: it was early this week, the food markets usually sent their circulars on Wednesday: and their bank statement. She handled this proudly. They had opened a checking account. They'd never had such a thing before. For years Belle had taken the bus into Jamaica and gone around to the electric company and the telephone company to pay them in cash. But now there were all sorts of bills. It made her feel very rich, somehow, to have a checking account. Poor people didn't have them, at least, none that she had ever known.

She decided to refill her coffee cup before she sat down with her cache. She then sat down and lighted a cigarette and picked up her reading glasses. She would save the bank statement for last. She opened the Goodyear circular and examined it carefully. Tires were on sale. It could be that Ed needed a new tire. She scrutinized the rest of the sheet, but there was nothing she needed. She would keep the circular, though, for Ed to see. He liked to look over the mail too, and maybe he needed a new tire. She put it on the seat of the couch across from her: they had no tables in this room either. Then she opened the A & P flyer.

Legs of lamb were on sale this week, only nineteen cents a pound. They hadn't had a leg of lamb in a long time. Her mouth began to water a little as she thought about it. She could buy just a half, that wouldn't be so expensive, and stretch it to get two meals out of it. She'd make gravy and heat the leftover meat in gravy. She loved that. Chopped meat was fifteen cents a pound, and so were chickens. Maybe she could make a meat loaf. One-two-three-four — she could surely get two meals from a meat loaf — five, if she bought a chicken. The other two meals — maybe they could just have a vegetable dinner one night, creamed spinach and poached eggs and home fried potatoes. Then . . . well, she'd see how her money held out. Anyway, the other circulars would arrive tomorrow and maybe something cheaper would be appealing. She laid the A & P flyer carefully on the couch seat.

Finally, she picked up the bank statement and slit it open with her hard fingernail. She glanced down the list: the mortgage; gas and electric; oil company; telephone company; Dr Hartley, the dentist; Lord & Taylor . . . Lord & Taylor? Lord & Taylor, $25. A mistake. She couldn't afford to shop at Lord & Taylor, she never went there. She shuffled through the checks clumsily, her hands shaking. There was the check. Check number 17, Lord & Taylor, 12/15/44. Signed: E. C. Stevens. E. C. Stevens. It couldn't be. E. C. Stevens. It was.

Belle laid the statement down on the footstool; some of the checks fluttered to the floor but she didn't notice. 12/15/44, Lord & Taylor, $25, E. C. Stevens. She puffed on her cigarette, but it had gone out. Her pack was empty. She stood up. She walked into the kitchen and threw away the crumpled pack and searched for a fresh one. She tore it open and pulled out a cigarette. It broke in her fingers, and tears sprang to her eyes. She pulled out another and lighted it. She inhaled deeply. Her face fell in deep creases as she smoked.

Then, tiredly, she climbed the stairs to the bedroom and sat on her chair and picked up a fresh organdy cap and began to flute it, pressing down hard, one flute after another, all around the cap. She finished it and picked up another. She would flute ten and then cut out some fresh caps. She liked to alternate jobs, it was less tedious that way. But as she worked, her face set in deep sad lines and her mouth drooped. Ed would be working late tonight, he'd told her. Yes, that's what he'd said. She kept working. The girls came in, she hardly heard them. She heard herself respond to their greetings, but from a great distance. The money she earned from this batch — she would make more this week, she'd work constantly, she'd make three hundred. She had forty dollars under the drawer. She'd make another thirty. Seventy dollars. That would be enough to get her started.

She made dinner in silence, the girls were, well, they were always concerned with their own affairs, they helped though, that was good: Anastasia washed the dishes, Joy dried. She could go upstairs and make some more caps. She saved a pork chop and some mashed potatoes and string beans on a pie plate and put it in the oven. She put the applesauce back in the refrigerator; he could have it if he wanted. Anastasia was going out to baby-sit. Joy had homework to do. She barely heard them. She went back upstairs.

She heard him come in; it was near twelve. She had stopped working and put on her nightgown and robe and gone downstairs to sit in the porch. She had left only the front door light on. He came in, smiling as always, 'Hello, Belle,' big hug, but she pulled away from him, she wouldn't let him touch her. She walked stonily into the kitchen and laid his dinner out for him. She asked him if he wanted applesauce. He did. He sat and ate; she went back to the porch and smoked. When he was finished eating, he came out to the porch and sat down across from her.

'I'm leaving,' she said.

A Christmas present. He bought her a Christmas present. It was still going on, despite his promise. Never, in the nearly sixteen years they had been married had he given Belle a Christmas present, or a birthday present, or any other present, but he had bought one for her. And he had paid for it by check! When he knew she reviewed the checks! WHAT WAS THE MATTER WITH HIM?

Never given her a present. Yes, once, on Valentine's Day, before they knew she was pregnant, maybe before she *was* pregnant, he had bought her a box of chocolates. Nothing more.

Same girl, or a new one? Had she moved to the new company with him? What was her name? Irene. Sweet face.

Older now. Still single. Waiting for him? She could have him!

Oh, my house! Oh, my stupid futile dreams! Why do I bother? Me, sitting up there bloodying my fingers to make those damned hats, and he had the money to buy her a Christmas present! He didn't buy one for me! We could barely give the girls anything! What is the matter with him?

Out, out, out! She had to leave, to go away, to leave them all, all of them hanging on her, devouring her energy, her substance, giving nothing back, taking, taking, taking. Demanding. Away, they could take care of themselves, she had had enough, no more, she could leave and get a job and get herself a little apartment somewhere, make a new life. Enough.

'I'm leaving,' she said in the dark room, smoke drifting above her head.

'Why, Belle?' he asked, sounding genuinely puzzled.

Lying there, her bones aching through her flesh, listening to the silence, she waited. A bad fight, she could feel it, even though she couldn't hear much. Dad arguing with her. Softly, a few sentences. Her, silent. Divorce. They're talking about divorce.

Anastasia moved her body slightly. The hard wood of the stair landing sometimes squeaked and she didn't want them to hear her. Why not? Divorce, they're talking about. She should charge downstairs and scream at them, scream, 'Get a divorce, get it! Get it! Anything to change the way things are now, anything would be better than this!' She thought about it. She would charge down and yell at them. The last time she had done something like that, Mother had been very angry, had hit her. She didn't care if she hit her. She would do it. Couldn't hear what they were saying. Murmuring. This was the third night. Well, the third night she had been aware something was going on. Who knew how long it had been going on? What was it about?

Mother's birthday last week, and I'd saved all my baby-sitting money since Christmas to buy her that wallet and she hardly looked at it. It was as if I'd given her nothing. She hates us. I used to think she loved Joy, but she doesn't, she doesn't love anybody, she hates us all.

I won't go down. What's the point? They should get divorced. I wish I could still pray, I'd pray for them to get a divorce. Maybe they will. We'll leave here. Dad will find a girlfriend, he'll be all right. We'll move to an apartment, we'll be poor but maybe she won't be so miserable all the time. I'll work. I'll go to college at night. I'll take care of her. Maybe she'd be a little happier. The tension will go away. We could move to Jamaica, I could get around there there are buses and trains oh god please let them get a divorce I can't stand anymore. . . .

'I had my bag all packed,' Belle said in a foggy distant voice. 'I was all ready to go. I could have gone, I could have found a way to support myself, I was still presentable at forty. I could get a job and find a room somewhere. I had seventy dollars. I didn't have to struggle the way I was struggling, working, slaving, for what?'

She sipped her drink, puffed on her cigarette. She was not looking at me.

'But I couldn't leave you girls. Who would take care of you? Joy was still a child, she was only eleven, she still wasn't strong. I knew he wouldn't take care of you. He'd probably just have gone to her, wherever she lived, and abandon you. I had to stay.'

She stood up unsteadily.

'What is it? Do you want another drink?' She nodded. 'I'll get them,' I said, taking her glass.

'Oh, will you, Anastasia? Thanks,' she said with relief, as if I had saved her from some horrible ordeal. She sat down again and waited until I returned with fresh drinks. We sipped. She was silent. I knew she would not speak again unless I did.

'But how did you feel about him?'

'I couldn't get over it.' She sipped and held the scotch in her mouth for a long time. I did the same. I didn't swallow until after she did.

'He'd told me he'd given her up, but all the while . . . I

guess when he moved to Bunnell, he offered her a job there too and she took it. Maybe he'd been seeing her the whole time, I don't know. She was a secretary, she could always get a job. . . .'

'What had he bought her?'

'A nightgown.' Her mouth twisted.

'After you caught him the first time, taking her out to dinner, he started taking us out to dinner, remember?'

She didn't.

'Yes, when we were looking for a house. We'd go out every Sunday and have dinner in a nice restaurant.'

She shrugged. 'I guess so.'

'And it was the following Christmas that he gave you a present for the first time. Remember?'

She shrugged again. 'If you say so.'

In the fall of 1945, Anastasia was a senior in high school, walking around in an emotional limbo, not knowing anything. She could not go to college, but she wanted to go to college, she would have to find a way, she couldn't think about it, she couldn't think about anything. She hung out with her friends and came home to eat, and wash the dishes. Then she either went out baby-sitting or went up to her room and read. When she turned out the light at night, she couldn't sleep, and would daydream. She'd imagine she lived in a beautiful place with her parents suddenly happy together, and she was meeting brilliant sexy boys who would immediately fall in love with her. She dated boys at the high school, but they were not anything much, they were not brilliant or sexy or even specially fun, and they all wanted to neck. She didn't.

She hardly knew what was going on around her. Her father, working late, her mother, hunched over the hats, Joy in and out. The tension was not as bad as it had been in the early part of the year, but it was not gone either. They had not gotten a divorce. Dad had gone on seeing the woman he'd been in love with, and Mother had found out because he wanted her to find out, just like the last time. Such a coward, he wants her to know but he doesn't come out and tell her, he manages for her to find out in sneaky underhanded ways. Then the fault for starting the argument is hers, and he can be silent. And she's silent anyway. Silent. Silent.

Still, her mother's plight hurt her: and although she used the money she had earned over the summer to buy her own clothes, she saved as much as she could in the fall to buy her mother a really nice Christmas present. She wanted to do something that would cheer her up. She had decided on a pocketbook, and went to the nicest store in Hempstead, Franklin Simon, to find it. She bought a beautiful black suede bag with a gold clasp, big enough to hold all Mother's eyeglasses, and her wallet and keys and handkerchief and everything. It cost $25, really expensive. You could buy a lovely bag for $4.95.

They no longer went to Jean and Eric's on Christmas Eve, since there were no longer any small children for whom a Santa had to be provided, and besides, she thought Mother had invited Jean to her new house and Jean had refused to come and Mother was angry about it. But about that she was only guessing. She had presents for Daddy (a belt) and Joy (fireman red Dr Denton pajamas) as well. She knew she was getting clothes. She would probably not get presents from anyone else. Jean and Eric wouldn't give her a present unless they came over at Christmastime; and Eddie and Martha no longer came down from Boston every Christmas since Grandma died. This year they were not coming. But she didn't care what she got: she was so excited about the bag she bought for Mommy. It was a truly grown-up gift, a nice gift, one she would have to love. Anastasia wrapped it carefully.

They waited to open their presents until they had had breakfast and were all nicely dressed. They had decorated the tree the night before. But when Anastasia stooped under it to lay down the gifts she had brought downstairs from their hiding place, she noticed a box with Belle's name on it. She stood up sharply: Daddy had bought Mommy a present! Her heart began to beat a little faster than normal, and her color rose. He'd bought her a present! Maybe she'd be really happy this year! Anastasia began to sing 'Joy to the World,' and Joy, giggling, joined in. Even Mommy was smiling when she sat down on the couch. Dad sat in the chair on one side of the fireplace, and Anastasia sat on the other. Mother said Anastasia should be Santa Claus; she was very pleased. She bent and picked up a present for Joy, and Joy's present for Dad, and handed them their boxes. Joy found a sloppy joe sweater, and cried out in delight. It was peach. She already had a pale blue one, so now she was rich. And Dad smiled over the socks that Joy had bought for him – although Anastasia knew that Mommy had given her the money, because Joy was too young to earn any by herself.

Then Anastasia bent and picked up the present marked 'Belle'. It was very heavy. She walked across the room and handed it to Mommy, her eyes gleaming, her face hot with happiness.

'Oh, for me?' Mommy said in a little voice. 'Oh, my.' She put on her glasses and started to tear off the wrapping paper. She had it only half off when she threw the box on to the couch and suddenly she stood up. She walked through the living room and up the stairs. She went into her room. They heard the door close.

Daddy and Joy and Anastasia sat. They did not look at each other. Then Daddy got up sighing and walked heavily up the stairs. They could hear him open the door and say 'Belle, aren't you coming down to open the rest of the presents?' They could not hear what she said, but he closed the door and came back downstairs.

'She doesn't feel well,' he said. He sighed heavily. 'Oh, my,' he sighed. He left the room and walked through the house and went down to the cellar.

Anastasia jumped up and darted across the room and tore open the rest of the wrapping paper on Mother's gift. There was printing on the box. It said: GE ELECTRIC IRON.

'So he gave her a nightgown and the next year he gave you an iron. You were furious.'

'Oh, maybe, Anastasia, I don't remember.' She was beginning to sound annoyed, and I knew it was time to stop. But I couldn't.

'That was the year I saved and bought you a beautiful black suede bag. I paid twenty-five dollars for it,' I recalled.

'Did you? You should have told me. I didn't know it was a good bag. I just used it for everyday.'

She hadn't opened it at all until late at night. She lay in her bed all day. Anastasia made Joy open the gift from her, and she opened her presents – a pair of slacks and a sweater from Mom and Dad, and a string of fake pearls from Joy. The sisters looked at each other helplessly. Joy went to the telephone and called a number of her friends. No one could come out today, it was Christmas. But she stayed on the phone for several hours. Anastasia cleaned up the wrapping paper and went up to her room and lay on the bed and read. When the light began to fade, she became aware they hadn't had lunch, and she was hungry. She got up and knocked at her mother's door, but Mother couldn't hear her. She was lying on her good ear. Anastasia opened the door a little. Her voice was cool.

'Do you want me to start dinner?'

Her mother was a dark lump in the bed; the shades were drawn, the room dim. The lump stirred slightly. A weak voice spoke. 'You can peel the potatoes and turn on the oven to four hundred degrees. You can peel the onions and string the beans. I'll be down in a little while.'

Grimly, Anastasia did as she was told. Then she marched back upstairs.

'What do you want me to do now?'

'Ask Daddy to cut the turnip.'

'Daddy's out in the garage working on the car.'

Silence. 'I'll come down.'

For Christmas dinner that year, they had rib roast, mashed white potatoes, creamed onions, mashed turnip, string beans with browned breadcrumbs and homemade cranberry sauce. They had an apple pie with a choice of cheddar cheese or vanilla ice cream to top it. It must have been a delicious meal if you could taste it. No one spoke during the meal, or afterward, during the cleaning up. When it was over and her mother was sitting in the dark porch, Anastasia carried her present to her mother.

'Oh, thanks, Anastasia,' Belle said in a weak voice, barely looking at it. 'It's very nice.'

This little story has what is known as a happy ending. Belle and Ed stayed together. He never again, as far as anyone knows, strayed from the marital bed. Beds, because as soon as there was more money in the house, Belle bought twin beds, and refused ever again, even if they were staying in someone's house, to sleep in a double. If there was only a double, Ed slept on the couch, Belle being, it was understood, a poor sleeper. And every Christmas after that, for a number of years, Ed bought Belle a present. The year following the Christmas described above, he asked Anastasia to help him: he didn't know Belle's taste, he said, and she did. She took him to the best jewelry store in town and selected a dainty silver bracelet with matching earrings. When Belle opened the present on Christmas Day, she looked over at Ed and said sharply, 'So you had Anastasia pick it out'. The following year, he tried on his own. A Saks had opened in Garden City, and there he bought her a beautiful hand mirror, gold-plated with an ornate border. She opened it, picked it up and looked in it, and put it down. 'It's too weak,' she said. 'The handle will break.' It was returned.

But, lover of happy endings, they stayed together. Isn't that worth everything? They grew old together, they are together still. They have together, if they care to dredge them up, a lifetime of memories. Ed no longer attempts to buy her presents: for years now, he has given her a hundred-dollar check in a box with some handkerchiefs. She buys him a large article of clothing – a coat or suit – and they go together to shop for it, usually after Christmas, when there are sales. It is now impossible to buy either of them presents: they have everything. Another happy ending: immigrant family makes good in the second generation. For they all did, my parents and their siblings. They all joined the middle class and sent their children to college and had cleaning women and gardeners in their later years. They all drove shiny cars. Isn't that what you want to hear? Hard work, sacrifice, and energy, especially when matched with intelligence, can still, or could still make one's fortune in America.

They stayed together and things improved for them. Slowly, but steadily. They did not change. Ed still has his gift for contentment, she has hers for misery; he is still unaware of what is going on around him; she is still aware, if no longer interested. His drawers are crammed with unworn shirts, sweaters, pajamas; hers with handkerchiefs, nightgowns (not one of which he bought her), slips, bras, panties, stockings, jewelry. Now she sighs when gifts are presented: Where am I going to put it? The time has long since passed when any gift could make her happy. *Was* there ever a time when it could?

There was, at least, a time when I thought gifts could make her happy, before I was able to give her much at all. And there were times, I think, when she enjoyed a gift – a few, anyway. I kept trying, though, for years, after she no longer cared, shopping, searching for just the right whatever, something that might make her smile. I still do, to tell the truth.

As if, as if . . . Oh, I sit here now knowing things I didn't know years ago, didn't know even when I began to compose this account. . . . Because we, Joy and I, for whom as she saw it she had given up her life, were not separate beings in whom she could sometimes take delight. We were like the brothers you find in fairy tale and romance, who, when they died, transferred their strength and energy to the next brother. This magical power made the third brother (they always come in threes) superhumanly strong once the other two have died in battle (they always die in battle). This fairy tale is another male usurpation of a female power – for the brothers are a magical imitation of the process of motherhood. A mother gives birth, drains herself to keep her daughter alive, and succeeds, but the mother, worn out by hard labor, dies young; she leaves her daughter in better circumstances than she had, and when that daughter gives birth, she also struggles to keep her child alive, and succeeds, leaving the granddaughter in strong circumstances. It is the granddaughter who questions the giving of birth, who wonders whether she should continue this process which sent her grandmother and mother to early graves.

Joy and I were all the vital identification Belle had. Having given up so much, she had nothing left to love with, and in any case, saw no need for something she had survived without. And having lived all her young life without it, she did not remember the need, and could not receive its symbols. Her neck refused to bend to a loving chest or shoulder; as if to take anything so little, so late, would make her sacrifice meaningless. To take anything from us – a gift, of whatever sort – would be to reverse the process, send the energy and strength backward through the 'brothers,' allowing the dead to quicken, and since, in the fairy tale, all three brothers invariably love and desire the same woman, allowing competition and jealousy to enter their otherwise sealed and perfect bond.

In my innocence, or call it by its true name, stupid willfulness, I imagined I could escape from all this, could break the chain of mothers, could free myself from the clinging fingers of a ghostly fate. The times permit such delusions – there are buses and railroad trains, jobs in distant towns, telephones for intermittent contact, apartments for single women. What I wanted to escape from was not the past, but the pain, and for me they were identical, because by the time I was sixteen, I knew my mother's story, and her mother's, and I saw the bloody cord connecting us. I set my teeth to bite myself free. I would not take my place in the sacrificial ranks, would not live the way they did, would not pass on to my children – if, indeed, I ever had any – a legacy of suffering selflessness. I would not repeat their experience. Above all, I would construct a new personality for myself that did not, like hers, absorb all the light and air surrounding it and turn it into darkness, into a hunched-over shadowy mass in a dim room, surrounded by the proofs of my enslavement.

Having no model for the new person I intended to become, I drew from the culture around me, which in my day contained figures like June Allyson and Doris Day. I would be cheerful, 'relentlessly cheerful,' full of jokes and light of heart. I would be my mother's opposite: I would not care about the things that mattered to her, I would be sexual, open, full of laughter. I would also be intellectual and imaginative, I would give every part of myself full expression. I would allow nothing to depress me.

With such a determination, I puzzled my mother by being nonchalant about the fact that there was no money for me to go to college, despite her efforts over all the years. By my junior year in high school, I had begun to work every night, baby-sitting, and every summer as a telephone operator, and to save every cent I earned. I went to a local college, Riston, so I could live at home and save the cost of room and board. And once at Riston, I plagued the employment office until it found a job for me in a college office. Things were informal in those days, and every two weeks, when I collected the fruits of my labors at fifty cents an hour, I applied some dollars to my tuition bill of $250 a semester. My mother helped. She gave me $100 the fall and spring of my first year, and the next year she was able to give me $250. She worked extra hours to earn this money for me, long hours in the dim room with the white piles around her. Her fingers were often bloody and covered with Band-Aids. Her face was always pale and drawn. And even as I acknowledged, silently, with profound gratitude, her labors and sacrifices for me, I was repelled by them, I pulled away in a kind of horror, I didn't want to see, I didn't want to have to know, I didn't want to feel the guilt that drenched my body like the sweat from menopausal hot flashes, every time I thought about her.

I pushed it all away. I went off to college and became Stacey the wild girl. I never much liked that nickname, but it seemed too hard to ask Americans to pronounce Anastasia properly. One of the reasons I loved Brad right from the first was that he did pronounce my name correctly or shortened it to Stahz. But for most people I was Stacey, too classy and too smart to be considered a tramp, and thus requiring some new category – bohemian, rebel, free spirit. I rebelled in every way I could: I wore pants to school – still forbidden on many campuses – and my father's old white shirts over a cotton knit shirt. I refused to be involved with girls, and surrounded myself with boys, with whom I went out drinking beer, jabbing, telling jokes. Skinny, quick, nervous, contentious, I had a reputation but admiration as well; most of the other female students were frightened of me, which pleased me. I was not going to be a woman, I had decided that. Since I clearly was not a man, my only alternative was to be beyond sex, or at least gender. I deluded myself that was how others saw me too. The delusion didn't last long, though: it's hard to make a claim for being beyond gender when your belly is sticking out a foot in front.

Stacey grew almost independently, because later in life people again called me that. She became a finished product, in the full sense of that phrase: polished, and complete. She was finished at least a decade ago, and I have been living since in a dark little room behind the store that sells her replicas. I've been living like a body that has fallen from and is being dragged by a sled, pulled by the momentum of something I set in motion but am no longer a part of. But this time, I am old and too tired to manufacture a new me, to devise someone I'd like to be and try to become it. That takes an energy and drive I no longer possess. Yet the only alternative is to let myself live buried alive.

Clara says I'm depressed. I say I have damned good reason. It's an impasse.

four

We moved into the apartment in time for the kids to start school in Lynbrook. It looked shabby and bare, especially by comparison with the furniture store we'd been living in, and we were all a little irritable despite Mrs Nowak's pot of stuffed cabbage, sent up for our first evening meal. I found myself concerned with the placement of furniture and knickknacks in a way I hadn't been since Brad and my first little one-room household – strange, given the little I had to work with here. It was almost as if having so very little to work with inspired me. I, who never in my life had been able to sew on a button once (it took two or three attempts before I got it sewn on the proper side of a garment), found myself shortening curtains and using old drapes to make swags for the living room and my bedroom windows. I suddenly began to pay attention to food prices and set myself challenges to make wonderful meals out of nothing – and succeeded, too. I was doing this for the children.

Because they were a couple of wrecks. They squabbled all the time, burst into tears at nothing, were surly and sulky and as relentlessly grouchy as I was cheerful. I tried to jolly them out of the blues, to make an adventure of poverty, but they were having none of it. They came near to killing each other in arguments about whose T-shirt got accidentally tossed into the dark wash and turned pink (they both wore the same size), or whose nickel it was that was found in the hall on the floor outside the bathroom. Their worst fight was over who would take which of the two small bedrooms; one was a little lighter than the other, but the other had a closet. The choice was impossible.

And there was I, only I, alone. I knew the divorce was my fault – it doesn't matter how you try to work things out on a moral scale of judgment – my feelings, my behavior, had cost them a father and a nice big old house with a huge yard full of big old trees. Most of all, it had required them to leave a school they knew and enter a new one as strangers, to make all new friends, to suffer the initial loneliness and fear. Everything was my fault. They felt that way, and truthfully, so did I. It was up to me to make things better for them, however I could. I tried; I violated the old Anastasia as far as I could imagine. No longer a wife, I finally became a domestic.

Still, although I learned to be firm and quash their vituperation of each other, I couldn't touch their unhappiness. I could keep them quieter, but not content. Billy would come home from school every afternoon scowling and turn on the television set; when I forbade watching television in the afternoon, he went into his room and lay on the bed staring at the ceiling. (I could remember doing that, feeling unloved and unhappy; so when he did it, I would go in there and put my arms around him and ask him what was wrong and tell him I loved him and kiss his cheek: but he'd turn away, turn his back on me and whine at me to go away and leave him alone. And I thought of my mother giving us what she hadn't had, and our finding it insufficient; here I was, giving them what I hadn't had and they wanted something else, domestic security, a father, popularity, whatever . ... and I felt a turn of despair in my stomach.) Billy would lie there all afternoon, unless I scolded him and made him do his homework. He'd usually do it, but not until I scolded; and then insist he be allowed to watch television. I'd let him.

Arden stalked home early too, at first, and would walk in with her head high, eyes glaring, a surly answer to my sweetsie cheerful 'How was school today, honey?' She'd refuse even Oreos and milk. She'd go into *her* room and slam the door (they'd ended by Billy taking the lighter room and Arden taking the one with the closet) and sit and read all afternoon, another thing I remembered doing. I'd knock on her door and enter at a growled (insofar as a ten-year-old can growl) reply, and sit on the bed and ask *her* what was the matter. Proud head still, 'You wouldn't understand,' she'd shoot at me. 'Try me, I was a kid once,' I laughed, but she was having no laughing. Glaring eyes: 'I don't care to discuss it!' And that was that.

The house seemed very empty after they'd gone to bed, though: odd, since they'd barely been in it while they were awake. I missed them after they were sleeping. I guess it was when they were sleeping that I could conjure their old selves, and miss those. I'd be reading, or looking through some old prints; sometimes I'd get out my equipment and do some cropping. But the house got quieter, and colder too: Mrs Nowak went to bed at ten, and turned the heat down when she did. And finally I'd get up and go into the kitchen and pour myself a rye and soda and carry it back to the living room and turn out all the lights except the one over the desk, and sit down by the window (wherever did I learn that?) in a soft old armchair I'd found at Goodwill, and try to think things through.

I was overwhelmed by how little I had done for my children. Here my mother, with zilch money and little education, had thought to and managed to take us kids to the Prospect Park Zoo and the Bronx Zoo, the Barnum and Bailey Circus, and the opera. She persuaded my father to drive us to Floyd Bennett Field, and paid one dollar apiece for us to go up, with Daddy, in a two-seater Piper Cub airplane, first me, then Joy. Belle herself stayed on the ground. She took me to Carnegie Hall to hear Nelson Eddy sing, and to Town Hall to hear Ruth Sczlenzinska play. She'd saved enough one year so that we went to the Catskill Mountains for a week, staying in a tiny cottage that was the equivalent of today's motels. We swam in Silver Lake, crowded as it was, when we could. Mostly we sat in the cottage, because it rained all week, steadily. Belle cooked on a kerosene stove while Joy and I lay on one bed, playing memory, and my father fiddled with something that was broken, and she opened cans and put food on plates and the smell of kerosene permeated the tiny room and made me ill. Another year she got us to Washington, D.C., for two days, and my father drove us to see the monuments and the Capitol.

And what had I done? These past four years or so Brad had earned a lot of money, but the only trips I'd taken my kids on were to the railroad yards or the back of shopping malls. I hadn't even taken them to a zoo – well, I hate zoos, I can't bear seeing animals in cages – although Belle and Ed had. They'd taken them to the circus, too, and reported on both occasions, that the children were not very interested in anything except what they would have to eat. They wanted frankfurters and orange soda and cotton candy, and had got them. I had given my children piano lessons, but that was all. I let them go to the movies on Saturday afternoons with their friends, but only in the past year or so. We'd never taken them on a vacation – well, that was Brad's doing, he didn't want the hassle – and anyway, we'd barely gone on vacations ourselves. A three-day trip to Niagara Falls, and another to Lake George – that was all.

I had been selfish and self-involved. I was a rotten mother. I was a rotten person. Such thinking made me squeamish with self-hatred and I tried to find ways to comfort myself. I had always been affectionate with them, physically and otherwise; I had always listened to them. I had answered their questions. Wasn't that worth something? I hadn't sighed, or turned away from them; I hadn't treated them as troublesome burdens. That was good, wasn't it?

From the looks of them just then, it didn't seem so.

I couldn't even really fall back on blaming Brad, because my mother had managed all of what she'd done without much help from my father. But at least he had been willing to spend his weekends driving children to Floyd Bennett Field, or to the slums, or the beach. Brad had always worked weekends, and had been unwilling to go much of anyplace en famille except to his parents or mine.

It stared at me, my failure of them. And now what was I to do? The money Brad sent was barely enough to keep us alive. I wasn't even sure I'd be able to keep the car, because I had nothing set aside for the insurance which would come due next year, and no way of setting anything aside. Even if I now had had the imagination to come up with some project that would cheer up my miserable children, I couldn't afford to realize it. Nor did I see much point in appealing to Brad. He didn't have time for them, what with his new wife and selling the house and buying another, one with Greek pillars and a pretentious front lawn (never used) and no yard, in Garden City this time. He took the children out for dinner once a week, to a place where they could get hamburgers and french fries, and they always returned from seeing him more irritable and taciturn than usual.

I had to do something. Having had no luck talking to them separately, I would talk to them together. Maybe being together would give them the courage to speak. I waited until Sunday morning, after making them a nice breakfast of waffles (which they barely touched. Why hadn't I got them the kind you make in the toaster, as I usually did, they wanted to know.) It was raining out, a coolish day in early October, the leaves just beginning to turn. And now being driven from the trees by wind and rain, so we would not even have the little beauty that resides in that part of the year. I poured myself another cup of coffee.

'You know, kids, you've both been awfully grouchy and unhappy since we moved. Since Daddy and I got divorced. Would you tell me what's bothering you?'

Silence. Hostile stares.

'Do you miss the old house? Your friends?'

'No, of course not,' Billy drawled sarcastically. 'It's fun to have to make all new friends in the third grade. And have a room without any closet and hardly any room for my toys.'

'I hate my room!' Arden announced.

'I'm really sorry,' I said sincerely. 'Sorry you don't like your rooms, and sorry you have to start in a strange school. But you know you will make new friends. It's hard, but you will.'

'I won't!' Billy exclaimed. 'I hate all those kids.'

'They're stupid!' Arden agreed.

'They're not all stupid,' I said calmly.

'Yes, they are,' Arden said authoritatively. 'The kids in Rockville Centre are smarter because there are more Jews.'

'Where did you hear that?'

She shrugged. 'Everybody says so.'

I knew 'everybody' probably had a name like Joan or Eileen, but I didn't probe. 'There are some Jews here, too,' I suggested. 'What about the Lench children? Aren't they Jewish?'

Arden nodded sullenly. 'I guess so.'

'And isn't there a really smart girl in your class – the one that got a hundred per cent the day you got ninety-nine per cent on the arithmetic test?'

'Math, Mommy, math!' Billy corrected me with contempt.

'Yes, math.'

Arden shrugged again, pulling her shoulders close into her body as if I were pushing her inside herself. 'Mmmm.'

'What's her name?'

'Joan Tebaldi.'

'And didn't you go to Joyce Lench's house to play one day last week?'

She nodded, even more uncomfortable.

'See? You're making friends.'

'She has friends!' Billy exclaimed, his face red with the strain of letting his anger out. '*I* don't! It's different for girls!' The word *girls* dripped with contempt. 'They talk all the time, talk and giggle. Stupid!'

'Girls are more friendly than boys, usually,' I said, still calmly, trying hard not to smile. 'But boys make friends too, just more slowly.'

'He'll never make friends!' Arden spat at him, returning contempt for contempt. 'He's too scared!'

'I am not!' Billy was full red now. 'You . . .' He began to rise from his chair.

'Calm down, Billy' I ordered. 'Maybe she's right. Maybe you're shy. But most people want to make friends. You have to try. You have to talk to them. They'll want to talk to you.'

'They don't! They don't! I have so tried! What do you know about it?' His eyes began to run, and his cheeks were splotchy, and he jumped from his chair, toppling it, and tore off into his room and slammed the door.

Arden watched him with fury. 'Baby!' she muttered.

'So what are we going to do about your room, toots?'

'It's horrible. There's nothing you can do.'

'Maybe we can paint it. Or put up some posters.'

'Oh, Mommy!' Contempt and disgust.

'You know what we could do? We could paint a mural on the wall, the long wall beside your bed. We could paint a big window, with the sun coming in, and trees outside, and flowers, or whatever you wanted.'

'That's stupid! It's stupid!' She was near to tears too.

'It would be fun!' I went on cheerfully. 'You and I could do it together, and you can order anything you like to go in it. You could have houses, or animals, or children playing . . . whatever!'

'Train yards and factories! That's what *you* think is pretty! That's what *you'd* put in it!' She jumped down too then and ran into *her* room and slammed the door. The house reverberated with silence.

I cleaned the kitchen.

I was no more successful at finding a job. The only one

available in the stores in the Lynbrook village was at the Kent dry cleaners, for minimum wage. I almost took it: almost let myself spend my days taking in soiled clothes and handing out receipts; handing out cleaned clothes and taking in money: for eighty-five cents an hour: but the hours available were 1–5 six days a week, impossible for me. (Saved!) In the end, I drove toward Rockville Centre, where the *Long Island Herald* offices were, and wheedled and wormed my way into a part-time job as file clerk, receptionist and switchboard operator. I'd never worked a switchboard, but claimed I had, sensing it would be easy to learn. I couldn't claim to know typing, since my method when writing term papers was hunt and peck, and not very quickly, either. They too paid minimum wage, but were willing to have me 9–12 five days a week, and I was close enough to home to drive back hurriedly so I'd be there when the kids came in for lunch around 12.10. And I told myself that the job might help me get work as a photographer.

After taxes and deductions, I took home a little over eight dollars a week. I thought about my mother making hats. Maybe she had known more than I did. Still, the eight dollars helped: it paid, for instance, for the paint needed to decorate Arden's wall. She came home from school a few days after our talk and asked, 'Well, when are we going to do it?'

'Do what?'

'Paint my room. I want the other walls pale pink, and the mural with a blue sky and yellow sun.'

'Oh?'

'You *said*. You said you would!'

'I thought you didn't like the idea.'

She sniffed a little and pulled her shoulders in, a gesture that remains characteristic of Arden to this day when she feels attacked. From picking and probing at her, I discovered she had mentioned my idea to some other girls, and all had oohed and aahed and said they wished their mothers would let them do that. She'd started by describing the idea as stupid, but had listened to them and decided that maybe it would be all right. 'They want to come and see it, so when can you do it? Today?'

We started it over the weekend, but didn't finish for a month. Then there began a parade of ten-year-old girls marching through the house to view with awe a large window on the wall beside Arden's bed, a tree outside and sun pouring down from above, billowy white curtains on either side of the window frame, a beagle (like Joan's) a cat (like Joyce's) and some flowers. After this was done, Arden stared at it thoughtfully. 'It needs something here,' she pointed to the horizon on the right. She was right. The tree dominated the left foreground.

'What would you like?'

She wanted some factories, squat buildings with tall smokestacks rising from them.

'Why would you want things like that?'

'You seem to think they're pretty, you keep taking pictures of them,' Arden said haughtily. 'So maybe they are.'

Eventually, Arden's irritability diminished, although she was not the carefree child she had been. When I asked her what she wanted for Christmas, she said billowy white curtains, like the ones in the mural, for the window in her room. So I went shopping with my mother and bought white organdy, and made, yes *made* broad billowy white curtains on Mother's sewing machine (and with her help). I also painted the bookcase and bureau in her room white; and made a billowy white skirt for her inner spring, and bought her a red-and-white patterned quilt. By the spring term, it had become a mark of great favor to be taken home by Arden Carpenter. And she would often say to me, 'You know, I was lying on my bed thinking last night, and . . .' whatever. And I told her how I had lain on my bed beside two windows, staring out at moon and clouds and the patterns they made, and the occasional star.

'I wish I could see the moon and the stars,' Arden mused, not complaining.

'Maybe I could make it do that.'

'You could!' Mommy was turned heroine.

I drove to Brooklyn, to a discount art-supply store, and bought a roll of heavy blue film: then I went to a hardware store and bought fixtures for a toilet paper roll and a heavy-duty stapler. I went to a lumber yard and bought a three-foot wooden cylinder one inch in diameter. I stapled the film to the cylinder, attached the toilet paper holders, and slid the cylinder into their openings. I attached a cord to the bottom. Then I began to paint.

This was really hard because I wanted to paint the film on the wrong side, but what I painted had to match what was already on the wall – perfectly. I shadowed in the animals; I put in a moon just emerging from gold-edged clouds; and a few stars; and I added dots of light around the factories. When the shade was down, it showed the tree and plants eerily, just as they look at night. It wasn't the sturdiest job in the world, even if it took me hours and hours to finish. It didn't last: of course, it got a lot of wear, being pulled down and raised many times every day. In two years, the film had torn and shredded. But that was all right. Art had served its true purpose: to nurture. By then, Arden was the most popular girl in her class.

Things were harder for Billy. He remained friendless, surly, and sulky. I kept (cheerfully) making suggestions: Boy Scouts (Nah! Boring!), my old stamp collection (that occupied him for a few weeks), basketball (there was an old hoop still attached to Mrs Nowak's garage, a remnant from her son's youth. That was a successful idea until the hoop, rusted with age, fell off the garage. Several requests that Brad put a new one up for Billy went unregarded). Finally, I suggested music lessons: 'Maybe you could play in the school band.'

This appealed, I don't know why. Billy went to see the math teacher, who doubled as bandmaster, who received him with open arms and handed him a sousaphone. A sousaphone! Billy was given a free lesson every week, and was allowed almost immediately to play in the band. All that was required was that he and I manage to shove, stuff, and slide the monster into the back seat of my two-door car every Thursday and Saturday; and that I listen daily while Billy practiced. It did not seem to me that my son was a budding musician. But I was patient. I never complained. And if I was grateful when, the following school year, he decided to switch to the trumpet, I did not let him know it. By then he had found a couple of friends, and played basketball in front of their garages every afternoon, and practiced his instrument hardly at all.

If I've been implying that things improved, I don't want you to think it was a steady thing. With kids, things never improve, they just change form. You never know what's ahead, and if you allow yourself to fall into complacency, you will be disappointed. For instance, there was Christmas the first year after our divorce. We had to split the kids – which split us. I took them Christmas Eve, the traditional time for my family's celebration, and Brad took them Christmas Day. We had reinstituted Santa Claus on Christmas Eve when the children were born, my father playing the role for my children and Joy's when she got home for Christmas. But we had Santa arrive at eight, and served a supper around eleven. There were only a few of us, far fewer than in the old days when Eddie and Martha and Wally and Jean and Eric and their children had all waited for Santa with our family. But the children were just as excited.

And my kids were happy with the event. The first year after the divorce, Arden got a doll from Grandma and Grandpa, and another from me (her wish) and a book: she got a doll's crib (her old one had broken) from Joy. Billy got a cowboy outfit complete with boots and hat from my parents and me combined; Joy gave him a gun and holster. Fine. They went to bed late, I admit it. They were tired and cranky when Brad honked his horn at seven the next morning – his parents like to have Christmas at daybreak if possible – and he was cranky about having to come in and sit in the messy kitchen and drink coffee while waiting for them to get dressed, and he yelled at them because he wasn't allowed to yell at me anymore (one benefit of divorce), and they got crankier. I admit all that.

Still, the reason they came back glazed and incredibly

irritable that night was not just tiredness, I think. Brad had to make four trips to carry up all the stuff they'd been given. There were a football, football shoes and pants and helmet (Billy hated football); a set of trains; an erector set; new roller skates; several games; a punching bag; two pairs of school pants, two pairs of pajamas, and two shirts. That was for Billy. Arden whined in with three more dolls (two replicas of those she'd received). A doll carriage, another doll's crib, a doll's highchair, a suitcase of doll's clothes, a jigsaw puzzle, ice skates, a skirt, blouse, and matching sweater, a nightgown and slippers. These children were unspeakable to; and next morning, as I tried to slog through toys to raise the living room shades, so was I. Oh, and an ironing board. She got. Arden. But no iron. She whimpered about that, but she didn't even want what she got.

They played on the floor with their new toys, shrieking at each other regularly, trampling things. Billy's plastic submarine (I forgot to mention that) broke the first day. He didn't care. He carried it to the kitchen and dumped it into the garbage. There was no room in our house for this many toys. I secreted two of the dolls, and one crib, intending to try to return them. Still, I praised their gifts, trying to make them appreciate the onslaught.

Arden turned her (even then) noble head on her neck and said quietly. 'He tries to buy us.' Then she kicked the doll carriage. 'I hate it all! Everything!' and stormed to her room. When I looked in on her fifteen minutes later, she was sleeping. Billy fell asleep among the trains, which he couldn't quite manage to set up by himself, and which I hadn't the energy to help him with. It took them several days to recover. By that time, I'd gotten the trains set up, but Billy had lost interest in them. That was the way it was. It was like that every Christmas afterward, too, until they were grown up.

I just sat there, the night of the day after Christmas, and stared at the mess. Even with the lights turned down, the room was hulking with things. Waste, I thought, and tried to avoid a spasm of jealousy. Here was I, down again to two pairs of underpants, and there was this floor full of waste. I'd packed away whatever I could salvage before it was crumpled, but even so, all I'd be able to get would be a credit against more toys. Unless I took them to a department store – and bought myself some underwear with the credit. I decided to do that, but it didn't comfort me.

I'd spent Christmas Day alone. I'd chosen to stay home. I sat in that apartment staring out at the grey winter sky and drank coffee and let things wash over me. I'd been so busy being cheerful and a good mother that I hadn't let myself think about myself at all in months. What kind of life did I have? Was it any better than when I was married? Mindless work five mornings a week; afternoons spent doing laundry, marketing, cleaning the house, errands; evenings at home at home at home until I thought I'd go buggy. Some of the guys at the *Herald* flirted a bit with me, but most of them were married, and I still had scruples. There was one younger guy who was single, but he was ugly – no chin, pop eyes – and callow to boot. I really loved one of the editors, but he was fifty and had a potbelly, and I loved him for his character, not his body. Besides, he never asked me out. The others did, occasionally, but I always refused, as gracefully as I could. I mentioned my children. Continually. That is a great deterrent with men, I've found. Anyway, it wasn't sex I craved. I felt no desire. My body was numb.

But if I'd thought I was among the living walking talking dead when I was married to Brad, where was I now? At least when I was married I'd gone out occasionally to a movie or a play, to dinner. I'd seen people in the evenings. Even if I didn't like them, they were a change from myself. Even hating Brad took my mind outside myself. Now there was only the children, the children all the time. I was narrowing myself to a circle of three. They were all I had to care about; they were all I had to think about. Except myself. And the last person on earth I wanted to think about was myself.

Hopeless, hopeless. I kept wiping my hand across my face. I drank so much coffee I felt ill, so I switched to rye until I felt ill with that as well. I never did eat. I didn't feel like opening a can of soup for Christmas dinner. I was too busy feeling sorry for myself. At some point, I caught myself hunched over in my armchair by the window, in the dark. I hadn't yet turned on the lights. I knew who I resembled. I pulled myself up and shook myself, I went into the bathroom and washed my face. I went into the kitchen and munched on some Saltines. I went to my desk and pulled open the picture file that stood beside it.

I'd been taking pictures, if less and less often (film is expensive), during free afternoons. I decided that day that I would experiment in a methodical serious way, with different cameras, lenses, films, lights, angles. I would begin to keep records of my experiments, teach myself photography in a scientific way. That decision sufficed to pull me together at least enough to embrace my cranky babies when they came home, to give them a sandwich and put them to bed lovingly. It kept me from tears. It even kept me going for some months. But it was a decision made in despair and I knew it. It was a stopgap. I was doing make-work. I, who had joked contemptuously at ladies' needlepointing, knitting, crocheting. Make-work for the idle, I'd snorted. Yes.

It was in April, about eight months after my overnight flight to Mexico for a quickie divorce, that I went on my first date. I was still feeling dead in my body. I didn't go out for sex, only for company. I was dying, drying up, craving adult companionship. The guy I went out with had worked at the *Herald* years ago, and had been hired by the *Daily News;* by *Herald* standards, he had made it. He lived in Lynbrook, in a big old white house with wonderful gardens. His wife had died of breast cancer some months ago; his beautiful gardens had gone to seed and overgrown; he had started to drink a bit, and taken to hanging around with his old cronies at the *Herald* office.

He was nice-looking, in his forties, and the drink didn't yet show. It might be a temporary aberration. I heard all the gossip in my central position in the foyer of the newsroom. By now, I had a 'rep' here too: only here I was the ice queen. That's what they called me. They liked me though and I liked them, the guys in the newsroom. Since

438

I wouldn't go out with any of them, no one had a special gripe against me. I was a good guy, one of the boys, just frigid. But I'd see Jimmy Hanna once in a while, sloping in to seek out company for a liquid lunch. I don't know what was happening with his job – maybe he was on a leave. He'd always stop and chat with me, and despite his depression and his habits, he still had an erect posture, a tight body, and he wore his hat at a jaunty angle. But he had a mournful look about him that captured something in me (oh mother!), he acted sweet and yearny, and I have to admit, I was drawn to him.

One morning, as I was cleaning up my desk preparing to leave, he stopped to chat, and asked me if I'd have dinner with him that evening. I looked at him for a moment, then heard myself say yes. I kept looking at him: I was sending him a message. But he didn't receive it, because a few minutes later, when I already had my hat and coat on, I heard a great howl go up in the newsroom, and the lunch crowd came out slapping Jimmy on the back, and looking over at me with leers. I was so cross I turned my back on them and left the office without a word, and I thought about canceling the date with Jimmy. I even called his house a few times that afternoon to do so. But there was no answer, and when the evening arrived, I found myself thinking that it would be really nice to go out to dinner. I hadn't been out to a restaurant in nearly a year. So instead of continuing to call him, I went down and asked Pane Nowak – that was what I called her now, to her enormous delight – to come up and sit with the kids that evening.

She folded her hands against her chest and rocked them back and forth – a gesture my mother made also, kind of a prayer crossed with a football cheer – and smiled 'You go out, eh? Is good! Young girl should go out. Get a better husband, hah?'

I knew she meant well, but it crossed my mind that there was little to choose between the newsmen's lascivious assumptions and her economic ones: for marriage preeminently meant financial security to women like Pane Nowak.

'I go out, yes,' I laughed. 'But not to find a husband.'

She nodded sagely. 'Yes, yes, I know.' She didn't believe

a word of it. 'I come, sure. We watch the Howdy-Doody together, hah?'

Jimmy had said we'd go to the Arbor Inn. I have to admit that had been half the attraction. The Arbor Inn had been a hangout for the boys and girls in the Christian clique when I was in high school. Their parents ate there; they drank there. I'd never been there. It was a pretty little place south of Merrick Road, and it had seemed to me in those days something like what the Waldorf meant to my young mother – something stylish and rich and far beyond me.

He appeared at the dot of seven-thirty. I'd fed the kids a little early and cleaned up the remains of the canned spaghetti Boyardee which was one of their favorite meals, and thrown out the homemade salad they left, and washed the dishes, and dressed up in a skirt and sweater which was one of the only decent outfits I owned. The children were agitated – a little excited with interest at this new development of Mommy's, and a little disapproving, a little resentful. They both fixed themselves firmly on the living room floor, where they were sitting in front of the television set prepared to swivel to examine whoever would walk through the door.

You'd never have guessed Jimmy had spent his lunch hours drinking. He must have spent the afternoon sleeping it off, because his face was as fresh and pink as a boy's, and he held his hat in a humble manner as he walked in. His eyebrows went up when he saw me in a skirt, and his mouth pursed, and I thought for an instant, with sinking heart, that he was going to whistle. But he turned his head toward the children and his eyebrows went up farther, and his mouth opened:

'What are you doing watching television? What about your homework!'

The children just stared at him without answering. They couldn't believe he was talking to them. I had been going to remind them of their homework, which they always started at eight o'clock, when the adult television programs began, but I didn't. I walked toward them, bent, and kissed them.

'I won't be late,' I said, loudly enough for Jimmy to hear. 'Be good, now, okay?'

''Bye, Mom,' they both said and turned back to the television set, not granting Jimmy so much as hello or goodbye. Nor did I prompt them. I didn't even introduce him. We walked down the stairs together.

'You leave them alone?' he asked disapprovingly.

I just looked at him coldly, and knocked at Pane Nowak's door when we got downstairs. Her head poked out and gazed not at me but at Jimmy, examined him from head to foot.

'I'm leaving now, Pane.'

She beamed at me. Jimmy had passed inspection. 'I go up just now.'

We walked out of the house and Jimmy held my arm as we descended the steps to the sidewalk. At that point I wanted to ram him with my elbow, but simmered silently instead. He opened the car door for me, and closed it after I had slid in.

'So!' he said in a hearty voice as we set out. 'Nice-looking kids.'

'Um-hum.'

He glanced at me. 'I can tell you're a good mother.' That, I presumed, was his form of apology for imagining I would leave them alone and reproving me for it.

'You have children?'

He had to. He hadn't learned that pompous bossiness at the office, not in his line of work.

'Yeah, two, great kids!' His voice was hollow. 'Both at college now, the house is empty.' His voice caught a little at the end of that phrase.

I know you, I thought. Heavy drinker, scolds wife and kids, demands perfection from them, is never home, wife dies, and suddenly he realizes how much he depended on her, something he never knew before. Thinks of himself as one of the guys, good buddy, always ready for a laugh. Now full of self-pity, wants to talk about his suffering. I wondered how I could sit over a meal with someone I hated as much as I hated him at that moment. I sat silent, debating what to do. Finally I opened my mouth, and my voice creaked, as if I hadn't used it in years and it was rusty.

'Look, Jimmy, I think you'd better take me back home. This was a mistake. I don't want to go to dinner with you. I'm sorry.'

He didn't seem surprised. 'Yeah, it seems we got off on the wrong foot. I don't know how.' He turned his head and looked at me appealingly, innocently.

'I can tell you how.' My voice was suddenly hot. It occurred to me that I had been so long out of male society that I had no idea how to behave anymore, and more than that, no idea about how I really felt. I knew I disliked him, but what was coming out of my voice now was pure fury. 'You started by announcing our date to the entire newsroom, never considering how that would affect me. I have to work there, every day! You followed that up by presuming to reprimand my children, something you, a stranger, have absolutely no right to do, and never will! You polished it off by daring to judge my ways of caring for my children, when my instincts tell me *you* probably never took care of your *own* children for an hour in your entire life. That's how!'

He drove, his mouth twisting. His silence impelled me further on. How could I have been so furious?

'You are pompous, presumptuous, inconsiderate, and selfish, full of self-pity, and I made a mistake in agreeing to go out with you. My fault. I'm sorry.'

He turned to me wide-eyed. 'How can you know me so well so quickly? It took my wife years to say things like that.'

'You were younger when she met you. It takes some years for things like that to show,' I said bitterly.

He considered. 'Yeah. You're divorced, aren't you. He the same way?'

'Close enough. And he had lots of friends like you. Can we turn around now?'

But he didn't turn. We were nearly at the Arbor Inn. He hit the steering wheel with his open hand. 'Look. I'm a clod. I haven't asked a woman to go out in twenty-two years, and I don't know how to behave. I seem to be acting like a cross between an adolescent ninny and a pompous ass. My wife always said I didn't know how to talk to the kids . . . I hardly see them since she died. . . .' He didn't choke up or let tears come into his voice, none of the expected tricks. He seemed really to be feeling bad about himself. His voice was resonant with sorrow. 'It's like starting all over again, and I'm not good at it, but I want to learn, I want to try. Please just have dinner with me. You never have to see me again if you don't want to, but at least sit and talk to me and you can berate me all you like. Will you?' He turned to me a boy's face, large-eyed and feeling.

How could I say no?

The Arbor Inn turned out to be a nice enough steak house, a neighborhood place where people knew each other, with a very active bar. Nothing like the Waldorf, my mother's Waldorf. But fine. We both ordered steaks. And Jimmy proceeded to tell me his life's story: his authoritarian father and brutalized mother; his rebellion; his wife, who slowly dwindled as a person over the years, who complained about his absence, his drinking, his inability to show affection to his children, and who then stopped complaining and sank into pale pain and death. It wasn't until the end that he let himself cry. The evening was proceeding exactly as I had feared it would. It was his nickel, and he was going to have things his way. I picked at my steak, wondering which was better, sitting home alone or this? I had dropped a few remarks about myself along the way. I mentioned that I'd been a rebel too, and offered a few laughing comments on my adolescent self. He passed right by them, didn't hear them. He was deeply serious about his own rebellion; nothing in it seemed funny to him.

He looked up at me with the appealing boy's face and wiped his cheeks with his napkin. 'I never realized how I depended on her. Just being there, listening to me when I got home, whether I was raving or furious about some stupidity perpetrated by that rag I work for . . . I don't know. But now I'm so lonely. I could die.'

'You'll find someone else,' I said calmly. I refused to act

moved by his story. I refused to show any compassion. If I felt any, it was for his dead wife.

He cheered up immediately. Maybe he expected compliments. 'You think so?'

'Yes. Men can always find a woman to bandage their wounds.'

He blinked at that, at my tone, which was cool and distant. Maybe it occurred to him that he was being inconsiderate, selfish, full of self-pity . . . 'You been divorced long?'

'Not quite a year.'

He grinned lasciviously. 'A looker like you, you'll be married in a year.'

'No.'

'Whaddya mean, no? Sure you will.'

I didn't feel like discussing with him my objections to marriage from the female point of view. So I just shrugged.

'Listen, I know it's tough, with two little kids and all. But some guy will fall head over heels, you watch, and he won't care if you have five kids.'

That took my breath away, so that what I said next came out all in a rush.

'Speaking of whom, I have to get home.' I looked at my watch. 'I promised to be back by ten. Pane Nowak goes to bed at ten,' I lied.

'That's her name? Panay? What kind of name is that?'

'Pan-e.' I spelled it. 'It's Polish for Madam, Mrs.'

'She's a Polack?'

'She's Polish. Like me.'

'You a Polack? With a name like Carpenter?'

'I'm *Polish*. Carpenter's my married name.'

'Oh, yeah, I keep forgetting. You seem so young.'

I had to acknowledge that he was trying to compliment me, so I laughed, putting my napkin beside my coffee cup in a final sort of way. 'Well, those two kids didn't come from the Holy Ghost.'

He howled at that. 'You're somethin', Stacey, you really are! You're a hoosher!'

My back tingled. (What did *hoosher* mean?)

I stood up.

'Okay, okay, just let me get the bill, okay?'

'I'll be in the toilet.'

'Ha? Oh, the ladies' room! Okay. I'll get the bill.'

I got him out of there a little before ten, but he drove not to my house, but his. He stopped in front of it. 'That's where I live. All alone.' It was a huge house, it looked to have ten rooms. 'How about a little tour and a nightcap? It's quite a place, my wife fixed it up really swell. Americana.'

'Some other time, thanks, I have to get back.'

He slid toward me and put his arm around me.

'No, Jimmy.' I unwound myself from him. 'I'm serious. I want to go home.'

I couldn't believe what happened next. He thrust himself on me, wound me up in his arms, pressed his chest against mine, began to kiss me, seeking my mouth no matter how I turned my head. It was quite literally, a wrestling match. I'd never encountered anything like that even from the boys in high school. I pushed against him with my hands, squirmed my body out from under, but there was no place for me to go. When I could get my face free, I shouted 'STOP!'

Shocked, he did.

'Take me home! Now! If you don't, I'll walk! And I'll tell everyone in the newsroom that I did, too!'

He pulled away from me, looking at me with shocked contempt, a sense of betrayal.

'Okay, okay.' He started the car. It was only three quarters of a mile to my house and we were there in a few minutes. When he stopped the car – leaving the motor running – in front of my house, he glanced at me resentfully. 'How was I supposed to know?' He asked in a hurt angry voice. 'You took the dinner, didn't you?'

I glared and opened the door, got out, and slammed it; he almost knocked me down pulling away from the curb suddenly, with a shriek of tires. Adolescent, I thought, and wearily climbed the stairs to my apartment. The kids were in bed and Pane was nodding over some detective drama flickering in black and white on the tube. I paid her and saw her downstairs, chagrined at having had to spend money for the evening I'd just experienced. Then I turned off most of the lights and settled myself in my soft cozy old armchair with a whiskey, and thought about my future.

I was worried about how Jimmy was going to describe his evening with me to the guys in the newsroom, and what my situation there would be. If he spit hate at me, they might start to look at me suspiciously, coldly. And given that their fellowship and camaraderie was all that made my boring job bearable, I would be unhappy if they turned against me. I tried to see it from his point of view – what would serve his interests? But I couldn't. I kept imagining him pretending we had a great time, because he wouldn't want to admit his own failure. But what would he lead them to believe about sex? I cursed myself for having accepted his invitation in the first place. 'I should have known better,' I kept muttering.

Suddenly I felt a movement in the air and looked up to see Arden standing a few feet away from me in her pale nightgown.

'Hi!'

She smiled and came toward me. I put my arm around her. 'Still awake?'

'I couldn't sleep,' she announced seriously, although I could see sleep creases in her cheek.

I lifted her to my lap, and wonder of wonders, she allowed it. She nestled against me. 'Why not?'

'I didn't like that man. I was afraid of him.'

'You were afraid I'd keep going out with him and he'd start bossing you around,' I suggested.

She looked at me, raising her warm pink face. 'How did you know?'

'Oh, I just guessed.'

'Well, will you?'

'No. I won't go out with him again.'

'Promise?'

'Promise.'

She settled her head down again. 'Mommy?'

'Um-hum.' I was rocking her now.

'Will you go out with other people?'

Oh-oh. I considered. Right at this moment, she wanted me to say no, and would be comforted it I did. But she might remember it, and think I'd lied to her. She was ten, after all.

'Probably. Someday.'

Her body stiffened. 'Oh.'

'But I won't let anybody boss you around. Ever. Only me,' I laughed.

'Okay.' She laughed. 'We could go out on a double date.'

'WHAT?'

She giggled wildly. 'Yes. Bobby Lench asked me to go to the movies with him on Saturday. Can I go?'

I was amazed. I'd thought she was at the boy-hating stage. 'Do you want to go? What movie? At night? No, certainly not.'

She was still laughing. 'No, not at night, silly, in the afternoon. And then have a soda or something. Maybe go to McDonald's. I want to go. Joyce is going with Huey Ashe. And Joan is going with G. G. McKerrow. I want to go too.'

I breathed again. A social occasion. 'Yes, honey, you can go.'

'We're going to go dutch, Mom. So I need money. Do you know what that is, going Dutch?'

I nodded. 'How much money?'

'A dollar.'

She had no idea how precious a dollar was to me. I'd been careful that she have no idea. 'Sure.'

She jumped down. 'I'll sleep now,' she said happily, and went off, still a child in body, but oh my god, what next?

My life continued as it was through Arden's eleventh birthday in November, and almost to Christmas of 1959. I didn't go out again with anyone, but my status at the office remained the same. I gathered Jimmy Hanna had told everyone we had a nice time, that I was a good kid and devoted to my children, so he felt as if he were out with his kid sister. I looked like somebody's kid sister, so they accepted his story, at least to his face – and mine. That was a help. But Arden, now in sixth grade, had started to menstruate, and suddenly she needed things – sweaters, money for Cokes, movies, fashion magazines, records. I didn't have it. I explained that I could give her only $1.50 a week allowance, and that at her age, that should be enough. Saturday movies, I had found out, were fifty cents, a Coke was ten cents. That left ninety cents a week; she would have to save up to buy the things she wanted.

'Mommy!' (Three syllables.) 'The other kids all get three dollars a week. It's not fair! A magazine is seventy-five cents alone, and records are eighty-five cents! I have a Coke in the afternoon after school, all I have left is forty cents. I can't live on that!'

I turned softly so she wouldn't see me laugh: I can't live on that, indeed! 'I'm sorry, Arden.' I turned back. 'But you're getting to be grown up enough to understand that I don't have much money. I can't afford more.'

She glared at me uncomprehending. 'Daddy has lots of money. Get it from him!'

'I'm not calling him up and asking for money, Arden.'

'Then *I* will!' She turned on her heel and stalked – with dignity; she no longer stamped, tore, or flew – into her room.

Billy stood there watching. 'Arden's a spoiled brat,' He commented.

'It's just her age, Billy. She wants what the other kids have.'

'But hardly anybody here gets three dollars a week allowance. Lots of kids in this town have hardly any money at all.'

Yes, I know that. But not many of them have a father who lived in a near-mansion in Garden City either. I hugged Billy. 'Well honey, you try to remember that next year or the year after.'

'I'll never be like her,' he muttered fiercely.

Arden got her three dollars a week from her father; he gave it to her on Wednesday nights, when he took the kids to dinner. This was fine with me, except some weeks he was busy and didn't take them out and completely forgot about the allowance. Then I had to listen to shrieks and tears, accusations of no one loving her, and end up shelling out the three dollars myself. This happened often enough to be annoying, and I told her to ask him to give her double allowance whenever he thought he'd be busy the following week. She told him that I had said this, in a way that sounded as if I had ordered him to do this. He reared up, refused to give her any allowance at all, and called me up and screamed at me. It took me a long time to calm him down, to explain. I told him that what he was hearing was *Arden's* resentment about not sharing in his luxurious style of living, not mine, and that he ought to think about it. He reinstated her allowance and began to buy her presents — usually clothes. He'd even take the trouble to find out what she wanted, and she soon enough caught on and began to hint. He bought Billy things too, but Billy would come home from seeing him, stuff his new shirt or whatever in a drawer, and walk around stiff-mouthed for a day. Arden was different. Something new came into her face. It worried me.

In my year at the *Herald*, I submitted photographs to the picture editor from time to time. I could see it upset him to have to reject any, so I didn't show him anything unless I thought it was exactly the sort of thing the paper wanted. They had bought a half-dozen of them in the year I'd worked there, at fifty dollars a shot. I kept that money apart, for myself. It paid for my film, for developing fluid, printing paper. I'd moved out into landscapes, having bought a wide-angle telephoto lens, and would occasionally take the sort I knew the picture editor liked — two lovers wandering along Silver Lake in Baldwin, in spring, a pretty girl sunning herself on the grass in Hempstead State Park. Cheap shots, but I wasn't thinking about integrity. I needed the money to continue my . . . what was it? Certainly I couldn't call it my profession. Hobby, I guess. Hateful word.

I took many pictures for myself, though. I was experimenting still, trying different points of view. Sunrise Highway was being widened, and was torn up. There were huge machines parked along the sides of the lanes, but men still worked with pickaxes and shovels. I took a series of shots of those men, looking up toward them, emphasizing their arms and bared chests. I kept the light down, and used slow film to get depth, sharp contrasts that would show up every muscle and sinew in their bodies; and I shot them huge against a background of sky. What I was thinking about was, I guess, my own life, so full of arduous tasks despite the mechanization of the world. I knew better, however, than to show *women's* labor. No one was interested in that. No one believed women labored.

The *Herald* liked these shots, and used one of them, the one with the best composition: one man was lifting his pickaxe as the other rose from bending to shovel away debris, and the sky was soft with gold-edged clouds behind them. You could see the brilliance of the edging even though the print was black and white. The dichotomy set up was false: smiling nature, the simple life, versus the huge task of creating civilization, man's work. But it appealed to the *Herald*'s editors. It appealed to others too, because about a week later I got a phone call from a secretary saying Russ Farrell of *World* magazine was calling.

They'd gotten my number from the *Herald*, Farrell said. They liked my work. Did I have a portfolio?

'Yes,' I said between heartbeats.

They'd like to see it.

Reader, they hired me. I couldn't believe it either. Yes, it was a leap into space. It was arriving at a longed-for destination when one hadn't even known one was on the road. It was being transported into dreams one hadn't even dared to think about dreaming. My future had seemed to me for a long time now a grey space, empty, just more of the same. I hadn't even dared to imagine some Prince Charming arriving to carry me away from the tedium and sense of waste that filled my days. I had never let myself think about photography as a career because I didn't see how I could accomplish that, and like the Indian women I met years later, I believed it was better not to think about what is impossible.

I had assigned no category to myself – not professional or amateur, not commercially, or artistically, inclined.

Except I did have a drawer in my photograph file labeled just A; and it was in that drawer that I had filed prints of what I considered *Art* – pictures that made my heart catch a little, that came out to meet the eye, that felt like some kind of truth. And it was the contents of that drawer that I sifted through, culling forty pictures to blow up or crop, to mount, and finally to lay carefully into my newly purchased portfolio the night before I drove myself, frightened that I'd have an accident and never really arrive, to the Long Island Railroad Station, where I purchased a ticket for Pennsylvania Station in New York.

I had had enough wits about me to set the interview a week away. This gave me time to go through all my drawers, considering. I rejected all the pictures of angry or dismayed mothers; and most of those that were interesting, odd close-ups of unusual objects like a stack of sewer pipes or a train wheel, or the inside of an iris. All baby pictures were taboo. I ended with a set showing men working, machines, and a few splendid landscapes. After all, I knew what *World* liked. I saw it every week in the *Herald* waiting room. It was the best picture magazine – and the best paying – in the world. At the time, I regret to say, I did not think at all about concealed censorship; about how, if you want to get ahead in the world, you take your cue from what is established, and shoot the things the establishment enjoys seeing, and avoid those it does not. I didn't think about the ways we are taught, outside the church and the schoolroom, what to value, or about my being manipulated by the power world. I just wasn't thinking: I wasn't a political person. All of that sort of thinking came to me much later, and from other people. I didn't even think about how I automatically knew what photographs to include, or the meaning behind the choice of what to exclude. That seems remarkable to me now, since I had in my youth been a questioner. I had forgotten my youthful self.

I walked into a small office with big windows in a huge anonymous building, and shook hands with Russ Farrell, a grey-faced paunchy man with a fringe of hair, and his two assistants, who were younger, thinner, somewhat hairier versions of him. I sat on an anonymous black leather couch and stared at the pictures framed and hung on the white walls – some spectacular ones, like Margaret Bourke-White's shot of London being bombed – and watched as the three of them stood over a long table on which they had placed my portfolio, and turned over prints, saying nothing. I believe that not a single muscle moved in my body during the time they scrutinized my work. The only sound came at the end, a breath expelled by one, an approving murmur by another.

'Umm. Umm,' Farrell said, turning. 'Nice work. How long have you been doing this?'

'Oh, I took pictures as a child. I've been working professionally for about ten years now,' I exaggerated.

'Really? And what have you been doing?'

'I've worked for a newspaper, and had some work in a local magazine' (two pictures in *Long Island*, a Chamber of Commerce magazine for tourists, but I didn't say that. Seventy-five dollars a shot), 'and I've done a lot of portraits.' (I didn't think it necessary to add that they were portraits of babies.)

'Umm.' He took a pipe from his jacket pocket and spent considerable time getting it lighted. The assistants had settled themselves on side chairs and were looking up at him. One of them was holding a print, holding it out, then bringing it in close, getting his greasy fingerprints all over the white mounting. I wanted to yell at him to put it down I was so nervous, I just wanted to yell, period.

Farrell sat down behind a long white desk and leaned back in his swivel chair. Over his head was a huge framed Ansel Adams. He was not staring, yet I had the feeling that he was managing to look me over carefully. I'd worn my sweater and skirt, stockings and heels – well, low heels, but not my usual sneakers. I'd put considerable thought into how to present myself, and I'd decided slacks would be a mistake. I'd seen some photographs of Margaret Bourke-White in which she was wearing a skirt even while she was *working*.

Farrell examined the application I'd filed in while I was waiting to see him.

'Umm. Thirty. You look younger.'

I smiled sweetly. 'Thank you.'

'And still unencumbered, huh?'

He was looking at the box I'd checked: there was one box for married, and another for unmarried. Actually, what it said was Marital [*sic*] Status: ☐ married ☐ single. I'd checked single. It had no box for divorced. But I knew what he wanted to know.

'Well, I was married, but I got divorced last year,' I said with a slight edge of sadness to my voice. 'There was no box for divorced,' I explained, demonstrating my desire to be totally honest.

'*World* requires its photographers to do a fair amount of traveling. That wouldn't present a problem, then?'

'None at all. I'd love it.'

Travel! Travel! When all my life my soul had been salivating to see the Baptistry Doors in Florence and the Duomo; the Medici Library; the Place de la Concorde, the Louvre, and Saint-Chapelle; and Westminster, and Charing Cross, and the Inns of Court, and Haworth, and the Lake Country, and the Alps, and Hong Kong, and Bangkok, and and and.

'Well, then, we'd like to have you aboard. You won't be staff; we'll send you out on assignments. You get paid only when you work, but we'll keep you busy.' He then gave me a spiel about wage schedules and per diem allowances and expense accounts; he talked about special pouches for delivery of film, and how many rolls to take for an article (that many!), and when to use color. I listened with a face full of attention, but my heart was beating too loudly in my ears for me really to hear much. I stood up with as much poise as I could pull together making my voice as inexpressive as I could, trying to copy them. I kept my face still, too, and my legs, and I didn't dance at all until I got safely home in my own living room.

I danced into the *Herald* the next morning too. After all, they knew me a little; I was allowed to dance there. I danced in and quit my job. They were all happy for me, those guys, a little surprised and a little envious, but on the whole generously happy. There are advantages to life in the slow lane, among the mediocre, the failed, and one of them is fellowship. I didn't realize then that I wouldn't have that again. They took me to their watering hole for lunch on my last day – I gave the *Herald* a week to replace me, and came in during that time singing every morning – and tried to get me drunk. But I had to drive home and take care of the kids, so I only sipped the martini they kept urging on me.

I look back on that me and shake my head. I can hardly remember her: that woman who could feel such elation, such surging power and hope, who could imagine a wonderful, brilliant, exciting future. And most of all, who didn't know what she was doing, what she was getting herself into. Not that, had I been aware, I would have refused the offer. That's the point, I guess, that even if you know what an experience will do to you, you want the experience.

I knew I was implicitly disavowing my children; and I knew I didn't want them to know I was doing that. The morning after I was hired, I called an answering service and had our telephone number hooked up to it, and turned off the bell in our house; and ordered a new phone for us. That way, if *World* called me, they would reach a nice professional-sounding service that would take the message and convey it to me. There would be no risk of a young voice answering the phone and yelling out 'Mommy!' It was an extra expense, but necessary, I told myself.

I told myself plenty. In fact, I didn't know and don't know now whether my acrobatics were necessary. I simply wasn't taking any chances. Would they have hired me if I'd been married? If they knew I had small children? Maybe. Would they have hired me if I'd worn pants to the interview? Twenty years later I heard some men talking about not hiring a woman because she showed up for the interview in pants. But they weren't the same men. I don't know, didn't know. I only knew I had a deep persuasive sense that women had to be extremely careful in the public world, that the smallest thing could be used as grounds for rejecting them. And having kids is not a small thing. I had kids; but I also had Pane Nowak.

I also had, only a seed then, but it would grow, a hot hard pebble of shame lodged near my navel. But I was too excited to notice it.

five

Belle and Ed had one more ordeal to pass through on their road to secure status in the middle class. The recession that followed the end of the war sent many businesses into decline, and Bunnell was one of them. In May of 1949, it finally shut its doors. Along with many other men, Ed was out of work, and could not find a job at his rank.

Arden was six months old, and had been sick with a fever for a week. Anastasia was feeling cooped up in the one-room apartment, and had asked Brad to come home in the afternoon, pick her up, and drive her to her mother's house, then pick her up there in the evening. She didn't call first. Belle was always home. Brad dropped her in front of the house, and drove off, not noticing the long ladder propped in front of the house. Ed was standing on it, scraping peeling paint from the clapboard on the upper story. Anastasia peered up at him, Arden in her arms, her paraphernalia on the sidewalk beside her.

'Hi!'

He turned and waved.

'How come you're home?'

He just waved again, and turned back to his work. Anastasia rang the front doorbell. Belle answered it, her face drawn.

'How come Dad's home?' she asked cheerfully (as always).

Belle grimaced, turned away, and walked into the living room. Anastasia followed. Belle turned back after the door was closed. 'He lost his job.'

Anastasia paled. 'He was fired!' This seemed inconceivable: her careful, efficient, methodical father, fired?

Belle didn't answer. 'Take off your coat,' she sighed. 'Do you want some tea?'

Not until she was an older woman did Anastasia discover that her father had not been fired, that the company had failed. Belle spoke rarely about the event, but always appeared to blame Ed for what had happened to him. Ed did not speak of it at all. The heavy dark counterpane of grim depression so usual in that house settled once more.

Who but Ed would set about repainting the house the day after losing his job? But in a week he had regained enough presence to go looking. There was nothing, and after a month, he took a job on the night-shift assembly line at Republic Aircraft for two dollars an hour, and a day job repairing vacuum cleaners for fifty cents an hour. For a year and a half he continued in this schedule, five nights a week at Republic, six days a week at Hoover, earning altogether eighty dollars a week, not quite enough to get them through. He never complained. When he was home, he painted the house or worked on the car. Belle made hats, managed to make 250 a week now. Joy was finishing high school, was a member of a clique, and needed this certain sweater, this skirt. But she asked for little, as little as she could. Nor could Anastasia help her parents.

In November of 1950, the same month Billy was born, Ed found a good job with a manufacturer of complex instruments like gyroscopes that paid him $100 a week and gave him good bonuses at Christmas. He was forty-four. He would remain there until his retirement in 1971, on his sixty-fifth birthday. By then he had a good salary, but one not commensurate with his value: the company had to hire five men to do his job after he was gone. He went immediately to work part-time, off the books, in various electronic firms, and continued to work until Belle demanded that he stop, when he was seventy-six. By then they were comfortable; their house looked like other people's houses, they had imitation Sheraton in the dining room, new rugs, lots of tables and knickknacks; their car was a Cadillac and not more than six years old. Belle had a sable stole and a mink jacket, both already out of style; and a spotted-cat coat that was only ten years old. They had taken two three-week trips to Europe on tours; and many vacations in upper New York State and Maine. Everyone they met found them a lovely couple.

Belle had made hats for over ten years, stopping only

after she had paid the bills for Joy's wedding, which took her a year. She stopped at the end of 1955, and settled back to enjoy herself. By that time, Ann Gwyn was dead of breast cancer; and within two years, both Gertrude Grunbacher and Mildred Bradshaw had also died. Only Elvira was left, settled into a grouchy old age. Rollo had died, and she missed having a man. She picked up with her old boyfriend, but he drank too much now, she said, and kept talking about 'Whitey' as if whites were his enemy, something she couldn't comprehend. *She'd* always been his friend. Only Jean and Eric were left, and the two couples still played bridge every Saturday night, and a few times went on vacations together. That old relationship had always been strained: Eric holding forth pompously, looking down at Ed; Jean sweet, complacent and complaisant; Belle quietly resentful; Ed silent. But they were all either couple had. The heavy mantle of gloom lifted in the middle years, but descended again as Belle entered old age. Eric died then, and the bridge games ended. They were still together, she and Ed; and alone, as he had wished, without noisy interfering children. Ed mellowed; he showed affection to his grown daughters. There was never dust on the many side tables now; nor radios playing nor Coke bottles lying around. There was order and peace and stillness in the large house by the water that they had acquired, the two of them, together, alone.

Part 3

*Arrangement in
Grey and Black*

Chapter X

one

Sunday, January 12, 1960. Emplaned.

Emplaned: A word that couldn't be expected to drop into my day like a package through a mail slot.

My day, my days: getting the kids off in the morning, driving over back suburban roads to a three-story brick building, a boring job: smile, yes sir, I'll see if he's in, smile, sorry sir, he's gone for the day, smile, oh yes, sir, I'll be glad to buzz him for you. Then the drive back, the woman's lunch – an apple and a cup of yoghurt – the supermarket, trying to find meat that costs less than thirty-five cents a pound, decent vegetables the kids will eat, tight-lipped, anxious; then unloading the heavy bags that really hold so little; then the laundry – down to the basement with a heavy straw basket full of smelly clothes, standing there waiting for water to fill the tub before pouring in the bleach, feeling itchy in the dark cobwebbed dank space lighted by a single bulb with a metal string hanging down, checking water temperature, soap, then back up two flights, back down in half an hour, transfer the whites to the dryer, put in the dark things, back up two flights back down in half an hour . . . oh I know I shouldn't complain, things were so much worse for my mother, but why is it that half the human race never has to do things like this and the other half never has time to do anything else?

Then the kids are home, noise, confusion, sometimes laughter, often squabbling and sullenness, even tears. Then commands, authority, that's not fun, why do you have to force them to do things? Change clothes, only one Scooter Pie apiece, eat fruit if you're still hungry, be back by five to do homework, an hour's respite for me until I have to start dinner, time to fold the clean dry laundry (more trips downstairs), to do some dusting, vacuum the living room rug, shabby and discolored, ugly, it's hateful to clean it . . .

Hate cooking, but dinner is a good time, the kids calmer, they love to eat, we talk, joke, tease, tell about our days, make things up sometimes. We all clean up after dinner now, they're old enough, that's not bad except they're in a rush to turn on that Thing, that Box, that Noise that fills my life with plastic – plastic joys, plastic violence, plastic adventure, oh god the noise of it. To escape it I have to go to my bedroom, and the kids feel abandoned so usually I sit with them trying to read while they sit on the floor like two hypnotized robots believing everything they see there. That Box is manufacturing their dreams, forming their imaginations . . . but to deny it to them I'd have to make a point, take some dramatic or moral or intellectual stand, make them different from their friends . . . Sometimes, if the program is too paralysingly awful, I do leave and go into my room and sit at the table and start to go through some pictures, but then one of them will come in and stand quietly beside me and ask if I dislike the program, and say they'll change the channel if I want, if I'll just come back in. And sometimes I say no, it's okay, I just don't feel like watching television tonight, and I go on working but I can't concentrate because I feel so guilty, I keep seeing that pale face saddened by my defection. Or am I imagining the sadness? Brad said I wasn't as important to them as I liked to think. But I have to go by my feelings, don't I?

I wonder sometimes what will happen to me when the children grow up and leave. There I'll be, after all those years of being central to them, years of feeling that my every gesture, facial expression, tone of voice, has an impact on them, a significance I may not intend – given my own history as a sensitive plant, how can I not know how important such things are to a child? – years of feeling responsible, and suddenly I won't matter or not in the same way. I'm not worried about being bored, about not knowing what to do with myself after the children are gone, the empty-nest syndrome that all the magazines castigate women for these days. No, that part's fine, I'll have more time to work. It's the other: by the time they're grown up, my reactions will be fixed. I will have been trained the way they say mothers who toilet-train their children very young train themselves, not their children – I'll be a creature that has been trained for eighteen years to anticipate and respond, to calm and console, to avert tears and anger, to spend my energies on the people around me, to be the axle, the selfless center that holds everything together.

I'll do that automatically – I already do – but suddenly they won't *want* me to act that way, they'll feel I'm treating them like babies, they'll blame me for doing what now they would blame me for *not* doing. It's impossible to be a woman, you have to keep readjusting. Like sex: you're supposed to be cold as ice, chaste and inviolable until you're married, then suddenly you're supposed to be ardent. Oh, why am I thinking this way, it just makes me grouchy. . . .

My day: yes. Then bedtime: making sure that teeth are brushed, bodies washed, windows open, blankets tucked in according to idiosyncratic tastes, kisses, hugging, much giggling now, settling them in, a sweet time. Yes. But then only a couple of hours of quiet when I can do some cropping or make entries in my records to get them up to date: last Saturday I photographed a stand of birch trees at 10 a.m., 2 p.m., 3.30 p.m., and these f-stops with these lenses, each example slipped into plastic and placed beside its data in the album, studied, thought about. You can't do much in an hour and a half, and by ten-thirty I'm yawning, exhausted, ready to shower and brush my teeth and check the kids, pink and warm with sleep, then slide into cold sheets, having set the alarm for seven. . . .

But now into the middle of this life, this regularity, drops this event, something not to be anticipated or even imagined: EMPLANED! Nothing in my experience has led me to believe that you can love your children, *have* your children and still have this, feel the lift of heart that is like the lift of the airplane itself as it rises from the ground and tilts off into another realm, another life. VROOM!

This is my first trip in an airplane except for my trip to Mexico for the divorce, but I was too numb to notice anything. But, yes, there was that ride over Floyd Bennett Field in a Piper Cub in 1939, my father in the seat beside me, both of us elated. His first airplane ride, too, and he tried to act protective and assured, to make me feel safe, but I didn't need calming, I wasn't afraid, I was soaring. And this is the first entry in the first journal I have ever kept.

I have written my name on the first page: THE JOURNAL OF STACEY STEVENS. A glamorous name, also fake: Stacey Stevens. The people of *World* don't like Anastasia, they think it sounds foreign, they didn't want me to use it. But to me, Stacey Stevens sounds like a movie star – blond curly hair, bright red lipstick, always plays a gal Friday, good all-round kid, cute grin, husky voice, good sport, ends up coupled with the second male lead.

Chapter 1, page 1 of a new blank book: Stacey is flying. Anastasia is emplaned!

Oh, the ascent, the engines accelerate so high I think they will explode, the plane gathers speed, the speed itself seems to make you rise, like water boiling up into the air, becoming air. And the earth tilts, moves farther and farther away, buildings get smaller, they are crooked like the cottages in children's picture books. Here I am, bold, adventurous, looking down at a tiny earth, low and dear, buildings like foolish little assertions, mounds carved by a timid earthbound species.

I am up here, above the earth! Like gods who can see earth and all man's works in perspective. And besides, we have seats that go back and neat little tables you can let down and write on, and then they push this cart through the aisles and serve drinks!

It's a slim book covered in marbleized paper – lavender, pink, purple, pale mauve lined sheets, faded watery blue ink in the large sprawling hand I had then, not so long ago was it? Twenty-odd years. Twenty years! How I filled those pages, dozens of them at a clip!

I remember. I had gone to the film lab in Chelsea, the first time to pick up film for my assignment. And across the street was an office-supply store, long since gone, narrow aisles, metal shelves piled with pads, folders, envelopes, everything covered with dust. The floor creaked as you walked through the aisles. And I saw these books, they were dusty, I had to blow the dust off them. It was hard to find pretty blank books in those days, and I bought this one, on impulse, delighted with not having to watch every penny for the first time in my life. . . .

You can't see much at this altitude. Sometimes the clouds break and you can see earth the color of clay, it looks close unless there's a building, and then you can tell how high we are, the building's only a spot. You can't tell from this land that it's January. Around New York there was snow, patches of it broken by dark soil. For a while we flew through a huge valley of clouds: we were at the bottom, the clouds were all around us, we were drowning in them. Like a picture in a children's book, cute, round little tots tumbling in a featherbed of clouds, screaming in joy as they career in whipped cream, float in egg white.

Nature uses the same forms, the same materials over and over, clouds like islands, sky like sea. Mozart too reused themes, stole from himself. Now the clouds are hazecolor, white shot through with rainbow pastels. Ahead a wash of deep pink, we keep flying into sunset, it's dark behind us, we go west, young woman.

I hope people can't tell I am not cool and assured. There is no one sitting beside me in the middle seat. A man sleeps in the end seat. Every once in a while he snores. But maybe someone else is looking at me, the way I stare at them, surreptitiously. A *World* photographer should be cool and assured. I try to remind myself that I am a person not entirely without importance.

I'm glad I bought this book: writing in it makes me look professional, *busy*. I've never really been busy that way – it isn't considered busyness when the kids are in the tub splashing water all over the bathroom floor, the phone rings, and the pot on the stove decides at that moment to boil over. Now I look busy in the other way, the important way. But it's also helpful to have this book to write in so people can't see that I am terrified this plane is going to crash just so I won't be able to have a career. Funny I never realized before how utterly self-centered phobias are. . . .

Career. Is that what I'm having? Eighty rolls of film they issued me, eighty rolls! Short rolls, twenty shots apiece, half black and white, half color. Do they really expect me to use it all? So wasteful. They must not care, they have money to burn. If we crashed we would burn . . .

We won't crash. Pretend you're in a boat. The clouds bump and rock the plane just as waves rock a boat, up down up down. All nature is similitudes, people knew that once, the Middle Ages, all things connected, interlocked, significant. That's the rub, significant. God my mind is racing, I feel as if I've been given an injection of something, all my pores open and everything is crowding into them . . . The world seems new, as if my eyes had been washed and I can finally see.

The truth is I *haven't* seen very much of the world: where have I been? I've had to imagine the world, or see it in photographs. The camera never lies. But of course it does, who knows that better than a photographer? The angle, the selection, the isolation – the camera shows what the photographer wants it to tell, children's game, show-and-tell. I don't know why I keep thinking about children's things . . .

Like that Indian woman at the airport. I thought I knew all about her: hadn't I read about women like her, seen pictures of them? I recognized the slender body, the meek posture, she'll have a dowager's hump when she's old, those large dark eyes. All those bundles and two children, one just a baby. She sat there bent over, listening to the man, her husband probably, give her orders over and over. She nodded, showed no impatience. The truth is *he's* nervous sending her off alone, and so he scolds her, peremptory as if she were a child or an idiot. Then he looks at his watch, he gets up, he picks up the little boy, hugs, kisses him, puts him down. He ignores the baby, he leaves. I look at her with all those bundles, those little children, I think – she needs help, maybe I can help her. But when the call comes to queue up, she gathers everything together swiftly, you can see she is used to doing that, and rises, she doesn't trip on the folds of the crimson sari, she almost runs. She charges the people in her way, elbows them, elbows me hard, she reaches the head of the line first.

Of course, she should have been first, it is only right, but she warred her way, she was prepared to fight the world, and I'll bet she never fights like that with her husband. From a distance she looks so graceful, the sari outlining her body in an S, emphasizing its flexibility, the softness and submissiveness of the woman. Lie. She's a fury with a ring in her nose. Doesn't a ring in the nose betoken subjection? On the other hand, there's not much difference between a ring in your nose and one in your ear, is there. Still, she *is* meek, too.

I can still feel it where she elbowed me. I'll bet I have a bruise. I'd like to look, but I can't do it here.

I am drinking. I am having a Bloody Mary, I figured I could spend seventy-five cents of the expense money *World* gave me. But I am getting a little drunk on it and my excitement. And now they are wheeling the foodcart through and handing people dinner trays covered with foil, there is a smell of food. Isn't this neat? It comes all by itself, you don't have to cook it. Such a neat little tray! How wonderful, how ingenious, oh I love it all!

It is embarrassing to have evidence – for I certainly don't recall feeling this – of once being excited by airline food. This whole account is embarrassing. What a naif I was! It's humiliating. I can't believe I was so horribly bubbly, that I could be excited by such stupid things.

Still, that girl sounds happier than I am. I was just a girl, even if I was thirty. God, ignorant. Did I really sound that way? Did I see life as a great adventure waiting to be discovered? Expected Elysian fields I suppose. Got the Slough of Despond instead. The question is: Does everyone? Are there people who do find Elysian fields?

Well, it wasn't very good, but it was fast.

Before I left, I tried to give myself a cool assured appearance. First, I cut my hair. It used to hang down to the middle of my back, usually in one thick braid, but now it ends where my ears end and flies out sharply when I turn my head quickly. Delilah liked it and so did Mother. But the kids were horrified. They said they liked my hair long – but they never said that when it was long. They say the short hair makes me look like their sister.

But then they've been rotten about everything. They were not even nice about my getting this job. Not that it's a real job. I'm not on staff, I'm a stringer, but god I was happy, I couldn't contain myself, it meant so much to me. But I don't really have words for what it meant to me and besides, if I tried to tell them, it would have sounded as if they were not enough for me, as if they weren't my whole life. Well, they aren't. But they expect to be, that's what they think children are to mothers. I couldn't tell them that I felt I'd suddenly been recognized as a person, as a human being and not just a woman, a mother, which is to say, nobody at all, a cipher. . . .

I can't concentrate, my mind refuses to stay in one place.

They dashed my happiness. There I was dancing around the damned ironing board I'd pressed my blouse on that morning, to wear into the city, and they stood leaning against the sink, both of them, staring at me with eyes so hard you'd think they were Puritan judges about to sentence an adulteress. I tried to think of what *they'd* get out of this, and told them we'd have more money now. They showed no interest whatever.

'You said you'd have to travel. Who's going to take care of *us?*'

'Pane. You love Pane,' I pleaded.

They glanced at each other, their faces expressionless. They were out to punish me, and I felt guilty enough to let them.

'You're going to go away?' Billy asked, incredulously. 'You're going to leave us alone?'

'You won't be alone. Pane will be with you.'

'Will she sleep up here? Or downstairs?'

I hadn't thought that one through. 'Up here,' I decided swiftly.

He turned away from me as if I had already abandoned him: martyred, tragic, little boy blue. Selfish monster is more like it. Arden crossed her arms and began to question me like a drill-master about whether Pane knew she was allowed to go the movies on Saturday afternoons, and have a soda afterward, and to do her homework in the afternoon with Joyce on the living room floor. Miserable creeps. Not in the least concerned about me, or what this job meant to me. *Their* little privileges and rights, *their* well-being, that's all they cared about. Monsters!

I started to fold the ironing board up, to put it away. I slammed the legs down and caught my finger between a leg and the board and cried out in pain. Neither child did more than glance at me. Little bastards. Horrible brats! They acted as if I'd done something wicked to *them* when I cut my hair. What do they want me to look like, for godsake? Good god, I'm only thirty! They want me in a rocker with a shawl over my shoulders and an amplifying horn held up to my ear. Damn them!

The trouble was I *needed* them to be happy for me. They were all I had. I decided to call my mother, but not in front of them. I waited until they were in bed. And my good mommy was as excited as I, she was really proud of me, impressed. She'd given up on me, I knew that, and here I'd gone and done something after all. My face had a smile plastered on it when I hung up the phone, it didn't fade even after I'd lain back against the bed pillows and started to imagine my exciting future.

Well, partly I was laughing, too, because Mother sounded so tense at first, worried about who would take care of the kids when I traveled. As soon as I said Pane she breathed out, 'Oh that's *wonderful*, Anastasia! How wonderful! And she's right there, it's so convenient for her, she doesn't have to get in her car and drive there, and she can go downstairs into her own house any time she wants to.'

So, I'm just like my kids, I expect my mother to live for me, don't I. And the night before I left, last night – was it last night? – they gave me a party. They invited Pane Nowak and they served pizzas made on English muffins, and they gave me a present. They chipped in to buy it, but they must have used their Christmas money, or else Pane gave them a lot, no, she wouldn't, she couldn't afford to. Because it was expensive. They both held the box as they handed it to me, and stood so close to me when I opened it that I could hardly move my arms. It was a camera case – a snappy leather one big enough to hold several cameras, lots of film, lenses, and all the small paraphernalia. I have to carry only the one case and my tripod. It has a shoulder strap and when it is filled, it weighs enough to give me bursitis. I love it.

Tears came into my eyes when I saw it. And they both hugged me at once. Oh god. No one has ever given me a gift like that before, something for *me*, not something I needed or asked for, but something they thought about, that would please me. They are good kids. They're adorable. I love them, my sweet babies.

Everyone is either watching the movie or sleeping. I'm going to get up and get myself another Bloody Mary. Anastasia, you're being corrupted!

My babies. They were pink from excitement and the hot kitchen, opening the broiler door every few seconds to check on the pizzas. So proud of themselves, grown-ups, buying a present with their own money, preparing a meal. Making those little pizzas was a major achievement for them. I understand that firsthand. First they had to decide what to serve. I can imagine the tentative suggestions, scorned proposals, arguments, the irritated voices rising, then Arden taking charge, deciding. Then they had to find the recipe and make a list of what to buy, and go to the market and find it all. They had to make tomato sauce, something they've never done before. And lay all the ingredients out on those little muffins, and broil them. They forgot to toast the muffins first, but I didn't point that out. There was brownish tomato sauce under Billy's fingernails, and melted cheese on the end of some strands of Arden's hair. They got into it, body and soul. So sweet, so dear. Oh god I hope they're not unhappy.

I had no shame in those days. I should have worked for a greeting card company photographing fat-cheeked tots in pink and blue, madonna-calendar girl mumsie with divine light in her eyes. Mumsie never guessed her little darlings would grow up to become . . . what? Bruises on a heart, pinched nerves.

Pane Nowak was overjoyed when I asked her to stay upstairs and take care of them while I was away. She said, 'Oh, yes, what I make? They like my stuffed cabbage, no? Or potato soup?' Maybe she thinks I don't feed them properly. And maybe she's like my mother: food is love. Is that inherent in a peasant culture?

She's lonely, poor soul. Sad that she's alone after raising five kids. She says it's because she had no daughters: a son is supposed to go away, she doesn't blame them. A daughter would have stayed near her in her old age, live next door or across the street. Mrs D'Antonio's daughter lives down the block from her mother, and Mrs Schneider's is next door. Law of nature. She never asks, but I can see she wonders why I don't live near my mother. She wouldn't understand if I said my mother doesn't want me next door, doesn't want my kids running in and out of her house, doesn't want to sit with them while I have my hair done – if I had my hair done – or go to the A & P. I think she misses Joy, but she's always far away on three-year tours. The trouble with marrying an Army man. In the Philippines now. I stop in to see Mom one afternoon a week and have coffee with her, or iced tea. She's happy I come alone, without the kids. She has her own life now, finally, as she should. Pane doesn't understand any of that.

She comes from a different era, or a different culture. She's a saint, like my grandmother. There are no more women like Pane. Terrible loss to the human race. But who'd want to be one? Still, these days children with mothers like Pane tend to flee to the other end of the continent. I wonder why that is? All of her sons live far away. Antoni lives in Ohio, Jan in Detroit, and Paul lives in California. I had a hard time keeping her from calling him when she heard where I was going. She *never* makes long-distance calls, she can't afford them. Paul's an engineer and makes good money from what she says, but he only calls her on Christmas and Mother's Day.

Her sons never call on her birthday. Funny. They don't seem to realize she has one. They probably think she has existed since creation like an eternal verity. My kids are like that too. They were surprised to discover a couple years ago that I have a birthday just as they do, that I was actually *born*. But once they realized it they were darling – Billy lugged a big leafy plant home from Woolworth's in his little red wagon, and Arden painted a beautiful card for me, of a mother with two children.

Last year, I gave Pane a birthday party. I invited her two friends, nobody Polish, there are no Poles around here except us, and I baked a cake. I made it from scratch because I know how she feels about packaged cake. It was a little gluey, and tasted of baking powder. Pane is like my grandmother, mother, too, she makes only yeast cakes. But she liked the party, she was happy, she kept hugging me. We had balloons and sweet wine.

She was convinced that Paul would be deeply hurt if I went to California and didn't stay at his house. She said that when someone comes to Poland on a visit, a relative or a friend of a relative, the whole village comes to meet them, bringing food and staying to drink vodka and to talk about the ones who went away and dance to Pan Zborowski's accordion. I wonder if they still do that. What would that be like, to be there? I wish I could see that, be part of that. Oh, I have such longings, I know they will never be filled. . . .

I'll never experience that kind of world, the kind that made Pane Nowak what she is. I wonder if they are all like her, so kind, so loving, so giving, so sweet, a different kind of people. No meanness in her face. Like my grandmother's face. Watery pale blue eyes, like my grandmother's. But Pane's eyes are still bright, she hasn't wept the light out of them as Grandma did. She can still feel pleasure, she loves the kids, she really gets a kick out of them, out of me too. And she asks nothing. She's overjoyed if you just pay attention to her. She'll spend half a day making stuffed cabbage for us, and all she wants, her only reward is your liking it.

Oh, I'm stupid to worry, they'll be fine and here I am headed for Los Angeles, I've never been there, well, I won't be there this time either, but still, LA! I have to find Coast Air, I hope it's not too far from the American terminal, where will it be will there be a bus will I have to walk miles carrying this equipment? I'll ask the stewardess. Coast Air to Fresno, then a little plane some funny name to the Sierra Nevada, Sierra Nevada! Just the name is exciting! What can it be like? A new hydroelectric plant, I wonder why *World* thinks that's important enough for such an expensive plane trip, eighty rolls of film, $100 a day for me . . . I wonder why they gave me this assignment? It sounds more like a man's thing. Will I know how to shoot it? hydroelectric plant, I don't even know exactly what that is . . .

And then I bought some New Clothes. I haven't had New Clothes since long before Brad and I . . . Three pairs of khaki pants, I bought them in the men's department, the salesman was really irritable with me when he realized I was shopping for myself, as if my trying them on would defile the clothes. I couldn't help giggling. And a khaki jacket, and some cotton shirts, women's because they have more flair, but in a large size, I love to look as if I'm wearing my father's clothes. And a wool skirt and a sweater and some hiking shoes and loafers. I have a hat too, a cap with a visor. Men's department. It looks cute on me though. I think.

Cute! Oh! Anastasia!

Three men gave me a real look-over as I sat in the terminal waiting for the plane. That hasn't happened to me in years, maybe it has never happened to me at all. I had kids so young. When you are with children you are invisible to men. One of the guys was good-looking, too, he looked like Dana Andrews, all-American bland, but still . . .

Maybe I should break down and buy some makeup. Just a light eyebrow pencil, a pale lipstick maybe. I used to use makeup once in a while, on nights when Brad and I went someplace fancy. He didn't like my looking different from the other women, he kept telling me to dress myself up. But I liked my hair long and straight. I like simple clothes and I can't wear high heels, I can't walk in them. His friends' wives wore lots of makeup and beehive hairdos and dresses with sequins and tottery high heels. They looked glamorous. To please him, I did darken my eyebrows a little, and put on some lipstick. I wonder if those things are still lying around the house someplace. I seem to remember the kids finding them one rainy day and decorating themselves. They were so cute then.

The truth is I never tried it – being a woman the way women are supposed to be, the way the magazines teach you, wearing the makeup, the elaborate hairdos, the girdles and stockings and high heels, the bras with wires in them, the waist pinchers or whatever they're called. Something in my stomach reared up at the mere thought of doing myself up that way. I WOULDN'T. I felt I – me, who I am – would die.

The way I *looked* disturbed Brad, but should it have? I wasn't ugly, or dirty, or even sloppy. I just didn't adorn myself much. Could a thing like that wreck a marriage? I don't understand men. I remember Brad's friend Lou coming up to me once at a party and looking me up and down in an evaluating way. I was outraged at his presuming to look at me that way but he went further: he scolded me. He said I looked like a kid, that I wanted to be a kid, that I didn't want to grow up, didn't want to become a *woman*. The way he pronounced *woman* made my stomach clutch, especially since he was a fat slob, his belly hung over his pants, and he had a mouth like a porpoise's. I wanted to smash his teeth in, but of course I didn't. But before he could tell me that *he* could make a woman of me, I snarled (I couldn't help it. I didn't plan it, it just came out that way): 'Who would want to be a woman if you were the man?' and stalked off.

He glowered at me the rest of the night and he must have told people I'd said something rude to him because soon his wife was glaring at me too, and later on, Eileen asked me why I was so rude to Lou. I told her what had happened, but she didn't seem to understand why I felt insulted, she said I was neurotic. And one day at the newspaper, Arthur Wurtz, the arts editor, came up and ordered me to put on some lipstick: 'You look like a ghost!' he cried, looking appalled. And I did it. *I did it!*

It's strange that men feel they have the right to criticize a woman's appearance to her face. Women don't go around telling men they're getting too paunchy, or suggesting they buy a toupee. Do they? Or suggesting they use deodorant, or even tell them they have egg on their tie or spinach between their teeth. I never even criticized Brad's appearance, and I was married to him. It's true I hated seeing him all dressed up in a three-piece suit. I liked him with long hair and a fancy shirt, standing on a stage. . . . And I wouldn't have liked him to grow a mustache, I wouldn't have liked to kiss it.

But maybe I have missed something. Maybe I was neurotic, as Eileen said. Maybe I was trying to insist on myself, on my difference from other women. Maybe it wouldn't hurt to try it. After all, here I am with a job women don't usually get – how many women photograph for *World*? None except me. And I don't have a husband, so it's not as though I were obeying someone, like Cheryl, whose husband insisted she dye her hair even though she was allergic to hair dye. She ended up losing all her hair and having to wear a wig.

Maybe it would be fun to use makeup, to dress up a bit.

I feel like a fool, I'm so excited, my heart is racing, my blood is speeding through my veins.

They were *really* looking at me. I felt . . . what would you call it? . . . desirable. *That's* what it was. I've never felt desirable before. I've felt desire, but that's different, desire consumes you, it takes you over, you forget yourself completely. All you can think about is the other, the one you desire, your *self* is just a fire.

But when you feel *desirable* – well, that's not so pleasant either. I felt very self-conscious when they were looking at me, as if I were a set of parts, each of which is supposed to be polished to perfection. Legs, breasts, hips, hands, feet, stomach, mouth, eyes, hair, voice, posture, clothing – is my slip hanging? is my nail chipped? I was being watched, someone was looking to see how I disposed my legs, if I shave them, if my stockings were wrinkled at the ankle, if they had a run. And how are your eyes? Is there red among the white? is your mascara smeared? And your hair: is there silver among the gold? I felt a little as if I were living in a country that had been invaded, as if enemy soldiers were exercising surveillance on me.

You are under surveillance and any flaw can earn you a One or a Two in some man's book, can turn you into a dog, a cow, a sow, a slob, a slut, a slattern: an undesirable woman. You must correct all your flaws. Aline once told me I had to change the way I walk. How can you change the way you walk? Models do, she said. Train yourself. Why do you think they have those girls walking with books on their heads? You must be erect, graceful, and sway your hips, very slightly, not stride along the way you do, unaware, uncaring of how you appear, like a man, like a truck driver.

I didn't see the purpose of all that bother. Back in the old days, I felt Brad desired me, in the days when we were young, before the world got us. But he desired me the way I was. Then. I thought. I know.

These men in the terminal were different. They don't know me, how can they desire me? They desire an image, me but not-me. As I sat there feeling them look at me I suddenly remembered my bewilderment as I'd watched other women walk along carrying themselves as if their every movement was being photographed, as if they were expensive pieces of merchandise that might break with a sharp gesture, an unselfconscious expression. And for the first time I understood what they were feeling. And I understood why in a corner of my heart I have always despised women and not wanted to be one.

Oh, I'm learning so much, just sitting on this plane, just being out in the world, I feel as if my head will explode.

Still, it's nicer to be noticed than to be invisible. Besides, it aroused me in a funny squirmy way, as if I had worms in my intestines. It made me feel . . . powerful. As if I had something that other people, well, men at least, want. And would give something to get. And I have the power to confer or deny it.

I haven't been aroused in a long time.

Maybe that's the way it really is, sex – conquering and surrender on both sides, a tacit battle that each one feels they've won. Maybe my love and Brad's was just puppy love, as his mother said. . . . Oh, everything's beyond me.

Get off that. Russ Farrell said that usually they send a reporter with the photographer so they can coordinate their material. But the reporter they hired for this piece couldn't make it at this time, so they were sending me alone and the reporter would use my contact sheets as a guide. It made no sense at all to me, especially since I'm new and the reporter is an old hand. He'd resent them giving me the right to select what would be covered. My theory is they want to be sure my pictures are good enough to warrant the second expense. They don't really trust me yet. But maybe I'm paranoid.

Anyway, I'll be on my own out there. A man named Mike Bostwick is to meet me, he's in charge of Liaison and Public Relations, he'll be my guide while I'm there. I can see him: late fifties, liquor-reddened nose, sun-reddened neck. He'll talk in spurts of disconnected syllables. Hard r's, elongated diphthongs, 'The ay-e's fahn, may-am,' A man's man. Oh, Anastasia, you need to sleep.

*

January 13. SIERRA NEVADA!

It's night now, thank god. I'm in a shabby motel which is all there is within forty miles of the dam site. Plastic furniture and a hideous patterned carpet that hides dirt. But a nice big clean bathroom, a shower, lots of hot water.

I don't care that it's seedy. This is my first trip away from home alone, and one of the damned few times I've ever been away from home at all. I AM ALONE. No kids, no TV, no one hogging the bathroom. It feels wonderful. It is luxury. It is freedom.

Yes, I remember that, the luxury of aloneness, like silence you can stretch your body into. When did traveling stop feeling like a luxury? When did it turn into weariness, one more metal and plastic motel, another anonymous corridor with fifty identical doors, another anonymous plastic room, a view of a parking lot, or the concrete wall of the next building? The only thing to be grateful for is the bathroom, a clean toilet, a hot shower. American talent like Joyce's Romans: It is meet to be here. Let us construct a water-closet. You hope the bed will not be too soft, the pillows not lumpy; that the windows will open and there is not too much street noise, or if there is street noise, that the air-conditioning works. By now, you know when you first walk in and set down the camera bag, the tripod, and your knapsack, how bad this room will feel when you return to it later that night, much later — after the high of shooting in the shifting lights, seeing, seeing, jumping from place to place, bending and lifting tripod, cameras, every part of you stretched — then drinks, dinner, surrounded by admirers, How thrilling it must be to photograph for *World*, How does it feel to be the only woman, How did you manage that wonderful effect in the pictures of the oil refinery, the Verrazano Bridge, the Greek islands, the Berlin Wall . . .

Then it's over and silence clasps you as the door to your room shuts. Life is still going on out there, somewhere, but you can't hear it, there is nothing but this room, not even ugly, just bland. Not even any room service so you can call down for a last drink to calm yourself, to keep you company. There's a television set, but in most cities even that is dead by the time you get back to your room. Nights when the dread of isolation is so strong you invite a man back to your room with you rather than go there alone . . . No, Anastasia, don't use that as an excuse. You sound just like a man.

I am tired. Landed at LA after a six-hour flight, then had to hop over to another terminal where I boarded a small commuter plane for Fresno, then another long walk to meet the turboprop plane that brought me here. In the mountains, the turboprop plane would drop every once in a while, several hundred feet in an instant, leaving my stomach on the ceiling of the cabin. Terrifying.

Arrived around six my time high afternoon here. Met by Mike Bostwick, who is BEAUTIFUL. Tall, muscular, trim, blond, hair thinning but still there. All-American grin, eyebrows that rose in the air when he spotted me and stayed there. Like the men in the terminal at Idlewild. I didn't know what to do with myself; I sort of wanted to cross my legs at the groin, put a finger in my dimple (if I had one), and bat my eyelashes. I also wanted to slap his face at his arrogance, at his unthinking appropriation of my body. . . . But I knew – how do I know these things? I am an inexperienced woman. Have I always known these things? – I knew that whatever I did or thought I was doing, he would read in his own way, and that I could never pierce his way of reading enough to make him see *me*.

What I did was act like a man. I blanked out all expression from my face except an empty smile, I strode forward and stuck my hand out to shake his. I hollowed out my voice, and acted a little cool and a little weary as if I had made hundreds of trips like this. It helped that I was so tired; I didn't have the energy to be expressive. He responded to this; he wiped that look off his face and began to treat me professionally. But every once in a while he'd glance over at me to check out the image, to see if the inexpressive professional was still there.

He wanted to drive me to the dam. I was tired: I would have loved a bath, a hamburger, and a bed. But I didn't want to seem in any way weak, and it would save time the next day if I got a sense of the layout tonight, so I said sure. We threw my things in the back of his Jeep and took off on an incredibly bumpy ride around the massive project. Mike reeled off statistics: I hope he has them all written down somewhere and will give me a PR packet, because I couldn't possibly remember them. I was having trouble keeping my face from showing disgust: the whole thing looked so ugly to me.

Not the mountains: the sun was low, dyeing the lower sky a burning coral, casting purple swathes far across the hills behind us, darkening those ahead. The earth was dry, the color of clay, and the Jeep spit up dust as we traveled. And there, in the middle of all this serious nature, was this huge white thing, a monstrous bathtub surrounded by machines that dwarfed the men who ran them. He stopped when I needed to jot down some notes about the light, and Mike waved to men in white helmets who peered at the Jeep, waved, and turned back to their blueprints, their machines, their Cokes. Mike's voice was full of awe at the size of the project, at its difficulties, all being overcome. I tried to see it as he did. I know that's what *World* would want.

The sun set suddenly – it just slid down behind a mountain leaving us in a purplish twilight. Everyone seemed to know that was coming; they'd already packed up their gear; Jeeps and vans started up from all around the project as the men headed to the shantytown of prefabs they live in. Only the executives live at the motel, and they, Mike said, were planning a dinner in my honor that evening. I had to act pleased, even though my eyebrows felt stuck to my forehead with clayey dust, my mouth was dry from it. I'd been up since five in the morning, and by now it was eight at night for me. But I took a hot bath and lay down for an hour before dinner, which is the only way I got through it.

I 'dressed' for dinner – that is, I put on a skirt. This was probably a mistake. They hadn't expected *World* to send a woman to photograph their dam, and I think they were a little outraged about it as if having a woman shoot it diminished it somehow. And the skirt emphasized my sex. On the other hand, they were starved for female companionship, and had slicked themselves out in suits and ties and haircream and were as courtly and polite as Southern Colonels. The problem was that after they had flirted as far as decency permitted, they had no other conversation. After all, men flirt with the ladies over cocktails; after that, they talk to each other. And they had me for the whole evening. We were all relieved when dinner was over, and I know they blessed me for pleading tiredness and going to my room after coffee, leaving them to each other and their after-dinner drinks.

Breakfast was at 5.30; by 6 Mike and I were out in the Jeep in hard hats of our own, bumping along the clay mountain roads worn into ruts by huge trucks. I was glad then for my introduction to the place the night before, because I was able to direct Mike to places I had noted then as offering spectacular prospects. I walked along narrow paths and catwalks, lugging my tripod and cameras; I rode up the side of the dam in a makeshift elevator; I got up on top of machines; I climbed over railings that edged the cliff-like sides of the dam, while I hung over and shot down. I grew more and more excited. What seemed ugly and uninteresting last night seemed complex and challenging when I looked at it through a camera – the way color suddenly blooms when you bring a blurry slide into focus in a projector.

The difficulties of photographing it excited me about the difficulties of constructing it. For example: a gorge they needed to cross was impassable; they spent days trying to come up with a way to cross it. Finally, they set an archer to fire an arrow across. The arrow was attached to a heavy line of wire. On the other side of the gorge, men waited until the arrow hit, caught the wire and attached it to a heavy reel, and presto, they had a washline, a ski lift. They needed to get a truck to the other side of the Feather River, so they devised an aerial ferry and hoisted it across. Brilliant!

There were other wonders, and before we stopped for lunch – dry ham sandwiches in waxed paper and beer, consumed in the shade of a foreman's shack – I was sharing Mike's enthusiasm. I had trouble staying awake after the beer, and napped for a while, just lying back on the hard ground (clearly if I was going to work with the men, I was going to have to drink like the men), but when I woke up, I was full of energy and a newborn belief in the miracles wrought by Man.

Oh, what shots I got! Mythic: man against nature: mere muscle and brain challenging the enormity of a vacant mindless nature, full of traps and wiles, offering death at every step, hindering the Fisher King from bringing water to the wilderness. I shot the men's faces full of strain as they stared upward watching to see if the aerial ferry would in fact work; I shot their sunburned arms, muscles straining to turn a wheel, to work the handle of a reel, or relaxed, lighting a cigarette. I shot the machines that dwarfed them, but which they controlled; I shot the gigantic apparatus itself, the dam, from all angles in many lights. By evening, the dam had been transformed for me into a massive basin of holy water shimmering in the sun, the redemption of the arid hills . . .

I was so busy leaping around doing gymnastics, I kept forgetting my professional, my *masculine* act, and by late afternoon, Mike and I were giggling together like high schoolers – after all, it was Mike who tied and untied me from the railing, who reached out a hand to help me back from my perches. And each time he touched or grabbed me, something felt – well, it contributed to the excitement of the day – for both of us. So it wasn't a surprise that when we reached the motel in the sudden twilight, he asked casually whether I had enough stamina to drive another thirty miles that day, to a little town in the mountains where there is a restaurant that serves great steaks.

He's really a nice guy. It's just the way he talks that put me off – those bursts of technical language, everything said in as complicated a way as possible. Like he says 'aircraft' instead of plane, and 'personnel carrier' instead of minibus. But I guess he can't help it, they all seem to talk that way. He's okay. I am still tired from yesterday but I hated to admit I don't have as much stamina as he, so I said yes. And besides, he's attractive, and he'd fluttered me, we'd had fun that day . . . So after a shower and a shampoo to get the clayey dust out of my hair, and an hour's nap, I met him in the motel lobby where we had what he called a 'camel stop' to prepare us for the long dry ride – a Bloody Mary for me and two bourbon old-fashioneds for him (the things these men drink!).

We drove the curving dark mountain roads for nearly an hour to a log cabin with red-checked tablecloths and candles in bottles and had a dinner that was anyway better than the one the night before. The food wasn't that important: here I am, the me, the mother of two from Lynbrook, Long Island, in a strange place in the Sierra Nevada with a handsome exciting man. I am having an adventure!

On the way back, I worried the adventure might be my last: Mike had three more bourbon old-fashioneds with dinner, and although he drove back a lot slower than he drove there, the road seemed even more treacherous. But the canvas top of the Jeep was down, and Mike kept glancing up and saying 'Will you look at that goddamned sky?' and I leaned my head back and stared. The sky here is huge and black and the stars stand out against it so brilliantly that they reach out and include you – you feel part of the same universe with them . . . And I thought, I have never seen stars before. I didn't say it, though. I didn't want to seem touched, or touchable . . .

The motel lobby was empty when we returned; there were no sounds even from the bar. I turned to shake Mike's hand, to thank him for the dinner, and he looked at me and pulled me – hard – toward him and held me close against his body. For the first time in my life, a man's acting proprietary did not offend me. My body didn't stiffen, it didn't pull away. I remember when boys – for they were boys, back then – acted this way, how I became stiff-spined as a cactus tree, how I pushed them away.

But it was different this time, and what was different was my *body*. It let itself be held, it leaned into his, it thrilled to his. My mind let itself down into dark warmth, a smell of body, and the rhythm of pulses. We stood together for what felt like a long time. I knew he wanted me to ask him to come with me to my room. But I didn't. I said I was tired and walked down the long hall alone; feeling him watching me, feeling his body chilled by the loss of mine.

I guess I was feeling desirable, desired, self-conscious, but all I was aware of as I walked away from him and into my room was what I imagined *he* was feeling. I put myself into his mind, what I imagined was in his mind. I fantasized him fantasizing about me – about pushing me hard against the wall, taking the key from my hand and opening the door and insisting, in an urgency of desire, on deep kisses rooted all the way down in my clitoris . . . I don't know what I would have done had he done that. I don't know why I turned away. It's true, I am tired, but here it is after midnight and I'm still writing.

January 16. 2 a.m. Emplaned.
Well, of course the next night I did and he did and we did and now I am on the plane again reeling from exhaustion, from too little sleep, I feel I've aged ten years in three days. And now I'm numb. They've served some rotgut in tinfoil, and my belly's full so now I'm going to sleep all the way to New York.

two

I barely remember that trip. What surprises me most as I read this diary is the excitement, the flush, the thrill. I don't remember myself ever feeling such things. Probably I was just high with the new experience. Maybe I was infatuated with the idea of being desired – it was new to me then. I didn't yet know that women fall in love with themselves through the agency of male desire – see themselves gorgeous, taunting, challenging men into uncontrollable passion; or that men fall in love with themselves through the agency of female admiration – see themselves powerful, wise, knowing, in control, twice their size in the mirrors of women's eyes; that most of what we call love, romance, desire, happens in a mirror, is a kind of cooperative masturbation. I was still a child at thirty.

Still, she's not so bad, that girl, she's kind of sweet. So why have I gone to such lengths to bury her? To hide her under my present truly cool and assured exterior, the facade of a person who has never known fear or embarrassment, who knows herself too well to fall in love with herself, and men too well to look up to them. Some of that facade is true, though, all the way through. Is it reality itself that has made me old and tired?

What is really embarrassing is the way I bought the whole message – Man Against Nature, Progress, Better Lives Through Industry. Oh, I suppose even that is understandable. That *World* should, in 1960, think enough of a new hydroelectric plant (it wasn't the first, after all) to send me on such an expensive trip gave the project huge importance in my eyes. I didn't know then that *World* regarded my expenses and wages as peanuts, that they had and would discard material for which they had paid five times as much if it didn't suit them. To me in 1960, a plane ticket in coach, a motel for five nights, meals and cab fare and eighty rolls of film represented a significant investment, even utter commitment. I also knew that my work on this assignment would determine my future at *World*. And that must have influenced me; led me to feel what they wanted me to feel. I was bought. I let myself be bought.

The evidence is there in the notebook, in the wide scudding handwriting, in pages of excited descriptions replete with exclamation points and underlinings, of underground generators, geyser fields, machines; there are even drawings of machines with the names of their parts attached by sloppy swiftly drawn arrows. Excitement was the form my nervousness took. I had never, in school, felt frightened of failure; nor did I now. But fear fueled my interest, my absorption in the materials.

And that rhapsody about the housing development planned for a huge tract a few miles from the dam, that ideal community of neat little houses for the maintenance crew, larger houses for the managers, schools, shops, an enclosed swimming pool, a movie house. My heart was moved to an outpouring of praise for the men who thought this up, who planned and designed it, for the happy people who would live in it, this community made of papier mâché complete with tricycles in the driveways and wading pools in the backyards.

It is embarrassing. But how could I have known then the kind of lives that would in fact be lived in those developments, the blank stupor that was the realization of the American Dream: alcohol, drugs, and TV to numb empty hearts, empty heads . . . I was too young to know then that when people plan the lives of other people, the result can only be a robot world. No one knew. They thought they were doing something good.

Strangely, what I do remember is what I *didn't* write about – the mountains, one after another, on into eternity, all different colors – sienna, purple, deep grey-brown, black. Sun-bleached or shadowed, they were still and empty and majestic against a sky blue and empty as a slate, things given, not to be argued with. Yet what was happening there, then, was that men *were* arguing with them, manipulating them, altering them, calling it Progress. Maybe it was progress. Maybe those little houses are better than wherever the people who bought them might have lived. I do know that it was ugly, all of it, and that I no longer believe that anything ugly can benefit humankind. My first reaction endures: that splendid vast landscape with a huge white concrete bathtub broad as a town set in its middle.

Wallace Stevens wrote about a jar in Tennessee – about man's art giving meaning to meaningless nature. Insurance executive. That has to do something to you, to spend your life in an insurance office. Well, I've spent mine as a photographer, and I know that the intentions of the maker are imprinted on the thing made as clearly as fingerprints on a murder gun, or character on a forty-year-old face. And that dam even in unfinished state revealed the heavy fistprint of the conqueror who claims to be bringing water to the wasteland, but who is actually branding with his own insignia the rumps of the slaves who pass the buckets. The water comes with his name on it, writ in water, that's true triumph, conquering nature. So massive, so seemingly impregnable, so intimidating, like the tombs of the pharaohs decorated with massive statues of the man, his face imprinted upon the desert.

I don't recall Mike What's-his-face either. He must have been the first man I screwed after Brad . . . He's gone. I can't even summon up his face. Doesn't matter. He wasn't important.

Tuesday, January 20. Lynbrook.

I've decided to keep up this habit of writing at night even when I'm not traveling. It's a relief, like talking to an adult in the evening. Of course, there's no response from a blank page. Still, it *feels* almost as if there were. As if the act of writing things down on a piece of paper summoned some other presence, critical, carping, the voice of a gargoyle, saying Liar, Liar, forcing you to sit up straight, correct yourself, abandon all pretense . . .

These last few days have been chaotic. I'll try to recoup them . . .

Friday, yes, I got in at nine New York time, having succeeded in sleeping most of the way from LA, and went straight to the film lab. I took a cab from the airport: it was *World*'s money, but I still felt guilty. From the lab I walked to the subway, drooping. It was 6 a.m. for me and my equipment seemed to have put on a huge amount of weight in the past week. Horrible Long Island Railroad home. Awful!

Then home, finally, The kids were at school so the house was quiet. Pane, of course, wanted to talk, but it's always easy to escape from her, it takes only a kind word. The fridge held the remains of Pane's wonderful meals and I munched on cold kielbasa, dipping it into a container of beets and horseradish. Then I went to bed and slept until the kids came home. They were really happy to see me! They asked questions, I told them about the plane trip and the little table and the meals in aluminum foil, and the mountains and the arrow shot across the gorge and the truck hoist and my brilliant camerawork. They didn't even go out to play that afternoon, just hung around me. Their news – 98 on a math test (Arden), 95 on a science test (Billy), Joan got a dog, can we get one? Mrs Morton, the second-grade teacher, was pregnant and refused to say whether she wanted a boy or a girl – led climactically up to its heart: what Pane let them do (MOM, TAKE NOTE): stay up to see the eleven o'clock news, have dessert even if they didn't eat their carrots; leave their shoes in the living room overnight; and what she didn't let them do (MOM, DO SOMETHING ABOUT THIS!): go out to play without sitting to chat with her over chruściki and milk; leave for school on a cloudy morning without galoshes; sleep over at a friend's house on a school night (something they know perfectly well I don't let them do either).

I couldn't keep my hands off them, I kept touching their shoulders and stroking their heads and rubbing their cheeks and hugging them. I let them have as many cookies as they wanted, I broke my own rules. And they babbled on, eyes glistening, cheeks pink and a little chafed from the cold. I smoothed almond cream on their cheeks. I felt we were closer than we'd been in months – maybe ever – and that my guilts were unwarranted. I asked them what they wanted to do over the weekend. I suggested ice skating on Silver Lake, sledding in Hempstead Park. Their faces fell: actually, they had plans to do just those things, but with their friends. They didn't come out and say I wasn't welcome to join them, but the message was clear. I subsided back into motherhood.

Guilt reasserted itself: of course you can't expect to go off and leave them for five days and have them hang around waiting for you to go ice skating. It was no more than I deserved that they should desert me over the weekend. I reminded myself that they usually spent weekends with their friends, that it was good for them to do that, and that for the most part I welcomed those desertions because I could go out by myself too and photograph. But some vague anxiety seemed to have just settled in me, like the dull ache of arthritis.

As it turned out, it was just as well they were gone all day Saturday. Lou Glick, Farrell's assistant, called around ten to say the contact sheets had been delivered to *World* and that he'd glanced at them but was waiting for the color prints, and that Farrell would call me on Monday. He said nothing about them. This planted an insane anxiety in me. Did Lou like them or not? Would I be dropped by *World* as swiftly as I'd been picked up? I couldn't be sure myself how the pictures had turned out. I sat on my bed, my hand still gripping the telephone receiver, the dial tone buzz screeching in the empty room.

I imagined pictures of blurry machines, sunburned streaky film, fogged mountains, distorted human figures. I kept hearing Lou's noncommittal voice tinged with disapproval, even contempt: stupid broad can't even hold a camera right. I imagined a heap of contact sheets, forty rolls worth, all worthless. My heart kept panging as if the Sierra Nevada archer were sending arrows all the way from California. I should never have slept with Mike, it made me too tired, I wasn't as sharp as I could be, I should have stayed more alert . . .

I tried to pull myself together. First, I put the phone down. Then I started to unpack, but every item of soiled clothing I pulled from my smelly bag made me sink down on the floor. I was gasping, I could hear my own breath. Maybe I was having a heart attack.

In the next hours, I managed to get the laundry together and pile it near the stairs. I didn't want to go downstairs where I might meet Pane, who would want to talk. I didn't feel capable of speech. My heart hurt from all the banging going on inside it. I straightened the living room a little, and washed the breakfast dishes. Then I sank into a chair and sat. I didn't notice when it got dark; I didn't realize the children still weren't home. They did come in eventually, happy with bellies full of soda Joyce's mother had bought them after the skating, and they made enough noise and had such high spirits that my stupor just got steamrolled and I was able to go through the motions of getting dinner and cleaning up after it.

All Sunday morning I was a cranky wreck. I couldn't concentrate, I couldn't even read The *Times*. I did the laundry and started to iron. The kids went sledding: Tim Moroney's mother drove them and I was to pick them up at four. I turned on the radio. I was standing there, the heat from the iron rising into my face, listening to a soupy WPAT rendition of 'Somebody Loves Me' when it occurred to me that somebody did. Into my poor battered mind slides the memory of this gorgeous man who had looked at me with urgent hunger, with passion.

And like water flowing through an opened tap, passion flows into my heart and flushes out the anxiety. The arrow-strikes turn into ripples of pleasure as I remember Mike's eyes caressing my body. A rosy memory of closeness, embraces, kisses, the body's memory takes over my mind. I begin to hum with the music. The ironing goes faster. I keep hearing him at our parting, promising, it seemed, eternal devotion, the kind of passion that could transcend three thousand miles and the fact that (I suspected) he was married. (I didn't want to ask because I didn't want to seem to be on the hunt for a husband. And he didn't say.) My mind – all by itself – begins to invent scenarios in which we meet at Idlewild Airport and clutch each other with the desperation of fated lovers.

By the time I picked up the kids, I had washed my hair and put on fresh clothes, nicer clothes than I normally wear around the house. I was humming. I was not fully present, I was floating in a romantic dream that required the continual accompaniment of Mantovani violins on the radio or in my head. The kids complained about the music playing on the car radio. I said they always got to listen to what they liked, that today was my turn. They made disgusted retching sounds as violins swooped up and shivered down, but I was impervious. They headed straight for the television set when we got home, and I let them. I went into my room and turned on my radio and began a careful survey of my wardrobe. It was apparent that there was not a single item there suitable for meeting a lover in Idlewild Airport.

Yes, well that was Sunday. Monday I woke up with anxiety clutching at my heart; the romantic dream seemed to have slipped a bit. I immediately turned on WPAT, and the kids looked at me as if they thought I had become peculiar. And then, at ten-thirty, the business phone rang. I let it ring three times before I picked it up; then my hands were so slimy that I dropped it, it clattered on the uncarpeted bedroom floor, and Russ Farrell's voice came on stiff and formal and my heart prepared to stop. But the words he was saying were *magnificent, spectacular*. He said he was going to give the pictures six pages in the March 12 issue, *with a byline for me*! Only the top people got bylines, the great photographers and men who'd worked for *World* for years. I soared. I listened as he discussed the photographs – which we should use, how, cropping, color, layout – but I just kept saying 'Um-hm'. He told me he wanted me to come in for a picture conference. I had to write down what he was saying because it wasn't going into my brain.

Yes, that part I recall, I remember too how impressed they were with a device I used on that assignment – I'd do a close-up, then move the camera farther and farther away from the same person or object, gradually placing it in a larger perspective, giving it a broader significance. They loved that, and although they didn't use any of those sequences in this article, they asked me to keep on doing it. Over the years they printed many such sequences. I liked them myself: for some reason they gave me peace. I had done my best to make my pictures show truth.

I floated up from the bed and into the kitchen and turned off some kitsch music playing on the radio. I rummaged in the cabinets for a bottle, I wanted to offer myself a toast, but I couldn't find anything except apple juice, so I drank that. I wanted to call someone up. I tried my mother's line, but she was out. I tried Delilah's but hers was busy. Then it occurred to me to call Mike. This led to a swift re-evaluation.

First, I had no telephone number for him – I had the number of the main office, but Mike was probably out on the site, showing around some politicians or journalists. Then I thought: why should I call him? He doesn't really know anything about me: I was so careful to appear confident, assured, on top of everything, I wanted to seem tough, impervious: there is no way he could understand how important this is to me.

That made me sit down.

I forced myself to recall our . . . whatever it was. How he'd gotten himself quite drunk the next night (as he had the night before); how he knew hardly anything about lovemaking except screwing, and was utterly oblivious to my gestures, my murmured suggestions. How he simply leaped on top of me when he adjudged me juicy enough, lunged and came and rolled off and fell asleep with his arm across my stomach.

I slid out from under his arm and went into the bathroom and drew a bath and masturbated. I let him sleep for an hour then roused him and made him leave. I didn't want him coming from my room the next morning, and I didn't want to sleep in the same bed with him, either. The sheet had dried by then, but I put a towel over it anyway.

Next day he acted sheepish, as if he didn't remember exactly what had happened. He made a lot of jokes about getting soused. He wouldn't meet my eyes and acted distracted all day. That night, as he brought me back from the site, he apologized: he was tired and hung over from the night before and was going to grab a sandwich and go to bed. And this infuriated me.

If he had wanted to sleep with me again, I fully intended to refuse. So why was I furious? I wanted him to feel so madly desirous that he would not want to give up a single moment with me – especially since Wednesday was my last night there. I wanted him to feel that way even though I didn't. I didn't know what to call my attitude, except bad. Still, I wanted to get even, so when some of the managers invited me to eat with them and sit around in the bar after dinner, I took them up on it. I flirted my tail off, and so did they. By midnight we were all buddies.

Next day I had to work intensely – it was my last chance. I had to make sure I hadn't missed any opportunity for a terrific shot, and I wanted to retake certain shots in different lights. Mike was attentive and sweet, much as he had been before, but I had no time to worry about him. When he left me at the landing strip where I'd get the turboprop, he put his hands on my shoulders and looked deeply into my eyes, and murmured, lovingly, 'Stacey, darling,' as if we'd been soul mates, deeply intimate. Then he kissed my forehead lightly and said he got to New York sometimes and would call me if he did and we'd find ourselves a fantastic steak.

This is what I'd used as the basis for a romantic dream.

How had I managed to convince myself, between Thursday and Sunday, that Mike Bostwick was the lover I'd been waiting for, the mate that fate had me created for? What's more serious, what worries me, is the question of how I'll ever be able to trust myself again if I imagine I'm in love with somebody. What should I have done if *World* hadn't liked the pictures, if my 'career' had ended yesterday morning? Would I have turned *him* into my meaning, my success? Would I have wept on the phone to him every night, having leaped every hurdle to find his telephone number, confessing passion and need? Humiliating myself, embarrassing him?

Just the same, the romantic dream helped. It got me through Sunday. It slid me gently back into the old round of marketing, dishes, laundry, and cooking, which now seem even more tedious and puny than they did before. After all, I am a person who flies to the Coast, who climbs up on huge cranes to photograph dams, who meets important people, who has glamorous love affairs! My mind is a mess. It is full of delusions and even though I know it, I can't clear them away. I don't know which to mistrust more: my heart or my mind.

three

June 1948.

Nothing left to hope for. It was in her, I knew it was in her, something special, something I wanted but didn't have, what I would have given to have it! and yet she let it go, and so young. It isn't as though I didn't warn her, she knew what my life was like, I told her what would happen, having to get married, the shame and then nothing, the end of your life . . . We never spoke of sex in this house, but she knew, she knew what happened to me. And even so, she did it.

Belle's memory of desire was thin, like trying to remember what your mother meant to you before she grew old and senile. At least she had waited until she was mature, twenty-five, it was understandable that she would have . . . But Anastasia was only eighteen, too young for a girl to feel desire. And the worst of it was it happened in the same month, February, the baby would be born the same month Anastasia had been born, it was as if her own fate had been imprinted on Anastasia, as if Anastasia herself could do nothing about it, it was destined.

Pregnant. Mom, I'm pregnant. What was there to say? Ed would have liked to scold, I wouldn't let him. How could he? How could either of us, given what we . . . I'll remember that priest in Washington forever, shrieking at him that he was depraved, filthy, a miserable sinner, a tool of the devil . . . The only time I saw Ed almost cry. Turned me against the church. So now she's married too, married the same way, furtively, a quick trip to someplace, even the date of it lost, why bother to remember, you don't remember the date your life ended. All that intelligence, so brilliant she was, talented too, she could have been anything, all her teachers said so – pianist, painter, teacher . . . Not like me, no education, no culture, nearly deaf, blind in one eye, no chances . . . I gave her everything, my whole life. Nothing, all for nothing.

Belle sits pleating hats. She is forty-four, but looks older. She is attractive with her fine pale hair, her delicate features, noble, even. Her face is the face of a lady, not a woman – important difference in 1948. But close up you can see how her face will age – how the ends of her eyes droop and fold into a pocket of puffy flesh, how the lines around her mouth are deepening, and the hundreds of tiny lines slivering her fine pale skin. Her long fingernails are thick and yellow, ugly, she thinks. She keeps them coated with polish, a deep old rose. Pleating the hats wears off the polish from the tips of her nails. But her hands are still beautiful, the fingers long and slender and graceful. Her best feature.

She has no shame, Anastasia. You'd think she'd be miserable, humiliated that people were talking about her. You'd think she'd walk about with bowed head and cry, like her, like Belle. Jean had sighed in sympathy, 'Oh, Belle,' as if Belle were the one in trouble. It was humiliating to have to tell them, their daughters would never get in trouble like that. Eric, of course, immediately reminded them that he had told them not to send Anastasia to college. Ed should have put his foot down and insisted she go to work, she was such a willful girl, it had been a waste to send her to college. Girls *will* get married, he said. It's nature. She'd hated him at that moment, sitting there smug and self-satisfied, pronouncing about nature and girls as things that he would never have to worry about, safe and superior in his impregnable body. And what about *his* children? He gave them everything money could buy and she'd bet he'd send them to college too. Looks down on us, one law for him, another one for us. Ed might not be as good a provider as Eric, but he'd never say a thing like that.

Girls! What about boys? Anastasia didn't do this herself. But she did seem – how could she be? – happy with this Brad, unstable boy, funny eyes, pale, that don't seem to see what they are looking at. No shame at all, you'd think she wanted to be pregnant, end her life so young. She even acts delighted with that stifling little one-room attic apartment, you have to walk through a stranger's living room even to get to the stairs, horrible, she wouldn't go there. No wedding, no wedding gifts, nothing to start life with. They didn't even have a toaster, and when Belle lamented this, Anastasia laughed and said you could just as well make toast on the gas ring.

Horrible. Her life will be one long slavery. When she could have married a big doctor, a big lawyer, she's attractive, she plays the piano well. If she had just . . . Well, at least they have their own place, that's more than I had, but no money, Brad not even finished with school, the only decent maternity dress she has is the one I bought her.

Belle's head ached. She set the hat down gently on the pile of finished work: ten, she thought, then counted them again. Yes, ten. She rose and went into the bathroom and swallowed two aspirin. She avoided her face in the mirror. She went back to the bedroom and lighted a cigarette. She sat down in the chair she worked in, but did not pick up another hat.

I'll just have a cigarette. A little break.

Ten. And it was only eleven-twenty. She could finish forty hats today, although her fingers got sore from the pleating after a while, despite the calluses that protected the tips. Pleat ten more, then sew on ruching for an hour, prepare another twenty. Then cut out some fabric, size 6, to work on tomorrow. A decent day's work. At this rate, 200 this week. Except she had a dentist appointment on Thursday, that would be time lost. Maybe 190. Not bad. Since her raise . . . what would that be? She couldn't multiply 12½ cents in her head. She set the cigarette in an ashtray and picked up the pencil that lay on her vanity. 190 x 12, she scrawled swiftly: $22.80. then half a cent each on 190 caps, that would be 95 cents. $23.75.

What would that be by the hour? Minimum wage, they said on the radio yesterday; there was a minimum wage. How many hours do I work?

She laid the pencil down. She wasn't going to keep track of her hours, she didn't want to know.

Suppose it was terribly little, way below minimum wage? Better not to know.

So now there were just the bills, keeping things afloat until something happened. Save some money for Joy, if she wants to go to college. She probably won't. Likes to have fun, be with her friends, throws up when she has examinations, not a student. Cute and funny though. But she doesn't have what Anastasia had. Wasted. Three years yet before Joy would need it. Unless she too . . .

No. She tamped out her cigarette with a grim mouth. No, it was Anastasia who was destined to repeat my fate, not Joy.

June 1951.

When they moved in Joy had loved the little wall fixtures in the bedrooms, two in hers and Anastasia's, three in Mother and Daddy's. They were made of porcelain Mother said and they had flowers painted on them and little etched glass chimneys enclosing the light bulb. But now she hates them because they cast so faint a light, they make shadows on her face when she looks at it in the mirror, like now, and they make her skin look yellow, but she isn't really yellow, Kitty and Linda said she wasn't, and she made them swear they were telling the truth, too. Anastasia had put all kinds of lamps in her room, four of them, it looked silly, six lights in one little room, of course they were all small, two on the bureau and two on the old green metal kitchen table Anastasia used for a desk, Anastasia hated darkness. But Anastasia had taken all her lamps with her.

Joy doesn't have a desk, she does her homework at Linda's every afternoon on the floor under a standing lamp with the radio playing. All the girls love the baritones, Dick Haymes and Frank Sinatra and Bing Crosby and Joy especially loved Vaughn Monroe. The best singers were all men, it was funny. They said the best cooks were men too, but Joy had never seen a man cook. And all the best athletes were men. Even though Kitty and Linda and Joy played soccer and basketball pretty well, no one ever came to watch them. They didn't really even have a team. But they loved to play it, running, your legs felt so great, then leaping up and tossing the ball, as if your body could fly, it was great. . . .

She wonders if they will have sports at college. Real colleges have sports, but Joy is going to a junior college Hilton Academy in Virginia. Mother speaks of it condescendingly, she says it's just a finishing school but Joy knows Mother is impressed just the same – impressed that she was accepted at all with her grades and because Alice Warren and Eleanor Staples two of the really rich girls in her class were going there too. But Joy feels that if it is really a finishing school, that is okay because she badly needs finishing. She is sure she went up in Mother's estimation, now Mother has to picture her in a fancy school with those rich girls, the idea excites her it frightens her too she would have liked to do something like that when she was young but she probably would have been too scared. Not that Joy isn't.

She tried to speak to Anastasia about it to see if she thought it was the right thing to do but Anastasia is strange these days all she cares about is photographing babies, not even her own babies, them she just drags along wherever she goes. Anastasia acts almost as if she thought that Joy is so stupid it doesn't matter what she does. Maybe Anastasia isn't the right person to talk to even though Joy has always looked up to her. Maybe Anastasia didn't understand. She seems different or maybe she wasn't different maybe Joy just never knew her. She always looks so shabby, her hair long and flying or done in a long braid down her back like a kid you wouldn't think she was a married woman with two children of course she doesn't have any money . . . but still . . . Anastasia doesn't seem to care about how she looks or maybe she cares but she won't admit it because she's mad she can't afford clothes and things. That's what Joy thinks.

Joy thinks it is important how a person looks. She always tries to smile when she looks in the mirror. She is smiling now even though she doesn't feel like smiling, not at all, she'd like to cry but she won't. Sometimes – oh it was terrible – she would catch her face in the mirror when she wasn't intending to like when she stood up straight and turned around after making her bed and then a terrible chill would come into her spine. So she'd smile to make it go away. But it would last a few seconds long enough that she was forced to register the new pimple on her chin or a right cheek aflame with them or even if there were no new pimples there were all the other things her yellow skin her full round face her slight sloping shoulders her long neck her broad hips. She hates her body, she hates her face! They all do Kitty and Linda too, she can't understand it Kitty is so pretty and Linda has such a cute body.

But everybody has always said that Joy has a great smile, so she resorts to that, it is the only thing she knows to do. You can hate the way you look and you can try to change it with make-up and stuff but you can't really change it. So you have to make people like you anyway. So you smile. Like now with no make-up on, in the red flannel Dr Dentons she wears even in June because she is always cold, the smile works, it makes her feel better the brightness of her large blue eyes the broad delighted smile welcomes her in the mirror as if she were a stranger meeting herself . . .

Kitty is so pretty with her blond hair like a puff of gold

around her face sweet delicate little face heart-shaped not big and round like Joy's; and Linda has so much personality always full of energy and she is witty funny she cracks them all up all the time. And Penny is *very* smart Joy wants to introduce her to Anastasia Anastasia would enjoy Penny she'd see how smart she is even though she doesn't do all that well at school but she doesn't care she's beyond that, school and all that because of her mother so sophisticated she's taking Penny to Europe after graduation, three whole months traveling Paris Rome London all those places and Penny has her hair done by her mother's hairdresser and had lessons in putting on makeup Penny's really lovely although she's putting on a bit too much weight that's her mother letting Penny have cocktails with them every night Joy too when she eats there her throat so tense she can barely swallow sitting in the living room with music playing softly on the hi-fi. Penny's mother always wears long gowns grey silk peach silk red brocade and her hair is as blond as Penny's and swept up like a movie star's and Penny's stepfather pouring martinis from a tall glass pitcher so distinguished third husband Penny had seen a lot her father was an alcoholic and then the second husband too and he used to hit her mother too even though he was a big stockbroker.

All the other cheerleaders have something special Amy with her long straight red hair and Joanie with that creamy tan complexion that's because she's Italian and drinks olive oil and Kitty with her blond hair and Linda with her great smile they looked so great standing in front of the crowd yelling 'give me an *S!* Give me an *O!* Yay! Southside!' in their heavy white letter sweaters and short swingy skirts and saddle shoes and thick white socks folded over at the ankle. And Kitty and Linda always say she is the cutest of all of them. But they only say that because they are her friends and they love her. Joy loves them too and she will love them forever.

Joy switches off the wall lamp near the mirror and turns toward the bed. The room is dark now except for the moonlight streaming through the back window the one facing the garden. Anastasia got the bedroom with the window seat but Joy likes hers better because it overlooks the garden. But right now she wishes she had a window seat and could sit by the window and look out at the dark shapes clustered on the pale lawn. Anastasia told her she used to sit on the window seat and smoke at night blowing the smoke out the window so it wouldn't smell up the room and Mother would find out and she'd 'moon' she said laughing 'dramatizing body juices into the chemistry of tragedy'. Anastasia talked like that. Anastasia was smart.

She thinks she has a cigarette left in her purse. Maybe she will try it: the chemistry of tragedy. What would that be? Whatever it is, it sounds right for her now. She feels around on the chest of drawers for her purse, and riffles through it, finding a wrinkled pack of Luckies. She pulls over to the window the hassock that stands before her little vanity (which with the low wide chest and the bed are all the furniture that will fit in the room) and sits down on it. She doesn't really mind that her room is so small, Linda's room isn't much bigger. But Kitty has a huge room, of course she has to share it with her sister, but it is a room and a half, it has like a little sitting room alcove and they have their own bathroom too. But her favorite is Betty Brower's room her whole house is huge Joy would love to live up there in the expensive area the Canterbury section where the plots are all large and have huge old trees on them where Whit's parents live they have two lots their property fronts on two streets. Betty has two beds in her room so she can have a friend sleep over and a big bureau and a vanity and a desk and a long chair she calls a shez. And in one corner there is a great heap of stuffed animals, some of them huge some little elephants and bears and horses and kitties and bunnies all piled on top of one another.

Joy pushes her face against the screen and breathes in deeply trying to sniff the sweetness of the June night. But all she can smell is the metallic odor of the screen. She lights the cigarette. She coughs lightly. She is not a smoker she only smokes to be like her friends. She realizes there is no ashtray in her room, and flicks the ashes in the palm of her hand the way the boys do. They say it doesn't burn it doesn't but it makes you feel dirty. She doesn't want to be like the boys, she wants to be feminine. She gets up and tosses the ashes into the wastebasket, then wipes her palm along her pajama leg. That's something a boy would do too but she is too lazy to go into the bathroom and wash it. She sits down again and gazes out. She breathes deeply. She waits to feel the chemistry of tragedy.

Anastasia says Mother thinks Joy is pretty and popular and Anastasia is smart and talented. Joy knows this is what Mother thinks. And Anastasia said Mother had made her believe that she was ugly, and Joy that she was stupid. And she said it wasn't true, that Joy was really smart. Anastasia was mad at Mother for making them think that. But Joy feels that Anastasia was mad at Mother for making her feel ugly, but not for making Joy think she was stupid because Anastasia thinks Joy is stupid too. She just had to say that to be polite.

Joy wishes Mother would tell *her* she is pretty. It would make her feel better even if she didn't believe it. It would make her feel . . . oh . . . happy. But Mother has never said anything like that to Joy. And Joy can't ask her directly she'd be too embarrassed what would she say, 'Mommy, do you think I'm pretty?' Then Mother might say something that would make Joy feel terrible like that time Joy came home from Linda's house when they were in the fifth grade and they had been fooling around with their hair and Linda did Joy's hair in a pompadour just like the big girls' and Joy thought it was beautiful and couldn't help crying out to Mother, 'Doesn't my hair look great?' She knew Mother wouldn't let her keep it like that it was too grown-up but Mother just looked at it and turned her mouth down a little and said it looked cheap. Or the time she and Anastasia were playing Chinese checkers and she won and she cried out and told Mommy and Daddy, and Daddy said she was making it up, because she could never beat Anastasia. Or the time Mother acted as if Joy was . . . something awful . . . because she loved to play with Cetta, and Cetta's nose was always running. Undiscriminating. Yes. Or the time she looked at Joy and shook her head and said in that awful voice, 'Always running, always out, you're just like Mrs Dabrowski!' Joy didn't remember Mrs Dabrowski but she understood it was not good to be like her.

Still sometimes Joy just drops a remark like 'Kitty is so pretty isn't she?' and waits to hear something maybe she might say 'Yes but so are you' or something like that. But she never does. But she never yells at Joy for failing a test either the way Kitty's father does he makes Kitty cry. It is so unfair Kitty can't help it that she isn't smart can she? If you try to understand and you pay attention in class as well as you can and do your homework then you can't help it if you don't get good grades can you? Mother never scolds but she never smiles either. Most of the time it feels as if Mother isn't there at all as if the house is empty even though someone cooks dinner and washes and irons the clothes the way all mothers do but the person wasn't real, it didn't talk. Kitty doesn't have a mother and their maid Sarah does all the work but when we go to Kitty's house after school, Sarah sits on her high stool in the kitchen and gives us Cokes and potato chips and talks to us and laughs. But here it feels empty, as though there's no one home Mother is always up in her room making those hats it feels as if there's no air as if no window was ever opened and the smells of all the old dinners are hanging on the wallpaper and the curtains . . .

But sometimes when Anastasia lived here she would talk to her sometimes. But she never talks to me or Daddy we are the outsiders. And sometimes I try to talk to Daddy but he doesn't talk to me except to scold me for always saying 'You know?' after I say something. But I can't help it. Anastasia used to do it too. Because if you talk and talk to a person and they don't answer, they don't even say Yes, or Um-hm, or anything, you just can't help it, you have to get them to say something, so you say 'You know?' to get her to say something. You can never be sure Mother is even listening when you talk, sometimes she is looking far away out of the window or out at nothing.

But sometimes she's in a good mood. Some nights if Joy isn't baby-sitting Mother says 'How about a game of Chinese checkers?' They are good players Daddy won't play with them. They take turns winning the three of them Mother Anastasia and Joy they play with two sets of marbles each and fly across the board so fast that Penny said when she watched them one time that she couldn't follow their jumps. Mother likes to do the crossword puzzle in the *Sunday Times* too and she asked Joy to do it with her the way Anastasia used to but Joy couldn't do it so Mother doesn't ask her anymore. She knows she disappoints Mother and she wishes she didn't but she can't help it. She loves to play gin rummy she's really lucky at it she always wins really fast just a couple of draws and she has gin so now Mother won't play gin unless Joy is sick. She hasn't been sick in a long time, she's healthy now.

But once in a while Mother sits down in the porch and lights a cigarette and asks Joy a question and Joy knows she wants to talk and if Joy isn't going out she pours herself a Coke and sits down across from Mother. Joy knows she wants to hear about her friends and their mothers and fathers and how they live. Mother seemed happy when Joy told her that Linda's house was as small as theirs but she was impressed that Mrs Hale can support her three daughters all by herself working as a bookkeeper. She acted like she'd like to be Mrs Hale even though Mrs Hale is a widow. Joy sometimes wishes Mother was Mrs Hale too. Mrs Hale is fun she laughs and jokes with Linda and Mae even though she's much older than Mommy, she has grey hair. Linda's oldest sister Silvia is grown up and married and lives in Ohio.

But Mother especially loves to hear about Penny's family the Swopes although that isn't Penny's real name Mr Swope adopted Penny and her brother when he married their mother Penny's brother goes to Princeton he's much older he never even looks at Joy or Linda or Kitty when he's there he has his own car a red convertible but he's really stuck-up. Mother loves to hear about Mrs Swope's clothes and how they have cocktails every night before dinner and how the maid serves the meal and what they had to eat. She loves it when Joy says that their dinners are not as good as Mother's even though they have a maid *and* a cook. And neither are the dinners at the McArdles,

Kitty's family, of course Sarah is all they have. Their dinners are all like the Carpenters' Anastasia always makes fun of the Carpenters' Sunday dinners – one thin slice of London broil Joy didn't know what London broil was and a baked potato and one teaspoonful of canned peas and a salad made of lettuce with a peach half and mayonnaise. Anastasia says it's wasp food, Joy doesn't understand what she means, wasps don't eat do they? Joy is always starving when she eats at the McArdles' at home she gets three lamb chops or pork chops one time she had five they were small and big heaps of vegetables and potatoes and no salad but she doesn't really mind because you don't eat dinner out to eat, you do it to be with people you like and besides, she loves canned peaches and canned fruit salad which they have when they don't have peaches. But she tells Mother how awful their dinners are because she knows it makes her happy and she loves to make Mother happy when she can.

Never before has Joy sat by a window and smoked. Mother does but she does it downstairs in the porch in the daytime, but Joy vaguely remembers Mother smoking downstairs when it was dark and all the lights were out. Joy likes to be doing things, she likes to be out with her friends. They go to games, well of course they have to they're the cheerleaders and they go to movies and sometimes they go to bars at night with the boys in their cars and Joy has a rum and Coke and her ears start to ring. But when she isn't going places or sitting around laughing and having fun with her friends she sleeps. Usually, she falls asleep as soon as her head hits the pillow she can never even remember lying down. But for the last two days, ever since, she can't sleep. So tonight she thought she would try what they do, Mother and Anastasia. If she could find a way to think about it maybe it would go away. But nothing has happened. Now she feels funny, nervous sort of and the cigarette is smoked down. She gets up and goes into the bathroom and runs cold water over it and throws it in the wastebasket. She wonders, as she returns to the dark bedroom, what Mother and Anastasia would feel if they were she. She can't imagine it. They are not like her.

She is not like them. This could not happen to them they wouldn't let it happen to them. Whatever the chemistry of tragedy was, she would never feel it.

four

August 1953.

It felt strange to be back here in this tiny room, so shabby with its one tiny throw rug and the old white pull-back curtains and the faded Indian bedspread. First thing she'd do when she saved some money was fix up this room – after she bought some clothes, she had to have really great clothes for this job, after all she was meeting the public. And Joy knew CBS had hired her at least partly for her looks, that's what a receptionist is, someone who looks pleasant and attractive. She feels surer of herself than she used to, she knows she presents a pleasant appearance but she will definitely sign up for that course in modeling, they teach you how to do your hair and makeup and all that, things she feels nervous about but everyone always tells her she's pretty, maybe if she gained confidence she could even be a model someday.

It was so exciting to sit there and watch people go by and wonder if they were someone famous, the other day she was sure she saw Kathryn Grayson, and Alison, who sat in the secretaries pool said she was always seeing stars, she saw Jayne Meadows just last week. So she wanted to be well-dressed, she had planned it all out, two good wool dresses, one basic black just in case she met anyone and was invited to the theater or something like that, and two suits with different blouses. Her school clothes were not really appropriate in this job although she has to wear them for a while longer.

It felt great to get that pay envelope every Friday too, of course thirty-five dollars and sixty cents which was all that was left after taxes and all the things they deducted wasn't as much as she thought it would be well of course she thought she was getting forty-five dollars a week she didn't realize about the deductions. And the commutation alone was over five dollars a week, and there were lunches too and Mother insisted she give her ten dollars a week for food, that hurt her feelings as if now that she was grown up she didn't belong to the family anymore. Still she had determined to set aside ten dollars a week for clothes and to fix her room, and when she and Alison went shopping last Friday night – oh, that was fun, they had dinner in Schrafft's and walked through all the big stores, Macy's Altman's they even went into Lord & Taylor's – she saw a suit she really loved, a creamy wool in a soft blue color that matched her eyes, it was beautiful, maybe it would be reduced thirty-five dollars was sort of a lot but maybe she'd try to save up for it . . .

If she wanted to buy clothes, it would be a long time before she could afford to fix up her room. Maybe for her birthday in October Mother would make her new curtains and bedspread and a vanity skirt, that one was really faded and limp, she could ask her, she'd made a bedspread and curtains for Anastasia's sweet sixteen.

It was sort of hard to stay in this room now. Expecially after visiting Pam's house in Palm Beach, only their summer house too, and they had another one someplace in Switzerland, some funny word starting with a *G* and an *S*, she couldn't pronounce it. And their main house was in Connecticut, she'd seen pictures of it it was even bigger than the one in Florida. Pam's room had its own verandah, with chaises and little tables and even a radio and she had a TV set in her bedroom, white wall-to-wall carpet, and all those windows, oh it was gorgeous! She felt lucky to be liked by someone like Pamela, so far above her, it was so nice of her to invite Joy, she knew Joy had no money but she liked her anyway. And Mrs Johnson was always very nice to her too, and Mr Johnson always made a great fuss over her, of course he was practically never there.

But still she was more comfortable with Kitty and Linda, and her own house, even this room, well, she wasn't in it much, only at nights and she always fell asleep the minute her head hit the pillow, she never even remembered lying down. The rest of the house looked better now since Mother had bought some end tables and a new dining room set and rugs, it was starting to look like other people's houses, that was nice. Funny she wasn't tired tonight though. If she just hadn't gone into Schoelerman's, they could have had a soda anywhere, it was just like last time only that was at Eckhoff's. It just didn't go away even though it had been four years, almost four years, she and Whit started to date in her sophomore year in October, yes, just before her birthday, 1949 and this was 1953, a long time. But it was still there like a burr sometimes people put a burr under a horse's saddle to drive them crazy cruel but that's exactly how it felt only it was in her heart. She knew she must have changed color, it was humiliating, but she couldn't help it, her heart started to pound and the ache, oh the ache was terrible, like a burn, a poker stuck right in her heart. He seemed to blush too so at least she wasn't the only one, he was embarrassed, but he said hello as if he hardly knew her, as if they'd just been in the same home-room or something five years ago.

Joy rose from the bed and switched on a small lamp standing on her vanity. She fished in her purse, found a cigarette, and lighted it. She picked up the china ashtray with little pink roses on it and carried it back to bed. Sheets are rumpled, maybe that's the trouble. She leaned back against the hard wooden headboard of the bed and smoked, gazing toward the window. Moonlight paved the floor and the foot of the bed with pale light, but from this angle she could see only the roof of the Gwyns' garage. She could hear the crickets though, and sense the soft dampness of the night.

Duke, he said, that was an expensive college, maybe it wasn't too hard, Whit never got good grades, he was like her. He looked older, his face had a strain in it that wasn't there when they no not even two years ago when she ran into him at Eckhoff's. All the kids still hung out at the same places, Eckhoff's, and Schoelerman's for Cokes or milk shakes and the Arbor Inn and the Shamrock for drinking. Buddy Raft and T.J. had a terrible accident after leaving the Shamrock, last Christmas they said, Buddy was killed. Funny to think of him dead. Fat, round, always boozing but he was really sweet, he was frightened I think, that's why he acted like such a bully sometimes. But he was always sweet to me, I think he liked me. He never asked me out though but that was just as well it would have been embarrassing I would have had to say no, I couldn't have brought myself to go out with him imagine kissing him ugh! But now he's dead it's so sad. And Penny's brother too, his convertible turned over on the New Jersey Turnpike, Penny's mother was in a sanitarium someplace, they stuck Penny in some fancy boarding school in Switzerland, but she ran away. The postcard she sent me was from Paris, I wonder if she's there all alone god I'd be terrified.

And I had a letter from Jane Selby too, I have good friends, I love my friends, she hates being back in Iowa, she wants to come to New York and get an apartment with me I'd be scared and Mother wouldn't like it but maybe who knows. Her parents won't let her go but she says after she's twenty-one in September that's just next month she can and will do as she likes. That's exactly what she wrote: 'As soon as I'm twenty-one, I can and will do as I like.' She's got nerve, she's terrific. Her brother should be finishing West Point soon, time I went up there with her, gala weekend, blind date for her brother, a dance no a ball Saturday night and riding the next day, that was fun, I had a ball, it was such a beautiful place, and the ball, all those uniforms, it was like a movie. She was so sure he'd like me, I thought he did but then I never heard from him. Jane said he was failing physics she said if I wrote him not to mention that he'd be embarrassed that she told me. She said he had to cram so that was why. But I couldn't write to him if he didn't write to me, I just wouldn't do that. Anyway, he's had plenty of time to write and he hasn't, the gala weekend was last April, a long time ago, six months nearly. And it's summer and they don't have to take physics in summer do they? I wonder if they get a vacation, I should have asked him, I was so nervous with him, he's so much older than me, he's been in the army and everything, that's why he's still in college even though he's twenty-four, he enlisted and then the war ended, he was really disappointed Jane said but then they sent him to Korea there was another war there too but then he got into West

Point so he was really happy. He has a wonderful name, Justin. Unusual.

Yes he was nice, all of them are nice but it's not the same, I just don't feel the same way about them. Maybe I never will, my whole life long, maybe that's my fate, could that be? Kitty and Ted, going together since sophomore year and they're going to get married as soon as Ted finishes school Georgia Tech, and both their families are happy about it, they like the other one, of course Kitty's father is rich too. Not rich rich, like Whit's family, but pretty rich, they have a maid and that nice house. And Linda too, pinned to John Burton that she met at college, he was a senior, but he's only four years older that's not too much, it's just right. They're going to get married at Christmas. Kitty has to wait two years but they've been going together so long I suppose it doesn't matter. They'll both be married then. Who knows. Whit might be too.

She wiped her wet face with the end of the sheet, then shook her head, got up and went into the bathroom, pulled a long string of toilet paper from the roll and blew her nose over and over. She dropped the sodden wad into the toilet and flushed it. But her mouth was wobbly and she felt she might be sick, so she bent over the sink and took handsful of cold water and sipped it, then she cooled her face with it.

She went back to her room, stopped to light another cigarette, and climbed into the damp rumpled bed. The last time it was June, finals week, she couldn't study, couldn't concentrate. That's why her marks . . . His school must have let out earlier than the public schools. He looked the same but not the same. His face was the same except a light had gone out in him. He said 'Hi Joy' but his eyes stayed pale, the light didn't go on in them the way they used to when they saw her. And his body didn't look as if it wanted to move toward her and she had to hold her own body back so it wouldn't embarrass her. She knew she'd known for a long time. Still, to know something is one thing, and to see it is another. To see it right in front of you, to feel it . . .

That time she didn't know what to do, she felt so terrible.

Her friends all talked about their boyfriends even when they hurt them but she never talked to anyone about Whit not even when they were together in their sophomore year he and she always together, people talked about them because they were always together. Sometimes they held hands but they didn't make a show of things the way some of the kids did Betty Brower and Bill Binns always with their arms around each other he six feet she five feet tall so that everyone laughed at them but it was kind laughter it made them feel important they thought they were cute and they were even if they were always kissing for an audience. Whit was tall too and she was short but not as short as Betty Brower but they didn't hang on each other that way. They walked quietly side by side.

They were quiet and private. They hardly even talked very much. They talked a little they laughed at things but mostly they just looked at each other their beings tremulous like tiny hairs trembling in a faint wind Whit's eyes so blue just the same color as hers identical eyes everyone said. They saw their own eyes in each other. 'They can do anything they want,' Whit had said 'but they can't separate us they can't make me forget you.' And he had written her every week for the first few months he was at Concord. It was after Christmas that he changed, what happened? Because he came over at Christmas, they went out for long walks together, they were the same, even more so, they said they would love each other forever, that nothing could come between them. He had to sneak out of the house, he had to lie, he hated it, he was near tears sometimes, he said they made him feel like a kid or a prisoner the way they kept after him. And Mother always said hello to him so politely as if it wasn't a surprise to see him, as if nothing had happened, maybe she didn't know anything had, she didn't notice, she wasn't interested. She wouldn't understand, that could never happen to her, Daddy bends over backward to please her . . .

Then they took him away skiing, yes, someplace in Iowa or Idaho, and she didn't see him again that vacation and after that he didn't write so often and his letters didn't have the same feeling. And when he wrote in May he said they were going to Maine for the summer and he wouldn't be in Rockville Centre at all but she knew that wasn't true, he had to come home to get his summer clothes and to leave his books and things from school. And that was his last letter.

She always went around the block when she was going anywhere near where he lived so she wouldn't meet him accidentally he'd think she was trying to catch sight of him, unless she was in a car with one of her friends, then she'd keep her head straight ahead but strain her eyes at the corners trying to see the house always looked empty, the drapes hanging straight, sometimes a gardener was working there and once she saw his mother's Cadillac in the driveway but usually there was nothing you couldn't tell anyone lived there his sister was gone and married and Whit was their only son, one and only, they expected everything of him.

And then after all that she'd bumped into him at Eckhoff's. And now again, two years later. Maybe they'd meet every two years at Eckhoff's but Eckhoff's was going now, Mr Eckhoff was retiring, too bad he had such good ice cream such a tall man with his shining bald head shaped like an egg, he was nice even if he was stern with the kids, once he threw Forrest Kelly right out on the sidewalk but he deserved it he was throwing spoonfuls of milk shake at all the guys in his booth, he had to be a little stern the boys were so wild. Not Whit. He was never loud or wild, just sweet, always, gentle he had a soft low laugh that sounded like a faint rumble, still he was a terrific basketball player, he hated to leave Southside it broke his heart he was a letterman in his sophomore year, he was going to be captain of the team the next year even though he was only a junior.

Joy got out of bed again and dug in her purse for a tissue and blew her nose. She gazed at the rumpled mess of sheets and thought about remaking the bed. But she felt too tired. The alarm clock read twenty of two. She turned out the light on the vanity and climbed back in and lay down and closed her eyes. But nothing happened.

I have to sleep, I have to get up tomorrow. 7.50 train,

Mother drives me, it's nice, I feel so grown up on the train with all those men with their newspapers. Tomorrow I'll wear my navy blue cotton skirt, the wide flaring one, with the short-sleeved white blouse Mother ironed today and my wide navy belt. And white heels and bag and earrings. That will look nice. Mrs Hooper came up to me this morning and said 'How pretty you look, Joy, just like a ray of sunshine!' And last week she told me my typing was excellent. Still, I don't think I'd want to stay at CBS forever, I'd just go on being a receptionist or a secretary. That modeling course should be fun and maybe it will lead to something. Because I probably won't ever get married now.

Just because we were poor. They were that frightened of a pimply-faced fifteen-year-old girl from the wrong sort of family not their kind. So frightened they were willing to make him miserable, sending him away. But they won, he forgot me.

I never really knew before that that we were poor. Or I knew but I didn't know that it mattered. Or how much it mattered. Or was that all it was, was there something else? Something about me?

Seeing him standing there today, paying his check, oh if only we'd gone a half hour later, they'd have been gone, I wouldn't have had to see her, I wonder who she is she's not from here, she looked rich probably some family friend, oh, who would expect him to be in Rockville Centre on a Sunday afternoon, August, why aren't they in Maine, maybe they feel he's safe now, they don't have to take him away. And I had to be with Kitty and Linda, not even with a boy any boy, well not any boy but some presentable boy why did that have to happen?

But that wasn't the worst thing, the worst thing was that when I looked at him it was just the same, just as if we were still sophomores in the same homeroom, and one of us who was earlier was watching the door until the other came in and then when we smiled at each other the whole world got brighter as if our smiles brightened darkness. W.T.C. Whitman IV he signed himself I used to tease him about it. He must have been in Maine sailing he loved to

507

sail I've never been on a sailboat, he was going to take me sometime, he probably takes her, they were both so tan, he was bronze his blue eyes so pale in his bronze face he still has freckles, he isn't quite as thin, his long hands are still beautiful.

She ran her hands across the skin of her belly and up her sides. Whit's hands. They never. They were too frightened but it was what they wanted, would always want, forever. . . .

He never told her what they said, why they were sending him away. He was crying. He just spattered words, his father, his mother, all they care about, well they had such expectations, he was the only son, what expectations? she had wondered, but he never said it straight out but she knew, she heard, even though it was unimaginable to her, who would go out with a boy just because he was rich? Well, put that way, maybe someone would, but she Joy she'd never thought about it except she did like his house, so huge on such a big plot with all those big trees but she was only in it once or twice they never went there that was funny their crowd always hung out at Ted's or Kitty's or Linda's, but Whit always came to her house and they went for walks. She only saw his mother once, a blond lady in a mink coat.

The last summer before he left they gave him some freedom, they weren't worried, they were getting him away from her, and they would walk for hours, over to Hempstead State Park and then wander around it. And he gave her a chain with a pearl on it and said that was for constancy. And she cried. And he cried. And they swore.

Forever. She sat up and reached over her head for the switch on the little wall lamp over her bed. She got out of bed and opened the bottom drawer of her bureau and removed a box. It was heart-shaped and made of satin, and smelled of chocolate, his gift to her Valentine's Day their sophomore year. She opened it. Thirty-three letters. She knew them all by heart. There was no place here she could start a fire. Hands trembling she set the box on the floor and sank down beside it. No place in the house she could start a fire now. She'd have to wait until winter when they had a fire in the fireplace but then they'd ask they'd want to know what are you burning why are you burning them? The box was a knife her hands were cut across it would be forever for her.

It was no different now. She felt the same way and she still couldn't talk about him, not even to Kitty and Linda, although they knew, they were right there walking in the doorway with her when she stopped, he was at the cash register, they must have seen her face, and after he was gone, Linda put her arm around Joy's back and made a joke about something she couldn't really hear it, and they paid for her soda, they said it was a celebration of her getting the job at CBS, but she'd gotten that three weeks ago, she'd started work last week they knew that but it was all right, they understood and she understood.

She bent her head and reached up and pulled the thin chain over her head and threw it in the box. Then she picked it up again, gently, apologizing, and tried to look at the pearl but she couldn't see it her eyes were too full. She replaced it in the box and a great deep sob came out of her mouth, as if she were a ghoul or a spirit, and then more kept coming and she tried to keep them quiet even though she knew that Mother couldn't hear her because she slept on her good ear and Daddy slept soundly and even if he heard her he wouldn't think anything of it, he wouldn't get up. It was silly to worry about making noise when there was no one who cared.

June 1954.

So.

Over.

Morning light, leafgreen, revealed the dust on the wooden arms of the porch furniture, settled on the cheap tweed rug. Belle sipped her coffee and reached for her cigarettes.

Over. Finally.

Oh of course not really over, it will take a year to pay off the bills, but now I can imagine an end, plan for it, have my own life. Not so old, only fifty. My hair is still blond, there's hardly any grey and it doesn't show. I haven't gotten fat. And I did well. She looked lovely, really lovely, and she was happy, I think she was. I wasn't sure it would ever happen, I wasn't sure she'd ever get over that boy, rich boy, sent away to separate him from her, we were too poor for them, too low-class. She never told me. But I saw the pain in her eyes, heard the hysteria in her laugh, she's a funny child, she keeps everything in but things go deep in her. Loves. Kitty and Linda her brides-maids, still her best friends, all married, living far from each other, clear across the country, but they're still as close as ever, they love each other.

Beautiful dress. I wish Anastasia could have had one like it, could have had a wedding like that. She could have, I would have borrowed, I would have given her a wedding like Joy's. Still, you can't predict, here they are married only five years and they have a house like that in this town, Brad's a better provider than Ed, it took me over forty years to get to Rockville Centre. Nice place for the kids to grow up in, big yard, big old trees, quiet street, good schools, they can stay in one place and have friends and grow up and know everyone. Anastasia never had that, neither did I. Joy did, we moved here while she was young enough, she makes friends. And Joy will be comfortable too, West Point graduate, he'll always make a good living. Stationed in Germany, they'll have servants there she said and a nice old house. She wants me to come and visit them there, maybe I will.

Oh how I used to long to travel, I dreamed of seeing Europe, Paris and Rome and the Alps and here she is, only twenty years old, with such an opportunity. Justin said they'd take trips when he has leave, I wonder where they'll go, he'll have a car, an officer. His family has money. Iowa. They invited me, well, us, Ed and me, I don't think I want to go to Iowa, they'd probably look down on us anyway.

But maybe they couldn't tell, the wedding was lovely, it looked expensive, just the way she wanted it, ceremony at 'The Point' – what an affectation – swords crossed over their heads, silly, but I suppose when you're young it seems glamorous. Joy cares about things like that, well, who knows at her age I might have been impressed by that too, still she's not like me. I never had a wedding at all, that cruel priest screaming at Ed . . . Usually the bride's family decides where the reception will be held but what could we do, she wanted to be married at that place, well it's pretty I guess, all those stone buildings, and that monument in the center, what did Anastasia say, an inflexible pillar surrounded by cannonballs, she was making some kind of joke but only Eric laughed, no not pillar, fallar or something, I didn't hear, my hearing is so bad I miss everything, everyone is laughing but I sit there like a stupid lump. Brad looked at her so coldly when she said it, well of course, she was mocking because she was jealous, she never had a wedding at all, she pretends she doesn't care but she does. But he's different now that he's making money, acts like a big man, pompous, very different from the way he was when she married him, there seems to be something, maybe she doesn't want to sleep with him all the time, who could blame her? but she doesn't seem to care even when he snaps at her the way he did when she was dancing with Eric for such a long time. She doesn't notice anything though, all she cares about is taking pictures. Expensive hobby.

Expensive, twelve-fifty a person for a hundred people and the Selbys wanted to invite more, they were even willing to pay for them themselves but I wouldn't allow it, it was insulting. I can't believe that many of their friends would have come all the way from Iowa, you wonder how they could even have that many friends. Then the flowers and the music and our wedding gift to them, lucky Joy was able to pay for her own gown but mine was fifty dollars and the hat, so lovely, a shame I'll probably never have another chance to wear it, that was eighteen ninety-nine. Well, I'm not going to worry about it now, I'll add up the bills this afternoon, but it will probably be over fifteen hundred. That will take me two years to pay off unless Ed gets another raise, he might, he's doing better now, he made almost eight thousand dollars last year with his bonus, maybe we'll be able to save something from his pay too. But he has another year of payments on the Cadillac, three-year loan. And he had to have a Cadillac, well he should, he deserves it, he works hard and he doesn't have anything else, there's nothing else he wants . . .

She has what she wants, I hope, the roses and the champagne and all her friends there, honeymoon in Bermuda, Anastasia never had a honeymoon, neither did I of course. I don't know why I should feel sorry for her. *Wages of sin.* What a ridiculous thing to say, that's what Anastasia would say if she heard me, I don't know why I thought that myself.

Belle turned her head slightly at a sound from outside.

Mrs Brand's going to the grocery store. They've had that car ever since we live here, it's so old. I wonder how she feels, if she's embarrassed when she looks around at her neighbors.

Belle gazed at the shiny sleek six-year-old beige Cadillac parked in her own driveway. As she looked, the corners of her lips tilted down slightly, and she raised her chin.

We looked good at the wedding, no one would be able to tell. Jean said I was the best-dressed woman there, even though his people have money, you can see that they do, but Iowa, well, there probably aren't any good dress shops there. Good thing Anastasia was matron of honor and had to wear a nice dress and shoes. She even had her hair curled, she looked quite pretty, both my girls are lovely, Joy looked so beautiful, they're lovely girls.

And now they're both married. Off my hands.

Well, of course, Joy hasn't been a burden since she finished college, well, not really a college, what a thing, to teach girls how to walk and how tables should be laid, 'No, Mom, the flatware is placed according to the order in which it will be used, you put the small fork on the outside only if you are going to serve a salad first, see?' As if I cared. How long did it take me to pay for that silver, sterling, saving all the while the baby was growing inside me, crying every day every night, living at home so I could save . . . Still, I'm glad I have it, I could see the Carpenters were surprised when they first came to dinner, they probably thought we had nothing, so snooty, members of the country club, and if the Selbys ever come to visit, it will make a good appearance. By then maybe I'll have a new bedroom set, I'm so thankful I bought that dining room set when it was on sale, prices have gone up since then. At least there's something in the room, not that old wooden table and the sewing machine painted grey and the wooden chairs that used to embarrass Anastasia when her high-school friends came, I knew even though she never said anything, she'd consider it beneath her to care what they thought, but she did just the same.

She tries to be superior, she acts as if she doesn't notice things, but she notices everything. When I said the Selbys were rich, she said maybe they were but they hadn't always been and I was astonished. 'How do you know that?' And she pointed to Mrs Selby's hands, it's true they were red and swollen, much worse than mine, and when you think how hard I have worked in my life, cooking dinner on a wood stove since I was nine years old, washing clothes on a washboard, wringing them out, how that used to hurt my hands, and all the dishes I've washed in my life, although Ed did help at night, and all the peeling and cutting and handling hot pots I've done, it's true my hands have stayed fairly good, but it does make you wonder, as Anastasia said, what Mrs Selby has been doing with hers . . . But I think she was trying to make me feel confident, she's always doing that, manipulating me. She should know how I see through her.

Joy doesn't do that. She doesn't care. But she can be fun, she makes me laugh with her stories. She's never been close to me, always out with her friends, I've hardly seen her the last year since she's been home. Glamorous job in the city, all dressed up every day, her whole salary on clothes. I did the same thing when I was her age. A place like CBS must have thousands of girls who want to work there, so if they chose her, that means she was really something special, well she has such a beautiful smile, she always did, she could melt my heart when she was a baby when she'd smile at me . . . She had fun, as she should, now she's married, she'll be married the rest of her life, she should have one year of fun.

Maybe I'll just have one more cup. Belle rose, went to the kitchen, and turned up the flame under the coffeepot.

She sat down heavily on a wooden kitchen chair and waited for the coffee to heat.

Empty house, now. Quiet and peace. No one else to think about. Not that Joy was noisy, not at all, she was never here. And when she was here, always ready with a smile, not sullen like Anastasia, and she always gave me her ten dollars board without my asking, and somehow she managed to save some money too, I have good girls. Nice that Kitty and Linda could come all this way for her wedding, and Pamela too, so rich, her father's a billionaire, came all the way from Paris for Joy, she must love Joy, she made a lot of important friends at that college. You could tell she came from money. Her hair was so smooth and such a beautiful color and she was dressed so beautifully, you could see she'd always had servants and never had to worry or scrimp or feel stupid the way I have. But she was very nice to me, gracious, and when Joy and she were standing together, they looked almost the same, of course Joy doesn't have quite the same confidence, the same polish . . .

I wonder whether she really loves him though. Ach, what difference does it make? After a couple of years all that is over anyway. I remember how I felt about Ed oh that was such a long time ago, it doesn't mean anything. As long as he is a good provider and isn't cruel to the children, Ed wasn't a good father but I wouldn't let him hit them or yell at them of course he mumbled and muttered, he thought I couldn't hear, but I knew, I knew. Still I didn't let him act the way my father acted.

He seems a nice boy, quiet, stable, both my sons-in-law are good boys. Brad is quiet and stable now too. They'll be back from Bermuda next Sunday night, they'll stay here until they ship out, is that what he said, ship out? what shall I have for dinner? A roast, maybe lamb, with browned potatoes and green peas and some other vegetable that everybody likes, I wish I knew what he ate, maybe I'll invite Anastasia and Brad and the kids, she won't see Joy again for a long time, three years they have to stay there, I wonder if she'll get lonely, but she makes friends every-where she goes, she's gregarious, she's like Mrs Dabrowski not like me. Not green beans, that would be two green vegetables, maybe carrots the way I make them in butter and sugar. Is that too boring, peas and carrots? Maybe cauliflower with cheese sauce if it isn't too expensive. Beets. No, Brad doesn't like beets, and Arden really hates them, that funny picture Anastasia took of Arden in her high chair spitting out beets.

Joy will probably see Paris before I ever do.

Well, I wanted my girls to have every chance, everything I didn't have, and they do, it's the best you can hope for with a girl, marriage to a man who will provide, life that isn't utter slavery day in day out the way mine has been.

She finished her coffee, and set the cup in the sink. She looked at the clock. She walked into the dining room and stood still. It was really a lovely room. The new Chinese wallpaper was beautiful, and the pale blue in the rug picked up the pale blue shading on the bottom of the cherry branches. Her dining room. What would Momma have said if she had known I would ever have a room like this in my house?

She put her hand on her heart. Sometimes she thought her old bad heart was acting up again, so often she felt something sore there, as if she had a wound that had never healed, a cut or something, right on her heart. But that wasn't possible, was it. You've done well, she told herself. Both your girls are married to nice boys and they are going to have opportunities you yearned for, oh longed for, oh how you longed! They would have better lives and their children would not lack for anything even though of course Anastasia had a bad start and they had to live in that awful little attic room, and then that tiny apartment, but it was all over now, she could be proud of both her girls.

A motion in the street caught her eye and she walked to the front dining room window. A car had pulled up in front of the Lynches'. She peered out without moving the curtain. She wasn't wearing her glasses, and she had to squint. Yes, it was Rosemary, she visited her mother every day, imagine! With both the children, so little, just babies really, and Rosemary looked as if she were pregnant again. And every day Mrs Lynch had them there! Anastasia had a friend who had seven children, it was disgusting, she told Anastasia it was disgusting and Anastasia looked at her so funny, as if she were crazy or something, and said 'Why should you care? Why should you get so upset?' She wasn't upset, she was just disgusted, it was revolting, why should you need to put out that many children, like a disgusting animal putting them out putting them out putting them out . . . But Anastasia didn't like to visit her friend, what was her name, some Irish or Italian name, Catholic, of course, she didn't enjoy spending time in a house with seven little children well who would?

No, two, and then no matter what a struggle it is they grow up and they're gone when there's still time to think about yourself, you have a little life left in you. Poor Mrs Lynch, she was so pretty once but no teeth in the front of her mouth, it is shocking really, such a nice house and he certainly spends money on his fun with that red nose, but she can't afford to have her teeth fixed, and she's young still, younger than I, I'll bet she isn't forty-eight yet.

Maybe, if Ed gets a nice bonus this Christmas and I can spread the wedding payments out over a year and a half, we could go. Heidelberg, it is supposed to be beautiful there. And maybe we could go to Paris too. How much would that cost?

A familiar dread closed in around her heart.

She stopped herself as she was mounting the stairs. No, really, how much? Two thousand dollars for three weeks? That was all the vacation Ed had. Maybe fifteen hundred. So if he got a thousand-dollar bonus this Christmas and she made more hats than usual and saved every penny . . . they could eat more cheaply now there were only two of them, and she always watched every penny . . . Maybe by the spring, she thought, and something in her heart carried her up the stairs like wings, maybe we could really go.

To Europe!

She reached the bedroom. It was hot up here, it was a hot day. She walked across the room and drew the shades down two thirds of the window length. Hot. She would work in her slip. She pulled off her blouse and skirt, and sat down on her work chair facing the sewing machine. She looked over at the small pile of white organdy hats standing near the corner of Ed's chest of drawers. She'd love to get a new bedroom set too. But if they went to Germany next year, she would be able to visit Joy. She could see where she lived and how, it would be easier to think about her if she could picture it.

She sat utterly still for a moment; her body wanted to slump, it felt tired already and it was only eleven in the morning. Oh, if only . . . she reached for a cigarette. She took a few puffs, raising her head to blow the smoke out. Then she pushed her chair closer to the machine, laid the cigarette in an ashtray, and switched on the small lamp on her vanity. She tried to pick up a circle of organdy, but the thin fabric made several circles stick together, and she had to wet her fingers with saliva before she could separate one. Finally, she laid it on the machine, under the needle, and reached down into a cardboard carton for a length of ruching. She laid the ruching on the organdy, bent her head over the machine, put her feet on the pedal, and gave the wheel a sharp tug to start it. Then she began to work.

five

August 1957.

Rockville Centre. Outdoors.

Kodak 135 Color film, ASA 100, bright afternoon sunlight, apertures as marked, fifty-foot zoom wide-angle and portrait lenses on the Leica.

Photo 1. Taken at twenty feet with w/a lens. In the foreground are two people. Belle Stevens is looking well-to-do and fashionable, wearing a white linen halter dress with a full skirt. Sequined appliqués adorn the pocket of the skirt and the borders of a fine white wool sweater that matches the dress but is presently hanging over the back of the freshly painted white Adirondack chair on which she sits. Her shoes are wedgies with twisted leather straps crisscrossing the instep. The straps are white and brown. Belle's blond hair is short and softly dressed, and kept in place by hair spray, a relatively new invention. At this distance, it is difficult to see facial details, but Belle is smiling, leaning back, and holding a tall glass with ice in it. Sitting opposite her in an outdoor chair made of aluminum with pale green plastic strips interwoven on seat and back, but leaning forward, talking, is

Joy Selby, her daughter. Joy is also well-dressed. She has chosen for this occasion a pale blue cotton so highly brushed it looks like satin. It has tiny straps over the shoulders, and a narrow bodice, with horizontal pleats and a single small button at the center. At the waist is a two-inch-wide matching belt above a full skirt. Joy is wearing white high-heeled sandals, and carries a white leather handbag. At present, the bag is lying against the chair leg, in the grass, which in this picture is very green. Her hair is very short and very blond. She looks smart, even glamorous with her white button earrings, her well-applied makeup, and her broad smile. She is so attractive she could have stepped right out of an ad in *World* magazine, any of the ads propagating a new postwar image of domestic bliss which can be achieved through the purchase of a certain make of car, breakfast cereal, soap, or sanitary napkins. Joy could pose in any of these ads, because although her attractiveness verges on glamor, she looks wholesome, a girl you would not feel intimidated by, a girl who would not threaten your family stability.

In the rear right hand of the photograph are several figures, some of which are a bit blurred because they were in motion when the picture was snapped. Those in motion are Billy, aged seven, who is in the act of throwing up his hands and opening his mouth in what appears to be a huge guffaw, after having gently tossed a softball to Jonathan, aged two, who has reached so far forward for the ball that he has tilted, like a board, clear over into the grass. Jonathan is about to ruin his beautiful little blue suit, a handknit from Germany with a matching coat and hat which presently lie upstairs in a drawer in Joy's old bedroom which also holds several suitcases, a crib and a cot, as well as Joy's makeup, hair spray, curlers, setting lotion, hair dryer, comb and brush, and her large bottle of Joy perfume, one of many purchased recently, duty- and tax-free, at a PX near Heidelberg, Germany. Billy is wearing jeans and a red-and-white-striped polo shirt, with sneakers. No one has made a comment about his attire. Similar clothing is being worn by his sister,

Arden, who as a girl and an eight-year-old, might be expected to have worn a dress, dainty white socks, and Mary Janes. It is true that such clothing would be ruined by her present activity, lying on her stomach directly on the grass, reading a book in the slight shade offered by a flowering crab apple tree not presently in bloom. This tree will, a decade hence, be struck by lightning in a storm, and be cut up for firewood. Arden occasionally looks up and toys with

Julie, a tiny girl, six months old, strapped into a slanted baby-carrier, who occasionally wakes and looks around blinking. She is wearing a hand-embroidered dress of fine handkerchief linen, in an appropriate pale pink, with lace trim around the round collar and the cuffs, also purchased in Germany. This tiny work of art is somewhat soiled by stains under the child's chin where she dribbled some of the orange juice she was given an hour ago. Her mother sighed.

Several persons present at this gathering are missing from this scene. One is the picture taker, Anastasia Carpenter, who is also dressed inappropriately in short white shorts and a man's shirt tied below the waist, with socks and sneakers. Her long hair is braided into a thick plait that hangs down her back, and she wears no make-up. Her mother greeted her with a silent survey and a proffered cheek. She greeted Arden and Billy with the same survey, although in their case, blame did not adhere to them but to their mother, the picture taker. Therefore Belle kisses the children and hugs them. They like her and they hug her back with energy. This information cannot be found in this picture, nor in any of the pictures. It resides gnawingly in the picture taker's mind.

The others absent from the photograph are Ed Stevens, Wilton Bradley Carpenter, and Justin Selby, Jr. These people are at the moment inside the house, in the kitchen. Ed is fixing drinks. He works silently and efficiently, he seems to be concentrating. From the way he has lined up the bottles, the mixers, a blue glass bowl holding ice cubes, and glasses of various sizes and shapes, an onlooker could deduce that he is trying to perform his task in the same way a machine would – with efficient repetitiousness and economy of movement. Indeed, once he has set up his materials, he does accomplish the task in record time. However, it takes him a long time to set up his materials in the proper order, partly because – and he swears under his breath at the fact – Someone – unquestionably not he and certainly not Belle, who knows that ice cubes are his domain and would not think of interfering with them, but Someone – probably one of the two adults presently residing in the house as guests, and most likely the male adult who can if he wishes hear the smothered curse, standing as he is only a few feet away – Someone has replaced in the freezer a half-empty tray of ice cubes. With noisy angry gestures, Ed empties the five cubes left in the tray into the blue bowl, refills the tray with water, and replaces it in the freezer. Then, sighing audibly, he returns to making drinks. The two other men in the kitchen are talking, but not to Ed. Nor, after the exchange of a short greeting, does he look at them. They are discussing the new jet airplanes.

Photo 2. The men have come outdoors and joined the women. All of them, with the exception of the photographer, are sitting in the aluminum chairs, or the Adirondack chairs softened with yellow-and-white-striped plastic-covered cushions. Now that we can see them, it is clear all of them could appear in an ad for the good life in America. Ed is wearing pale blue summer slacks, a fine white pima cotton shirt, with a silk tie, blue with a red paisley figure, given to him last Christmas by his daughter Anastasia. He wears this tie although he prefers more striking and dramatic patterns and colors, because he has been told his daughter has good taste. His shoes are cordovan moccasins, either brand-new or rarely worn. His socks are old-fashioned, navy blue ribbed cotton and lisle, therefore it is just as well that only a glimpse of them can be caught between his shoe and the cuff of his slacks. Bradley Carpenter is wearing beige linen Daks with Hush Puppies in the same shade, matching his socks and his light knit shirt, short-sleeved, open-collared. Although he is on leave, Justin Selby wears proudly the uniform of the United States Army with a captain's bars on his shoulders.

This shot focuses on the group of adults. Belle is leaning slightly forward as Brad reaches out to light her cigarette. He is smiling at her flirtatiously, and she has a pleased wry expression. Joy's bare back is to the camera — a lovely slender back, tanned by the Mediterranean sun during a week's vacation in Torremolinos which immediately preceded the departure of the Selbys from Germany at the end of Captain Selby's tour of duty and was made possible by the reliability and trustworthiness of their three German servants — maid, cook, and nanny — who will be sorely missed. Justin appears here in profile, his straight black hair combed firmly back, his cheek, smooth and unlined as a statue's, even darker than usual because of the Spanish sun. The blur in the right background is Jonathan doing a somersault.

Photo 3. Another shot of the same people, taken, obviously, after the photographer had hailed those who were turned away from the camera. This time, Belle, Joy, and Justin are facing the camera. Joy is smiling broadly, and appears to be concentrating on her smile. Justin is staring impassively, even sternly, at the camera, concentrating, it would appear, on avoiding any imputation of frivolity. Belle is distracted, she had turned at the last moment to call something out to her husband, who is just barely visible as he leaves the scene to fetch Belle's sunglasses from the house.

Photo 4. Billy, crowing with laughter as Jonathan creates another blur.

Photo 5. Someone has managed to stand Jonathan still, probably Billy, whose hand he holds. They are both smiling with delight. The front of Jonathan's pale blue knit suit is stained with green and brown streaks.

Photo 6. Arden, on her stomach, deeply engrossed, with her legs up in the air swaying to the music of whatever she is reading.

Photo 7. Arden appears to have been summoned, for she

looks up from her book and around at the camera. There is an expression of annoyance and disdain on her face.

Photo 8. The three children stand together. Billy is looking down at Jonathan with great sweetness, smiling, and Jonathan is half-turned, looking up at Billy. Beside them, her legs touching at the knees and feet pointed outwards, Arden glares at this interruption of Laura Ignalls (Arden's pronunciation) Wilder's *Little House on the Prairie*.

Photo 9. Jonathan, in a rare still moment. He is sitting in the grass looking dazed, having just somehow collapsed from his cartwheel, hitting his head. He has a round pink sweet face, big blue eyes, and at the moment, a puzzled expression. These children are very beautiful. The older ones are beautiful too, but their expressions are already clouded and shadowed in ways that prefigure adulthood. There is a tinge of sadness in Billy's face; in Arden's, of anger.

Photo 10. Joy is speaking and gesturing, her smile gleams, her eyes are aware of Justin beside her. He listens, as erect in his chair as if its back were not slanted, his face expressionless except for a slight upturning of the sides of the mouth as he gazes straight out into the camera. Belle is leaning forward in her chair, straining to hear her daughter. Ed is gazing into space.

Photos 11–22. Julie, in various phases. Pictures taken over the course of an hour or two. She has a round pink sweet face, large blue eyes, a happy smile, and a dab of hair poking out from under her fine handkerchief-linen bonnet trimmed with lace. She is caught by the invasive photographer asleep; drooling; with one eye open and one closed; smiling a broad toothless grin and reaching out to someone (her father) whose arms alone are visible; perched happily in her father's arms (his head turned to her, only the back of it visible in the photograph); held more formally and a little uncomfortably, by her mother, who is smiling broadly at the camera; by her grandmother, who seems to be tickling her tummy, and whose face is hidden, although the baby is laughing uncontrollably; on all fours on a small white blanket placed on the grass, head up facing the camera, mouth open, eyes wide, awed, discovering, an explorer.

Photo 23. Justin holds up for the camera a map of Germany and is pointing to the area where Heidelberg is found. Attending upon him are Brad and Ed, both absorbed in the map, Brad holding a glass in his right hand, Ed not. You cannot see Justin's face in this shot.

Photo 24. Joy is presenting Belle with a box, wrapped in flowered paper and a bow.

Photo 25. Belle has opened the box and is holding up a large (one-ounce) bottle of L'Air du Temps, her favorite perfume. In the background, Justin's face is hidden by a movie camera with which he records this scene. The movie camera and the perfume were purchased in the PX at Heidelberg. The movie camera will go on to record other openings of other gifts, Ed holding up an enameled penknife with a nail file, bottle opener, screwdriver, can opener, and other attachments cleverly contained within it. The movie camera will focus on the opening of each of these attachments. It will, briefly, show Anastasia with a strained smile holding up a bottle of Shalimar, Billy holding up a knife similar to Ed's but a little thinner, and Brad holding up a German beer stein. Since the movie camera neglected to record Arden's gift, its nature has been irremediably forgotten.

Photo 26. This is a close-up of Justin with his mouth open. He is speaking. He does not gesture as he speaks, nor does his facial expression change. It is not recorded what he was saying.

Photo 27. The picture taker has changed, and this and the following few shots are not as clearly focused or well-composed as the earlier ones. They are, however, just as cherished by those who received copies of them. Here is Brad, standing smiling behind Anastasia, whose face looks strained and who seems to begrudge the camera a smile. He has a glass in his hand and is toasting the camera. His face is a little lopsided.

Photo 28. Here are Brad and Anastasia standing with their children. The children look off into the distance – Arden's foot is up at the toe, suggesting she is tapping it.

Billy's face is extremely sad, his eyes sunk into their sockets, they seem to grip emptiness: it must be a trick of the light. Anastasia has her hands resting lightly on the children's shoulders, but her face is stiff and strained, its lines deepened and darkened by the sunlight. She looks disdainful. Brad stands behind them, taller, they conceal his emerging potbelly, but not his receding hairline. He is smiling, but here too, his face seems puttylike, unfinished, like a clay head molded by a sculptor who then changed his mind and has begun to change his work. You feel you should throw a cloth over it until it is done.

Photo 29. Belle stands in the center, a stiff smile on her face. Joy stands to her left, smiling broadly at the camera. Anastasia stands to her right, her arm about her mother's shoulder, looking at her with an expression of tenderness.

Photo 30. The original photographer seems to have returned to the job. This picture shows Joy and Justin standing together, Joy smiling broadly, Justin brown and smooth and erect, without expression. Joy's head is turned a little toward her husband as if she is watching to try to catch his reaction. He looks straight at the camera.

Photo 31. Joy and Justin with Jonathan and Julie. Justin holds the baby; his profile seems to smile. The baby's mouth is open, her eyes veer wildly. Her bonnet has come off and her wisp of hair stands straight up. Joy is trying to smooth it down when the picture is shot, and her head is turned away from the camera.

Photo 32. This is the one picture that shows the photographer's skill, having been taken with great speed after photograph 31. The group is the same, but in this picture, Joy has turned back to the camera and appears to be crying out with surprise. She is smiling and protesting at once, in a good-humored way. She is clearly a person who finds herself as well as the world amusing.

Photo 33. Belle and Ed standing formally but smiling side by side. Despite the sun hinted at by the shadowing on their faces, Belle has the sequin-trimmed sweater draped over her shoulders. Ed's hands are clasped behind his back in the manner of the Prince Consort. He holds his head at a precise angle so the sun will not reflect on his eyeglasses and turn his eyes into two round silver dots. He had learned to do this after many experiments.

Photos 34 and 35. Both of these are group shots taken with a timer, and include the entire family. In the first, Ed is standing on the end, where he ran after setting up the camera on its tripod. It is Anastasia's camera and her tripod, but Ed wanted to take the shot so she has left the arrangement to him. In the picture, he is tense, strained. This setting up of camera, tripod, and timer has taken him nearly twenty minutes (during which the children fidgeted, fussed, and the baby cried; Belle sighed loudly and lighted a cigarette. Brad went to the kitchen to refresh his drink and Justin's, and Anastasia whispered in her daughter's ear a plea for patience). The operation seems to Ed a miracle, the work of a master controller, and he is not sure, although he has checked everything twice, that he possesses the skill to work it.

In the picture as it is finally shot, Belle is in the center, smoking, her face arranged in a sophisticated, knowing expression; Joy is (after all) caught unprepared, looking downward and trying to arrange Jonathan's hair, which is wild as a halo around his sweet face. Brad also seems unaware that the moment has arrived finally, and is looking to the right, his face appearing a little angry about something unknown, but at the same time he seems not to want to be angry, so that his expression is unclear. The children look overjoyed – an accident, because just before the timer snapped, Arden announced that it had better hurry up or she would wet her pants, a remark that made the two younger ones burst into uncontrollable giggling. Anastasia too is smiling broadly, unselfconsciously, perhaps also giggling at Arden's crack. The baby, in Joy's arms, looks uncomfortable. Only Justin is unmoved, spare and erect.

Photo 35 is similar, having been taken the same way, but since the camera was already set up, people were more prepared. Belle smiles directly at the camera, but she must be thinking something she does not say, because her smile is a sarcastic smirk. Anastasia is smiling with the strain always apparent in her face when she knows her picture is being taken. Joy is smiling happily. Ed, perhaps sensing what Belle is thinking, looks sober and thoughtful, gazing down at the grass. The children are tired and have seated themselves on the grass with their arms entwined, smiling sweetly, Arden in the center, one boy on each side. Justin, strangely caught unprepared in this shot, is looking down at the children with a worried expression.

They are, overall, pictures of a happy comfortable American family. There is the golden glow of summer sun filtering through green trees on green lawn, a green thought in a green shade; and although skin tones range from Joy's fair skin to Justin's dark one, none is *really* dark, and all of the skins have the golden tone which indicates a standard of living that permits vacations at beaches, or at least sunbathing or sitting of an afternoon in a garden.

The picture taker would like you to consider also the names Stevens, Carpenter, Selby. You would never know from such names that there was an ounce of anything but WASP blood in any of them. Nor could you tell this from their appearance. Whether blond and blue-eyed or dark-haired and brown- or hazel-eyed, they have the look of people raised in privilege. They are certainly middle-class Americans. Belle looks almost aristocratic, and there is a look on Anastasia's face that makes her unsuitable dress unimportant, that gives her the appearance of being a person who sets her own standards. The background is equally impressive – green lawn, a bed of brilliant flowers, trees. The shot is so focused that the garage does not appear, nor the driveway that separates this 50' × 100' plot from its neighbor. These happy smiling people could be living on a small estate on the North Shore of Long Island, or in the wealthier exurbs of any large American city. These are Americans who have *made it*.

Photo 36. To the sociologist-historian, this photograph appears to have been taken somewhat later than the previous ones. In support of this hypothesis, we offer first, the fact that it shows all the adults with the exception of the older daughter, Anastasia, seated in a rough circle. It is therefore likely that she is again the photographer. A half-filled glass stands in the grass, tipped precariously against the leg of her empty chair. Second, this picture is somewhat less sharp than any of the others. We may deduce from its fuzziness, as well as its lack of sufficient light, a lack that could have been alleviated had the picture taker opened the aperture, that the photographer was at this time somewhat less clearheaded than earlier. In addition, the facial expressions of all the subjects (with one exception) are more animated, less controlled, than before. And finally, the writing on the tag accompanying the negatives is nearly illegible. It would appear the photographer wanted to finish this roll of film regardless of her condition.

In the picture, we can make out a low wooden table, yellow with blue trim, at which three children sit on low matching benches, eating. It is not possible precisely to discern *what* they are eating, although they seem to be eating *on* paper plates. One child, a boy of about two, is holding up his face for the camera, grinning in delight with what appears to be chocolate smeared clear across his chin and mouth; a sight which has a girl, aged perhaps eight, with her legs drawn up on the bench as if she were about to kick something, laughing uncontrollably, with one hand hiding her mouth and the other grasping firmly a large leg, probably from a turkey or large chicken; while a boy of about seven rolls his eyes at the table just in front of him, on which there is a large spreading purple stain, apparently spilled grape juice. The baby who was earlier part of this group is no longer visible, having been placed upstairs in a crib in a small hot bedroom, in clean diapers with a bottle in her mouth. She is well out of it, for this is an extremely poor photograph, with blurring that suggests the photographer's body or arms were moving uncontrollably up and down.

Beside the table of children is a group of adults. The youngest adult female sits on a kind of Adirondack love seat next to the man with the putty face, her head lying on his shoulder; she is smiling and holding up her glass toasting the picture taker. The putty-faced man is smiling in uncertain, puttylike pleasure. His expression is open to complex interpretation: he looks as if he is feeling himself to be utterly depraved, something of which he is deeply ashamed and yet at the same time, proud. He has his arm around the female, whose simple happy smile betrays no recognition whatever of her companion's state of mind. A man in uniform sits stiffly in an aluminum outdoor chair placed to the right of the Adirondack love seat, glaring at something outside the picture. On the other side of the love seat, a woman in her early fifties, unaware of the camera, is glancing around her with a look of panic, wildly, as if she had suddenly realized that she has lost, is missing, something terribly important. Her mouth is open in what looks like a cry of alarm, there is an anxious line between her eyes, and there is panic in her bodily position as if she were preparing to leap to her feet. And bending toward her from his chair, his face caught only in profile, is a man who looks five to seven years younger than this woman, with a look of concern on his face, or rather, concern blended with anger, outrage even. Perhaps what is lost was something precious, and the man blames the woman for its loss, but does not wish to express reproach. Or perhaps the woman is blaming the man for the loss of whatever was lost. It is difficult to tell from this poor photo precisely what was occurring. There is a problem of haze, and the picture is too dark, although there is a brilliance on the right side, which suggests a setting or near-setting sun, a huge red flame on the verge of the horizon, just outside the frame, that causes glare and seems to threaten to burn the film, and even, if the sociologist-historian were to abandon her professionally objective posture for a moment, to threaten to set fire to the picture even as I hold it in my hand.

Chapter XI

one

Reading those old journals of mine is like reading a graph – sharp ups, swift downs, predictable: the ups come when I'm on an assignment, the downs when I'm home. On assignment I am full of excitement, I write tens of pages, odd accounts, because often I pay less attention to the thing I'm photographing, the thing I'm there for, like the dam or – years later – the Berlin Wall – than to the feeling of a place, its ambience, or to people I meet – not important necessarily, just interesting or odd people. I spend whole paragraphs on small details like the graffiti on some statues in Pittsburgh, or the meaning of the fact that a pigeon perched on my shoulder in front of the Baptistry in Florence – God dwells in the details, someone said. I spend a whole page of outrage on a young Algerian boy who tried to pick me up in the Métro, and screamed at me that I was a lesbian when I rejected him.

My returns home are not so much excited, as exercised – page after page lamenting the behavior of the children, and detailed accounts of my attempts to deal with the latest crisis, paragraphs heavy with tiredness and patience. They read as if I were trying to prove to a blank book or to myself that I was a good mother even if I spent time away from home. Or maybe I wasn't trying to prove anything, maybe I found being a mother a difficult and thankless occupation.

As the kids settle down again and life returns to what we called normal, as things begin to perk along without serious distress in a contented way, the mood sinks down, the entries grow briefer and further apart and eventually dwindle into a single bored paragraph once or twice a week. For example:

Saturday, February 9. Lynbrook.

Nothing new today. The kids are both out tonight, Arden at a pajama party at Lily's, Billy at David's. Mom home alone. Spent the day photographing a new tract-housing development out on the island, a place that used to be a potato farm, maybe one of the farms my mother and grandmother walked through to reach the orphanage. There is something so terrible about these tracts, although I'm not sure what it is, why I feel as I do. Certainly the people who sold the land are having an easier life than they did before – almost anything is easier than farming. And what's wrong with these houses? Why am I such a snob? I wouldn't mind having a decent kitchen with a dishwasher, a laundry room, a dining room, a fireplace, a little yard of my own, a garage to keep the car in. Last week somebody smashed in the side of my car while I had it parked in front of the house – not badly, but I don't know who did it, it must have happened in the middle of the night, and I'm worried about what it will cost to repair, maybe it will be over a hundred dollars, well, maybe I can afford that now. Meantime, I have to get in and out on the passenger's side, since my door can't be opened. Still, there's something awful and ugly about those tract houses. Maybe it has to do with the intentions of those who made them. Like the dam.

Anyway, here I am alone and quiet, no TV set blaring, no squabbling kids, so bored I could cry. I've been working on my pictures tonight, but after two hours of that I've had it. Maybe I'll go to a movie. I haven't been anywhere in ages.

Thank God Monday I go out on another assignment.

By the time of my next entry, on the following Friday night, I was hyper again.

Friday, February 15, Lynbrook.

What an absolute bitch of a week! I'm exhausted and beside myself, so furious I've broken out in hives, I could kill, I'd love to put my hands around something's neck and wring it. Oh, for the old days when you killed your own chickens for supper! I'll bet those farm women got their rocks off just preparing meals. Whereas I have to carry my rocks around. Luckily, I stayed in the city while I was shooting, so the kids didn't have to put up with me those four nights, but I was so exasperated, I went out and bought a bottle of rye and kept it in my hotel room. And I drank nearly the whole thing, so much that I didn't bother to bring the remains home. I look horrible, my face is all puffy and I swear I gained five pounds. I'm going to have to buy a scale. The only good thing I can say is at least I can afford it now. This is a terrific job – it enables me to afford to buy whiskey so I can drink myself into something resembling sleep and a scale to weigh the damage the drink did to my body because of upset about the job. Thank god I'll be home now for at least a month before they send me out again. Russ promised. Except once they see the pictures I took, they may never call me again.

The assignment was New York, the unseen side. I loved the idea. I had visions of shooting quiet tree-lined blocks in Queens, ethnic neighborhoods in Brooklyn with Chinese, Italian, Jewish, Russian and Syrian or Armenian restaurants and shops all jumbled together. I imagined stopping for lunch where you can get grape leaves stuffed with rice and nuts, lamb cooked with artichokes in a lemon sauce, umm, I'm hungry, all I had for dinner tonight was a little bit of meat loaf that was left over – Pane wasn't expecting me for dinner and the kids are greedy pigs – and some mashed potatoes and peas, an old-fashioned dinner, the kind Momma used to make, but there was only a tablespoon of each left . . . Yes, and gorgeous old houses in Harlem, facing the park – carved moldings along the ceilings, beautiful windows, paneling, fireplaces in half the rooms, and staircases with curved wood banisters. And little dockside streets in Brooklyn or Queens, with the masts of sailboats standing like the spears in Uccello's bedstead for Lorenzo de Medici or whoever it was, and shacks where you can buy bait, and an old fisherman, resonant of Maine or Gloucester, sitting on a keg . . . Oh, I was seeing it in a romantic, clichéd way, I suppose, but I thought the assignment would be fun. I asked *World* to do research for me, and they sent me a long list of suggestions. *World* wanted to call it 'The Real Naked City', as a commentary on some television program that shows mainly murders.

But this time I was supposed to work with a writer, a well-known writer, well he wrote some famous books and he is the darling of critics who like manly, virile prose. He comes from Chicago and he is supposed to write well about cities and under-world people, to be tough, like Hemingway; he's praised for his realism. I've never read him, but I was very excited, here I was going to work with Orson Sonders and it was only my second assignment!

I was to meet him at eleven at the Oyster Bar in Penn Station. I knew I'd be walking miles and clambering over barriers and climbing up on things, all the while lugging my fifty pounds of equipment, so I wore pants and a sweater and a heavy jacket and a wool cap to keep my ears warm – we are having a cold February – wool socks and lined boots against the snow that is still piled up along the curbs and buildings.

So I walk into the Oyster Bar at AM, clutching my camera case and my mental picture of this man. The place was empty except for one guy standing at the long polished mahogany bar, everything shiny and clean on it and behind it, except this guy who looks as if he has been standing there all night. He is medium high and medium fat, with a flabby unused body and rumpled clothes. You can see he was good-looking once except his face is as rumpled as his clothes and he hasn't shaved in a while. I just stand there: this couldn't be Orson Sonders. He looks at me with a surly expression, but he doesn't say anything. He leans back against a barstool; his thick hand is around a glass of beer.

It feels strange to me to be in a place like this at all, but especially when it is empty and I am alone. I don't know what to do, I know I have to wait for Sonders, but I don't want a drink at this hour of the morning and I'm too embarrassed to order coffee. So I sort of sidle toward the bar, and get up on a stool and sit on it facing the door. This is an unsuccessful ploy: the bartender immediately approaches me and asks what I want. I stutter, I blush, I can feel the hot pulse of blood in my cheeks, I explain I am waiting for someone and don't want anything at the moment, thank you.

A gravelly voice blasts me: 'Who you waiting for?'

I turn with hauteur. What the hell business is it of his? 'Someone I have an appointment with,' I say coldly. Is he going to try to pick me up, this bum? How dare he! (Damn it! Why am I frightened?)

'What's all that stuff you're carrying,' he continued, unperturbed by my haughtiness.

'My camera equipment.' Cold as an ice cube in the hand, proud as an empress.

'Your camera equipment,' he echoes in a mincing little-girl voice. (I don't sound like that!) 'Your camera equipment! Don't tell me you're a photographer!'

I turn and give him my worst glare, a look that says I am preparing to do murder, a look that has reduced shopkeepers, waiters, Brad, and men who whistle at me or make propositions on the streets to paralysis followed by expostulation! 'Okay, lady, okay! I'm sorry, okay?'

He lays his flabby face in his thick paws, resting his elbows on the bar. He cries out 'Don't tell me you work for *World!* Don't, please don't! A girl photographer! A baby girl dyke yet, they send me! No, No!' The sobbing is loud and it takes me a few seconds to realize it is fake. Now he is pounding the bar, sobbing. 'No, no, no, no, no!'

The bartender has a shit-eating grin on his face as he watches the man; he glances over at me to see how I am taking this. I do not know how I am taking it. I am filled with dread, horror, hatred, and embarrassment, and I do not know what to do. I can't help staring at the sobbing drinker, who pounds the bar rhythmically now and the bartender swiftly goes into action, pouring a double of bourbon into a pony, and replacing the empty glass with a fresh beer. The sobber raises his head and tosses the shot down his throat, then grabs the beer and drinks deeply, getting foam on his upper lip. He does not look at me at all. He puts his head back down in his hands.

'Oh, the little girls, how I hate the little girls!' He raises his head a little, like a bull about to charge, and looks at me. 'Always running home to Mommy, always crying, "I've been raped! I've been raped!" If you have to have women, give me a whore any day!'

He sobs, pours half the glass of beer down his throat, then glares at me furiously. 'But worst of all are the dykes, my god, girl, didn't your mother teach you how to dress, or was it your father, did daddy give his ittoo dirw his fly to play with, or are you trying to convince the idiots of *World* that you're a man, is that why they hired you? they must be blinder than even I thought, you don't even have on lipstick, for Jesus' sake!' This outrage reduces him to tears again and he knocks on the bar for another drink, which is promptly supplied.

Deep in my stomach there is a sharp throb of dread. This guy is crazed with woman hatred. What am I going to do? I have to work with him, I can't blow this, I know that. *World* is the kind of place that hates trouble and gets rid of troublemakers, and if things go wrong with Sonders, I will automatically be considered the one at fault. He's famous, I'm not. Russ reveres him, I heard the tone of his voice when he told me of my great good fortune in working with him. But I can't stand this, I can't stand his insults . . .

'Are you Orson Sonders?' I ask coolly.

He doesn't answer. He's busy mimicking me, making me sound like a prissy little girl. I can't, I can't put up with this, I can't, there's no way I can just accept this abuse calmly like a slave, a person with no rights, no dignity. I can't.

But what am I going to do?

I open my mouth. 'I'm Stacy Stevens, the photographer assigned to work with you, Mr Sonders.' I feel my voice about to tremble, and stop. I know instinctively that it will be fatal to show this man any vulnerability. I try to focus my mind on his outrageousness, instead of my hurt, and collect enough anger to keep my voice steady. 'I'm sorry my sex and my appearance offend you. But I'm a professional, and I know you are, and I suggest we get to work. One thing I can assure you of: you won't hate working with me any more than I hate working with you, so we're even.'

He raises his head and looks at me with glassy cold eyes. 'Oh, you're a professional, are you, I'll bet you are, but you don't cut it, girlie, the women *I* know who are professionals look like *women!*' He cackled.

He pounds the bar and mutters to the bartender, and lays some bills on the bar. He pulls himself upright carefully, holding to the bar with one hand, watching his feet. He stands up. He lets go of the bar. He takes a step. He looks at me triumphantly. 'Well, are you coming or not?'

I don't answer. He walks toward me unsteadily. 'I needa eat something,' he growls.

We walk out to the station, and find a hot-dog bar and he gulps – disgustingly – two cups of coffee with three teaspoons of sugar apiece and eats a hot dog with mustard. 'All right,' he says as he chews, 'the underside of New York. You going to be able to stand it, missy? Drunks and dope addicts and whores? Streets so filthy the dust comes right up between your legs and dirties your nice clean panties that your mother told you to wear every day in case you're in an accident so the ambulance driver won't see shit stains. Guys with shivs and guns, whores with VD. You ready for this?'

'That isn't what we're doing,' I say coldly, I pull out my list.

'The hell it isn't!'

'That isn't what they want. They want charming, or interesting, or especially lively corners, places most people don't see. Look!' I point to my authority, the list. He doesn't bother to glance at it.

'Oh! Charming, interesting, lively corners!' he mimics, sounding like a priggish British spinster. 'How sweet!' He swings his head around as if he were going to charge and butt me with it. 'They hired me to write it, right? That means they want what I do, and Hell's Kitchen is what I do.' Truculent, dug in. I know there is no point in quarreling. I pick up my bags and start out of the dump.

'Where the hell do you think you're going!'

'To call Russ Farrell,' I say, and leave before he can say anything more.

I know I may be endangering my job. But I *will* not, *will* not be bullied by this man. As I run for the phone, I think I can present the situation in such a way that Farrell will see it as a legitimate question rather than a challenge. I hurry because it's almost noon and although I don't know what time Farrell goes out for lunch, I do know that once he's gone, he's gone for hours. I reach Farrell's office: he's at a meeting, I'm told. I find myself shouting at the poor woman on the other end, crying Urgent, and Important, and she says she'll try to interrupt it and call me back.

By this time, Sonders has sidled up to the phone booth, fiddling around inside his mouth with a toothpick.

We stand there waiting. I feel like crying, I want to go home and get in bed and I have to breathe the foul air of the place and feel it on my skin, and there's nothing to look at except Sonders examining the stuff he manages to extract from his teeth, and the crowd of harried miserable-looking people who rush by. At that moment I hate my life, I hate my job, I hate the world.

The phone rings: it's Russ. I explain that Sonders and I have different notions of precisely what the assignment is, and need some clarification. All the while I'm talking to Farrell, Sonders is yammering at me, 'Tell him I'm insulted to have to work with a dyke cunt,' and muttering about my general idiocy and the way I'm dressed, and his own misery in having to work with such a creature. I keep my hand over the speaking end of the phone except when I talk, and then I put my mouth right up against it. I know it will be fatal for Russ to hear Sonders.

Russ hems and haws, typically. He speaks abstractedly, in a low voice I can barely hear over the noise of the crowd and the ceiling fans and the loudspeaker announcements. In the end, there is a compromise. Russ did want the kind of piece I described, but clearly he wants even more that Sonders write what strikes his fancy.

At a quarter of one, we stagger up the stairs and into the New York air, which is not a whole lot better than the air in the station. I am hungry but will be damned if I'll admit it. Sonders is grinning, pleased with himself: he's won, he's had a victory over me. We stand on the sidewalk while people stream around us.

'Okay, where first?'

'We have to sit down someplace and work it out. We have to decide where to go when, what light I'll need, and try to get some order in our itinerary so we're not crisscrossing the city for the next three days. We have to choose eight or nine sites from this list.'

'Okay, okay, you go sit down someplace girlie and figure it out with your little brain. Just don't forget the nights belong to me. I'll meet you here in half an hour.'

I know he is going to catch another drink. I look around. Now's the time for me to get something to eat, but there isn't a decent-looking place in sight.

'No. You'll go with me to find a coffee shop. I'll go into the coffee shop and you can go booze yourself up some more – not that you need it – and come back to the coffee shop for me in half an hour.' I talk to him like a mother to a naughty child. He shrugs.

I walk on and he follows. We walk five blocks before I find a coffee shop I am willing to enter. And there is a bar just two doors away.

'Okay,' I bark at him like a sergeant. 'Half an hour. If you're not here then, I'll go without you and you'll have to go to the sites on your own, another day.'

He raises his eyebrows. He looks at me appraisingly. He turns and shuffles off.

I look at my watch. It is one o'clock of the first day, and we have not even started. I go into the coffee shop and order a sandwich and coffee. I am still trembling and I need to cry. But I can't do it here. What I have to do is all by myself pick out what look like the most interesting places, decide the time of day when they would be at their most characteristic, and the kind of light they'll look best in. Knowing that he should be helping me with this, knowing that instead, whatever I decide, he will mock and attack, make fun of me for choosing it. That I can't win.

I feel horribly abused. I look at the waitress: I would like to blubber to her as if she were a momma, that it wasn't fair of him to expect me to wear spike heels and hose and a beehive hairdo when I was going to have to be walking and climbing and bending and carrying, but I see she is wearing hose and a beehive blonded hairdo despite her hard job, and she might not sympathize. She isn't wearing spike heels though. I suppose I should have worn makeup, but you need your entire concentration when you photograph, you can't worry about eye makeup smearing and dripping and reapplying lipstick whenever it gets worn off and it's not fair, it just isn't fair. . . .

I move from defense to attack. Look at what *he* looks like! No one says boo to him! He could wear anything and no one would say anything. But immediately back to defense: It isn't fair! How dare he, anyway, talk to me that way, a complete stranger, and innocent, I'm not a bad person. I never meant him any harm, I was even excited about meeting him. . . .

But at the same time all this is going on in my head/heart, another part of me is looking on with a kind of appalled shock. *Why do you care!* it exclaims. *Why do you feel you have to defend yourself against this man's attacks! Why do you feel that what he says about the way you look matters at all! Why does anything he says or does hurt you, he is a drunk, a bully, an infantile tyrant!*

But I can't just dismiss him as a drunk and a bully.

He is a man. And automatically, because he is a man, he has a kind of authority. Over women. Over me.

WHY! shouts the other part of my heart/head.

I feel the way I used to feel as a child when my mother treated me with disinterest or contempt. I want to die. I feel everything is too much for me. I want to quit this job, go back to Lynbrook and get some office job that pays a little better than what I was getting at the paper, and just live for small pleasures. I want to move to the country, to some quiet rural spot where you can see the sunrise and the sunset, and live quietly with the kids, raising a garden, taking pictures of the landscape. Forget this business of career, success, the big world.

I can't manage this world. I'm not strong enough. I hate myself, I feel weak and teary and victimized and I don't want to feel those things, I want to be able to deal with whatever I have to deal with. But I know that most women, maybe all, would feel what I was feeling. I have to recognize that despite all my resolutions, I am just like other women.

My lunch arrives and I take tiny bites and chew them a long time. Even worse is swallowing. I drink three glasses of water; the waitress is looking at me strangely. I wipe my mouth finally, I can't finish this food, and I pull out my list and a pad, I work intensely, and in a half hour I am able to plan out the first day. It looks as if it will take more than the three days allotted to us. I figure I'll do the rest of the schedule that night in my hotel room. There is a sharp pain in the muscles of my shoulders and it hurts to turn my head.

I pay for my barely eaten sandwich and two cups of coffee and leave an extra tip for all that water. I go outside, my stomach tightening, expecting the worst. But he is there and together we walk to the IRT and set out for Queens.

I didn't come to like Orson Sonders in the time I spent with him, but I learned how to manage him. I spoke to him coolly and only in the imperative mode. What I resented most, apart from my problems with myself, was that the relation between Sonders and me was stipulated only by him, that I could not change it or even affect it very much. I could choose to be bullied by him and fall apart; or to be bullied by him and bully him back, something I didn't like to do, something that didn't fit into my image of myself. But there was no other choice.

He forces me to be someone I don't like no matter which role I take – just by being who he is – because he sees relations between men and women, or maybe between all people, to be power struggles and nothing else, ever. I feel exhausted by this thought, it reminds me of my marriage, of what happened to Brad and me, and that crushes me.

But I went on. I don't know why. I didn't make a decision to go on, I just did it, plodding, in the same way my mother went on and on, plodding to the supermarkets and lugging back the heavy bags, doing the laundry, the way I too went through my days doing the work that had to be done, not-feeling, not-thinking, no matter how demeaning or boring the work was. Maybe I went on because I had no one to run to, no one who would hold me and sympathize and pat my head and tell me I was good and Sonders was bad and it was all right. Or maybe I went on because it was my nature and training to do so, and someplace inside me I recognized that if I could get over this problem of mine – having respect for the male for no reason – the job was no worse than any other I could do.

On Monday, I quit shooting around four because the light was gone, and we went together back to the Pennsylvania Hotel, where *World* was putting us up because it was convenient to subways and the Long Island Railroad. Sonders of course headed immediately for the bar. I went up to my room. We agreed to meet at the bar at ten, 'There's no action in this burg until then.' I ordered a large pot of coffee and spread out my lists and a pad. I knew, from what I'd been able to accomplish that afternoon, that the assignment would require at least three more days. I roughed out an agenda, then began to plan tomorrow's shooting in detail.

I ordered a whiskey and a sandwich from room service, and after three hours, I stopped working, having done as much as I could do in advance. You simply can't plan these things completely – a chance view, the weather, a badly placed garbage truck – things like that can delay and divert you. Then I showered and took a nap, having called the desk for a wake-up call at nine-thirty. I wondered what shape Sonders would be in by then.

In fact, he was sober, the only time I'd seen him that way all day. Maybe he'd eaten or slept. But he was as wretched as ever, more so, he was in command now. He had decided to start in the immediate area, Seventh and Eighth Avenues, where he knew every gin mill, every arcade, every hangout. I appreciated his knowledge – it must have cost him a lot to acquire, in time and money, not to speak of the state of his liver.

I was careful about what I shot, 'casing' the territory first so as not to waste film on second-rate material, and he was impatient with me, he kept pointing to one or another depraved-looking face and saying 'Look at that mother, by the pinball machine.' I didn't know what 'mother' meant but I could tell it was an insult. This enraged me: I knew that almost every word in the English language that referred to women had an obscene meaning, but I didn't know then even motherhood had been vilified.

We worked until two in the morning, by which time Sonders was staggering and I was yawning, despite my nap. I wanted to quit, he wanted a nightcap, and he was so desperate, he asked me to join him. I said he could stay, but I was going, and he yapped 'Go ahead, girlie, whatta you ashamed to be seen with me? Ittoo dirw don wanna get swunk with old bum, huh?' He turned angrily away toward the bar, which had already closed, and loudly insisted on being served. I packed up my stuff and left while he argued with the bartender, who was surely as tough as he was. And there I was, on a filthy dangerous street, all alone, and not a cab in sight. Not that it made sense to take a cab for so few blocks. I walked back to the hotel in terror, clutching my heavy case so that I could use it as a weapon if I needed to. I decided that despite my loathing of this man, I should have stayed with him. Although what help would he be? Why do I assume I'll be safer with a man than without one?

I had told Sonders I was going out at six the next morning, and he said 'You fucking are not,' and I said 'I fucking am'. And he said he was no such idiot as to get up in the middle of the night, and that he'd check out the areas I photographed later. I gave him a copy of the schedule I'd made up, but warned him I might deviate from it if I saw something special. He said, 'You do that, girlie. You can fill me in tomorrow night. I'll meet you at the bar at ten, like tonight.'

I left before six the next morning in a rented car and got some great shots of sunrise over Flushing Bay, with sailboat masts in the distance near a few little houses still left along the water. I shot alleys and cracked sidewalks and old windbeaten trees and a bench, still and empty in the first light. I worked my way around the bay, searching for picturesque spots the researchers hadn't noted. Then I drove east along Little Neck Bay, sometimes getting out and walking, shooting as I went.

After lunch in a diner, I drove west to Flushing, then southwest to Forest Hills, the Gardens, not the section where I'd lived once upon a time, and then down to the water again, Jamaica Bay this time. It was getting late, the light was going, but I could not stop myself from driving into South Ozone Park and looking for my old street. The neighborhood was now completely colored; most of the trees were gone, and the houses were in disrepair. The house we'd lived in had been re-sided in asphalt shingles imitating brick. The hydrangea bush was gone, and so were the poplar trees that had bordered the backyard. Black boys wandered through the empty streets looking angry, and I locked my car doors. There were as few cars on the street now as there had been when I was a child – only a couple of dented, rusted cars left to rot in driveways. It was sadder than ever – no *World* shots here.

I was morose and frustrated by the time I reached Howard Beach – which had been on my schedule for the afternoon – and the light was no longer good. I walked down to the beach, but there was nothing interesting, or maybe I just wasn't in the mood to see what there was. So I drove back to the city, and fell asleep the minute I got to my room. I didn't awaken until 8.30 – I'd forgotten to ask for a wake-up call – so again I just called room service for a hamburger.

Sonders wanted to check out some joints in Brooklyn. He'd gotten hold of a book called the *Amboy Dukes*, so he had me drive us to Amboy Street which is in Greenpoint or Williamsburg or Red Hook or someplace. The population here was different from last night's – younger and rawer, just as hard-surfaced, but somehow less corroded inside. But the consequence of the softer inside was that these guys were trigger-happy, ready to offend or take offense at almost anything. I felt we should have had a bodyguard, but of course the mighty man mocked my fears, claiming to have wakened up bruised in alleys many times, and to have nothing but contempt for someone like me who was, as he elegantly put it, 'a scaredy cat'.

I calmed my fear by concentrating on my work, and it is true I got my best pictures in these dumps – smelly, dark, grotesquely lighted, noisy with jukeboxes, tough talk, and Sonders slurping black Russians or rusty nails, or whatever his drink was called. I used color film to catch purple shadows on the sides of young smooth faces, or the crimson cheek and neck on a fat one, the color of smoke drifting around heads like dispersed halos. I had brought my small telephoto lens, so I could get close-ups of people without their being aware of the camera – although of course, we had to get releases from everyone I shot. But, whatever my success, I didn't want to remain there any longer than I had to, and when Sonders started to whine and bully me to stay on for a nightcap, I said in a voice as tough as any around us that I was driving back, with him or without him, and he came meekly enough. He didn't realize that I didn't know how to find my way back to the city alone.

I spent the next morning in Staten Island, which is still country-like, really rural in places. It would be an ideal place to live if the trip there took less time. I even saw cows grazing, and a house with chicken coops. I drove around leisurely, deviating considerably from my list, and chuckling vengefully about the fact that Sonders would have to spend an extra couple of days finding the places I was shooting.

That night Sonders wanted to 'do' the Village, and we went in a cab. There was a more interesting population down there, largely homosexual men and lesbian women who mostly did not look like drunks or addicts – although some people did – but just as if they liked to dress differently from the rest of the population. I got some interesting eccentric shots: women in twenties' outfits with turbans on their heads, women dressed in men's clothes, men dressed in women's and wearing makeup, and worn-faced Negro musicians, and quiet types who hung over their glasses as if they were drinking Pernod in Paris in 1925.

It came to me that many of these people were *acting* – not for us, not for anyone perhaps, but for themselves. And then I thought that maybe the kids on Amboy Street were acting too, acting out an image – and maybe the crowd on Seventh and Eighth were too. But if that was true, was there anyone who *didn't* act? Who lived the way they lived because they wanted to live that way, enjoyed it? Or did everyone act, just taking their images from different sources? Did *I* act? What about all those people in Penn Station, those men in suits, all alike? Was Sonders acting? This thought disturbed me, so I dropped it.

Sonders had plans to meet some friends for drinks at two, in a jazz club on Bleecker Street that stays open until four. His pals began showing up around one-thirty, while I was still shooting, and by the time I was finished, and went over to him to tell him I was leaving, there were four men and five women sitting at a scarred and shaky round wooden table with him. Sonders had to introduce me. The men stood up as they were introduced. All of them were journalists, I'd heard their names. One of them, Mike Boyle, dark, heavyset, and thick-faced, leered broadly. This was no doubt Sonders's first intimation that there was anything about me that anyone might find attractive, and his eyebrows shot up and he invited me to sit down. I excused myself – I was tired, it had been a long day, I'd been up since five. But Boyle grabbed my arm, and Sonders wanted to please his friend, so growled, 'Wattsa matter, we're not good enough for you,' and I felt coerced and joined them.

The talk was of cities and city editors on large newspapers. The men talked to each other, in a kind of guffawing shorthand, spattered with banter. They did not address the women at all, nor had any of them been introduced. I looked directly at them, wanting to smile and introduce myself, but they were all focusing on the men, and never looked my way.

'Yeah, old Baldy Salvucci, remember him?' Sonders was yelling. The men laughed loudly, repeated fondly, 'Sure, old Baldy Salvucci.' They continued to speak about old Baldy, although what it was that made him noteworthy, I could not tell. 'Baldy was bald at fifteen,' Sonders continued, 'balder than Joe here!' Great rounds of laughter.

One of the men got up to use the john, and I moved into his chair, which was on the women's side of the table. I introduced myself to them: 'I'm afraid we weren't introduced, I'm Stacey Stevens.' They smiled and told me their names, showing no annoyance at all about the failure of courtesy. But then I didn't know what to say. I fell back on work: 'I take pictures for *World*, what do youall do?'

Theyall were in journalism too – one did obits, two wrote 'Lonelyhearts' columns, one covered society events, and one was a secretary who had worked for the *Daily News* for thirty-two years, and knew everything about everybody. They started to talk about the differences in working for various New York newspapers – differences in editorial policy, and editorial personalities. The men went on with their banter, ignoring us. The man whose chair I'd stolen sat happily down in mine – the table was now divided, four men on one side, six women on the other. Boyle was telling a story about a thirty-five-year-old stewardess with a cunt as big as a bucket who went around lamenting her dissatisfaction until she met a big black male stripper named Ten-and-a-half. Such howling went on throughout this story that the women were drowned out, and turned to look at Boyle, all smiling sweetly. When he was through, I turned to the woman next to me. She was the secretary, about fifty, with flaming red hair set so the curls stood up by themselves like tiny fingers.

'That man is disgusting,' I said in a low voice.

'Oh, I don't know,' she said sweetly, nevertheless managing to convey her disapproval of me. 'He's such a poor soul.'

'How can you say that when he talks the way he does? I suppose you have to deal with guys like this all the time, but I don't know how to stand it.'

She looked at me as if I had just made an anti-Semitic or anti-Negro remark. 'Oh, I don't think that about them. Not at all! I only hear their pain, their yearning, their suffering!' She smiled benevolently at the bastards on the other side of the wooden board.

And I thought: yes, and those guys couldn't be such bastards if the women weren't complicit.

Sonders was really drunk by now, his head nodding slightly. The other men had their heads close together, and were howling about something. Sonders directed his gaze to the women.

'Whattya think, when I'm finished with this stupid job, should I take the plane or the train back to Chicago?' he asked loudly.

The women stopped talking. They gazed at him. They glanced at each other. One asked him what his problem was – short of money or time? Where exactly in Chicago did he want to end up? He rambled on about the fucking airlines, exorbitant rates (I knew *World* paid his plane fare). They advised him to take the train and returned to their conversation.

He nodded, his head bobbed, he yelled loudly to the waiter for another drink. He turned again to the women.

'Lissen, whattya think, should I take the train or the plane back to Chicago?'

Again the women stopped, looked, listened, and advised. Again they returned to their conversation.

This sequence was repeated, with only slight variations, *six* times. By then, the men were looking at their watches, declaring important destinations. It became clear thet the women had been brought along and were not there on their own, for when their men stood up, so did they. Boyle left with the secretary *and* the obit writer. I tried to imagine the three of them naked in bed together, but it was so unattractive a picture that I banished it.

'Let's go,' I said to Sonders.

"Nother drink,' he slurred. He waved his hand over my glass as if that would suffice to refill it.

'I'm going.'

'Who's better, men or women?'

I was startled. 'I thought we were equal,' I said prissily. My mind was whirring, trying to outthink him: where was he heading now?

'Men!' he announced, inadvertently spitting in passionate assertion. 'Men are better, you know why? There's this eighty-year-old man can still get it up, my friend tells me, not just for her but for two of the other girls too, friends of hers, you know. They laugh and pat him on the back when he finishes, pretty good, huh? But women are finished at sixty. All men want big firm tits, firm asses. Who cares if they're young and stupid, callow. Now a nice mellow thirty-five-year-old you might take her over a young one. I'm not saying youth is everything. But a woman of sixty – her tits are hanging down, her belly's slack, who wants her? She's finished. But a man of eighty, he can still get it up!'

I leaned back in my chair. Sonders's wave had summoned a waiter and another drink. I gulped it. I couldn't speak. The whole evening revolved in my mind.. I felt I was living in a version of hell, yet everyone around me, everyone in the world, was smiling and saying 'Sure, sure. Right,' like the bartender that first morning in the Oyster Bar. I took another gulp. I leaned toward Sonders.

'Your comparison is illogical,' I said in a quietly lethal voice. 'You can't compare unlike things – men's desire for older women with potency in an older man. You don't ask if women desire eighty-year-old men. You don't consider that if there were male prostitutes, women could also get it off at eighty!'

He didn't hear me. His eyes were wandering around the room idly, seeing nothing. They returned to me.

'I got three girls, you know? My special friends. Two of them are nineteen, one is eighteen. Nice and firm and ripe, you know, sweet. And they know their place. Whenever I want, I just call and they're there, day or night. If they're out and I call, they come in for me, ah, they're sweet. And Nichi, I call her Nichi, she's a Jap, she's exquisite, what skin she has, she's the best. And they know me, see? So they know what to do. See most of the time I can't get it up, it don't work right, see? and they really are great, especially Nichi, and they never try to make me feel bad, they make me feel good, they know how, see, they know their business.'

I stared at him: this was the tough guy, the manly man? But of course he can't get it up, he's always drunk.

Still, he was not ashamed, that was something, I admired that. On the other hand, he was so drunk who could tell whether he was ashamed or not?

We left the club together, and I had to sit in a cab with him stinking of booze and me terrified that any minute he was going to vomit all over me or the cab. I handed him a list of the areas where I intended to photograph the next day – the Village and Harlem. Actually, I tucked it in his handkerchief pocket since I doubted he would remember tonight tomorrow. He staggered off to find out if the hotel bar was still open, and I headed for the elevator. Halfway across the lobby, he stopped and turned and called out to me in a plaintive, frightened voice: 'Hey, Stevens!'

It was the first time in our time together that he had called me by anything resembling my proper name: usually he addressed me as 'girlie'. I stopped and turned.

He was standing there in his rumpled suit, his trouser cuffs drooping over his shoes. His pants beneath his jacket were probably hanging below his stomach, distended from all the liquid he'd poured into it. From this distance, the way the light struck it, his grey face was wizened and infantile, screwed up like the face of a baby in pain.

'Should I take the plane or the train back to Chicago?' he bawled.

Now I'm home. I feel as if I have spent the last four days in a sewer. And I don't even know whether I got good pictures. His world is totally self-created; he is the realization of existential man. He carries hell with him and projects it around him and so strong is his vision that it eradicates all others, no other vision can live beside his. I feel filthy. First thing I did when I got home this afternoon was take a bath and brush my teeth, but it doesn't feel like enough, I keep feeling I should wash my mouth out with soap. I'll gargle, I'll make some salt water. I wish I could wash my mind as easily.

Wednesday, February 20. Lynbrook.

That bloody bastard! That shit-faced buzzard-dropping! God how I hate and despise that man, there is no end to my loathing, I want to kill him slowly, Indian-style, tied over a fire, slowly turning! I'd grin in glee at his cries, I'd laugh when he moaned, and I'd even go over every once in a while and poke him with a hot stick.

Because the bastard took the credit for my work, and that fuck Farrell believed him! Well, at least the pictures turned out to be terrific, I should have trusted my skill not to desert me even though I was shooting from inside a toilet bowl. They were good. Soft afternoon light on a quiet block of neat little houses, snow on the front gardens, an evergreen tree in the right foreground of the picture, softening the rest. A busy intersection in Brooklyn with signs for restaurants and shops in six different languages, all within feet of each other, and all kinds of people walking past, every color and shape and size. A mews in the Village, little Georgian houses that have been kept up, snow along the path, a Federalist lamppost. An exquisite set of houses in Harlem. *World* didn't want the interior shots, of course – I should have known. (I did know. I took them anyway.) I wasted five hours of work getting pictures of carved moldings and cherry wood banisters and parquet floors surrounding people hollow-eyed from poverty, living in rooms with lathe showing in the walls where the plaster is missing, using filthy ancient toilets and sinks a century old. I can't even add those shots to my personal collection because *World* owns them and won't let me have them back even though they won't use them. Maybe someday they will. But they should use them, really. If they're going to sell the American Dream, they ought to show its cost.

But I really aced the night pictures, I really showed him, except of course he didn't realize it, but I showed this world he finds so glamorous, I showed the pimps and the druggies and the prostitutes and the drunks, and they aren't glamorous or gorgeous or dangerous or even interesting-looking, they are miserable and empty. If you look at my photography you might pity them but you certainly wouldn't want to emulate them, they have bad skin and bad color and tense expressions, except for the occasional Negro male who manages to convey a look of triumph – and who knows, maybe life on the street is better than ordinary life for him. I used to think that if I'd been born a poor girl in the nineteenth century I'd have become a prostitute rather than a mill girl.

Anyway, most of the people I photographed look as if they will be able to stand up only as long as a strong wind doesn't come through. Oh, they're tough, I guess, they don't let on that anything touches them, but in that they're no different from Brad's businessmen and lawyer friends. All they have is faddish clothes, but I photographed through the clothes, I showed the bone. Well, that's what I tried to do, that's what I thought I did. No one else mentioned it.

Farrell called to tell me the pictures were great but that we wouldn't plan a mock-up until Sonders's manuscript was in, and when Sonders delivered it they had drinks together and Farrell praised the pictures, saying the choice of sites was brilliant, and that fucking lousy stinking bastard said he'd chosen the sites because I was young and inexperienced, a little girl, and he was glad he could be of help. Well, Farrell didn't use Sonders's words, I had to translate what he told me into Sonders's language. I was so outraged I couldn't speak.

And I didn't speak. I didn't tell him that bastard was a liar, that that work represented hours of my time each night while Sonders was out drinking or out cold, that Sonders never even went to some of the places I'd shot, and certainly never saw them before the shadows in the place got too heavy, before human footprints defiled the new-fallen snow. Oh, AGGGGCH!

Oh, he adored Sonders's prose, so lyrical, so evocative, so subtle! (So drunk!) 'Sonders never imposes himself or his values, he draws out the spirit of a place, soaking it up to reproduce the poignant life of the underside of great cities.' (What values? Soaking it up is right!) 'Like Ernest Hemingway, he is a sophisticate of unspoken feeling, barely gestured action; but his style could not be more different. Sonders is a literary impressionist, using vivid dabs of color with a profound understanding of light to create his sensitive, evocative portrayals. Yet despite his many journeys into lost worlds, he has not lost a feeling for the healthy, fundamental part of life. Sonders managed to find, in a great metropolis, little-known corners showing the peaceful, contented world of ordinary people who make up the majority of those who live and thrive in quiet corners of The Real Naked City: New York.'

This is what appeared in the editor's column, but I could tell that the paragraph came from Farrell, because he was already practicing phrases to send up to William Carney, the editor, when he spoke to me. The drivel about Sonders was followed by a sentence on the photographer: 'The photographs were taken by one of *World*'s most brilliant young beginners, lovely Stacey Stevens.' A stamp-sized picture of me was inserted in the column.

It is not surprising that no one commented on what I thought I had expressed in my pictures, because the text accompanying them, Sonders's 'masterpiece', as the guys around *World* referred to it even years later, sentimentalized and idealized the street people, making them sound like the poets of a fallen world, and made the people who lived in the 'quiet corners' sound like slightly better-off versions of the same thing. I have to admit it is well-written in a sentimental kind of way, but I hate it because it is dishonest.

It isn't that I don't think that we are all in some way alienated – a word Sonders is fond of – from our world. Lots of us feel disconnected. But Sonders romanticizes that disconnection, rhapsodizes about it, instead of showing it for the wretched jarring feeling it is. Like everybody is 'half in love with easeful death', as if that is admirable somehow. He turns the misery of aloneness, disconnection, a sense of not mattering, into heroism.

He idealizes sensitive young men (they are always men, he isn't interested in women) who cannot find a way to live inside the narrow precincts of middle-class life. My whole life has been a struggle to find a way to live outside those confines, but I just struggle, I don't dramatize myself. His writing is basically self-aggrandizement. Like the Beats – good name: I'm beat, I was beat, I've got the beat. Male self-aggrandizement and self pity. On the other hand, it's an alternative image to the usual one of men as conquerers of the wilderness, of the machine, the kind of thing that was my stock-in-trade. I cannot condemn them I guess, without condemning myself.

But why is it they have to counter one false image with another?

---

two

Reading this journal now, more than twenty years after I wrote it, I began to understand something of how I got the way I am, how I got sick, essentially. Oh, I suppose I was always a little – what shall I call it? Neurotic, my mother would say. I think she thinks that means *nervous*, in the way the old ones used that term – sensitive, delicate, in need of special care. But she doesn't think I'm neurotic, she thinks she is, and that I am the epitome of health and sturdiness, self-sufficient hardiness. I guess I would say just that I was always unhappy, seriously unhappy, no matter how cheerful I acted. But I got worse as I got older.

The Sonders incident brutalized me in exactly the same way women these days are brutalized by their jobs, making them want to quit and move to Vermont and grow herbs. There were many such incidents over the next few years, and with each one I grew another layer of callous – not insensitivity to others, but to myself. Until I reached the point where I couldn't hear my own heart crying, where my body had to falter and fail before I noticed . . .

Oh, enough of that.

In March and April of 1960, I had short assignments, one in Detroit, a photoessay on high-school dropouts which I probably drew because of the photographic attitude – which they must have perceived, although they didn't mention it – of my pictures of street people in New York. This time they wanted a pathetic message. I was gone four days. In April *World* sent me to the end of Long Island to shoot an idyllic set of pictures about Montauk Point. And it was probably these that gave them the idea to give me a major assignment – a month in Scandinavia, for a long photoessay, in June.

The kids were good kids. Pane spoiled them a little, she let them have their own way about most things, despite my injunctions about homework and bedtime. I couldn't blame her, she was a *babushka*, and grandmas aren't supposed to have to provide discipline. When I returned from Detroit, I had to settle them down a bit, let them yell at me a bit, get rid of their anger with me for leaving them. That was okay. And I took them with me to Montauk. We went over the Easter vacation and stayed in a motel for the four days I shot. That wasn't easy, I had to keep an eye on them and photograph at the same time. I was harried by the end, and decided not to repeat the experience. The time was gone when I could mix motherhood and photography.

But the trip to Scandinavia was another thing, and it made me cranky. First of all, I couldn't enjoy my success. I know it seems self-indulgent to complain, but it does seem a shame that I couldn't exult, couldn't dance around maypoles and put up flags of self-congratulation in this period when things were going so well for me. If I acted pleased the kids would interpret it as delight at being away from them. They'd gotten used to my being away for four or five days at a time, but a month seemed a huge gap to them. And to tell the truth, to me too. So I felt resentful that I couldn't take a perfectly normal pleasure in what was happening, and guilty because I felt a month away from them was too long, and I shouldn't go, but I wanted to.

So there it was, staring me in the face: which came first? I did then what I've done many times since, what, I expect, men do all the time. I didn't put it into words, I just felt it: that the kids would always be there, but the job wouldn't. This way of thinking was worse than taking things for granted – a euphemistic way of describing things anyway. I was assuming that having kids was simply a biological act, something that didn't require intelligent and feeling attention. Like having plants and paying somebody to water them once a week. Even plants don't do well under those conditions. But on the other hand, if I'd turned down the assignment, I'd have resented the kids horribly. There was no solution, except to take them with me, which I couldn't do. In June they had their final exams; with our new prosperity, Arden had begun ballet lessons, and her class was giving a recital; Billy was to play a bicuspid in his class play; and the school was showing exhibits of social studies projects in the lobby on a special parents' night. And in any case, *World* wouldn't pay their way, they didn't even know I had kids.

But worst of all was the fact that Brad's new wife was pregnant, and due to deliver in June.

It's funny, I'd completely forgotten this whole period until I reread the entries in my journal. It's clear from what I wrote that by late April of 1960 I knew I was going to Scandinavia, but hadn't yet found the courage to tell the kids. Brad never found the courage – or never bothered – to tell the kids about the pregnancy. They had learned it by the evidence of their eyes, and had asked Fern when the baby was to be born. Since Brad hadn't mentioned it, they couldn't bring it up with him, and they didn't feel comfortable talking about it with Fern. I imagine they were sullen and withdrawn when they saw Brad, but he either didn't notice or didn't care. At least I *hope* they were sullen and withdrawn around Brad, because they certainly were around me.

I tried talking to them the way the advice columns in newspapers and magazines suggest – reasonably, kindly. From my journal, April 18:

Over ice cream in the kitchen I offered them pious verities like 'When Billy was born, I didn't love Arden less, I just added Billy to the people I loved. Nor,' I drew it out painfully, 'do I love Billy less because I have Arden. I just have two people to love.' They watched me over their spoons. 'And it will be the same with Daddy. When the new baby arrives, he'll care about you just as he does now, he'll just have an extra person to love.'

Oh, those eyes of theirs! I felt such anguish as I looked at them, as if my heart were being crushed between rocks. Because you never know what's going on in a child's mind, even when they are as nearly grown as these two, and looking into their eyes reminded me of how I had tried to interpret their feelings when they were babies, gazing at their eyes, trying to read them. They'd said nothing then, and they said nothing now.

I tried again. 'Daddy was probably too embarrassed to tell you about the baby . . .'

'Yeah, he was probably afraid we'd ask him where babies come from,' Arden interrupted in a cynical drawl shocking in an eleven-year-old. I almost expected her to cross her legs and light up a cigarette. After I blinked, I pulled my face back into shape and continued.

'Maybe. He's probably embarrassed altogether, you know? He left us, he got another wife, and he probably feels guilty about that. . . .'

The spoons were set down in their bowls. They both peered at me with intense interest.

'But in a way, he isn't responsible, I mean, we left each other, Daddy and I, we stopped loving each other long before he started to see Fern . . .'

'So, you *can* stop loving somebody you used to love,' Arden concluded, a child again, with a child's hurt firmness.

'Yes, adults. But not your children. You never stop loving your children. Any more than you ever stop loving your parents.'

'No matter how bad they are? No matter how they treat you?'

Dread made my stomach hollow. Were they going to attack me now for leaving them?

'Well, you know, some parents are really terrible to their children – they hit them and punish them for small things, sometimes they're very stern. . . .'

'Like you when you make us go to bed at nine o'clock,' Billy shot in.

'No, not like that. You don't know what stern is!' Why was it I could never stay on track when I was talking to these kids?

'Yeah,' Billy agreed, stirring his melting ice cream, 'like Mr McFee, he hits all of them with his belt. Even the baby.'

'How do you know that?'

He shrugged. 'Everybody knows it. He just whips them all, they're really scared of him.'

Arden urged her face at mine. 'It's true, Mom. All the kids know. You can hear them yelling sometimes.'

They were looking at me in a fixed instense way. I could see this was a moral quandary for them. And, without thinking, I just burst out, 'How horrible!' They glanced hard at each other; something had been resolved.

As I read this over, I search inside the words to see where, how I went wrong, how things came to be the way they are. Did I tell my children that they didn't have to obey their parents? Because it is clear that Arden at some point felt it unnecessary to obey me. Did I undermine my own authority? But what was I supposed to say? Mincing lies about some parents being stricter than others? Shit!

The other thing that comes through as I read what I wrote about the business with Sonders, arguments and discussions with the kids, is how I gradually trained myself not to show my feelings, and because feelings kept in are terribly painful, how I also trained myself not to feel them . . .

Because I know, yes I do know, that the worst thing about my present life is not the way my kids are, not even my loneliness (oh, are you admitting you are lonely, Anastasia?), or maybe those things are simply reflections of the worst thing about my life – which is the heavy heart I carry through it.

'Anyway,' I continued, 'I've known people whose parents did terrible things to them, and who didn't like them or want to see them when they were grown up, but they still love them, it's almost tragic, it can't be helped, the love is there. . . .' I stopped myself, I didn't like the morass I was getting into. I tried to get things back on track. 'And I don't know any parent who ever stopped loving their child. . . .'

'What if they didn't love their child to begin with?' Billy asked in a faint voice. Arden looked at him tenderly, then turned a furious glare at me.

'I don't want to talk about this anymore! And I don't know why you *do*! Does it make you feel good to upset him?' She left the table, forgetting the ice cream, mostly melted by now anyway, and went into her room and slammed the door.

'Do you think Daddy doesn't love you?'

Billy moved his head: I couldn't tell whether he was nodding yes, no, or maybe.

I took his hand. It was sticky and small and soft. 'Daddy loves you,' I whispered. 'I know he does. He doesn't know how to show it, is all.'

'He kisses Arden.'

'That's 'cause she's a girl. He doesn't kiss you 'cause you're boy and . . .' I caught myself. I couldn't go into *that* now. But had to finish the sentence. 'A lot of men think you shouldn't hug boys. It's silly, but . . .'

He looked up at me with those eyes which are so much like

mine but bluer, greenish blue instead of greenish brown. 'Why, Mommy?'

Oh god, then I did it. I launched into a lecture about the way things are; I told him a little about the way Orson Sonders had treated me because he thinks women should wear high heels and makeup, and how Daddy's parents didn't want him to be a musician because they think men should make a lot of money and live in a particular way, the way people have fixed ideas about what girls and boys should be like, I went on and on, stumbling deeper into territory I should have avoided. But if I didn't know when to stop, he did. He took what he could handle, then began to let his eyes close in tiredness and asked if we could go to the carousel in Baldwin. I agreed with relief.

I went to Scandinavia. I was a little disappointed that my first European trip wasn't to Paris, Rome, London, or Florence, but Scandinavia was a good introduction to travel on your own – even then, many people spoke English, and since it was summer, daylight lasting until midnight, everyone was joyous too. I spent time in the capitals, but also went to the countryside, up the fjords in Norway and all the way to Tromsø at its northern tip, into Jutland in Denmark, and around the southern part of Sweden – landing at Malmö after a swift trip from Denmark, and driving to Göteborg, a college town. I made friends everywhere; one guy took me flying at night toward the north Pole, so I could see the northern lights; a group of journalists took me bathing on little islands that dot the coasts of those countries. I'd take a quick swim, then lie out on a rock under the sun. I went walking through the old castle at Elsinore, wondering if in fact Shakespeare had seen it. People took me to the opera, the theater, the ballet, to dinners; I even ate once at the Operakällern, one of the world's great restaurants, on some man's expense account. I traveled by train, plane, and boat, and even by cart.

I took wonderful pictures. From the deck of a ship cruising the fjords, I took panoramas with my new telephoto lens. The water – opaque, silvery, calm – blended with the sky, which was the same color and just as opaque. Huge bare stone mountains rose up all around, one silence speaking to another. I had fun, I played with my camera shooting the mountains reflected in the water instead of the actual mountains. Occasionally we'd pass a village curled in the crook of a mountain arm, houses made of what looked like yellowed old stucco, all orange-roofed; stone streets, and the masts of sailboats swaying gently at the pier that was lapped quietly by the still fjord water. The masts moved me, they were beautiful but they were also necessary, people could always look out from their windows to make sure their lifeline was still there.

I shot Tromsø, a frontier town with windbeaten wooden buildings and wooden sidewalks to protect you from the mud that was the main sign of summer. (Years later, visiting Siberia, which suffered from the same problem – permafrost – but which didn't have wooden sidewalks, I remembered Tromsø. As I sloshed in the mud of Irkutsk searching vainly for orange juice, tomato juice – anything with citrus in it, since I couldn't find fresh fruit anywhere – I figured the Norwegians couldn't be smarter than the Russians, and there were certainly plenty of trees around, so why didn't they have wooden sidewalks? I decided that the Russians devoted all their resources to making weapons, to keep up with us. But that was later.)

In Tromsø, even in June, people preferred to spend most of their time indoors. The wind was still fierce, and the sun lacked warmth. In the cafés an aromatic fire always burned in the hearths, and people climbed wooden staircases noisily, laughing, and settled themselves on wooden banquettes that lined the walls, around long wooden tables covered with blue checked cloths, and called for beer. Conversation was loud and lively, political and intelligent. Everyone seemed to be worried about the world situation. I was unused to such concern, people at home did not talk about politics or morals.

I took my share of festival pictures – people in traditional costumes, dances, flowers heaped on carts – and cityscapes, although I felt that these cities were really built for winter, especially Stockholm, massive, grey, stony, its buildings presenting to the grey cold river a facade of equally ominous impermeability. I used black and white for the cities, the cobblestoned roads, and an occasional small farmhouse standing in utter isolation on an island surrounded by grey mountains. I took pictures of people – wonderful faces, especially the old, who have character no longer found in America. American faces are the faces of children who have somehow aged.

I found friends everywhere. Of course there were journalists and photographers, built-in 'contacts' who were supposed to help show me around. But there were professors and publishers, doctors, lawyers, radio personalities as well, people who were friends of my 'contacts'. And lots of students, whom I liked best – I felt they were closest to my age, although that wasn't literally true. There were formal dinner parties with members of the government that ended with people down on their hands and knees pretending to be bears in games of charades; and quiet evenings sitting in austerely furnished farmhouses around a kerosene lamp, drinking aquavit. The silence of the countryside was amazing – no trees to break the wind, only the house itself and its barns and outbuildings, nothing really grows in the north, even in June. The wind, the quiet water, people breathing: that was all. A creak in the house shocked like a thunderclap. I would lie in a featherbed, a puffy duvet around me as if I were lying in a nest, and think that I could get used to that silence, that in it I might hear myself again. At home I put on the radio as soon as I walk in the door.

But the deep-carved faces full of character, that I saw in these places, did not recommend silence to me. Maybe what you hear when you hear yourself is not altogether cheering. And I did so want to be cheerful.

Many nights my friends and I went pub crawling, drinking into the morning. We'd go from place to place, running under the trees along city streets as bright as early morning, singing, cracking jokes. We talked completely impersonally, but once in a while, someone would, without preamble, confess some deeply intimate fact. I have heard confessions of marital infidelity, bisexuality, homosexuality, impotence, incest . . . But painful as these often were, they were not the most painful. No, the worst confessions to come in the early hours of morning, whispered across a table – sometimes the speaker would stare at me as if in my face he read his destiny, and sometimes he would not look at me at all – the announcements that were like moments of sudden intelligence that turned the face and knuckles white and cracked the voice were: 'I hate my father!' Or: 'My father hates me.' Then, often, tears, helpless, inconsolable. Or sometimes, a furious disquisition on papa.

My friends were almost entirely men; it wasn't easy to meet women, there were almost no women in journalism then, they were all home with the kids or working in jobs so low-level that a relation between them and me, an honored professional visitor, would not be considered appropriate, by them or me. Yes, I was like that.

I met a few men who hated their mothers, or felt their mothers hated them, but this knowledge didn't devastate them. Men who hate their mothers, I have found, generally feel perfectly right in doing so. Hating your mother is acceptable, but hating your father is not, it seemed. They uttered their hate explosively, like something retched up, something that should be hidden even from the self. That they hated their fathers, or felt their fathers hated them, was a ravaging new knowledge, discovered, perhaps, that very night.

It was not until years later, when I began to know more women, that I heard similar utterances from them, although it was hatred of their *mothers* that ravaged them. And women tell their tales differently – with drooping faces and sad voices, or expressionless faces and brittle voices. The main difference is that women are never surprised by their knowledge. They recite the cruelties visited upon them by their mothers in simple language, like my mother saying, 'When I was nine years old, my father died,' as if they were telling old stories, known forever. Some make jokes. Women do not tell these stories late at night, drunk, startled by a sudden awareness. They tell them casually, on beaches, or sitting comfortably on wicker sofas in summer rooms gazing out at the water, or in the plush luxury of a flowered armchair in a hotel lobby surrounded by the clatter of tea being served, piano music drifting in from the cocktail lounge, oblivious to the luxury around them, oblivious to anything outside, encompassed by memories they are used to, bitter knowledge they have lived with forever.

Sometimes a night of drinking would end with my having company in bed. Drink usually created a maximum of desire with a minimum of capacity, but there were many good nights in bed after lingering dinners with guys with shining faces, shining eyes, and what passed for uncontrollable passion. I liked to screw men who adored me, who were outside themselves, ecstatic. I loved making love, even though I rarely had orgasms. I didn't care about that: I loved being there with them, being who I was, loved the rolling, transient feel of it, the freedom, the exhilaration. I loved feeling like a high-spirited, smart, energetic, sexy, brilliant photographer, always on top of everything, utterly understanding and compassionate, but still gay, still in control: Stacy Stevens, the Rosalind Russell of real life.

Even disasters – there are always disasters when you travel – can be turned into adventures. You miss a plane – so you have to charter your own; or you charm someone who owns his own and get him to fly you into the very field where the event you have come to shoot is being held. An airport closing down because of bad weather – something that happens often enough in Scandinavia – can lead to the adventure of searching faces for a new companion who will invite you to dinner, and perhaps a bed for the night; cars breaking down in the middle of wilderness means hitchhiking with a new acquaintance, the joys of exchange and new knowledge, or maybe, tramping together for miles over barren land until you spot a farmhouse, knock on a strange door, eat strange food, and sleep in a strange bed. I joined forces with people I would, in normal course of life, never have met – a French couple, backpackers with weak English, who shared my chartered plane, watched the ceremony on the castle grounds, and afterward took me to dinner; Japanese businessmen (all of course with cameras hanging from their shoulders, fascinated by mine) with whom I spent an evening talking in the Göteborg airport, and who later sent me a wonderful Japanese telephoto lens; people of all ages and kinds with whom I became friends on no more basis than that we were together in trouble. And of course, anything that happened could be an opening to photograph, a chance for a special picture . . .

Coming home was a letdown. I left Stockholm on a Friday, before noon, went to the lab from the airport, and didn't arrive at my house until after six. Pane saw me getting out of the cab and met me at the door with her hands clasped as in prayer. Sorry, so sorry, she said, she had told the children I was coming home this afternoon, but they had things to do, and no one was there but they would be home soon, she was so sorry, she knew they wanted to see me, she could not always get them to do what she wanted them to do . . . I knew this meant there had been trouble. She apologized for the house – her legs were all swollen up with rheumatism (which is what she called all her aches and pains) – she had not been able to clean up. She lifted her skirt to show me her swollen, blue-lined puffy limbs. Tired as I was, I had to exclaim, to insist she go to bed and I would bring down some dinner for her. Oh, no, she cried, no no, you tired, she would be fine, she had already eaten dinner, she was sitting in her wonderful reclining chair watching the television, I was not to worry about her. I was relieved, I didn't want to worry about her. I was worried enough.

The house was a mess – stuff was scattered everywhere. I walked through it like a woman in shock, I'm sure my face looked like the faces of people you see in photographs, who return home after the enemy has bombarded their village. Only the kitchen was relatively neat, and that, I suspected was because Pane kept cleaning it up. I could not see the floor of Arden's room, it was littered with dropped clothes, books, toys (although you're not supposed to call them toys when a kid is nearly twelve). Billy's was not as bad, but there were food-soiled plates on his desk and bed table and empty soda cans on the floor.

I went into my room. It was dusty, but neat. It looked as if neither of them had entered it in the last month –

except for a deep dent in the middle of my bed, and a slightly disordered pillow. Someone had been lying there. My throat thickened. I couldn't swallow.

Billy came in at six-thirty. He smiled when he saw me, he hugged me, but his color was poor, he looked pale. I asked him how his exams had gone, did he know any of his grades? was he a great tooth, did people praise him? had he seen Daddy, had the baby been born? had he tried out for the Little League team? I got answers from between locked teeth – okay, no, okay he guessed, no one said anything, no he didn't know, yes. Great, I said: and did you make it? He didn't know.

Since I'd put myself through the emotional upset of asking Brad to spend more time with them than usual, while I was away, I was upset at that answer. 'You haven't seen him? Why not?' Billy just shrugged. He stood there looking limp, and when I, silent with dread, said nothing, he left the room. I sank down on a chair in the kitchen. I was trying to keep myself from pouring a drink. Then Arden walked in, cool and distant. She said hello as if she'd last seen me that morning, and we'd had an argument. I tried my questions out on her. She didn't even bother to answer. She glared at me, and started to walk out of the room.

'Arden, I'm talking to you!'

She stopped in the doorway and partly turned around. 'Well, I'm not interested in talking to you. You go away for a whole month and don't even come to my dance recital or help me study for my math test, you leave us completely alone with just an old woman you pay to take care of us, and now you want to talk. I don't.'

'I had to go away! I was upset about it too! I called you! It's very expensive to call from overseas, but didn't I call you? I called you the day of your recital, and before your math test! I called Billy and gave him ideas for his social studies projects, didn't I?' I was near tears.

She didn't answer. She simply disappeared. I poured the drink. It got later, but I just sat there. I couldn't think. Around eight, both of them wandered into the kitchen. Arden opened the fridge door and rummaged around among the containers of leftovers. There was a package of hamburger sitting on a shelf – Pane had been considerate and bought some food – and something easy. But I couldn't think about cooking. Billy drifted in and peered over Arden's shoulder. She was eating something – leftover mashed potatoes, it looked like – with her finger out of the container.

'Aren't we going to eat?' he asked me.

I burst into tears. 'I can't cook if you're not going to talk to me!'

Both children froze. They stared at me. I was sobbing in my hands. Billy's hand touched my shoulder, then slid around my neck. Arden put the mashed potatoes back in the fridge (with the cover loose) and came over and took my hand.

'We'll talk to you, Mom,' she said. Billy's face was wet against mine.

'Don't cry,' he whispered.

'Well, will somebody tell me what's going on around here?' I yelled. 'I know you're mad at me! But I love you and I have to do what I do, I have to have some kind of life too, I need it! Can we please be normal again?'

We cooked dinner together – cheeseburgers on buns, creamed corn out of a can and salad made of iceberg lettuce, a grainy tomato, and bottled dressing. We all drank Coke. (I could hear my mother's voice in the back of my head: 'Is this what you feed your children, Anastasia? Carbohydrate, fat, sugar? Do you realize that in America they put sugar even in salad dressing?' 'Shut up!' I roared silently. 'I can only do what I can do! I know you would have managed somehow to cook a good meal for them, but you wouldn't have talked to them! Would you!')

The children talked a little warily. As things went on, I understood that they wanted to avoid certain subjects. Most of all they did not want to talk about their father, and we never did. They also didn't want to admit, to me, but mostly to themselves, how they counted on me without even knowing it. It mattered that I was there to kiss them good night, to tell them they were good and wonderful children, to listen to their daily litany of miseries.

At that time I felt they – I – none of us should have miseries. Weren't we fortunate? Weren't we living in greater ease and comfort than our parents, well, my parents had? What right had we to feel miserable about our small misfortunes? Only because they were children did I let them have sorrows. I smoothed their foreheads, I told them things would look brighter in the morning. (You can see why Brad called me Pollyanna: but the truth is, things *do* look brighter in the morning.) But this luxury I allowed them I did not allow myself. I had no right – after all, look at me, the most fortunate of women imaginable! – no right to be anything but pleased with my life.

It is Clara who made me see this, who has been trying these last months to make me see that everyone has the right to feel bad about the things that happen to them, the right to complain and even cry about them. I haven't quite managed to accept it though. For me, the only people entitled to cry about their lives are my mother, my grandmother, and people whose lives were as miserable as theirs.

And maybe even though I was allowing my children to complain and cry, maybe in some subtle way I was also telling them they were being childish and petty. So what if Arden was the only girl in the dance recital, and Billy the only child in the play, whose mother did not show up to applaud, to hug afterward, to bestow praise, to beam? (I should have been there, of course. I wish I had been there.) Life is hard all over, and they *had* a loving mother, even if she wasn't present. They had enough to eat, a decent place to live, and they weren't abused, beaten, or even yelled at.

What I said was, 'I told Daddy to come and see you. I told him it was important.'

'Well, he didn't.' Not only had he not attended their play/recital, but he hadn't taken them to dinner except for the first week I was gone. He had said then he might be busy for a while, and when they asked him why, he'd evaded them. Arden had said 'Because Fern's having a baby, right?' and he'd been startled and suspicious.

'Who told you that!' he glared.

'Our eyes,' Arden said.

He admitted it then. She was due in a week, and because

she was nearly thirty, the doctors were worried about her. He'd see them if he could, but he couldn't promise. Then silence. He never so much as called the rest of the month.

'Did you call him? Did you call him Tuesday night to see if he was taking you to dinner on Wednesday?'

Two heads shook no.

'Did you call him after that to ask him where he was and why he hadn't come?'

Two heads shook.

'Why not!' I screamed, something I rarely did. And strangely, they understood, because they did not get upset at my screaming.

I was shocked. I understood Brad had been punishing me for going away, but that he would take it out so cruelly on them passed my line of understanding.

There were tears in my eyes when I said I was sorry – sorry that Daddy wasn't there, but sorry most of all that I hadn't seen them, that I had missed seeing them at a moment of their lives that would never be repeated. I don't think they understood what I had lost, but they understood that I was grieved. I wiped my face and cleared the table. I proposed a hot game of hearts. I promised them we'd go away for a vacation in the summer, and told them to think about where they'd like to go.

That night, after they were asleep, I called Brad, I screamed at him, I told him he wasn't fit to be a father. He said I wasn't fit to be a mother. I told him he was cruel, he said I was. I told him he'd better pay some attention to them fast or I'd see a lawyer about denying him visitation rights. He laughed. He said no visitation, no child support. Then I cried again: I asked him how he could do such a thing to them. He said he'd been busy okay? He had a new daughter and a sick wife to worry about. I said maybe the kids would like to meet their half-sister, and to be reassured that even though he had a new baby, he still cared about them. That seemed to surprise him. I guess he never thought about how things seemed to them, how his behavior affected *them*. I hated him.

School ended, the kids got their report cards, and they did well except that Arden had dropped from a ninety-five to a seventy in math. Billy got into Little League. And one Sunday, Brad came and got them and drove them back to his house to meet Annette, their new little sister. They came home quiet and pale, although they were enthusiastic about the baby – so little, such tiny fingernails, so beautiful, so cute, so sweet, she kept smiling at Billy and clutching Arden's finger. They said nothing about their father.

I made arrangements to rent a little house on the bay side of Cape Cod for August, when Little League would be over. Slowly, the children healed. Only their rooms stayed a mess. I had wanted to charge in like a field marshal ordering a mop-up operation, but guilt or love stopped me. Their rooms stayed sties until we came back, all of us tan and strong from swimming and horseback riding and playing ball, to get ready for their return to school. And then they cleaned up their rooms without my saying a word.

three

All through that summer, my stomach worried. I knew that I could not again leave the kids for so long a time; but the best assignments, the major ones, often involved staying away a month or more, sometimes three or four months. It was conceivable that I might take the kids with me if I were going to be away for four months, but how was I going to explain that to *World*, which didn't know they existed? And I knew how hard it was to work when they were with me.

My anxiety wasn't serious – it was just that I'd find myself chewing the inside of my lip at odd moments, or I'd have indigestion after eating a perfectly innocent pizza. I'm not writing a heroic tale, a tragedy or an epic. I'm trying to recount a life, my life, a woman's life – and lives are made up of small events that wear us down. It is not great crises that mark us, that make us what we are, but the small details of ordinary living that stiffen us into shape gradually. And the shape once formed: can you change it? That's the great question for me now. Not then: I hadn't yet been molded, molded myself.

After my return, we had a good, easy summer, marred

only by one problem. I discovered it on a Tuesday night (no date in the journal, just, 'Tuesday'. But it had to be sometime in July).

I'd made a good dinner for a change, a lamb stew with big chunks of carrot and rutabaga and potato and the cheap cuts of lamb that are my favorites, breast and neck, and we'd all eaten too much and were dallying at the table talking and joking, when Billy made a nasty crack to me, and I flailed out to slap his hand. His remark was a signal, telling me he wanted to play our old game. We hadn't played it since Brad and I got divorced. My flailing out at him was my acceptance of the challenge.

We both leaped to our feet; Billy darted to the other side of the table; I lunged for him. He darted in the other direction, and I reversed mine. Around and around we went, both getting dizzy, beginning to howl with laughter, panting. He took off for the living room, me in hot pursuit. Once I caught him and began to tickle him; he let out a bloodcurdling scream and eased out of my grasp, running back to the kitchen, tossing chairs as he went, to impede me. We darted back and forth at opposite sides of the table again, then, by faking my direction, I caught him again and grabbed a handful of his hair. Again he let out a wild shriek, escaped, and again headed for the living room. By this time, we were both laughing so hard we had trouble running at all. Of course, at any time Billy could have darted into his room, or the bathroom, and locked the door, but the point was not to end the chase, but to prolong it. This game of ours always ended the same way – I'd catch him, and bend his middle finger backward – not hard, not enough to hurt him, but just enough so that he felt legitimate in crying out 'I give up! I give up!' and then we could cease, our hearts pounding, our cheeks red, our stomachs aching from the laughter. Billy would throw himself on the floor panting, and I'd lean on a chair to catch my breath.

Billy and I had been playing this game since he was little, five or six. We played it only at home, but sometimes in front of my parents or the Carpenters. It made them uncomfortable. I think people felt it to be incestuous, but because they didn't allow themselves even to think that word, they simply sat there, silent, not laughing, bewildered and inarticulately embarrassed. I *knew* it was incestuous, but I thought it was a harmless way of expressing incestuous impulses. It was fun, and innocent, and besides, I sensed that Billy only asked to play – it was always Billy who gave the cue that he wanted to play – when he needed something from me.

Arden had always been unhappy about this horseplay of ours. At first I tried to get her to join in with us. If Billy pinned me, as he somtimes did, I'd cry out 'Arden! Help me!' but she'd sit at the table sour-faced with disapproval and glance over at her father. She had the comfort of seeing her father looking as disapproving and uncomfortable as she felt. This time her father wasn't present and as I glanced at her, she looked forlorn, alone at the table. So I called out to her, and she leaped up and joined in. Billy wasn't too happy about *that:* this was *his* game. (No way to keep everybody happy.) And besides, Arden wasn't as gentle as I, there was some animus in her playing. She caught Billy and pulled his little finger back, but she did it too hard and he cried out in pain, 'You nigger!'

That was the end of that game. Arden was angry about being called a name, but she saw the tears in Billy's eyes and was sorry she'd hurt him; Billy was angry at being hurt, but felt guilty at his name-calling: comforting was required on both sides. After we'd all calmed down and cleared the table and I'd suggested a game of hearts, and we were shuffling the cards, I asked Billy why he'd called Arden that name. He shrugged.

'Do you know what that word means?'

'It means the same as kike,' he responded promptly.

'And what does kike mean?'

He shrugged again and looked to Arden, who, called upon to be the authority, tried to fit the role.

'It means people who are dirty and nasty,' she said with assurance.

'Who told you that?' I could see that my insistence was making them nervous and guilty without understanding what their fault had been. But I couldn't let it drop. They looked at me, they looked at each other, they looked at the table.

'I mean, where do you hear these words, from other kids?'

'No, Pane says them,' Billy said, glancing at me uneasily. It was inconceivable to him that Pane could do something seriously wrong.

Oh. Oh no. Now I'd have to speak to her. Shit.

I went into a long rap about how people have different backgrounds and skin colors, how some people looked like Mr Ferguson, pinkish white like the gladiolas growing in the Lenches' garden; and some were like their father, a reddish color that turned copper in summer; and some like me, a bluish white like Grandma Belle's freshly laundered sheets. There were people the color of pale caramel, tan like Arden's friend Joan Tebaldi; and some the color of dark caramel, like Mrs McCabe, the lady who cleaned the Lenches' shouse, and some were even tanner than that, the color of chocolate, and some the color of polished ebony wood. I explained that there were other people who were the color of lemon taffy and some like the walls of our apartment where they were clean, under the pictures, which was called ecru. They were smiling with delight by now.

So I went further and said that some people whose parents hadn't let them know they loved them, did not feel good about themselves, and because they did not feel good about themselves, they had to make themselves superior to other people. And sometimes they used their color as a reason to claim they were better than all the other colors, and that this was ridiculous. I told them there were even colors they'd never seen, bluish browns and shiny dark browns that were almost black, and pale pale whites, like skimmed milk. And that all these differences were wonderful, part of the rich variety of the world. And how not just the color of skin, but other parts of people varied – some had straight hair, some very curly, some in between, and hair was all colors too. And noses were different. We had a giggling session then while the kids came up with examples of notable noses – among them mine, their father's, and each other's. And that people believed different things too, and some people believed in gods, and there were a lot of different names for their god, and some people worshipped one and some another and they sometimes killed each other because of this. The children stared at me incredulously.

'That's stupid!' Billy announced.

'Yes, well, I don't think people are stupid, but they believe a lot of stupid things. And they have nasty names for other people, intended to make them feel bad just because of some difference or other, skin color or religion or even the place where they were born.'

Then I listed all the pejoratives I could think of, together with a translation. I could not come up with a single term that demeaned the English – their father's heritage – except cockney, which referred to class more than national background, and WASP, which wasn't really pejorative. But I ended with 'stupid Polack,' the only term I knew to refer to Poles, and informed them that it described them.

'I don't like the *stupid*,' Arden said, considering. 'But the other word doesn't sound so bad.'

'No word is bad inherently. I mean, words can't be bad or good in themselves.'

'Not even *damn* or *hell?*'

'No. Words are just sounds. It's the meaning people put on those sounds that makes them bad or good. The words we call bad are bad because we mean them to hurt someone.'

'Who gets hurt if I say *damn?*' Billy had been experimenting with cursing recently.

'Those words are supposed to hurt God.'

'What *is* god?' Arden pounced.

Well, that was the end of the card game. We sat around the kitchen table talking until it was time for them to go to bed. I had a bad moment when Arden suddenly piped up: 'Didn't Pane's mother tell her she loved her? Is that why she talks that way?' Otherwise we had a good night; but I was left with a gnawing stomach that kept me awake until dawn. Not wanting to spend another night like that, I went down to see Pane soon after the children left for summer school, a play and crafts program they ran at the local public school. She was, as always, thrilled to see me, which made me feel even worse.

She opened her arms to me and cried 'Ah *kochany*, come in, come in!' There was homemade almond yeast cake, and she started a fresh pot of coffee in my honor, although the old dull aluminum drip pot on her stove always had coffee in it. We sat in her breakfast nook, on old-fashioned high-backed wooden chairs, like pews. Sunlight poured in from the back window on the faded blue-and-white-checked tablecloth, showing a week's worth of crumbs and spills. There were crumbs on the windowsill too, because Pane kept a box outside this window for the birds, and simply brushed her ends of bread into it. She also put in chunks of fat cut from pork chops or ripped from a chicken, so sometimes there were ants on the sill as well. Consequently, Pane's yard always had the most birds of any in the neighborhood, which was wonderful except that the patch of yard beneath this window was always thick with bird droppings.

She told me all the neighborhood gossip, I told her bits and pieces about my trip to Scandinavia. Then she began to tell me anecdotes about the children, and how cute they were. Often her anecdotes were testimony to how much the children loved her, but that was harmless, I felt, she did love the children and they did love her. I grew more and more tense; I drank coffee and smoked cigarettes and listened as her voice lilted up and down with laughter and affection. After three cigarettes smoked in a chain, I began.

'Pane Nowak, the children are using some words that are not nice.'

'Oh!' She stared at me. Then she shook her head. No, no, it was not possible, they were good children, they would never use bad language.

'Well, last night, Billy said "nigger" and "kike". I wonder if you've heard any of the children in the neighborhood using those words?'

She looked at me. I could see her debating. But then she decided. She took the noble course. She claimed responsibility. She opened her mouth and out came a tirade.

She hated Jews. She'd been a servant when she first came to America, and the wealthy Jewish family she worked for treated her like a slave and fed her the scraps from their plates. She understood Yiddish, she could hear them talking about goys, especially Poles, they hated them, they looked down on them. She hated the colored too: her sister had had a fine house in Brooklyn, but the niggers had moved in and trashed the neighborhood. When her sister had to sell the house, she got almost nothing, after her husband's funeral there was nothing left, she had to go live with a daughter-in-law who treated her miserably, and she died in just two years. In real Polish neighborhoods, they were too smart to sell their houses to niggers – or to Irish or Italians or kikes, or anybody except other Poles. Those people were savages, animals, they should go back to Africa, all those people, they should go back where they came from.

I have no excuse for what I did except that I was a lot younger.

'Should we go back then, too?' I began, calmly. 'After all, the colored people have been here longer than we have. My grandparents didn't come here until about 1900. When did you come, Pane?'

She drew in her breath between her teeth, almost whistling.

I then pointed out her illogic: Some Jewish families were unkind and exploitive, but so were others. Unkindness had nothing to do with Jewishness: my Polish grandfather had abused his own children, and what about her own Zbishek, hadn't he made her weep beating their sons? It wasn't the fault of impoverished colored people overcharged for a house in a decent neighborhood, and finally unable to keep up the payments, that Pane's sister had ended her days in misery. I used reason.

Now, just thinking about this makes my face hot with shame. What did I think I was doing? Did I think I would convert her?

After a time, I saw the uselessness of my words. All I had accomplished was to make her feel uneasy with me. And I needed her. I told myself that didn't matter: a person of principle doesn't allow personal need to interfere with the transmission of truth. I told myself it was more important to insist upon just sentiments than to avoid hurting the feelings of an ignorant prejudiced old woman.

But I could not avoid seeing her eyes.

It was done, though. I couldn't take it back, wipe it away, give her a hug and tell her to go on being herself, and go back upstairs and tell the kids they simply weren't to use those words, and that was that.

I made my face compassionate. 'I understand your feelings,' I said. Water sprang to her eyes. 'But I do not want my children to use words that cast contempt on other people.'

She folded her face. She stood up, and walked around the kitchen, drying and putting away the dishes resting on the dish drain – something she never did, she just used them again. She turned the heat off the coffee, another act rarely performed in this house until she was about to go to bed. As she walked, she talked, in a cracked old voice, never looking at me. She explained that God himself, as the priest himself often said at Mass, perhaps I should go sometimes, it would benefit my children, whose religionless upbringing she worried about, God himself had decreed that only Catholics would be saved, that all others are damned. It could not be an offense to damn those whom God had damned. She knew what she knew. She was muttering now. I stood up, with a firm severe expression on my face.

'Pane, you must not use such words around my children.'

She stopped, she turned, she looked at me. She heard the voice of authority, and saw the posture of a man giving orders. She lowered her head, hunched her shoulders: the change was slight, subtle yet in front of my eyes she was being transformed into my broken grandmother. And I was doing the breaking.

'Yes, Pane,' she said. She had never so addressed me before.

I thanked her for the cake and coffee, and left. I went upstairs and sat down in my breakfast nook shaped just like hers, just lacking the crumbs on the sill and the birdfeeder. I sat there for a long time, thinking. What *should* I have done? What was right? I wasn't just worried she wouldn't take the children again. Just then, that seemed unimportant.

I had loved her, I still loved her, and she had loved me and my kids. She was a good sweet woman in most ways. It came to me that the price of her sweetness, her complete acceptance of anything we did, was this hatred for the alien. To keep us always in the black in her moral bookkeeping involved keeping those who were not of her group always in the red. She couldn't tolerate the near-blacks, the greys, the off-whites that were the joys of my profession. For a photographer, pure whiteness is a scorched photograph, a blanked-out spot; and pure black is just as useless. But I had always known how her mind worked. I had understood that the corollary to the fact that the kids and I could do no wrong was that the other people got charged with the anger she felt at our failures, that the only way she could offer absolute love to the people she loved was to offer absolute hate to the stranger. I'd been happy enough to go on bathing in her warm acceptance. I'd been willing to consider her a saint. It was convenient.

Why hadn't I seen my own complicity in her bigotry before I charged down there and ruined not just her day, but her year, tainted the last years of her life, her pleasure in my kids, in me? Was it worth it? Had I advanced truth or justice an iota?

I knew that if she took the children again, she would obey me. But she would never again trust me not to hurt her.

So I was the more surprised when, one afternoon in July, as the kids and I clattered into the house laden with beach chair, blanket, cooler, umbrella, thermoses, and heavy sandy wet towels, after a day at Jones Beach (we could not go to Zach's Bay, where I had gone as a child – it was too polluted. I had to sit on the beach, a nervous wreck, watching my kids disappear and reappear in the rough and dangerous surf, trying not to transfer my fearfulness to them), that Pane swung open her door – she must have been waiting for us, watching from the window – her face radiant.

'Anastasia! *Kochany!* Guess who is here! My grandson, my Antoni from Ohio! He come to see me, his *babushka*, to visit!'

Her hands were clasped as if she were praying. She was in a state of beatitude.

'I not see him since he is twelve years old, now he comes!'

I crowed, I hugged her, I acknowledged her triumph – her grandson had not forgotten her, which meant maybe her son had not either.

'Just two hour ago he come! I not know he coming, I could might be at market, at coffee with Pane D'Antonio! But he!' she giggled wildly, 'he say I am out, he sit on front step all day until I come!' She laughed in unshadowed delight, and I saw that for today my sin against her had been forgiven because of this grace that had descended upon her. It was easier for her to forgive me just as it was easier for me to see her as a saint than to question her goodness. We had to live together, literally in the same house.

'And he come, and he go – swoosh! – to A & P! I want to go, I say I go, but he say I not carry home heavy Coca-Colas. He American, Coca-Cola!' she laughed. Since Pane believed most American food was nothing short of poison, especially its soft drinks, it was clear that she had had to make another mental shift. Grandson was inside the charmed circle, therefore so were his drinks.

'He college man, *kochany*! Educated!' she cried out, turning in a circle, a kind of dance, then put her hand on my arm. 'You come for coffee and cake after dinner, *kochany*, yes? Bring the little ones.' She noticed them then, standing smiling at her joy. (I gazed at them intensely as she hugged them: You see what children mean to us, kids? You see how much Pane loves her grandson that she hardly knows? How could it be that your father does not love you?)

'You come, hah?'

We all agreed, nodding, smiling, and trooped upstairs, Billy wondering if the big boy would fix the rusted basketball hoop on the front of the garage, or throw a few balls with him, and Arden wondering how Pane could recognize

572

him as her grandson if she hadn't seen him in a long time. 'How old is he, Mommy?'

'I don't know. He must be eighteen or nineteen if he's in college.' I had no desire whatever to sit for a couple of hours making conversation with some midwestern college boy, but I was grateful that she was allowing us to make peace.

We went down about seven-thirty; Pane ate early. She was wearing her very best dress, a rayon floral print with a white lace collar and her Sunday shoes, the shinier of her two pairs of tie-up black midheel oxfords. Pane's living room – she called it the parlor – normally looked a bit dusty. There were hundreds of photographs on every old-fashioned surface, sitting in places of honor on lace scarves and doilies, and these rarely felt a dustcloth. But tonight the room smelled fresh, and there was a vase of roses on the table by the wall. She saw me notice them, and smiled radiantly and spread out her arms.

'My Antoni! So good he is!'

Antoni appeared in the dining room, carrying a heavy tray with a rum babka on a footed glass plate, plates and silverware, and Pane's good linen napkins.

'Oh, NO!' Pane cried, running toward him. 'You not do. Not man, woman do!'

She tried to grab the tray away from him, but he smiled and said, 'No, Gramma, it's okay,' and set it down on the table, and turned to us and smiled.

He just smiled.

I just stood there.

I still can't think about Toni without awe at his beauty, and I still remember him as he looked at that moment. He had a broad Polish face with high cheekbones and his skin was smooth and golden. It was the color of golden caramel, and shiny, but the light wasn't on him, it was in him, coming from his skin, his eyes, his smile . . . Oh, that smile!

He came forward to shake hands, and I could see that his eyes, large, but with a little slant to them, were a deep blue. His mouth was shaped just like a Cupid's bow, the kind of mouth movie stars of the twenties used to paint on themselves, and it looked like a child's mouth, so sweet it was.

'Hi. Gram's told me a lot about you. She says you're a photographer for *World*. That's really great!'

I know I said something or other.

He couldn't be eighteen.

Pane introduced him to the children, and he said we should call him Toni, and as we walked toward the table, Billy was asking him if he played basketball, and he laughed and said he'd noticed the rusty hoop, and that he'd put up a new one if he could find a ladder, and then Pane was insisting he must not exert himself, but he said didn't she have a ladder and she said Zbishek – her husband's nickname – had kept one in the cellar and maybe it was still there but it must be old, perhaps rotten, he must be careful, he must not fall. And Arden asked him how old he was and he said twenty-two, and my breath started to come again in light quick drafts, and she asked Pane how she recognized him, and out came the photographs, and in short, there was no trouble whatever in making conversation over coffee and cake that evening, for hours and hours. But whatever was said, even if I said it, washed past me like water in a gutter when you're walking along the sidewalks. From my exalted perspective four inches above the road, all I was conscious of was the way Toni kept looking at me – and the way I knew I must be looking at him.

When there was a light rap on my apartment door the next morning before nine, my heart did a peculiar stop-start routine, but I didn't even have time to run into the bathroom to comb my hair because Arden opened the door to the only person who could have been standing there. There was the smile again, and the blinding brilliance of light that came from his face. I was wearing my usual morning attire – a discarded shirt of my father's that hung down just far enough to conceal my underpants, and bare feet. He noticed.

'I hope I didn't come up too early.' There was a suspicious pink tinge at the edges of his cheeks.

'Not at all, I've been up for minutes,' I laughed. 'Come in. Want some coffee?'

He had some trouble getting his eyes to detach themselves from whatever they were fixed on, to look at my face. The pink grew deeper. 'Oh, no, thanks, I've had breakfast.' Billy came wandering into the hall from the bathroom, his hair tousled, with sleep in his eyes. He brightened when he saw Toni.

'I just came up to ask if it would be okay if I took Billy with me to the sports store to pick up a new basketball hoop.' He turned to Billy. 'If you want to, that is.'

After the clamor waned – considerable clamor, since I insisted Billy go to summer school as usual, and could go with Toni only afterward (I wasn't having any college kid here on a two-week visit wreck my entire summer schedule) – and the argument that followed my insistence on paying for the hoop (after all a boy right out of college probably didn't have much money) – there was more small talk, and the door closed, and my heart gradually returned to its normal rhythms.

Then I let the broad grin that had been itching my mouth emerge, walking toward my room so the kids wouldn't see me. I knew what I wanted to know.

I spent special care of my self-presentation that day. I wore clean navy shorts that made me look as if I had hips, and a V-necked white cotton jersey over the only bra I owned that made my breasts look as if they belonged to someone over twelve. I brushed a smidgeon of brilliantine into my hair and carefully applied the new makeup I'd bought but rarely used – a light eyebrow pencil, and a pale pink lipstick.

I had to go marketing that day, and set off soon after the kids left for summer school. I was not shocked when, as I struggled with three heavy sacks and the front door key, the door was thrown open and there was a smiling face attached to a body I hadn't cared to examine. Ready for him this time, I was sure my smile was as radiant as his, and I managed to convey the proper degree of surprise and delight at the suggestion that I might want help carrying the bundles.

I didn't ask him to stay, that time, offer iced tea or coffee. Once a day was enough. He was young and I didn't want to push him. Still, he lingered in the kitchen after he'd put the sacks down, reminding me of his arrangements with Billy. When the kids came in a couple of hours later, I was still humming.

I watched from the window as Billy held the old rickety ladder steady and Toni climbed up and worked at removing the old hoop. The screws were rusty and stuck, and the job took some time, but he did not seem to lose patience. Then, since the new screws were a different size, he had to drill new holes in the clapboard garage pediment for the new hoops. This all took more time, but when it was finished, he was not too bored to throw baskets with Billy for almost an hour. I hadn't known I had such an account book in my head, and became aware of it only because he was earning such high marks in it.

In the next week – we were leaving for the Cape at the beginning of August – he became a hero to both my kids, since he was willing to sit and talk to Arden at length about serious matters like the habits of dogs, cats, horses and dinosaurs; and to play three-way catch with them out in the street that still in those days had little automobile traffic. He and I did not spend any time alone together. It would have been difficult, because Pane would certainly not approve of any hanky-panky between her innocent grandson and the divorced, world-traveled sophisticate I seemed by comparison. At least, that's how I felt, and as I found later, so did he.

He helped us load the car the day we left for the Cape, and he and Pane stood on the sidewalk waving goodbye. I was irritable, as both kids pointed out indignantly. But they were too excited about the impending holiday – they'd never gone anywhere far away before – and too generally happy to let my bad mood disturb them. They chatted and argued about spelling in the backseat, the Scrabble board set up between them. I turned on the radio, low. Of course I chose WPAT and let my mind drift.

Billy's voice intruded. 'Mom, Toni says he'll take us rowing at Belmont Park when we get back. Can we go?'

'Oh, I don't think he'll still be there when we get back, honey.' I wondered if they could detect the real sadness in my voice.

'Yes, he will,' Arden said knowingly. 'He's going to stay and help Pane for a while, he told us. We told him we'd be gone a month, but he said the lake will be wonderful in September. So can we go?'

My mood improved enormously. I began to hum with the radio.

four

Toni had been graduated from Ohio State that June, an English major with plans to be a writer. I said nothing when he told me this, having unhappy memories of people who wanted artistic careers, and I never asked to see his work – and was relieved when he never offered to show it to me. He was a beautiful boy, and sweet, but I had a feeling that he might not yet – or ever – be a writer. I don't know why. I guess I think people who are really artists are so intense as to seem a little mad, or strange, and Toni was entirely too healthy and happy to fit my image.

He had come to New York with thoughts of going into publishing, and during the month we were away, he did trudge into the city every day, looking for a job. But his degree was not only not from Harvard or Yale, it was from a school not highly regarded in New York; he knew no one; and I guessed that his self-presentation was not polished or arrogant enough to impress publishers.

He perked up instantly when we returned, Pane commented, attributing it to his affection, so swiftly developed, for her two little *kochanies*. Still, he remained anxious – his money had almost run out, he couldn't live off his grandmother, who had little enough as it was, and he didn't want to go back to Ohio. But he finally found a job as manuscript reader for a small house that specialized in western and adventure novels, Cimarron Press, which Billy always called Cinnamon Press. After Toni started working, we did not see much of him. He left early in the morning and came back around seven at night; Pane ate at five, and put a plate in the oven for him. Weekend mornings we could hear his old Royal typewriter clatter sporadically in the downstairs back bedroom.

Occasionally on a weekend afternoon, he'd emerge from what I thought of as his lair, and look for the kids and me – for a walk, a drive to the park, a game of catch. When his eyes actually raised themselves to mine – which was rarely – he looked pale and faint. He reminded me of the helpless heroine of a Victorian novel, yearning for the hero to save her, but unable to ask. I knew he hated his job, although he never said so, only shrugged when I asked him how it was going. I knew it paid little, but his expenses were low. Pane was outraged when he offered to pay for his room, and accepted only ten dollars a week for his food. He did not own a car, and when he took the kids over to the merry-go-round, or to Belmont, or took Pane to the market, he borrowed mine. Whatever charge there had been between us was neutralized by his misery – or his inhibitions. I forgot him – well, I sort of forgot him, I let him rest in a puzzled and slightly hurt back pocket of my mind – and got on with my life.

In September I had two short assignments, both in the States – one in New Hampshire, photographing a town meeting, and one in Cincinnati, photographing the University of Cincinnati basketball team and their star player, Oscar Robertson. At the town meeting, I focused on the most unusual and impressive faces I could find, faces with strong lines of personality or character. I used the close-up/distance technique, capturing people in action, as they protested or yelled or argued or pounded the backs of the chairs in front of them, or cried out with laughter, or applauded, or, afterward, gossiped and smiled with their neighbors over coffee and cake; then gradually moved away to catch the whole, the communal participation of a bunch of eccentrics at a meeting or a village social. There were no motels near this town at that time, so I stayed in a private house. It was a fine old New England farmhouse owned by an outspoken, not to say opinionated widow of sixty who amazed me by the depth of her understanding of the political issues in the town, and her cynicism. I made her the center of my piece, and she so charmed Russ and the others that they called the article 'Gingham Curtain Politics'. Not my choice of title, but it got the attention they desired.

The second assignment was even more of a challenge, since I'd never done sports photography: damn few women did. It was a challenge to capture those long-limbed guys jumping for baskets, leaping in circles to hedge the opposition, running, passing, dribbling the ball. I shot them at practice, and they let me get right on the court with them. I was nearly run down a few times, but I got a great shot of Washington from below, as he leaped for a shot. It made him appear nine feet long, with huge thighs and feet and all of him in motion. *World* put it on the cover. What a coup! Here too the close-up, zoom-out technique worked beautifully, since of course each player was unique and had a slightly different technique, yet the team worked together like a corps de ballet.

Here I stayed at a motel, and after the game with Penn, the team ended up partying in my room clear through the night. Two of them fell asleep there, but it didn't matter, since I never went to bed at all, just kept on partying until it was light, packed my bags, and called a cab for the airport. Slept all the way back. Fun.

I was nervous when I had to ask Pane to watch the kids while I went to New Hampshire. I went downstairs during the afternoon when Toni was at work, and instead of my usual cheery announcement of where I was going and when, I asked her diffidently if she would watch over the children for the four days. A shadow deepened on her face and she looked at me sadly. My heart stopped, my mind whirred: my mother would surely be willing to take them for four days, but she'd have to drive them all the way to Lynbrook to school each morning, and pick them up each afternoon, and they'd be unhappy away from their friends. I wondered if Mom would be willing to stay in my apartment. I was wondering how to ask her when Pane said, 'Yes, Anastasia, I will do, but soon no more. I am old, too tired for such big ones.'

I was relieved and burdened at the same time. 'Okay,

Pane, thanks. I'll have to look around for someone else. If you'd just do it until I find someone, I'd appreciate it very much.'

She nodded soberly and turned away from me.

So she hadn't forgotten or forgiven! Why was she so pleasant to me then?

The next time I called around, culling numbers from friends, from cards on the supermarket bulletin boards, from ads in the newspaper. I found a woman, a widow, who was willing to baby-sit at my house for days at a time. I was nervous about her. She sounded prissy over the telephone, I sensed the kids wouldn't like her, I foresaw months of problems, difficulty in getting away, worry while I was away, and kids unhappy while I was gone and furious when I returned. I only hoped she had a stiff uneasy telephone manner, and would be better in the flesh. But she would be visiting her daughter in California during the time I needed her.

I had to make another trip downstairs. I assured Pane that this would be the last time I would ask her, and she, she let tears creep into her eyes! I wanted to shout, to smack the wall. What did she want from me? I was only doing this because she had instructed me to. Did she want me to apologize? I couldn't. Maybe I should have let the whole issue go and just told the kids to ignore her language, but once I had broached it, I couldn't retreat, couldn't say I was wrong. Because I wasn't. Why did I feel so wrong?

I stamped back upstairs and tried to calm down. I told myself her attitude might not have anything to do with our quarrel. Maybe she had been happy to take the kids because she liked the extra money and she was lonely and enjoyed being with the kids. Maybe now she had Toni for company, and to bring in a little extra money – because he did buy things for the house apart from his board – she could let herself feel her age and tiredness. Maybe she was feeling worn out – she was only sixty-eight, but she's had a hard life since childhood. But with a woman like Pane, you could never hope to find out the truth of her feelings. It occurred to me that although Sonders and Pane were opposites, both of them were in different ways tyrants. Both permitted only one sort of relation; their way of being was the only way of being. And then I thought: but my mother is like that too. And then I thought maybe we all are. And then I decided to stop thinking.

On the way from the train station, I wasn't thinking about anything except wiping my silly smile off my face – a smile that had covered it all the way from Cincinnati. I was tired but quiet and glowing the way you are when you've had a wonderful time and people have made you feel good about yourself. My car was not in front of the house when the cab dropped me off, but I assumed Toni had taken it to go marketing or to take the kids someplace – it was a Saturday afternoon.

So I was shocked when Toni met me at the front door, and even more shocked by his face. Immediately I thought something had happened to one of my kids.

'What is it?' I gasped.

He shook his head. 'Nothing. It's all right. The kids are fine.'

I held onto the molding of the doorway, which looked as if it were moving. 'Then where's my car?'

Nice, selfish question. I wasn't thinking clearly. I shouldn't have had so much to drink last night. The fun of it – the night itself – had completely vanished from my memory.

He grinned a little. 'I cleaned out the garage. Thought it was stupid for you to have to park in the street with a perfectly good garage back there. Some of that junk was old when my grandfather collected it. Why don't you come inside?' he laughed, grabbing my duffel bag and camera case.

I stepped into the small hallway. 'Well?'

'It's Gramma.'

I could feel my face grow cold. Pane! Sweet good Pane!

'Had a stroke. It's not too bad, they think she'll recover, she's in the hospital now. Her right side.'

It was only because I was tired and still had alcohol in my blood, but I burst into tears. This – it occurred to me later – gave Toni a perfect excuse to embrace me, and placed our relation in a slightly different mode – but I swear, I insist, that wasn't on my mind at the time. (I'm almost sure.)

The kids came out of Pane's apartment at the sound, and they began to cry too, and embrace me, and we all walked back in there as if it were our home, and pushed away the Scrabble board and Toni brought me a drink (I didn't tell him how little I needed it), and we sat together until dinnertime as they told me the horrible details of the day before.

Pane recovered, but she would never be the same. The right side of her face drooped a little, giving that sweet accepting visage a cast of malevolence. Her right eye protruded slightly, and she had almost no vision in it. And for months, she could not walk. She needed a permanent caretaker.

Her sons arrived to visit her in the hospital and decide what to do with her. Knowing how little they cared about her, I was sure her sons would stick her in a nursing home for the rest of her life and sell the house and split the proceeds. I would have to move. By now I had some money in a bank account, but I was saving it because I didn't believe that my job, my good fortune, would last. I would need it again, I felt, to tide me over after *World* bounced me, until I found another way to earn a living. And I didn't want to move – my kids liked this town, had friends nearby, would be unhappy moving. But all that was secondary.

I was terrified for Pane. I went to see her every day; I talked to her even though she didn't seem to hear me; I stroked her hands, I told her everything the kids were doing. If one of her sons were there, he would glare at me, sitting in a corner reading a newspaper. She improved. It was obvious she could get better, to some degree anyway. But she wouldn't get better in a nursing home.

And a nursing home is precisely where the family intended to send her, I discovered later. Toni stopped them. He argued – passionately – I know because when he described the arguments to me later, he was still passionate – how much they owed her, how good she was, and how she deserved a chance at whatever life was left her. They countered that she would need continual care, that that was expensive, that they could not afford it (having so many car payments, so many kids in college; one was still paying off a new swimming pool; another had two little ones with braces on their teeth), and besides, who could they trust? They would have to send checks, the woman would have to be able to cash them, how could they be sure she wasn't boozing it up and leaving Momma to rot in her own pee? Who would take care of the house, see to it that the leaves were racked, the snow shoveled, the oil delivered, that the roof didn't leak.

Toni had an answer: himself. Would they trust him? He wanted to write, he hated his job, it was mindless, and it left him little time for writing. For a stipulated monthly payment, he would take care of Pane, and be able to write. Her Social Security check would continue to keep up the house, with his help. They were aghast. It would have been different if he'd been a girl, a woman. Then they would have given her the bare essential in payment, and gone home and forgotten her. 'They would have gone home, boozed it up, and let her rot in her own dust,' Toni said bitterly, later.

But Toni was male, the first child in the entire family to go to college, and *this* was what he proposed to do with his splendid masculinity, his college degree? What in the name of heaven and hell was wrong with him? Was he a man or wasn't he?

Toni won, but not because they ever accepted his case. He won because they didn't want to be bothered. They had wives who wanted them to come home, jobs or businesses to attend to. None of them wanted to take the time to search for a nursing home, or a companion – in fact, one of the brothers, Louis, came up one evening and asked me if *I'd* do that. I would have, of course, if Pane had been alone and in need of that, but I was furious.

'I have a job, Louis! Surely *you* owe her this!'

He sat there, a beer can in his hand, chewing on his thick lower lip. 'Well, you owe her too. You used her enough, I guess. Baby-sitting.'

'I always paid her.'

'Uh-huh. Fair recompense for her time, on the open market, I suppose?'

God, I hated him.

'I paid her ten dollars a day for every day or partial day I was away.'

'Barely covered their food, I'd think.'

'I paid for their food.'

'Where I come from, we pay our baby-sitters fifty cents an hour to stay with them when they're *asleep*. Don't sound like fair recompense to me. A lot of responsibility she had, wachin' kids all day long.'

'*My* kids sleep too. Ten hours a night. And they are in school for five. That means I was paying your mother over a dollar an hour for the hours they were awake. And they were often not here.'

'Yeah. That's a worry, ain't it.' Louis's grammar did not come from ignorance – the other brothers were well-spoken enough except the one who worked at the GM plant near Detroit, who spoke in a calculatedly tough 'masculine' way. Louis put on the folksy accent to disarm. He'd probably adopted it when he moved to Missouri where he sold real estate – adopted it to hide the fact that he was a Yankee. He was the most prosperous of the brothers. 'Worryin' about where they are when they're not here?'

I stood up. 'It appalls me that you are trying to shunt the responsibility for your mother on to me. I guess you've noticed that I care about her. I guess too that's more than you do – given the way you've all ignored her for years.'

'Well I guess we don't need you, little lady, to tell us what we oughta do. Any good woman'd be honored to repay some of what you owe her.'

I couldn't control myself then. 'And the problem with you is you've had too many good women in your life: you've learned to be a bastard! Get out!'

He rose lazily, heaving his great belly out of the chair. 'Yeah, well I guess you're throwin' me out of a house I own, little lady, at least one-fifth of,' he chuckled in his folksy way.

'You don't own this apartment as long as I have a lease and am paying rent on it. And she isn't dead yet!' All my life I'd read about people talking 'with gritted teeth,' and I never before understood what that meant. Now I was doing it.

I flopped in a chair after he'd gone and I'd noisily locked and chained the door behind him. I sat there trying to relax my neck and shoulder muscles. I could hear them arguing downstairs. They were really yelling; they'd subside, then one voice would rise through the floorboards like a sonic boom. I knew it was Antoni, Toni's father, and I knew that he was showering contempt on his son as a pansy and a weakling, and I understood why Toni did not want to go back to Ohio. The argument rumbled and roared for nearly two hours. The voices began to sound drunk. The front door slammed. I guessed it was Toni, gone out just to get out of there, and I ran to my front window. He was walking, head down, hands in his pockets, fast. Where could he go? I felt awful for him, I wanted to throw open the window and tell him to come upstairs and sleep in my bed with me, warm and safe.

Suppose the kids had heard and were lying in bed in terror? I got up and tiptoed to their doors, pushed each one open a crack, and peered in. They seemed asleep. I whispered their names; neither one moved. Asleep.

I poured myself a drink, formally, sometimes I do when I am preparing to Think. I flopped in the chair again. Would Pane hate the way I treated her son? I know she would have hated the way he treated me. How could it happen, this good woman, this saint, this sweet loving person, how could she have sons like Louis and the others?

I knew her husband was domineering. I could hear it in her voice when she talked about him, even though he'd been dead for over twenty years, and I'd seen it in her posture when I bullied her into submission about her language. He may have been brutal, cruel, to his sons, probably was. But that would not account for the way they treated her, the way they must feel about her.

I thought about Pane's sins. Not being honest, that was the main one: all that sweetness and all those smiles, when god knew what was going on inside. But I'd known Pane for quite a while now, and I had no sense that inside she was very different from outside. She wasn't brittle and angry, covering it over with a smile like the glaze on pastry. She wasn't calculating or mean or envious. She was really good: the only serious fault I'd ever seen in her was her bigotry. Maybe she whitewashed her sons' behavior and blamed everything on other people, especially if they were not Polish, not Christian, not white. Was that enough to account for them?

I finished Thinking when I finished my drink. I always ended that way – since I could never find my way out of the mazes I built, I simply had to pull down the shades on them. But the questions didn't disappear; they crumbled in a heap like cobwebs in an unused barn, dark, thick, frightening grey masses lying along the floor and climbing the wall in a corner of the room.

One by one, the sons left. Three of them were staying in a motel – the nearest one was in Rockville Centre – so they had to rent a car as well. That cost money they would prefer to spend otherwise. There was no one to cook for them, so the men had to eat their own cooking (hah!) or spend money to eat in restaurants.

Antoni left with a roar, slamming the front door with his heavy Gladstone bag, stamping down the front steps to the waiting cab. (Toni never, while they were visiting, asked to use my car. And I never offered.) Paul and Jan stayed to bring Pane home from the hospital. Toni told me when they were going to pick her up, so I was ready. I ran downstairs thinking This much I would do. Pane didn't clean often and the men certainly hadn't, and her room, the room she would be confined in for a long time, was filthy.

The curtains – I had known this and prepared for it – were too disgusting to be saved. First thing I did was take them down, dust flying out from them and making me cough. I bunched them up and tossed them in the garbage. Then I found a mop, tied an old towel around it, and mopped the ceiling, the tops of the walls, especially the corners, which had cobwebs as thick as those in my brain. I lugged my vacuum cleaner downstairs and it gulped up several years' worth of dust from the faded rug; I got down on my hands and knees with a damp sponge and wiped up the wood floor around the carpet. I dusted every surface with lemon oil and washed the windows and the mirror. I checked the bed, but someone – Toni probably – had lain fresh sheets on it. Then, with a soapy cloth, I sponged all the knickknacks. I unwrapped the fresh curtains I had bought at Woolworth's and hung them. Finally, I brought down a jug of chrysanthemums and set them on the chest of drawers across from the bed where she would see them. I ran back upstairs – I didn't want to be there when they came in, and I was hoping they wouldn't notice what I'd done. They'd think they had me; they'd think I was another one of those good women they could cozen into doing their work for them.

I watched from the window as they helped her out of the car; my cheeks felt as if they were bleeding, but it was just tears. She looked so frail, so tiny in the wheelchair, like a baby in a carriage. Her hair, which had been that colorless greyed brown, was almost white, and she was wearing the same shabby old black coat she wore every spring and fall. There was silence downstairs for a long time, and I smelled coffee. I would not go down until they left.

At last they did, and I went down and knocked lightly. Toni must have been expecting me because the door opened immediately.

He kissed me. 'Thanks for cleaning Gram's room. I wanted to do it, but my uncles were in there until just before we left. It was sweet of you.'

'It was nothing. How is she?'

'Sleeping. She's exhausted. But she noticed the flowers. I told her you'd brought them. She smiled and fell asleep.'

My eyes filled up. I was getting goddamned soupy with this business.

'You want to see her?'

He led me to her room and pushed open the door, which was ajar. 'I want to be sure I hear her,' he explained.

A stranger with white hair and a twisted face was lying in the bed, making a high hump for such a little woman.

The shades were drawn. The room smelled of soap and flowers. She was breathing evenly.

Toni and I sat for a while in the living room, talking in whispers. He told me a little about his uncles, and apologized for Louis's intrusion on me. 'I couldn't stop him. They don't listen to me.'

'I understood.' I sipped the coffee he'd poured for me. 'So you're really going to do it – take care of her?'

'If I can. She can use a bedpan. She only needs pills now, not shots. And if she needs a shot, a nurse will come. Mainly, she needs to be fed, kept clean, and kept company.' He smiled like a mischievous boy.

He was going to keep her clean? Empty her bedpans? Was he another saint? Ugh, the very thought . . . But of course I'd do such things for my children, had done them for years, without thinking. . . . Well, I wasn't going to start pasting gold stars on his forehead. Maybe he was really strange, and got kicks out of things like that. A weirdo. Maybe his father knew him better than I did. I got up.

'Thanks for the coffee. And anytime you want to use the car, just yell. And if you need to get out, go to the market or anything, I'll be glad to spell you.'

'Thanks. Mrs D'Antonio and Mrs Schneider have offered too. I think everything will be fine. They even brought over a casserole and a ham and a couple of cakes, so Gram won't have to eat my cooking for a while.'

'Good.' Yes, women do gather round to help. 'I have a pot of chicken soup on the stove, I'm making for her. I'll bring it down later.'

'You all are saints,' he smiled.

'Don't say that!' I cried out sharply, and frightened myself with the loudness of my own voice.

Toni quit his job, and settled in immediately as Pane's caretaker. Little by little, she improved. At first she stayed awake only for minutes at a time; then she began to sit up for a half hour, so Toni carried the television set into her room and set it up on the bureau across from the bed. Then she began to stay awake for several hours at a time. She loved the game shows. The kids visited her every day, and on rainy days one of them would stay with her and play gin rummy or checkers. I visited her every day too, and her friends came in several times a week.

But she could not speak, and that grieved her. She would try to talk, she would gesture with her left hand, and roll her eye. But she would give up in frustration. Sometimes a tear appeared on her cheek after one of these efforts.

Because she went to sleep for the night around nine, Toni was free at night. And of course so was I. So it came to pass that he would come up or I would go down, one night out of three, one night out of two, and spend an hour or two chatting. He was writing well, he told me, putting in four to five hours a day.

We talked like friends, like women friends. After all, we were both 'women' – we took care of the relatively helpless; we washed dishes and did laundry, marketed and cooked, worried about others. We also both had work of our own, creative work which did not lend itself to discussion but was simply there, like validations of our personal existence. The current of desire that had struck up between us at our first meeting resurrected itself with this togetherness, this privacy; but of course Pane was always in the next room or my kids, and just knowing they were there inhibited us. At the same time, the repression of our feelings acted as a great stimulus to them – for there is no aphrodisiac like tension, taboo. I'd be startled to find myself staring at his hands while he was talking; or catch him staring at my mouth – I could tell it was my mouth, not my face he was looking at. But something had to happen to carry us over the barrier we had created.

I had several assignments during this period, all of them in the States, none requiring me to be gone for more than four days. Each time, Toni took care of the kids, working it in easily enough with his care for Pane. He was upstairs and down, just as if we were all one family living in a two-story house; Toni slept downstairs so he could hear Pane if she wakened during the night, but left the door to our apartment open. The children adored him. He treated them more like an older brother than a parent; he taught them to play poker; he read Arden's stumbling attempts to write

poetry, and bought her some paperback books of poetry –
Gerard Manley Hopkins, Emily Dickinson, Robert Frost.
He played ball with them, played chess with Billy, watched
TV football games and talked sports with him. He was
gentle and his authority was always couched in a tone of
'C'mon guys, you know you gotta do this, you know I gotta
do what I'm doing too.'

After a while, he told me something about his parents.
He hated his father, hated his dominating, bullying manner
with his children and his wife. Antoni was a table pounder,
a bigot, and mean with money. He was already, only two
months after Pane's return from the hospital, dragging his
feet about contributing to the small check the brothers sent
Toni each month. But worst of all, he drank. Not every
day or even every week – but when he drank, he drank
until he was drunk, and then came home violent, beating
his wife or any child who was handy. 'My two older
brothers got out of the house as soon as they could. They
got the worst of it, he was younger and stronger, and there
were only the two of them. My oldest brother just ran off
when he was sixteen – after my father whipped him. The
other one enlisted during the Korean War and never came
back to Dayton.'

Toni loved his mother, but his voice sounded thin and
lemony when he talked about her.

'You don't respect her,' I ventured.

'How can I?' whined the lemony voice. 'She lets him
beat up on her, her poor bones are frozen in a cowering
position. And when he used to beat up on us, she would
just stand there and cry and wring her hands.'

'He doesn't hit the children anymore?'

Toni looked over at me. 'Can I have a drink? I mean, a
real drink, whiskey. Do you have any?'

Since I had been a 'success', I'd taken to keeping a bottle
of rye on a shelf. I poured a drink for each of us.

Toni settled down again in the old shabby armchair
facing the equally old shabby couch. He sipped.

'I studied to kill my father,' he said. 'When I was ten, I
was short for my age. The neighborhood we live in, in
Dayton, is blue-collar, rough enough without being really

dangerous. When I was about ten, I told my father I wanted to take boxing lessons. I was small for my age, and I told him I wanted to do something to protect myself. That was the one thing I ever did that pleased him. He signed me up at the local Y, and I trained myself to fight. I worked hard, for years. I ran, I jumped rope, I learned judo; later on, I did a lot of weight lifting, to strengthen my muscles . . .'

(So *that's* how he got those arms, that chest!)

'I worked out every afternoon after school for a couple of hours. My father was surprised at my dedication. He started to talk about my possibly training to be a fighter – bantamweight, that's all I'd ever be able to be. But he didn't know the real reason I was training. I wanted to turn myself into a superman so the next time my dad started in on my mom, I could level him. I knew it would take years – you've seen my dad.'

Antoni weighed over two hundred, although he was only about five feet ten. Toni was no taller than that now.

'As it turned out, though . . .' he wiped his hand across his face, 'I didn't defend her, I defended myself. I'd done something he didn't like – I can't recall now even what it was – he didn't like most things I did. Maybe I'd dared to defend my friend Brian. My dad hates everybody who isn't Polish – and lots of people who *are* Polish, too – but the people he hates the most are the Irish, I guess because there are a lot of them in our neighborhood, and they were moving up a little faster than most of the Poles. Anyway, he didn't like something I said, and he swung his arm out to deck me, and without thinking, without even realizing what I was doing, I grabbed his arm and turned it back. It happened so fast . . . it made him fall right out of his chair. I was thirteen.

'It's funny. You can hate your father, but there's something – I don't know – a mystical taboo on him. I felt terrible, seeing him on the floor like that, I was overcome with guilt and terror, I felt that God would reach down from heaven and strike me dead on the spot. My dad saw all this on my face as he sat there on the floor staring at me. He looked at me – the only word to describe his expression is malevolently. And I must have looked terrified, so he knew he could get away with what he did next.

'He stood up real slow and started to take off his belt. "Hit your father, will you?" he said. I stood there. I didn't say a thing. My mother didn't say anything either. Her face was dead white. I guess she thought he'd kill me.'

Toni gulped some rye.

'He reached over and grabbed me by the hair and pulled me down the cellar stairs and told me to let down my pants. Then he threw me over a low table and began to belt me. I didn't try to stop him, I felt he had the right to do this after what I'd done. But I wouldn't cry out either, and he kept hitting me, he said he was going to hit me until I cried. And I wouldn't cry.'

There were tears in my eyes, and I wanted to go over and hold him, but I didn't move.

'My mother had come downstairs too, I don't know when. She walks silently and speaks in a soft low voice. But suddenly, along with his grunts and the whack of his belt, I heard her voice, low and sad.

'You will kill him, Antoni,' she said, No crying, no tears at all. His arm held for a moment. I was half out of it with pain, but my heart was whirling. I thought, yes, and then he'll kill her, but he didn't. He stopped. He walked upstairs.

'I was sick after that, for quite a while. I couldn't go to school. But he never raised his hand to me again. I don't know why. Maybe he thought the next time I'd feel justified in killing him. And the next time he started in on my little brother, I just stood up and looked at him, and he stopped.

'But he kept on beating my mother. I wasn't able to stop that. He'd come in late at night, after a boozing session, and just whack her. For no reason. She always cried softly, so as not to frighten my little brother and sister and me. Sometimes I'd hear something and go running downstairs, but by then he'd have stopped and fallen into a chair, passed out. Once I went over to wake him up – I was about sixteen, and as tall as he by then, and a hell of a lot stronger, even if he had sixty pounds on me. I was going to wake him up and punch him out. But my mother wouldn't let me. She held on to me, weeping, begging. I gave up then. I was going away to college soon, and I vowed I'd never return to that house, that craziness.'

He wiped his face again; I could see it was damp. Not with tears, just with sweat. 'Summers I got jobs far away from Dayton – I'd do anything. I worked on a ranch – funny, because I'd never been on a horse in my life, I'd hardly ever seen one. I even worked on an assembly line, just like my old man. But not in Dayton.

'After the fall I left for college, I never went back except for holidays. And I didn't always go back for them. I can't stand that house. I'll never go back. They can have it, they seem to like it. Fucking insanity.'

He put both his hands over his face and cried a little. I did not move. I didn't want to embrace him that way, as a mother. Soon, he raised his face, apologized, got up and went into the bathroom. He came out with a washed face, eyes moist and deep, and walked toward me. I stood up and walked toward him, a few steps, and we closed each other in our arms as easily and naturally as a morning glory closes up at night. Then we went to bed.

five

Belle smoothed the meringue carefully over the pie, sprinkled granulated sugar on it lightly, and put it back into the oven. She set the minute timer, and sat down on a kitchen chair and lighted a cigarette. She did not like to sit in the kitchen, but browning the meringue took only a few minutes, there was no point in going out to the porch. She was making this pie for Mr Campanella, her piano teacher. Every time she took him a pie, he became ecstatic, he started to speak Italian, he said he and his wife believed Mrs Stevens made the best pies of anyone in the world.

She smiled a little, thinking of it.

Her lesson was at three; the pie would be cool by then. And between now and then, she had nothing to do! She would practice her lesson again, and take a bath, and remove the pins from her hair and comb it, spend time on her makeup. She would make a *toilette*, she, Belle! Just like a lady of leisure. She liked to look nice when she went to

Mr Campanella's, they were such cultured people, Mrs Campanella sang at the Met even though she was over fifty and very fat, and he – oh, he was so elegant, and their house was full of antiques, all the tables covered with photographs of famous people they knew, and that wonderful piano . . . Bosen . . . Bosensomething.

She felt always a little let down when she returned from her lesson. She would go over and over everything in her mind – the way he looked and sounded, the way he looked at her, everything he said about her performance. He was very kind to her, but she knew she wasn't good. After all, she'd listened to the girls practicing for years. Here she'd been taking lessons for three years, and she still couldn't play any of the pieces Anastasia was playing after two. She was too old. Fifty-six. The girls had started at seven. But maybe she'd never have been a good pianist, even if she'd started young. She lacked something . . .

Still, he was kind to her. He knew she knew she would never be good. She just wanted to play some songs, songs she liked, play them really well. But she could never seem to get the songs to roll out from under her fingers, the way they did when he played them. They were easy enough. She must do exercises, he said, get her hands strong. But she practiced her Hanon every day, and her scales too. Arpeggios were harder.

Anastasia hadn't practised in years, but sometimes when she came to visit, she'd sit down at the piano, and she could still make the piano sing, play Chopin so beautifully, it was beautiful even if she screwed up her nose when Belle told her so. She didn't like the way she sounded, she didn't know how Belle wished *she* could make the piano sound like that, well, Anastasia always looked down her nose at things . . .

Anastasia. Belle's mouth set in a grimace. Her birthday was in two weeks. Thanksgiving. What to give her. A book on growing up. She loved lemon meringue pie. Belle sighed. She would probably bake one for her, but she didn't want to.

The timer buzzed. She got up and put on a mitt and removed the pie from the oven. Perfect – golden brown tips on waves of white meringue. She set it carefully on the cake rack to cool. The she rinsed the soiled dishes and put them in the dishwasher. She loved her dishwasher. It was still new. They had remodeled the kitchen last year, put in lovely new cabinets and drawers that slid open easily, and a new floor, a special kind of linoleum – or maybe they didn't call it linoleum anymore – that stayed shiny all the time without being waxed. Except once in a while. Ed did it two or three times a year. It was very pretty, shades of white and ivory and cream in little boxes shaped like mahjongg pieces.

Ed didn't like her to put pots in the dishwasher, so she scrubbed them by hand and laid them on the drain. Then she smoothed cream on her hands. They weren't bad, considering what she'd done with them all these years. She wished they were as white and slender as they had been years ago, but still, they weren't bad. Setting her face in a smile, she went upstairs and drew a bath.

Nowadays, she took a long leisurely bath several times a week. She even had bath salts Joy had sent for her last birthday. She leaned back and let the water lap around her. When it stopped, she moved, to set it in motion again. The water sloshed high up at the tub whenever she moved her body. There was more of her than there used to be. She watched her weight, and all the salesgirls said she had a wonderful figure for a woman her age, but she wished she could be thin again, as thin as she had been, of course her legs and hips had never been what you could call thin, but since they'd been playing golf, her legs were thinner. Anastasia commented on it, she said Belle's legs looked good. But Anastasia would say anything to make her feel good. You couldn't believe her, she was always trying to get Belle to do things. Joy too: always telling Belle to go out and meet people and play bridge at the church on the corner, not understanding, not knowing.

Playing golf was good. You were out in the air, in the sun, and walking over greenness, that was nice. And the other people on the golf course were nice, well-dressed, not fancy of course, you don't get dolled up for golf, but it was nice to wear neat cotton wraparound skirts and light jersey tops, to have soft-soled low-heeled shoes on your feet, it felt good, and she had several outfits and three different cotton golf hats, and some neat poplin jackets, white, pale blue, and yellow, they were comfortable too. She looked just like the other women out there, and they all always smiled and waved, and Belle and Ed smiled and waved, and sometimes they even stopped and chatted, and they were beginning to make some friends, Peggy Helder, she was an interesting woman. She didn't get married until she was fifty, and then *she kept her own apartment*! She lived on the West Side of Manhattan and he lived on the East Side. Anastasia laughed when Belle told her about it, she cried 'How to keep a marriage happy!' Her husband was an important man, he imported something, something like machinery. And Peggy had a little house in Long Beach, that was how she came to play golf at Jones Beach. Her daughter lived there, grown daughter, nearly Anastasia's age. She must have been married before, then . . .

Her husband didn't mind if she went to Long Beach every weekend, well, he traveled a lot himself, and besides, they didn't even see each other every night, she went home from work to her apartment on what was it? Well, Eighty-something Street, and he went to his. I wonder if he cooks his own dinner, or if he eats in a restaurant every night? He must be very rich. And Peggy liked Belle and Ed, and invited them to have drinks one evening after golf. The house in Long Beach was small, but it was a summer house, how many people could afford to have two residences?

Peggy had been to Europe many times. Belle sighed and splashed herself up and out of the tub. So many years she had dreamed of it, seen it in her imagination! And there were beautiful things, that square in Brussels, the Rhine River, the castles. But she wasn't impressed by London, it was dirty and grey, depressing, all that rain! And Paris was so cold it was a nightmare. Anyway, it was all too much for her. Anastasia said you shouldn't see thirty countries in fifteen days, well, she was exaggerating of course, looking down her nose as usual, they only went to six countries, that time, not everyone could do what Anastasia did, she just went and stayed someplace, but she had jobs to do and people to meet her and take her around. She didn't understand how hard it would be to go by yourself if you couldn't speak a language. When Belle and Ed went, the tour people made all the arrangements and did the tipping and handled the travel from one place to another. How would they have gotten around without the tour? They couldn't read the signs or tell the taxi drivers where they wanted to go.

But she had to admit the tours were exhausting. Up at six, suitcases outside your door by seven, all that waiting in the lobby, the bus never left until eight, and then so many hours on the bus, driving, driving, all day sometimes, the guides spouting into the loudspeaker, she couldn't understand a word they said, and sometimes it was so hot, or else it was cold, Paris was very cold, she froze, she hadn't brought a warm jacket, she was miserable. Even the hotel was cold, oh it was a beautiful hotel, all three-star hotels the travel agent had said, but freezing and the coffee! horrible! she couldn't drink the coffee, and the bed was hard and lumpy and the pillows felt as if they were made of board. The second time they went she wanted to take her own pillows but hard as he tried, Ed couldn't make them fit into the suitcases, only two apiece they were allowed.

Tired, so tired all the time, from getting up so early and those long bus rides. She was too old for Europe, for travel. But she had wanted to see it. The Eiffel Tower, well, it wasn't pretty, not really, although she tried to make herself feel it, she said to herself, the Eiffel Tower, the Eiffel Tower, I am in Paris, but it didn't do any good, she was cold and the food was awful, tour food Anastasia said, but it seemed like any food to her, just meat with gravy on it and french-fried potatoes and overdone vegetables, it wasn't as good as Howard Johnson's. She hardly ate it, Ed always finished her dinner and her ice cream, every night they had ice cream for dessert. She could see other people in the restaurant having interesting-looking pastries but they never got one. The Arc de Triomphe, that was nice. They took an elevator up, she wouldn't have walked, she couldn't, she was too tired, and stood there, and the whole city was laid out below them, broad avenues like spokes emerging from an axis, tree-lined. Beautiful. And there was a woods nearby, right in the middle of the city, the Bois de Boulogne, something like that, she couldn't really hear, her hearing was so awful . . . She sprinkled perfumed talcum powder – good quality talcum, with a lovely scent, Joy had sent it with bath salts and cologne – over her damp body, and padded barefoot into her bedroom in a long heavy white terry-cloth robe. So nice to have a robe just for when you're wet. She let it fall off her shoulders as she sat at her vanity table looking into the mirror. She raised her chin a little. Not bad. Not good. She examined her body. The flesh on her upper arms was thick and flabby.

Arden: she was only four, maybe even younger. I was wearing a sundress, my arms exposed, I must have been in my late forties. She was sitting beside me, and she turned and looked at my arms and lifted one of them up and jiggled the flesh of the underarm, and sat back appraisingly, and said, 'Not yet. But soon.' Funny kid. Smart.

She opened the drawer that held her girdles and bras, immaculate, folded neatly, in piles, and chose her undergarments. In the next drawer were underpants, and the one below held slips, all ironed and folded neatly. The new chest of drawers was wonderful, so much room, and so beautiful. She gazed around her. She'd done the room in a Chinese style, because of the Chinese lines and fittings on the furniture. She'd bought a jade green rug, and made drapes and bedspreads of a darker green damask. Her prize possession was the white Kwan Yin lamp that stood on her vanity, but there were other lovely Chinese pieces in the room, prints, bowls, ashtrays. It was lovely and cool. It could have been in the house of a wealthy woman. Her old habits of watching pennies still worked to her benefit – she'd done a great deal on a little money. Anyone seeing how they lived now would think Ed made much more than he actually did.

Throwing a Chinese satin robe Ed had given her for Christmas over her underclothes, she walked into Anastasia's room. The one problem with the house was closet space. She used the closet in Anastasia's room, and Ed the closet in Joy's room, and he had put up a rack in the lower part of the hall linen closet for his jackets, but even with the big closet in their own bedroom, their clothes were a little crowded. She opened the closet door and surveyed her dresses and suits. She liked to look nice for her piano lesson. She chose a classic beige wool knit three-piece suit: the jacket was trimmed with black. She'd wear her new camel's hair coat and black heels and carry a black bag. Yes.

She laid the clothes carefully on Ed's bed, and removed the robe. She did not want to spoil it with makeup. She sat down on her vanity bench in her slip, a pretty one, plain but nice, a pale peach satin with a tiny embroidered flower in one corner of the bodice and removed the metal pin curlers from her hair and combed it. Then she applied makeup, slowly, carefully, leaning close to the mirror to do it. It was hard for her to see her eyes when she was putting on eye makeup. It was awful. Her eyesight was getting worse. Her throat filled, and she sat back and blinked back tears.

Joy was always telling her to go out and make friends. She didn't know. Anastasia knew, she saw, sometimes. But now! She'd been proud of Anastasia, getting that important job, flying all over the world, having her pictures in *World*, having love affairs in exotic places – such a glamorous life! Still, every time *she* saw Anastasia, she was wearing pants and a shirt and those shabby old huaraches. But it was fun when Anastasia dropped in while the kids were at school, and they had a couple of drinks and Anastasia told her about her adventures, she'd get Belle laughing, all those men! But this one wasn't a man, he was just a boy, and it wasn't as if he even had any money or even a job. Imagine a man spending his life taking care of an old woman, of course it was nice of him, and it helped Anastasia, what would she do with the kids when she traveled, Belle would probably have had to take them, or maybe even stay at Anastasia's house, all those stairs up and down every day! But did she have to invite him for Sunday dinner? When Belle and Ed were coming?

Of course, Belle was always happy to see Pane Nowak,

she loved Pane Nowak, she was so much like Momma, even looked like her a little, not her features but the look, the round wrinkled face, the grey-brown hair pulled back in a bun, but Pane Nowak had more hair and it kept escaping from the bun. The same shapeless body, the cotton housedresses, the tie-up black shoes, the shabby black coat.

Belle's throat filled again. If only I'd been able to do something for Momma before she died. Get her a beautiful coat. I couldn't even afford clothes for the children. The tears overflowed this time, and she pulled a paper tissue from her vanity and blew her nose.

I could never do anything I wanted to do.

Pane Nowak, poor woman, her face all distorted that way, but at least she had lived. More than my poor mother did. She's sixty-eight, Momma died when she was sixty-two. I was still young, I had nothing.

She's young too, not even thirty-one, she looks twenty-five, all those men she meets, important men, couldn't she find someone better, someone who can take care of her and the children? I wonder if Pane Nowak knows. She's not herself, maybe she never will be again, she can't talk. She used to be so happy to be invited to my house for thanksgiving, she would cry when she said goodbye. She appreciated good cooking, good ingredients, fresh sweet butter not margarine or Crisco, heavy cream. She always used to bring a babka or a strudel when she came for dinner, they were delicious, they tasted just like Momma's, I wish I'd asked her for the recipe before . . . I don't remember how Momma made them. Well, but at least she's walking now, even if she has to use a cane.

Maybe the boy won't last long, maybe Pane Nowak will recover completely. Oh, he'll get fed up with that life, what can it be for a healthy young man like that? It's like taking care of a baby all day, who would do that if they didn't have to? He'll go off, and then maybe Anastasia will find someone else, she should get married again, how is she going to take care of herself? You need a man. She could find someone, a big doctor, a big lawyer, she's attractive and intelligent, what's the matter with her?

At least Joy has done well for herself. Justin is a bit stiff, but he's a major now, an important man, he has security, a wonderful pension when he retires, and he could retire in fourteen years, and at least they were out of the Philippines, so far away, primitive, Joy said there were constant little wars going on, bullets flying over the military compound where they lived, horrible! A nightmare! The children, I couldn't have stood it, I would have had to come home. But what can she do, she has to be where her husband is assigned. She wants me to come to California, maybe I'll go next year when Ed gets his vacation. But then we wouldn't be able to go to Valeria.

So nice there, lovely old stone buildings, neat rooms, wonderful meals, the little nine-hole golf course, just right for me, the lake. All the people are lovely, and they're like us, middle-class but not rich, there are no low-class people there, all neat nice people, the Harmons, they sent a card last Christmas, they missed us last summer when we went to Europe, Greece, the islands, Santorini, ugh.

Joy and Justin went to Hong Kong, that must be interesting. Justin is a good husband, he's a good provider and he doesn't drink or gamble or run around. Joy seemed tense her last visit, more hysterical than usual, but of course it's hard with two little children, it will be better for her in California even if she doesn't have servants there, safer, healthier. Jonathan's a handful, so active, climbing up on the roof of their house when he was only a year and a half old, getting stuck in that pipe, always in motion, but now he is in kindergarten, and Julie is no trouble, such a good child, both good kids, so were Anastasia's kids, good kids, I have wonderful grandchildren.

Maybe I will go to California. It's hard, seeing them only once every three years, and then when they come they stay a week, and Ed gets grumpy with kids underfoot, he doesn't like kids, the house a mess all the time. It would be nice if they were posted nearer, maybe next time. Ed might want to drive out there, too far, I couldn't take it even with the air-conditioning in the car, crossing the desert. Better to fly and rent a car, but that would be expensive, still it would be expensive to drive – all that gas, the motels, meals out for so many days.

They were still living in quarters, Joy had written, they hadn't yet found a house they liked. Maybe it would be better not to go next summer, she might just be getting settled in a new house. The letter is downstairs, in the porch.

I'll have to save up for it in either case, maybe I'll go the year after next, go to Valeria next summer.

If I'm still here. If I can still see. Her eyes filled again, and she dabbed them with a tissue. She stood up, slid her skirt, then the top, over her head, and surveyed herself in the mirror. Her hair was a little mussed, but she'd fix it later, before she left. She straightened up the room and went downstairs, into the kitchen, found her reading glasses, and walked to the porch. She sat down gracefully, enjoying the luxurious sound of her satin slip against her nylon stockings, and the soft feel of the wool skirt as she sat. Like a woman of olden times in many skirts, a lady, white hands and delicate feet, moving gracefully from room to room, sitting with upright back, pouring tea . . .

One cigarette on the porch, then I'll practice.

She lighted her cigarette, then picked up the letter luxuriously. Yes, quarters. What are they like, I wonder. He is a major, they couldn't be too bad, they had to be better than that horrible place Anastasia lives, all those stairs, the tiny rooms! She could move now, probably, she makes good money, but she doesn't want to leave that boy . . .

Five rooms it said. They certainly couldn't stay there. They would have to stay in a motel. Anyway, it would be better, two little children racing around the house, the noise . . . In Germany when she visited them it was hard enough, and that time there was only Jonathan. It was all right, the Black Forest, the Rhine, oh that was beautiful, those castles up on the mountains, the quaint little town, Heidelberg, but the guest room in Joy's house was cramped and she'd had to sleep in a double bed with Ed, the ceilings were so low, she was tired all the time . . .

Always tired. Always. She had always been always tired, but before she could understand it, she worked so hard, always working, trying to get ahead, make a decent life for the children. But now, she had time, She still marketed and cleaned the house and cooked and baked and did the laundry and ironing. But that was only half what she used to do. Why should she be tired now? So weary, down to her bones. Something wrong. The doctor said he couldn't find anything, he said she was just a little anemic, nothing else, vitamins, he said, she couldn't take them, they choked her. But she knew there was something wrong. She knew.

Maybe she'd get to California, and maybe she wouldn't.

Chapter XII

one

When was it she started to fall apart? Was it after she got a whiplash in an accident, when was that, which accident? there were several. Was that the time the crazy man forced her off the road? Maybe it was after she developed arthritis. She stopped playing golf, then she stopped her piano lessons. No, she stopped the piano lessons first. Or, no – she stopped the lessons after she lost the hearing in the other ear. She had an operation on her ears that was supposed to bring the hearing back. Did she have one or two? The operations didn't help so she stopped the lessons. Was it true she could no longer take pleasure in music? The hearing aid distorted it, she said.

Maybe there was no special point of beginning, just a gradual slide, a gradual articulation of pain like the knuckle that aches for years, then starts to throb; months later it swells up, and one day when you wake up you find you can no longer use it. I can't remember any time when she seemed well, although she had to be strong, the things she did, bending, lifting, scrubbing, carrying, walking miles with heavy packages.

She was always tired when I was a child, and her sinuses bothered her, I thought 'sinus trouble' was a serious disease. Every morning, for an hour at least, she blows her nose then hawks up phlegm and spits it into tissue, over and over again. It disgusted me when I lived at home, and I would wonder why a person as fastidious as she would do that in front of everybody. I would wonder, but I guess I knew the answer. This sequence – the deep hawking cough, the sickening expectoration, and the residue, masses of wadded-up tissues in every pocket of every housedress and apron she owned – was the visible emblem of her suffering, the one kind she was able to display. She never suffered from menstrual cramps, or if she did, she never complained about them. She suffered her headaches alone in a darkened room we were not welcome to enter.

She was able to stop making hats in 1955, after she finished paying for Joy's wedding. I was around then, I was even living in Rockville Centre, but I don't remember when she stopped, she didn't talk about it. I try to picture it now: all those long lonely years in that bedroom, cutting, sewing, pleating: over. What must she have felt? Informing old Mr Gwyn, what satisfaction! I no longer need to do slave labor for you. Not that she thought of it that way, she was grateful to him for giving her work. Closing the sewing machine and moving it into my old room; gathering leftover organdy and ruching into a pile to return to Mr Gwyn, cleaning up all the scraps of fabric, putting away scissors and needles and thread and thimble in a place where they must be looked for, taking the floor lamp downstairs to the porch, vacuuming the bedroom of slivers of organdy for one last time . . . Then surveying the room, her bedroom, a bedroom again, looking amazingly spacious and clean and bright now. Free. She was free. Did she feel free, released, delivered? Did her heart sigh with relief? Did her eyes fill with tears at the thought that now she could have a life? I don't recall her saying a word.

She set out to become a lady of leisure, but she had no training for it. She hadn't ever known a lady of leisure, so what could she model herself on? *Vogue?* Except when I was very young, and she occasionally bought a copy of *Woman's Daily* at the A & P – a magazine not intended for ladies of leisure – she never read a 'woman's' magazine. She had contempt for them. She did not read much until her later years, when she subscribed, bless her, to *Mother Jones*, and

The Nation. She never talked about what she read except when KAL 007 was shot down over Sakhalin. Then she called me up at ten o'clock at night in outraged pain, asking me what kind of government we had, what kind of country were we living in, did I know? did I understand?

I loved her that night.

Maybe it was the accidents. There were a couple, maybe three, four. She was an uncertain driver. It was hard to believe that a maniac with burning eyes would drive his car directly toward her, crossing from his lane to hers, so that she had to pull off on the shoulder of the road through Tanglewood, a small community near Hempstead Lake, making her crash into a tree. She was going only about five miles an hour, so the car was just dented, but she complained about severe pain in her neck and shoulders afterward. Or maybe that was after a different accident.

I already thought of her as sick. Maybe I always, after my first childhood, thought of her as sick. She dragged so with fatigue, her voice was so often drained of life, not teary but thick and soft, as if her tears had lodged themselves permanently in her sinus passages and her throat, occasionally venturing out in the daylight, but never departing. And then there were those days in which she lay in her room unspeaking, a cloth over her head, the shades down, the room smelling of slept-in sheets and soiled clothes.

After I got my own car, I would often drop in of a morning to have coffee with her while the kids were at school, and one day she opened the front door and staggered back from it as if she were falling, fainting backwards, and she cried out. I had to catch her, hold her up. I was frightened, but it turned out she had a cold and was feeling woozy in the head . . .

I remember a time – I was at college, still living at home – when she stopped talking to me. Several times I asked her what was wrong, but she only shook her head, pinched her mouth, and whispered 'nothing'. After a few days, in stiff anger, I attacked her. I said it was clear *something* was wrong, since she wasn't speaking, and it would be better for her to tell people what it was than to go around not speaking to them. Tears sheened her eyes. She cried out in a thick voice that she was no good, she knew she was no good, I was always blaming her, attacking her. I always misunderstood her, no one knew her suffering.

I did what I knew I had to do: apologize, express sympathy, and ask again what was bothering her, this time in a tone of deep maternal concern. She whimpered out her answer, she had been to see Dr Hoxton because of a flush that appeared regularly on her cheeks. He listened, and when she described it, asked if it was in the shape of a butterfly. It was. He nodded soberly, sadly, and said he'd have to take some tests.

There was, she said, a form of cancer that manifested itself in this way. The doctor thought she had it. She tried to keep things to herself, but she knew she was dying. Years later, I would receive such news from her more calmly, but that was the first time, and I was horrified. I tried to console her, but she was, as always, inconsolable, and after some time lashed out at me: 'All right, Anastasia, all right! I don't want to talk about it anymore!' The topic dropped into oblivion, was never mentioned again. I was afraid to bring it up, afraid of her anger, or maybe, afraid of my own. But after a few weeks, I couldn't contain myself, and asked. She shook her head in silence. When I pressed her, she admitted that the tests had been negative. She said this in such a way that I was left with the impression that she did not believe the tests and knew better. Luckily, I had my Pollyanna streak: I chose to believe the tests, so I forgot about it. I don't know when she did.

There was the time – how did she happen to tell me? I know we were standing in her bedroom, she was getting dressed, we were going shopping together, she always loved that, and she was cheerful. But something I said, or she said, something led her to turn to me and say . . . oh, god, of course. I was traveling and screwing around and I would tell her about the men I met and the places they took me and the fun I had, she loved to hear about these things, and she was sitting on her vanity bench, powdering her face and she turned to me and said, 'Good. Have fun. Have it now, when you can.'

I looked a question at her.

She turned back. She put the powder puff down. 'I went to the doctor last week.'

I armed my heart.

'I've been having this trouble. It hurts,' she whimpered.

'What hurts?' Ready to leap up, to put my arm around her, to console. But she seemed entirely too cheerful for cancer.

'Sex,' she whispered.

I stared at her.

'It's been hurting for a long time. It's horribly painful, it burns and tears, I could scream, it's a nightmare! So I went to the doctor!' There was satisfaction in her voice now. 'And he said it's true, that I'm very dry down there, it *does* hurt, so I can't have sex anymore.'

'Can't you do something about it?'

She shrugged. 'It's age. It happens to all women.'

I sat appalled. Would that happen to me? What about my poor father, who clearly loved sex?

'So . . . you don't have sex anymore?'

'I can't.'

End of subject.

We had almost the identical conversation years later, also in her bedroom, when she confessed to me in a whisper that she was going blind. I was not to tell anyone – not Joy, not even my father. No one was to know except me. (Why me?) I immediately went out and bought her several kinds of magnifying glasses and the large-type *New York Times Book Review*. She was annoyed. 'My sight isn't *that* bad, Anastasia,' she explained. 'Not yet,' she added ominously.

I guess I am making her sound wretched. I guess she was. I know *we* were, Joy and I, when we lived at home. But at the same time, I understood, I understood her. Or thought I did. I felt her life, her pain, as if it were my own, as if it were I who had lost everything before I, Anastasia, was even born. I took her side against myself – I was her burden, the event that ruined her life.

In those days, I thought that Joy was oblivious to her, to everything that went on in the house. We never discussed Mother, or Dad, or ourselves for that matter. The only talk was jokes and stories, anecdotes about one friend or another. Joy was always out with her friends, always laughing. But after she was married and went away, and we didn't see each other except for the few days every three years Joy and Justin spent on Long Island between tours, we found a new friendship. Whether absence made our hearts grow fonder, or marriage and children gave us a common ground we had lacked before, I don't know, but while she was on Long Island, she'd always take an afternoon and come to my place for a visit. The kids would play outside in the yard, and we'd have coffee and cake, and move into drinks, and sometimes she'd stay for dinner too. We talked a little about ourselves, our lives, but because we never told each other the truth, that subject was limited. So we talked about Mother. Even then we were unhappy about her, for her: we both thought she should get out and join things, meet some people, have some companionship. Joy kept urging her to do that, she continued to urge things like that until Mother was in her seventies. She couldn't help herself, she was frustrated by Mother's unwillingness to improve her life.

But I had stopped. I stopped from sheer hopelessness. I came to understand that it was useless to urge her to do anything because she was suffering from sickness of the heart, an incurable disease. My last suggestion was that she try therapy, but Belle refused. 'I would start to talk, and I'd cry, and I wouldn't be able to stop crying.' I guess it seemed to her that to open up her disease would be to let it thrive in the air, that the proper thing to do, the courageous thing – not that she would have used or even thought those words – was to keep it to herself. She had no idea that her sickness made everyone around her unhappy, and that if she had had someone to talk to, she might feel better. And truthfully, given the way psychiatrists were in those days before feminism, I felt they did more harm than good, so I didn't urge it strongly. In 1950 or 1960 the best cure for melancholia was the same as it had been in the seventeenth century – to write about it, endlessly, to write an Anatomy of it that was the longest book in the English language.

So I gave up exhortation and tried my own brand of therapy – I listened, tried to understand, sympathized, I broke my heart sympathizing. I came to understand that it was not just our poverty, her endless rounds of tedious arduous labor, my father's limitations, her worry about us, that had made her so miserable and depressed when we were children, that there was something more, something older and deeper. I didn't know what it was because she hadn't yet told me about my grandmother's crying over her orphans every night. She always said simply that her mother was a saint, but she had never been able to please her.

I came to believe that she had somehow felt better when her circumstances were harsh than she did now when she had a little leisure, a little money. Because when she had to work so hard and worry so much, she could attribute her state of mind to her state of life; but when her state of life improved, there was nothing for it but to attribute her fatigued depression to a slow-working, fatal, undiscovered physical disease.

She had many diseases over the years, and some of them were real. She had to have her sinuses drained every six months – a painful operation, she told me in hushed awed tones, amazed at her own toleration of pain. Her hearing deteriorated. The first time I suggested she get a hearing aid, she was sitting in my living room in the Rockville Center house. She stood up and walked out without a word. And I did not hear from her again until I called and apologized for upsetting her. In the mid-sixties, she had operations on her ears, but they did not help, so she had to wear a hearing aid, which she hated, after all. But even so she could not listen to more than one voice at a time, so the aid was useless in a room full of people.

One thing I am sure of, and that is she gave up golf because of a whiplash. After that, she would play only on minicourses, the little nine-hole courses at Jones Beach and Fire Island. I guess the whiplash pain left her after a while – she never wore a neck brace – but then she said her arthritis made golf too painful even though she never grew the swelled joints and knuckles that Mr Carpenter had in his last years, when, the kids told me, he had to climb stairs on his hands and knees. Still, she didn't give up golf entirely until after the emphysema. And I know it was after her hearing went that she gave up music lessons, closed the lid of the piano and put the sheet music up on a high shelf in a closet, out of sight; each renunciation performed like a religious sacrifice.

I did wonder about that. Was it penance she was doing? And for what? Maybe her sin was the same as mine, the sin of having been born.

Still, she never stopped trying to find the elusive wisp, pleasure, well-being, something she had been waiting for, working toward, the thing that was supposed to make it all worthwhile. wasn't that the promise of America? She and Ed took vacations in Valeria, a nice estate in Peekskill; they took tours of Europe; they went on a cruise on a windjammer, on car trips to the South, through the Smokies, to Florida.

But it was always the same – a nightmare. Something terrible always happened, she was always unhappy. The food was awful, everywhere, without exception.

Joy and I grimaced at each other about this, and at the end of our conversation, we'd shrug and give it up. It seemed so cruel – all those years she had worked so hard and now she could not enjoy herself. We were angry with her for her intransigence, her utter refusal to take pleasure from life. People say pleasure is selfish, but if she had enjoyed herself, she would have made us feel better about everything – her and ourselves. Still, if we had known what the future would be, we would have found some way to count present blessings. After all, she was only in her early fifties, she was good-looking and slender and well-dressed, and she sometimes acted almost cheerful. She gave dinner parties and played bridge and went to people's houses for an evening of talk or cards. Their trips may all have been 'nightmares', but they went on taking them.

But I – I put quite a few nails in her coffin. Not only had I been born, something I after all could not control, but I performed a series of unforgivable actions: I repeated her error in getting pregnant and having to marry; then soon after he reached prosperity and bought me a nice big house, I divorced the man. One of the nails dislodged when I got the job with *World* – she was proud of that, proud of me, and maybe she even began to forget the divorce. But even then, even after I began to make some money, she told me she had nightmares about the kids and me living in a Volkswagen bus. 'You need a man,' she insisted. Only a man could guarantee a woman's security once she had children.

But the nail got hammered back in and several more were added when I took up with Toni.

It was October 1960 when Toni and I became lovers. I was coming up to my thirty-first birthday, but I still felt like a kid: I was so wildly in love, and Toni was so much like the boys I had first made love with – shy, inexperienced, very tender, and untiringly passionate in the way only a young man can be. He had never made love before, so he had no preconceived ideas except that someone had told him women love to have their ears blown in, and I had to explain, gently of course, that that wasn't true for me at least. I taught him lovemaking, and he had a natural aptitude, so that our sex life was wonderful, marred only by the fact that he wanted to make love every night, and I didn't: every second or third night was enough to me, and he couldn't understand that. We had fights about it. But they were the only fights we had.

When I think back now to how it was then: oh, that mix of fierce passion and boyish tenderness! I say boyish because I've never found it in an older man, although people say men are changing. These days I wouldn't know . . . When we'd finish, he'd hold on to me, making little cries in his throat, like a puppy overwhelmed by the pleasure of being stroked. He didn't want to let go, and sometimes we'd fall asleep that way, which was dangerous. Because I didn't want Pane to know what was happening. I wanted Toni to get up and go back downstairs and sleep there, so he'd be there in the morning when she woke up. She woke up very early, before six, and needed help getting out of bed to go to the toilet. So I could not sleep soundly;

I'd have to remember to wake up and caress him awake and send him, forlorn and complaining in a high thin voice, back downstairs.

Still, I think she knew. Debilitated as she was, there was something in her eyes when she looked at me these days, something cold that had never been there before. She said nothing. What could she do? She was a helpless old woman, dependent on us. And that made me feel awful in a way I wouldn't have if she'd been able, strong. I felt I was shoving something unpalatable down her poor old throat, force-feeding her a fact she would never be able to digest.

The kids, though, didn't seem to suspect a thing. They adored Toni, and accepted him as one of the family without any question about just what role he occupied. He had dinner with us most nights; sometimes I cooked, sometimes he did, and sometimes we cooked together, which the kids loved. They'd join in crowding the little kitchen. Pane could eat very few things, mostly soups and stews with a little meat and vegetables cut up very small; and she ate early. So we took turns on that too. Every couple of days one of us would cook up a pot of soup or a stew and freeze it in Pane-sized portions, so she could have a varied diet. We'd do this downstairs in her kitchen, which was bigger than mine – we'd always have four or five different dishes in her freezer.

Those first months are hard to remember now. They melt together in a glaze of golden sunshine and autumn leaves and walks and furtive touches and smiles and cries of the kids running ahead, finding treasures, celebrating simply being alive. When I had to travel, I knew the kids were safe and loved and happy and hardly missing me. I paid Toni for baby-sitting, over his objections. He said the allowance he got from his father and uncles was enough for him – and god knows he didn't buy anything except books. I had to take him by the hand, the kids giggling helplessly, and force him into the car and downtown to buy a new pair of jeans.

The time came when I had to read Toni's writing. I managed to procrastinate so that I would read it when I was away from home, so that if I didn't like it I would have time to prepare my voice and my face – and my words. I got an assignment in England and Wales. I was excited about it: the piece was on stone ruins from prehistoric ages in England – at Stonehenge and Castlerigg and West Kennet and other places in the British Isles. Just recently I was reading that scholars think these ruins date back to a time when women were central in society. But in 1961 everyone was sure men and men only had built the things, and I simply accepted that opinion. If only I'd known! I'd have photographed them entirely differently – showing the democracy implicit in circles, the beauty of the arrangement, the wisdom of the builders, the knowledge they must have possessed about stars and moon. Instead, I focused on how imposing they were, how impressive, how huge a task it must have been to cart the stones to the sites, to build these structures.

Toni gave me a hundred pages of a novel. I took the typescript out on the plane, after dinner was over, and the plane dark and silent with sleeping passengers. I finished it on the flight back, relieved that there were lots of good things to say. The novel was about a handsome, brilliant, sensitive young man under the command of a sadistic top sergeant during the Korean War. Toni's knowledge of war had come mainly from his brother's stories and other novels and didn't ring true. And the hero was entirely too wonderful. But the sergeant really came alive. Shades of Daddy. And so did long passages when Toni forgot to idealize himself and just let his hero meander around in his mind, seeing, feeling. What this meant to me was that Toni did have talent and could write well when he forgot himself and his preconceptions and simply let himself observe, or when he was writing something he knew about. That he was talented pleased me enormously, and I was elated; not only did I have good words to say, but I might even be able to help him – if I spoke with great care.

I got home late in the afternoon – as usual I'd gone first to the city to drop off my film. As the cab pulled up to the house, the front door opened, and Toni and the kids stood there. I ran up the steps, and we all cried out and embraced and kissed, and went in, and the entire front hall was hung with balloons! They were strung up the staircase as well, and in Pane's living room there was a birthday cake with candles, and more balloons and Pane herself in a chair, smiling! I'd completely forgotten it was my birthday.

He'd bought me a present – a shocking pink nylon blouse, something I'd never wear, but it was a sweet thought, and I acted as if I loved it. I put it on right away, figuring I could wear it once at least, for him. The kids eyed it, eyed me, said nothing. They'd bought me a set of recordings of Beethoven's late quartets; but after all, they'd had a longer time to get to know me. The three of them had made the cake together, and Arden had decorated it with pink icing flowers that, she said laughing, were supposed to be roses.

Oh, it was a fine year.

I was extremely ginger telling Toni what I thought about his novel. I saved the best for last, and he brightened, loving my praise of his section where the hero is daydreaming on the firing range (although I didn't believe one could, actually), and the one where he meditates on what might have made the sergeant the man he is. I did not mention that I believed the sergeant was based on his father; I did suggest the hero could be a little more human, less godlike; and that he read some journalists' accounts of the Korean War. He took it all pretty well.

That hurdle past, the next one hovered: Thanksgiving. Oh, these holidays that are supposed to be joyous!

Brad had called early that month, announcing that he expected the kids to have Thanksgiving dinner with his family. I said I would ask them. I did.

Silence.

'Well, what do you think?

'How will *you* feel?' (Billy.)

I got up to pour myself a cup of coffee so they wouldn't see the tears in my eyes. Sentimental idiot!

'Look.' I turned around, realizing I couldn't fool them. 'I'm going to feel terrible. But I want you to see more of your father than you do. You hardly ever see him anymore. I know it isn't entirely your fault. But he *did* call last Sunday, asking you to dinner, and you' I eyed Arden –

'didn't want to go. Of – course I want you Thanksgiving. But I feel selfish, I feel wrong, as if I were keeping you all to myself.'

'We had it with them last year,' Billy said in a thin voice.

'You don't want him to get mad at you, to blame you. You think he won't send you any more money for us!'

'Oh, Arden, do you think that's the reason I want you to see your father?'

'Why else would you? He doesn't care about us! He only wants to show us off, to show his friends; or Grandma and Grandpa Carpenter that he is being our father, when he isn't.'

Her fierceness made my stomach tremble. What rage, what hurt, was lying there in my child's heart?

'Come on, Ard, you know Mom wants us to know Dad.'

'What for!' Her face was flushed and mottled, and I couldn't help myself, I got up and went to her and put my arms around her and held her.

She shook me off. 'Let me go, Mom!' I sat back in my chair. I watched her, aghast at her pain, my helplessness.

Billy put his hand on my arm. 'We'll go, Mom,' he said glaring at Arden, daring her to argue. 'If that's what you want, we'll go.'

'It's *not* what I want!' I cried. 'It's what I feel we should do, ought to do.'

'Why?' Arden asked coolly. 'Why, if not to give him value for money received?'

Twelve, I thought. Not even twelve. Three weeks away from twelve.

'Isn't it because you feel you owe him something? You owe him *us?*'

'I have you all the time, he doesn't.'

'He doesn't want us.' The same cool voice.

'Do what you want,' I sighed. 'But if you decide not to go *you* have to call and tell him. I don't want to be screamed at for something I can't control.'

Billy stared at Arden. '*You* have to call him.'

She shrugged. 'Okay, I'll call him, ' she said in that cool voice. But I could hear through the coolness that she didn't want to do it any more than I did, any more than Billy did. I knew she would put it off until Brad called me in fury.

'You have to call him now,' I said.

'I'll do it tomorrow,' she said, standing, her voice rising into anger.

'Now, Arden!'

She whirled on me. 'I'll do it when I want to! Okay?' The 'Okay?' was an afterthought, a half-hearted concession to my status as mother. She marched from the room, into hers, slammed the door, locked it.

Billy and I looked at each other.

'She won't call him.'

'I know.'

'He wouldn't scream at her.'

'No. But he'd sound hurt, he'd be angry quietly, he'd act martyred and blame me. It would infuriate her.'

'What it really is, is we're all afraid of him.'

I stared sadly at my boy. 'I guess so.'

'Is that right? I mean, if we let him bully us aren't we sort of . . .' He searched for a word.

'In collusion? I guess we are. Maybe I'm cowardly. But – oh, I don't know, Billy, maybe I'm deluding myself, but I feel he asks so little of me, of you kids – it seems the one thing we should give him . . .'

He stared at the floor. His little face was so sad for a child his age. It ripped at me.

'Not because we're afraid of him,' I burst out. 'Not because he'll yell. But because he'll yell only because he's really hurt, and if he's hurt, he cares, and . . .'

He nodded. We sat in a companionable silence. When Billy and I were together, we could be silent for long periods and yet feel close, so close that sometimes I felt we were thinking with one brain, feeling with one heart. I did not have that closeness with Arden.

Then I said, 'I have an idea! They have Thanksgiving dinner early, at midday, don't they still?' He nodded. 'So you go to them in the morning, stay until about five or six, and come home and have Thanksgiving here at night. I'll make dinner for around eight, or seven.' My mind was whirring: how would my mother feel about that, a big dinner late at night? Not good.

'Sure,' he said uneasily.

'What's wrong?'

'I don't think we can eat that much.'

I burst out laughing. 'Of course you can!'

I cooked Thanksgiving dinner downstairs. I had never had Thanksgiving before, we always went to Mom's. But I didn't want to leave Pane on Thanksgiving, and it was just too hard for her to go out. Mom was just as glad not to have to cook. But was I nervous, cooking a turkey! I got a twenty-two pounder and roasted it five hours. Mother said it must have been frozen (it was) because it was dry. 'And,' she said in a tone of voice that suggested I had done this to persecute her, 'the gravy is burnt!' (It didn't taste burnt to me – but what do I know?) She had me nearly crying at the table. I had tried so hard to please *her* – no one else was fussy.

She never hesitated to criticize my cooking – or my appearance, or anything else about me – but there was animus in her voice that day, she was angry with me. She saw instantly that Toni and I were involved, and she didn't like it. Toni didn't notice. She was polite to him, and he wasn't used to polite families. He was used to people screaming and shouting when they were displeased, upending tables, throwing crockery. He didn't realize people could smile at you and still hate your guts. He was my sweet innocent baby. Not that she hated him. She was indifferent to him, personally. She was angry with me for taking up with someone so unsuitable, someone without money or status, someone I could not marry, who couldn't support me.

But he loved her, loved the way she sat like a grande dame, dressed so beautifully, her hair so elegant, sipping a scotch and soda, expecting to be waited on. It was unique for him to see a woman in such a position, and he gloried in it. I'm sure he wished he could see his mother treated that way. To him, my mother was a creature from a more exalted world than he had known, and his voice crowed with delight every time he spoke to her. He didn't notice that she never addressed a remark to him. I did.

I did, but I said nothing. I hadn't expected her to like it. And I knew she'd be polite, and that if he didn't see her often, he would go on not seeing her coolness. But when, at Christmas, he broke out his bank account and bought her a silver gravy ladle, I had to say something. We were at her house. Toni and I had carried Pane, bundled in blankets, out to the car and set her in the front seat. The kids and I sat in back with the presents that wouldn't fit in the trunk. Pane was extremely excited at going out, and I worried a bit about her. But she was settled in high state in my mother's living room, and Toni had two queens to wait on – three, if you count me. He was overjoyed.

Mother and I were in the kitchen, preparing to set out the Christmas Eve feast that followed the giving out of presents, and I whispered into her good ear: 'Toni is sweet, isn't he?'

She squirmed. 'Ye-es. He's sweet,' she admitted, very reluctantly.

'He spent most of his savings buying you that ladle,' I said, knowing what hit my mother's core.

Her eyebrows rose.

'He adores you,' I added, finishing the job.

Eyebrows remained raised, shoulders shrugged. 'I don't know why.' It was a question.

'He just does. You're probably very different from his mother.'

'Oh, Polish men . . . !' my mother exploded in soft-voiced contempt.

She has a gift. She can convey so much in a phrase, in a tone of voice. All of it was there, years of watching men bully and abuse their wives, of watching the women, her own mother, shabby and shapeless in old housedresses, bent into postures of servility, smiling and cringing simultaneously.

'Yes, he hates his father,' I agreed, 'who is terrible.'

My mother nodded. And she did act a little warmer to Toni after that.

*

I discovered that the kids knew that Toni was my lover when Arden came down with scarlet fever. She woke up around midnight, one Tuesday night, felt hot and feverish, then was seized with nausea and couldn't make it to the bathroom. She cried out as the vomit propelled itself out of her throat, and I leaped up from bed naked, threw a robe around me and ran to her. Toni grabbed his jeans and followed. The poor kid was crying, she was humiliated and upset at fouling her room, and I had to calm her down as I helped her into the bathroom. Billy woke too and Toni pressed him into service cleaning up the mess.

'Ugh! Ugh!' cried my fastidious son. 'Why should I clean up *her* vomit?' The *her* was dyed in all the venom of sibling rivalry.

'Because she's sick and upset and your mother is busy helping her and I need you to help me,' Toni said firmly, and without a word, Billy went for the paper towels and the liquid cleaner. I should be able to command obedience like that!

She was so hot I was terrified. I cleaned her up and led her back to bed and got a basin of warm water and alcohol and washed her face and neck down with it. I kept this up for an hour or so until she felt cooler. I was afraid to give her an aspirin until I knew what was wrong.

For the next few days, things were chaotic in the house – the doctor's visits, medicine to be administered, chicken soup to be simmered, the busy unsettled quiet of a house where someone is ill. I sat for long periods beside Arden's bed bathing her with alcohol as she swam in and out of delirium. I kept Billy home from school; it figured he'd be carrying the stuff as well, and a few days later, he came down with it too. But he didn't run such high fevers, and I worried less about him.

It was a few weeks before they were more or less normal again, sitting around in the living room in pajamas and robes watching the tube, complaining about boredom, getting into arguments with each other at the least thing. During Arden's illness, I made Toni stay downstairs at night. He'd come up in the afternoons and – blessed relief – play chess with Billy and read poetry to Arden, allowing me a couple of hours to go to the market or just sit in my room working. And he ate with us. But I wouldn't let him come back up later on. I don't know why, exactly. Superstition – if I had sexual pleasure, my kids would die? – or maybe I just wasn't in the mood for sex with two sick kids in the house. So one night Arden turned to me during a commercial and said, 'How come Toni doesn't come up at night anymore?'

Billy looked over too, adding his look to the question.

I know I must have changed color. 'What do you mean?'

Arden gave me a knowing look. 'Come on, Mom, we know Toni comes back up at night after we go to bed.'

'Yeah.'

'Oh. I was trying to protect you from that knowledge.'

They both laughed. 'Us or Pane?' Arden chirped nastily.

I shook my head. 'You kids are too much.'

Then we all laughed, long and hard, out of relief I guess.

'Why doesn't he just stay up here with us after dinner, and go to bed when you do?' Billy wondered.

'Because you-all like to watch television and he likes to read.'

'You read. In your room.'

'Yeah, but there's only a hard-backed chair in my room and I have to read in bed. It wouldn't be comfortable for two.'

They gave each other a long considering look. I understood what it said, and was amazed: they so much wanted Toni to spend his evenings upstairs that they were considering giving up evening television. I held my breath.

'Maybe you could put the TV in one of our rooms,' Arden ventured.

I just looked at her.

'Yeah, you're right. We'd fight about which room.'

'And the one whose room it was in would start to treat it as if it was his – or hers.'

'And there's not too much room in our rooms either, Arden.'

'What about the kitchen?'

'On top of the stove?'

'Mmmm.' Heads were busy. No solutions.

620

'Couldn't he read while we watch TV? We'd keep it low.'

'It's hard to concentrate. But you can ask him.'

'We only watch till nine. Then you could both read.'

'I'll ask him,' I smiled.

The outcome, of course, was that the kids got exactly what they wanted. We *all* watched television until nine, then they went to bed and we read for a couple of hours. We did this every night. We were a family.

It wasn't until spring that Brad found out. In the middle of March, I was sent to Algeria, where the OAS – the secret revolutionary organization of the Algerian army – had declared open war against the French. Terrorism and bombings had mounted, and the French were arguing among themselves about what do to. During a lull in the action (some sporadic guerilla action was still going on), *World* sent me over to get some pictures against the future – for they expected either a full-blown war or the granting of independence soon. It was a dismal assignment, it turned out. As a woman I was denied entry to the male councils of the OAS, and I ended photographing mainly French buildings that had been or might be destroyed by the rebels, the souks, and the wonderful dark cobblestoned alleys of the Algerian quarter. But I did make some important Algerian contacts.

I was gone for two weeks during which Arden agreed, for once, to have dinner with her father – maybe because she missed me, but probably because he offered to take them to a restaurant, just the three of them, instead of having them to dinner at his house with Fern and Fern's daughter and the baby. Normally, when I was at home, Brad rang the doorbell and waited on the front porch for the kids to come down. He didn't like to encounter me. He had a grudge against me. You might even say he hated me.

Before she got sick, Pane usually opened the door to Brad, and he would stand chatting with her in the doorway. Since her illness, Billy ran downstairs to answer the door, ready to go, calling up to Arden that Daddy was there and to hurry up. But this time, Billy wasn't ready; he answered the door in socks, and without his coat. And Brad, knowing

I wasn't there, followed him upstairs. And he found Toni ensconced in an armchair in the middle of a chess game with Billy, looking completely at home with his shoes off.

Brad darted him one look of hatred, then stood silent, stiff, angry-looking, until the kids got themselves ready. I know all this because Toni told me: and it puzzled me. Because Billy was always nervous when his father was coming for them; he began to wash and dress far ahead of time, nagging Arden to get started, and usually, building into a frustrated rage at her.

I arrived home late Thursday night, and Toni came up and insisted on heating some pasta for me – I was tired and would have been happy to eat it cold – and made a fresh salad with one hand, his other around my waist, crowing – oh, only the young can be so happy – delighted to have me back. I glowed, happy to see him, to be near him again, to be home, warmed by his happiness, as if already my heart had started to cool, harden, petrify, whatever it's done, and needed warmth from the outside to get it pumping.

He was standing at the stove, turning the pasta with a wooden spoon, and he grinned at me, 'I met your ex the other night.'

My heart may have trouble pumping, but it has no trouble whatever in stopping dead. I moved away from him and let myself down into a kitchen chair.

'You did?' Even the expression on my face did not faze him. He told me what had happened.

'Oh, god.' The voice was much deeper than mine, I didn't even recognize it as my own.

Toni put the plate of linguine in front of me and sat down across the table. '*Mangia*, baby.'

But I couldn't – I fussed with it, moved it around, put a few forkfuls in my mouth, but couldn't swallow.

'Why, what's wrong?'

'I'm going to hear about this. I just know it.' My body was seized with dread, the kind of fear that debilitates because it prevents you from thinking clearly. I felt as if my blood had stopped moving through my body, had clotted, clogged, and lodged in my brain. Toni laughed at me: I was a puritan after all, a good girl despite what I'd said about my college days, and once a wife always a wife, I was overcome with guilt, while Brad ran around even before we were divorced and remarried and had a new child and paid little attention to his other children and thought nothing of that.

It didn't matter what he said. I knew Brad, I said, ominously.

But several weeks passed and nothing happened. Toni had the grace not to bring it up to mock me. I walked around holding myself tensely, expecting a disastrous phone call. Brad did call one evening to arrange a shopping trip with Billy – he was going to buy him a new spring jacket – but I didn't talk to him. The Saturday afternoon of the shopping trip, Billy came in looking very disturbed. He was short with me, and spent the rest of the evening in his room. When I went to try to talk to him, he was withdrawn and sullen, reading, he said. He didn't even come out to watch television that night, and my dread grew again, like a tumor that has started to shrink, but suddenly expands hugely.

Brad called Monday morning around ten. I knew he didn't need to be at his office that early, but I also knew that is where he was – with the door shut no doubt against the possible arrival of a secretary.

'You bitch! You slut! You whore!' were his opening words.

My dread eased as adrenaline pumped in: the worst had arrived, there was no further need for fear. What I had to do now was act angry, outraged.

'This is an obscene phone call, and I am hanging up now to call the police.'

He ignored that. He poured it out. My filth, my whoredom, having a young lover in the house with my children. He spent several minutes lovingly mouthing the language all men know and secrete away in a back pocket, waiting for a chance to use it: the extensive vocabulary indicting the vileness of women. There was no time for me to say anything, but it humiliated me to stand there holding the phone listening to it, implicitly granting his right to use it, so I hung up. He rang back immediately. I didn't answer the phone. It rang on and off for the next half hour, then stopped. But my dread now had returned. What next?

Next was a ring at the doorbell a few hours later. Why hadn't I gone out? He was standing there white-faced, his features standing sharply on his face like a line drawing. I was amazed at how lined he was – he was only a year older than I, but he looked forty. He charged in when I opened the door, ran up the stairs and went through the rooms searching, throwing open doors and slamming them shut. He even checked all the closets. Then he went into the kitchen and counted the dinner plates in the dish drain. There were four.

I followed him screaming. 'How dare you! What the hell do you think you're doing! I'm calling the police!' I went for the phone, but he leaped at me and grabbed my hand. Hard.

'You can't call the police. I'm paying for this place, remember,' he gritted out between clenched teeth.

'You pay child support, not alimony! I support myself and I pay the rent here. This is my house!'

'The hell it is! Any judge in the country would grant my right to be here! And any judge in the country would grant me custody of the children after what you've done. And I'm just telling you, bitch, that I'm taking the kids away from you. You're an unfit mother, whore!'

'Hah! You'll take the kids and make Fern take care of them? She'll like that, won't she, oh righteous one! Who's the adulterer around here, I want to know. If you're going to invoke conventional morality, Brad, at least get your story straight.'

'I never brought her home. I was married to her before the kids ever saw her,' he hissed. 'You bring a young boy into the house, it's obscene! Are you reduced to robbing cradles? Or is it that you've finally found someone your own age!'

I had all along been a little uneasy about Toni's age, but now I felt outraged. He was, after all, only eight years younger than I. How many men get involved with women half their age, or girls young enough to be their granddaughters? Hot running blood rushed to my head – a bad thing for me, because I lose the ability to think and fall back on mindless language.

'You fuck! You stupid asshole! Get out of my house! Get out now!' I reached for the phone again, and when his hand darted out to stop me, I thrust it off, hard. I pushed him as hard as I could. He was caught by surprise and rocked a little on his heels, and I shoved him toward the door. He caught his balance and began to move back toward me, but I gave him a huge shove – my arms are strong from holding and carrying heavy equipment – and he fell back against the front door and slipped down a step. It frightened him, although he caught himself, and he glowered and spoke like a movie villain, in a low threatening voice.

'Just you wait, bitch. I'm going to take your kids away. Any judge in the country would judge you an unfit mother. WHORE!' He turned and stamped down the stairs. He slammed the front door so hard the glass cracked. When I heard it, I ran down after him and threw the door open. He was about to get into his car.

'I'm sending you a bill for destruction of property! You broke Pane's front door glass!'

He laughed. 'Go ahead! Send all the bills you want! You won't see another penny from me!'

I stood there, tears welling in my throat, and watched him drive away. I felt utterly defeated. I knew he was right – the cops wouldn't have helped me if I'd called them, they'd defer to him without even checking when he said he paid the bills; and probably a judge would take my children away from me. And even if the whole thing was a ploy to enable him to stop paying child support – because that must be what he was up to, I couldn't believe he really *wanted* the kids, or that Fern would agree to take care of them – even then, he wins. Because what could I do about it? Who would help me?

I ran upstairs and put in a call to Steve Sindona, who had handled my end of the divorce. He was out. I called Edna Lench, who lived down the block, whose husband was a lawyer. When I told her what happened, her voice froze. She said she'd ask her husband, but she sounded as if next time I met her on the street, she might very well cut me. I cursed myself, because her daughter Joyce was one of Arden's best friends: would Edna stop Joyce from seeing Arden?

I wanted to die. I was no good. Everything I did, I did wrong. I just didn't think, I just didn't pay enough attention to the way the world works. And I was so panicked I couldn't reason out the situation.

I was sitting in the kitchen holding my head in my hands when I heard the light rap on the door that meant Toni was there. He came in. I was shocked at how completely I had forgotten him. And I wondered – briefly – why he hadn't come up earlier, when he heard – as he must have – Brad throwing doors open and slamming them shut.

'What's up?'

Strange how I forgave him everything, always. I never asked him to be accountable, responsible for me. It's only recently that I realized that, and Clara says, think about that, think about why you did that. At the time, I felt that it was love that wiped anger out of my heart every time I looked at him.

I told him what had happened. He sat beside me, holding both my hands in his.

'I heard a rumpus up here. I wanted to come up, but I didn't know how you'd feel about that.' He looked the question at me.

'It's probably just as well you didn't. It would just have made things worse,' I said with assurance that, at that moment, I felt. I smiled love at him. 'You made the right decision.' I caressed his face with my hand.

There was noise – clatter and chatter – on the stairs, and tears sprang to my eyes. I turned around in my chair when they came in. My heart kept pinging, ping pang ping pang, pain pain pain, and water poured down my cheeks. I memorized – not that I didn't already know them – every contour of my children's faces, their young bodies, the way their hair grew on their heads. They stopped dead in the doorway, looking.

'What happened!' they both breathed. Toni told them; they turned to me horrified. 'Can he do that?'

'I'm afraid he can. I've called some lawyers, but they haven't called back.' I wiped my face with a dish towel that was lying on the table, and Billy left the room, returning with a handful of tissues for me to blow my nose in.

'Well, we won't go. I won't go. They can't make me go if I don't want it!' Arden announced.

Billy glanced at her, then at me, seeking assurance, I grimaced. 'They can make you go,' Billy informed his sister in a low voice.

'No they can't! I'll run away!' I sat there admiring my daughter's spirit, her courage, her ferocity, but then – as always when she was upset – she turned her anger on me. 'You have to stop him, you have to do something! How come he can have a lover, he even has another baby, and they don't do anything to him?'

'He's married. It's legal.'

'Well, you can get married too!' She looked at Toni.

'Just what I was about to suggest,' he grinned at me.

'Oh!' I stood up. 'No! A shotgun wedding, 1960s style?' The truth was, I didn't want to marry Toni. *I didn't want to* – deeply. I didn't know why and I didn't want to think about why.

'I'm never speaking to him again!' Arden announced, stalking out of the room. 'And if they make me go to him, I'll run away! I won't live in that house!' Her door slammed.

Billy stood there, pale. His mouth was working. Then he too left the room. I heard his door close quietly, and the springs of his bed creak.

'How about it?' Toni was smiling up at me, his face shining. I could see what he was feeling: he was my savior, my knight on a white horse, he was going to save my children for me. The situation was open to that interpretation. Why did it feel so false to me, so wrong? Wrong.

'I don't know, Toni. Let me think. Let's not rush into anything. I don't want you to be pressured into anything.' Him: or me.

'I'm not. It's what I want. I love you.'

'I know. But . . .' I gestured with my hand.

'And I love the kids.'

I kissed him. 'Let me think. Let me talk to some lawyers. And right now I need to talk to Billy.'

'Billy?'

'Something's bothering him.'

'Well, naturally . . .'

'No. Something else. Something more.'

'Okay.' He stood up. 'I'm just downstairs. Do you want me to come up for dinner tonight?'

I considered. I knew I did not. I didn't know how to tell him so. 'Maybe it would be better if I had dinner with the kids alone. We need to talk together.'

There was only a momentary shadow on his face. 'Okay.' He took me in his arms and held me, kissed my cheek, and left. I went immediately to Billy's room, knocked lightly and went in. He was lying rigid, staring at the ceiling.

I sat on the edge of the bed. 'What is it, tootsie?'

His face was wrenched out of shape. He looked at me, then looked away. I could sense he did not want me to touch him, so I sat still and silent.

Eventually, his mouth opened and a hollow voice emerged. 'Saturday. When I went shopping with Dad. In the car. When he drove me home.' He stopped.

I began to see. 'He asked you questions?'

Billy nodded. His lips twisted.

'Like what?'

He stared at the bedspread. 'He wanted to know if Toni was up here a lot. And if he ate with us. And if you paid for his food. And if he stayed all night.'

His body was taut, as if it had taken an electric shock. He looked as if he would break if he were touched.

I didn't ask him what he'd said.

'I didn't want to . . . I felt as if . . . but I didn't want to lie to him. He's my *father*.' He looked at me then.

'He's your father, and he put you in an impossible position – you either had to do something you'd feel·was a betrayal of me, or lie to him, and feel you were betraying him. It was terrible of him. He was wrong, not you. You did what you felt was right.'

'No, I didn't Mom! I didn't feel what I did was right! I told him Toni ate with us most of the time! I told him sometimes you paid for the food and sometimes he did. And I told him that I didn't know if Toni stayed all night. I did! I did!'

He had got up now, and was standing in front of me, jerking his arms like a robot. 'I didn't know what to do! I didn't want to lie to him! But I didn't want to get you in trouble, and I knew it would! I didn't want to keep on being afraid of him, lying because we're afraid!'

I stood up and put my arms around him and held his body against mine. He was stiff. 'I understand. I do, honey. It was too hard for you, you aren't old enough to deal with a thing like that.'

He was watching my face intently, his own face wrenched in pain.

'And you have a whole lot of different feelings, and some of them you probably don't even know you have.' I was thinking about his being too engrossed in the chess game with Toni that evening to be ready for his father. I wasn't sure what was going on inside him; I was sure that he didn't know either. Maybe he wanted his father to know about Toni, maybe he wanted to make him jealous. Maybe he wanted to suggest that Toni was more of a parent to him than Brad was. But he could have had no idea what the consequences of his actions could be. And now that he knew — I suspected nothing I said could ease his guilt.

I caressed his cheek. 'We'll work it out,' I smiled at him and let him go. He stood there, stiff, his arms held tensely at his sides. 'Try to remember that you were put in a situation that would have been difficult for a grown-up, that was too hard for you. Because it was, honey.'

He nodded. His eyes were damp. That was good. I kissed him and he let himself relax against me.

As soon as I left him, I got on the phone. I wanted to reach these lawyers before five. But it took several days before any of them called me back, and the tones of disapproval in their voices, their complete identification with

Brad, told me as much as their hesitant opinions that it would be a long-drawn-out case, but Brad would probably win. All of them assured me they were far too busy at the moment to handle my end of it. I searched the Yellow Pages for a woman lawyer. There was one listed; it took me several more days to reach her. She sounded stiff and masculine, and told me somewhat scornfully that she did not handle marital disputes.

By then, a week had gone by. Monday morning a letter arrived with the letterhead of Lou Regan's legal firm. Lou had handled Brad's end of the divorce. I took it into the kitchen and poured myself a cup of coffee, and sat down. The letter said that he had been instructed by Brad to initiate proceedings to gain custody of the children on the grounds of my unfitness if my relation with Antoni Nowak did not cease immediately. So that was it. He wanted me to break with Toni. And he was serious. I sat there holding it, watching it shake in my hand. He must really hate me, far more than I imagined. He hated me so much he wanted me not to have any happiness. Because I knew, absolutely, that he did not want the children, and a picture lighted itself on the movie screen in the back of my head – them living with him, the way he would treat them, the way he would talk to them about me, and what that would do to them.

That was intolerable and I clocked the switch on it, sending it into darkness but not oblivion.

All right. He wins. I'll break with Toni, I thought. I lived without him before, I can do it again. But then what? I would miss Toni, I would really feel awful. But I could do it, would do it to keep my kids. But once he knew he could bully me this way, he would keep it up. For the rest of my life, or at least for the next ten years or so, I would have to remain alone. If I got involved with anyone, he would pull the same trick again. And again. He'd know he had me, he'd know what would work with me.

All right, so I'd just have my on-the-road romances, lovers in transit. He couldn't stop that. Unless I met a man I wanted to marry. But I didn't want to marry again. My reluctance to marry Toni had nothing to do with Toni himself but much to do with marriage.

And if I gave Toni up in the face of Brad's threats, my kids would hate me, they would lose all respect for me, they would blame me for the loss of him. They loved Toni, they didn't want to lose him. They *wanted* me to marry him. Shit. Shit, shit, shit.

I sat there for several hours, thinking. There was no one I could talk to about this. All of my women friends in the neighborhood were shocked at my relation with Toni. They all felt it was wrong, shocking, scandalous. Even my mother, who might be expected to understand, found my relation with Toni reprehensible. I felt utterly alone. Not alone in the social sense, but morally alone. Like someone who has survived a plane crash in the Andes and has to decide whether to eat human flesh, or someone in a concentration camp who has been ordered to work for the Nazis, with an implicit promise of survival for a few more weeks, months. Someone for whom there was no right and wrong, just survival. It was wrong for me to marry, I knew that. I did not wish to marry. Ever. I hadn't realized that until this moment. I felt like a woman who goes on the streets to feed her children. Years later, when I watched film of Saigon flash on the television screen, and heard about the thousands of women who became prostitutes during the Vietnam War, I felt like their sister.

It was in this frame of mind that, the next day, I asked Toni if he wanted to drive over to Hempstead and apply for a marriage license.

two

It wasn't a romantic way to get married, but our bond was romantic anyway. It went on being sweet and harmonious despite the hex of marriage license, law, roles. I sent Lou Regan a letter informing him that I was married to Antoni Nowak, and that he and Brad should drop dead. Oh, I didn't write that, but the tone was bitter. Because I was bitter. I was filled with shame at my cowardice. I was already ashamed at the way I concealed the kids from the guys at *World;* I was starting to feel that being a woman meant living in a continual state of shame.

Brad was shocked at what he had precipitated. I guess it had never occurred to him that Toni would be willing to marry a woman years older than he and with two kids. I know how he felt because after the letter, Brad stopped in again. He began by calling Toni and me names, and vilifying my behavior. How dare I give his kids a stepfather who didn't know how to wipe his own ass, who needed me for a mommy, who couldn't earn enough money to feed himself on dog food, and so on.

I told him to get out, wondering how many times people can replay the same scene. I felt so tired. He had forced me into a step I didn't want to take, and now he was vilifying me for it. He launched into a tirade about my rottenness as a mother, my whorish sexuality, my refusal to grow up. I wanted to go to bed, pull the covers over my head, and cry, and sleep.

But I did my duty. I was cold, hard, forbidding. I commanded him to leave my house. But this time, Toni, who had heard Brad shouting, came upstairs and confronted him. (Marriage does make a difference.) And Brad shut up. He just shut up. I couldn't get over it. This kid, the mere presence of this twenty-two-year-old boy, had the effect of silencing him, when I could not. Male territorial insanity yields only to another male. What a difference the possession of a penis makes! I thought then, maybe for the first time. This thought filled me with rage, I was overwhelmed with it, drowning in a purple fire that pumped through my brain. I was angry with Toni as well as Brad, something he couldn't understand, couldn't be expected to understand.

My pattern with Toni was set. I never tried to make him understand what he didn't understand. I never forced him to take the responsibility of being a partner. I let him be my boy-lover, my pet. Brad wasn't entirely wrong. He was just a pig.

It passed, of course, my anger, Toni's; we came together again with as much passion and joy as before, and life went on. But something profound had happened to me, I recognized it even though I did not choose to think about it. Life happens in the interstices of things; events are merely the visible reflections of processes buried and secret, like the frenzy of life that goes on beneath the earth, on the other side of silence, as the insects and earthworms and snakes and seeds and roots and air and pebbles join together or repel each other, move back to make space among themselves, while you see nothing until one day there is a mound, an antheap, where nothing was before, or a blade of grass erupts through the warm idle clumped soil. Allowing Brad to force me into marriage did something irrevocable to me. It was not Toni's fault. Nothing was ever Toni's fault. Except being young.

But life came back, the shame subsided, the choice came to seem right. Shameless I became: it was that or die. We were able, without shame, to tell Pane we were married, to avoid seeing the grotesque expression that crossed her face when we told her, to avoid letting ourselves know what she felt, to avoid caring. *I* was able to blind myself. I don't know if Toni needed to, I don't know what he saw. The innocent are ignorant. We were even able to leave Pane for two weeks, having asked Mrs D'Antonio to stay with her during that time, it was only right, we told ourselves, we were entitled to a honeymoon, a little vacation, we took care of her all year long. We were able to relax into a glowing well-being, lying together on the beach at Barnstable, on the Cape, where I'd taken a little house on the bay for August, sprawled in beach chairs in the sun, smelling of sun lotion and sea salt, sand, and mustard from our sandwiches, reading together, smiling at each other when the kids shouted in the water, him pouring me a glass of lemonade from the gallon thermos, happy to have me break his concentration by reading aloud from Robert Lowell's *Life Studies* – 'Tamed by *Miltown*, we lie on Mother's bed' – breathing his appreciation . . .

And later, after chicken cooked by Toni and the kids on the barbecue grill while I smile in the kitchen peeling avocado and tomato, washing lettuce, after lingering over coffee on the screened porch, listening to the birds celebrate sunset – clamorous, hot, sweet – the four of us breathing together in silent reverence for the concert, after dusk descends and the birds fall silent, the locusts continue the music, we rise, yawning, stretching, saying in hushed voices *time to clean up*, and do it together in lazy easy movements, quietly, even the dishes abiding by the decorum, not clanking as they touch the porcelain of the sink or the wooden shelf where they are stored after being dried – after all that, a noisy game of hearts which Billy wins easily, protecting his face against the thrown cards of the rest of us, after laughter and banter, and kisses goodnight, and sleepy sunburned faces pressed against ours, after all that, a midnight walk alone along the beach, and the moon rising and the water lapping our bare feet, and holding each other and stopping to kiss, and barely talking except once, one fatal moment when Toni holds me and whispers in my ear, 'I'm so happy. So happy. I've never been so happy. I love you. I love them. I want one of my own.'

And I kissed his eyelids.

What could I do? You can't go back on a promise like that. Useless to reason, cruel to suggest that that was a night when I'd have agreed to anything. My only hope was that I'd have difficulty getting pregnant. But I didn't. It took only a few months. I assumed I was pregnant when I missed my period in mid-December, but I said nothing to Toni. That sounds like something out of a sentimental novel of the thirties when men never seemed to know whether their wives menstruated or not, but there was so much confusion that December that Toni *didn't* notice. And I said nothing because I was committed to an expedition I imagined would be the most exciting of my life.

Somebody at *World*, a senior editor, had been contacted by a man representing Cuban refugees attached to Alpha 66, a revolutionary force intent on overthrowing Castro, who had ousted Batista a couple of years before. In April, a group of Cuban refugees backed by the United States, by the CIA I guess, had landed at Bahía de Cochinos, and been wiped out in three days. It was a humiliation for the new president – an unfair one, I thought, since Eisenhower had planned the whole thing and the guy I had voted for only continued his policy – but it's true Kennedy had promised not to send US forces to Cuba . . .

Anyway, a new invasion was being planned, and . . . well, the way it happened was, I was sitting in Russ Farrell's office, finishing our examination of a layout of some pictures I'd taken of a new bridge in Oregon, when Ron Bulstrode came tearing in, and blurted out, 'We've got it! State Department approval to cover the Alpha 66 invasion!' Russ leapt up, sent a fist crashing upward in air, and whirled around and saw my face.

'Oh no,' he said.

'Oh yes,' I said, standing.

'No. We can't. They'd never approve a woman.'

I stood up. 'Russ, who could do it better! Who's better at showing heroism?' I was embarrassed at selling myself that way, but the truth was I'd been dreaming of being a war correspondent since I was young, when Margaret Bourke-White was my idol. It was a dream I'd never allowed to crystallize into words, knowing how unrealizable it was. But the whole dream was glowing out of my face then, and Russ saw it and couldn't resist it. Besides, he knew I was right: I think that the guys at *World* felt odd in giving such masculine assignments to a woman, but that something about it pleased them – my pictures were like a testimony to women's adoration of heroic men. Still, if I hadn't been there at that moment I'd never have gotten the assignment. I know that, but I was and I did.

I did a bit of thinking about how to present this assignment at home. I would minimize the danger, and in fact, I wasn't sure I'd be in danger. I had little notion of what it would be like. I just *hoped* there'd be danger. And of course, I had to glide over the possibility that I might be pregnant, and the fact that I'd be away from home on New Year's Eve – our first New Year's Eve together. Luckily, Toni wasn't sentimental, and he got as excited as I about the trip. So on December 27, after the best Christmas I'd ever spent, I took off for Miami with my camera case and a knapsack.

Woody Hedgecock was the commander of the group I was

to cover; I was to meet him at the hotel we would stay in, La Fonda del Sol, in western Miami, in the Cuban section, far from the water. The hotel was a white stucco building, five stories, with wrought-iron balcony railings at some of the windows along its façade. Rust from the wrought iron stained its front in long tear streaks. The lobby was equally shabby, despite its high-backed wicker chairs and potted trees. The carpet, once brilliantly colored, was worn and faded; ceiling fans circulated the hot humid air. There was no one in sight anywhere, and I had to call out 'hello!' several times before a small man in a dirty white suit emerged from a back room wiping his greasy mouth on a paper napkin, the thin kind that come with take-out orders.

It all felt exactly right, even the note the man handed me with his greasy fingers after I'd registered.

'Where is Mi Tierra?' I asked after I'd read it. He gave me directions to a bar on the next block.

Then he led me to a wide staircase – the elevator was not working – and up to the second floor, to a bare, white-washed room, its walls stained with damp patches, and I set my things down. I went into the bathroom to wash my face and hands, and a giant cockroach darted for a crack between the tub and the floor. The sink was the old-fashioned type, with two taps. The towel was the color of dirty water. Even though there was no one else in the room, I tried to conceal my smirk of satisfaction.

I walked down the street and found the bar – dark, smelling of beer, with cheap metal-legged tables and chairs in the middle, and red plastic benches in booths along one wall. The walls were plastered with colorful ads, all in Spanish, and plastic grapes and bananas and pineapples hung from the ceiling. It was a true dive – something I hadn't seen before, even during my time with Sonders. I looked around. An old man hunched over a drink at the bar; and two men in work clothes were drinking beer at one of the tables. They eyed me when I walked in, kept eyeing me. I was uncomfortable. (That was right too.) I walked farther into the room and saw some men in a booth at the back. I approached them nervously, and one – a big

man with thick red arms and face and a ginger beard –
looked up and raised one ginger eyebrow.

'I'm looking for Woody Hedgecock. I was told to meet
him here.'

The red man stood up. 'Yeah, I'm Hedgecock.'

'I'm from *World*,' I said, knowing which name would be
important around here. I moved forward, hand
outstretched, my professional face on. 'Stacey Stevens.'

He didn't take my hand. He looked horrified. 'A *girl?*
They sent a *girl?*'

'They sent one of their best photographers, Mr Hedgecock,' I said confidently in my best brittle tough voice. 'Do
you want your mission covered or not?'

He glared at me, sat down, motioned curtly with his
head, directing me to sit down opposite him. I did.

He looked me in the eyes, hard. 'This is a dangerous
mission, miss. Too dangerous for a girl.'

'I'm not a girl, Hedgecock,' I said in my deepest voice.
'I'm thirty-two, experienced, and terrific. I've been in
dangerous situations before – I was in Algeria during the
revolution,' I lied. 'And it's me or nobody,' I threatened.

He stared at me. The man sitting beside him stared at
me. The man sitting beside me stared at Woody.

Woody raised his eyebrows. He looked questioningly at
the others. They shrugged. He shrugged. 'It's your funeral,'
he said.

Woody Hedgecock had a thick neck and a thick,
muscular body. His skin, roughened by weather and sun,
was permanently red and wrinkled. His eyes were pale
blue, the eyes of a visionary or fanatic; and his stiletto
speech, comprised mainly of facts and figures, emerged
from between barely opened lips. He was past his prime,
but still good-looking – very. He was my very image of a
soldier of fortune.

He nodded his head toward the bar, and miraculously,
the bartender appeared beside me. 'What'll you have?' I
looked at the table. They were drinking beer. 'A beer,' I
said.

'This is Alex, and that's Noel.' Again, he indicated them

with a mere nod of the head. A man used to command, I thought.

'You know the gig?'

I nodded.

He turned to the others.

'Fourteen letters probably means seven shows. Tomorrow's the deadline; by the day after we'll be able to blueprint it. Doesn't matter – we only need five six guys.'

'If they're good,' put in Alex, speaking in the same tight-lipped way.

Woody nodded. 'We got weapons for a dozen – four BARs, eight M–14s, and some satchel charges.'

'And the bazooka,' Noel grinned. He had a British accent.

They began then to talk a language I didn't understand, although I knew they were referring to weapons. They longed for M–16s, and things called Mark Twos, and Mac Tens, and more satchel things, whatever they were. They talked about laws, which laws I don't know, they didn't seem like men who worried about laws. And clips and belts and mortars and Colts (well, I knew a Colt was a kind of gun). I dearly wanted to know what they were talking about but felt I could not interrupt to ask questions without losing face – or what is nowadays called 'credibility'. I figured a man might know these things. And it was bad enough they had to have a 'girl' photographer, without my emphasizing my 'girlish' ignorance. So I pulled out a pad and pen – I was to do the reportage on this story – to take notes. I figured that would give me the clout I needed to ask questions. But when he saw the pad, Woody stopped dead.

'What's that,' he said in a cold voice. His eyes were slits. Had he practiced looking like that?

'What does it look like? I'm writing this story, you know.'

'*No notes!*' he ordered. 'Nothing written down! You'll have to remember what's important and write it later.'

'Okay,' I conceded with irritation. 'But it would help if you guys gave me a little information.'

In a monotone and with an expressionless face, Woody told me that he'd placed an ad in *Hero* magazine two months ago, asking for men who wanted to help overthrow Castro. In response to my questions, he explained with exaggerated patience that no, Castro couldn't trace them through the ad because the reply was to a PO box in Dallas, a crowded post office in which it would be hard to isolate his 'contact', the person who picked up the mail. Replies were carefully screened (How? I wondered, but was too intimidated to ask), and those that seemed legit were asked for further information. Twenty-two men had replied; nineteen were asked to send more data. Sixteen of these did so, and of those, fourteen were chosen and told to meet here, at this café, on December 28. Tomorrow they would know who their cohorts would be.

'But you have arms only for a dozen.'

'These guys are pros, like us. They have their own.'

I stared at him: A BYOB war! Bring your own bullets!

Woody returned to his former conversation. It seemed that although it was indeed a BYOB war, these guys had arms hidden in some tiny islands off the coast of Florida; and that they knew a man, whose name or code name was Luna, who had a boat big enough to transport us all to Cuba.

After a couple of hours, Woody nodded to the bartender. (I wondered if the man kept his eye on Woody so as to see his slightest gesture. He seemed to. I wondered what Woody did to earn this kind of attention.) The man came over, announced a figure – in Spanish – and Woody nodded to Alex, who pulled some wrinkled bills from his pocket and threw them on the table.

'Okay, let's go see a man about a boat,' Woody said as they stood up. I stood too, and lingered.

'Not you.'

I raised my eyebrows at him.

'You can know after. After,' he said emphatically, and strode out of the bar, Alex and Noel trailing him.

I felt like a child left behind when the grown-ups go to the movies, but I tried to pull my dignity around me, and I followed them out. They were getting into a red convertible parked in front – hardly a car for a secret mission, I thought. I stood beside the car.

'So what's the next move? When and where shall I meet you again?'

'You're at the hotel? I'll be in touch,' Woody said curtly, and drove away.

I walked back to the hotel. My room was hot. Nylon curtains the color of soot blew wildly into the room, but the wind was from the west, hot, humid, and dusty as the miles of Florida scrublands beyond. I closed the windows, pulled down the greasy yellowed shades, and turned on the ceiling fan. I lay down on the bed. It was five o'clock, too early for dinner, and I was tired, having gotten up at six to finish packing and say goodbye to the kids and get to the airport for a ten o'clock plane. I thought I'd have a nap before dinner, if it wasn't too hot for sleep.

But I can't sleep. I feel uneasy, not sure why. I'm pumped so full of adrenaline from excitement and fear of an entirely unfamiliar situation that I can't feel anything very strongly; I have to relax my mind and body to discover the source of my dis-ease.

I don't mind the grunginess, the shabbiness, the ugliness, the lack of luxury. I wouldn't mind it getting worse, getting hard. I want to experience hardship, to see what it feels like to be in danger, in a war, situations I've only read about. I want to see what hardship is like and whether I can take it. So it isn't the physical unpleasantness that is bothering me.

The men. Yes, something about the men, my heart starts to beat a little faster when I think about them. Am I afraid of them? Whoops!

I get up, search through my knapsack for my journal, and throw myself back on the bed. I will write it out. I discover things more easily by writing than by trying to think or feel. My hand knows more than my head does.

The men. No, it isn't fear. Not exactly. It's . . . it's . . . outrage. At the way they look at me, or don't look at me, as if I were invisible, well they look at each other the same way, it has nothing to do with me, but . . . But what?

I can't stand it, that's what! It's hateful, it's inhuman, oh it's intolerable and I won't stand for it!

Really, Anastasia.

And the way Woody spoke to me, ordered me around as if I were one of his hired help, how dare he!

I put down my pen and light a cigarette. I wish I had a drink. No room service in this dump and I don't feel like going downstairs and sitting in that disgusting bar and besides the men might be there . . .

Yes, Anastasia, go on.

Yes, the way Woody speaks to me. He makes an easy assumption of command, as if he has never known anything else. And that turns you on, Anastasia, doesn't it, just the way the guys did when you were in college, the older ones who walked around as if they had the secret of control in every situation, you would like to believe they did, wouldn't you, it would be thrilling, oh, ravishing, to give yourself up to someone who really was that powerful, like surrendering to god . . .

Yes, the way Clark Gable acts in the movies, wonder what he's like in life, certainly not in control all the time, but that's his movie role, that hateful knowing smile, one raised eyebrow that claims he knows every man's price and every woman's desire.

This assignment would make a great movie. Maybe when I get back, I'll tell Toni the story – the whole story, with all the psychological and emotional overtones, their hostility toward me, my ambivalent attraction and repulsion toward Woody – could I tell him that? I could say I was making it up, and he could turn it into a movie script. Plucky girl reporter (who hides the fact that she's occasionally near tears) wins over tough soldiers of fortune (who hide the fact that they find her attractive and likeable). Starring Rosalind Russell and Clark Gable. Or Audrey Hepburn and Gary Cooper. (Or had they already made that one?) Or – oh, yes! Burt Lancaster, beautiful tough tender Burt Lancaster, and me, Stacey Stevens! Ahh . . .

I woke damp and hot and terrified from a nightmare. Naptime nightmares are much worse than those at night because they feel so real – at least mine do. They always occur where I actually am, in bed in a particular room, and at the actual time, so it feels that what is happening is really happening. What was happening (I dreamed) was that I was asleep in a shabby hot hotel in Miami and the city was attacked by men in gas masks carrying rifles with bayonets who were at this moment at my door, about to knock it down. What was actually happening was that someone was banging on my door. I pulled myself groggily up, staggered to the door, had trouble unlocking the simple old-fashioned skeleton key.

Woody was standing there. I blinked.

'Dinner,' he announced.

I looked at him dumbly. 'Oh.' I looked at my watch. It was seven-thirty. It came to me that this mission must be scheduled like a military exercise: dinner at seven-thirty, bed at eleven, breakfast at six-thirty, like that. I felt apologetic. 'I didn't know . . .' I began.

He nodded, turned, and started to walk away. 'Where?' I cried.

'In the bar,' he said, and left.

I tossed off my sweaty clothes and ran into the bathroom and got in the shower. I ignored the cockroach who swiftly evacuated the tub as I entered it. I put on a clean, if somewhat wrinkled wraparound skirt and a cotton jersey and sandals, ran a comb through my hair, and ran downstairs, my heart pounding. Terrible to be so ignorant, to be late . . .

Woody was alone at the bar, in an alcove of the lobby. The desk clerk was standing behind the bar talking to him in a low voice. He must be one of them, I thought. My heart pounded. It was exactly like being in a spy movie. I approached Woody, who turned, nodded to me, and went back to his converation with the clerk. I looked around. Neither Alex nor Noel was in the room. The restaurant, a greasy-looking dark room just beyond, was empty except for a middle-aged Cuban couple sitting at a table against the wall.

I waited.

Woody motioned me to take a stool. I did so, thinking I was being trained to obey just as his men were, like the bartender in Mi Tierra. Still talking to the clerk, he gestured toward me with his glass and his eyebrows. 'Vodka and tonic,' I replied. The clerk fixed my drink, his head bent low to catch Woody's every word. He put the glass in front of me. The two men continued to talk.

Woody nodded once; the clerk walked away. An old waiter shuffled in on soft-soled shoes, and stood at the end of the bar, waiting. The desk clerk went over to him, poured two ponies of crème de menthe. The waiter put them on a tray and left the room. The desk clerk stood at the end of the bar, staring at the wall.

Woody was now sitting beside me, silent.

'How did things go with the boat?'

'Luna's a fool,' he spat.

I raised my eyebrows in question.

'Oh, it'll be okay, we'll get off all right. Just the waiting now.'

'Where are the others?'

'Taking care of some business for me.'

'Is this the dinner hour or something?'

He frowned.

'I mean, the way you summoned me I thought we were eating in the officers' mess, and I'd missed the gong.'

For the first time, he smiled. 'Just my way, I guess. Women tell me I'm peremptory. Too many years in the military.'

'You mean, that was really an invitation to dinner?'

'Thought I ought to fill you in.'

By the time we entered the dining room, a few other couples were sitting there, and more came in later – Cubans, like the Spanish, eat late. The greasy menus were an omen of the food – the meat was inedible and the salad was swimming in sweet dressing. But the rice and beans were good, and I could live on them forever, so I didn't care. All during dinner, Woody talked and I listened.

He'd enlisted in the Marines as soon as war broke out in 1941, and had fought in Europe and the Pacific in World War II. He loved the Marines; his eyes turned radiant when he talked about 'the Corps'. He loved the hardship of the training, the toughness required of the men. He rose to the rank of sergeant before he was sent to the Pacific, and while there was awarded a field lieutenancy. I thought as he talked: he was trained to kill just as women are trained to mother. After five years of doing nothing but fighting, preparing to fight, waiting to fight, recuperating after a fight, years in which he must have learned a great deal, he was completely a soldier, he was probably no longer fit for anything else.

I asked him why he didn't stay in the Marines after the war, and he let his eyes wash over me and a tiny smile dislocate his features. 'Money,' he said out of one side of his mouth.

He had to have practiced these expressions.

'You're being paid to . . . !' I burst out, astonished. What had I imagined? I pressed my lips together. I really had to watch it. If I betrayed my real naïveté about the world, these guys would dump all over me.

But at that moment, Woody seemed to enjoy my ignorance. He leaned one thick arm on the table, he smiled benevolently at me with all-knowing superiority.

'There's a lot of patriots in the States, ma'am,' he enunciated firmly, a government representative addressing a reporter. Then he winked.

'You mean private citizens contribute to what amounts to war against whomever they don't like?' It was hopeless for me to try to pretend: he already knew I was an innocent, and that knowledge was adding to his pleasure. 'Isn't that against the law? I mean, doesn't Congress have to declare war?'

He laughed. 'War? Who said anything about war?' He lifted his glass to toast me. 'You're a sweet kid, Stace, but you shouldn't be covering this story. You should be home having kids or something. This kinda thing's too rough for you.'

I wanted to say I was experienced in war, that I'd covered war in Algeria (but I'd already used that line, and besides it wasn't quite true), I just wasn't experienced about a new kind of corruption, the alliance of private citizens for private wars which the government seemed to tolerate. It had to: my assignment had been okayed by the State Department, which meant so had Woody's. But I thought it politic to shut up and listen.

'So tell me about this kinda thing, Woody. What's so rough about it?'

He did. For hours. He had fought in wars in places I'd never heard of, and he rambled on from story to story: I might have doubted the tales in which he was the hero, except that he told some in which he was the butt, and told of being frightened too. His way of describing fear was to say 'I wanted to shit in my pants'. Men often say things like that. I wonder if that's just an expression, or if fear really hits men that way. I've been frightened, but it has never made me feel like that.

I listened. I didn't try to believe or disbelieve. I was listening not just to the stories, which after a while grew repetitious, but to the way Woody saw the world. For him, all of life was power. He loved the marines – and the United States – not for reasons of principle or even just because he was at home in them, but because to him they represented the most powerful institutions on earth. Power was an automatic good, an absolute almost. There was no one in the world who didn't either have power or want it, and what fascinated him was watching the struggle for it, knowing the behind-the-scenes machinations, the ins and outs, who's in this year who was out two years ago, who was on top a decade ago and is now in the pits. Most of all, obviously, he loved being on the side of someone who won, but in a way, he didn't really care who won or lost, he enjoyed being part of the struggle. It *amused* him. Underneath the bravery, the heroism, the starkness of some of his stories – and I didn't doubt that part, he *had* known incredible physical hardship, he'd lived in filth, infested with vermin, sat in the blood of a dying comrade for hours, waiting for rescue – under that there was a hollowness that terrified me. Because if you weren't fighting for something that mattered – the only thing I could think of that I'd fight for was my kids, my home, my right to think and speak – then what was the reason to live in filth and vermin, what justified that dying comrade's blood, why was Woody's life heroic? As he certainly felt it was.

Oh, I know that governments always paste reasons on wars, label them so they'll appear decent, like whiskey bottles kept in boxes made to look like books one can properly keep on one's bookshelves. But didn't people know better, didn't the men who fought know better? Woody was fighting for fun. What kind of person finds such a life fun?

My ruminations kept me quiet – not that I had anything to add to the conversation (he would surely not be interested in my experience of childbirth). But he was enjoying himself, just like the boys I'd hung out with at college, who loved having me – or any female – for an audience.

We finished late, sitting over brandies. Woody smoked a cigar, still talking. Then almost in midsentence, he stopped, announced, 'Enough. Time for bed,' and stood up. Just like that. Orders.

He walked me to my room, patted my head as if I were a child and said ''Night, kid,' and winked and marched off with his military posture. I stood for a moment at my door watching him, partly regretting and partly relieved that he hadn't made a pass.

Woody had told me he would be busy the next day until two, when the newcomers were to meet us at the café; so I slept late, had coffee and a roll in my room and went out with my camera. I wandered the streets, staying within the Cuban neighborhood, looking for shots that would show the character of the place. I shot old men sitting in the sun, children playing in the streets or lolling, empty-eyed, on the front steps of shabby houses. There were no women around. They must all have been working – at home, in shops, factories, greasy spoons. They would probably appear later in the day, five or five-thirty, looking worn, shabby, shapeless, lugging string bags stuffed with vegetables, giant tins of oil, big cotton bags of rice. The few younger men on the sidewalks mostly paraded around in tight pants with great bulges at the crotch, looking dangerous.

I had lunch in a restaurant no better than the one in the hotel, then went to the café. Woody, Alex, and Noel were sitting with two strangers at two tables pushed together in the middle of the room. No one smiled or greeted me, but Woody made Alex move so I could sit beside him. Neither Alex nor Noel showed any reaction to this.

Woody introduced the newcomers, Philip and Cyrus. They were in their mid-thirties, both with deep tans and athletically trim bodies. I studied them, trying to figure out why they were here, what they did, but I sensed that questions about people's backgrounds were taboo. I listened. The men were talking with great familiarity about Indochina, Iran, the Congo. They were apparently soldiers of fortune, adventurers, mercenaries. But Philip and Cyrus looked classy in a way the other three did not; and they sounded as if they'd gone to schools like Groton or Exeter, Princeton or at least Dartmouth.

At two-fifteen, two more men drifted in, middle-aged Cubans in white suits: Clemente and Orlando. Jack, another American, tall, gaunt, with eyes that never met others', arrived a few minutes later. Three younger Cubans appeared at quarter of four, and one of them – Lope – told us that another man, Ettore, would arrive soon. Ettore arrived at five-thirty. I wondered if they would be this cavalier when the time came to attack. I was tired of sitting there, and I was bored.

From the conversation, I deduced that Clemente and Orlando had been prosperous before Castro expropriated their land, and that Lope had had some property. They may have exaggerated their wealth, but these men seemed easy in a way that comes with wealth – they were used to authority, or command, used to being seen as legitimate. Three of the Cubans were heavyset, all had mustaches. And they were intense, serious, driven, almost. Clemente said they had managed to smuggle out some of their money with them, and could afford to buy weapons. Orlando had brought along a paid subordinate, José, who came swaggering in a little after I arrived looking dangerous and suspicious, reached a hand inside his white jacket, and pulled out a package of cigarettes and handed them to Orlando. He was an errand boy; he looked like the boys out on the streets – young and tough, a cock looking for a barnyard to rule. Ettore was a small, plump, voluble man with warm brown eyes that filled with tears whenever he mentioned his wife, his children, his farm, and Cuba. His family was still living outside Havana, and they were to help us in some way.

I was interested in these men although their conversation bored me. It was an argument about the excellences and flaws in an entire range of weapons – semiautomatic guns, rifles, even tanks, planes, military boats. They talked as if they were outfitting a regiment, and I wondered which of these supplies they actually possessed. Woody rarely spoke, but when he did, announcing that C–4 was the best (what was C–4?), the others shut up.

We broke for dinner at six, and I went back to my room and napped; again I was awakened by a rapping on my door, and again it was Woody. This time I didn't rush getting downstairs. But we all had dinner together at a big round table in the center of the room. A seat had been left vacant for me next to Woody. A handful of hotel guests was scattered around the room. The guys drank and blabbed.

'Me, I gonna blow up the telephone company and after that I go for the radio station,' said Lope.

'Listen, we gotta prioritize,' Jack countered bitterly. 'The radio station is number one. We gotta get the police stations, they're up to their asses in weapons. We gotta split into three teams, get the radio station first . . .'

'What about the barracks?' Orlando screamed.

'The generator, that's the thing,' Philip put in precisely.

'We should get their water! Really fuck the bastards up!' cried Sebastián.

'No!' Ettore pounded the table. 'No water!' He had a family in Havana.

'You know how Alpha 66 contaminated all that sugar in the warehouses with chemicals,' Alex said between clenched teeth. 'Wrecked the fuckers' economy. We contaminate the reservoirs, water storage tanks, we got 'em.'

'No the water,' Ettore pleaded.

Cyrus laughed. His narrow teeth were yellow, which was unexpected in a man with the tan, the physique, the carriage of a California surfer. 'They gave the bastards swine flu, they gave them dengue . . .'

Philip picked it up, laughing too. 'They unloaded a ton of infested mosquitoes on them.'

'What about their oil pipelines . . .' Noel put in.

'You do what you like, I go for the barracks,' Clemente said to Lope.

'There is gasoline at dee pier,' Ettore offered ominously.

'Most important,' Jack announced, 'fuck off the soft targets, head for the hard stuff. We're only a dozen . . .'

'Oh,' Alex yearned, 'if only we could get some C–4!'

The argument broke into splinters, with two or three guys fighting one another in a set of nasty little groups.

'Yeah, you use a whole satchel charge when you only need a couple of sticks, I know your kind . . .'

'If we had pineapples . . .'

'We could make juice. Forget it.'

'Shit, there's only eight fucking BARs, everybody else'll have to carry M–14s.'

'But what I'd like to lay my hands on is some MK2. Think our contacts . . . ?' Woody looked questioningly at Noel, who didn't respond.

'I'd like an M–60 myself,' Jack muttered.

'Some mortars . . .'

'A satchel charge apiece, half a dozen bazookas, and some M–16s. We'd wipe 'em out!'

'No, a law! A couple of laws!'

I turned to Woody. I whispered, 'What the hell is a law?'

He gave me a disgusted grimace, grabbed a paper napkin, pulled out a fancy ball-point pen and scribbled 'LAW: light antitank weapon.' He passed it to me, I read it; he crumpled it up in his hand. He turned back to the men. 'Listen, if we are making up a shopping list, what I want is a couple of MACs.'

I knew MACs weren't Macintosh apples. I didn't dare ask him what they were.

By ten-thirty, they were no longer arguing. 'We blow it all up!' Huge laughter. 'All of it!'

They were too drunk to do serious planning – nor did this seem the place to do it. It would be safe for me to go to bed. I leaned over to ask Woody if we would be leaving tomorrow. He shook his head. 'Problem about the boat. Maybe the next day.' I excused myself, but I don't think any of them even noticed my leaving. They were having too good a time.

Before going to my room, I went into the phone booth – there were no phones in the rooms – and called Toni. I spoke to the kids, too. They were still up, playing Scrabble. It was a holiday week. My heart ached when I heard them laughing together, and I couldn't tell them anything except that I was okay and things were progressing, but we hadn't gone yet.

I went upstairs feeling uneasy. I had no idea how expeditions like this should be run, but it did seem that the guys should not talk so loudly about the mission, especially in a hotel patronized by Cubans. But maybe they were all on the same side. The *way* they talked bothered me too – it was like sitting over coffee, listening to a bunch of women moon over their dream houses: what would yours have? A dishwasher, a dryer, a stainless-steel sink? A garbage-disposal unit? These guys wanted bigger and better killing machines. But they had about as much chance of getting them as most women did their dream houses: that much was clear. Could these men really be professional soldiers? Was this the behavior of professional soldiers? They were so *silly*! Oh, what did I know about such things? Only what I saw in the movies. Maybe *World* should have sent a man. Maybe a man would know things like this . . .

I thought maybe I was uneasy because I felt like a traitor. I admired Castro, who had saved his country from Batista, that hideous dictator. In my heart I didn't support what the men I was covering were doing. And that made me feel guilty, an intruder, a person acting in bad faith. I reminded myself that I was a photographer, impartial, a professional, and that there was no reason not to cover what one didn't agree with, that you couldn't do news that way, but still . . .

Eventually, I fell asleep.

The next afternoon, we all met in Mi Tierra again. Most of the guys were wearing khaki trousers and T-shirts, but Woody wore a freshly pressed safari suit and the rich Cubans wore immaculate white linen. We were drinking beer and the guys were repeating the conversation of the night before almost word for word, arguing over the respective merits of the radio station, the reservoir, the police station, the barracks, the telephone company, and yearning after dream weapons, when two men came in wearing suits and ties and wary expressions, and I thought, oh-oh, CIA or FBI, what's going to happen now.

The men in suits looked around, stared at Woody, nodded; he nodded back, and they asked if they could join us. Much noise, scraping of chairs as half the guys at the table got up to make room for them. They acted as if they were in the presence of royalty. The men in suits accepted this as their due, and sat down next to Woody. The one closer to him turned and said something in a soft voice I couldn't hear. Woody nodded and in an equally soft voice sketched his plan: the boat, the hidden weapons, the point of landing, the points of attack. I was surprised – I hadn't realized that while the others were going on and on, Woody, Alex, and Noel actually *had* a plan. As Woody talked, he occasionally glanced at Alex or Noel for confirmation or addition, and that one would lean forward and fill in what was needed. For once, everyone was whispering. The men in suits listened, nodding.

I looked around the room. There was an old man at a corner table, nodding over his aperitif. He looked harmless, but who knows? And two toughs were sitting in a booth drawing plans on paper napkins, looking as if they were planning a robbery. There was a handful of men at the bar. I felt extremely agitated; but the men in suits paid no attention to the others in the room. I must be foolish, I thought: after all, these guys really were experienced.

The guys in suits nodded, eyes lidded, expressionless. When Woody was finished, they whispered to him for a few minutes. I only caught 'Alpha 66' and 'Dominguez'. I was thrilled: I imagined they were laying out the master plan and filling Woody in on it. He kept nodding, his eyelids down too, face expressionless. After a time, they stood up. Woody nodded at them, they nodded at the table, and left.

That night, Woody and Alex and Noel and I drove in a borrowed car – an old dented, rusting, rattly Buick – to a stucco bungalow set among blocks of similar shabby peeling houses on the outskirts of the city. Everyone was quiet, tense; we were going to a secret meeting set up with a defector, Castro's former minister of defense, Dominguez. He had information on where things were located – arms, tanks, airplanes, men. This was an important meeting, and they had included me!

Alex parked the car a block away from the house and we walked down the poorly lighted street to number 27, which was completely dark. Alex gave a signal knock. The door opened on a dark hallway; we couldn't even see who had opened it, but we entered. Noel closed the door behind him, quietly, then a thick, short figure shuffled along in front of us and threw open a door to a lighted room. The light illuminated the figure – a woman, aged, ageless, shapeless, grey. She pointed, and we entered.

The room was heavily draped so no light showed outside. It was also hot, stifling, and filled with cigar smoke. In a shabby easy chair a man sat in a bright blue bathrobe that fell open from the belt tied at his waist. He waved us in, asked – in Spanish – if we wanted a drink. Alex translated for us. (Woody spoke Spanish too, I knew; but he was the commander, not the translator.) The men asked for rum; I requested a Coke. The man rapped out the order to the woman, who was wearing bedroom slippers. After ten long hot smoky minutes, during which we sat in silence, she returned carrying three cloudy glasses half full of rum, and a glass of cola with one small melting ice cube floating in it.

We drank. Woody took over. 'Excellency,' he began deferentially, 'we are honored to have you with us.'

Alex translated.

Dominguez nodded, then began to talk. He spoke for a long time, rapidly, with passion, pounding the little rickety table beside him so that it shook, pounding his chest, rolling his eyes. His statement was translated rather cursorily by Alex, who probably could not remember all of what was said. His Excellency had believed in the revolution, had believed in Fidel; his heart was entirely with the cause. But now Fidel had become a betrayer: he was imprisoning people, murdering people, putting people in camps like the Russians, expropriating property (including Dominguez'), making dictatorial laws. He had betrayed the revolution; he was ruining the country.

Tears ran down the old man's cheeks. He did not bother to wipe them away.

He, Dominguez, had probed his heart, his conscience, his soul, and out of loyalty to his homeland had finally defected. He now believed The Devil was ruining it. The Devil had betrayed him, and was now betraying Cuba, his motherland, his sacred soil . . .

Woody's face lifted in exaltation as Dominguez spoke. His chin lifted, his eyes began to flare.

'Excellency, you inspire us, we who are about to die, for Cuba, for your cause, for FREEDOM!' Then he took a sip of rum – after first toasting Dominguez with his glass, which, when he held it up to the light, was really very dirty and smudged. Alex and Noel lifted their glasses too, and His Excellency, who was already drinking, thrust his glass toward them slightly, sloshing rum over his bare knee.

Then Woody began to speak, and this time he spoke in Spanish. His speech was long, and from the bobs of his head at its opening, I gathered he was offering kudos to the minister. Later, he seemed to be asking questions, and Dominguez answered, but then something seemed to be wrong. Alex joined in the conversation, and the three men looked around as if searching the room.

At last the minister shouted something, and no one spoke until the silent woman shuffled to the door and opened it. He gave her another order, and ten minutes later she appeared again with a large ordnance-type map of Cuba. The men all got down on the floor on their hands and knees. Dominguez began to pinpoint important sites.

I didn't join them, I knew they would resent my intrusion, that Woody would act as if I were trying to pry into State Secrets. Besides, I didn't speak Spanish. I told myself my job was to absorb the atmosphere totally, to study the minister, to try to read his character on his face. It was a fine face – deeply lined, sad, with traces of sensuality – but it is difficult to be confident about a face when you do not understand the words that come from it. I yawned. I felt overwhelmingly sleepy. It came on me that I was bored. Again. How could that be? I was almost never bored. Well, there is so much waiting, I thought. And this room is airless.

I sat there sipping my lukewarm Coke, head spinning from the heat, while they argued and exclaimed and pounced on spots on the piece of paper on the floor.

I was feeling faint. I tapped Woody on the shoulder and told him I'd be outside on the doorstep, getting some air. He looked alarmed, and turned swiftly to Alex.

'Ask him if it is safe if she goes outside!'

Alex did. Dominguez shrugged. I got up and left the room, I peered down the dark hallway, searching for the woman, but did not see her. The back rooms of the house were dark. (Did the woman sit in the dark? Why? Did she have lights, and a television set on in a cozy back room with all the drapes drawn? I hoped so. Was she his sister, his wife, his servant? Maybe just his landlady. I knew these questions would hold no interest for the others.)

I opened the front door, went out, sank to the step. I lighted a cigarette, inhaled deeply. I looked up at the stars, brilliant in the southern sky. I waited.

It was after midnight when they came out, silent, tense with elation and a sense of importance. We walked back to the car in silence. Only when we had driven well away from the house did Woody explode: 'Great! Just great! We got it now!' and Alex and Noel assented, all of them laughing, lighting up cigarettes, relaxing. Woody glanced at me. 'We leave tomorrow,' he said between clenched teeth. 'Be ready at six.'

three

At six o'clock of the morning of December 30, 1961, I was sitting in the lobby with my knapsack and camera case, wishing I had a cup of coffee. Woody, Alex, and Noel appeared and disappeared. They were making telephone calls, sending messengers, trying to find a car. It seems José had not got the message, and Orlando's car had broken down. At seven, the hotel restaurant opened, and I went in and ordered coffee. We did not get on the road until eight. Eleven of us crammed ourselves and our gear into two cars, a Ford station wagon and the rattly Buick from the night before. (What had happened to the red convertible? Whose car was it?) Sebastián and Ettore were to meet us with a third car at a Mobil station near the road to the Everglades. Some people from each car would move to Sebastián's, so we would not be so crowded during the long drive to Key West. It suddenly occurred to me that there were thirteen of us.

It was a beautiful day, and lovely driving down the two-lane highway to the Keys. Sand, sky, narrow necks of land connected by bridges threaded water blue, blue-grey, Winslow Homer blue-green, depending on the sky, the clouds. There were only a few poor shabby settlements along the road, but they were – to me, at least – utterly appealing: shacks along the beach, small trailers with tattered canvas awnings, people in straw hats, barefoot, sitting on the bridges or piers dangling a fishing line. Sun. Silence.

We reached Key West in the early afternoon. We drove straight to the pier where the boat was anchored. It was a cabin cruiser with sleeping accommodations for six. Its name, somewhat faded, was the *Argo*. An unshaven Cuban was standing by the boat, smoking a cigar. We all clambered out; Woody and Alex went to talk to the man – Luna? – while Noel supervised the unloading of our gear from the trunks of the cars. The other men disappeared.

There was a bar/bait shop at the pier, and I went in to get out of the sun. The three Americans were already sitting at the bar, drinking beer, and Lope came out of a door zipping up his fly. I assumed he was coming from the john and used it myself. The toilet seat was wet and covered with old dark stains. The room stank, and flies buzzed, hovering around the toilet and the floor around it.

I joined the others at the bar and ordered iced coffee and a ham sandwich. The bread was so dry its edges had curled up. A radio was playing, reminding me it was New Year's Eve. I longed to call Toni and the kids, but didn't dare.

I'd been told over and over how secret this mission was, especially now that we were actually embarked. I sat there imagining I was going into battle, trying to feel what soldiers feel at such a time. I managed to develop some sentimental thoughts about the kids and Toni, although I had no sense whatever that I would be in danger.

I went outside and wandered down to the boats. No one was around, and one of the cars was gone. I set up my camera on a tripod and began to take pictures. I moved around, walking as far from the scene as I could – there was thick scrub brush behind the bait shop – and took two more rolls. Then I plopped down in the sand, pulled my visor cap down over my eyes, and fell asleep. I woke up at voices. Noel, Alex, and José were loading our gear onto the deck of the boat. It was almost five. Woody emerged from the cabin and jumped the railing onto the pier. His shirt, face, and arms were smudged with heavy black grease. I looked at him inquisitively.

He shrugged. 'Problem with the generator. Had to replace it, don't make them anymore, had to find a rebuilt. Things take time,' he concluded in a resentful voice, as if I'd been criticizing him.

Maybe I was, I thought. Maybe it showed on my face.

What with other 'things', we did not weigh anchor until six. I stood on deck watching land recede. That experience always moves me, it feels mysterious and terrible, and arouses tragic emotions I savor. I was breathing deeply, the suffering of loss thrilling through my nerves, when there was a terrible crunch and squeal and the boat stopped.

It was hours before it became clear what had happened. Immediately after the crunch there was the usual harangue; we chugged slowly back to the pier; something was wrong with the propeller. José donned a frogman suit and dove under to examine it. It seems we had rammed a coral reef. (Where were the maps? Who was the navigator?) Usual chaos – argument about what was wrong and what to do, checking the maps, starting up the motor and listening, discussing the matter – that's a polite way to put it – with Luna, who glared at Woody as if he would kill him. Time passed. I sat on the deck, smoking, with Philip and Cyrus, whom I suspected of giggling behind their hands.

The sun was sinking into the water behind us, a great red ball falling into the sea. Then it was dark. Philip made daiquiris and served them in real cocktail glasses he had found in the galley. The Cubans joined us, except for José, who was still under the boat. The men began to grow mellow. Then Clemente gasped, sat up, pounded his fist on his knee.

'Iss New Year! New Year! I must call!' He stood up. 'Where iss phone?'

Philip pointed to the ship-to-shore telephone.

Clemente went into the cabin and called someone – his wife, I suppose. He talked for a long time, expostulating, laughing, wishing her *felices ano nuevo*. When he finished, Sebastián got up and used it. One by one, they trotted over and called, all a little high from the daiquiris, the sun, the excitement.

After several hours, Woody appeared all cleaned up (where had he found a shower?) and announced that it had been decided we would go ahead without repairing the propeller. We would make slow progress, but the Cuban coast was only an overnight trip. It was true we had to make two stops to pick up the weapons Woody had hidden, but to wait for repair might delay us several days, even a week. Then Woody relaxed with a bacardi, and called *his* wife in Houston. And I could *understand* what *he* said. He told her everything! Where we were, the trouble we'd had, the fact that we were leaving as soon as José was cleaned up and ready! And *I'd* been afraid to call!

We left near midnight and sailed all night. I slept on deck wrapped in a blanket because I could not bear the gasoline smell below decks, it made me seasick. Around noon the next day, Philip and Cyrus spotted some mounds of earth in the distance; they yelled and waved their arms, and everyone on board grew animated. Ettore, who was running the boat under Woody's orders, had difficulty in steering toward the right ones. We sailed around them, Woody and Alex passing binoculars from hand to hand, others scanning the view with hands held as shields over their eyes. Woody cried out, 'There! There! That turtle shape! That's Dannyboy!'

We pulled in as close to shore as we could, and Alex and José lowered a large rowboat. Noel and Orlando were delegated to stay with the ship, José and Alex to row. The rest of us clambered down the rope ladder and rowed to shore.

It was hard to walk on the wet slimy rock. You'd take a few steps up, then slide back down. It was especially hard for me with my heavy camera case, and José would sometimes reach out a hand to help me. Eventually we gained dry rock, a narrow flat surface, and followed Woody around to a spot that offered footholds for the rest of the climb up. The older men were red-faced and puffing when we reached the top, a plateau that stretched for a mile or so, offering a clear view of the few groves of scrub trees that grew on this 'island', which was really just a rock in the sea.

Woody and Noel began to argue about precisely where the bazookas were hidden. It was hot. The other men threw themselves down on the baking rock and passed around the canteen. I took some pictures. We waited. At last they came up with a plan: they broke us into groups, sending each group to a different grove of trees, with orders to call out if we found the guns. I was assigned to go with Sebastián's group. We set off across the rock.

It took about twenty minutes to reach our grove. We all bent and searched beneath the trees, unsure of just what the cache would look like. Suddenly Woody gave a long triumphant yell that stopped short as if his throat had been cut. We all rushed to where the sound had come from – the scrub trees right in the center of the island. Woody was standing there holding a small box in the air.

'We been robbed! Robbed! Somebody's been here and taken them!' he cried. 'The fuckers left a clip behind just to be sure we'd know they were here!'

There *was* a rough spot beneath the trees where conceivably something had been stored. That and the box – a clip, he said. Bullets. Nothing else. Woody kept screaming 'It was here, it was! Look at this, somebody got here before us!'

There was muttering, cursing, kicking of the dust. Not all the hostility was directed at whomever had robbed Woody. I slumped down again – I was tired – and lighted a cigarette. Who? I wondered, remembering all the people who could have overheard us at La Fonda del Sol, at Mi Tierra.

Woody read the mutiny in the faces around him and mustered us together swiftly. 'We got to get to the little island before they do,' he insisted, and hurried us back to the boat. We climbed back aboard and set off again, again winding in and out of small rocklike islands, again having trouble finding the right one. Philip and Cyrus made sandwiches in the galley and shared them – tuna fish and mayonnaise. They tasted good. We hadn't eaten much that day.

About four-thirty, we anchored again near a small friendly-looking island: it had a wide beach, a forest beyond, with some pines and cypresses among the scrub. Some of the older men remained on the ship this time, while the rest of us rowed to the island and headed for a tall pine at its north end, where the four BARs – Browning automatics – and the two satchel charges of dynamite (I had learned something listening to these guys) were hidden. Had been hidden. Only a weatherbeaten tarpaulin remained.

Woody sank down onto his heels cursing. The others threw themselves on the ground. I smoked.

'Okay, war council,' he announced, finally. He looked at his watch. It was almost six, and the sky was nearly dark. 'It's getting dark. Maybe we should camp here tonight – it'll be more comfortable than that tub. And we need to have a meeting, decide what to do.'

We were all pleased by the decision to camp on the island; we were irritable from our cramped uncomfortable sleeping arrangements: even by day the boat was overcrowded. So José and Alex and Noel rowed back to the ship, and ferried back and forth conveying people and equipment – sleeping and cooking gear. Woody ordered Philip and Cyrus to gather firewood, sent Jack and Ettore to find water, and ordered me to help him find places for the sleeping rolls. When everything was done, and a fire was started, he passed around a bottle of bourbon.

'War council,' he announced.

The men attended with seriousness broken only by the passed bottle, and they even tried to rouse themselves to their usual level of debate and argument. But their hearts weren't in it.

'Okay, men,' Woody said in a particularly solemn, portentous voice. 'How many weapons we got with us?'

They had seven handguns, three Springfield rifles, and a hundred cartridge clips.

Woody tried again. 'What kind of handguns? Anybody but me and Alex and Noel got a Colt?'

Most of them had Smith and Wessons, they confessed mournfully.

Long silence. We were camped among trees, sitting on blankets over a thick layer of pine needles and leaves of scrub oak. It smelled clean and green, and through the trees we could see the sky, still a deep purple. No stars yet, and just a pale moon low on the horizon. It was peaceful.

Woody sighed.

'Well, let's get on with it. Stevens, you cook.'

'What?' This was the first time during our expedition that I had rebelled, but rebel I did. 'I can't cook! And I'm a photographer, not a member of your team to be ordered around!'

The Cubans murmured. 'Of course you can cook,' Woody laughed. 'You're a dame, aren't you?'

'Oh, come on, luv, give it a try,' Noel smiled at me. 'It can't be any worse than what we do.'

Sullenly, with a bad grace I was ashamed of, I got up and searched the food locker. They had brought four boxes of spaghetti, four large cans of tomatoes, two cans of kidney beans, two of baked beans, and a giant can of tuna fish. There was dried onion, dried garlic, dried parsley, salt, pepper. There were thirteen of us. There was a large pot and a medium-sized one, neither big enough for cooking for thirteen people. I groaned.

Feeling wretched – exactly like the old slave in slippers who waited on Excellency – I poured two cans of tomatoes into the middle-sized pot with some spices and set the big pot full of water on the fire. We went on drinking. After half an hour, I poured one can of kidney beans and half the tuna into the tomatoes. I cooked spaghetti in batches, lifting the cooked strands out with a fork and spoon so I could save the water from the first batch to cook the second. Then I served the glop on seven plates and started a new batch of sauce, and after another half hour, served the rest of the guys, who by then were pretty drunk.

They ate it, sloshed it down. They were on the second bottle of bourbon. I managed to swallow a few strands. I refused to clean up.

'That's not the cook's job,' I announced imperiously, trying to recapture some dignity. 'I'm not your servant. Share the labor.'

Woody assigned the chore to Noel. I was grateful to him for finding a way to save my pride, I got up and helped him. Most of the men were completely drunk now. Only Woody and Noel seemed sober, and maybe Alex and José – they weren't saying anything, so I couldn't tell. Jack and Clemente and Orlando and Cyrus were talking about their exploits, past glories, the ones that got away and the ones that didn't.

I didn't listen. I had heard it all before. I sat, leaning back against a tree, watching the sky turn blacker, the stars appear. It was a rich black with stars like a whole pouch of diamonds poured out on a velvet cloth. I tried to appreciate the beauty.

When it got dark, it got cold. We wrapped ourselves in blankets and burrowed into the layers of dead leaves. The fire was dying. Several men were already asleep, I could hear them snoring but I couldn't see them anymore. I could see only the small light of the embers and the tips of cigarettes, moving in darkness like fireflies.

I let myself slide down a bit against the tree trunk and tried to close my eyes. But the sky kept me awake in a way no sunny bright sky could ever do. Then, suddenly, I felt an arm come around me. I turned, but I knew by his smell who it was – Woody.

'What, you get me to cook so you think you have me domesticated?'

He laughed, nuzzling my neck. 'That really got you, hey, kid?'

He laid his head against my breast.

'Knock it off, Woody.'

I wriggled away from him. What in hell was he doing? Did he expect to make love here, in front of everyone? I glanced at him. He was leaning against the same tree with me, smoking. I could see the dark bulk of his profile, the tip of his cigarette.

The problem was part of me did find part of him attractive: much as I detested it, I was drawn to that assured command, that assumption of superiority of his. Once, when I was married to Brad, I dreamt I was Leda, being overpowered by the swan, and I awoke hot and horny. But the swan *was* Zeus, King of the Universe and he had to be Zeus for me to accept his acting as he did. Woody was not Zeus, he was not even superior; by now I seriously doubted that he had any intelligence at all.

Thinking about him as a lover reminded me of a gorgeous Italian I had met in Zurich, who seduced me languorously, with much show of passion and adoration, and then, in bed, leaped on me from behind, thrust and came before I even had time to yell. And if Woody made love disgustingly and I turned against him, he would feel it and that would wreck the relationship I needed to maintain to fulfill this assignment, and that would be bad. Fine: problem solved.

Still, when he put his arm around me again, I let him, and I was relaxed enough that I was drifting off when Ettore appeared above him and cried in a whisper, 'Woody, Woody, they come back, they come back!'

Woody leaped up, reached for his gun. Alex was already waking the others. They sat up swiftly, reached for rifles, guns, loaded cartridges. We all strained our eyes gazing out to sea. A group of small boats was approaching the island from the northeast, coming fast. Our boat was anchored to the south, hidden from them by a curve of the shore.

'Jesus!' Woody exclaimed. 'Now's our chance to get

them! Get our weapons too!' He darted forward, from tree to tree, waving his arm wildly to the others to follow his example. They did, a covey of bodies leaping in the dark night, scurrying, grunting. The boats anchored near the shore; some men leaped out and waded to land, guns held above their heads.

'Get back among the trees!' Woody hissed at me. But I was rooting around by feel in my camera case to find my camera and flash. I had brought my Nikon, because I could hold it above my head and look upward when I was shooting – something I thought might be an advantage. Adrenaline was pulsing blood through my veins, my hands were shaking as I loaded the film in the dark, praying that I'd get it in fast enough to get some photographs. A skirmish! We were nowhere near Cuba. Who were these invaders?

'Save your ammo,' Woody whispered loudly. 'Wait till they're closer.'

But someone hadn't heard – or panicked – and a shot rang out, then several, then there was the swift sound of bullets from a repeating rifle. I edged back into the grove ready to shoot *my* weapon. I stood beside a tree and held the camera as high above my head as I could, and peered up. I wanted to shoot above the heads and bodies and capture the shape and fire of the invaders. The sights were eerie – like flashes of lightning penetrating the darkness. I kept shooting. I heard something thwack into a tree near me, and I felt something sharp, as if I'd been stabbed in the arm. Then a submachine gun strafed the ground around our camp, and someone shouted 'Hands up! Throw down your weapons!' The accent was clearly American.

'Identify yourselves!' Woody commanded.

What a guy! I thought. Even with his hands in the air he gave orders. I edged away from the tree: it seemed, in the darkness, that our men were all standing with hands in the air facing an uncertain number of men carrying much larger weapons.

'Alpha 66,' the enemy replied, and our side howled and jumped in the air cheering and hugging each other.

So this was war.

*

The newcomers were really Alpha 66; they had been sent by the men in suits who came into Mi Tierra that day; except for the two in charge, who were CIA, these men were Cubans, but *trained* – unlike our guys. They had brought our group automatic weapons, dynamite, and grenades. Our team was overjoyed, they leaped in the air, they hugged their deliverers, they kissed their brand-new BARs, their 'pineapples', and the satchel charges, they held them against their bodies crooning the language of love.

Alpha 66 also brought booze, and Noel built up the fire again and everyone gathered around it to drink and talk, prepared, I thought, to get drunk again. Most of them had slept off their last drunk for the past hour, and were eager to start over. Now they could drink in celebration, because of course the weapons had saved their mission.

My arm ached; I thought I must have jabbed it against a sharp branch, too concentrated on photographing to notice. So this time I shared the passed bottle. One of the CIA guys came over and sat beside me, acting with professional curiosity about a female presence, but also turned on by it, I could hear that in his voice. And he couldn't even see me in this flickering light!

My head was aching too. After I told him what I was doing there, he told me he ran a used-car business in Miami, and that his buddy did a little business in dope, and when this mission was over I should come and visit his shop and he and his buddy and I would go out and get high and see the town.

I wanted to cry. My head was aching, my arm was aching, and something awful had happened, I didn't know what, but I didn't want to be there anymore, I wanted my mommy, I wanted my own cool clean bed, I needed to sleep. I swigged some more scotch. I felt myself swaying a little. The CIA guy put his arm around me and I cried out. Woody leaped up and came over, his face – even in that light I could see it – hard and mean, ready to pounce on this guy as if, as if . . . Then his face changed and he crouched in front of me.

'What is it, kid?'

'My arm,' I gasped.

I put my hand on my arm; it was wet. Woody frowned at me, and blew out a long whistle when he looked at my hand – it was bloody. He eased me gently closer to the firelight. My upper arm was covered with blood. He peeled away my torn shirtsleeve – there was a deep cut, like a stab wound except it was more jagged. Suddenly everyone was in motion. Noel was washing my arm, Philip was applying some kind of cream from our first aid kit. Alex was twisting some bandage into a tourniquet, someone was forcing some pills down my throat – only aspirin they said – along with some more scotch.

They wrapped me in several blankets and helped me to lie down again. Then they returned to drinking and talking, this time about me. The CIA men took flashlights, our guys tried to remember where I was standing during the shooting, I tried to tell them which tree it was, but my voice didn't come out loud enough. They beamed their lights all around the area where I'd been seen, then moved away from it in a circle. They found a tree that had been hit by a bullet, missing a big chip of wood and bark. They deduced that when the bullet hit the tree it sent a sharp shard of wood flying at high speed into my arm.

After they had found the cause, they returned to me. I felt hot and funny, a little dizzy. They examined my wound, announced it had stopped bleeding, and removed the tourniquet. Then Woody bound it in a bandage, very gently, and sat down beside me and cradled me in his arm. Noel brought me a tin cup with whiskey in it and I sipped it. My arm throbbed, and I was grateful for the whiskey. I was even grateful for Woody's arm. I leaned against him, listening to the guys talk. They were off again on the radio station versus the electric generator versus the barracks . . .

I fell asleep in Woody's arm, and woke up wrapped in three blankets – others had sacrificed theirs. I felt a little feverish, but I didn't let them know it. I didn't want to be sent back with those CIA guys. I had some aspirin in my knapsack, which I took with the coffee Noel served me. I said I felt fine, much better. We all packed up and trudged back to the boats. We said goodbye to Alpha 66, stowed our gear on the *Argo*, and set off for Cuba.

We reached it mid morning of the next day, in full light. We anchored in a cove that seemed uninhabited, and Noel rowed Ettore ashore. He had telephoned his wife from the ship; she was supposed to meet him at a spot beyond the rocks and trees that rimmed the cove. She was to bring a car, and lead a friend with another car; they would transport the guys and their weapons to Havana. The question was, would I accompany them.

I watched him go in a feverish daze. I fully expected a company of Cuban soldiers to charge out of the trees heaving grenades and firing at us. How would the Cubans not know our plans, advertised in every possible way? I took some pictures, then sat in the shade of an overhang, half-asleep, in so much pain that I didn't mind the thought of being killed. But nothing happened. Noel rowed back to the boat, Alex made sandwiches. We waited. Some of the men cleaned their new weapons; others dozed on the deck.

We waited into the night. Since I was well (I claimed), I was expected to cook dinner: it had become my job. (Once a woman waits on a man, that's it. There's some saying about elephant dung . . .) I opened cans of Spam and potatoes and green beans, although I could barely move my arm, it was red and swollen. We drank. We slept. We woke. We waited through the next morning. At eleven, an unmarked plane swooped over us. Everyone looked up, silent, pale. We all thought we were going to be bombed. But it hovered for a while, then flew away. We waited into the evening.

By then I knew I was in trouble. The swelling on my arm had spread, and a thin blue line showed on it. It was infected. I slathered disinfectant cream on it and swallowed aspirins every few hours. I slept on and off all day. It crossed my mind that I could lose my arm. I vaguely remembered that people died of blood poisoning. But there was nothing to be done.

On the morning of the third day, Philip spotted Ettore on the beach, waving his arms, and rowed out to fetch him. He was distraught, his face was dirty with tears. His wife had not appeared at the meeting place. He waited eight hours, then hitchhiked into the suburb outside Havana where his family lived. His wife was gone. His children were gone. His *house* was gone. None of the neighbors knew what had happened – the house burned down in the middle of the night, they said, no one saw his wife or the children. He crouched on a crate, holding his head in both hands and rocking it back and forth, weeping as he told us about it.

'Maybe they dead, dead! Where do they go?' he lamented.

Of course they're dead, you idiot, I thought. You signed their death warrant yourself, calling them on the phone and telling them to bring a car to pick up weapons. But at the same time I kept picturing his wife and his four children pronged with bullet holes, sprawled on some scrubby hillside; or even worse, not dead but in some prison being tortured. Horrible images kept invading my mind, and I wanted to hit Ettore, go over and pound him on the head in fury for his stupidity. And I wanted to hold him, he was so grief-stricken, I wanted to put my arm around him and assure him they were safe, healthy, happy.

It was all too much for me. I was sick and dizzy and I wanted to go home. The men held a conference. I slept. They concluded that if Ettore's wife had been picked up, Castro had anticipated them and there was no hope: this mission would fail. They decided to return to Miami, regroup, and try again. When Woody finally told me about this, I nodded. I was too sick to talk, but I wanted to tell him that was the first intelligent move he'd made in two weeks.

Sometime that afternoon we chugged out of the harbor and when we were far enough away from the Cuban coast, Woody telephoned for help. At dusk we were met by a Coast Guard seaplane, to which I, no longer conscious, was transferred on a stretcher. They flew me to a hospital in Miami. For days I lingered in delirium. When I woke one afternoon, Russ Farrell was sitting by my bed. He was smiling. 'Great shots!' he said.

They told me later that because of the circumstances

surrounding their rescuing me, the Coast Guard called the State Department, who sent a man to 'debrief' me. He searched my bag, found my *World* ID, and called Russ Farrell. Russ flew down, collected the film I'd shot and had it developed. The pictures of the attack by Alpha 66 were dramatic. The sky looked purplish black behind dark hulking forms which seemed to emit by themselves flashes of light that burst at different rates, so had different sizes. They were not informative pictures – you could not know from looking at them what the scene was, who the men. But the mystery of it added to their power: they were simply terrifying, anonymously terrifying, like the invaders in Bergman's *Skammen*, a modern 'Disasters of War'.

By the time I had recovered, Woody and the others had already left on another adventure. The State Department man, some FBI and CIA guys – and Russ – (that's the way secrecy worked) had heard Woody's and Alex's account of the mission. (For some reason, Noel did not appear with them and his name was never mentioned.) The story they told was that they had spotted several companies of Cuban soldiers dug in around the cove where we anchored, so they pretended to be a fishing party. They had landed Ettore at night, he had evaded the encamped soldiers and worked his way around them and into Havana to make contact with his wife, who would suggest another possible landing site. But she too had been discovered, was gone, the children were gone, the house burned down, etc., etc.

It was Russ who reported all this to me. 'Somebody leaked, huh?' he whispered, crouched over in his chair, his mouth close to my ear, talking between his teeth exactly as Woody did. It was Russ too who told me that Woody's wife, who had inherited millions from her first husband, was the central figure in a right-wing group that financed his operations. And, laughing, that Woody had urged them not to send women on dangerous assignments in a way that suggested it was my presence that had ruined the mission.

'He said,' and Russ began to imitate Woody, talking between his teeth even more pronouncedly, 'we were thirteen, and the thirteenth was a *woman*! Thing was jinxed from the start!'

World never ran the pictures: the shots of the *Argo*, the islands where the weapons were supposed to be hidden, the cove where we'd anchored (photos the CIA blew up and studied microscopically for gun emplacements) might present a security risk, might endanger future expeditions to Cuba. I winced at the thought. But there were a couple of positive consequences to this assignment; my work impressed the editors at *World;* so did my wound, and what they called my 'moxie'. Russ quoted Woody again (I could see Woody would be the font of stories Russ would tell for a decade): 'That kid – she never shed a tear.' I was never again given a trivial assignment, nor was there any resistance in the future to my being given any assignment, no matter how dangerous.

So I suppose I should say it was a fruitful experience. *Fruitful* is a neutral enough word. There are cactus fruits that sting the lips, berries that poison. The Cuban experience curdled my mind. While I lay in the hospital moving in and out of delirium, I remembered things I should have paid attention to but hadn't because I didn't trust my own perceptions. I *had* recognized their sloppiness about the secrecy of their mission. But I had doubted my recognition because it seemed to me that secrecy would be the most important element to boys playing games: they would love the whispering, the sense of exclusivity, of knowing something others didn't. So why would they not observe secrecy, even if they were not embarked on a serious mission? I concluded that secrecy was inessential, that it figured so largely in spy movies because it added to the suspense.

But there were other things I'd sensed and lain aside. The way Woody told me his stories, for instance. It felt to me that he'd told them before, and to a woman. He had them down so pat, like a performer's routine, a speech frequently given. I could imagine Woody sitting with his wife over cocktails on the poolside terrace of their Houston house, telling her the same tales in the same way, making her feel part of an exciting secret organization, commander of her own personal army, creating her own foreign policy right under the nose of the electorate, the government. I could see how it might appeal to her. All she had to do was believe her swan was Zeus.

And the others: I'd heard Philip say – in contempt – that Jack had been a high roller in the Havana gambling casinos before Castro deprived him of his livelihood, and was with the group in an effort to regain his old livelihood. It wasn't his motivation that Philip held in contempt, but his amateur status as a soldier. Philip and Cyrus claimed to be soldiers of fortune; they'd fight anywhere for anyone, they proclaimed, laughing. But they were amateurs too or they would have seen that this expedition was ridiculous, that no one knew what he was doing. Or maybe they saw and didn't care: adventure stimulated their erotic life together.

I also remembered how good Alex and Noel, and Woody too, had been to me when I was hurt. Two of them – who? – had given me their blankets. And Woody had held me that night until I fell asleep. But I didn't forget that he tried to hold me earlier, that I had thought he was on his way to trying to seduce me. As I lay in that hospital bed musing, it came to me that Woody had not wanted to have sex with me at all. If he had, he'd have made a move in Miami. What he wanted was for the other men to *think* he was having an affair with me, to mark me off limits and himself my proprietor. But then it occurred to me that Woody's 'protection' forced the men to treat me decently. He might have realized that, maybe that was why he acted as he did.

No. Woody would not have cared what happened to me.

Then I started to think about what it could have been like if Woody had not marked me 'his'. Twelve crazy men and me. There was no way they would ever have accepted me as one of the guys, as I once deluded myself my college friends had.

The thought of what could have happened was terrifying, and I was glad I hadn't allowed it to come to consciousness while we were on the mission. God.

I had lost other illusions. My hero, Castro, had preferred to arrest, torture, maybe murder a woman and her children rather than spend bullets and risk his men's lives against an invading bunch of idiots. It made sense, economically. But I couldn't bear it. In later years, I came to see Castro as one more tyrant, with his camps, his decrees – not that that made Batista seem any better.

In later years, I photographed real wars, wars that were the result, the *flowering* you could say, of deeply planted seeds – wars that were cries of despair from entire peoples. But I never again was able to believe that war served any good human purpose. In every war I saw mostly absurdity, stupidity, delusion, the ridiculous spectacle of boys playing games. I never got over the sense that trip to Cuba gave me, that war was a stupidity that could be avoided if men were not boys who wanted to play games in which they could pretend to be men, could pretend that they cared about something more than creating a self-image. I never forgot how I felt when Woody was telling me his adventures, a feeling I couldn't name then but did later. Horror. Kurtz's horror. Not the fascination of the abomination, nothing grand, demonic, evil: no.

It was just emptiness, a horrifying emptiness at the heart of things. Because nothing mattered – who won, who lost, who was up, and down – except the game. And the fact that real people, with real blood streaming down an arm they raised as they cried out over the body of a dead child, real lives that involved things like buying vegetables and washing their hands and stroking the head of a child and arguing with their spouses, the fact that this was destroyed as the game flowed inexorably across cities, countryside, across the whole fucking world it seemed, that fact was irrelevant.

Our whole expedition was a joke. I was the only one wounded – and that by accident. Ettore's wife and children were the only ones killed. The CIA must have known how incompetent this group was, but the agency didn't care – they would aid and abet anything that might cause Castro trouble. And the men themselves, except Ettore, would quickly transform the incident into a tale of adventure, add it to their repertory.

I retreated from politics, from opinion. I pulled myself inside a shell; I became a suburban liberal, one of those people who argue that right and wrong were relative and could only be judged with full knowledge of personalities and the context of a situation. Since it was rarely possible to know much, judgment was essentially impossible. It was an unassailable moral position, and furthermore, cost nothing to maintain.

I did tell part of the truth to Toni and the kids – making the whole thing a joke, a sitcom war. I left out what real shooting there had been; I minimized my wound, saying I fell on a sharp stone, cut myself, didn't take care of the wound, which became infected and I developed blood poisoning. For a few weeks the kids chanted a rhyme about me, 'Mommy is a Clumsy Clown, went to war and she faw down!' but then they forgot that too.

The doctors saved my arm.

four

Long ago, all that. Not just twenty-odd years ago – a different life. Or maybe, that *was* my life before I died, years ago. A thousand, even a hundred years ago, I wouldn't have lived past forty, if I made it that far; few men did and even fewer women – women worked so hard, they had less to eat and less nourishing foods than men, and they died in childbed. So maybe the years after forty are a bonus, nature's reward to women for surviving that long. Most men are dried up, grey and weary after forty; women aren't. Their children, if they have them, are grown, and their careers, if they have them, are well-launched, and they have their friends, and they still have living juice in them.

But if I am any example, well, and lots of other women I know too, we are alone, we have only our work. There are no men for us, there is no love waiting to happen. And I figure maybe nature intended us to use these bonus years for the well-being of others, recognizing in its wisdom that somebody's got to do something about the world the men are transforming into their own image – rigid, sterile, mechanical.

That's what I try to do now, do for others. I can't do

anything for myself because there's nothing I want. Clara says the truth is that I don't want anything because there's nothing I want that I believe I can have, when in fact all I have to do is reach out my hand. She really gets on my nerves sometimes.

Whenever I am not on an assignment, I sit here hour after hour writing this account of my mother. This room is the best thing in my apartment. The window in my studio looks out over the city. The view is just rooftops and the long open tunnel of Eighty-sixth Street ending in a triangle of shimmer that is the Hudson River; and a wide swathe of wounded city sky retreating, gauzed and vacant. I am alone. I don't mind being alone, I like it. If I wanted someone here with me, I couldn't think of a name. There is no one I want, nothing.

I have few resource materials: my journals, which I kept only intermittently, a stack of yellow envelopes stuffed with family photographs, pictures I didn't file and label, didn't paste in albums. I leaf through account books I used to keep a record of my expenses in those days. They are my only help in recalling where I was at times when I wasn't keeping a journal. And there are a few letters. That's all. That and my brain, in which the past is registered, my brain and the kids', except they forget things, it's amazing how they forget. Oh, I guess I forget too.

Yet my memory for some things is keen. I remember vividly that my first thought when I arrived home after the Cuban trip was that I might be pregnant – something I'd managed to forget during it. I didn't know if I'd had a period while I was unconscious, so it wasn't until I missed in February that I brought the matter up with Toni and went for a pregnancy test. It was positive. Toni was overjoyed; the kids were thrilled. I tried to be positive about it, but I was mostly worried. How would I explain this to *World*?

The baby was due – by my reckoning – in August, so I told Russ I wanted to work on a book, and needed to take a leave of absence from June through the end of September. He wasn't angry – in fact he seemed impressed; he was happy to give it to me, he said, I needed it after my 'ordeal'.

He paid me for the Cuban trip, paid for all my time in the hospital, and threw in a bonus. I was touched. It was the first time I'd seen anything kind in him. With that and the money I had saved we'd be okay for a few months even though I wasn't working.

And then – feeling grateful that I'd kept my arm and my life, and feeling content with my life – even with the pregnancy – something happened that made me believe the old saw that those who have get. Russ Farrell knew lots of people in publishing; his favorite pastime was gossiping. And over his many lunches he mentioned that I was going to work on a book, although he had no details. So the story went out, but no one could figure out who I'd signed with or if I had, and this caused interest, and by the end of April I'd had four calls offering me advances on a book of photographs. The advances were small: money wasn't the issue. Legitimacy was. I signed a contract with Focus Inc., the most prestigious publisher of photography books at the time, for a book to be called *Power*. And then I settled back to a relaxed pregnancy, careful only not to gain much weight.

In the middle of August of 1962, my third child, my baby, my little Franny was born; and early in September, *World* called and begged me to break into my leave and fly to Algeria to cover the elections. I couldn't refuse: the reason they'd sent me there in March was to get to know the place, to make contacts, to gain an informed view. And they wanted a heroic slant on the outcome of this struggle for independence. I didn't tell them I no longer had a heroic slant. I was fascinated to see what had happened there, quite apart from heroism.

Toni did most of the caretaking of Franny right from the beginning, assisted by Billy and Arden. I didn't even nurse her because I knew I had to go back to work and didn't want the mess that comes when you stop nursing. I felt fine. My figure had bounced back to normal after her birth, my arm had regained its strength after a summer of swimming, and my book was finished.

So a little over a month after the appearance of Frances Nowak, named for both our grandmothers, Toni's and mine, I took off for Algeria carrying my usual knapsack and camera case, feeling utterly secure that she would receive great care and even greater love, knowing my book was good and that my family was happy. I was on top of the world.

Or was I. Maybe that's just the story I told myself. Maybe I was anxious and guilt-ridden about leaving the baby, and upset at Toni's dismay at the thought of taking care of her *alone*.

'But I've never taken care of a baby! I won't know what to do if you're not here to tell me!'

'You'll learn! I had to learn, you will too.'

'But you're a woman!'

'What in hell does that matter? I never took care of a baby before.'

'But you saw other women taking care of babies . . . your cousin or something.'

'I did not. I learned. I read Dr Spock. I used my perceptivity. I sympathized. I made mistakes.'

He moaned. 'Suppose I make a mistake!'

'I turned off the cold tap first, once when I was bathing Arden. The hot water almost scalded her back.'

His head was in his hands. 'Ohhh,' he moaned.

'But not really, not badly. I mean the water hurt her but she wasn't really burned. She just cried.

'And when Billy was little, I put him in his Grandmother Carpenter's bed one afternoon for a nap, and he woke up and got into the pills she kept in her bed table. I found him sitting on the floor, pills dotting the carpet all around him, while he chewed and babbled and grinned happily to see me. I didn't know what he had taken or how many.'

Toni was mock-sobbing now, his head on the table in front of him.

'I fed him Syrup of Ipecac. He threw up for hours.'

Toni sobbed louder.

'Toni.'

He raised his head.

'You will be fine. Just pay attention to her.' He looked doubtful. I took his face in my hands. 'Darling, love is attention. *Attention*. Just give her that. She'll be fine. I'll be back in ten days.'

So maybe the whole time I was away, I worried. But I should have been feeling good: those were happy years. Why didn't I realize that then? I always let myself be distracted by small details, the troubles that can fill any day, any week, if you let them. I neglect to sit back and enjoy the overall experience. I keep thinking that once this and that is repaired and this is solved and that is explained, *then* I can sit back and relax, savor the air, the scent of roses. As if life were a garment that had to have every minute wrinkle ironed out of it, that had to be perfectly smooth before it could be worn. Knowing that nothing is ever perfectly smooth.

Yes, I was filled with guilt about leaving a newborn baby, even for ten days; and there was something in me that didn't want to leave her, that missed those clutching tiny fingers, the baahing cry startling me in the middle of the night, those sudden smiles that came from nowhere and made my heart, just as suddenly lighter than air, float. I missed her smell, that baby smell of milk and talcum and pee and fresh new skin.

I missed the scent of roses, too: the spring before Franny's birth, Toni dug up sections of the backyard and planted a garden. He put in lilacs and daffodils, tulips and rosebushes, some annuals. Only the roses bloomed that year, and he and the kids would cut bouquets and carry them into Pane. She had improved some – was able to move around with a cane and to eat by herself. Although she could not speak, she did understand much of what was going on around her. When I came back from the hospital with Franny in my arms, I held her out to Pane, and tears rolled down her poor old cheeks, the wrinkles so deep in them, like channels for the tears. I wondered if her tears had always run down the same way and that was what made the wrinkles. We didn't dare to let her hold the baby by herself, but Toni pressed the tiny form against Pane's body, and she put her arms under it so she felt that she was holding her, and she gleamed at her. We told her we'd called the baby Frances after her and my grandmother, and she hugged me. Maybe she'd forgiven me for scolding her, for marrying Toni.

Belle had not. She didn't say much but the look on her face said everything. But what mother would be different? Would like the fact that her daughter had had a third child when her first two were nearly grown, with a boy eight years younger who couldn't support himself much less a wife? She said nothing. She simply withdrew from me, treating me formally, like an acquaintance. She did the correct thing: she visited me once in hospital, and once at home, bringing a new bathinette as a gift – the old one had rotted out. She called to invite us to dinner once every month or six weeks. The following year, she got as far away from me as she could – she moved.

I suppose it is egocentric to imagine the reason she moved was because I had had a baby. She'd been wanting to move for a long time and she and Ed had looked at new houses. She wanted to live near water. But new houses were expensive, and Ed was to retire in ten years. They worried they might not then be able to afford large mortgage payments. So they stayed where they were.

Summers they went to Valeria, a resort in Peekskill open only to families with incomes below ten thousand a year. They played golf and took walks and drives and ate three large meals a day and chatted with other people like themselves, the genteel low-income middle class. Valeria also had a lake, rowboats, and canoes. Ed had always loved canoeing; they had taken a canoe trip up the Hudson on their honeymoon. With age and a touch of arthritis, Belle had become nervous about getting into a canoe – still, on one stay, she agreed to go.

She dressed for their canoe ride as she dressed for everything – in stockings and heels and a freshly pressed outfit – a stylish cotton dress with a heart neckline and a full skirt. Ed too was dressed well, in lightweight wool slacks and a freshly ironed sports shirt. (Belle always had Ed pack a travel-iron when they went anywhere.) But he wore canvas shoes with rubber soles. He got in the canoe first, holding onto a pier rail to steady the craft. She was carrying her handbag and the camera he had handed her when he stepped into the canoe. She hung both over one arm, holding to a pier rail with the other, and put her stockinged leg forward tremulously. He cried out in alarm, angry-sounding, 'Not there, in the middle!' and she looked up in terror and put her weight down where she was and the canoe tipped and she screamed and they both toppled into the water, along with handbag and camera.

After their return she told this story in an aggrieved tone. Anastasia laughed. Belle set her lips and silently determined never to tell her another thing. Anastasia saw her mother's face.

'But it *is* funny, Mom. Didn't you laugh when you got dunked?' She searched her mother's forbidding face. 'I mean, it wasn't *dangerous*, Mom.'

Her face stiff with indignation, Belle almost sobbed. 'We were sopping wet! We had to walk all the way back to our room sopping wet. Everybody who passed us laughed! They laughed at us! It was humiliating!'

'They were probably laughing with affection. Everyone knows how easy it is to go over in a canoe. It's probably happened to them too,' Anastasia argued, hating her own tone of voice, patient, tolerant, preaching.

'I was so humiliated. I've never been so humiliated. And Daddy's camera was ruined. I'll never get in a canoe with him again. If he hadn't yelled at me, I wouldn't have fallen that way. He knew I was nervous! Why did he have to yell?'

'Well, he shouldn't have yelled,' Anastasia tried to placate, 'but he was probably nervous too . . .'

Belle glared at her. Betrayal.

'He always yells!' she cried, close to tears. 'He didn't need to yell! Oh, such humiliation! I'll never get in a canoe again,' she concluded with grief-stricken resentment, as if he had taken from her one last pleasure.

The next thing she lost was Valeria itself: Ed's last raise put him over their limit. They began then to take trips – they drove to the Maine coast, through the Blue Ridge Mountains, explored the Poconos. When Ed was given three weeks vacation they started to take winter vacations in Florida, exploring both coasts. Belle loved the sleepy shabby villages in the west, little low houses made of wood and screening, resting on a neck of land jutting out into a river, overhung by swamp trees. They priced them, and perhaps she pretended they would buy one but they could not afford two houses. Although they appeared to be well-to-do, Ed still did not earn a high salary. They lived as comfortably as they did because they knew how to economize.

Then, one spring, Belle got a job. She did not tell anyone she wanted a job or was looking for one; she simply announced she had one.

'Wonderful!' cried Anastasia. 'Where?'

There was a plant in Rockville Centre that packed and distributed sheet music. In one large airy room of this plant, a dozen women sat on high stools from eight to four five days a week for minimum wage, folding and packing the sheets.

'Oh,' said Anastasia. 'Do you like it?' Incredulous.

'I *love* it!' Belle glowed. 'The women are so lovely! We have such a good time. They know I'm hard-of-hearing, and they just speak up, and they laugh all the time.'

Anastasia tried to picture it; her mother in her expensive outfits, matching shoes, bag, and gloves, driving up in the four-year-old but new-looking Cadillac, parking beside the plant, entering, laying aside her coat or jacket and putting on a smock, sitting on her stool. How did the women greet her, how did she behave to them, poor women, large of body or very skinny, greying hair pulled back in a bun, or frizzled with a permanent, wearing cotton housedresses and slippers, some missing front teeth, some unable to speak English. What did they think of her, the grande dame? They must like her or she would not be so happy there. And if they liked her, that meant she was not putting on her grande dame act. She was comfortable enough with them to tell them about her hearing.

She was back in the sweatshop, back with the women she'd known in her youth, women she understood and did not fear. For all she had acquired the armor that charac-terizes the middle class – the neat house in the expensive suburban town, the fine clothes, the well-tended hair and skin, the polished nails, the Cadillac – nothing had changed inside her head, she was still the big gawky shy girl in the sweatshop.

Whenever Anastasia visited her, she would talk about 'her ladies'.

'So skinny, and she works so hard, and that boy! Now he's in the hospital, he may lose his leg. And Josephine has worked so hard for him, he's her whole life! He *had* to have a motorcycle! She's heartbroken. Boys, they're so wild, it makes me grateful I never had a son . . .

'Sophie doesn't talk much about her husband – well, I think he drinks. She doesn't say so, but he's never home, and he's Polish – you know. She has such a sweet face, she reminds me of my mother, she pulls her hair back in a bun like Momma, of course Momma was never that fat – not while she was working. But Sophie is always smiling, nodding her head, so agreeable, Momma was like that too with the women she worked with. Even though things are hard for her, she is trying so hard to earn enough to send all her boys to college. She hides her money, the other girls tease her about it, she has to, I guess . . .

'Awful, hardly any teeth in her mouth, she lets her own teeth go so she can save money for her daughter, she's really talented, Katie brought in pictures of her, she's very pretty, in her tap outfit. Twelve years old. She needs dancing shoes and costumes and the lessons, of course . . . It's hard for Katie, her husband drinks and plays the ponies, that daughter is all she cares about, she talks about her all the time . . .'

These were the same women we'd known in South Ozone Park, the women she'd always known and understood. Did she too show pictures of her daughters? Boast about the famous photographer for *World*, the well-married one living in the Philippines, waited on by seven servants? Did they envy her that her children were grown, that she didn't have to worry about them any more? That her children were *safe:* that's what all the women wanted, I knew that, I understood it, I felt it too. Absurd: as if the possession of a mate and a job, a place to live, children of their own, somehow put them over a line, within the paling, protected for eternity, armed against their own fragility. As if your children could ever be safe.

Occasionally Belle was invited to visit one of her 'ladies' at home. No nasty comments about the scantiness of food offered, the thinness of the sandwich filling, the store-boughtness of the cake, the lack of taste displayed in the furnishings. Yet their houses must be poor, shabby enough, but maybe the food was good and plentiful – the poor are generous with food, it's the middle class who aren't. These women were in a different category for Belle, not to be judged as middle-class women were judged. I understood that too: these women had no pretensions.

Then she quit.

'But why!'

'Dad and I want to go to Europe this summer, and they wouldn't give me three weeks off. I only started in March, they said I could have a week in October. So I quit. You can't work and take vacations when you want them. You know, we want to go to Florida next winter again. So,' she spread her hands.

'You'll miss the women.'

She nodded. But she never mentioned them again.

That summer they took a three-week tour of five European countries, including a cruise among the Dodecanese Islands. Belle was pleased that their tour entitled them to a superior double accommodation on the ship. But one night, the porthole in their cabin accidentally swung open and seawater washed in, drenching their clothes, all their possessions, and frightening them both. Belle swore she would never get on a boat again.

The ship stopped at Santorini, where the tourists would ride donkeys to the top of the mountain. Belle was afraid to get on the donkey. She did not even consider it, she shook her head hard, 'No!' Ed offered to remain with her, but she urged him to go, and he was eager; he laughed as he mounted, his camera slung around his neck. She could see he was a little frightened too.

Belle sat on a stone wall and watched the procession wind up and up around the steep curves of rock and out of sight. It was a little after ten. It was hot. How long

681

would they take? An hour up, an hour back? They should be back in time for lunch. She sat, looking around her. The scrubby hillside, the stone wall; off in the distance some white houses with red-tile roofs. And down that way, a street with cafés and shops.

He was so eager to go, he just clambered on that thing, he didn't even worry about what she would do, where she could go to get out of this terrible sun. She was glad she had thought to wear her golf hat but it didn't make her any cooler. What time was it? She should have worn a watch. But she hated watches. It seemed an hour had passed, they should be back soon.

It seemed that hours passed. She was nearly crying with thirst. *They* had canteens with them, she'd seen them. They probably stopped to drink along the way. And at the top too. Suppose it took two hours to climb! Suppose they had lunch up there! Why why why had she urged Ed to go? Why had he gone? Why hadn't he thought about her? She wanted to cry. She gazed toward the main street with longing. There were cafés, they looked so pretty with their striped awnings, the green chairs and tables. They might have drinks, orange juice, lemonade, coffee, oh, how she longed for some lovely ice-cold lemonade! They were not far away. She thought about going, but her legs felt wobbly, she felt faint, she was not sure she could walk that far, a block and a half, she was too hot and upset. And she could not speak Greek and she was afraid to walk down a Greek street, to sit in a Greek café. How would she order? Suppose they asked her a question? She wouldn't hear. She couldn't explain to them that she was hard of hearing. They might humiliate her, insult her.

Hours and hours passed. The sun had passed the zenith. It was afternoon. Belle's stomach was tight and growling, she was starving. It must be one o'clock, and not a bite since breakfast, and she only had orange juice and a tiny bit of roll with butter and coffee in the morning. She wanted to cry. To go off like that and leave her, helpless, knowing she was helpless, terrible, terrible, how could he do it? She bit her lip to keep from crying. The . . . *selfishness* of him! thoughtlessness! He hadn't even given her any Greek

682

money! She couldn't buy anything if she wanted to try! He hadn't even found out where there was a toilet for her. Suppose she had to pee! The sun was so hot, she felt dizzy, faint, she thought she would collapse . . . She would collapse and they would have to fly her home, and she would never get to see Constantinople, all that money for nothing, such a waste!

The scene blinked and spun under her vision. She would have lain down on the wall, but she would have been embarrassed, tourists kept passing by, strolling along the walk, coming from the shops with packages, sticks of souvlaki, ice-cream cones. Oh, what she would give for an ice-cream cone! Deprived and helpless, she watched them.

She was seeing spots now. Maybe that was the caravan, coming back down the mountain. She could not keep her eyes on the spots, they shimmered in the sun. There were dark little explosions in her eyes. She was losing her vision! She looked away. She wanted to die.

But next time she looked, she saw the caravan returning. Her lips set. *He* had had a good time. It was long past lunchtime. He'd had *his* lunch; she was starving, she had had nothing. The spots got bigger and bigger: she could make out the leader with his wide-brimmed hat with the colorful band on it. She couldn't see Ed.

Then, somehow, she turned around, and Ed was standing there at her side, smiling broadly, his arm open.

'Hallo, Belle!' he cried out, settling a kiss on her cheek. He was cheerful, he had had fun.

She wouldn't look at him. 'What time is it?'

He checked his watch. 'Four, Belle. Twenty minutes after four.' He looked at her. 'I didn't know it was going to be so long. I wouldn't have gone. Did you get some lunch?'

'Of course I didn't! How could I get lunch! I don't know where to go, I can't speak Greek! And I have no money, you didn't leave me any money! Six hours you were, six!'

His face cringed. 'I only had a sandwich, Belle,' he said, as if that exonerated him. 'We should get you something to eat, what would you like, Belle, some fish?'

'Oh, Eddie!' she cried with contempt, disgust, despair. 'It's too late now! It's four o'clock!' She was shrieking now, and Ed looked around him furtively, embarrassed. 'We have first seating for dinner, six o'clock, it's too late to eat lunch!'

'Maybe we could just get you a snack to tide you over, Belle,' he ventured. 'Here, let me help you.' He put his arms around her waist as if to lift her from the wall.

He helped her to her feet and she tottered beside him, leaning on his arm. They began very slowly to walk toward the main street. The group leader ran up to them.

'Folks, we've got to get back to the ship by five, so if you want to do some shopping, now's the time.' He spread his arm to indicate the shops, winked, and moved on. Belle, whose hearing was always worst when she was upset, looked to Ed for translation. He leaned toward her and barked in her ear. 'He asked if we want to go shopping! We have to go back to the ship at five.'

'You don't have to shout!'

'I wanted you to hear, sometimes you don't hear!' he defended himself. 'What do you want to do?' Anger seeped into his voice. He stopped on the side-walk.

Her voice emerged as a cry, petulant, helpless, a whimper. 'I don't care! I'm hot, I'm exhausted, I just want to go home!' She hated herself. Why was she like this? Why was life so awful, why was everything such a nightmare? Ed looked around again to see if people were listening, watching them. 'I want to go back to the ship,' she said quietly, with the dignity of martyrdom.

Solicitously, Ed took her arm and helped her as if she were ill, and led her to the pier. 'I'll just run and get you a cold drink,' he said, leaving her again, and she cried out to him not to go but he was already gone, and she turned her suffering face toward the water, sitting on the bench hunched over, patience on a monument. Never, never again would she let Ed go anyplace without her, never! Oh, what a horrible day, a horrible day! Horrible.

'Horrible, it was a nightmare,' she told Anastasia. 'I'll never go to Europe again.'

She was bored. She was tired of the neighborhood, where she no longer had any friends. Ann Gwyn had died; Belle had befriended Mr Gwyn's second wife, another woman of intelligence and refinement, who took on the twins as her own, and who suffered, as Ann had, from her husband's tightness with money, and, presumably, everything else. But then the old man died, leaving Charles Gwyn rich, and they moved to a large house on the north shore. The Bradshaws moved to Florida, to St Petersburg. For a few years, they sent postcards and Christmas cards and in January, boxes of oranges. Then the messages ceased. Belle presumed they had died. New people moved into the houses on either side of her.

'So young, Anastasia, to have houses like that, such lovely houses. I don't think they're more than thirty. They're Jewish. The father of that one, Mrs Halpern, must be in the garment business. At least once a week he drives up in his big Cadillac and gets out of the car carrying three or four brand new dresses in plastic bags. Can you imagine? Without lifting a finger she gets so many dresses! Every week! She changes her clothes four or five times a day, I know she does because I see her. In the morning she walks the dog, and drives the children to school, and she's wearing one thing. Then around ten she goes marketing and she's wearing something else. Then she comes back and goes out again for lunch or after lunch, and she's wearing something else. Then in the evening, when she walks the dog around five, she has on something else! And they go out at night – a lot! And I'm sure she wears something new then too. Can you imagine?'

When she spoke of those neighbors there was an edge in her voice that I had never heard in it before.

'Awful people! Their children use our yard as an alley! Dad went out and scolded them, but they didn't pay any attention to him. I made him go to the parents and complain, but the children *still* run back and forth. They ruined all my flowers – the petunias, the zinnias, the marigolds – I worked so hard planting them and those children just trampled them.'

The Halperns and their friends on the other side, the Allens, did not speak to the Stevenses. 'I suppose we're not good enough for them, poor little Christians with their six-year-old car!'

Ed put up a high fence of wood palings behind the pine trees that lined the driveway. That stopped the children.

One late afternoon in winter, on her way to pick up the kids from ice skating, Anastasia stopped in to visit Belle and found her mother distraught. 'I feel so awful,' Belle moaned.

They settled in the porch with scotch and water. The street was bleak, bare branches under a muted grey sky.

'I sit here,' Belle began, her eyes looking damp, 'and look out. Mrs Brand goes to the market and comes back, she still drives that old Plymouth, she must be having a hard time since her husband died. Sometimes Margery stops in with the baby. Sometimes on a Sunday she comes with her husband, for dinner I guess. Mrs O'Neill has visitors all the time, the girls with their children, one two three blond heads in the back seat of the car, they must all have a child every year. She has practically no teeth in her mouth but Mr O'Neill is never home, he has the money to booze it up with his pals.

'I don't know any of the others, the Wilsons have moved, and the Peakes. Just these Halperns and Allens, and they don't speak to us. I feel surrounded . . .' Her voice rose.

'Mrs Halpern – so young to have such a beautiful house, can you believe it, Anastasia? She even has a girl to clean it twice a week, a colored woman, I see her coming and going in a taxi. And her clothes, oh, her clothes! And her dog, she has a little dog, it looks like a rat, it yaps all the time, and she walks it three times a day, she walks it up and down along the sidewalk, and then, when it's ready to do its business, she brings it over here, to the curb in front of *our* house! Where *we* can step in it!'

Anastasia's face, bent toward her mother, kept pace with Belle's account, registering sadness, pity, outrage . . .

'This morning she did it again! Every morning I watch her do it! And I wanted to run outside, Anastasia, I almost did, I was going to shout at her, "you kike! you yid! Keep your filthy dogdo on your own property!" Oh, Anastasia, can you imagine?'

The glisten of her eyes grew thicker.

'You didn't do it, though,' Anastasia said very calmly.

'No.' The tears overflowed, and Belle wiped them away with a tissue. 'But I almost did. I wanted to. Maybe tomorrow I will!' she added, a willful petulant child. But then she cried again. 'Can you imagine that, Anastasia?'

Anastasia reached forward and took her mother's limp cold hand. 'Tonight you'll send Dad over to tell them. You didn't do it, that's the important thing. Everybody's prejudiced, Mom. I'm sure the Halperns make nasty cracks about goys, everyone has these feelings. The important thing is you didn't do it.'

Anastasia hated the sound of her own voice preaching at her mother. Belle hated it too. But this time, she did not respond, she looked blank. And that weekend, Belle and Ed began looking in earnest for a new house.

So it wasn't really Anastasia's pregnancy that led Belle to flee from Nassau County to Suffolk. It is simply Anastasia's habit of mind to assume that she is responsible for every sorrow her mother suffers. It is to be presumed that this habit of mind gives her pleasure or she would give it up.

Months passed before they found a house they liked, and more months before they moved in. The house was far out on the island, in Brightwaters, on a small lake. They moved in the June after Franny was born, and for several years after that Belle was occupied with decorating, shopping, furnishing her new house on a small budget. There was carpeting to be bought, drapes to be resewn to fit the new windows, new furniture to fill the 'family room', something they hadn't had before, and iron furniture for a broad summer room on the back of the house facing the lake, a real porch, finally, where Belle could sit every afternoon and study the animals, the birds the foliage, in their seasons. Anastasia told herself her mother was finally safe.

five

Remnants found in a box.

October 20, 1963.

Dear Anastasia – or should I write Stacey – hah!

Thanks so much for the silver spoon and fork you sent Jennifer. They are darling! I love the little animals on the handles. She can't use them yet, but soon – I hope! It's really not that bad because we have a wonderful nana for her, she doesn't speak English but she loves babies. But it's so hot and humid here all the time, you can't blame a baby for fretting, she has prickly heat.

Yes, I flew to California to have her. The clinic on the base is very good but they're not really set up for obstetrical matters, hah! And I thought I'd feel more comfortable in an American hospital, and the Army was willing to pay for my flight. Justin flew over the day the baby was born, and helped me going back so it wasn't bad at all. That way the kids were only alone for a couple of days, and we have this nana and the housekeeper speaks English and my friend Annette looked in every day to make sure they were alright.

The children are great. Jonathan started third grade this fall and Julie started second and they're a couple of eager beavers, doing projects for social studies and Julie's going to be in the school play, she plays a tooth. Some fun making her costume! The American school here is really great, and they have great teachers, the wives of officers stationed here. So it's nice because they're our friends too and everyone knows everyone else.

How is your new baby? Frances. It's nice you named her after Grandma, Mother must have been pleased. I hardly remember Grandma. Is she walking yet? It will be so much fun this Christmas with two babies to look at, children really love Christmas, I remember I did when I was a child. I'm looking forward to it. It will be my first Christmas home since I got married. I'll be glad to get out of here too although our next tour is in Panama and I don't think that's much better. Not that it's bad here, the Army is really great, as Justin says the Army takes care of its own. We have the PX and the Officers' Club and excellent Medical Care and cheap Help. Justin loves his work, he loves the Army. But it is hot and humid all the time and there are so many bugs and outside the enclave there's nothing to do, no place to go really, it gets a little boring after a while always seeing the

688

same people and doing the same things all the time. But my tennis game is getting pretty good.

I guess Mom and Dad's new house is really beautiful, I'm dying to see it. It will seem funny though not to drive to Rockville Centre the way we always have. We'll fly to California December 1. Then we'll fly to Iowa to visit the Selbys for a couple of weeks, and then to Long Island. With three kids, and all their stuff, that's a big deal, as you can imagine, all that packing and carrying, but it'll be great, we'll have a ball.

Love,

Joy

P.S. Mother tells me you're having a book published, pictures of power. What does that mean? Anyway, congratulations! Maybe I'll get to see it when I get home.

Mass card, picture of crucified Jesus.

Pane: Yes, the card says Frances Nowak, January 12, 1964. She was only seventy-one when she died. They don't have long lives, those old ones, I wonder why. You'd expect them to live long – they don't have careers that give you ulcers and heart attacks. Of course they all worked so hard for so long, were poor for so long, probably lived on bread and coffee. Pane worked in sweatshops too, like Grandma, for years. They didn't buy the house in Lynbrook until she was fifty and her sons were grown. She brought the boys up in a railroad flat, three bedrooms, Bedford-Stuyvesant. She worked in the sweatshop all day, worked at home all night: marketing, cooking, cleaning, washing, ironing, and dealing with the kids and husband. They could afford to buy this house because they could rent the apartment upstairs, a good investment, Zbigniew said. Smart – he only lived for five years after that. He left her a thousand-dollar life insurance policy and this house. The insurance money buried him; she survived on social security and the rent.

I wonder how she felt about her life. The old ones never say. They act as if they are not entitled to have feelings about their lives. Their only concern is to survive. That's all they allow themselves to want: survival, their kids' and their own. I wish I'd talked to her more. I used to talk to her a lot, but after what I did she wasn't open to me anymore. I could understand that.

She left her house to her sons. It didn't matter how they had treated her; blood is all that matters to the old ones. They came to Long Island to bury her and immediately put the house on the market. It wouldn't fetch much, and after taxes and the real-estate agent's percentage and division by five, they would not get more than a few thousand dollars apiece, but they were hungry for that money, you could see it. They told Toni it was time he got out and got himself a man's job.

It didn't snow the day we buried her, but the sky looked like snow, heavy and grey like a bag of tears frozen solid. They laid her beside her husband in an old unkempt cemetery in Brooklyn. It had hardly any trees. Only at a distance you could see some barren brown sticks suggesting them. There were miles of old marble stones, tilted and greying, dotting the frosty earth, and lots of dull grey crosses, some askew. We cried. We couldn't stop crying, the four of us – I'd left Franny with a neighbor. The sons were grey and heavy. I like to think they would have liked to cry, but couldn't anymore. Like me now.

I invited them all back to the house for a buffet lunch. They trailed in, heavy and grey, looking around as if they were assessing the value of Pane's poor possessions. I could see them making mental notes – who was going to insist on getting the old silver sugar bowl, who the china, who the old – maybe antique by now – thin, dented silverplate flatware. They barely spoke to me, even Toni's mother, even after she saw Franny. They drank up two half-gallons of our vodka though, and devoured the food. I worked in the kitchen, or serving, and sat talking to Mrs D'Antonio and Mrs Schneider, Pane's friends, who kept sighing and stroking me and wiping their cheeks.

And I thought: they are her children! But we are the ones who loved her. How many sacrifices had she made for them, how had they wrung her heart? For what, I thought, for what! I slid into a rage, I wanted to throw them out of my house. But it was their house. It was Pane's friends, not the Nowaks, who helped Toni and me clean up the mess, put leftover food away, wash and dry the dishes. Then they embraced us both, and the children, and left. The sons were still sitting around the living room drinking. Their wives, heavier but less grey than the men, sat talking in soft voices, desultorily, drinking coffee. I went upstairs to my own place, lease to run until the end of June, mine, they could not dispossess me or intrude upon me. I left Toni to deal with his family. I didn't even say goodbye to them.

Yellow envelope of photographs of a house on an old street lined with chestnut trees.

Yes. That was our house. I took these just after we bought it, we hadn't moved in yet. It had four bedrooms – one large, two medium-sized, and a tiny one for Franny; a garage; a finished basement with a wet bar – water! – that I could turn into a dark room; and a small room off the kitchen that the previous owners had used as a sewing room, that Toni could use for writing. It had a 100–by–100–foot plot, big for that neighborhood, and a wonderful garden. We bought it. That is, I bought it. I paid for it and I put it in my name. I don't know what Toni thought about that. He said nothing.

We moved at the end of June, when my lease expired. We left Pane's empty, still unsold – the brothers were asking a very high price for it. I felt a little sad at leaving Pane's house desolate, but pleased at the thought that the brothers now had a non-income-producing property that would swiftly erode if they didn't come and take care of it. The hell with virtue, it's revenge I love. Of course what they did was to call Toni and ask him to watch over it. I had anticipated this and told Toni he should say he was busy writing, and would do it only if they paid him. But of course he didn't.

We had fun in the new house. We spent some time on it, some money, making it pretty, pleasant. Toni was restless, though; he was ragingly frustrated at not publishing anything, and maybe he was tired of being a housekeeper. He started to pressure me to buy him a sports car. I did buy a new car — we needed one. But I bought a station wagon that could hold all of us.

He was a wonderful father to Franny. He took her with him everywhere. He complained that being at home all the time was making him fat, so I urged him to take up a sport, tennis, maybe, and he did, taking lessons at the private courts in Rockville Center, while Franny sat in her baby seat, watching, in a diaper and sunbonnet. I had never toilet-trained my children, and we didn't toilet-train Franny either; she was in diapers until she was three and trained herself.

Every once in a while Toni would fall into a depression and talk about maybe getting a job. 'I'm getting older and nothing is happening. Maybe I should give up. Go back into publishing. Make some money. It's obscene, a guy my age sitting in a playground all afternoon.'

I urged him to keep trying. I told him he had talent, that one day he would write something wonderful.

I meant it. I think I meant it. But I also knew that I was terrified that he would go to work and dump Franny on me. I had *had* this baby for *him:* he promised that he would take care of it. But memories are short, and I didn't, after all, have it in writing. I felt I had done my service to the future of the human race, I had raised my two. It was enough. No more.

A beaded bracelet, African, from Kenya.

Yes, I remember this. I bought it from a woman who stood all day in a gas station (a rarity in Kenya) waiting for tourists. I bought her entire stock and handed them out as gifts when I came back, but I never wore my own. Forgot about it.

Those were great years for me. I was hot. I took photographs of everything I could dream of shooting – mountains and jungles, dams and deserts, the winding stone-paved streets of old cities, the boulevards of new ones. White on white in the Himalayas; green on green in island rain forests in Hawaii, Puerto Rico, Antigua; black and white in tens of cities. I shot people everywhere: a man unaware, sitting bereft beside a railroad track, bent over, wide-brimmed straw hat pulled down over his eyes, under the Mexican sun; a skeletal Indian mother staring vacant-eyed as a two-year-old child sucked her thin dangling breast; a very old Japanese man sitting on the curb of a city street, playing with a small child in his lap; heavy-bodied women in Siberia, crimson babushkas on their heads, offering paper cones of raspberries to passengers on a train; wizened, shrunken Chinese women sweeping the streets with straw brooms. Some of these became *World* covers, but the greatest pleasure for me was *seeing* – and trying to capture what the inner eye saw.

I traveled everywhere, and everywhere I had adventures. I went by plane, train, car, and once, rushing to the scene of a carbombing in Algiers, by motorcycle; I took trams and cable cars, sailboats and motorboats, and floated in a hot-air balloon across the Masai Mara, shooting the shadow we cast on the rust-colored plain. I went by canoe to shoot a camping site in Canada; rode an elephant up the side of a mountain in India; and in a haycart outside Peking, I sank in the soft hay along with two sleepy kids who had been haying since dawn. I shot the afternoon rainbow over Victoria Falls from a two-seater plane; sat in a quiet-running motorboat, its sound the drone, beat provided by the clicking of my cameras, awed by the mountains rising on either side of the Navua River in Fiji, my heart resting in the silence, the flowers that climbed the mountainside, and like larger flowers, a group of copper-colored women in brilliant wrappings washing clothes on some rocks at a bend of the river. And around that bend, a bunch of boys playing in the water, their eyes like the eyes of no western child – alive, joyous, friendly, unafraid.

I shot a pride of lions sleeping in the sun on a giant rock in the Serengeti; and a giraffe poking its face over some high foliage right beside me; and the lake in Ngorongoro, shimmering in the sunlight, pink with flamingos; and spent hours shooting a whole tribe of monkeys scurrying back and forth across the limbs of a banyan tree, chatting excitedly, grooming each other, babies clutching their mothers, who held them, stroked them.

In Greece I shot white villages climbing up mountains,

houses bleached by the sun, with red-tile roofs; and in Spain, adobe villages with the same red-tile roofs, clustered together, their backs to the dry hot wind. Always, everywhere, clustered together, like the monkeys, for comfort, safety, company. I shot wattle-and-daub villages in Ireland, England, Wales, Germany, low cottages with thatch roofs, some with half-timbering and diamond-paned casement windows. And in those places, too, streets of plain-faced houses rising uphill, connected, all the same, but each painted, a different color, bright pinks and yellows, lime green, azure, brightness challenging their own homeliness. And in Samoa the quiet waiting emptiness of wood platforms and columns holding a thatch roof, set among hibiscus and banana trees, the blue sky, the blue-green water showing through the open house, the house a receptacle for the beauty around it. But sometimes a television set on the floor, and the log houses of Siberia, each with a fenced garden brilliant with broad-faced sunflowers.

All of it beautiful, filling my eyes that ache with need to *see, see*. Even the ugly and afflicted have the beauty of variety, the richness of difference: the one-roomed tin-roofed shacks of Addis Ababa almost on top of each other (how can you tell which is yours?), divided only by narrow muddy lanes smelling of urine. The settlements spread, sprawl over miles of the city; people emerge from them, tall, slender beautiful Ethiopians, barefoot, walking slowly to the bus stop, to work if they were lucky enough to have it. Old men naked in the streets – no one turns to look, they are not trying to shock, they simply own no clothes. And the half-naked boys in the marketplace, orphaned, abandoned, living by begging, bright clear eyes of once-loved children, asking for pennies, selling matches, plastic bags, whatever you want, eyes that are sure that love will be renewed. I want to pour out money to one, about twelve, whose tattered jeans are held together at the waist by a safety pin, who is barefoot and without a shirt, whose eyes meet mine in recognition – I *am* his mother, long-lost. My companion, an Ethiopian who works for a state-controlled newspaper, says don't. The other children will beat him to get it from him. I want to take him home, this child. The reporter shrugs. 'It is not possible.'

Hovels in Mexico City, too, and muddy streets. But here there are a few trees, a beat-up car rests askew in a rut, there is not the same look of starvation. Is even that relative? But here you cannot breathe, the air and water are foul, poisonous. I shoot Coalicue the Filth-Eater, deposed Mother of the Aztecs in her skirt of snakes, majestic and ugly, dominating the Anthropological Museum, dominating the city, still alive. And wonderful ugly sexual sculptures in a children's playground in Stockholm, penises digging up vaginas, reaming a mine, harrowing hell. And a tall cross bearing an ivory Christ bleeding, along a deserted country road in Normandy.

And everywhere, men. I always packed my diaphragm. I never even thought about it, I didn't try to conceal it from Toni, it was simply natural, normal for me to take it. Ah, I had wonderful times, in wonderful places – a grove in the Alps above Geneva, grass studded with edelweiss: at the edge of the water, one day at a strangely deserted Walden Pond; coming out from a hotel to the Grand Canal and looking across to the lights of San Giorgio, unable to part – so sitting down for a late night coffee in the Piazza San Marco. Beautiful boys, men, I recall making love with a beautiful blue-eyed Irishman named Shane among the reeds by the lake at Lissadell. I'd never before made love on a beach, and my body luxuriated in the sand, the sun, the reeds, sibilant, all around us. There was a handsome Pole named Adam who took me to his mother's apartment in Krakow, and pulled out a sleeping couch and heaped it with immaculate white lace-trimmed linens and a comforter and lay me in it as if I were a baby; and a sweet-faced blond hotel clerk in London who tried to act cynical and knowing, but was as sweet at my breast as a baby.

There was a jolly red-bearded German who took me to a wood-beamed, smoky restaurant in the old town of Frankfurt, where he gorged himself on spareribs and sauerkraut and a whole pitcher of beer, then chugged whisky in bed and laughed through sex; and a delicate blond French boy, who made love as if he were creating a work of art, and who had the most ecstatic orgasm I have ever witnessed.

Not everything was pleasant, of course. Shane, a puritan without knowing it, begged me to be true to him at least until the next day, when we were to meet again. I laughed. Did he think I screwed every hour on the hour? Or that I didn't know he was married? And the Venetian merchant marine cried out at the moment of climax, 'You are a virgin, I know it, is first time for you, beautiful Stacey!' And a kind-faced, gentle, middle-aged Greek, also a reporter, who courted me by taking me to restaurant after restaurant, all filled with men, no women anywhere (the men ate out alone, he said, because they were unmarried, having had, like him, to spend their youths earning money for their sisters' dowries. Since I saw hundreds of women – and only women – rushing through the streets of Athens marketing, shopping, every evening, I did not believe him.) When we finally went to bed, he immediately got on top of me and kept shaking my body, while he thrust his penis at me hard, repetitively. The thrusts were hard; the penis wasn't. At some point, he shuddered. That was it. I wondered if he'd lost the knack, or if he'd never had it.

There was the guy in Florence, nice-looking, in his thirties, who suddenly fell into step beside me on the sidewalk and said, 'How did you enjoy the Bargello? And Dante's house, it is wonderful? But your favorite was Santa Maria Novella, no? You stay there the longest time.'

Astonished, I turned, yes, I would have a coffee with him, I was curious. I questioned him. He had been following me since eleven o'clock.

'How can you keep a job and follow women all day?' He was wearing a nice suit, he was not penniless.

He shrugged. 'I work for insurance company.'

That did not explain anything, I felt, and questioned him more, but he dismissed my questions with a shrug. 'I see the big cameras and I know you are important. I follow only the important ones.' He told me Florentine men had a scale from one to ten to rate women they fuck – of course he did not use so obscene a word – and that I was a One.

'Americans are Ones?'

'Americans are Twos. Important beautiful women are One. Ethiopians are Ten.'

'Why is that?'

He spread his hands. 'They are fat and ugly.'

'Ethiopians are beautiful,' I argued.

'They are easy.'

'Ethiopians are easy and Americans are hard?' I couldn't believe this, given what I knew about the two countries.

'Scandinavians are also easy. But they are beautiful, so they are Fours. Or sometimes, Fives. French and Germans are Five or Six, depending. And British are Three.'

'This seems to have less to do with hardness and easiness than with coloring,' I suggested. 'Are Italians prejudiced against dark coloring? They are dark themselves. And what about Italian women?'

'Oh!' He was horrified. 'No Italian women! They have the brothers, the fathers. . !'

A crumpled airline ticket to Saigon.

Oh god. Grant. Yes.

That was after Toni and I had been married for a while, two or three years, I guess. And our life together was contented, we and the kids together, we were happy. And then Grant . . . when did I first meet him? In some city, unpleasant, show-offish, tall buildings topped with huge neon signs, yes, Berlin it was, West Berlin. His name was Grant Michaels, and he was a reporter for *Worldview*, a news magazine, a sister magazine of *World*. Yes we were both in Berlin covering Kennedy's visit there, so it was 1963, June, I think. Our paths crossed a couple of times, we sat around the same tables with other reporters and photographers and local journalists, eating or drinking, and our eyes met in an electric way, but we never really spoke. I liked his face. He was in his forties, and every year he had lived was written on his face, it was deeply lined, but there was no petulance or anxiety on it, only understanding and sorrow. He was tall, and walked as if he had no relation to his body, but he had been married three times, some guy told me.

I met him again in Saigon in 1965, after Johnson had

ordered heavy bombing of the North. The military wouldn't let me – or any other journalists I knew – go out on bombing missions or raids, so most of them sat in our very American hotel all day, drinking and gossiping, waiting for the official bulletins, the official photographs we sent home as news. So we all knew each other. I spent time wandering the city taking pictures of ordinary people, not action shots but depressing enough – the lack of young Vietnamese men; the heavy American military 'presence'; the hundreds of maimed bodies; the young girls whose bodies were whole but whose spirits were being maimed, for there was only one way to get money; the sense of corruption and disease . . .

One afternoon, feeling especially guilt-ridden and rotten because I had gotten some wonderful shots of a café hit by a bicycle bomb – the finished photographs showed the lower half of an arm flying off amid the smoke of the blast – I went back to the hotel early, resolved to get drunk. I went up to my room and took a shower and put on fresh clothes, but nothing helped, I felt dirty, my mouth had a bad taste in it. I went down to the bar, said hello to the regulars, and a head turned, and it was Grant. I moved toward him as if he were a magnet and I an iron filing. He pulled the barstool beside him closer to him, his eyes never leaving mine.

I ordered a bourbon. 'I'm going to get drunk this afternoon,' I confided.

He said nothing. He simply looked at me as if he already knew everything I would tell him, as if his heart was breaking for it, as mine was.

I told him, it spilled out – the suddenness of the noise, the loudness of the noise, how my entire body, every nerve in it leaped, blood leaping too in rage at the assault to my senses, then becoming conscious of the screams, the screaming of one person in particular, it didn't stop, was it the person whose arm I'd seen go flying out to the curb? The chaos, the sirens, the crowd, the voracity in some of the faces looking on, wanting to feel, needing the sensational to feel . . .

And worst of all was me, my own reaction, my instantaneous pulling of my camera to my eye, setting the f-stop, checking the light, clicking, clicking, the shutter. Humanity? Where was mine? Did I rush to help, to heal, to console? They shot their weapons. I shot mine: what's the difference between us? Complicit. I was complicit in this hideous world I lived in.

Tears were spouting out of my eyes and even my nose. I tried to hide them, I was wary of these journalists, they were all men and they were tough and they had contempt for emotion, especially tears, especially in a woman. For a man to cry would be dramatic, the source of a grand confessional moment; for a women to cry was simply ordinary, expected, exactly like being home. Grant suggested we go have some dinner in a little restaurant where few foreigners ventured because it was on the outskirts of the city and the menu was in Vietnamese. I agreed instantly.

He had a car there. He'd been there for weeks, he said, but outside Saigon. He'd been there before, many times, he had contacts, he sometimes was able to go along on a mission, he couldn't say more . . . Except he told me about the mission he'd been on last week. The bombing was over, the planes had to get out of there, enemy anti-aircraft guns were homing in on them, and the plane still had a bomb left and needed to get rid of it. The pilot fretted about it, but didn't drop it although they passed over a range of arid hills. He waited. And then he saw, far below him, a little old man in a donkey cart heaped with crates, a refugee probably, and called out to Grant, 'Lookee, man, you wanta see some fuckin' A aim,' and signaled the bombardier, who dropped it, plop, on top of the little old man, whose cry couldn't be heard, nor his arm seen, who exploded in a dusty cloud, vanished, leaving the entire road empty and barren as it had been for miles before. There were tears in *his* eyes too, and my hand crept over his lying on the table, and we touched glasses and drank, and kept drinking.

I guess we ate something. I guess the food was good. But between the upset of the day and the excitement of his presence, I was dazed even without the three or four drinks I'd poured down. We went back to the hotel and got in bed and passed out in each other's arms.

After that, for the rest of the time I was in Saigon, Grant and I spent our evenings together. We talked, held hands, looked in each other's eyes. We made love, but his disconnection from his body and the sorrow he carried with him like his body smell affected his lovemaking. He would make love for a long time, but he came as soon as he entered me; and once he came, it was over, he did nothing to help me. Still, he made me feel cherished somehow. Sex can be so many things . . .

He was from a Greek family that had suffered under the Nazi occupation, then in the civil war, and had finally given up and emigrated. Grant had been studying at Penn when World War II broke out, when his family was still in Greece. He immediately enlisted in the Air Force, went to OCS, became a pilot. Now, some of the Air Force officers felt he was one of them, had the right background to be allowed to participate in bombing raids. The other journalists who lacked this regarded him with envy or admiration, but they all treated him respectfully to his face. He was between wives – he'd had two, not three, although he would have a third before he died. For he is dead. I read about it two years ago in *The Times*. His heart. I could have predicted that.

For Grant was like me, his heart hurt him. My heart was starting to ache regularly, who knows why? I say, I insist, this was a happy time of my life. I had a rich and contented family life, I loved Toni, my career was really hot, I was successful in a way I had not been before, nor have been since. I suppose, really, it was the best time of my life. *My* life. The lives of others were not so fortunate. The world was cruel, and I could not avert my eyes – I existed to *see*.

It was after that first coming together with Grant that I had the dream about Poland. I was walking through newly tilled fields, brown furrows spread off into the distance as far as I could see, ending in masses of green foliage that framed my view like the frame around a picture. The air was fragrant with the sour smell of new-turned earth, and I knew this was Poland, I had always known it looked like that – at the time, I had not been to Poland.

I walked happily, I was filled with joy even before I spotted a rough-built wooden vegetable stand a few hundred yards away on my left.. The back of the stand had a narrow roof covering a counter; there was a parallel counter in front, with room in between for her to stand – it was Grandma's vegetable stand, I knew that. Oh, Grandma! I was overjoyed to have her back again. I began to run, crying out 'Grandma, Grandma!' I could see now that there were huge pots – soup, I knew – simmering on the burners on the back counter, and that Grandma was working – but not too hard, it was work she enjoyed – cutting up vegetables to add to the soup. She heard my cries and looked up and came out from behind the counter to greet me, my grandmother, small and shapeless in a cotton housedress without a belt. She threw her arms around me as I threw mine around her. I was breathless from running, warm with happiness. 'Grandma, guess what! I'm going to be married!'

'Ah! Ah!' She kissed me many times, hugged me, held me, she couldn't let go of me, she was so happy. 'We must tell Papa!' she crowed, and raised her voice to call him. We both stared out acrosss the brown fields toward the trees. A small figure appeared, running. He got larger and larger and then my grandfather was there with us, a small brown man, smiling, happy. 'Papa, our Anastasia is going to be married!' Grandma cried. And he embraced us both, we embraced him, it was ecstasy, it was bliss, it was coming home.

I woke glowing with it, and glowed all morning as I prepared to leave Hawaii, where I'd spent a night to break the journey from Saigon to New York. Because of the dream, I didn't carry the horror of Vietnam home with me.

I didn't see Grant again for a long time. He called me when he got back to New York, on the official phone that no one but I was allowed to pick up, but I couldn't meet him in the city, how could I? He sounded disappointed, but I didn't want to tell him the truth about my life. I was too afraid the word would get out. I just said I was completely tied up. He didn't understand, obviously, because next time we met, in London, in the fall of '64, he acted cool. He was there doing an in-depth report on the new Wilson government; I was on my way to Zambia to shoot the independence ceremonies. He'd been there for a while and would stay several weeks longer; I had a night's layover in each direction. We were both staying at Morrow House, where all the *World* people stayed, and met by accident, one leaving, the other entering an elevator.

He colored, then paled when he saw me, and we talked for a moment, the usual excited 'How have you been, it's been so long, we must get together' sort of thing, and then he turned to walk away, cool and detached. But I slid my arm through his and walked along with him through the lobby, teasing him out of his pique.

'Don't be mad,' I cajoled. 'I have a private life I can't talk about. I can't see you in New York. But we could have wonderful times meeting each other in exotic places, couldn't we?'

He gave an unwilling smile, and almost whined. 'It's just – it's not enough, Stacey. I want more . . .'

I nodded. Men did tend to want to be married. 'You'll probably get more,' I said. 'But in the meantime, can't we be friends?'

He gave me an anguished look and I suddenly realized that he'd fallen in love with me, that our separation was painful to him. That stopped me short. I freed his arm. 'Oh!' I cried softly, and stood still. I don't know what he thought, seeing my stricken face, but he moved toward, me smiling and said, 'Sure we can, sure! Are you free tonight?'

That was really the beginning of our affair. We cherished each other from a distance, and when we were together, we had deep affectionate conversation, affectionate *sex;* and a shared knowledge of work, shared attitudes toward what was going on in the world. What we didn't have was intimacy on the day-to-day level, we didn't talk about our troubles with the oil burner, the check that bounced, the kids' newest revolt. And that was great. It was freeing. We went on meeting for several years – we met in Manila, Paris, Ottawa, Perth, several times in London – other places too. I don't remember. Sometimes we'd even make an effort to get assigned to the same places.

I had the Yeats dream – that's how I think of it – in Zambia, a couple of nights after our reunion. Probably it was influenced by the pageantry of the celebration in Lusaka, the colors, the feathers and banners. And it was a happy time, I had so much hope for the new African nations . . .

I was walking through a huge park, deep green lawns carved by neatly tended paths, woods at a distance, with two men. We all had our arms around each other, I was in the center. One man was older than I, the other was younger. We were full of joy, we were going to the opening of an arts complex and all of us were artists – our work was going to be performed, shown, read. As we turned into the low fence marking off the exposition, we were approached by a man wearing tight black pants, a short flared black cape, and a wide-brimmed hat with a great feather, the kind worn by seventeenth-century cavaliers. He was carrying an open book, reading softly aloud to himself. When he saw us – me – he stopped. He did not bow or remove his hat. He stared at me imperiously. He gazed down at his book and read:

'For death does not end life but is part of it, one of nature's transformations as we work our way through its cycles. Death informs life. It is not, as *your* poet says, simply the mother of beauty; it is the mother of life itself for how could we conceive of life if there were no death? And it is only because we conceive of life that we know we must taste it lingeringly, try every flavor and nuance, drink in experience while we can. Death and life are dependent upon each other, like order and chaos, neither concept being possible without the other. So there should be no fear of death, which is omnipresent, part of life. Welcome it into your arms, for it is but rest: For you lie in nature like a heartbeat.'

This sounded profound to me, and I breathed 'Oh, thank you, Mr Yeats' – I knew he was William Butler Yeats. He nodded peremptorily, closed his book, and walked on. My companions and I continued, with the lightness of heart that follows an aesthetic liberation, and entered the first building on our right. It was all glass – its high roof, its sides. Through the glass we could see an encompassing green blur – the trees that surrounded the building. Sunlight reflected on the floor, bright and cool at once. We walked directly to William Hull, my college English teacher, the poet, who was standing on a ladder painting glass panels. Below him, ranked in parallel rows at a forty-five-degree angle to the side walls, were glass panels, all painted in Rouault-like patches of brilliant color so they resembled stained glass but had more fluid, freer forms. The panels are making rainbows of the sun that pours in through the glass roof; the room glows like jewels, glistens with light, I am speechless at the beauty. I knew that I was home, had come home. William smiled, my companions embraced me, I embraced them, smiling. We were encased in bliss.

Yes.

An envelope of photographs dated August 1967. Twelve prints made from Kodachrome slides, shot on Old Hodge's Road, Huntington, Long Island. Four shots: various aspects of a house built about 1930, in some disrepair, pale yellow clapboard with peeling white trim, trellises (paint flaking) with climbing roses (overgrown), a suspicious-looking dark patch on the roof. Eight show a garden; two distance shots show it to be fairly extensive for a suburban plot. It too is overgrown, but full of peonies and honey-suckle, clematis and foxglove, delphinium, and low, delicate pale purple heatherlike flowers at what used to be the edges of the beds. One bed has been weeded and tended, a long rectangle filled with rosebushes in shades of yellow, peach, salmon pink.

Several of the garden shots contain the figure of a woman, pretty, slender, with browning blond hair, in her early thirties. She is posed like a model by the rosebushes, wearing white cotton shorts and a navy and white horizontally striped cotton knit shirt with white sandals. She has good legs.

'Beautiful! It's all beautiful!' Anastasia gushed for the fifteenth time.

Joy smiled in pleasure. 'I love it! I loved it the minute I saw it! I just loved it! It needs work, but I think it's just great!' She pushed open the swinging door to the kitchen.

Dim afternoon light from two windows above it brightened the stained porcelain sink and the well-scrubbed wooden counter, softened the outlines of the old-fashioned appliances, the open wood shelves that lined two walls, stacked in a lovely homely way with dishes, cans, boxes of cereal, rice. The floor was covered with old, cracked linoleum. On the windowsill were two small green plants, thriving.

'What a lovely room!'

'I love it! We all just love it! It's bright in the morning when we have breakfast.' Joy walked to a bare wall that stood at a right angle to the sink. 'And here,' she pointed, 'I want to break through and put a door, and lay a terrace outside. Wouldn't that be terrific? Then on summer mornings we can have breakfast out there, looking out at the garden.'

'That would be wonderful, beautiful!' How are you going to pay for it?

Joy smiled happily. 'Shall we have coffee or tea? I got in the habit of drinking tea when we were in the Philippines.'

'Tea is fine.' Anastasia sat on a wooden kitchen chair painted bright blue and yellow, one of a set that looked antique, and watched her sister prepare tea.

'I'm so glad you could come!' Joy cried heartily. 'It's been such a long time since we talked, had an afternoon alone together.'

'Years.'

'We have so much to catch up on!' All Joy's statements emerged as pronouncements, loud, absolute, as if by speech alone she was trying to create a reality she feared did not exist. 'We couldn't really talk at Jenny's birthday party.'

'Not with all the competition from paper bugles, burst balloons, and spilled ice cream,' Anastasia laughed. 'Not to speak of screaming kids.'

'Weren't they? But I'm glad I had it. She's so disorientated. She was six months old when we left the Philippines, we spent the next three years in Panama, in California, we lived on the base, she's not used to playing with children, she was always in the compounds, she had a hard time adjusting, it's hard for her.'

'The house is nice, but . . . I don't understand it. Has she told you anything?' Bitten lower lip. 'No.' 'I wonder what's happening. Do you think Justin has left her?' 'Why don't you ask her, Mom?' Bristle. 'Oh, I couldn't do that.'

'I knew I wanted to live in this town. I just *love* this town, it's so pretty and country like, I love it! I wanted Jenny to get to know other children. Well, it turns out there aren't too many kids her age in the neighborhood, but she'll meet kids in school, when she starts school.'

The official version, the story she tells: kids disoriented by continual moving about, need solid stable home, neighborhood, friends, American friends. But why here, why not in Texas, where Justin is? Of course, everyone accepts the story because easterners think that to live in Texas is to drop off into hell. But is it, if your husband is there? She has left him, that's clear. 'You found a really beautiful house.'

Joy returned, her face glowing. 'Isn't it?'

And will Justin live here too? And if he doesn't, how will you afford it? It needs work. How are you going to pay for it?

'Let's have tea in the living room!' she suggested gaily, proposing a party. She stacked cups, saucers and teapot on a tray. She opened the refrigerator. 'I have some pound cake, and *one* apple tart!' She gave her loud, hard, forced laugh.

'Just tea for me,' Anastasia said quietly, feeling that her every utterance was a damper on her sister's enthusiasm.

'You too? I don't seem to like sweets anymore, either. Neither does Mother. That's funny! The three women in the family don't like sweet things! And all the men do! Daddy loves his ice cream, and Justin gorges himself on chocolate. And Billy and Jonathan will eat anything as long as it's sweet!' Laughter.

Anastasia smiled, a strained smile.

Everywhere, dirt-darkened walls were cracked, the ceilings were peeling. There was a dark patch on the ceiling in the upstairs hall. Joy had seen Anastasia glance at it, and had said, tense-mouthed, 'Yes, I have to get the roof fixed. I just haven't had time to get around to it.' But everywhere, too, light poured in through the generous windows, light and intimations of the luxurious wild gardens beyond, green and aromatic.

Anastasia stopped at a living room window. 'You can smell the honeysuckle, even indoors!'

The room reflected Joy's travels. There were two low brass-ornamented Korean chests, a Chinese carpet between the couches in front of the fireplace, Chinese vases, and on the walls, scrolls and ink drawings. Chinese? From Hong Kong, probably. And Hummel figurines from Germany on a carved shelf, and a German grandfather clock in the hall, sending a steady inexorable recounting of time passing clicking up the wide curved staircase.

'Yes, we did go to Hong Kong, several times, when we had a four- or five-day pass,' Joy was saying. 'It's really great! The Peninsula Hotel! Mmmm! Yummy! When you first get your room they come in with this big basket of beautiful soaps and let you choose the one you want. They're all done up in these gorgeous packages! You hate to open them!' Laughter.

The teatray was set on a large round brass tray table. Joy, her legs crossed neatly at the ankle, poured.

'So what loot did you bring back from Panama?' Watch it: envy creeping into the voice.

'They have the most beautiful linens, Anastasia. Made of rice cloth, I'll show you later. Embroidered tablecloths, tea towels . . . oh, you know! I gave Mother a tablecloth for Christmas!'

'Oh, yes, that was gorgeous!'

'Oh! And these!' She dangled her tea napkin in the air.

'Yes, I was noticing them. They're Panamanian too? Beautiful!'

Tea sipped. Strong, smoky Lapsang souchong. Silence.

'So how are the kids?'

'They're great! They're really adjusting! Jonathan went out for Little League this summer, and he's the star of the team! He really loves it! Julie's not so outgoing, but she made a friend last term, and she goes over to see her on her bike just about every day, and they talk on the phone, they're never apart, I call them the Siamese Twins,' laughter, long long laughter, 'so she's okay.' Joy wiped her eyes, which were damp from laughing. 'It's Jenny who's having a hard time, but there are two kids her age just two blocks away, so she'll be great!'

The enthusiasm, the emphasis: to make what she wants to happen seem to have already happened.

Carefully, Anastasia set down the delicate porcelain cup. Carefully, making her voice sound easy, relaxed, she asked, 'And is Justin going to be able to get up to see the house?'

Joy set her cup down too, and wiped her lips on the lace-edged linen napkin. 'He's in the middle of a big project, very hush-hush, some new plane they're testing. He's in charge of all the test pilots, it's a big job. He's always busy,' she finished, with an especially bright laugh.

'How does he live down there?'

'Oh, he lives on the base, they have quarters for unmarried officers. I mean officers without wives. I mean, if their wives are someplace else or they don't have one. They eat at the Officers' Club, it's really great, they can have steak every night, their rooms are cleaned for them, and their laundry done, the Army is very good to their own, they take good care of the officers. He doesn't miss me at all!' Protracted laughter, very bright.

Or the children either? Officers' quarters: is that why they don't visit him there? He didn't come last Christmas, well his tour didn't end until the end of the year but surely they would have let him take the last week of December off. Joy came, alone, with the kids. She doesn't want me to ask questions about him.

Joy burst out, 'And how is Arden? She excited about going back to college?'

'Oh, very.' Try to think of something good to say. 'She got a job in a fast-food joint and spent all her money on new clothes. Four pairs of jeans and twenty-five tops!' Anastasia laughed.

Joy howled. 'Aren't they something?' She wiped her eyes. 'She still at Cornell?'

'Yes. She wants to be a poet. She has talent. But you can't earn a living writing poetry.'

'Well, once upon a time they might have told you you can't earn a living taking photographs, and now look at you!'

Anastasia smiled wryly, nodded. 'Except I never imagined I'd earn a living taking photographs.'

'But you didn't want to do anything else, either, and you *wouldn't* do anything else.'

Anastasia gazed at Joy. 'That's right.' Profound. When had that happened, that Joy became profound?

'And Billy's a senior?'

Anastasia nodded. 'Going into his senior year this fall. And Franny's going,' she shifted to a childish accent, 'to kindergarten!' They both laughed then, together. Why am I laughing? Just the thought of her, so cute, looking up at your with those eyes, so serious and self-important. 'She's full of self-importance,' Anastasia went on. 'She feels she is now an adult, going to school like her big sister and brother, she has a pencil box and notebook, never mind that they're going to make her cut out paper dolls.'

Again the sisters laughed together.

Got past Billy safely.

'And Toni's fine?' Joy poured fresh cups of tea, adding hot water to the strong brew from a beautiful little pewter kettle set on a stand with a candle.

Where did she get *that*?

Anastasia nodded, sipped. 'He's a little frustrated. All these years and he's only published four short stories in little magazines that don't pay anything. He's talking about changing his style.'

Changing his style: silk shirts and martinis before dinner.

'What about that novel he was writing? About the Army or something? I remember he was asking Justin questions the last time we came home at Christmas . . . was that 1963? Did he ever finish it?'

'He's given up on that, wisely, I think.'

Joy registered dismay. At the fact? Or at a wife criticizing her husband?

'He just didn't know enough about military life, war, any

of it. He's started another, about a boy growing up in a town rather like Dayton, Ohio, in a Polish family,' Anastasia grinned. 'Not all autobiographical, of course. But I like it, I think it's really terrific. It *is* in a different style from the other one – spare, plain, no dramatics, there's the continuity of chronology but it's really a set of vignettes strung together, each one a pow in the eye, it hits you, hard, it's true and powerful . . .'

Joy was nodding her head with a fixed smile, glazed eyes. Enough of that.

'And tell me what you've been doing! Have you been travelling?' Joy's voice was strained; she emphasized each word as if she were talking to a child, asking about first grade. Why was that? 'Where have you been recently?'

'Oh – well, last week I was in Nigeria . . .'

'Nigeria! Now, where is that?'

'Africa. There's a war going on there . . .'

'Oh, my! Did you see any of that?'

Why did she sound as if she were speaking a part in a play?

'Well, yes, of course! I was sent there to photograph the war.' Why does my voice sound so tight, so angry?

'Isn't that dangerous?'

'A little. But they're not especially interested in Americans, they're fighting each other, Christian and Moslem, it's terrible, it's causing such starvation, you might have seen my pictures of Biafran children.'

'Oh! Right! So Nigeria is the same as Biafra?'

Change the subject. Change the subject. How, gracefully . . .

'So those children . . . but it's terrible! Terrible! Oh, my heart just ached when I saw those pictures! I just wanted to scoop those little babies up in my arms and pour milk into them, it was terrible. . . .'

'Yes.' No more. Change the subject. Put down the tea cup. Yawn. Stretch. Look out the window. 'How lovely the garden is from here.'

Joy looked out, smiled. 'Yes.'

Forget jealousy. Forget anger. Think about her. 'It must be comforting to you after all these years, to have your own home. A place you chose, a place you can fix up as you like.'

Tears sprang into Joy's eyes. She pressed her lips together. She nodded.

'How did Mother like the house?'

'We-ell . . . you know Mother.'

Anastasia smiled broadly. So did Joy.

'She liked the house, she loved the garden, but she said it was too much for me. And she *hated* the kitchen!' Joy laughed. 'Guess what she hated the most!'

Anastasia considered the old-fashioned sink and stove, the cracked linoleum, the non-self-defrosting refrigerator. 'The wooden shelves and counters,' she guessed. 'My favorite thing in the whole room.'

'Right! I love them too! Why do you think she hates them?'

'Because,' Anastasia announced authoritatively, 'they remind her of the houses of her childhood. They didn't have sinks and stoves and refrigerators and linoleum, they had cast-iron tubs and huge iron stoves and no fridge, but they did have wooden shelves and tables, scrubbed clean by generations of women.'

'Wouldn't you think she'd like them, then?' Joy asked, a puzzled look on her face. 'I mean, they'd be familiar. And they're so pretty.'

Anastasia gazed at her sister. Did she know their mother at all? 'She hated her childhood, so she hates anything associated with it. Like she hates antique furniture – all she sees is that it's old.' *She* hated the tone of her own voice, superior, patronizing. Why did she sound like this?

'Oh!' Joy breathed out slowly. 'So that's why she hated the kitchen table and chairs! You know, they're Mexican, antiques, Justin and I bought them when we flew to Acapulco one time when he had a week's pass. We rented a car and we drove out to the countryside and saw them in a little cantina and I fell in love with them and Justin bargained with the owner, and we bought them!' Great protracted laughter. 'I love them. But she told me they should be heaved out in the trash, they were old and ugly.'

Anastasia caught her breath. 'Oh, I'm *sorry*, Joy. She can

be so cruel. They're beautiful,' she offered sincerely. Why did she feel responsible for Mother's behavior?

Well, that certainly sounded as if she and Justin were getting on, no bitterness of a cast-off wife, which Mother is sure she is, or a wife who's left her husband, which Anastasia thought she was.

Joy's face was a little twisted – anger? grief? She was looking down at her thin hands twisted into a knot. Anastasia looked them too: they were clenched, white with tension. Oh god.

'She just always tries to make me feel – oh, I don't know – as if nothing I have is any good, as if . . .' She raised her eyes to her sister. 'And she's always praising you, like bragging, really.'

'Oh, Joy!' Anastasia cried. 'You know what my house is like!'

'It's not your house. It's your career, your book, the famous people you meet . . .'

'She criticizes me, too. All the time. My house, with my money, why don't I have something grander, my furniture, why don't I have fancier furniture. My clothes. My cooking,' Anastasia grinned.

Joy gazed at her. 'I know.'

She knows. So Mother criticizes me to her, just as she criticizes her to me. Yes. But we both know something else, something that cannot be spoken. Whatever she has to give, she gives to me, not Joy. Oh, Joy! Her hands clenched and white in her lap, long nails digging into the flesh, just like Mother's hands. And Arden's! Arden's!

'She said I'd need twenty thousand dollars to fix this house up!' Joy exploded with laughter. 'Can you imagine?' Laughter, hard, stiff, forced-air, tears on the cheeks. Was laughing a way of crying?

It *would* cost that much. But Anastasia laughed as if the statement were ridiculous.

'Oh, my!' Joy wiped her eyes. 'But she really was wonderful while I was moving in. She and Daddy came over and helped me put things away and get settled. And she took Jenny home with her for a couple of days, until I got everything in order. And she takes her whenever I ask.

She's really great! Jenny's there now. I'm going over there for dinner tonight, after the kids get back from the pool, and pick her up.'

Relieved, Anastasia sank back against the chair back. 'That's great.'

'But I feel so bad for her. She's so miserable. I think she's just bored, I keep telling her she should get out and make some friends. I've been telling her and telling her, I'm sick of it! I swear I won't say anything, and then, the next time I see her, it just comes out of my mouth, Mom, you need to get out.'

'I know,' Anastasia sighed. 'Now she's stopped piano lessons.'

'I know,' Joy sighed. 'She tells you about it as if she were telling you somebody died. 'She sat up brightly. 'How about a drink? It's nearly five.'

'Sure.'

The two women rose and carried the tea things back to the kitchen. Anastasia sat on a high stool watching Joy mix drinks, as they complained of and bemoaned Mother, their favorite subject, the person who ripped them apart, the person who bonded them, the only thing in the world that told them they were sisters.

Chapter XIII

one

Now accidents are of two kinds: necessary . . . and non-necessary . . . Although privation is an accidental principle, it does not follow that it is unnecessary for generation. For matter is never lacking privation: inasmuch as it is under one form, it is deprived of another.

Thomas Aquinas, The Principles of Nature, II, 9

This quotation is the backbone of my life. I have typed it on a three-by-five card and pasted it up over my desk. I read it every day. I use it to calm myself, to make myself firm, to keep myself from crumbling. Arden saw it one day – years ago – and asked me what it meant. She could not understand its abstract language. So I made a joke of it; I told her that inasmuch as a carrot is a carrot, it cannot be celery. The carrot may crave to be a celery; it may wilt and sag in its singular, lonely life, and long to live pressed tightly to its fellows the way celery stalks do: it may sicken with the desire to live above ground in the light, and to have pale green delicate leaves; but it will never have them. It will have, instead, dark green feathery lacy leaves, and spend its life in the warm dark earth, a creature of darkness and isolation. It can have only what it has, be only what it is. Always. Until it dies.

I did not tell her what it meant to me. I try to tell myself that I have much. And must be reconciled to having what I have, being what I am and nothing else, until I die. Because all things being under one form are deprived of all others.

Still I find it hard. It is hard while you are alive, breathing, sentient, to know that your heart is dead, that it has died inevitably because you are what you are, that you cannot resuscitate it.

Clara says, 'You're just like your mother. You don't see alternatives. You close down shop and cry, instead of opening the door and looking around.'

'For what? At what?' I counter. 'And,' angrily, haughtily, 'I never cry.'

Looking back, rummaging through these dusty boxes full of old photographs, letters, bits and pieces – the children's class photos, a certificate decreeing Arden Carpenter of the fifth grade winner of the Poetry Prize for Linden Street School, a scrap of newspaper, saved . . . why? Toni's and my marriage certificate, two yellowed report cards for William Carpenter, grades two and three – looking back, my memory triggered by these fragments that would be meaningless to anyone else, mere detritus, I remember good years, I remember happiness. What happened to change it, and when it changed, I can't figure out. I suppose it didn't end, but just ran down, the way my mother gradually slid into her present state. No way to mark even the beginning of the end: when was the first time Arden was sullen and furious with me and I looked in her eyes and saw real hatred? or noticed that Billy was rarely home, and realized he was spending all his spare time with Brad? Or the first time I noticed that Toni – but, yes, I do remember that.

We had become prosperous enough that we could afford a woman to come in and clean, do the laundry, iron, straighten up a little – always a hopeless task in our house. It relieved me to pay someone to do this work. I hated doing it myself, but I felt squeamish and guilty about Toni doing so much housework. I don't know if I'd have felt that way if he'd been a woman and I a man. But as it was, I did.

And one week Mrs Landors had to leave early, I don't remember why, some appointment, and she didn't have time to put away the ironed clothes. So I did it. I am no housekeeper, but I love ironed clothes, so there was a stack of them, pajamas and tablecloths and knit shirts, and blouses and shirts hung on hangers. I was happy that day, I remember, I was humming with the record player, Billie Holliday, 'He's My Man', as I went from room to room putting clean fresh pressed clothes away in closets and drawers. I avoided Arden's drawers, they were a mess, I just laid her things on her bed (after making it), and went into our room, into Toni's chest of drawers to put away some knit shirts, and there, glistening and luxurious in a pile in the bottom drawer, were three silk shirts.

Nowadays, that might not be shocking, but in those days you could still buy a fine man's white shirt on sale for two ninety-five, whereas silk shirts cost seventy-five dollars. And Toni never went anywhere much – we occasionally spent an evening with neighbors, or went to a party, but he didn't go to work, to business dinners or cocktail parties, to events that required such formality. So why these shirts? And how did he get them? I ran downstairs and looked into my desk and pulled out the charge statements for the past few months. I paid all the bills, but I didn't check them over.

And there it was – Lord & Taylor, three silk shirts, two hundred and twenty-five dollars plus tax.

I was appalled. But I didn't know what to do. Toni and I never discussed money. We had a joint checking account, I put a regular sum in it. When he needed money he cashed a check, and he carried our few credit cards – this was before people lived on them – because he did most of the shopping. I had never said to Toni, you may spend only this much, or you may buy this and this but not that. How could I now say to him what in fact I did say when he walked into the room.

'Why on earth did you buy silk shirts!'

He looked at me in a way he never had before – can't describe it – *distant* – as if he didn't know me. Pale.

'Why were you snooping around in my drawers?' is what he answered.

Snooping! Snooping! I was putting your fucking clothes away for you, you shit!'

He turned and left the room. He went into the kitchen. I followed him like a fury. 'Toni! I asked you a question!' He turned away from me and went back to the living room, sat on the couch, and started to leaf through a magazine, casually, as if he were unperturbed. But his body was taut, I could see he was ready to spring. He'd sprung before when we'd had fights, leaping up and throwing a glass across the room, smashing a vase.

I sat down across the room from him. He lighted a cigarette. I lighted a cigarette. 'Toni,' I began in a quieter voice, 'you buy whatever you like. You know how much money we have. But do you need silk shirts? At seventy-five dollars a throw? When we're still paying Arden's orthodontist? Why?'

'Do I?'

I stared at him.

'Do I know how much money we have?'

My face grew hot.

'Or do you have money stashed away in accounts in your own name, money in investments you never bothered to mention to me?'

'You went in my desk!'

'It was an accident. Like your going into my drawer. I was looking for the orthodontist's bill, he called, he was annoyed, he claimed we still owed him four hundred dollars. And I find all this stuff – bank accounts, investment reports, everything mailed to you at *World* so I wouldn't see it.'

I sank back in my chair.

'I didn't say a word when you bought this house and put it in your name. Or when you made the kids the beneficiaries of your life insurance. Those things made a kind of sense to me. And I wouldn't even mind your having bank accounts in your own name, or investments . . . I mean, there's a kind of logic, you earn the money and I'm not a wife even if I do the work of a wife . . . I could have found a way to accept everything, if you'd told me about it. You didn't.'

'No,' I admitted miserably.

'Why?'

I could feel that my face was all scrunched up. 'Oh, I don't know.' I did, of course. But I couldn't say it. How could I say: you are not really an equal partner, you do not take equal responsibility. Everything is up to me. So everything is going to be in my control, not yours. I temporized. 'You know . . . you're young . . . you're a male. We got married under pressure . . . I guess I never believed it would last, never really felt married . . .'

His taut body sprang forward, his face ghostly. 'Is that why you take your diaphragm everywhere you go?'

I was dead. I just sat there. After a while he got up. I heard him moving around in the kitchen. He came back with a drink, it looked like straight Wild Turkey. He sat, gulped it.

'I've had to do a lot of thinking these past couple of months,' he began.

'How long have you been sitting on this!' I cried out. I couldn't bear thinking he'd been feeling this way about me, knowing these things and hating me and still making love to me . . .

He raised his eyebrows. 'Oh, *I'm* the villain?'

I got up too then, went into the kitchen, and fixed my

own fucking drink. I plopped back down in my chair. I was pissed. 'Look. You're angry with me and you have a right to be. But I won't be played cat and mouse with. I'm sorry if you feel bad about the money, but it *is* my money, I earned it, and I am going to save it or invest it as I see fit! You were screaming you wanted a sports car! Who knows what you'd decide to want if you knew there was money for it! I'm in a tricky profession. I don't know how long this job will last.'

'Ditchwater! They love you there. Is that what you think of me? I don't think I want to be married to someone who thinks my pretty little head isn't smart enough to understand money, who can't be trusted with it! Who gets a little allowance to buy food and clothes and gas for the car and everything else!'

'You don't buy clothes out of weekly expense money! You use the charge accounts!'

'And what about my work? You used to pay me for watching your kids, but after we got married you stopped. Once you're a wife, your labor is free?'

'*My* kids?' I roared. 'You can cash checks whenever you want, what is this about an allowance, for all I know you've been cashing checks for more than you need and socking money away in a bank account of your own all these years! You had one when we got married, I never asked you about it, I didn't demand to know what you had!'

'You're damn right. And I have. Been socking money away. Whatever was left over at the end of the week. All these years. Just like a housewife.'

'You bastard!' Then I laughed. 'How much do you have?' I asked, wiping my eyes.

'Not as much as you.' He grinned. 'But I have got twelve hundred dollars.'

'Oh, you bastard,' I moaned, still laughing.

We sat smiling at each other across the room for a moment until he recalled his other grievance. 'So how many have there been? – lovers. Do you screw everyplace you go? Are you a regular little whore?'

'Don't you dare call me names, Antoni Nowak, I won't stand for it! I do what I do, I live as I live, I like living

718

that way! I've never pretended to be anything but what I am!'

'And that makes it all okay?'

'Toni, do I ever check up on what you're doing? Do I ever ask you to account for your time? You could be having affairs with all the women on the block for all I know.'

'You forget the kids,' he lashed out. '*Your* kids. And yes, they are *your* kids. They're not mine.'

This really hurt. 'You love them!' I cried, and blew my nose.

'Whether I love them or not, kids are the greatest impediment to fucking around ever invented. That's why guys who screw around all the time when they're away from home can leave home with total impunity – they know their wives can't do fuck-all because the kids are there, there, there!'

I peered over my handkerchief. 'Sounds like you've felt the itch.'

'Whether I have or not, I haven't acted on it. I can't. Couldn't. Even if I wanted to. But I *didn't* want to, damn you!' Now his nose was full, his voice thick. 'I love you, I've loved you so much, I couldn't even think about another woman, no one else ever swam into my eyes the way you did.'

Silence.

I thought about Grant. I loved him, I couldn't bear to give him up. I didn't want to give up spontaneous sex either. It was *important* to me. I couldn't explain this to anyone. It was so contrary to the accepted code of morals for women, especially for a married woman . . . yet I knew that if I had to give it up I would not just feel deprived but would dwindle into grey aridity, I would die. 'I'm really sorry,' I said.

He sighed and lighted another cigarette. 'I don't know what to do.' He raised his eyes to mine. 'I suppose it would be useless to ask you to give it up.'

'I could try. But if I didn't succeed, I'd feel guilty and angry at you. And if I did, I'd hate you for it. I really would. I don't know if I could forgive you.' I blew my nose again.

'I guess we could pretend we had one of those open marriages, where both people do what they want,' he said tentatively.

My heart jumped right up in my chest: a way out? 'What do you mean *pretend*?'

He leaped then, his small muscular body tight as a fist, and flailed out at the coffee table in front of him, sending everything on it to the floor with a huge crash. '*Pretend* because I won't be doing it and you will! *Pretend* because I, one, don't want to do it, and two, can't get away from the kids in order to do it!'

'*My* kids are hardly ever here. It's *your* kid who is. The one you wanted. The one you swore you'd take care of. Don't lay that on me!'

He fell back onto the couch. He was white and drained. I got up and went over to him. His face pained me. I sat beside him, I put my hands on his cheeks, I kissed his forehead.

'Ah, Toni, I'm sorry I am the way I am. I'm sorry I hurt you. I do love you.'

He started to cry. 'When I think about the way you acted seven years ago, how jealous you were, how possessive. I thought you adored me!'

I fell away from him. 'Jealous! Possessive! Me? What are you talking about?'

'One night Drew Linden was here, don't you remember? Your friend, with that pompous asshole husband, Courtney. They moved. You said she was putting the make on me and I was eating it up. Don't you remember? And you cried, and you said if I ever had an affair with her it would kill you. Don't you even fucking *remember*?'

I hadn't. I did now. Vaguely. 'I cried? I asked you not to have an affair with her?' That part was gone. I remembered them making goo-goo eyes at each other all night, and her kicking his foot under the table, I remembered my disgust. Not the rest.

'Oh, Anastasia,' Toni wept.

We made it up. I don't know how, it wasn't through words, it was through our bodies, which still clung to each other apart from our wills. And, I suppose, Toni was trapped. He adored Franny, he couldn't bear to leave her, but what would he do, how could he leave and take her with him? He couldn't move. And his novel was nearly finished, and it was very good, he knew that, and he'd have trouble finishing it if he went out and got a job to make himself independent of me. He was in the situation of a married woman with children. And I, god help me, was in the situation of a man.

I went to visit Mother. Toni's father had a heart attack and he went out to Dayton for a few days. I wasn't on assignment, and the kids were on vacation, so I packed us all in the car one summer morning, and drove out to Suffolk prepared to stay a couple of days. I saw my mother rarely and the kids liked to go there, it was near the beach and they could play croquet on the lawn and eat Grandma's wonderful meals. Every night Mother and I stayed up late and talked.

I asked her about her life, over and over, asked her for stories I'd heard many times before: how her father threw the creamed spinach, how she'd known how to cook without being taught, how she'd worked in the box factory, how she had been sent home from school the first day because she couldn't speak English. Her stories came late at night, after we'd both had quite a few drinks, when she was willing to go back into the place where those stories were buried, the place where the tears were.

But early in the evening, she would ask me and I would tell her everything about my life. She was avid for stories about my 'social life'. She loved hearing about my travels, any compliments I'd received, anything at all that could pass for a triumph, and the men in my life, especially Grant. She always asked after Grant, and always in an approving tone of voice. I could see she hoped I'd divorce Toni and marry Grant – he was older and had a prestigious job, she thought he must have money; in any case he'd have more than Toni.

One night – I'd been there a couple of nights – we watched the evening news and there was a story about

Elizabeth Taylor, she was marrying number, oh, I don't remember, one of her many husbands, and I said, 'I wonder why she marries them. She must be a romantic, she believes in marriage.'

'She lives like a man,' Mother pronounced.

'What do you mean?'

She shrugged. 'Like a man. Men aren't satisfied with one woman, they want more, more, more. They always want another woman.' She turned to me. 'Like you. *You* live like a man.'

I had been feeling bad about my character, but when she said that, everything became clear to me. I was built, constituted, the way men were. I couldn't help my sexual urge, it was built-in. And like men, I was clogged and tied down by the domestic, the day-to-day. I wanted freedom, total freedom. Maybe everybody did, women as well as men. Maybe it wasn't that I was like a man, but that only men were permitted to live out their desires. I turned to my mother.

'Would you have liked that? To live that way?'

She shrugged. 'How would I know? I always lived like a woman.'

'So how am I different from you?'

'Oh, you!' She slapped at me in the air.

'Well?' I was amused.

'You,' she sighed, 'you always wanted everything.'

'Well, how about you? Would you have liked to live like that?'

She tilted her head; she inclined her eyebrows; was there a tinge of a fraction of a glint in her eye? 'Oh, I don't know, Anastasia,' she said in that voice that told me I'd gone as far as she'd let me – any further and I'd get the disgusted, 'Oh, Anastasia!' I was so used to, and she'd get up and go to bed, abandoning me to my questions. I dropped the subject.

Driving home the next day I kept imagining what she would have been like if she'd been sexually free – and what it would have been like to have a mother like that. On the whole, I decided, it would have been good for her but not for us. Situations like this make me wonder about nature's

722

economy: why had nature planted so much desire in us if it harmed our children. *Did* it harm our children? I didn't consider the effect of my behavior on my children, because, after all, they knew nothing about it, they never had to witness it.

My problem with Billy started sometime during his last two years of high school – 1967, 1968, around then. Billy worked hard, he had to, because he wanted to get into medical school: he had to do well at calculus, physics, organic chemistry, subjects that required study. He had few friends. Several afternoons a week a boy in his class who lived near us would walk home from school with him and they'd throw some baskets in our hoop for an hour or two; and sometimes they'd go to a movie on a Friday night. But he didn't hang out with a crowd the way other boys did, and he never dated. I worried about him a little, but remembered being shy and unsexual in high school myself, so I told myself to wait and not to worry.

He was still close to me, although not as close as he had been. Billy was always my baby. That was, perhaps, an accident. Brad had more tolerance for the girl than for the boy, and when he was kind or playful, it was always with Arden. And his parents had not had a daughter and had wanted one – so they lavished attention on her, at least when she was little. And my mother seemed only to *see* girls, boys somehow didn't really exist for her. So no one paid much attention to poor Billy, and I tried to make up for that, picking him up, holding him, nuzzling him, kissing him more than I did Arden. I tried to make him feel as loved as I knew she already felt. Or thought I did.

Oh god.

Anyway, he *belonged* to me, *adhered* to me in a special way. He wanted to go with me no matter where I was going: a trip to the supermarket with me was for him a happy occasion, and when we walked together we had a closeness hard to describe – as if there were only one will, one heart between us, as if whatever I said or did or wanted was his most fervent wish.

It was when he entered puberty that things began to

change. When his voice began to crack and deepen. He'd always been a sore loser at chess, but now he played it in a savage way, almost as if he hated Toni, whom he had loved the year before. He didn't stop going to the supermarket with me, or going shopping and out to lunch together on days when Toni was immersed in work; but when we were together there was a certain strain in his face and body, a self-consciousness. I could feel him wanting to touch me as he had as a child, to hold my hand, to lay his head against my body, to throw his arms around my waist – but restraining himself. I missed the old ease, the innocence. I missed my baby, my sweet good boy, my darling. But I knew it was right, even necessary, that he should move away from me a bit. I even – I could stab myself remembering this – urged him to get to know his father better. For a long time, he made no such move. He went on seeing Brad once every week or two, usually having dinner with him, with Arden or alone, on a Tuesday night. (Tuesday was a bad television night, the kids said. Maybe Brad thought so too.)

It must have been near the end of his junior year when he told me his father had offered him a summer job. Real estate boomed in the spring and summer, they always needed people. Billy could help out with the paperwork, Brad said, and answer the telephones when the salesmen were all out. He could learn about the business.

'Why should you need that?' I bristled. 'You're going to be a doctor, not a real-estate salesman!'

Something inside of him shriveled at my tone, I could see it on his face. 'Med school's expensive, Mom. I just want to earn some money,' he mumbled.

Still I couldn't be gracious about it. I didn't like it, I didn't want it. But I had nothing better to propose. So I mumbled consent, and that summer I hardly ever saw Billy. He grew golden from playing golf with his father mornings – Brad even bought him his own clubs. Trying to turn him into himself just as his father did to him, I thought, and set my teeth. Of course I knew Brad wanted him to go to medical school, was enormously proud that he wanted to be a doctor, everyone wanted their sons to be doctors in those days, I don't know why except doctors made a lot of money, but I couldn't get over the feeling that Brad wanted to . . . brainwash him . . . to wean him away from me . . . to turn him into . . . a *Republican*.

Brad opened a bank account for Billy, and one day he showed me his passbook – he'd saved most of what he'd earned over the summer and had nearly a thousand dollars in the account.

'You've earned that much? What is he paying you in, gold bars?'

'Oh, Mom.' He slumped. I went up behind him and put my arms around his waist. I lay my head against his back. 'Don't pay any attention to me, honey. I'm just jealous.' He turned around and put his arms around me. He pulled my body against his. 'Don't be, Mom.'

'I'm just stupid, I guess. I keep feeling he's trying to turn you into him, and I don't want that to happen.'

'It can't, Mom,' he said quietly but with such conviction that I couldn't doubt it. 'He's my *father*, Mom. I don't want to be like him, I see what he is. But I love him.'

I closed my eyes. Isn't this what I had wanted? that they should see their father for what he is but love him at the same time? Why was I so ripped with jealousy? Jealous and possessive, Toni had said. I didn't recognize myself in those words.

I looked at Billy's face; there were tears in his eyes, his expression was as tender and sweet as a lover's. I was stricken. Could it be that I was turning into one of those jealous possessive mothers who want to hold on to their sons forever, who find in the son a satisfaction they have never found in any other man? I smiled at him and let him go. He was more cheerful after that, but as time went on he was never home – now he was having dinner with Brad and his family once or twice a week at 'The Club', Brad's country club (oh, how Arden and I mocked him about 'The Club', which we saw as the height of pretension), besides playing golf . . . and then school started, and I thought it would end but it didn't, he spent every weekend working for his father.

I simmered, I seethed, I developed a bad stomach from

all the grating going on inside me, and maybe I showed how I felt; in any case, Billy felt uncomfortable around me, I could see that. I attributed his discomfort to his guilt not at the fact that he was moving away from me, but the reason he was. For I attributed his wooing – that's how I saw it – of his father to a calculated campaign to get Brad to pay for the many years of training ahead of him.

I also noticed his attitude toward Toni had changed – he was distant with him, almost hostile. But Billy buried his hostilities so deeply they didn't show as anger so much as inwardness, withdrawal, depression. Still it was perceptible. I blamed it on Brad, who, I was sure, was brainwashing my son, the child I had raised alone, with little financial help and no emotional help from him. My bitterness seeped into my face, my voice. Here I had done all the hard work and now that Billy was nearly grown, Brad was taking him away from me – and Billy was letting it happen.

Still, all that occurred gradually and it didn't feel as bad as it sounds because I didn't know then that I was really going to lose him: when you don't know the disease is lethal, your suffering isn't so acute. And other things were going on too, like Arden's new attitude toward me. That probably started even earlier than Billy's defection, maybe even in her sophomore year of high school, but I was less aware of it. There were just flashes, now and then, of rebellion, that I took to be normal for a girl her age – she'd always been passionate, fiery. They became more frequent, and reached the point where everything I said was a challenge to battle. Yes, now that I think of it, the problem with her started way back, at the very beginning of what I was a minute ago, like a blathering idiot, calling the 'happy years': oh my Pollyanna soul!

Yes, at first just childish rebellion. She started to wear jeans to school, even though that was not permitted. She was sent home. She participated in a student strike over dress rules. They won, an unusual victory in those days, but a harbinger of the permissive era that was beginning. It was a long time afterward that she stopped putting soiled clothes in the hamper, insisting on wearing the same filthy jeans every day. For a long time, she was a slob about her room, but would clean it under my pressure; and left messes around the house and had to be nagged to help with the housecleaning, or to throw her own empty soda cans in the trash; then she refused to clean her room at all, refused to do anything at all in the house. Even Toni, whom she adored, couldn't get her to wash a dish or rake some leaves or put her soiled underwear in the washing machine. And my kids had been trained to help around the house.

'Arden's getting difficult, isn't she?' I asked Toni one night. We were in bed, having a nightcap. I was leaning against pillows stacked against the headboard, he was stretched out across the foot of the bed, stroking my feet. 'And she's peculiar around you, too. Tonight she sat down right in your lap. You were embarrassed.'

Toni's glance was wary and a little absent, as if he were considering some other subject.

I sat up alarmed. 'What is it?' But of course, as soon as I asked, I knew. There had been hundreds of tiny signs. I sank back, my face sagging I guess, because he looked at me in sympathy and said, 'Honey, she'll get over it.'

'What does she do when I'm not around?'

He squirmed. 'It's like . . . like she tries to be you when you're not here . . . she does the things you usually do, you know, like she makes the salad. She dries the dishes when I wash them.'

I sat up outraged. 'You mean, she *helps* when I'm not here!'

He laughed. 'Well, more than she does when you are.'

I scowled. 'What about this lap business.'

'No,' he frowned, 'not at all. She . . . well, she sort of flirts . . . but it's sweet, she's sweet, it's fine. She never sat in my lap before. She does hug me, but she's always done that. It isn't that so much. It's everything else – I think she cuts school. She doesn't seem to do homework. She won't clean her room. And sometimes . . .' he looked at me guiltily, 'she doesn't come home when she's supposed to.'

'At night?'

'Day and night. You know, she's supposed to come home afternoons when she has an orthodontist appointment, but sometimes she forgets. Well, you know, she plays hockey and the girls all go for a Coke afterward. You can understand it. But sometimes – well, you're not often away on weekends, but when you are and she goes out, I tell her she has to be home by one. That's what you said, right? And she isn't. Sometimes she doesn't come in until after three.'

'What do you do?'

He shrugged. 'What can I do? I reproach her. She just grins at me. Sometimes she hugs my arm and begs, "Don't tell Mom, Ton'." And I don't.'

'For god's sake, why not?'

He rolled his body up and sprang to his feet. He liked to use his muscles. 'I don't know.' He went to his bureau and found his cigarettes and lighted one. 'It's hard. You know, I'm in a funny position. I feel almost as if . . . the kids and I, the four of us . . . are conspirators or something. Like I'm one of them, not of you.'

'All kids together. You're their big brother, not their father.'

He looked alarmed. 'I don't feel that way about Franny. I scold her, I discipline her. Not that she needs much, but when she does . . . like the time she decorated the living room wall with lipstick.'

I pondered. I knew he was asking me for permission to act like a father – to scold, punish, discipline my kids as well as his own. The idea was a stone in my throat. I couldn't get the words out. Why? I wondered, sitting there looking at this beautiful boy – well, he was a man now I guess, he was twenty-six – whom I loved and who loved us, and yet . . .

I moaned, 'Oh, god, Toni, what am I going to do?'

'I think you should beat her.'

'WHAT?'

'That's what my father did. We were terrified of him and that kept us in line. We were a wild bunch in my family, four boys, we drove my mother crazy. But when my father was around, we stood straight.'

'I can't believe you're saying this! You did *not* stay in line, you and your brothers were always in trouble, probably in rebellion against his brutality! And you hate him now! And besides, you can't *start* beating someone at the age of fifteen who's never been beaten before, it wouldn't work, it's a crazy idea, it's stupid, I can't believe you're saying that . . .'

He shrugged. 'I don't know what else to do.'

I considered. 'I'm glad she loves you. Especially since she hates Brad so. She needs to like one man she looks up to. I don't want you to become a big bad wolf, a Father . . . But, oh god, I'm worried about her.'

He sat up and turned away from me.

'What? What?' I sat up again. 'What are you telling me?'

He put his head in his hands. 'An . . . oh, hell, I don't know.' He got up and started to leave the room. At the door he turned. 'You want another drink?'

'No. I'm exhausted, I'll just finish this and sleep.'

I heard the light ripple of his stockinged feet running down the stairs – such a young, buoyant walk he had – and I looked at my fingernails thinking I had to give them a good brushing and I knew, suddenly, that he was going to tell me. So, to save him the agony, I said, as soon as he walked back in the door,

'You're going to tell me you think she's screwing, aren't you.'

He stopped dead, stared at me. 'You knew?'

'No. It just figures, somehow.'

His body was rigid. 'I didn't catch her . . .'

'Catch? No, of course . . . why do you think she is?'

He kept watching me as if he expected me to spring up and murder someone. If I hadn't known better, I'd have thought he felt guilty. But I knew he was terrified of my response because of what he knew his father would have done if he'd 'caught' his sister at such an activity. 'Oh, sit down, man, I'm not going to explode!'

He relaxed back onto the bed. He shrugged. He gulped a huge mouthful of whiskey. He's drinking too much, I thought. 'Just the way she looks when she comes in at night, like on a Friday night when she's been to the movies with her pals and comes in around two in the morning. She looks . . . you know, her eyes are big and liquid . . . she looks . . . voluptuous.'

'You don't think she's on drugs!'

'No, no!' Heartily. 'Oh, no, sweetheart.'

I *was* exhausted. I was still jet-lagged from a four-day stint in California, taking the red-eye, going on to the *World* office without sleeping. 'Well,' I leaned back against the pillows again, putting my glass, not yet empty, on the bed table, 'I'll have to have a talk with her.'

I turned out my light. It was early, not yet eleven, and Toni went back downstairs to watch the news on TV. I was exhausted, but I couldn't sleep. I kept thinking that I couldn't do what I had to do alone, that I needed a partner, that Arden needed a father. It never occurred to me that this father could be Toni. He took care of the kids when I wasn't there but I never thought of him as their stepfather, as someone *responsible* for them, who shared with me the weight of worry, the need to act – for them, about them. I never thought of him that way and I never allowed him to feel that way: he took care of them.

But what could I do? How could I trust him to know what was good for them, give him the right to scold, to impose punishments? How could I trust someone so young? Oh, it wasn't just that – I hadn't trusted Brad, and he was old enough to be their father, he *was* their father, and so of course he didn't need my permission. Maybe I didn't trust any man to raise children. But hadn't my mistrust been justified? Hadn't Toni just said his idea of dealing with a recalcitrant child was to beat her? And I knew lots of men, I'd heard them talk about their kids, I heard the toughness in their voices, the rough expressions as they bragged that *they* knew how to keep kids in line. There were men I knew far older than Toni who would have said what he said. *Brad* might have said the same thing, for god's sake.

The truth is I felt men were unfit to raise children. It was a belief I had imbibed young: my mother felt that too. On the one hand, I've always thought it was convenient for men to be so lousy at parenting, maybe they even play up their incompetence, so the women will dismiss them, tell them to go away, and deal with the mess themselves. Then they can go out and play golf or poker or whatever other games they liked to amuse themselves with. They can have fun or make money while the women do the dirty work, deal with the really hard stuff, like this. On the other hand, I also believe – it's strange, I never realized this until that moment – that women *are* more selfless, more sympathetic, more empathetic, more sensitive, more fun – all the things you have to be to raise kids – and that it was just as well that men kept their noses out of it. I didn't want to believe these things. I hated believing these things. I didn't want them to be true. But when I looked around me at the world I knew back then in 1964, they seemed true.

I finally fell asleep and didn't even wake when Toni came to bed. The next day was a Saturday, the kids were home. Billy was going to a baseball game with Brad at Shea Stadium, and I asked Toni to take Franny to lunch at the carousel. Arden was angry – she was always angry when Billy was to do anything with his father, she snorted contempt all around – at the furniture, the food, the *air* – anything Billy passed or touched. He raced out of the house, eager to get away from her. I told Arden she had to clean her room.

She 'Oh, Ma'd' me, she groused, she banged things, she stormed. She was supposed to meet her friends and go to a movie that afternoon. I insisted her room was going to be cleaned that day or she was not going out. It was only eleven, there was plenty of time before the movie. I added that I would help her, which calmed her a little – enough so that she sidled into the room behind me when I called and watched me pick things up off the floor. I had to order her to do each task.

'Pick up that sock over there.'

'There are crumpled papers under the dresser. Pick them up and put them – no, Arden, don't *hurl* them, *put* them in the wastepaper basket.'

'Start on that pile of clothes in the corner. Pick up each thing, shake it out. If it needs to be washed, put it in this pile here on the floor – *this* one, Arden, are you looking? If it needs to be dry-cleaned, lay it on this bench, like this, neatly, so I don't have to unroll it before I take it to the cleaners. No, spread out and folded, not in a heap. If it is clean but wrinkled, put it in a third pile. You can press these things tomorrow.' This direction was entirely too complicated for the 150+ IQ of my daughter, and she gave me a look of the most appalled disgust.

Teeth clenched, she hissed, 'The way you're doing this I'll never get done. It will take all day! I want to go out this afternoon! To meet my friends!'

'You'll go. As soon as this room is clean.'

I had hoped we would move through conflicts to harmony – as we might have six months earlier, after she'd become a slob but before she decided she hated me. I had anticipated giggling comparisons of her smelly socks with Billy's, or long martyred descriptions of her wardrobe, ending with an extracted promise of a new pair of boots. Then, good feelings restored, we could have thrown ourselves down on the newly made bed and I could have talked to her about boys, sex, and birth control. This was my plan.

That isn't what happened. She worked with me reluctantly, angry, white-faced, throwing things in drawers, slipping them over hangers so sloppily that they immediately fell off, then turning in fury on me when I pointed out that the newly hung blouse was now on the floor. At one point, when I pointed to some dirty socks stuck in sneakers, she strode to the closet, pulled the socks out furiously, tossed them on the dirty-clothes pile, and put her hands on her hips. 'If I miss that movie, I'll never forgive you.'

'It's up to you whether you miss it or not, Arden. Not me.'

She began to scream, yelling that it was *me* making her do this on this day at this time, *me* who was preventing her from going, and therefore my fault if she missed the movie. She didn't – not then, not yet – suggest that she was going to the movie whether I liked it or not and what could I do about it? Was I going to restrain her forcibly? And how could I, when she was stronger than I from playing hockey? No, she didn't say that then, that came later – another year? Six months?

There was a limit to the neatness I could demand. Her

732

drawers were her own: at least, she felt they were and so did I. Despite her hurling of the clothes replaced in them, it took hours to complete the task – to dispose of all the clothes, mop and dust and vacuum the room, put fresh sheets on the bed, wipe up spilled talcum powder and mascara stains from the glass top of her vanity table. They were cold silent hours, the only sounds my nagging – because I had to nag – and her occasional outburst, under her breath, 'Shit!' At last she turned on me with clenched teeth: 'May I go now please? I'm already half an hour late.'

'The movie doesn't start until two,' I snapped. 'It's only one-thirty.'

'We were going to have lunch first! And I'm filthy, I have to take a shower and change my clothes.'

I let her go. She banged around for a while, washing and dressing. I went into the kitchen and hung over a cup of coffee. After she'd banged the door – yelling, 'I'm going!', no goodbye, no kiss – I dragged myself upstairs and looked at her room. Dirty clothes were scattered on the floor and there were fresh mascara stains on her dressing table.

. She didn't come home for dinner. She called, the kids were all going out for pizza, could she go? Her tone said it would be a criminal act to deprive her of this and I had no desire to, but . . . 'Be home by midnight, Arden,' Mother said firmly.

She wasn't home by midnight. Or by one. At two, Toni wanted to get in the car and drive around to all the pizza parlors in the area. I shook my head. I told him to go to bed. He sat up with me. At two-forty, the front door opened.

'I think it would be better if I talked to her alone,' I whispered to Toni. He nodded, kissed me, walked out to the hall and met her.

'You mean you actually came home?' I heard him say.

'I had to. I have nowhere else to go!' I couldn't see her but I saw her in my mind, eyes flashing at him, furious. He started up the stairs. She began to follow him. He turned. 'First, lock the door. Second, your mother is waiting for you in the kitchen.'

She locked the door. She stormed down the hall and flounced into the kitchen. 'Yes?'

I was sitting at the table drinking tea and pretending to read the newspaper. I looked up slowly. I didn't know how to be. Should I be angry, yell? Should I try an understanding approach? What was the best method of dealing with this child? I decided to talk about myself: 'Arden, do you realize Toni and I have been worried out of our minds? You were supposed to be home by twelve, and it is nearly three o'clock.'

'I couldn't help it. Jill got sick and Len took her home early and so I had to wait until the other kids were ready to go and they don't have these stupid rules and they dropped off Doris first and then Binky, so I just got here now.' (Indignant.)

'There is such a thing as a telephone.'

'I didn't have any money left after the pizza and the movie.' (Implicit reproach: insufficient allowance.)

'You do have friends from whom you could borrow a dime,' I said, exasperated.

'I didn't think of it.' (Leg thrust out, hand on hip, mouth angry, patience fading fast.)

'Arden, do you want us to be unhappy, fighting all the time? I don't like it. I don't want to live this way. If there is something bothering you, why can't you tell me instead of acting like an irresponsible child?'

When her patience went, it went all at once. What trigger did I press? For she was screaming suddenly, incoherent, teary: 'I don't like lots of things! What good would it do me to tell *you*? You don't care about us! You go away when you want to and come back when you want to! Why can't I? I'm *not* irresponsible! *You're* the one who tries to keep me a child with your stupid rules and regulations, you act as if I was eight years old, you just do it to be mean, you hate me, you hate us both, you're worse than Daddy!'

At which she raced from the room, up the stairs, and into her room, completing the scene with the obligatory door-slam.

Oh, that simmered down too. A week or two later, six

months even, she might be teasing me, lying at the foot of my bed watching me drink coffee on a Saturday morning, or cuddling next to me as I sat in bed – I never got over the habit of working in bed – adding up my expense account, or transferring notes I'd scrawled on bits of paper, about f-stops and light and shutter speed, to permanent record books. Toni would be downstairs writing, he wrote all the time then, he rarely came out of his study except to pee or get more coffee.

It would be late morning: a sweet light filtered through the trees outside my bedroom window, and it was quiet. All I could hear was the clatter of birds, Billy and Jonas throwing baskets out in the driveway; I could hear the ball hit the backboard, the boys yell scores, the ball bounce on the concrete garage apron and the shudder of the backboard again, and the call, over and over, like surf.

And Arden chatting and giggling, a cozy domestic scene, it made me happy . . . confiding in me (the boys all like Binky best they like Jill too but not is there something wrong with me I don't think they like me as much sometimes I feel jealous of Jill and I hate myself because she's my best friend and I don't want to feel jealous of her I love her do you think I'm ugly homely pretty *really* pretty, really? and it makes me mad that she's popular and I'm not but I don't want to be mad at her I hate feeling jealous why do I am I awful do other people feel jealous do you think she feels jealous of me is that why she said because that really hurt me why does that happen and what can you what can I what do grown-ups do about it?).

During those times I could occasionally get her to dry a dish or clean her room a little at least and she went to school every day and even did some homework. And then I'd go away and come back and she'd be terrible again and I couldn't understand it because here she was almost sixteen years old and acting this way, you'd think she'd be used to my traveling by now, what was the matter?

I asked her. She blinked, she shrugged, she denied she was angry about my traveling – she just threw that at me when she was angry about other things, she denied that she behaved badly after I'd been on a trip, denied that she was difficult at all. The only thing she didn't deny was that she was in love with Toni. She told me about this one evening, it was after her sixteenth birthday, Billy was doing homework in his room, Toni was working, and she asked if we could talk and she turned off the television and we poured Cokes and took them up to my room and sat on the bed and she began to discuss her sweet sixteen birthday party, who had said what and done what and what she felt and what did I think that meant?

So I was able to ease the conversation toward her feelings about boys in general, Toni in particular, and sex. Arden was describing Jill's relations with Len and Carey, and I listened carefully, and then said, 'It sounds as if you're telling me that Jill is having sex with Len.'

My directness took her breath away for a moment. She tried to read my expression. 'What if they are? Lots of kids do it. You know, things have changed since you were young, Mom.'

'But Arden, how much do you all know about what you're doing?'

Look of disgust. 'Oh, Mom! We all know everything.'

'Really? That's amazing. I don't think *I* probably know everything.'

'Really?' What don't you know?'

I just looked at her and we both broke into hysterical giggling.

'So you-all think you're old enough, and know enough. But then why did you put it the way you did, asking me what I thought? I don't believe you're so sure of yourself. And tell me this: how many of you know anything about birth control?'

She shrugged. 'Jill's on the pill. Her mother took her to the doctor and got it for her. And Binky has a diaphragm. Her mother doesn't want her to go on the pill so young. But,' here Arden lowered her voice and her tone became hushed, awed, shocked, 'Gloria Caron, a girl at school, you don't know her, she had to have an abortion last year.'

'And what about you?'

'Well,' she was scratching a mosquito bite on her leg. 'I tried it once. With Len. One time when he and Binky had a fight and weren't speaking, and he was depressed and he begged me. I told him I was afraid Binky would get mad at me, but he said she wouldn't. But she did. She wouldn't speak to me for weeks until I cornered her one day and said we had to talk and we did, we went to the soda shop and I told her how it happened and that I didn't want to try to take Len away from her, that she was more important to me than Len, and she cried and said she was terrible because she was blaming me instead of Len and she knew that was wrong and she'd try not to, and after that we were friends again. Anyway, it wasn't much,' she concluded.

'That's too bad.'

'What's too bad?' Wary.

'That it wasn't much. I would have liked your first experience of sex to be beautiful.'

Suspicious. 'It can be?'

'It can be. But it has to be right.'

'What does that mean?'

'Well, it *doesn't* mean screwing some boy to make him feel better about his girlfriend. Or doing any boy a favor.' She stopped scratching. 'It is right when *you* want it, want it very much, and trust the boy you're with and know that you aren't going to get pregnant as a result of it.'

She pondered. 'Yeah.'

'Frankly, I think you're a little young for sex to be right.'

Straight back, angry eyes. 'Mommy! That's not true! All the girls are doing it!'

'I doubt if *all* of them are doing it. And even if they are, that doesn't mean they are really enjoying it. I don't know if this is true, but it seems to me women develop desire later than men. I'd bet most of them are doing it to please the boys.'

'Mmmm.'

I had her. It was a tricky business, capturing her interest and trust, and I couldn't be sure I'd keep it, but I tried by remaining honest. So I was able to convince her – not that this was made explicit – not to have sex unless she deeply, profoundly, *wanted* to have sex. I was able to extract a promise that she would let me know if she were seeing someone she desired so much that she would really enjoy sex with him, and we would go together to get her measured for a diaphragm. Things *had* changed, even young girls could get them now. When I was young, you had to be married.

In time, I moved us onto the subject of Toni. She was relaxed now, my old little girl, lying across my legs fiddling with her hair.

'Yeah. I do, you know. I love him so much. And he's so cute. I think about it a lot. And you know?' she sat up and smiled at me with astonishment, 'I think I could do it, I could get him if I tried. I think he loves me too, and would like to!' Showing the delight of a little girl who one day realizes she is attractive, I thought. I did not let myself think about how I felt about all that.

'I'm sure you're right. He *does* love you,' I smiled.

'But,' she sank back down again, 'then I think that if we did I'd keep thinking about who was better, you or me, and that would drive me crazy.'

'That's an extremely intelligent perception,' I said, every inch A Mother. 'That's exactly what would happen and it wouldn't be good for you, it would make you anxious.' Not a word about how it would be for me, or for Toni, or whether he even could under such circumstances, or would, although I suspected that if I gave him tacit permission, he yes he would have, no wonder he didn't want to screw around, he had all the turn-on he could handle right at home. Arden was beautiful.

We got through that, and afterward Arden seemed to flirt less with Toni. I think. We got through everything in the sense that we went on living together, getting up and going to bed, banging on bathroom doors, eating meals together, talking, cleaning up. But the feel of things changed, was changing, the texture of our lives, the color. Because nothing dramatic happened, we told ourselves – or maybe it was only me – that things were all right. Yet beyond my thought, beyond my awareness, things pulled at me, wore on me like weights; it's more than time that pulls down the facial muscles, the flesh inside the upper arm. It isn't just age that makes you walk more slowly, slump when you walk, look weary.

We survived. In the fall of 1966, after a hellish year – late nights, marijuana, failing grades pulled up at the last minute – Arden went off to college. I felt it was a miracle that she got in to Cornell with her grades, but she had a high IQ and high SAT grades. Many youngsters were failing in those years, drugs were becoming rampant in the schools, and she wanted to be a poet, so maybe they judged her by less rigorous standards than, say, science majors. Before she went she was happy with me: I was buying her clothes, I was helping her pack, I drove her up to Ithaca.

Still, I breathed out when she was gone. Even the good times between us were poisoned, because I never knew what would set her off, could never forget that she could be set off, so I was always edgy with her. It is hard to live with hatred. But after she'd been gone a month or two, I convinced myself that all that was wrong was that she needed a space of her own, and college gave her that. Things would be fine in the future, I thought: because she called me regularly, she sounded cheerful, happy, there was love in her voice. And she was excited and loving when she came home for Thanksgiving and for Christmas – for a few days. Then things deteriorated – as if she went around a corner and found herself suddenly in a sharp dark place, or fell over an edge – she'd lash out and move into a morose rage, in which she took every remark addressed to her, every plan that involved her, every reference to her, or any omission of her, any plan that didn't involve her, as a slight, an attack, darts aimed at her, lethal. Then she would retire to the corners of chairs using her eyes to shoot poison darts of her own at all of us, especially me. And these states would last for days, would not end until it was time for her to leave again.

In the spring of '67 I went up to visit her at school. She stayed in my motel while I was there and we sat up late at night talking, laughing. She had gone for a diaphragm by herself, and had tried sex many times by then, each time out of desire, she said. But something always happened, she didn't know what it was, the enchantment faded – fast. She averaged two weeks with each new boy. I tried to understand this. I remembered my own high desire at eighteen, my belief that love and desire should be untrammeled, free. Still, something felt wrong. But by then I was totally intimidated by my daughter, afraid to say a critical word lest she go into one of her black moods. I didn't know this then, I couldn't have said it in those words. I was still in the place where my thinking was entirely practical – what to do about . . . I never examined myself, I simply tried to cope.

She didn't come home that summer. She had met a new man, Bill, and at the end of her freshman year she moved with him to a commune way out in the country. It was a small farm without electricity or running water or a toilet. There were eight other people there, some living in a main cabin, some couples in smaller ones. They made music and wrote poetry and raised vegetables. They kept goats and a cow and a horse, and ate only vegetables and cheese and bread, and smoked pot and participated in antiwar demonstrations. She wrote me long passionate philosophical letters, sometimes with a poem enclosed. She was studying wildflowers, and becoming an expert on herbal brews and how to dry flowers, and she picked up spending money by selling bouquets of dried flowers and herbal teas on a grassy corner of Ithaca.

I hoped Billy would stay home more after Arden left. Arden and he hadn't got along well for the last year or two. But he didn't. I didn't think much about it. I was immersed in my career, which was really soaring in those years, and the truth is, I was grateful for the rest, the space. It is arduous work, being a mother – you are constantly overwhelmed by the voices, needs, weeping, arguing, demands of others, you have little or no space of your own. With Arden gone and Billy away from home most weekends, there was some space, some silence in the house. There was only Franny. Toni too was quiet in those years, spending most of his time in his little room near the kitchen, typing, erasing, tearing up papers, typing again. And Billy did spend some time with Franny, he adored her. He taught her to ride her tricycle, how to tell time, and he often read to her. Franny missed Arden, who used to take her for walks and talk about trees and flowers and the look of houses and people, and make up songs about them. But she was a happy kid – she'd had four mothers, and still had three.

Arden came home for a couple of weeks at the end of the summer, but she brought this boy with her, Mike, and expected me to let them sleep together in her room. I said Mike whatshisface had to sleep on the daybed in Toni's study. Toni was pissed at that because the boy didn't wash, he smoked pot in bed, and he smelled up Toni's study, and besides, he didn't get up until eleven and Toni couldn't work. So I told the boy he'd have to sleep on the living room couch, and even though he sneaked up to Arden's room late at night (I knew this but pretended I didn't, learning through parenthood to be a hypocrite), she was angry at my treatment of him and wouldn't speak to me . . . oh, it was disgusting. The two of them left in his battered car, Arden and I not speaking. Yet when she called me a month later, affectionate and lighthearted, she'd broken up with Mike, was with a boy named David, and had forgotten the whole thing. . . .

I had become resigned to Billy's absence from home and the knowledge that he was with Brad. I couldn't speak to him about it anymore, I had such contempt for him. I couldn't get over the fact that my little prince had turned into a toad. To think I'd have a son like that! Oh, I wanted him to go to school and be a doctor if that's what he wanted. But it appalled me that he had such a slimy character. How had such a darling boy become a toady, a slimy calculating ass-kisser? Why had my sweet fiery girl turned against me so that nothing I said or did failed to arouse her rage? Like every other mother I know, I concluded all this had happened because of something I had done – or not done. In rage and guilt, I crawled further into a shell.

It turned 1968, the beginning – I know – now of a period when domestic conflict seemed just part of all the other terrible things that were happening out in the world, as if we were all experiencing an earthquake so huge that it shook the entire globe and toppled, not buildings and hillsides, but ways of life. I wasn't so attached to our traditional way of life that I fought to preserve it, but on the other hand, it was all we knew, and we didn't know what to put in its place.

That fall Billy joined Arden at Cornell. She'd come home for a few weeks at the end of that summer too, wisely alone. I drove them both up to Ithaca, vainly trying to calm the furious squabbles that erupted throughout the trip. The first one was over whose baggage occupied more space, and it set the tone for the rest:

Billy: Arden has too much gear, there's no room for mine, she has lots of stuff up there already; I'm going up for the first time! It's not fair!

Arden: I don't have that much and I need everything I'm taking. He's the one with all the junk!

Billy: Yeah, you need that guitar!

Arden: And you need all that stereo equipment! At least a guitar is a musical instrument, something artistic, whereas a stereo is just another concession to bourgeois consumerism.

Oh? cried Billy. And what was that rug she was taking back with her, *Mommy's* rug that she took right off Mommy's floor!

Arden bristled into fury then, screaming about the cold floor of her cabin, and that Billy wanted her to develop pneumonia (the same argument she'd used, more quietly, to persuade me to give her the rug). There was a long argument about where to stop for lunch, and Arden pouted and refused to eat because we could not find a vegetarian restaurant. After that no one spoke at all. Arden sat in the backseat smoking furiously, as angry with me as with Billy. Billy and I spelled each other with the driving, silent.

We planned to drop Arden off first, at the commune, and have tea and cake there. Following her directions, I turned off the main road at a place unmarked, a narrow rocky dirt road, and bumped along it steeply uphill. After a couple of winding miles, we came out into a green plateau surrounded by hills, with four or five old wooden buildings set randomly among trees. It was beautiful, I could see why Arden loved it. There was a fenced meadow for the horse, another for the goats; and in a sunny field protected by a high fence, there were corn and potatoes and cabbages and lettuce and tomatoes and green beans.

As we got out of the car, some young people drifted out of the house. They greeted Arden without enthusiasm, except David, who bounded out of the house and ran and hugged her. The others stood staring at Billy and me. Billy and I looked at them and – I could feel his feelings – drew back into ourselves. It wasn't the men's beards or the women's long tangled hair, the shabbiness, even filth, of some of their clothes, or the long print skirts the women wore, their headkerchiefs, their plain, unmade-up faces, all suggesting a kind of submissive role – no. It was the way they stood, the way they looked at us, with angry suspicion, wariness, as if they believed that we were there to destroy them or at the least, disapprove. They were embodiments of the paranoia Arden felt when she was in her black moods. Was it generational, then? Or had a group of paranoiacs simply found each other? Was Arden mentally ill?

We didn't stay long. Arden did not seem disappointed that we decided not to stay for tea. She did not kiss either of us goodbye. As we drove back down the dirt road, Billy and I looked meaningfully at each other. We both had the shivers, and once we were back on the main road, we got quite silly, joking and giggling the way we used to. We went straight to the campus and I helped him settle in his dorm room – hang drapes, make up his bed, hang some pictures on the wall. When we kissed goodbye, we clung together. All the way back to Lynbrook, I felt dead around my heart.

Billy behaved in college as he had in high school; he was quiet, hardworking, with few friends. Arden wanted nothing to do with her brother. Neither of them told me this, but I could hear it in Billy's tone of voice if Arden was mentioned when we spoke on the telephone, and hear it in hers on the (now) rare occasions when she called – I couldn't call her, there was no phone at the commune. She ignored him, she never invited him to the commune – not that he wanted to go there. And since they were in different colleges of the university, they rarely met on campus. That hurt me. It hurt him too.

*

Two weeks before Christmas, Toni had his thirty-first birthday and I gave him a party, invited some of our friends from the neighborhood, served dinner, champagne. He was withdrawn and abstracted all evening, and after we finished cleaning up, he told me he was going to work for a while longer. I didn't see how he could work after six glasses of champagne, but I went to bed. When I woke at three and he still wasn't in bed, I got up and went downstairs. The house was cold; the air hung cold, still, and fetid from the cooking, the smoking, the spilled drinks. It was dark, and I tripped against a chair entering the living room. Toni was hunched up in a corner of the couch, smoking.

I went over and sat beside him, put my arm around him. He put his hand over mine, draped over his shoulder. We were silent. We sat there for a long time.

'It was a nice party. It was sweet of you to have it for me,' he said. 'It isn't that.'

'I know,' I said. We sat on.

'You can't solve anything now. Come to bed,' I said. And without a word he rose and followed me.

He had finished his novel a year and some months before. It was good, I thought it was good, I thought it was *very* good, and he did too, so far as he could judge his own work. He probably thought it was a masterpiece. And who knows? Maybe it was. I had inquired about agents among my journalist friends, and he sent me to a man named Jay Waxman who was reputed to have excellent taste. Jay was enthusiastic about it, but it had been making the rounds of publishers ever since. Whey Jay first took it, Toni was elated – Jay's enthusiasm fired his own: he was sure he'd be published and acclaimed in mere months. But the novel plodded from office to office, and he sat waiting for the phone to ring, and he lost heart. One day he got up wearily and went into his study and closed the door. Every day after that he went religiously to his study; there would be a furious spate of typing, then a palpable silence. Three hours later he would come out angry at a noise, an event (garbage collection, a neighbor at the back door) that kept him from concentrating. He would remain sullen and unspeaking for an hour or more afterward.

After some weeks of this, he stopped trying to write, and spent his days in the living room reading men's 'adventure' and western magazines. He bought them by armfuls. Research, I thought. Despair. Soon he returned to his study and was clacking away on the old noisy portable Royal that he'd had since college. He told me he was writing stories, but he did not seem cheerful and did not offer to show them to me. Finally I asked him what he was writing.

'Trash,' he said bitterly. 'If I can't sell my novel, I'll sell trash. I don't care.'

But he didn't seem able to sell 'trash' either.

Then – it was three days after his thirty-first birthday, three days after his bad night (was it suicidal? Had he thought of dying, or just of leaving me?), Toni's novel was accepted by a New York publisher. And while he was still elated by that, he got a phone call from *He-Man*, one of the magazines he'd been submitting stories to: they loved his work, were going to publish the story he'd sent them, and wanted more.

He floated. He walked through a doorway into the Big Time. When I suggested that achieving a degree of worldly success did not make you a different person (it hadn't me. Or had it?), he looked at me as if I was crazy. He began to go into the city regularly – for lunch with his editor in an East Side restaurant; for lunch with Jay in an East Side restaurant; for lunch with the editors of *He-Man*. Jay was sending his stories to film agents, and that excited him more than anything. He talked wildly about what he would buy with the money he was earning. The stories – he sold five of them in three months – each earned him more than the novel that had taken five years of his young life to complete. I read only one. He snatched the pages out of my hand after I'd finished reading it, before I had a chance to say a word. He snarled: 'So it's crap! So what! It sells! You think what you do is so exalted?'

Oh, Toni.

Still, he was high, reading the editor's comments on the novel, editing it himself, then waiting, wondering about reviews. I knew he was walking around the house composing reviews in his head, and that whatever the real ones said, he would be disappointed.

The book was published in early September of 1969. It was dedicated to me. 'To Anastasia,' it read, 'sine qua non.' It was reviewed, in short but admiring notices. It sold 2,500 copies. 'Well at least I earned back my lousy thousand-dollar advance,' he muttered in a new harsh voice. He sent copies to his family, but I imagine they were offended by what they had to see as a family portrait and only his mother wrote to praise him – and she, clearly, hadn't read it.

A few weeks later, Paramount optioned one of his adventure stories. Ironically, it was the story of my Cuban adventure, considerably altered. It had a plucky but naive reporter as heroine and a stupid, venal leader commanding a bunch of trigger-happy ignorant Cuban émigrés. They actually land in Cuba, get into serious trouble there, but a wise and skillful CIA man who had been tracking the raiding party comes in with a group of Alpha 66 men who save the lives of most of the Cubans and the girl. The CIA man ends up with the girl, but of course must immediately leave her to go out on another adventure. The venal leader is captured by the Cubans and left to his fate.

They loved it. They told him it blended humor (the stupid Cubans), drama (the invasion), romance (the girl), and irony – for the entire adventure is pointless and accomplishes nothing. Irony was in fashion in film just then. They said it would make a great film. It did, too. They paid him $10,000 for a year's option and guaranteed $50,000 more if the movie was made. After that he spent hours on the phone with Jay every day discussing 'deals'. He spent the option money on a red Corvette. He wore his silk shirts into the city for business lunches, and bought a suit at J. Press.

two

It is February 1970; grimy remnants of the last snowfall are piled up along fences and curbs, ice-hard, unmelting. Ribbons of ice crisscross each other in the roads of the suburbs, sending automobiles weighing tons shimmying across them. Ice still hangs on some branches of the trees that surround a house with a large garden on Old Hodge's Road, Huntington: it glistens in the sun like frozen tears.

A six-year-old Ford station wagon curves round the bend into the street, slowly, carefully maneuvering the ice tracks. It stops in front of the house with the large garden, and a woman emerges from it, in pants, a ski jacket, and high fur-lined boots. She reaches into the back seat of the car and pulls out a large shopping bag filled with what appears to be clothing. She struggles with it, trudging up the icy walk to the front door, slipping several times. She rings the bell and the door is opened.

The hostess greets her guest in a low voice, affectionately but intensely, in the kind of tone one uses after a death.

Her guest replies in a similar tone and sets down the bag.

The two women kiss lightly and embrace each other, standing close to each other for a long minute, each patting the other's back. Each of them is aware that the usual constraint between them is missing.

'Come on in. Take off your coat. I was so glad you called.'

'It's good to see you.' The visitor removes her gloves and coat. The hostess takes the coat and hangs it in a small closet near the door.

'It's been a long time! Christmas, I guess.'

'Yes.'

The visitor reaches for the shopping bag. 'I brought some things. Franny's just shooting up – she needs new everything! I was going through the clothes she's outgrown, and I thought maybe Jenny could use these.' She points to the bag. 'They're in good condition, just too small. They're probably too big for Jenny, though,' she concludes apologetically.

The hostess gazes at the bag as if she were calculating a sum. 'Oh, let's see. Come in!'

The guest removes her boots. In thick wool socks, she pads after her hostess into the living room, carrying the bag. The women sit near each other on the couch; the visitor pulls out one item of clothing after another and spreads it out for examination.

'Oh! Oh great! Oh, *that* she could wear right away! Oh, that's terrific, she'll love that! The kids really love those thick sweaters these days. She'll probably want to wear it right away, but she'll swim in it. But next year!'

The visitor hears the strain in the voice, the effort to sound cheerful and pleased.

The hostess smiles, folding the clothes up again and setting them on a side chair. 'Well! How about some coffee? Or a drink?'

'Coffee would be great.'

There is a tension between them now.

'I hope you don't mind my bringing them,' the visitor apologizes as the two women walk to the kitchen. 'They were just too good to throw away, and I thought Jenny might like them . . .'

'She'll love them!' the hostess replies, but her voice is loud, there is an edge in it. 'So!' she announces as she runs tap water into a kettle, 'whatcha been doing?'

The visitor, who sits on a high stool near the sink, shrugs. 'Same old stuff.' She lights a cigarette. She is pale, wearing eye makeup but no lipstick; her short hair hangs limply – it could use a shampoo. 'You?'

'Yeah.' The hostess pulls open a drawer in a cabinet and pulls out a nearly-empty package of cigarettes. She lights one. Arms akimbo, each hand clutching the opposite elbow as if she were cold, cigarette dangling between two fingers, she walks across the room and sits in a wooden chair. 'I have a day off today – teachers' conference. Otherwise it's the usual round.'

The two women look at each other. The hostess is wearing no makeup and her hair is pulled back severely and clipped. Her face looks tired and washed out; she is wearing baggy wool pants and a pilled Orlon sweater.

'So how's Toni?' the hostess asks in her loud voice. 'Doin' okay out there in Hollywood?' She seems to find something wanting in her utterance, because before the other can answer, she blurts, 'It's really great! Writing a movie! That's terrific! How wonderful!'

The visitor smiles a little as if she understands something that has not been said. 'It's great for him.'

The hostess leans back in her chair. Her voice softens but there is still strain in it. 'Not for you?'

The visitor shakes her head.

'Why, Anastasia?' the hostess asks quietly.

The kettle whistles and the hostess starts to get up. Anastasia waves her to sit and turns off the gas. She pours boiling water into the filter cone of the coffeepot. Her back to the other, she says, 'He left me with Franny. He promised when I agreed to get pregnant that he'd raise the child. But he went off without her.'

The hostess sits up sharply. 'You wouldn't have wanted him to take her!'

'No.'

The hostess leans back again, there is something sagging in her posture. 'Yes. I see.' She exhales smoke. The tension in the room decreases. 'But at least you can afford to hire someone to take care of her.'

'Yes. But it's awful for her. You know, Arden and Billy are gone, Toni's gone. When I go away, she's left there with a stranger. She's in a state of shock, she has nightmares every night.'

'Oh! Oh! Maybe . . . no, you couldn't bring her here, she goes to school . . . but maybe . . . you could afford it . . . you could move, buy a house near here and then when you went away, Franny could stay with us. The kids are always around, there's always something going on, she'd feel more as if she were in a family. Well, she'd *be* in a family!'

'Joy, that's sweet. Really. But you have your hands full as it is.'

Joy's head sits up erect on her neck. 'We manage,' she says stiffly. 'Everyone has to help out.'

Anastasia hears the anger in the voice. She tells herself it is not directed at her. She directs herself toward *it*. 'Oh, that's wonderful!' Warm voice, smile. 'Do your kids really help? Mine weren't too good about it.'

'They have to,' Joy snaps. 'They have to! I can't do it all. I just can't!'

The visitor ignores the anger, continues warmly, 'What do they do? I'm impressed.'

'Coffee's ready.' Joy walks across to the stove, removes the filter cone from the glass pot and pours coffee into two waiting cups. 'You want to go inside?'

'No, let's stay here. I like kitchens.'

'Me too.'

They carry their cups across to the table and sit down. Anastasia gets up.

'What is it?'

'Milk.' She opens the refrigerator door.

'Oh!' Joy's lips narrow. 'I don't think I have any. I ran out this morning. I meant to go to the store but . . . I forgot.'

Anastasia returns to her chair.

'I'm sorry.' Joy studies her face. 'Can you drink it black?'

'Sure! It's fine. I often drink it black.' Her voice is tight.

'I don't have any coffee cake or anything,' Joy says miserably.

'You know I don't care about that.'

'I was so grateful to have the day off to work on my term paper. It's so hard for me to do big projects like that. Usually I work on them over the weekends, and that's when I do the marketing and picking up stuff at the cleaners and getting things for the kids . . . you know how it is . . . so I just sat down at the dining room table this morning and cracked the books and it slipped my mind . . .'

'Oh, Joy, of course I understand. Don't apologize. Maybe I shouldn't have come today. You could have had a whole day of peace and quiet.'

'When else could we visit? I'm glad you came.' Joy sips coffee and leans back in her chair. She unclenches her left hand. It is dead white. She tries to smile at her sister, but her mouth is stiff. She clears her throat, trying to gentle her voice. 'Anyway, I guess Toni won't be away for too long. It doesn't take long to write a screenplay, does it? How long will he be gone?'

Anastasia shrugs. 'Can't tell. Six months, a year.'

'How long ago did he go?'

'He went in October – a little over three months.'

'So, it won't be much longer.' Warm voice, returning warmth received.

Anastasia smiles. 'So tell me about these wonderful kids of yours.'

Joy smiles too. 'They really are good kids. Well, Jonathan is supposed to do the laundry, clean the toilets, and alternate with Julie washing and drying dishes; Julie vacuums and dusts the downstairs rooms and cleans the kitchen. I'm responsible for everything else. Jenny – well, she's supposed to keep her room clean and set the table,' Joy laughs. 'They're all supposed to clean their rooms . . .'

'And they really do it?' Anastasia sounds amazed.

'They have to if they want clean clothes and a clean house!' Sharp. Then more mildly, 'Oh, they're careless, I have to remind them. But they're pretty good except for cleaning their rooms. They know we all have to pull together . . .'

'What's your schedule like?'

'You don't want to know.'

'I do.'

'Really?'

Anastasia nods.

Joy recounts it as if she were reading from a manual for single parents: Rise at 5.30, make coffee, set table for breakfast while the coffee drips, take a cup upstairs, shower, make the bed, dress, put electric-curlers on head, make up face, wake the children, prepare their breakfasts – frozen orange juice, cereal or muffins, marge a muffin for herself and eat it while making sandwiches of peanut butter and jelly or bologna and dealing with the kids' questions arguments complaints, remind them of their chores for that day, go upstairs, help Jenny get dressed for school, make sure she has her books, her homework, her lunch, throw a scarf over head, put on coat and boots, put on Jenny's snowsuit, walk her to bus stop, return to house. (Variation: in snowy weather: start car, turn on heater and defroster, leave car running.) Reenter house, remove coat and boots, try to stop Julie and Jonathan's argument, make sure they have lunches, remind them of dental or doctor's appointments (variation), kiss them goodbye, run upstairs and remove curlers, leave hair uncombed, putting scarf over it, go downstairs, clear kitchen table, wipe up crumbs, place all dishes in sink and run water over them, turn off heat under coffee, take last sip of coffee, place cup in sink, run water in it, put on coat, boots, gloves, take books, papers, lunch for herself, leave house, lock door. (Variation: in very cold snowy weather: remove ice from windshield with scraper.) Drive five miles to Manners School, park. (Another variation, a crisis: car will not start. Procedure in this case too complicated to be included here. See notes.)

Anastasia sighs. It is only 7.45.

'Go on,' she says.

'Are you sure?'

'Yes.'

Enter school, greet coworkers in office, go to female workers' lounge, remove scarf and comb hair, touch up makeup. Return to office, make or pour coffee (the office workers have their own machine), light cigarette, chat briefly with coworkers, prepare to begin work promptly at 8.00.

From 8.00 to 12.00, typing, filing, answering telephone, taking dictation from school principal, always chosen for this task because quickest and most accurate, making coffee and carrying it in to principal. More typing. From 12.00 to 12.45, lunch. Eaten in office-workers' lounge, with coffee carried from office, while reading and trying to memorize French verbs, the names of generals and important battles during the American Revolution, or the names of the parts of paramecia and amoebae. Brief cheerful chat with coworkers. From 12.45 until 3.00 – except it is never 3.00, more like 3.10 – more typing, dictation, filing. Put on coat, scarf, boots, return to car. (Variation in snowy weather: clean snow off car, run engine and defroster.) Drive at high speed the five miles to the corner of Mill Lane and Hobart Street. Three possibilities: 1. No school bus or child visible: turn off engine, sigh, wait. 2. School bus not visible, but child is: turn off engine, leap from car, prepare to calm down distraught six-year-old. 3. School bus visible but child not: get out of car and walk to bus stop, take hand of small girl who descends from it, lead her back to the car.

(Variation 1: at least once a week drive three miles to supermarket. Get out of car, enter market, pick up: package of hamburger or hot dogs; lettuce; milk; margarine; bread; cookies; any staple needed. PAY for purchases (this action is omitted from the recounting but both speaker and hearer are keenly aware of this step). Variation 2: occasionally, drive small child six miles to next town to doctor's office, escort child into office, attend her there, speak with doctor, PAY doctor by check, leave. Variation 3: same, except office belongs to dentist. In this case, sit in waiting room, reading textbook, no need to PAY immediately.

Drive three miles to house on Old Hodge's Road, get out of car, lift out packages (if applicable), see that child has books and gear. (Variation in snowy weather: mutter self-reminders to sand or salt walk), enter house, remove outer clothes, help child remove outer clothes, offer child cookies and milk. Sit with child, ask about her day. SMILE.

Agree to let child go to play with friend, send up to change clothes. Spread textbooks out on dining table, complete homework. Time allotted to this task varies from none (worst case) to one and a half hours (best case) according to Variations (see above). During this period, older children appear. Hour of appearance varies enormously, as does mood of children. Sometimes books thrown down; doors slammed, voices raised; at other times, smiles, good-natured offers of help. But invariably at some point in this period, argument arises between at least one child and another, one child and parent.

Two nights a week: at 5.15, start to prepare evening meal. Since this must be ready by 5.45, preparations are hasty, meals simple. Best case: leftovers. Small child returns home at 5.30, sits down to eat with mother. Older children may or may not join them. If not, they will prepare their own food, or heat it up later. Gulp down food. Clean away dishes, put in sink, yell at older child for not having yet washed breakfast dishes. At 6.05, prepare to leave: instruct small child to do homework, call out to older children with instructions, run to toilet, reapply lipstick, comb hair, put on coat, boots, gloves, place books in canvas bag, kiss small child, *leave house by 6.15*. Drive twenty miles to local college, park in huge parking field, walk half a mile to classroom, enter, remove coat, sit, chat briefly with acquaintances, bell rings, instructor appears, class begins. Sit nervously in class, unsure French verbs generals battles properties of one-celled animals properly memorized, very nervous when instructor gives quiz, gratified no deeply relieved when quiz papers returned with grade over 85. At 8.20 bell rings: put on coat and gloves, walk to building three hundred yards away, enter, go to classroom, repeat above.

9.50. Leave building with other students but do not stand and chat with them. Walk more than half a mile back to car, enter. (Variation in snowy weather: clean off car windows with scraper first.) Drive twenty miles to house on Old Hodge's Lane. Leave car, locking it; enter house. Pray that all is well there: no arguments, homework done, chores done, children smiling. Prayers rarely answered. Situations often must be dealt with. No capacity left to SMILE. As soon as possible, undress, throw clothes on chair, fall on bed, SLEEP.

Three nights a week: same as above except meal may take somewhat longer to prepare, and after dinner, books taken up to bedroom where sound of television is muted, and homework done there. Many interruptions by children, a long one overseeing small child in bath and to bed.

Weekends: rise at 6.00 or 6.30 out of habit. But a luxurious cup of coffee at table, sometimes accompanied by a cigarette. Ease and quiet, ability to set own schedule marred only by intermittent but regular presence of (always) noisy (often) wrangling, complaining, weeping, angry children.

Invariables: bank: cash check; major marketing; cooking of roast to produce leftovers for week; taking clothes to dry cleaner, picking them up; children requiring delivery service to wide variety of sites; homework, homework, homework.

Variables: shopping for necessary clothes or school supplies for children; shopping for birthdays, Christmas, other occasions when gifts required; medical or dental appointments; crises, internal (child has accident, requires hospital care; child falls ill requires tending; parent falls ill, throwing entire household into confusion; car trouble: see notes) or external (friend calls weeping, requires consolation; friend falls ill, requires assistance; friend rarely seen calls, requiring long telephone conversation). Other: friend or relative drops in; parties or dinners on Saturday night: attended, never given.

'Let's have that drink,' Anastasia says. She thinks but does not say: Her life is worse than mother's was.

They have moved to the living room, where they sit on love seats placed opposite to each other. Joy is less tense, the weariness around her eyes has relaxed a little. Anastasia is warmer. She can ask now, in an easy way, without sounding judgmental or prying, 'So what is it, Joy, what's going on with Justin?'

And Joy can answer, without brittleness or anger, 'Oh, god. I don't know, An.'

Anastasia watches her for a few minutes. 'Are things very bad?' she asks finally.

Joy sighs. 'Pretty bad.' Her head comes up. 'I don't want Mother to know.'

'Why?'

Joy's mouth hardens. 'I just don't! I don't know why, I just don't!' Her eyes are glistening.

'She knows something . . .'

Eyes flare with alarm. 'What did she say?'

'Oh . . . not much. She was putting out feelers to see if I knew anything.' Anastasia's tone is guarded, she is being careful about what she is saying. 'Just that you look tired, that it was strange that Justin went back to Texas so soon last Christmas, that she's worried about you.'

'*I don't want her to know!*'

'I won't say anything.'

'Promise?'

'Promise.'

Joy looks around, finds a crumpled pack of Camels. 'Can I bum a cigarette?'

Anastasia hands her one, she lights it nervously. She blows out smoke and begins to scratch her hand. Her thumb is red and raw. 'It was true, what I told everybody when I first came back to Long Island – I did want the kids to have a real home, I wanted a permanent home too after all those years of moving, moving . . . And I didn't want to live in Texas. I don't know a soul in Texas, I wanted to be near my family, my old friends, not that many of them are left . . . But I do see Kitty occasionally, and Penny Dyckman – you remember her, Penny Swopes – she lives near here, in Old Westbury . . . And Justin was only going to be in Texas for three years.

'I talked about it for a long time, he got sick of hearing it, he finally said okay, go ahead, but he wanted me to settle in Washington because he figured he was in line for a post there, he had some inkling they were going to assign him to a high-level job in the Pentagon . . . But I don't know anybody in Washington except some Army wives I knew in Germany or the Philippines, whose husbands are assigned there now, and I don't like them, I didn't want to be with them, I *hate* them, I *hate* the Army!' Her eyes fill.

'He still isn't sure that's going to happen, he won't know for another few months. Anyway, the understanding was I'd come here and settle and he'd come up whenever he could and then if he was assigned to Washington, he'd commute, he could drive or fly easily between here and there, it would be fine and I said it was about time I had my way about something, for fifteen years I moved and moved and dragged the kids around and I'm *sick* of it! *Sick* of it!' Her eyes fill again and she inhales deeply, leaning her head back against the couch.

'I suppose I'm wrong. Justin's mother, Amy – you know how I loved her . . .' Tears appeared again. 'Awful to say, but I loved her more than I loved my own. Well, in some ways. She's been so kind to me. Well, he must have told her something because she flew out here last month, she said she wanted to get out of Iowa in January,' Joy laughs, 'but what she really wanted was to teach me how to be a proper wife. She kept talking about it – you know, what wives have to put up with, it's the nature of the job, she says. She does have a firm character, she's great . . . And how Army wives have to be especially dedicated and oh all that garbage I can't stand it I could care less I have to have some life of my own or I'll go crazy! Those women, those Army wives, all they do is play cards and drink, drink, drink, half of them are alcoholics, well you can see why, they can never do anything of their own, they start and get settled and then boom! they're moved halfway around the world. I just couldn't stand it anymore!' Joy stares straight ahead.

'I completely sympathize, Joy.'

Joy shifts her eyes to her sister.

'You know I do, know I would. I couldn't stand being someone's wife as an occupation even *without* moving around.'

Joy expels a forced hard laugh. 'That's true!' She sips the last drops of her drink. 'Maybe I am weak or selfish or whatever. Maybe I don't have a great character. But you know I just can't worry about that anymore, I can't stand that life . . .'

'I understand. So Justin's angry?'

'Angry!' She leans back tiredly. 'He's in a rage! Well, you know, he came at Christmas . . .'

'Yes. He seemed strange.'

'Well, he was already angry – at my moving here without him. But, you know, he's so unfair. *He* goes off for months at a time. If I'd stayed in Texas with him, he wouldn't have been home for Christmas – last year, I mean – because he was on a secret assignment, I think he was in Iran, because he sent me that vase as a Christmas present when he came back,' Joy nods toward an exquisite Persian vase sitting on one of the Korean chests, 'and when he came up at Christmas, we were arguing, and he said something about Moslem women and how they're kept in line, it sounded as if he knew what he was talking about, as if he'd seen something . . .

'Anyway, the kids were supposed to go down and visit him over the summer, but he had no place to put them up, so in the end we decided he'd come up the following Christmas, this past Christmas.

'And I don't know . . . maybe it was because he was angry with me . . . or maybe it was because . . . you know, every other place we've lived has been for him, around him . . . you know Army housing, usually right on a base. We were surrounded by Army, everything was Army . . . so in a way, wherever we lived, the house, the surroundings, it's all been his turf, sort of . . .

'But this house wasn't. Isn't. It's *mine*. I mean, he paid for it but I *feel* it's my house. I bought it, I've arranged it . . . well, not around *him*. He wasn't here. So I arranged it for *us*, for our comfort, our pleasure, the kids and me. And when he walked in the door last Christmas, he looked all wrong in this house. He just *did*. Well, I thought he did. I couldn't help it, that's how I felt. He *looked* wrong and he *acted* wrong. The way he walked, I mean. I couldn't help it, he looked so ridiculous the way he walked, like an automaton . . . ordinary people don't look like that. When you're on an Army base, you don't think anything of it, everybody walks like that, but in a real house it looks so strange. Have you ever noticed the way Justin walks? Does it seem strange to you?' Joy appeals to her sister.

Anastasia keeps her face as expressionless as possible. A fight isn't a separation, a separation isn't a divorce. 'Well,' she temporizes, 'he's a soldier, of course . . .'

'And the way he talked. I'd got out of the habit of hearing him. He doesn't talk, he *barks*. Barks orders at the kids, at me. Like he's talking to his men. Subordinates. And it made me dizzy. I couldn't look at him, I couldn't talk to him, I just felt dizzy, faint, all the time. I couldn't eat. I'd forgotten what mealtimes were like, the silence, because he never let the kids talk at the table, so mealtimes are silent, so silent, all you could hear was his chewing . . . oh, I couldn't stand his chewing, chomp, chomp, so *thorough*, a couple of times I just got up and ran upstairs, I couldn't sit there . . .' Her hands are at her sides, lying on the couch, clenched and white.

'So . . . he could tell something was wrong. Well!' she hoots, 'it was pretty obvious! I couldn't sleep with him either, I said he snored, I went and slept with Jenny, we slept with our arms around each other . . . So of course he was furious. And I didn't know what to say. I mean, I didn't want my marriage to break up! How would I manage? And I didn't want to be a divorced woman, it's . . . oh, I'm sorry, An, but it still seems terrible to me, divorce.'

'You were aghast when Brad and I divorced.'

'Yes, I guess I was.' Reluctantly. 'I guess I wasn't much help to you. But I couldn't understand it. Brad was such a doll.'

'In your eyes. He liked you. He always flirted with you.'

Joy bristles. 'I don't know about flirting, but he was always nice to me. But I know you never know the truth about people, how they are with their kids, their wives . . .' She moves her hands, uses one to scratch the other. Her red thumb blooms redder. 'But I *couldn't*, I just *couldn't* go on living with him. There was no way. I couldn't stand anything about him. The way he talks, those chopped phrases, all the numbers, he's always talking about numbers . . . I felt he was a robot, sex was like sleeping with a robot with moving parts . . .'

Anastasia reaches across the cocktail table and picks up her sister's glass, cocks an eyebrow. Joy rises too, nodding. The sisters move toward the kitchen, Joy still talking.

'What I really want . . . well, of course it's impossible, I know that, so I couldn't do or say anything, I couldn't propose any arrangement because the only thing I want is to stay married but not live together, to have him go on supporting us, but never see him.' She explodes with laughter. 'Crazy, huh?'

They reach the kitchen, Joy fetches ice and begins to refresh their drinks. Anastasia sits on the stool.

She sighs. 'You're constantly blaming yourself or defending yourself. As if you were required to do all the bending – which I guess women are. But the situation is simple enough. You don't want to live with Justin anymore, you find him intolerable as a husband and as a father. But you know that once men get divorced they don't support their kids, and you know *you* can't, and so you are paralyzed, you don't know what is the best thing to do. If you were alone, if you didn't have kids to take care of, you'd just leave.'

Joy stares at Anastasia. 'What do you mean?' She hands

Anastasia a glass, sips her own drink. She leans against the sink.

'Think about it. Think about yourself. You don't look too great right now, you're worn out, but you're still terrific-looking. If you were alone, you'd hie yourself into the city, get a high-paying job as a supersecretary, get yourself a neat little apartment, buy some great clothes, have fun. You make friends wherever you go, you might even meet another man.'

Joy closes her eyes. 'I never thought about it like that. If I were alone, if I didn't have kids!' She thinks for a moment, then shakes herself, shaking it off. 'Oh, what's the point of thinking about it? I can't even imagine it. I *do* have kids.'

Anastasia sits silent, staring at the sink.

Joy moves. 'Let's get out of the fucking kitchen! I *hate* the fucking kitchen!' They return to the living room, sink into couches, light cigarettes.

'So what happened?'

Joy breathes deeply. 'Well. Let's see. It's hard to remember the order of things. Where was I? Yes, so I wouldn't sleep with him and he was furious, and all I could do was cry because I couldn't tell him how I felt . . . you can understand that . . .' She glances up, and Anastasia nods.

'And I said I was confused about things and he had to give me time to think and I didn't know what to do.' A frown settles on her face, meditative. 'You know, the *kids* had forgotten him too! They didn't like the way he talked – barked – at them, the way they couldn't talk at the table, I let them talk at the table, it's crazy, what is the matter with him? Why shouldn't they talk? So they were acting strange with him too. They looked at him as if he was . . . an *enemy*.

'And I guess it finally got to him, maybe he finally felt it, noticed the way they looked at him, I looked at him. He doesn't usually pay attention, it's like we're all subordinates to him, he doesn't care if his men like him or not as long as they obey. But he sort of had to notice that I wouldn't sleep with him, or that the kids kept forgetting he was there and breaking into conversation at the table . . .

'He had a ten-day pass, but he left the day after Christmas, he had five days left but he just packed his bag and went to Iowa.'

'So *that's* why Amy descended on you last month! What did you tell her? I mean, how did you leave things, what was her understanding of the situation when she left?'

Joy stares listlessly across the room. 'I don't really know. She talked and I listened. I didn't argue except to say that the kids needed a home, some permanence, some continuity in their lives. I told her a little about how they'd been getting. . . .'

'How *had* they been getting?'

Joy's mouth tightens. 'Oh, I don't know. Sort of jangly and nervous, always arguing. Oh, they still do, I guess all kids do, but the last couple of years there's a different quality to it, a feeling of . . . I don't know . . . hysteria. They still are like that,' she adds, staring across the room, her face deeply furrowed, tight.

'It happens when parents aren't getting along, when there's a divorce, when things around them start to fall apart,' Anastasia says authoritatively. 'My kids did that too. Took them a couple of years after the divorce to calm down.'

'Oh. And Jenny bursts into tears at the least thing . . .'

'Franny does that too, since Toni left.'

'Yeah. And other problems . . . school . . . things like that. Getting along with other kids.'

Anastasia murmurs sympathy, falls silent.

'I can't figure out whether it was our moving around so much, or whether it was Justin, the way he treated them, the way he was. Is. But you think it's our separation,' Joy concludes in a cold voice.

A spasm of irritation crosses Anastasia's face. 'No.' Irritation in the voice as well. 'That's not what I said. I think all of it contributes, anything that gives kids a sense of instability. There isn't anything you can do about it, Joy. It isn't your *fault*, for god's sake! Most families experience problems, dislocations, crises at some point. Kids just have to learn to handle them, same as we do.'

'Oh.' Fists unclench. 'Would you mind if I had another cigarette?'

Anastasia tosses the pack across the table to Joy's lap. 'Help yourself.'

'I'm smoking so much. I shouldn't. But most days I only have two or three cigarettes, some days I don't smoke at all. Like tomorrow, I won't smoke at all. But then, in one night I can smoke a whole pack. I hope I'm not leaving you short.'

'I have another pack. You're lucky, not to be addicted the way I am.'

Joy's face relaxes a little. 'Yes, I am lucky.' She lights the cigarette, exhales deeply, lets her face smooth out further, and leans back luxuriously as if the nicotine were a shot of relaxant. 'Anyway, I don't know what Amy thought. She's really terrific, Amy, but she . . . well, of course she adores Justin – he's her only son. And Jane lives so far away, she's lived in London for years. I don't know what she sees when she looks at him – she probably still sees him the way he was, her baby, you know. She was sweet, she kissed me and hugged me when she left. But she probably left feeling that I wasn't going to change my mind.'

'So then Justin writes saying he wants a divorce, he doesn't intend to spend the rest of his life living in quarters, he doesn't want a frigid wife and kids who treat him as if he were a monster, what have I been doing to them brainwashing them to hate him . . . stuff like that. Oh, it was awful! And he said since I was working and not staying home like a proper mother, he wasn't going to support us anymore unless we all lived together and he gave me a month to decide.'

She stubbed out her cigarette, lighted another.

'It's so ridiculous! The amount I earn is ludicrous, thirty-eight hundred a year, what can you do with that? I can't even pay for our food, and after taxes it's even less!'

Anastasia bursts out angrily, 'Oh, that's terrible! Why don't you get a job in the city? Secretaries earn decent salaries in the city!'

'Oh, Anastasia! I'd be gone from seven in the morning until seven at night. I'd have to spend money on clothes and I'd have commutation . . . I just can't be away from the kids that long, and in the end I probably wouldn't have that much more money either!' Joy calms a bit. 'It won't be like this forever. In another two years, with the credits they're giving me from Hilton Academy, I'll have a degree, and I can teach. Teachers start at seven thousand. That's why I'm putting myself through this ordeal.'

Anastasia grimaces. 'It's ironic. He blames you for working, saying it isn't proper for a mother, and here you work for slave wages so that you *can* be a decent mother! They've always got you, coming and going. It's always been like this for women!'

Joy stares at the redness on her thumbs. 'My hands are all broken out,' she murmurs. 'Nerves, I guess.'

Anastasia waves her hands; Joy tosses the cigarette pack back to her. She lights a cigarette. 'Did you answer his letter?'

'Yes. I wrote that I could understand how he felt but I wasn't going to move the kids again. And that I'd give him a divorce if that's what he wanted, but he'd have to support his own children. And that I never tried to turn his children against him. You know, An, I never say a word against Justin! I never have, no matter what I felt. Even when he was strapping Jonathan for some little thing, and Jonny was only a baby, he was four or five, I didn't say a word in front of them. I've always supported him!'

'That's true.' At what cost, too: so brittle, edgy, you were.

'Anyway, I haven't heard anything since I wrote. It was only last week. I don't know what's going to happen. But he didn't send me the usual check on the first of the month – he only sent me a few hundred dollars. Not that he's been sending me what he agreed to before I came. He says it costs him more to live than he thought – so the hell with us. It's been tight ever since I bought the house. *Don't tell Mother!* That's why I got the job in the first place. And I figured things weren't going to get better with him, so I started school – I can't go on working for such measly wages. But this month I couldn't pay the mortgage. I told him in my letter – after all, it's his money we put down on this house, does he want to lose it? But I haven't heard anything.'

'It may be time to hire a lawyer.'

'Oh, Anastasia, how would I pay him?'

Anastasia's mouth is grim. 'I know. Christ! Always the same fucking story! All they're good for in the end.'

'What?'

'That's what Mother thinks. She never says it straight out. That all men are really good for is to bring money into the house. That's their entire function once they impregnate women.'

Joy lifts her head, laughs. 'It's true, she does believe that!' She wipes her eyes, sighs, folds her hands in her lap. 'I hope she's not right,' she says in a small voice.

'It's what she thinks, it's not how she lives. Dad is more to her than a paycheck.'

'That's true.' Joy frowns. 'At this point, though, I'd settle for a paycheck.'

The sound of a key turning in the front-door lock startles them. The door opens, both women focus on it, alert. Jonathan enters, his face pink and puffy. He glances into the living room, sees his mother and his aunt, turns away, and starts for the staircase.

'Jonathan! What is it? Why are you home so early?' Joy cries.

A muffled voice retreats up the staircase. 'I got sent home. I got expelled!'

Joy rises, white-faced. Anastasia rises, moves to Joy, puts her hand on her arm. 'Wait. Don't get upset. It could be nothing. Arden was expelled a couple of times, just for a day or two, an argument with a teacher, lateness, they may just want him to apologize, it may not be serious.'

Joy turns her drained face toward her sister. She utters a tiny moan. 'It doesn't matter. It's one more thing and god, I'm so tired. I can't take any more. I don't understand how I got into this mess. How did I, Anastasia?'

'By caring about the kids,' Anastasia says bitterly.

three

Women: caring about the kids or ending up with them, somehow, willy-nilly, refusing to leave them. We cannot give them up. So rare is it that when we do newspapers report on it.

Like me, lying on my bed wondering why I ever got married to anyone at all, and my kids informing me sweetly that if I hadn't I wouldn't have them.

I scoffed, but that was cynicism. I adore them, I would not be without them. Then and now: I still . . . what can I call it? Not love. More than love and not excluding hate. My heart is tied to them with unbreakable cord. The cord is scarred, pulled thin, has been hacked at, but it does not break, it is a towrope stronger than what it is attached to, strong enough to rip apart the heart before it break.

There we were, the two of us, my mother's daughters, not yet her shame (but that would come: 'What did I do that both my daughters are divorced? No other children in the family are divorced. Is it something about me?'). We were already bitter, even before we knew that Joy had only a few months left in her beloved house: Justin refused to pay for its upkeep and she had to sell it, give up the one prize she had garnered from what was it? fifteen, sixteen years of marriage.

Then she had to tell her mother. But Belle did not judge her, raise eyebrows, ask prying questions; she and Ed closed around Joy as if our family were celeries instead of carrots, clung to her tightly to keep her up, to keep her children up, helping her with money (all they could spare) and child-tending and moving to a small apartment – Belle washing and drying all the dishes and putting them away in the tiny kitchen with its few cabinets ('Well, at least these have doors, Joy'), Ed putting up curtain rods and pictures, moving chairs from one side of the living room to the other as Joy, face strained, voice tense, trying to fit the old dream into a shrunken reality, says, 'Well there will be less housework now,' and sells off whatever she owns that is of value. Within months, we are both recognizably, publicly, without men, raising children on our own.

But I knew already, that February, about Toni.

I know that Toni isn't coming back, no matter what he says or thinks. I imagine he tells himself he is because otherwise he would lose all self-respect. He does not intend to be a bad person, he does not want to feel like a bad person. He is having fun and does not want self-contempt interfering with his pleasure. Toni is out in Hollywood writing a screenplay, earning hundreds and hundreds of dollars every week, driving his red Corvette, living in a rented house on the beach in Malibu, he's on top of the world, his family is even speaking to him now, now, suddenly they're proud of him.

Trouble brought Joy and me closer too. Finally one day she asks *her* questions and gets answered truthfully: 'How long did you say it takes to write a screenplay? He's been gone an awfully long time.'

So I tell her. The truth. For the first time in our lives, we are telling each other the truth. Will this last?

I told her about the day Jay called and told Toni Paramount was picking up their option and would like him to write the screenplay. I'd just come back from a longish trip, and I was doing my laundry. I heard the phone ring and when I came up from the basement Toni was standing in the kitchen with his back to me, he was staring at the window, and I asked who had called. He turned around, the light behind him. His hair was on fire, his eyes were like flares. The only time I'd ever seen him look like that was the first time we'd embraced each other, the first time we made love: burnished. Rose-gold. Body taut, afraid to move, afraid a shift in position will shake the dream loose.

He spoke just above a whisper, afraid to move the air. He told me. And in that instant I knew it all, saw it all.

Or did my sense of it impel me into making it happen the way it did?

Screenplay. Hollywood. Money. Fame.

I didn't move immediately to embrace him, sensing his need to be inviolable just then. I waited until my exclamation, the congratulations, the felicitations, all that was over, before I embraced him. But he wasn't there. His body eluded me. It was inside my arms, but he was not present in it, it was living on some other plane. Although a second later he hugged me back, he tried to hug me back, he tried to be present. But I knew.

How long, I wanted to know. I asked this with trepidation, not wanting him to perceive the ground of my fear. It wasn't separation from him I feared: he'd been gone from me for a long time. I was terrified I was going to lose Franny. But I didn't want him to know this, I didn't want to ruin his moment of exaltation by intimating that his leaving would not devastate me, nor to give him any more weapons than he already possessed. There is, after all, vengeance in every heart, and I knew he had never forgiven my betrayals. My guilt was weapon enough for him.

A couple of months, he thought. Not long. And he'd be making so much money, we could afford to pay someone to take care of Franny when I traveled.

I turned away so he could not see my face. I pretended to be looking for my cigarettes. I was looking for my cigarettes, but I couldn't find them because my eyes were all blurred. He had told me what I was afraid to ask: *he was not going to take her with him*. This late child, this burden, this baby I had not raised completely as I had the others, this almost unwanted young life in the house: I could not have borne losing her.

I yelled enthusiastically, 'I want to hear all about it! I just have to pee, I'll be right back!' And ran into the bathroom and blew my nose and washed my face with cold water and tried to calm down. He wasn't going to take her. I wasn't going to lose her.

When I came out, he was pouring champagne into two glasses, grinning, full of delight in himself. He was himself again, and I could hug him more spontaneously, and he could hug me then the same way, we could be children giggling in pleasure. And sit down across from each other in the breakfast nook, two people who love each other, or who live on the memory of having loved each other, and talk about plans and hopes and break in with congrats and self-congrats and all the excesses of elation, and smile at each other until we wore down into silence, only our hands clasped across the table. In the stillness I saw us as a photograph, framed by the window, the afternoon light tinged green by the shrubs beyond, our heads haloed with sun, the softening colors, yellow and red burnishing the trees in the garden, a portrait of something momentous, what is happening in this photograph? an arrangement mysterious, unreadable, opaque.

I was happy for him. It was the right fate for him, the right future, although I had not realized it before. I could see now it was what he had always really wanted. And why not? The austere dedication to art alone comes late, after the realization that the ability to make art is all one is going to be given; that the acclaim and the reward, the world-hand stretched out to receive what one knows one has to give are not contained within one's portion, that in the eyes of the world, except for ten or a hundred people, one is a failure. Who wouldn't want everything, if it were available?

The slight, beautiful, poignant book about his youth had cost him much and given him little beyond the satisfaction of making it. And I thought: drop your snobbery, Anastasia. You know by now what you never learned in school, that art is what nourishes, what feeds: art is food. The oversweetened or over-spiced food that is most of popular cultures makes a society sick, thin-blooded and vacant; but the wan delicate work of the self-engrossed nourishes not at all, is papery dry as communion wafers offered as body and blood. Maybe Toni's story would make a wonderful movie, maybe it was in its way art.

And maybe he did not have another book in him like the one he'd written. What could he write about the last nine years of his life that would not be received as a joke? A diary of a house-husband, like accounts of housewifery, offering the tragicomedy of the quotidian in the self-deprecating humor of those who realize their insignificance? Could he lavish pathos on the last years of Pane's life? On learning to love somone else's children? On having, finally, his own baby? On what it is like to take care of them, every day, every day, what it costs, what is repaid, what it really feels like to hear a child scream in the middle of the night, or the other feeling that comes after they've been crying on and off all afternoon? Fear and rage and absolute love are matters for tragedy, but how could the man write tragedy with no prince or king, no sword or gun, no castle or palace but only someone wearing an apron with a diaper thrown over one shoulder, only the dailiest of scenes, the kitchen, the nursery?

In truth, it was no life for a man, the life he'd been living for the past nine years.

That's what I thought, sitting awake in the dark living room that night, Toni in the deep sleep of the drunk. He'll have a hangover tomorrow: champagne. Thought — and then caught myself. If it was no life for a man, then why was it an acceptable life for a woman? Everyone thought it was, even women. Not me, though, I'd always hated it. I'd evaded it, scrunched down along hedges, shimmying through sewer pipes, finding ways to avoid the main highway. But it was crazy, all mixed up, because partly I liked it. But wasn't everything like that? I loved my work and my worklife; I loved being away from home, traveling, photographing, meeting people, carousing, going to bed with whom I felt like, living 'like a man'. But I hated it too, often — the tedium of travel, the anonymity of most hotels, the need to wind yourself up like a mechanical toy to meet new people, to converse, to impress, to act alive when you simply want to feel at rest. You can't feel at rest when you are traveling, even when you sleep. For that you need home, the kids, Toni, the contentment of tedious eternal recurrences.

No life for anyone, maybe, stuck in one or the other. And Toni deserved his chance, any chance. Still: a part of my heart petrified that day, even as I congratulated him and he congratulated himself, as we celebrated, as he crowed, pouring more champagne. As if I'd had a stroke and a part of me ceased to feel, stopped moving.

What I couldn't understand, was *how could he do it*?

I didn't say a word, I didn't show a thing on my face, I didn't question or challenge. Because if I did, he might feel guilty and decide to take her with him. And then I would die.

So *how could he do it?*

I hadn't really wanted her, a child twelve years younger than my youngest, a baby when the older ones were almost grown. I hadn't had her fully voluntarily, I had had her as a gesture of love to Toni. For Toni.

She was his. But he could leave her.

How could he do it?

Oh, I know how he managed it on the surface – claiming he was going only for a few months, that he would be back by Easter, maybe even by Christmas if things went well. But how could he not know that he was lying? He even talked about it, explained that he'd thought of taking Franny with him, but had decided against it. She had just started first grade – he had walked her to school himself that first exciting day; in California he would have to find a place to live fast, maybe just a small apartment or even rooms somewhere, it would not be a home for her. And he would be gone all day every day, working at the studio, she would be left with strangers, she would be lonely, frightened, she would miss her sister and brother, her mother. It would be bad for her. I agreed. But still I wondered how he could stand the pain of the wrench of the unbearable loss of . . . and the even worse pain, the knowledge of her agony in losing him . . . How could he pack his bag and load his car and drive off leaving her behind? She watched him pale-faced, in shock, her little six-year-old body stiff and aghast on the sidewalk, waving furiously even after his car had turned the corner. I knew he would never come back: did she? Did he?

Yes, Toni packed his J. Press suit, his silk shirts, some new Italian shoes and a new Brooks Brothers blazer and slacks with the best of his remaining clothes into the back of the Corvette: his plan was to drive to California and see the country. He made a point of the fact that he was leaving behind his old manual Royal, as if that were proof he planned to return. He took a thick envelope of photographs of all of us but mainly of Franny. I felt sure, although he didn't mention it, that he'd make a stop in Dayton, Ohio, to show off that Corvette and maybe the clothes. He left at the end of October, when the kids were supposed to be at school, but both of them came home for two days, to say goodbye, to hug him one last time. Arden cried, and even Billy had tears in his eyes at the parting, but Toni was hearty in his assurances that it was only for a couple of months, that he'd be back before they realized he was gone. They chose to believe him, or act as if they believed him, and they were used to separations, so they did not mourn. Except Franny, who had never before been without her father. Then Arden and Billy went back to school and Franny that night crept up to bed bereft in the deserted house.

So what I had to think about, that night in October one month before my fortieth birthday, the night I sat up in the cold living room smoking, thinking about long ago when I used to do that while Brad slept the sleep of the blessed, the dense, or the drunk, was what was I going to do? what was I going to do about Franny? With whom I would not willingly part. But whom I had unwillingly to care for.

I wasn't sure I wanted Toni back. Not that I didn't love him, not that we didn't have, together, a sweet intimacy and acceptance that kept us both warm. But I had broken his trust in me, and he had remained but withdrawn from me – I could feel his furious need to get out. I don't believe he doubted my love for him, no matter what my sexual habits. I don't believe my sexual habits even really bothered him. I think he felt that a real man, a man as men are supposed to be, would not accept such behavior from a wife. So the sight of me made him feel diminished, less of a man. And he already felt unmanly.

We live in a world that requires something other of men than that they raise a family and love a woman and write sensitive delicate prose in a small back room of the house. At the beginning, when he chose that course, he was still a boy and thrilled by his rebellion against the world of men: it made him feel strong. But whatever either of us might think or feel privately, we could not escape the world's judgment. As the world judged us, against our will, willy-nilly, we judged ourselves and each other. The world gets you. It got Brad, it got Toni, and through them, it got me.

It was time for Toni to move on. If he had not, his contempt for himself would have spilled over onto me and he'd hate me for his jailer. And I would in time – did I already? – feel contempt for him for passively accepting himself as a failure.

It seemed strange to me as I sat there, cold, a blanket draped over my shoulders, that neither of us had mentioned the possibility that we would remain together, he in California and I in New York, occasionally commuting across the country. Or that I could move to California: 'It Never Entered My Mind': I began to hum that song, always a favorite. No. It had reached its full organic growth, our union, and had to end. I had no right to quarrel with whatever he did, I had forfeited that right. He was young, unimpeded by children now, he would find a new woman – he had to have a woman – and make a new life.

My fortieth birthday came and went. Toni called and sent flowers. Billy called the following day – he'd forgotten under the pressure of a chemistry exam. Arden called a week later saying thanks for the sweater, but she was no longer celebrating her birthday, she was renouncing bourgeois occasions like that. She didn't mention mine.

Without realizing it, I settled into a permanent state of woundedness. Toni had phoned the night he left (from Dayton, and the bastard reversed the charges); then four days later, from someplace in Indiana, two days later from Wyoming, and two days after that from a hotel in Los Angeles. A week went by before he called to announce he'd found an apartment. After that he called every week, Sunday evenings. I will never forget the first Sunday he neglected to call. I let Franny stop up very late – she was so anxious, so sure something terrible had happened to him, that she was afraid to go to sleep. I put in a call to his apartment, but there was no answer. I let her sit on my lap and I turned on the television to distract her. Around eleven, she finally fell asleep, her body heavy against mine, damp, sodden with sorrow.

Franny got in the habit of sleeping in my bed. I didn't have the heart to forbid it, but I worried about what would happen when I had to go away again. I ran ads in newspapers and interviewed people, but every woman – only women applied – seemed wrong. Franny nestled beside me on the couch when I interviewed them, and I could feel her reactions, feel her body tense or withdraw. I trusted her. The women were either puritanical, cranky, sloppy, mean, or unreliable. I worried.

Russ called me with an assignment to go to Belfast to do a photoessay on Bernadette Devlin, and I still had not hired a housekeeper. I asked my mother. She came. She and my father lived in my house for a week: he went to work as usual and she took care of Franny. Mother seemed really happy when I came back and an idea lighted in my head. But every time I spoke to her in the days after my return, she told me how tired she was after a week with a six-year-old, and I knew there was no hope even though having Franny with her would have made her happy. I kept looking for a housekeeper, and finally found a kindly responsible woman, Mrs Czepiel (another Pole! It was amazing).

Franny turned my heart. She was so brave, so sweet. She'd apologize for waking me up by crying out in her nightmare. She was pale and seemed to be holding herself together by will. She had after all, lost three people – her father, her brother, and her sister – in a space of two years. She grew inward, quiet. She had no friends. She sat home and read, or played the piano. She was taking lessons. When I was away for more than three days, my mother would drive over one afternoon and take her back to their house for dinner and the evening, then drive her to school in the morning. She was very good when she was at Grandma Belle's house – angelic.

She mentioned Toni less and less. Sometimes he wrote to Franny, or to me. But intimacy requires continual contact (is your cold better? Did you try those pills? So you didn't sleep at all? Why don't you take a nap while I do the dishes? Did the washing machine repairman come? Was he able to fix it? How much did he charge? Outrageous! So how did Franny manage at show and tell? Was she happy with herself? And what did teacher say? And what about the other kids? Did they like it? Were they good? Were they funny? Oh, Belle got a new couch? What color? What does it look like? Does it look good? Yes, I went to the dentist and I need an inlay, two or three appointments, five hundred bucks, but it's worth it. You know, in the store today I saw a necklace, thick and gold, well, not real gold of course, a sort of collar, I guess, and I thought of you, it looked like you, but you don't wear necklaces. Still, I wondered . . .)

It wasn't long before we were out of touch with each other. Once that happened, there was little to say – we'd lost the feel of each other's lives, and only major events – triumphs or disasters – were worth mention. He had some triumphs, so did I. Franny's, which she continued for over a year to report religiously, were the occasional A on a test, gold stars on test papers, compliments from her teacher, her birthday party and all presents received (Toni sent her a doll with her own suitcase and wardrobe), her part in the school play (she played a tooth), promotion to second grade, her mastery at day camp over the summer of the Australian crawl, the reopening of school, her new school clothes, the occasional A on a test, gold stars on test papers . . . eventually, she flagged. It was too hard: so often when she begged me to phone him, he wasn't home; when he was, he could only repeat the same words, Wonderful, Franny, Great, honey.

I photographed cornfields in Kansas, a bridge in Seattle, the outback of Australia, rioting in Gdansk, two massive peace marches, and the prison at Attica after the massacre. Arden was graduated from college and Franny and I drove up to the ceremony. We stayed at a motel, not at the commune. Arden was going to remain there with Jacob, her newest lover; she would write poetry and sell dried flower arrangements. She was distant, edgy with me – with both of us, really. Franny cried on the trip back; she'd been so excited about seeing her beloved older sister. We went back without either Arden or Billy: he was staying in Ithaca to take some summer courses. I wondered briefly, what my life would have been like then if I hadn't had Franny. I let a glimpse of a neat little apartment in Manhattan, of no more responsibilities, no more concealment, an easy life, cross my mind, then fade. I did have Franny: and I would not give her up. She was my darling.

I still screwed around when I was traveling, but less often and with less joy. It wasn't the same. Before, extracurricular sex had seemed an overflowing, an exuberance, an adventure. Now there was a shadow on it, an edge; it felt urgent, a seeking, a need, desperate. I was looking at every man I met, not with an eye to pleasure, but with an eye to – oh, not marriage, but something permanent, something that permitted intimacy. I didn't like feeling that, and more and more I avoided looking at men at all. I felt old, abandoned, unwanted.

Toni, meanwhile, was having a great time. It took a year to come up with a screenplay they liked, but now the producers were looking at locations, directors, talking about cast, it was all so exciting, he loved it out there, maybe we could all come out and visit, or maybe Franny could, when he had time to spend with her, maybe next year when he wasn't so busy, when things calmed down. I told him I wanted him to come home that Christmas. He said he would if he could, but they were in the middle of all this important stuff. I said he *had* to come home. He came. I had the feeling that if I told him he had to come home for good, he would have done that too. I didn't.

He stayed a week. Franny was ecstatic. Arden had come home that Christmas, bringing Jacob with her (Mother by now having resigned herself to unlicensed sex). She recognized that Toni and I were finished and flirted wildly with him, which sent Jacob into a drugged withdrawal. I overheard her discussing plans to fly out and visit him. Billy, with the same recognition, barely spoke to Toni. I was in deep gloom, I don't know why.

I told Toni I wanted to sell the house and move into the city. There was no point to keeping it, with only Franny and me occupying it. There were too many rooms, the garden was too much for me. He said it was my house wasn't it: I could do as I liked. He said this without bitterness. I asked him if he understood that my moving to the city would mean Franny would have to go to private schools, and that I expected him to pay for that. I don't know why I did that. I could afford it myself. But his checks for Franny's care had been erratic. I guess I was demanding something from him for her. Something I could tell her about, something she would understand. I guess.

Anyway, he just shrugged: if he had to, he would. He made no demurral. He had utterly given over emotional responsibility for her. I had expected him to protest he did not want his child raised in the heat and filth of New York streets, like Brad a half-million years earlier, but he said nothing. I recognized guilt when I saw it: I should, after all. I asked if he wanted a divorce. He paled. He said he loved me. But he wanted his chance, and this was it and it was in California and he knew I wouldn't move out there. He asked if I wanted a divorce. I shrugged.

One night we stayed up late drinking and he told me about the women he'd been involved with out there. There had been quite a few, but right now he was involved only with Gail and Pauline. But he felt inexperienced, he needed advice, a woman's view: why did Gail act that way, what was going on? And how was it that Pauline had treated him like that? Did other men have problems sometimes . . . you know . . . ? What did I think he should do? I told him what I could. Mainly I listened. I knew that he wanted more than advice – he wanted to brag a little, to show me. I let him: he deserved it, he was allowed.

We agreed with enormous civility to grant a divorce should either of us decide we wanted one. When he left, in a taxi this time, we kissed affectionately, like sister and brother. Franny was more relaxed this time, her body leaned into mine. But this time she cried for a long time after he left. This time she knew he was not coming back.

'Saintly, weren't you!' Clara snorted.

'I am, you know,' I said coolly. 'You can be saintly when you don't want anything.'

'Oh, baby,' Clara sympathized (and I drew myself together like a clamshell at the word), 'don't you see? You were still insisting on control. You wouldn't let him know he mattered to you! You would be damned if you'd give him any sign you were jealous!' She said this passionately, leaning forward, touching my hand.

I pulled my hand away. 'Jealous? I'm not a jealous person. I didn't feel jealous in the least. Why should I? I was glad he had other women, it alleviated my guilt.'

'Even Arden?'

I could feel my mouth narrow. 'Arden? Yes. Well, I figured if she went out there and got involved with him – she'd be sorry. It doesn't work to screw Mommy's lovers. She'd find out.'

'Vengeance, saith the lord,' Clara laughed. 'Oh no, you're not jealous.'

'Is that vengeance? I think it's just common sense.'

'Look, whatever you did or were, you loved him and he loved you – once. And for years you believed in him, in his talent, his promise, and supported him, emotionally, financially . . .'

'Yes. But he was taking care of my kids, of me . . . it was so wonderful to come back from a trip and have them all so happy to see me, have Toni happy to fix something to eat . . .' I sighed. 'It was an even exchange as I see it.'

'Even if it was! You loved him and encouraged him and you *did* support him and the minute he succeeds he leaves you. That's a pattern.'

'Not *your* kind of pattern! It's not the typical male-female situation, Clara! Toni was the wife in our house!'

'A wife who leaves you high and dry with a small child to raise, a child he asked you, begged you, pressured you to have. Promising he'd always take care of her!'

'Mmmm.' That part *did* make me bitter.

'And he leaves right before your birthday. Your fortieth birthday! An important one, not to say traumatic. You gave him a party when he was thirty, and another when he was thirty-one. He couldn't hang around for one month?'

'He couldn't hang around period. He got the call; he made arrangements. He was gone in ten days.'

'And that didn't hurt you?'

'Clara!' I was growing exasperated. 'I've told you, he had to leave, it was time. He had to leave and go out into the world and be like other men. And after all, I had been screwing around and he knew that. I had forfeited my right to complain. Why shouldn't he have his chance at sexual freedom?'

'I'm not saying he shouldn't!' Clara was growing heated too. 'I'm saying he hurt you! I'm not saying he didn't have reasons to do so, maybe even a right to do so – I'm just saying that it hurt you. You keep talking about not feeling anything and I'm saying you did feel something, and you keep telling me you didn't because you had no right to! You are being impossible!'

'So go home!' I exploded, rising and stalking invisible enemies in my large, light, plain living room. 'Who asked you to interfere! Do I need you? What do I want to listen to you for?'

She stood up too. 'I won't! I won't go home until I get you to listen to reason!'

'Listen to *you*, you mean! And you are hardly the voice of reason! A person who eats peanut butter out of the jar for breakfast and crackers in bed? A person who rides a bicycle in New York City, breathing in truck fumes? A person who has dedicated her life to not making enough money to live? You are reasonable?'

She started to giggle then, and so did I. 'Oh, Anastasia . . .' She walked toward me, her hand outstretched.

I turned away, I walked toward the kitchen. 'I need some more seltzer,' I said. She sank down on the old shabby couch, sighing. From the kitchen I could hear her, yelling:

'You're full of pity for Franny, losing her sister and brother and father all in two years, but you don't even bother to mention that you lost daughter, son, and husband in that same period!'

I stopped, my hand on the refrigerator door. A memory had just pierced me, cold as the fridge, damp, metallic. Moving. I was moving from that house, our house, Toni's and mine, and I was packing the things from the medicine chest in a carton, and I picked up a bottle. Toni's after-shave. It was a cheap after-shave, but he liked it, and even though the kids would give him better brands at Christmas, he went on using this cheap stuff. And I started to hurl it into the trash, thinking, I don't need this cheap after-shave cluttering up my medicine chest, but it wouldn't leave my hand and suddenly I was bent over the bathroom sink, sobbing . . . I loved that he loved that after-shave, I loved it because he loved it. I sobbed myself dry.

'You keep on denying your feelings. That's why you suffer from zombiedom!'

I returned to the living room with my seltzer and a dish of candy. I handed it to her. I sat down. 'Zombiedom comes from pain. And pain comes from the things that happen. And the things that happen *do* happen, and maybe they're even inevitable. In any case, you can't change them. You have to accept your fate. And if your fate is zombiedom, or carrotdom, then you have to accept that.'

'Ah, Anastasia!' Clara breathed in lament, pushing the candy dish away. Then, face upturned: 'Carrotdom?'

four

In June of 1971, *World* folded. My world folded with it, and other people's. There were hundreds of us out on the street, dozens of photographers used to a high standard of living, out of work. Because I kept myself so removed from office politics and affairs, I'd had no sense that things had been going badly for the magazine. Its failure was a complete shock to me.

I went home – which by then was a light, airy, shabby two-bedroom apartment on the Upper West Side, with a view of rooftops and on clear days, a fingernail of river glittering metallicly – and collapsed in a chair. I'd had lunch with Russ at a little bistro near the office, and he'd told me that the magazine was closing down at the end of the month. There would be no more assignments.

The phone began to ring then, and went on ringing for weeks – other photographers and journalists out of work, wondering where to find work, asking what I was doing. I wasn't doing much. Because I'd always lived simply, I wasn't as desperate as some of them. I had enough money in the bank to carry me for six months and enough invested that dividends would cover the rent on my apartment for the foreseeable future. I had to find work, but I wasn't yet at the end of my resources. It was the shock that felled me – the fact that it was ended so irreparably – for there was no other magazine like *World* – so suddenly, so unexpectedly, the life I loved, the swinging around the world with a knapsack on my back . . .

I had only Franny to fall back on. But the truth is it wouldn't have made much difference (would it?) if my kids had been closer to me, if they had been part of my daily life, because when your work is your identity, people, even family, people you love, can't compensate for the loss. Still, I tried to reach them. I called Toni, but he wasn't home. He wasn't home for weeks. I could have tried to reach him at the studio, but I didn't.

I couldn't call Arden, but I wrote her, and a week later, she called. She was sorry to hear about *World*, but sure I would be all right, would find something, I was strong and independent and I would be all right, that was for sure. The great news was that she and Jacob were getting married, and she wanted me to help her plan the wedding. Where should she hold it? The commune was a bit hard to reach, wasn't it? What did I think?

I summoned up what heart I had and suggested they hold the wedding at Grandma and Grandpa's house out on Long Island. There was a broad lawn, water, it was lovely there, we could have a tent, maybe we could rent rowboats. Oooooh! That would be beautiful, would I help plan it, could she come down and stay with me next month to prepare? And would I check with Grandma to see if it was okay? I said I knew it would be okay but of course I'd call them. Fine: how much did I think it would cost? She and Jacob had only $350 in the bank, and now that I was out of work . . . Did I think Daddy would pay for it? That, I said firmly, she would have to discuss with him.

After that conversation – which occurred late in the evening – I dragged myself to bed and lay there unable to sleep, unable to think, feeling more alone than I had at any time in my life. Around eleven, I got up and dialed Billy. I hadn't called him yet. I don't know why. I kept putting it off. I wasn't worried about calling him late, I knew he studied every night past midnight even in summer school. But it happened I got him on a bad night – he was studying for an exam in organic chemistry and was tense. So I didn't tell him what had happened, I said I was just calling to say hello and I got off the phone quickly. He sounded really worried and I asked him to call and let me know how he did on the exam. He didn't call.

Days I hustled: I called people at photography agencies, ad agencies, travel magazines, even food and fashion magazines, I met them for lunches, dinners, drinks, coffee, I started to gain weight in my poverty. I picked up an occasional assignment, enough to keep me going if I kept on hustling. It was exhausting, but staff positions were not to be found. I spent many days sitting in the apartment. My office had never been so neat. I clipped and filed and catalogued things that had been sitting in manila folders for years. When I finished arranging my professional photographs, I started in on the family pictures. There were hundreds of them. And there were boxes of memorabilia, junk, the tawdry remnants of the past that one cannot part with. I began to sort those too.

It was then that I began to keep a notebook. I'd kept journals when I first started to work as a photographer, but after a few years, they'd dwindled into mere expense accounts. This was different. It was a record of . . . what? An arrangement of thoughts. Paragraphs, not necessarily related to each other, in no particular order . . . a photograph album arranged randomly . . .

Franny was nine, which seemed to be a traumatic age for females in my family. My mother was nine when her father died; when I was nine, I fell in love with my father and my mother wooed me away from him with her stories, making me her confidante, then killed him for me with those stories. And Arden was nine when Brad and I divorced.

Franny – oh Franny was a brave spirit, she tried to

comfort me. She was – like me – very adult at nine; but I remembered how I hid the child I was then. I tried to find ways to let her be a child. It didn't come easy for her. Nor was I able in any consistent way to be the mommy so she could be the baby. I had lost heart. I was a walking zombie. Something I know about sickness – it is utterly self-engrossed.

Franny was mature enough that I could count on her to evaluate the women we hired fairly when we first moved to Manhattan and lost Mrs Czepiel. Together we had found the perfect person – she was Alaia Registrando from Grenada. She was a bit slovenly in the house (so was I), but she possessed an ample lap, a large laugh and an accepting nature. And she was reliable. To find her was like finding a gift, like finding Pane many years before. I could relax, rest myself in the knowledge of her capacity. What would happen to the world, I wondered, when women were all like me and there were no more Alaias. Or Panes.

Franny went to a private school a few blocks from our apartment. Toni paid for it. He could afford it – he was a great success in Hollywood then, in demand – his movie had been a hit. I often wondered how he behaved out there. He couldn't have been the Toni I knew, delicate and tentative and sweet, and survived out there – could he? He called when he heard about *World*, offering condolences with a hearty assurance that I would be fine, I'd land on my feet, I always did. That's what everyone said. He went further, though: he said, in a swaggering voice, that if I needed help, I had only to let him know. It wasn't the offer, it was the tone that offended me. I countered with a tone as cold and haughty as I could manage, reminding him that I had bank accounts and investments of my own and would not need his help, thank you very much. There was a certain self-righteousness in *my* tone. You see? I was saying, you see how prescient I was when I invested my money and concealed it from you? Everything I expected has come to pass: you have left me, and left me with a child to support, the child you swore to care for always; and now I am out of work. Then I bit my tongue. I didn't really have that much – and I had burned a bridge, which someday I might regret. But I couldn't have done it – taken money from a swaggerer. Even if he was still legally my husband. Never. I left the phone and went into the kitchen to make myself some tea. My hands were trembling. I told myself what everyone else told me – that I would be all right, that I would survive.

And I stood there in the kitchen gazing out the window at the back wall of another apartment building, sipping tea, and it struck me with some force that I was a peculiar person, and had been, all my life. Things that seemed large, even absolute to other people were utterly unreal to me. Like cultural rules about sex; or the rules of the institution of marriage; or rules about the proper relation of parent and child. I didn't know if any of those rules were written down anywhere, part of a code, but they were binding and powerful for most people. But I had always had trouble remembering that I was not supposed to feel free about my feelings, about desire; and being married or not being married seemed to me a state of mind. I'd only been married once, according to my state of mind, and Toni was no more my husband now than Brad was, even though a piece of paper said he was. And I wondered if my troubles had come to me because I had ignored the rules.

Grant called often. He still had a job, and once I moved to the city and let him come to the apartment to pick me up, he understood that however I had been bound before, I was no longer. We had dinner, we went to some plays. He talked about marriage. But . . . oh, I don't know . . . I didn't feel the same way about him, or maybe it wasn't him, maybe I didn't feel the same way about myself. Thing was, he was fine as a lover – I enjoyed his moony sensitivity, his eloquent depression, his alienated stance. I loved, when we were in a foreign place, to hear him talk about things, as if he were a resident of the moon, looking down on a psychotic planet. His attitudes seemed utterly right. Things were, as they say, bad all over. The world seemed to reflect his personal state, his depression seemed justified – all the assassinations, the war, My Lai. Grant was sent to My Lai to do a story. Of course there was nothing there – some rubble, the dirt, the wind. Like Theresienstadt, which I photographed, barely able to see through the lens which reflected only my own damp eyelashes: some skeletons of barracks and the spread of brown plains, the wind . . . No sword shining high in the sun as testimony that God had seen and would remember. No god, no memory. All of that bore in on me when my own personal world fell apart. I couldn't even remember the girl I'd been, the girl I saw in my early journals, full of enthusiasm and energy, certain that her country and her government were benevolent, that happiness was part of what people could expect from life.

But if Grant made a wonderful wry feeling lover – not so great in the sack, of course – he would be impossible as a husband. Who could live with that depression day by day? The same hopeless shrug he took to My Lai would be brought to the washing machine when it broke down, a crying child, to my despair about my children . . . Besides, I had no desire to marry again. Why should I? What did I need from it? Only financial security, and it was not possible for me to marry for that. It wasn't my principles, it was my heart that kept me from doing that.

So I'd see him once in a while, and we even went to bed occasionally, but I felt nothing at all. Little by little, I stopped seeing him. He got married a year later, suddenly, to someone he'd just met. I didn't care. I didn't feel anything.

My life was hustling, an occasional assignment, Alaia, and Franny. Franny would think up things for us to do together. She'd pore over the newspaper searching for a ballet or a movie or a play she might enjoy and I could tolerate. She suggested walks and bike rides, a trip to the zoo. I always hated zoos. I saw in her the same despair I'd felt as a child, as a young woman, felt still if truth be told, trying to get my mother to give over her clutched melancholy, her hopelessness. At the same time I felt just like my mother, inconsolable. And I saw our inconsolability – mine, hers, her mother's before her – as the natural consequence of being alive for forty years as a woman. It was inevitable. The only choice was to feel it or not feel it, admit it or not.

784

Still, I didn't want to engender these feelings in Franny, so I pretended to be cheered up. Her efforts touched me as much as anything could touch me. She must have known – well, now I know she knew – that nothing could touch my cold hard core of sorrow, but she kept trying, and I kept loving her, caressing her sweet nine-year-old cheeks, that face full of yearning . . . But the world humped onward in its stumbling progress toward its termination, and I slumped every day further toward my own.

'It's easy to do that,' Clara swoops. 'Blame your depression on the world. Why not try your mother?'

'Oh, please,' I say, laying down my fork. 'If you get on that again, I'm going to get up and leave this restaurant.'

Her eyes fill with tears. 'I'm trying to save you!'

'Do I call you Jesus or Adonai?'

She paled, fell silent.

'Sorry.'

She looked up at me, damp-eyed. 'I love you,' she said.

We survived. All of us. They were hard years. Joy lost everything. Justin eventually followed through on his threat, and filed for divorce on grounds of abandonment. He was punitive about the child support. What else is new? Is it any wonder so many women believe women must insist on virginity and outlaw abortion, in order to force men into marriage and support of their families? But it is incomprehensible to me, one of the world's great mysteries, why men don't care about their children. But then, many men as I've known – known well, because all kinds of truths are uttered over the pillow – men themselves are a mystery to me. How can they get satisfaction from the games they play? How can they enjoy being violent, aggressive, and so utterly isolated?

Of course, I'm isolated myself now. Like a man I put all my worth into my career, and when I lost it, I lost everything. I lived like a man and I guess I'll die like one.

Anyway, Justin sent Joy two hundred dollars a month to raise three kids, offering her the alternative of his taking the kids and raising them.

'Look at him and tell me if any sane person would put helpless children in his hands! He'd teach them to be robots, just like him!' she raved.

We saw each other frequently until I moved to the city, we became friends. Sort of. I don't think I was a good friend to anyone then, not to her or to Mother or to my women friends in the old neighborhood, even though after *World* folded, I saw them regularly. I knew what was happening in people's lives, I told them what was happening in mine, if anything. But sometimes when people called and said how's your life, I'd say what life? Yet I was alive, I must have experienced something.

Joy moved into an apartment complex in Huntington – the rents were high there, but she was adamant about giving her kids a sense of permanence. I don't know how they got through those years. Mom and Dad helped her, and she had friends by then, who did what they could. She did not finish college until 1973. Her kids were giving her problems too – the high school was rife with drugs and Jonathan had been experimenting with them, well, at least with marijuana and mescaline. And Jenny was doing poorly in school. Joy's laugh grew more brittle. But she still laughed. That was more than I did.

And my mother was – what was it in those years? Was that when she told me she was going blind? Or when the arthritis got more severe? Or when she developed gout and had to stay on a rigid diet which curtailed her only remaining pleasure? She was miserable, got more miserable as the years stretched out. She lamented. I listened to everything as if between it and me lay the roar of the sea, as if I heard it over a transatlantic line with rhythmic rushes of static that sounded like wire being brushed by the tides back and forth, back and forth across the ocean floor.

My life ended when I was forty. Oh, I went on breathing and drinking coffee and preferring stew to steak. I even, sometimes, wanted things – a new pair of safari pants with lots of pockets, a neat pair of walking shoes. Once, when I was very broke, I bought a beautiful little velvet evening purse in an antique shop. I didn't need it, I had nowhere to carry it, it was anyway too small, but I bought it, I had to buy it. But wanting was faint in me, the weak cry of a sick infant, a mewling, easily ignored, easily stifled. It was a memory, a habit.

I would sit up at night – why sleep? There was nothing to get up for the next day – and try to recall the passions that had driven me. But I could recall only *facts*, not the feelings of things – my passion to save my children, *save* them from Brad's malignity, for instance. I could recall protecting my kids, I could remember my sense that they were threatened, my belief that I needed to embrace them to carry them away to someplace safe warm safe loving . . . I recalled that I had felt envy in the years of my youth when I heard about someone who was going to travel abroad, or had gone to the theater, or was having a show of their photographs. The most difficult things to remember were the feeling of loving, the conviction that I was loved; and the overwhelming possession of passionate sensuality. I could recall the burning heat in my groin, the pulsing of blood down my thighs, up to my breasts, the sense that if I did not have the person who was standing there (oh, beautiful!) I would die. But I could no longer get hold of those feelings – the clutch of envy, the unbearable pulsations of desire, hollow hungry devouring WANT – they receded tantalizingly like the events of a dream the next morning. Only I knew *about* them the way you know about crops and industry in a country you have visited for twenty-four hours in the middle of a long journey.

Oh, I made demands: I insisted that Franny be given a regular dinner, not fast food, when I was away; and that the lab get my contact sheets done on time; and that cabdrivers follow the route I gave them. I went through motions: sat at dinner tables with acquaintances, with my parents, with my sister, and made small talk. If I saw a man who seemed to be attracted to me I would survey him in the old way, I would try to dredge up a response, to pump up the blood that would flood my loins and mount to my heart and ears, drowning me, drawing him. It was useless, and the few times I went through the motions of sex, I ended as dry as I started, empty, staring at some kind of final emptiness.

Men's sexuality seemed to me meretricious. The reason men were so insatiable, why they went from woman to woman, was that they were repetitively going through motions to prove to themselves that they were still alive. Their lust, their desire, their hunger – it had little to do with the women they desired, little to do with me, it had never had anything to do with me. I was merely a convenient receptacle. Desire had to do only with self, self, self.

But if that was true, then what about me? What about all my passions, all the sweatings, the clutchings and cling-ings and explosions of love, all the tension and need and the long lovely painful stem of desire that rose from my groin, sending roots to my feet, branches throughout my upper body, a flower that had to offer itself to be smelled, plucked . . . was all of that too then just wild attempts to prove over and over and over that I was, am alive alive, present, here, breathing, heart pumping . . .

Only love was different. But love was not part of my portion. I did not deserve it. I did not know how to keep it when I had it. I had a career – I used to have a career – and that was all I was allowed. I had failed as a mother, failed as a wife, failed as a lover, all because I was a carrot and not a celery, I was an egoist, ambitious, willful, wanting my own in everything, insisting on my own will, way, desires . . .

Now all of it was gone. All my late-night hootin' and hollerin', my singing and laughing fests, all my falling on to strange mattresses ebullient with strange men, all of it had fallen away from me like wisps of cobweb in a wind, nothing clings to me, I roar too fast through life for anything to stick . . .

Only the work is left, and my pleasure in that. When I am working, I have energy, drive, I know what I want and I get it. I thank the powers who require thanking for my work. When I am not working, I am tired, I am bored, I am going through motions. I often want to die. I wake up in the pale sick morning light and lie there trying to force my eyes to remain open. Franny has gone to school and Alaia has brought my coffee in on a tray. I pull myself up and look at the clock. I don't want to get up. It is time to get up, but what for? What is there waiting for me out there in the day that is worth such an effort?

I do get up eventually, and go through the requisite motions to prove to the world that I am alive. And then I fall into bed at night, and if I have not drunk enough, or have not exercised enough, I lie there plunging into the black hole that is my heart, plunging deeper, dizzy, hoping that this time it will be permanent, that I will not have again to face the morning, not again have to face another night.

I cannot cry. I think of Arden and Billy and I feel I have a sponge for a heart, a sponge that is squeezed, so tightly it compresses to the size of a marble, cold and hard and impregnable in the palm, and the pain of that is unbearable, unbearable. Why do we do it, I wonder. Why have children, give them so much . . . Well, perhaps they would say I did not give them so much, I did not give them enough. But me, I feel as if I gave them everything, squeezed myself, my sponge heart dry over and over in worry and caring and attention, to make them happy, to make them able. But they swallowed me up and stayed hungry, they never had enough mother, there is never enough mother, don't I know? And they stand unforgiving, glaring at me. And I can't cry.

I want to die. It is true I lost Brad, but that was long ago; and true I lost Toni, but I conspired in that. And I lost *World*, too, but that was reparable. But to lose *them* that way, those babies who came out of me, who were literally fed by my body, my blood, no symbolic communion wafers and wine here, the real thing, body and blood, who went on being nourished by my body and blood, or at least heart and mind and soul and sweat, how could it happen, how can it be explained?

Why do we go on doing it? Why didn't Frances leave those children in the orphanage and go off and make a new life for herself? She was only thirty-two, hardworking and skillful and responsible, sweet, attractive to men. She earned her own living, she might have found a better man that time, or just forgotten about men and made herself a better life. Why? Why did Belle stay with Ed when he was showing her he wanted more, when he forced her to swallow the bitter pill of her need for him? Why didn't she leave him, us, go off and make a new life for herself, create a career? She was attractive, smart, able. Why? And here we were, another generation, why were we repeating this past? Why did Joy live as poorly as Mother, as Grandma ever did? Stinting on food, living in tight unpleasant quarters, scrimping on everything, wearing old clothes to keep her kids, keep her kids. Why didn't she send them to Justin and the hell with it?

For generations – for centuries – for millennia women have dedicated their lives to saving the kids and we were continuing the tradition. Sweet, martyred and sighing; honest, angry and yelling; tender, tough and mean, whatever, however they acted, women gave up their lives, any hope of a life, to raise the kids, to make things better for the kids, to preserve the children. And the children, in their turn, *turn*: the mother was martyr, screamer, a calculating bitch. She was not what was wanted. There is no end to the bitterness in their hearts against the mother, no end in mine, no end in yours, no end in theirs.

Why can't I leave my children who have left me? Why can't I find the right-sized knife to carve them out of my heart? or a potion that will make them fade, as Brad and Toni have faded, pass off into memory, become just two more portraits in my album? Why do I continue, in my crowded space, to reserve a space for them? to give them house room, who have repudiated my house? Why do they lie undigested at the top of my stomach, burning? How can I so much love them, who hate me?

I will not love. I will not feel. There is a place beyond pain and pleasure, I intend to find it, perhaps I have found it. My mouth tightens, my cheeks sag, my chin droops in disappointed sacs. I am developing my mother's aged face sooner than she developed it. Already my hair is greyer than hers. Perhaps I will die before her, too. It would be a gift.

Chapter XIV

November 21, 1977. I am forty-eight today. I have just opened this journal – the first time in over a year – and what I saw on the first page made me shiver: 'I feel that when I finish this volume, I will die.' The book – crimson covers with black leather edges, where did I get it? – is nearly full. When did I write that? The entry isn't dated. Why did I write it? I am not usually superstitious, but this prophecy makes me uncomfortable. Maybe because it is traditional for a book to end with a death – unless it can end with a marriage. Yet here I am, continuing to write, steadily, tensely filling the last few blank pages.

There are seven books on the shelf. The first one is not dated, I often forget dates, but I think it was in 1972 that I started writing down fragments of – well, feeling, I guess, although I was convinced I no longer felt. Just around the time that Billy started medical school: fall of '72. After my father retired – that was when? – '71. Arden was married in August of '71, a beautiful wedding on the broad lawn of my parents' house out in Suffolk, a white-and-green striped tent, rowboats on the lake. Brad was there, heavier, red-necked, face swollen, suffused with pink, biting his lip – I knew the look, it meant that he was controlling himself, keeping in the rage and sorrow he felt at what I'd done to him. But he had his wife with him and I was alone: he didn't think about what that meant. After all, he has had the life he wanted; as I did. What we have now is the consequences of having wanted what we wanted, and those are always sorrowful. *For matter is never lacking privation; and inasmuch as it is under one form, it is deprived of another.*

This journal-keeping isn't a regular occupation, months go by and I don't open the notebook, but then the day will present itself – there will be a little blue visible in the sky behind its usual pallor or maybe it will be an especially dark day on which it is impossible to take photographs – and I will sit down at my desk and write for an hour or two, lifting my head often to look at the closed-in sky. I would like to move away from here, to a place where the sky is huge and spreading and deep and you can see the stars at night, but I have to stay here, this is where I get work.

I get mostly commercial work; I have enough assignments to

get by. I still live simply, so I can afford to pay for Franny's school tuition, which is expensive. Toni isn't doing so well in Hollywood just now; he says he's nearly broke. Whereas we can live on three or four assignments a year. Last year I photographed an offshore oil rig for an oil company ad, and earned enough to live for six months. That was good, because I didn't get another assignment for six months. The great advantage to this moderate poverty is that I have time to do my own work.

My name is still associated – to the degree anyone remembers it – with the heroic, the large-scale, man's domination of nature. This makes me uneasy, I feel like a spy, a pretender, because I no longer find humans heroic. I find most of the works of human hands pathetic or absurd; only the beautiful – in whatever way – seems admirable to me. Shooting grandiose structures feels like prostitution, wage labor. I do it competently; I have enough experience to hand clients what they want. But I hate it and myself for doing it. I do only as much as I need to for survival.

I still photograph for myself, as I always did, and in my personal work, it is the private, the daily, the small acts that make up the texture of a life that interest me. I go to Harlem, the Bronx, or Little Italy, I seek out places where women still hang wash on the line, children play in the streets or sit, large-eyed and vacant, on the steps of ravaged brownstones; where the young of both sexes adorn themselves like tropical birds and flaunt themselves along the sidewalks. I photograph butcher shops where meat hangs on hooks in the front window, and vegetables piled with proud artistry on stalls in front of grocery shops. These become, daily, harder to find in Manhattan. They are completely gone from the suburbs.

I go to Coney Island and shoot elderly people sitting on benches on cold sunny days – I like photographing two old women schmoozing with all the sharp expressiveness of age in their faces and gestures. I take the ferry to Staten Island and shoot people coming home from work. I especially like to shoot people with children – talking to them, playing with them, ignoring them, comforting them, scolding them, raising their hands to them – when they are unaware of the camera. I feel I am recording the ethos of a time.

I think about things more now. I have the leisure and the solitude. Only Franny breaks in to remind me that I am not living in an isolation cell. We no longer have Alaia, alas. I couldn't afford her when I started paying for Franny's school. And once Franny was fourteen, she didn't absolutely need a woman of Alaia's great talent. But we were both distressed saying goodbye to her, and once in a while, she stops in to see us. Now when I have an assignment that takes me out of town, Franny goes to stay with her friend Jillian, whose parents are happy to have her.

I don't really have anything to write today, I don't know why I opened this book. Maybe because it's my birthday: one more. Franny is taking me out to dinner tonight to celebrate, if that is the right word. She is dear, as always. She clings to me, I cling to her. There is a great vacancy in my mind, in my heart. All I can think of are facts, the kind you write in a letter to be mimeographed and sent to all the old friends and relatives along with the Christmas card.

Dear————. (Name to be filled in by hand)

Billy did very well in college and has gone to medical school at Harvard. We are very proud of him.

Arden is married to Jacob. They live on their farm (social license) outside of Ithaca. Arden has had two babies, two boys, Jeremy and Jeffrey, who are now three and one, respectively. She is expecting a third child next month. The babies are adorable. We are very proud of her and them.

Joy has also finished college and has a job she enjoys as business manager in an insurance company in Huntington, which pays more than teaching. Her children are all fine. Jonathan got a football scholarship to Ohio State, and wants to be a coach; Julie got a scholarship to Stony Brook, where she is majoring in psychology. Jennifer is fourteen now, and a cheerleader, just like her mother! We are very proud of all of them.

Belle and Ed are still living in Brightwaters, and they keep busy. We are proud of them for managing to live so long.

Franny is fifteen now and a sophomore in prep school. She loves to play basketball and she makes excellent grades. We are very proud of her even if she is mad for the Rolling Stones.

I am fine too. I have just come back from photographing a plant in California, part of a new burgeoning business, computers, for a business magazine. It was interesting and *very* lucrative. We are very proud of me.

We are proud to announce that everyone is fine. Everything is great here. (Can you say the same? Aren't you jealous?) Have a happy Christmas!

Love, as always . . .

It sounds wonderful. I am impressed myself. It sounds like a happy ending. It seems you can always have a happy ending, no matter what really happens, simply by selecting what you choose to leave out. You leave out the fact that Billy and Anastasia see each other rarely, and that this grieves the mother; that the same is true of Arden and Anastasia, an even deeper grief because when they do see each other they fight, sometimes violently; and that Jacob is ethereal to an extreme, flaky is the word. He doesn't look Anastasia in the eye, ever, and rarely looks at anyone else either. He doesn't walk, he floats; his body seems attached to his head by thin, loose wire. When he speaks, he speaks to Arden, who translates for him to the world. And you leave out, entirely all of Joy's suffering and struggles, her problems with Jonathan (drugs) and Julie (hostility to her mother, sullenness) and Jennifer (a sense of not belonging, unhappy shyness).

Besides that, you must be careful to end your book in time, before terrible new things occur. I think I will end this one here. It seems right.

December 1, 1977. I've started a new book: Book Eight. I decided not to risk finishing the other one. Besides, it is time for a new book since I seem to have been given a second chance. It arrived last month, on my birthday, actually. This magazine called me, a feminist magazine called *Woman*, and asked me to fly to Houston to photograph the women's convention that was being held there. Because they called me so late, I figured I was their second or third choice, and considered standing on my pride and refusing. But I was feeling so low I thought it might do me good to get out of the house and shoot something that wasn't machinery for a change. And besides, even if I am not a member of any organization, I am certainly a feminist at heart. So I went.

It was spectacular. Partly it was a war, involving strategy, alignments, and regrouping. First A struggled against B, then where A was defeated it decamped; leaving B against C, then BC against D, while X waited over the next hill, preparing a massacre. Men are probably used to things like that, but women aren't. And partly, it was a religious ceremony.

The beginning was bad. A convention of furniture manufacturers, all men of course, had been meeting at the hotel where most of the women had reservations. When the men heard who was coming next, hundreds of them decided to keep their rooms an extra day. So when the women arrived, there were not enough vacant rooms for them. The hotel didn't want to offend the furniture manufacturers, who might want to return, whereas the women certainly wouldn't, so they were gentle with the men who were overstaying. The result was that for two days there were huge lines of women winding several times around the lobby, with their baggage heaped in the center.

This confusion was complicated by the fact that many of these women had never traveled far before and didn't understand the system. They were delegates elected by local women's organizations, and their way was being paid by government agencies. Many of them were poor, black, old, impaired, and/or did not possess credit cards. NO CREDIT CARDS! How can you expect to stay in a hotel without a credit card? the hotel clerks gasped. The women intended to pay in cash. That was unheard of, put a crimp in the system, and took hours.

Most of the women found beds. Only a few slept in the lobby, curled around their bags on the cold marble floor. The rest doubled up with friends or strangers, or took cabs to seedy motels on the other side of town. No room lacked a crowd, women slept on the floor without complaint. And they all stayed up all night talking, laughing, sipping wine. The next day, the women were incredibly bouncy – proud of their resourcefulness, joyous at sharing and from their talk sessions – tired as they were, and even though most of them had once again to stand on the endless lines in the lobby. They didn't get angry, they coped.

'Typical,' Clara said dryly.

Dialogue overheard: Standing in an elevator crowded with furniture manufacturers and their wives – the men wearing nametags on their lapels. Tom Brokaw gets in. The men recognize him.
    'Hey Tom Brokaw, nice to see you.'
    'Yeah, we watch you all the time.'
    He nods, agreeably.
    'You here for this bunch of broads?'
    'I'm covering the women's convention, if that's what you mean.'
    'Oh you poor guy!' Guffaws.
    'I don't know why you say that, I'm finding it fascinating,' he says stiffly, and gets off at the next floor.
    Silence.
    What are they thinking?

Fascinating it is. Thousands of women from all over the country, all ages, colors, sizes, shapes, classes, together in as democratic a spirit as I have ever seen in a large group, mixing, merging, talking, laughing, arguing about points in the document they are about to vote on, a document answering the age-old question, *What do women want?* This will be sent to President Carter to help him in making policy; it will be a public document, so anyone who really wants to know what women want can find out just by reading it. The women believe, utterly, that what they do there matters, that it will inform government policy-making for the next decade. They meet in caucuses, they argue, debate, weep, scream, fight each other, fall into each other's arms. They gather in the great hall, hushed, awed by their own participation in the democratic process. I am moved, watching them. They have so much energy, so much faith.

The two most debated points are abortion and lesbianism. The deck has been stacked by the right, which started early to form local organizations, so that as many delegations as possible be made up of religious women – Mormons, and those Catholics and Protestants who could be trusted to vote against these issues. Some of the delegates want to yield these points, fearing a walkout, a ruinous split in the convention; others accuse of cowardice, of selling out. Passions simmer, rise, boil over. For the delegates it is a struggle between life and death, good and evil.

The antifeminist forces have massed themselves across town, at the Astrodome, where Phyllis Shlafly is a puppet for the men. Man after man – low-level politicians, military men, born-again homosexuals – strides up to the podium to shout horror of sex, abortion, sex, homosexuality, sex, the devil. Families have been bused in by their churches from all over the southwest, from the west as far north as Utah, from the east as far as Georgia. They fill the Astrodome, they rise to their feet, stamping, cheering with ferocity. A woman alone, I feel frightened there, people are looking at me, where are my husband, my children? Why am I carrying a camera? Taking pictures? I am afraid they will mob me. I try to work my way out, slowly, no sudden moves or sharp gestures. But even as I walk safely, breathing slowly, deeply, down the last staircase, I hear their fervor. No positive chords here, no agenda for the future, only terror, knowledge of the anti-Christ. What constitutes life, the good, is not made explicit, perhaps it does not need to be spoken, presumably they all know, for they rise, thousands of them at once, screaming death to the devils on the other side of town.

Back to the Coliseum. Voting has begun. It is hard now to keep this hall in order. Calls for votes, gavel rapping, requests for silence, a chair who refuses to respond if she is addressed as 'Madame Chairman', insisting on 'Chairwoman'. Women line up in front of microphones to speak for or against each issue.

The abortion problem has been eased by renaming it so it does not come up first in the alphabetized list of resolutions and split the convention on the very first vote. Now it is called Reproductive Freedom. The vote is for, the hall explodes, everyone looks around to see who will leave, and women do, rows of them, how many? Will this destroy the convention? It takes twenty minutes for things to settle down. About a hundred women have left, a handful in that hall, there is more cheering, silent sighs of relief.

The next stumbling block is Sexual Preference – lesbianism. The hall falls as still as such a hall can be. The arguments begin. Betty Friedan, who in the past, fearing loss of mainstream women, opposed it as a plank, gets up to urge it. The explosion cannot be contained, it goes on and on, the chairwoman cannot stop it, women are jumping on their seats, whistling through their fingers. The resolution in favor passes and thousands of balloons are released, thousands of voices raised in cheers, no one leaves this time, the convention as a body has chosen to be courageous, to risk opprobrium, to support all women, even those traitors to the system who do not desire men.

I am very busy. I shoot fifty rolls of film that afternoon. I would like to feel superior to what is going on; I know how the men I know would see it, I know their thinking: they admire men with power, and adopt the way those men think. They call it being realistic. I want to be realistic, which in this case means having contempt for the naïveté and simplicity of these women. But I can't. Something is blocking my 'reason', something odd is happening inside of me. It feels like an unborn baby turning itself completely over in my uterus, I am dizzy but I keep my hands steady, my eye focused. I go back to the hotel exhausted, eat a sandwich alone in my room, lie back on the bed still dizzy. There is a sharp pain low in my gut like a baby wanting to be born.

I think about my origins as a photographer and the hundreds of pictures I took of babies and their mothers, of women caught, trapped, bewildered by motherhood, impaled forever on their ambivalence – love and resentment in almost equal proportions. How I did that coolly, with the eye of an outsider, as if I weren't one of them, caught in the same knot. As if I were *objective*.

And before that, when I was young, unmarried, a girl. I didn't want to be a woman, no, not at all. In the first place, I knew how men looked at women, talked about them, had contempt for them, preyed upon them. But more important, I didn't want a woman's life. And I tried not to have one, fool that I was, as if you could renounce your body, as if a woman who was drawn to men could escape. Even women not drawn to men can't escape – if you are a woman, you are treated like one. I had a woman's life in the end, no matter what Mother says.

I didn't want to be a woman because I didn't want to have a life like hers. I knew somehow, even very young, that lives like hers were built in for women, they had no choice about it. How old was I? When I set my teeth and swore to myself that I *would* have a choice, I would not live like her. I had watched too carefully her endless labor, the tedium of her days, the insufficiency for anyone's life of the tasks and worries that filled her days, day after day after day. Even her satisfactions – stretching a few dollars far enough to put good dinners on the table for her children and Ed, or to buy a cheap remnant of a good quality fabric to make new dresses for the girls for the first day of school or a coat for Easter Sunday; or saving dimes and nickels for months to take them on a week's vacation in the Catskills (and it rains), to pay for a small present at Christmas – oh, the farmwoman's joy at half a cup of milk saved, an extra egg, to bake a cake for her child's birthday, all the scraping and worry, all the labor, the painstaking work done by hand, all the planning and foresight, so pathetic, it makes me even now want to scream, to hurl something across the room: it is unbearable!

I leap up and run to the toilet. I have diarrhea. My head aches. I walk back, drained, and fall on to the itchy bedspread.

Oh god my heart aches thinking about it, about her. When in her there was a mind that needed something other, a body that needed . . . something. How she suffered the pain of something thrusting, like grass, that has to be pressed back day by day. I remember. I did it too when I was first married, when the children were small. It makes you tired all the time – constantly pressing back tiny shoots of impulse and desire, fixing your face, guarding your gestures, so they don't show, so you won't recognize them.

I wanted to avoid that but I didn't. I just didn't suffer from it as long as my mother. Mommy. Oh, Mommy, I slipped and slid, I evaded, and in the end, I escaped. But into what? I spent ten years of my life in a man's world, meeting, speaking to, dealing with men only. The only women I met were girlfriends and secretaries. It was a rich time, I saw the world, I learned how to behave in it. I learned utter self-control – not to cry, not to lose my temper hotly, only coldly, not to show I was hurt, and in time, not to feel hurt, and in more time, not to feel anything. I learned to deal with the Orson Sonderses, the Woody Hedgecocks, the Russ Farrells of the world, with whom it is fatal to betray the slightest tremor of feeling. I mastered my feelings so completely that they disappeared and now I cannot find myself.

I learned to function superbly in the system; I would never find myself ignorant and bewildered, humiliated, insulted, like the women who stood all night on a line in the hotel lobby, the women who were turned away. The knowledge made me firm and hard and I do not regret it. It also left me depleted, abject, alone.

I took my pleasure – warmth and closeness and fun – where I found it. I don't regret that either but it too had a cost. After how many? countless men, some sweet, some sexy, some fun, but some who raked my soul like the young man, Michael his name was, strange I remember that name, a man I met in a small town in upstate New York when I was shooting Lake Erie for a story about pollution. He flirted with me all night, then after we'd made love, said 'How do you know I won't leave here and tell everybody about you?'

'What?'

'Sure. I mean, it's a coup for me, fucking the great Stacey Stevens. How do you know I won't tell the world?'

I looked at him in disbelief. Who was he, anyhow. 'You won't,' I said. What was he telling me? That he had fucked me not out of desire but in order to score? Was he telling me he hated me? Hated women? Hated easy women? What was he? Oh, I didn't care what he was, I cared that he left me with a problem, because the next time, and the time after, ever after that I would wonder when a strange man flirted with me, *is he doing this because he desires me? or because he wants to brag about a coup?*

Or the man I invited up for a drink, it wasn't late, I didn't want to go to bed, I was high after photographing all day, where was I? Bologna, I think. There was no bar in the place I was staying. And I gave him a drink and we talked and I realized I didn't like him and I said I was tired and asked him to leave and he wouldn't. He said my inviting him for a drink was tantamount to inviting him to bed, and he wasn't going to put up with my being a cocktease. He was six foot five and weighed over two hundred pounds, and he stood, head down like an animal, threatening me. I put on the cold contemptuous act, and bullied him into leaving, but the memory of him didn't leave me.

Or the contained young Swiss, very stiff and formal when I met him, the representative of a company whose works I was shooting, who after dinner got a little high and stumbled speaking English and became charming, mixing German and English without realizing it, became funny, so I took him home with me. Who after we'd made love, sat up stiffly, suddenly, and announced in perfect English that he was married and expected me not to make trouble for him. Or the sweet Norwegian, who ran out the next day to buy me a piece of jewelry, as if I expected payment for my services.

The cost accrued. Spontaneous sex was fun until one day it

was no longer worth the trouble, when I could take one look at a man and know which form of injury he would do me.

I hadn't always put my career first; I had never treated my children as given, the way men do, ignoring them yet expecting them to love me. I hadn't. But had that helped? Worrying about the kids, feeling guilty at leaving them, missing them, being as concerned about them as about my career only helped to age me. And they turned against me anyway. Except for Franny – so far. I'd escaped nothing.

And now, here were these women. The men I knew would scoff at these women, would howl in derision at their impracticality, their delusion. I'd heard them belittle even *men* who talked about hope; and any woman was fair game for mockery – 'present company excluded, of course', with a laughing nod in my direction. They didn't think of me as a woman, but as one of them. And so did I.

Lying there on the lumpy hotel pillow staring at the carefully-chosen-to-be-inoffensive wallpaper and drapes which nevertheless offended me, my insides completely turned over. As if I had, from youth, been looking at life through a pair of bifocals and just now discovered there were two ways of seeing through bifocals: you could look up – or down – and things looked somewhat different. Suddenly it seemed that the occupations of my mother's days, the meat loaf, the lemon pie, the smocked pink dress she made me when I was eleven, were as important, more important, than all the dams and hydroelectric plants, the oil rigs, the highways, the articles, the photographs, the magazines that occupied the other world, the world I was part of. And that she was as heroic, more heroic than the men who built cars and planes, paved roads, shot bullets at each other, dropped bombs. Because what were they doing and what did it cost them? The highest price extracted from such men was their lives; they never had to pay the higher price, the price she'd paid – daily sacrifice, slow torture, day by day by day, the hard way.

Even forget sacrifice: I never worshipped sacrifice, never wanted to sacrifice, I wanted to *live*, to experience everything. And I had – everything that seriously mattered to me. No, we shouldn't judge according to sacrifice but according to what a person gives, what contribution they make to the huge intricate organism that is the world, and what is worth what. And there was no contest. To nourish children and raise them against odds is in any time, any place more valuable than to fix bolts in cars or design nuclear weapons or certainly, to take photographs for a magazine.

Oh, I know the world would say I'm crazy. But I have been

thinking about all this ever since I came back from Houston. Here I am, nearly fifty years old, looking back at my past and feeling as if I'm reviewing the biography of a dead person, yet I'm unable to say here or here is where I went wrong, this was my mistake. I don't feel I made mistakes: but if I didn't make mistakes, how come I ended up dead while I'm still breathing? I approve of what I had and how I lived given the information I started out with. It was that information that was flawed. Because I was taught that life was split into two parts, one for women, the other for men. If you were an extraordinary woman, you could take the man's role. And I was and I could and I did. Veni, vidi, vici.

But somehow, even though I was extraordinary and filled the man's role, I still had to be a woman. And even if I hadn't had kids, I still would have had to be a woman, because how many men are willing to be housewives for women? I had to be a housewife, somebody in the house has to, and even though for some years I had a man who did it, I had to do it too. And when I was being a housewife, I always felt resentful about it. I felt I was doing menial work, the damned laundry, the boring marketing, the dismal cooking. I was too intelligent, too talented, to do such stuff. That wasn't the part I'd chosen, I just had it dumped on me.

But seeing those women has changed the way I think about all this. Maybe it wasn't just seeing those women. It has taken me years, but now that there is only Franny and me and the kitchen sink, I enjoy cooking dinner with her. I won't say I can sew, but I do sew a button for her once in a while, or iron a blouse. It's no more tedious than cleaning all my lenses. Franny and I grow herbs in window boxes. We love watching them get taller. It's taken me fifty years to realize that domestic things, women's work, can be fun and has its own dignity. I'd not seen that when I was a child because it wasn't fun for my mother. And it wasn't fun for my mother because she wasn't doing it by choice.

That's the secret. Men choose what they do, or feel they choose what they do. And I guess lots of men's work isn't fun. But the kind I did, do, is fun, is wonderful. So how come it turned me into a zombie? That's what Clara calls me, Stacey the zombie-woman.

These women weren't zombies. They were alive, the short fat women in sweatshirts, the slender Asian women in brocades and satin, the leggy young women in shirts and jeans, the middle-aged, middle-class women with permed hair and neat wool suits and mid-heeled shoes shouting for Reproductive Freedom and aid to battered wives, the sixty-year-old women in wheelchairs, wearing baseball caps with huge pins proclaiming YES! SEXUAL PREFERENCE FOR WOMEN! were unafraid to appear naïve, were not worrying about their image, not even caring if people saw their emotions. Dreamers, imagining that what they did there would matter a damn to Carter or any president, idealists, imagining that the world of felicity and harmony they envisioned was possible; fools full of love and energy and hope. I loved them.

I wished I could be like them. Because it was better to stand with the women, better to rise and cheer believing in hope, faith, and charity, than to slump on a barstool or banter over golf with the guys with a heart full of despair, knowing The Great Game for what it is, unable to bear it, unable to change it, unable to go on looking at it and unable to look away: feeling noble and self-righteous in one's cynicism. Better to be a fool for god, whatever god might be – ourselves, maybe, the future, the children . . .

Better. But how can I change now? I'm so old.

December 2, 1977. The women at *Woman* are upset about my Houston photographs, and asked me to come down and talk to them. I went today. What a difference from *World*! *World* occupied most of a building: fifteen floors identical to each other, miles of corridors with hundreds of doors leading to neat anonymous cubicles, all the floors and walls the same color grey, you could never be sure where you were. This magazine is housed in a loft that has been haphazardly divided into small offices, erratic in shape and very crowded, with three or four desks jammed into each one. At *World*, you could always tell someone's status by their office, by its size, by whether it had a window or not, whether it was a corner office – the premium space. At *Woman*, the biggest office houses the four secretaries, who need more space than the editors because they have a wallfull of file cabinets and the only large electric typewriter.

I wound my way through the maze to what I was told was the editor's office, a cluttered cubicle with two desks and a filing cabinet in which a woman was typing on an old-fashioned machine. I said hello, and introduced myself; she turned and gave me a broad smile, leaped up and shook my hand, 'Oh, I just loved your photographs!' She is Lu Marcus, in her fifties, a little plump, a little grey, dowdy, but with brilliantly clear, intelligent grey eyes.

She put her head out her door and cried 'Margot!' and waved me to the other chair as she fished around on top of the filing cabinet and brought out a folder with several contact sheets. Then she sat and, leaning toward me, repeated herself.

'We love your pictures. There is so much humanity, such compassion in them. And the composition is superb!'

I could not help comparing this with my awed introduction to *World*, to the murmured understated praise, the barely polite smiles Russ and Lou gave me. Humanity and compassion were words rarely uttered there, and the need to impress was far greater than the desire to be agreeable. In this different atmosphere, I tried to act like a human being, pleased with praise, responsive. But I am too imbued with the *World* style. I smiled, it was the best I could do.

'But . . .' she paused, looked at me sharply, 'some of them are disturbing to some of the editors.' She put on a pair of eyeglasses and examined the contact sheets. 'This one,' she pointed. 'And this, and this.' She picked out about a dozen shots. A few showed women arguing angrily, there were a couple of the chairwoman looking fierce and grim, and several showed a small group of well-known political figures talking privately, their faces as hard and dark as any man's. Four showed women walking with their arms around each other.

I was confused. I understood of course why they didn't like these pictures. But why consult me? The pictures were their property, and they would do, magazines always do, exactly as they chose with their property. *World* never complained if I showed men looking silly: they just didn't use the shots. I often shot men grimacing in anger or strain, or looking hard and mean – *World* rather liked shots like that. They just didn't like to see men appearing foolish. I raised my eyes to Lu in question.

A tall, slender young woman with oriental eyes and pitch black hair entered the office. Lu introduced her – Margot Wong, one of the editors. She slipped past us and perched on Lu's desk. She regarded me with cool dark eyes and suddenly I saw what was going on – there was a quarrel within the magazine about these pictures.

'I've been telling Stacey that some of us are upset by some of the pictures,' Lu said.

Margot nodded. 'The pictures as a group are very fine – the best of their kind that we have seen.' She had a high delicate voice and an almost singsong delivery, as if she had been raised speaking an oriental language. Her speech was extraordinarily precise in sound and diction.

'I wish you to know that we do not object in principle to the portrayal of women in the full gamut of emotional expression. But for this piece, we feel it is important to emphasize the anger and hatred of the Eagle Forum women – ' she pointed to the contacts from the Astrodome – 'and the harmony and happiness among those at the conference. At the same time, we do not wish to impose our desires upon you, nor distort your intentions.'

WHAT? I didn't believe what I was hearing. A magazine that would not dictate to a photographer? Unheard of! They were both studying me. I wasn't sure what I was supposed to do.

'The photographs are your property. You can do what you like with them,' I said, surprised at the coolness of my voice.

'Yes.' Lu leaned forward even further. 'But we – I – wondered what you were thinking when you took these.'

A spurt of rage pumped into my forehead. And I spoke. But all the while I was talking, I was wondering what was wrong with me. For years I had sat in silence while *World* selected from my pictures those that would suggest the image of America, of manhood, that they were instructed to sell, to foster, to create. And I never said a word, I never complained, I simply accepted. And here these women were *asking* me what I was doing, giving me a chance to talk about my vision, and I was angry with them. Why?

'I admired the women at the convention, I thought they were great! And the most marvelous thing about them was their diversity. When you go into men's groups, whatever group you're in, the men look and act all the same: every male group is a club, whether they're all truckdrivers or all Harvard lawyers. But these women were every color, size, shape, age; they showed every style and every emotion, and I wanted to capture that. And I did!'

I could feel heat in my face, as I swung around to Margot Wong. 'Your idea of showing the Eagle Forum women as angry and full of hate is fine. They were, and I shot them that way. But the convention women were not, you have to know this, totally harmonious and happy. There were serious arguments in that group. It's because there were serious arguments that the final unity was so extraordinary, so moving. And there was power brokering going on among some of those women. To deny these things is just as bad as *World*'s showing an image of America with everybody happy and healthy except a few unfortunates who were going to be helped immediately! It's a lie just like men's lies.

'And readers know when you lie! They recognize truth! I'd like to show you the pictures I took the first few years I was photographing, all women with babies. Sweet smiling motherhood? Hah! The truth is deeper and richer and harder and not so pretty,' I wound down.

Then I stood up, and picked up my handbag. 'If you censor the truth about women in that way you might as well be putting out *Lady's Day*, or *Godey's Lady's Book*. You're not doing women a favor when you present them with a false image of themselves. That's all they've gotten all these years. I thought your intention was to be different.' My voice sounded tired. 'But do what you want. The pictures are yours.' I turned to leave, but Lu put her hand on my arm. I glanced at her: she was looking intently at Margot, who was frowning, staring at the floor. It was an argument they'd already had, obviously.

Margot looked at Lu. 'We have so many enemies,' she pleaded. 'If we give them ammunition, if we show our own when they are not their best selves, we defeat our own purposes.'

'If we act exactly the same way they do, how are we better?' Lu pleaded back.

Margot's head went up like a shot. 'Our *vision* is better! The world we want to build is better!'

'We can't build a better world on deceit,' Lu countered firmly.

'We can't build anything! – consider what we're up against! without getting women's support! And we lose their support if we show them images of angry, unhappy, hard, grim women. Or images of lesbians!'

'Always talking about me,' said a dour voice from the doorway. I turned. A tall, rangy, large-eyed woman in her forties stood there leaning against the frame in shabby jeans and an old leather jacket. Lu grinned, stood up and hugged her.

'Just the person we need in this argument.'

Margot groaned and put her head in her hand.

Lu said to me, 'This is Clara Traumer, who runs *Outsiders*. Why don't we all have lunch? We can discuss this further.'

Clara Traumer publishes a small feminist journal that takes its name from Virginia Woolf's suggestion that women constitute themselves a Society of Outsiders. Because women are excluded from the male world, they can see it in perspective, and, Clara said, because women are excluded, they have different values from men. They are outsiders in the world.

'Ah,' I laughed, 'now I understand.'

'You've always felt like one, huh?' Lu smiled.

'As we all do,' said Margot in her high delicate voice.

With such a name, it is understandable that Clara's journal does not have a huge circulation: people don't like to think of themselves as outsiders. It is a small tabloid paper that comes out once a month and seriously tries to work out feminist theory.

'It does what we cannot do,' Margot lilted.

Lu treated Clara with great admiration. Margot seemed to admire and resent her equally. It was obvious that Lu expected Clara to support her in the argument, and she did. I felt it was a little unfair to bring in an outsider as her second. Margot did not complain about that, but she set her mouth stubbornly, she wouldn't give in. I was uncomfortable, and wanted to leave, except that I was fascinated by this Clara, she was so unusual. And it was Clara who came up with a solution.

'Look, you only have room for six-seven pictures tops, right? So why not show the image Margot wants to show, women working together in harmony – all that. But Lu, you know Alison Tate, don't you? She's always looking for new stuff. Why don't you cosponsor a show with her? You can afford that. "Stacey Stevens: The women at Houston." All of them – the Eagle Forum women, the convention women, all their expressions, all the diversity – I mean, you seem to think these pictures are great.'

'I think they're magnificent,' Lu said. 'I think they show women as they really are in a way no other set of photographs has ever done.'

Clara turned to me. 'Would that satisfy you?'

I turned up my palms. 'I'm not a contender here.'

'Sure you are,' she insisted breezily, and turned to Margot. 'What do you think?'

Margot rewarded her with a brilliant smile. 'I think you're a genius.'

I was interested enough in *Outsiders* – and Clara – that after lunch I walked for thirty blocks looking for a shop that carried it. I had to walk all the way to Womanbooks on Ninety-second. They had back copies as well as the present issue, and I bought all they had. And went home and fixed myself a drink and curled up on the couch and read them.

I felt all over again the way I felt in Houston. I had to revise my entire view of things, of profound things, the most essential things, like what were women really like, and men, and life. This journal of Clara's dealt with real things that other journals shun, uncomfortable things like the reasons some women have for denying they are feminists, or the pros *and* cons of socialism or separatism. There was a gritty article about white feminist prejudice against blacks; in another issue there was a series of short pieces by women of color exploring their prejudice against other women of color. It even on occasion gave houseroom to rightist ideas. It is open, even if Clara isn't, as she said, laughing, over the lunch table.

'I even deal with them,' she tossed her head at Lu and Margot, 'the commercially successful insiders.'

Lu hooted. 'Have you seen our last statement?'

'Have you seen mine?' Clara countered, and they all laughed.

Outsiders, Clara said, is always on the verge of failure, saved so far by niggling grants from foundations with unusual levels of tolerance. 'Everyone hates us because sooner or later, we print things they don't agree with. We'd be in trouble if we maintained a straight leftish position, but we even offend the left.'

All the women seemed to find this hilarious. It didn't seem funny to me. I could imagine it: how many people did she have helping her? Two? Three? Working in dark cramped quarters, late into the night every night, drinking coffee from stained chipped cups, yoghurt for lunch, maybe for dinner too; days spent tramping city streets to find shops to agree to carry the journal, arguing with printers over late bills: all for a magazine so maligned that even I had heard of it. Yes, living in a fifth-floor walk-up, dark little room with a closet of a bath, falling in bed every night too exhausted to look through the mail. No life other than the magazine, nothing else . . .

So what did I have?

I picked up the phone and called Clara Traumer just to tell her how much I admire her.

December 7, 1977. I can never write December 7 without thinking: 1941. It was a Sunday, we had an outing, we went to visit some people Mommy knew who used to run a delicatessen but had retired to a farm. In the car after we left, Mommy said 'Now they work nineteen hours a day in the country instead of in a town.' We had Sunday dinner with them – twenty-six people at a long trestle table heaped with bowls of steaming mashed potatoes, creamed turnip, carrots, peas, stuffing (it wasn't as good as Mommy's), gravy, and chickens, many roasted chickens, I'd never seen so many on one table. It all looked delicious but none of it was as good as Mommy's, there was grease in it, and lumps.

And on the way home we stopped at Jean and Eric's and they opened the front door, usually only Jean came to the door, but this day they both crowded together at the door, their mouths were Os, their eyes too, 'We are at war!' Eric announced, his voice was, he sounded frightened and that was the first time that I understood that grown-ups were frightened too, and that even they did not know what was going to happen, that things made them upset and unhappy, even Eric, who was so smart and strong and big and who intimidated Mommy and Daddy . . . This day shall be marked in infamy, Roosevelt said, The President, and I believed him.

Had dinner with Clara last night at a cheap little Indian place in the Village. She is extraordinary! I found it exciting to talk to her, she has something fresh to say about everything. She went into a brilliant rap in which she proved that all our problems with the water table and groundwater shortage are caused by the adoption of the flush toilet; and another in which she proves conclusively that all the great media stars have been androgynous. And she seemed interested in me, her eyes sparkle at me and she asks me questions about my personal life, something people in New York rarely do.

She talked about herself too. She is a lesbian, has always been one. She's alone, and lonely when she has time to be. She comes from a well-to-do family, received a small inheritance, and blew it all starting *Outsiders*. But she doesn't know how long she can keep it going, the last five years have been a terrible struggle and she's running out of sources of help. Still, she's full of courage and heart and hope and enthusiasm. She makes me tired just listening to her. She makes me terribly aware that I have none of those things.

December 10, 1977. Lu called yesterday. She is trying to set up the show at the Alison Tate Gallery. But she also asked if I'd be willing to do a set of photographs of American women to be run serially in essay form over a period of six months. I am to go across country by bus, stopping wherever the spirit moves me, for six weeks. They can't pay a great deal but enough – they have a grant for this project. They want to show farm and factory women, executives and students, poor women, very rich women, middle-class women who work and who don't, women who head families in the inner city, itinerant workers, declassed refugees. Beneath this diversity they think there is a similarity of concern, an essential unity among women which will be developed in a written essay.

I said I'd think about it. Then I made a big salade niçoise and put it in an aluminum bowl with a plastic cover, went out and bought some French bread and a bottle of wine, and took the subway downtown to Lafayette Street, where the *Outsiders* office is. It's small but light, on the fourth floor of an old loft building, and as I expected, Clara was there alone, working.

'Time out!' I announced as she let me in, a little stunned. But she was delighted, and we ate right out of the bowl – I'd remembered forks but forgotten plates – and drank the wine and talked. I told her about the new series.

She shrugged. 'It's a good idea, but it's sure to come out fake.' Her speech is punctuated by her broad black eyebrows that almost meet, that rise and fall and arch in question, in disapproval, in delight.

'What do you mean?'

She put down her fork. 'Look, poor women and laboring women might be willing to say out loud to a reporter that they're worried about their children or about money, and middle-class women might be willing to say that they're having trouble managing a job and a family, or that they don't know whether to give up the job to have a family, or abandon the family for a job. But none of those women, none of them, is going to talk about the real ground of women's unity, is going to say that what upsets her most is men. But the truth is that it *is* men – his not working, his drinking, his abandonment of her, his refusal to take responsibility for daily living, for the child, for child-care payments, his resentment of her success, his self-hatred at her independence, her not being able to find a lover, not being able to find a husband, not being able to keep one . . .' She picked up her fork again and waved it around. 'Mark my words,' she said.

Or not being able to find one you want, I thought.

December 14, 1977. I have decided to do the pictures anyway. It's just too interesting an assignment to pass up. They can do what they want with them: I'll do what I want. Even though it's true, what Clara says: So you take pictures of things the way you feel they should be taken, of the things you believe should be photographed. And they sit in an editor's discard file. Or in your own files. What good do they do there? No one sees them. No one understands what it is you are saying.

No one does. That's true. But I have to survive. And survival means taking assignments and earning money, even though my work will be censored; but it also means taking the pictures they will censor. Taking them. Not refusing to see. Nor turning away. I'll take some just for myself, the way I did years ago. Just to take them.

What in hell else can I do?

*

December 16, 1977. I have a great plan. I'll leave the day after Christmas – I can't not spend Christmas with Mother – and I'll take Franny with me. Her school is closed for the month of January, so she can travel with me for five weeks and come back and stay with Jillian while I finish the assignment. She will miss a New Year's Eve party, but she's so excited at the prospect of seeing the country's backyards that she doesn't mind. I will miss nothing.

She asked me to buy her a camera for Christmas. I bought her a simple Canon. The thought of going on this trip with her makes me feel good, as if I maybe once am being a good mother. I'm almost excited. I'm happy I was able to work things out so well.

January 7, 1978. Portland. We stopped in Los Angeles to see Toni. He may think he's broke, but he lives in a beautiful little beach house in Malibu and he drives a red Porsche. He has changed so much – he's older, of course – he's forty, he kept mentioning that, bringing it up as if it were something terrible he had suffered that the rest of us knew nothing about. After the third or fourth time, I said, 'Yes, Toni, I know what it feels like to be forty and alone, you left me a month before my fortieth birthday.' He didn't bring up his age again.

Anyway, it's more than age. There are small fine lines around his mouth and eyes – the kind of lines you see on ageing actors and male ballet dancers and models, men who often smile when they don't feel like smiling, men who have to pretend because they have not completely obliterated their emotions. He embraced me and hugged Franny hard for a long time, but within an hour he was drinking and complaining about money. I had written him beforehand to ask if we might visit – I knew Franny would love to see him – and he'd asked if Franny could stay with him for a few days while I came up here to northern California, Oregon, and Washington.

I have left her there with trepidation. I hope he sticks around a little, does things with her. I don't trust him.

January 15, 1978. Laredo. God, it's hot! We spent the day standing out in a dusty dry farm under a sun that beat down, it must have been 110 degrees out there. Great shots, though, a great face on that woman – angry, twisted in physical pain, but strong, not worn down.

I'm worried about Franny. She's been silent ever since I picked her up. Toni wasn't there the day I arrived, he'd gone to the studio, and when she closed and locked his door and slid the key under a stone she did it in mechanical ritualistic gestures, holding herself stiffly, like a child burying her dead pet. And her mouth was thin and stiff, it still looks that way at moments. But she says nothing in response to my questions: everything was fine, is fine, according to her.

We are moving east this coming week, to Louisiana, Georgia, and Florida. I'm giving Mom and Dad a trip to Florida with the money I'm earning on this assignment, for Mom's birthday really – flying them down and putting us all up in Palm Beach for five days. I'll use Palm Beach as home base for forays into the poor areas around Glades. Then they'll drive over to the west coast, and we'll fly home. I'll get Franny settled at Jillian's, make sure she has notebooks and pens and whatnot for school, then I'll bus up to New England to finish the job. Oh, I'm glad all this worked out so well.

March 10, 1978. Brightwaters. Mother is sick. She has emphysema. That's what's been wrong all this while, why she's had trouble walking, playing golf, climbing stairs. She can't breathe.

I realized this when we were in Florida. It was hard being with her – she walks so slowly, she has to be helped in and out of cars, up stairs. You can't move with pleasure when you're with her. It was especially hard on Franny, but she's such a good kid, she held 'Gramma's' arm, she talked directly into her better ear in a soft voice. Mom is only seventy-four, but she moves and looks like a really old woman. Dad still bounces along like a boy.

I made a doctor's appointment for the week after their return, and went with her. But I spoke to Mina privately beforehand. Mina's first diagnosis was emphysema, but she took other tests, and yesterday all the test results came in. No cancer. I drove out here to 'celebrate' with them. I tell Mom she should be relieved, all she has to do is give up smoking and she'll feel better. But she doesn't want to give up smoking. It's almost as if she'd just as soon die as not smoke. I understand, I'm addicted too. She is very depressed. She sits in the rocker and looks out at the lawn, the lake. Sometimes she calls me to her, and I go eagerly, thinking she wants to chat, play Chinese checkers or gin rummy, something. But she doesn't want to talk. All she wants is a puff of my cigarette.

Today is Dad's birthday and I took them out to dinner. This morning we went shopping for a present for Dad – it's hard to find anything to give him, he has everything he needs or wants. I ask him what he'd like.

'Just that. Belle gets better, that's all,' he says, his forehead wrinkled with pain.

April 1, 1978. Well, it's on! My first show! It is in a bright broad space, framed beautifully, it looks wonderful, the kids all came in for the opening, Mom and Dad came, we drank champagne, it was . . . No. It wasn't fun. It should have been. What's wrong with me?

Well, for one thing, the reviews bothered me. They were so full of hate, outrage. As if none of the reviewers had ever seen an angry, grim woman before, as if it was an offense against public decency to show women that way. Oh, they were praising too, they talked about the power of the show as a whole. I begin to understand why I put my mother-child photographs away in an envelope all those years ago. I knew.

May 2, 1978. Alison has sold three-quarters of my photographs. This is spectacular, she tells me. We split fifty-fifty, but she is asking so much for them that even so, I'm becoming mildly rich. And moderately famous. Mom is very proud, she has hung the two I gave her right in her center hall.

June 4, 1978. The first photographs of women are in the June issue of *Woman*, which came out in the middle of May. They will run straight through November, and in December there will be a long summing-up essay. The pictures are very good, although the accompanying texts fudge the truth, just as Clara predicted. It's strange, this feminism that fudges. Is it conceivable that a socialist group would deny that capitalists were their main problem? Men have never hesitated to blame their problems on women. But men are somehow sacrosanct. I tried to bring this up with Lu, but it made her uneasy, she glided away from the topic.

Clara is intensely interested in this series. She wants to run a commentary on it, a piece about how and why women fudge the fact that men are their major problem. She wants me to write it. I won't. I can't. Whatever troubles men have caused me, my major problem is not men but the fact that I have become one of them, inexpressive and unable to feel, all tight inside like a sealed tank that threatens to explode if the safety valve is loosened. Clara says I suffered plenty from men and my refusal to admit it is another example of my mind dictating what I am permitted to feel, and ignoring what I really do feel.

'You know, you seem to believe you can't lament anything, that you have to be on top of everything – or seem to be. You say you just refused to be a wife so it's no wonder Brad divorced you, but goddammit, it had to hurt you when he changed, when he became a person you didn't like who didn't like you! He *betrayed* you, long before he had an affair: his father was the co-respondent! Why don't you admit that? And Toni broke your heart leaving you like that, just before your fortieth birthday, my god, what a thing to do! And he seduced Arden! What a thing! It's scandalous! And what about Franny's distress after she saw Toni? You were very upset about that.'

'He didn't seduce Arden. If anything, she tried to seduce him. She flew out to see him – she told me about it – she *planned* to have an affair with him after he left me.'

Clara's eyebrow went up.

I shrugged. 'No, she didn't. She said once he wasn't involved with me, he wasn't all that appealing to her. She said he seemed to be – nothing. I told her she ought to think about what that meant about her feelings about me. She gave me a filthy look and stormed out of the room.'

'That kid is really something,' Clara said.

'It's my fault,' I said.

She sighed.

'And what about Franny?' This woman refuses to give up.

Yes. She didn't talk about him at all while we were traveling. What a delight she is, that kid! Everywhere we went she was snapping away at my side or off somewhere, taking pictures of places. She is fascinated by places more than people; all sorts of places – even Route 1, as I call it, or Main Street – the same everywhere: hundreds of hamburger and pizza joints, used-car dealers, stereo shops, neon signs. She finds something fascinating in housing tracts, decrepit farms, the streets of small cities. She came home with fifty rolls of film and made me teach her how to develop it. She got some very nice shots, and now she has a sort of travelogue of the United States. She plans to write short comments on the scenes – comments poking fun at the scenes or at teen-aged values and preconceptions – and submit the thing to a publisher as A Teen-Eyed View of America. I can't get over her! But maybe she's too old too soon?

It was after we came back, after I'd taken my mother to the doctor, yes, it was the night after we saw the doctor and got the diagnosis of emphysema. I was feeling lower than usual, and Franny saw it and suggested that we just call and have a pizza sent up for dinner, and we did. While we were eating, she looked over at me and asked me how I felt.

My throat filled. 'I feel that my mother never had a life and now she's dying.'

'But she did, Mom,' Franny argued. 'I mean, she's had you and Joy and Grandpa all these years. And she has that nice house.'

'That isn't what she wanted from life. She wanted – oh, she had dreams.'

Franny looked puzzled. 'But if that isn't what she wanted, why did she have it? Why didn't she have something else?'

'Life doesn't always permit us to choose, Franny,' I said in my bitter monotone.

She regarded me for a while. Then, in a thin voice, 'Is that how you feel? That you didn't get to choose?'

'God, no! I chose!'

'Then why are you so mad all the time?'

'Mad? Angry? Is that what you mean?'

She shrank. She stopped chewing. Silently, she nodded.

'Is that how I seem to you? Angry?'

She managed to swallow what was in her mouth. 'Yes.'

I looked at her amazed. 'Franny, do you feel I'm angry with *you*?'

'Sometimes. I'm never really sure.'

Oh my god. *Mommy, are you mad at me? Did I do something? Mommy, why are you angry all the time? You're always angry, Mommy! Why!*

'Mommy?' Franny's voice was tremulous and it brought me to. I was leaning over, elbows on the table, my head in my hands. I raised my head.

'Yes, honey. I'm here. It's just a shock. I didn't know I appeared angry.'

'Well maybe it isn't angry exactly. It's sort of . . . tense . . . as if you're all coiled up inside, ready to explode. As if you're *looking* for something to get mad about. And, I mean, everything you say is so . . . so bad all the time, so . . . I don't know.' She was pink-faced ' 'Negative?' I suggested.

'Yes. That's it. Negative. Like Gramma. Like when she has a problem and she tells you about it and you say, why don't you do this or that or the other thing and to each thing she has an answer, nothing is any good, she just refuses to solve it. Like she *wants* the problem to be insoluble, you know?'

It was my turn to nod.

'Like that time in Florida,' Franny was gaining enthusiasm now, speaking with energy. We were off the subject of me. She took another slice of pizza and pulled her plate back. 'She said she wanted to have a brunch and invite the whole family but it was too much work for her. And you said she should serve some prepared foods, coleslaw and potato salad from the deli, cold cuts, things like that. And she said she wouldn't serve food like that in her house, she hated it. So you said, well, you could have a ham, that's no work, and make macaroni and cheese the day before. And she said she wanted to serve baked beans, her own baked beans, and they were a lot of work. And you said, so make them a few days before. And she got really annoyed with you and said "Oh, Anastasia, I know how to plan a meal! Besides, it isn't the cooking I mind, it's the cleaning up." And you said, and now you were being very careful, "Why don't you hire someone to help you?" And she said "Who would I hire?" And you said look in the telephone book, there were services for waitresses and people to clean up. And she got impatient, she waved her hand at you, she said "Oh, those people are no use, I'd have to show them everything, it would be more work than without them." And you closed your mouth.' Franny whooped with laughter.

I laughed too. 'What do you think she really wanted?'

'She wanted you to go out and help her.'

'That's what I thought too.' I got up from the table and went into the kitchen and poured coffee for myself. I carried the cup back to the living room and sank into an easy chair.

'But you didn't want to,' Franny grinned wickedly.

'No. I've done that. Lots of times.'

'I know.'

'I don't want to be her alter ego anymore.'

Franny's face looked hurt. 'I wasn't attacking you, Mom.'

'I *know* you weren't!' But I'd heard my voice too. 'That's what you mean? By angry?'

'Yeah.'

I considered. I don't feel angry, I feel sad. Why does it come out that way?

'I don't feel angry,' I said. 'I feel sad.'

'But why?'

You can't tell a child that every choice brings pain, can you. You can't send her out into life believing that. You can't tell a person of fifteen that what everyone inevitably discovers in life is that they are alone. So I tried to laugh a little. 'I think I inherited my sadness.'

'From your mother?'

I nodded.

'You have what you want, don't you?' she pleaded. She rose

and came toward me, she dropped onto the footstool in front of my chair. She leaned forward. 'Don't you?' She wanted, it was important, she needed to believe that life can be beautiful, that there are happy endings. 'You have your work and you love that. And now you're making lots of money again. And you have Arden and Billy and me.'

'I have you, yes, sweetheart,' I said, leaning over, pulling her close to me, enfolding her. For how long, though, I thought. I had never let myself feel about Franny as I had about the other kids, that she was mine, part of me, that we were bound together forever. I treated her like a gift lent to me for a while. Regularly I would look at her and wonder when it would begin, the turning away, the hatred . . .

'Franny,' I hugged her, 'I'm really sorry if I seem angry. I guess if I seem angry I must be angry but I didn't realize . . . sometimes I'm so blind. I love you, I'm almost never mad at you.'

'Except when I don't clean my room or don't come home at the time I'm supposed to,' she smiled.

'Well – that's not profound anger.'

'I know,' she said indulgently.

She was sprawled across the footstool, her arms around me, I leaning forward with my arms around her, and she dropped her arms and leaned her head against my breast and said, 'I feel sad about Daddy.'

I stroked her forehead. 'You do, baby?'

She nodded. 'He seems so . . . lost, somehow. Like he's always running to catch something he never gets. I mean, maybe he gets the thing he's running after, but it isn't what he thought it would be. He's always disappointed. He was telling me about the lady he married after you got divorced, Lydia? And his voice got so . . . husky, as though . . . and he felt so sorry for himself. You never talk that way about Brad or about him. And he's always complaining about money, but he has that house and lots of expensive clothes and that Porsche, and he eats in such fancy restaurants . . .' She sat up suddenly. 'Oh! He took me to The Brown Derby, did I tell you?'

She babbled – a child again, briefly – about this momentous experience, then stretched herself and stood up. 'I think I'll go start writing my commentary.'

I smiled at her. 'It must be hard for you. A lost father and an angry mother.'

'Yeah,' she agreed, yawning. 'But everybody has something.

I'm pretty fortunate compared to my friends. They think so, anyway.'

'You've discussed this with them?'

'Sure. We all talk about how things are at home.' She turned suddenly. 'You don't mind, do you?'

'I don't mind. It's good. I wish kids had done that when I was a kid,' I said. She drifted away, I sat there, and an echo sounded like a wind chime, my mother saying 'I wish I could have talked to my mother like that.'

I remembered feeling tense, my stomach tight every afternoon as I walked home from school, never knowing what mood Mommy would be in, whether she'd be angry or not . . . Is that how Franny feels?

Ah god.

What is the matter with me?

I thought I had reconciled myself to being what I am. And after all I'm fortunate. I *do* have Franny and she's wonderful and healthy and cute; and these days I don't even worry about money anymore. Offers have been flooding in ever since the show and the *Woman* series; and it is for the kind of thing I love to do. I have more work than I can take and I can charge top rates. I'm making three times what I earned at *World*. I'm really now what people call successful, I have *money*, money enough to buy Mom that mink coat I dreamed of getting her – too late. Now there is nothing she wants. The money sits. I should spend some of it. Fix this place up, maybe. But I don't have the energy.

The school term is almost over. I have to make up something to do, make up a life. I have an assignment to photograph a computer plant in California for an investment brochure. Boring, but such money, five times as much as I earned on the *Woman* job, women's things never pay, women have no money. There's no rush on this, so maybe I'll push it to the end of the month when school is out and take Franny with me and send the contacts back and go on to Mexico. She'd love the Yucatán, pyramids in the jungle, turquoise waters. It would be nice for her. And who knows? Maybe I'll get some pleasure from it.

August 30, 1978. Spent an evening with Joy. Out on Long Island to see Mother, who is mad as hell at life and everyone around her, but so grateful for a visit from me that I feel guilty I go so rarely. But it's depressing to be out there. They keep all the doors and windows shut, the air conditioners running, there's no air. They draw the blinds and drapes the minute it starts to get dark, close everything in. The two of them move silently around the stuffy house, encased by it like old tortoises in their dark prisons, pretending to a world of outer threats that they are rocks.

Mother's day: She gets up around eight, shuffles into the kitchen where Dad has made coffee and squeezed orange juice for her. She slumps into her chair, sips her juice, accepts a piece of toast which she breaks into tiny pieces as if she were not going to eat the whole slice. She butters each fragment, spreads a little marmalade on it, and slowly chews it. Her teeth are bothering her, she has continual trouble with her false teeth. Still, she eats almost all the pieces.

After breakfast, she helps Dad clean up the kitchen, and gets out the vegetable she intends to serve at dinner, peels it and sets it in cold water. Then, saying nothing to anyone, she disappears. She has gone back to bed. She gets up again around eleven and goes into the kitchen and peels the potatoes or a second vegetable for dinner and sets it in cold water.

Then, if the day is fair, she dresses and they go out for lunch and a little shopping. Each purchase requires a day to itself. One day they might go to buy new batteries for her hearing aid; on another they might drive up to the farm stand in Smithtown to buy some vegetables; on a third they might drive all the way out to Ronkonkoma, where a Polish butcher sells homemade kielbasa. On rare occasions, they will drive into Nassau, to the Five Towns, where there is a shop that sells high-fashion clothes at reduced prices. She always returns from these expeditions in a foul mood, on the verge of tears, because nothing fits her anymore, nothing looks good on her.

When it is raining or cold or snowing, she dresses and makes some lunch for them – scrambled eggs, grilled cheese sandwiches, tuna fish. Then she goes out to the porch and sits there looking out, doing nothing, for hours. Or some days she will have a project – to make a pot of soup the long careful traditional way, or a pot of stuffed cabbage to be eaten that night and frozen in small containers that hold just enough for the two of them. They eat little now.

But when they come back from an outing, or if she has cooked, or even if she has done nothing, around four o'clock she is exhausted and goes to bed. She sleeps for an hour or two, gets up and while she finishes the preparations for dinner, she sips a weak scotch and water. They eat on trays in the TV room, watching the news. Ed cleans up, she helps. She sits in front of TV for another hour or two, and goes to bed for the night. She no longer smokes.

Dad tries to keep busy. He doesn't work away from home

anymore, she is afraid to be alone. He will not leave the house without her. When she sleeps, he finds things to do, cracks that need caulking, fixtures that need polishing, bushes that need pruning. He is nervous and restless, he tries to read but only flips through pages and sometimes falls asleep in the rocker. He waits for her to get up again, and is relieved when she does, but nothing changes. They speak little, but his eyes thirst for her. He thinks only of her, only of her.

I tried to cheer her up. I chattered all one night and she managed to stay up past midnight, she was lively and curious; the next morning Franny showed her her photographs. That afternoon we played Chinese checkers for a couple of hours, and I took them out to dinner that night. She doesn't complain about the restaurant, no matter how bad it is, if she has chosen it. When we returned, she asked me to help her decide where to hang some photographs I'd had framed for her. She'd been withdrawn and surly all afternoon, and barely livened up even for dinner. We talked about places, and decided on the TV room. Dad was sent for tape, hammer, hooks, and agreeably fetched them, looked eagerly toward her. 'Where do you want them, Belle?' he asked in that loving solicitous tone that sets her off so dependably. 'Oh, I don't know, Ed!' she snapped, and I jumped up and pointed to the height. We went through the ritual – stepping back, how is that? Too high? A little to the right? and finally Dad was able to mark the height. Then he measured carefully for centering. He takes a lot of time. He is extremely precise. He does a beautiful job. But Mom was tired, or bored, or irritable, whatever, and she sighed irritably, 'All right, Ed, you're not hanging a chandelier!' and he expostulated, sputtered, 'Well, I have to center it, I can't just hang it anywhere,' murmured further, defending himself under his breath. He tried to hurry, and as he went to hammer in the hook, it slipped from his fingers, it fell, it rolled, and he burst out cursing, 'Goddamn it to hell, goddamn nail, goddamn, sh – sh – !'

Shocking. I stood up and went to him, I put my arm across his back, I said, very calmly, 'It's all right, Dad, we'll find it.' I bent down with him searching for the tiny nail, stroking him with one hand all the while. There were tears in his eyes.

By then I was exhausted too – from the pain of seeing her like that, him like that. I had nothing left to offer. I couldn't stand any more. The next day I drove up to Joy's. I haven't spent time with her alone in several years, and we had a lot to catch up on – as we both said when we greeted each other, determinedly cheery as ever. She is home, on vacation.

She is still living in the apartment, which looks cute now, she has been able to spend some time on it. When she finished college, she got a better-paying job, still local so she'd be near the children, who were nearing college age but still needed her presence, she felt. College was going to be a problem: Justin was unwilling to contribute toward the kids' education, but he earned a decent salary, so they were not qualified for financial aid. They would probably not have gone if Joy had not been utterly determined that they should. She unhesitatingly admits she drove the kids so they would be able to get scholarships.

'I don't care what they say about pressuring kids! They had to, they had to! I told them, do you want to work in a garage, be a waitress all your life? If not, WORK!'

How is it her children still love her so much?

They got into good schools, they got scholarships, but even so, the expense was too much for Joy's woman's wages. So she wrote Amy, who sent checks whenever she could. It was not easy for Amy either; her husband had been retired for years, and although they were well-to-do, James Selby, true father of his son, was incredibly mean with money.

Years ago, late at night when we were a little high and silly, Joy and I would make up stories about James dying. He would die and leave his large estate to Amy; she'd get out of Iowa and have some fun. We invented wonderful lives for Amy the widow – we had her in rickshaws in the Orient, logging in Alaska, spending winters in Monaco and falling in love with a prince. Small p. But it was Amy who died first, in 1976, of pancreatic cancer, a cruelly painful way to go. The next year James remarried, a woman in her forties – he was close to eighty – who will no doubt inherit the lot.

'There's no fucking justice, An,' Joy said, frowning.

I was shocked by her language. Joy never used to talk like that.

Joy didn't hear about Amy's death until a month afterward, when James finally wrote her.

'Justin, the son of a bitch, could have let the kids know their grandmother had died, couldn't he?' Her face was thin, ravaged. She was starting to get grey. Well, she was forty-four. I'd blown up into a moonface, Joy had burned away to a wand, charred and electric. 'But I couldn't have afforded to fly out for the funeral anyway, and besides, Justin would have been there . . .' She fished for a cigarette, then suddenly threw the pack away from her. 'Damn! Why don't I stop? When I look at Mother . . . Oh!' She lay her hands beside her on the chair. Her fists were clenched tightly. Her voice was thick with phlegm. 'You know, Amy flew out here to see me once, years ago.'

'I remember.'

'I told you? Did I tell you what she said?'

'Generally. Something about a wife having to be solid and strong and uphold her husband in everything no matter what he was like. Duty, devotion, that sort of thing.'

'Yes.' She pondered, then looked up, a sweet child's face again for a moment, the Joy I remembered. Then the moment passed – an aged child's face it was. 'An, do you think she was right? I think about it, I wonder about that a lot.'

'No, of course not! She was lovely, you could see her character on her face, and she was sweet, I remember her although I only met her once, at your wedding. But her way of thinking – well, she was trained in it, she believed in it, but it seems crazy to me. I mean, what is the reason women are supposed to sacrifice their own lives – you know, to *not* say what they think and *not* argue for what they want and believe – why should they? Why, what is the reason they are supposed to support men in whatever men want to do? It's a kind of slavery.'

'She kept her family together.' She raised her hand to wipe her nose with a tissue, lowered it mechanically, a plebe eating square meals. Dull phlegmy voice, a tissue crumpled into a ball in her tense fist.

'Well, I suppose that's one way of looking at it. It's true her husband didn't leave her, her son still phones on Christmas Day. But god knows what James was doing all those years, she may have been dutiful but he didn't treat her well from what you say, and he sure didn't wait long to remarry. More important, I wonder how he was to her when she was sick, when she was dying . . .

'But the other way of looking at it is to see that her submission enabled her husband to go on being the bastard he is, and maybe even become a worse one. It also gave her son an example he has not seen any reason not to follow. After all, you've kept your family together too.'

'I've paid a horrible price. I'd hate to tell you how my life has been these past ten years. You know,' she gave a short hard laugh, 'it's really charming. I spend the first fifteen years of my marriage with Justin a nervous wreck, I was broken out all over, all over my body, I had a bad stomach, I was so tense, well I was miserable, I see that now . . . so I leave him. Great, huh? So then I spend the last ten years in hell, worrying about the kids, about money, about how we're going to survive. *If* we are going to survive! The only good thing about the last ten years is that Justin wasn't in them.

'I'm forty-four years old and I don't know anything. I don't know what's right or wrong, what's smart or stupid. I feel like a blind person. Whose life was worse, Amy's or mine? See, she said – I've never forgotten it – she said, "Joy, dear girl, this world belongs to men. Women are here only on sufferance. It is essential that you recognize this. I urge you to do your duty was a wife, not because I believe that it is right that you do so, but because I believe it is necessary. If you do your duty, then no matter what Justin is or does, he will respect that. You have the right, and he knows it. And if he tries to leave you, or refuses you support, the law will support you. But if you abandon Justin – well, he is my son and I love him, but he is very like his father, and I know . . . I know," her voice broke then, and she was so dignified, so controlled, I was really shocked, "I tried to raise him differently, he was a sweet little boy, but I don't know what happened, it must be the nature of the male . . ."

'She stopped to blow her nose and clear her throat, she had a lace-edged handkerchief, I remember that, I couldn't get over that, I don't even own a handkerchief. It was blued and ironed and everything! That's what she did, that's what was in her life . . .'

'Like Mother.'

'Even Mother doesn't blue her handkerchief anymore. She washes and irons them, but she doesn't blue them.'

I laughed. 'You're right.'

'Anyway, after a while she continued, she said, "I don't know exactly what he will do but I am sure he will make you suffer. I don't know exactly how because I never took such a risk. But my vision, my nightmare – is you and the children penniless, homeless, in desperation."

'I was crying by then, and she came over and put her arm around me. "I hope that will not happen. I love you and I adore my grandchildren," and she started to cry again. "And I sense I will not be allowed to see much of them if you and Justin – if you cannot make it up. But if you can't," and by then she was sobbing, "let me know. Write me. I always see the mail first in the morning, even when James is home. I can help you, a little, and I will. I have my own little nestegg. I may seem totally subservient to you . . ." '

Joy broke off. 'Remember how he used to snap his fingers at her at the dinner table when he wanted something?'

I shook my head. 'I never saw that.'

'Well, he did. Totally subservient!' She shook her head as if she were trying to shake a flea out of her ear. 'Yes, well, she said she wasn't. She said she had her own way of protecting herself. She said that tight as he was, she was able to put away a few dollars in a bank account every week, and that she'd been doing that for thirty years. She used to hide her bankbook in with her Kotex pads, because she knew he'd never look there.'

Both of us giggled.

'But after she went into menopause, it was a real problem where to hide it!'

We both burst into laughter.

Joy laughed long and hard, a laugh that moved into hysteria. Tears came into her eyes, laughter-tears. Then she stopped, wiped her eyes, and continued: 'So she said, "So my dear, I have something, and I want it to go to you and the children. Promise me you'll let me know if you need it. Promise!" I promised. I was sobbing by then, we were clinging to each other. I felt as if we were conspirators or something. I felt that we could have been living in 1600 or 1000 or anytime at all in the past, that it was always like this for women, that we were simply repeating what had happened a million times before . . . it's always the same, it never changes.'

'And did you? Ask her to help?'

Her ravaged face sank further into tiredness. 'I had to. I didn't want to. But I had to.'

Amy had helped, just as Mother and Dad had helped, and Joy's kids went to college. But Amy died before they finished.

'By then, the kids were in gear. They *knew*. They had summer jobs and part-time jobs, and they managed to work themselves through.'

There was a provision in Amy's will that her savings were to go to her grandchildren, but when she died there was nothing left in the account. James did not offer to help his grandchildren. It was as if they were not his grandchildren. Justin by then had married again and had a new baby.

'That money was for her protection – in case James left her, or left most of his money to Justin,' Joy whispered, 'and she broke herself helping me.

'Someday,' she was blowing her nose now, 'I told the kids we're going to drive out there and go to the cemetery and say goodbye to her properly. And lay roses on her grave . . .'

Another bout of nose blowings, clearings of throat. 'She loved her grandchildren more than Justin loves his children! I can't get over that!'

I pondered. 'The thing is, you got out. Amy didn't. So you went through hell for twenty-five years; she went through it her entire married life. A different kind.'

'I suppose.' She didn't sound convinced. She stood and poured more coffee in our cups. She spilled it, her hand was trembling. 'Mom and Dad have been wonderful to me too. Great. Terrific. Couldn't be better. It's sort of reconciled me to . . . everything.'

'Reconciled you?'

She shrugged. 'It made me feel she cares about me after all. Maybe even loves me. You know, I never felt Mother loved me very much. I was like Daddy. There was Mother and you – and Daddy and me – and we were outside.'

'Yes.' I couldn't lie. 'Mother isn't great at loving anyone. She wasn't given love – oh, that isn't true, I know Grandma loved her, I remember how she used to look at her – but she wasn't given something, she wasn't given emotional sustenance I guess. And so she couldn't give it to us. Like the baby rat that isn't washed clean, you know?'

She didn't.

'Well, if a female rat has a baby, the first thing she does after it is born is lick it clean. But experimenters have taken away the baby rat before the mother has a chance to do that . . .'

'Cruel!'

'And if the baby is female and has babies of her own, she won't lick *them* clean. They're imprinted so early! Anyway, I guess what you don't get you can't give.'

'I didn't get it and I gave it.'

I stared at her. This was true. 'But you had problems. Remember, years ago, after Julie was born, you asked me once if I was afraid I didn't love my children? And I said no, I was afraid they wouldn't love me?'

She laughed. 'But that was before Jenny was born.' She stretched her arm toward me and I handed her a cigarette. She leaned back and lighted it. Her face was calm, smiling. 'My kids were so wonderful! I didn't know how to love them, really. I was always anxious, like I had to be told what to do, how to be a mother, or read it in a book, because it didn't come to me naturally. But when Jenny was born, my kids – well, they'd spent summers with Amy, often, and she loved them . . . so they'd learned, I guess. Anyway, the kids just loved her up, they held her and cooed over her and played with her and loved her so much and I watched them and I saw . . . and she loved them back, oh god how her eyes would light up when they came in from school! That's how

I learned, I learned from my kids. Thank god I had a third child, I never would have known . . .

My voice came out low. 'I was too jealous of you to love you like that when you were little.'

'Well, you would be!' she flared. 'Given the way Mother is. She sets us against each other – you know, she praises you to me and me to you. She's really possessive of Dad. You know for a while there, he was coming over here all the time to fix things for me, just for something to do, you know, he's so bored. And she'd come too, but she couldn't stand it. He was so happy, and of course I was very nice to him, I made a fuss over him, well it is great the way he fixes things . . .'

'Yes.' When I was nine years old, I began to love my father . . . We sat in silence.

'Mother loves you,' I said finally.

'I know. She just makes me feel I'm shit. All the time.'

'Well. If it's any consolation to you – I'm not sure it is, I'm not sure anything could be – there's a cost for what she gives me. She has me in this bind: she wants me to do things for her, be something for her, but if I become attentive, if I go out often and stay for a few days, she gets as nasty to me as she is to Dad. And whatever I do is not enough, she makes sure I know it is not enough, it can't help. And I die, it does something terrible to me to look at her looking at me that way: saying did you imagine this could help? Well, you know.'

'Yeah. Like that dress you gave her for her birthday. That dress is gorgeous! What is it? Feracci or something?'

'Lucca Ferelli. I mean, I knew it was very dressy, but I thought she'd have something splendid to wear on Christmas, or some special occasion, and I knew from the cut that it would fit her.'

Joy twisted her mouth. 'It was really beautiful. And what did she say? "What do I want with this?" Something like that.'

I nodded. 'She said, "What do I want with this?" as if it was a piece of shit. Then she saw my face and said, "Where would I ever wear it?" '

Joy sighed.

'But she keeps asking me in her own silent way, to do something, to save her . . . and I want to, I would if I could. But she's inconsolable. Oh, I love her. You know that. You love her too. We all do. Profoundly. She doesn't know what she does to us. She thinks she doesn't matter, she is sure she doesn't matter to us. And so she makes you feel it doesn't make any difference to her that you love her . . . . And it doesn't – her sorrow, her desolation are all that exist . . . She lies cold in the center of my heart like a gravestone.'

'She does in mine too,' Joy said quietly.

But does Joy lie in bed at night whirling down down into a black abyss of pain? Does she lie there wishing to get to a place where nothing matters, where she can sleep deeply, restfully, and never wake up? Does she spend her nights fighting off the desire to die and her days pretending she doesn't feel it? Does she whirl down into the black hole, lie there in that pain, that incredible pain, sharp and aching at once, piercing every organ starting with the heart moving outward through the body, flowing into the arms and legs, penetrating the genitals, shoots of pain, of aloneness, knowing the aloneness, recognizing it, it is familiar from child-hood, it is the only thing that feels safe . . .

It seems unfair that even after you lose the capacity for pleasure, you go on feeling pain.

Maybe she does, though. Maybe I should ask her. No. She doesn't. No. No.

October 20. Dinner with Clara. Very upset. I had too much to drink. So did she. She wants us to be lovers. She loves me, she says. I can no longer love, I have no love left in me. I told her that. I've told her that before. She says I'm sick and won't help myself. I shrug. How can I help myself?

But it pains me to see her tormented for something she feels I could so easily give her. But I couldn't, easily. How can I offer desire I don't feel? Promise to compromise, to have a life together, when I am so rigidly committed to doing what I want to do when I want to do it.

I love Clara, in my fashion. But whatever I feel nowadays doesn't go deep, the way my feelings used to, before – when I was young, when I was in love with Brad, when I was falling out of love with Brad, when I was falling in love with Toni. In those days, emotion was so overwhelming that nothing mattered beside it, it was a whirlwind, a tornado. Now my feelings are swift birds skimming the surface of the water but never plunging in, vanishing, colorless, into the grey sky.

The only deep feeling I have is sorrow.

She says, 'You want to die first. Before your mother.'

Mother: a splinter in the heart that cannot be extracted. I cannot think about her without pain. I think about what I can do, what I can give her. I drive out there with offerings. They are accepted with that grim smile, the one that says what makes you think this can fill the void? Love. The hardest thing, no wonder philosophers urge against it. Much harder than hate, anger, aggression. They are cheap, facile, next to it.

But it isn't just Mother. The kids pain me just as much. All except Franny. Billy finished medical school last year, and I thought he'd come to New York for his residency. He did well, he must have had some choice. But he took an internship at Mass General. These years I see him at Christmas and for a few days in the summer. He is never going to come home again. It is not their physical presence that I need, but their presence in my life. Home is where the heart is, and their hearts are not with me.

December 29, 1978. Billy was here! He had five days off for Christmas, and he came and stayed here! He left this morning. He had to be back at the hospital at noon.

I didn't expect him. He spent Christmas Eve with our family, out at Mother's. I did what I have been doing for the past few years – since she likes to have Christmas at her house, but it is too much for her to prepare it – I go out there with Franny a few days before and we do the cooking with Mom's help. This doesn't entirely please her either – she likes to be in command of her own kitchen. But she prefers it to driving all the way into the city and sleeping in my room, in a double bed with Dad; and Joy has to prepare Christmas Day dinner and can't do both. So this seems the best compromise. But Mother doesn't like compromises, and she was grouchy with me for getting her oven messy.

Billy came out to Long Island the night before Christmas Eve. Oh he is beautiful, tall and slender and sweet-faced. We played bridge that night and he teased Mother out of her ill humor; the next day he and Franny went out for a long hike, and came back red-cheeked and bright-eyed and he made cocoa for them. He is a sweet boy. I was tousled and pink in the face myself, from cooking, and he made me sit down and he finished the sauce for the seafood ragout. I've graduated to things like that, hot dogs are no longer my only accomplishment.

Christmas Eve was nice enough, although as usual I was in pain because Arden wasn't there. But Billy was so sweet it almost eased the Arden-ache. The next day he went to the Carpenters', taking the train, and we went to Joy's. We drove home, got here around midnight. I didn't expect to see Billy again, I thought he'd go straight from the Carpenters' to LaGuardia and back to Boston. But at one in the morning the buzzer sounded and the doorman said one William Carpenter was below. My heart hasn't zagged up like that since . . . I don't know when. Maybe not since I realized that Toni loved me.

'SEND HIM UP!' I cried, and went to meet him at the door. Then it occurred to me I should be cool, not show too much emotion: I might embarrass him. I took deep breaths, and then opened the apartment door to wait for him. He smiled so broadly and easily when he saw me standing there, it was like the old days when no shadow fell on our love for each other.

He came in, easy, casual with his knapsack. 'Had a couple of days off and thought I'd spend them with you,' he explained. 'See a little of the city.' Did he want to be sure I knew he wasn't here because he wanted to see me?

'Sure, terrific!' I couldn't help myself. 'I'm glad you're here,' I kissed him.

Franny had been in bed, but heard something and came bounding out in her longjohn pajamas and leaped up directly at him, arms and legs spread apart. He caught her, grabbing her around the waist. She was astride his front and they whirled a little.

'What have you been eating, stones?' Billy laughed and put her down, red-faced from exertion. 'You're getting too heavy for this.'

Franny mock-pouted. 'Mommy!' she complained, 'I don't want to get big. I don't want to grow up! Do something, Mommy!'

'What can I tell you? You could diet.' She *was* a little pudgy.

'Give up hot-fudge sundaes? Never!' she announced haughtily, and threw herself like a five-year-old into an armchair. 'Hey, Billy, you gonna stay here?'

Yes, he announced, and sat down on the floor, leaning against an armchair, facing her. I sat down on the couch. The kids talked, bantered, we all talked, saying nothing substantial, just chatting. I was basking in his presence, it didn't matter what we talked about. Every time I looked at him my heart would give a ping – who knows what to call it, pleasure, pain, ecstasy? It was love, whatever else it contained. The room looked golden to me, sepia, like the old rotogravure sections of the newspaper, soft warm light cast by this boy's body – man, really. He was twenty-eight.

Franny wouldn't go to bed, and at some point she fell asleep in the chair. Billy and I were talking, I was telling him about the Houston conference, and for a while we didn't notice the sharp silence in a corner of the room. When we did, we looked at the chair, at each other, and smiled.

'Want me to carry her in to bed the way I used to when she was little?' Billy laughed.

'When she was little?'

'Yeah. Remember how on the nights when you came back from trips, we'd all sit up talking half the night? Toni'd fix you some dinner and you'd eat and tell us all about your adventures, and it would get to be midnight but Franny would refuse to go to bed? Usually she'd fall asleep in your lap, sucking her thumb. And I'd carry her up to bed.'

I'd forgotten that. It came back with a pang. Happy days. They had seemed to be happy days.

'I remember,' I smiled, but I could feel my mouth tremble. 'She's gained a few years and more than a few pounds since then, though. I'll wake her up.'

I tried, but she wasn't having any, the little fake! She kept her eyes squeezed shut and wouldn't move and finally Billy and I had to lift her and carry her – he at her head, I at her feet – into her room, where we swung her thrice and threw her on the bed with a vengeance, and she cried out and burst into giggles, and threw her arms around Billy and wouldn't let him go.

I kissed her good night and left the room, so she could have her brother to herself. When Billy came back into the living room, he asked if I wanted a drink, and went to pour them. It was like having Toni back again, a handsome young man who serves drinks and talks like an adult. Is an adult.

He settled down in the armchair near the couch and asked me how I'd been apart from the conference.

'Good!' I lied brightly. 'And tell me how you've been.'

He colored a little. 'I'm in love.' Her name was Livvy; he'd met her at Mass General, where they were in the same program; she was his age, with long dark hair she kept rolled up in a bun days and only took down at night . . . His eyes glazed over.

'I see,' I said, careful not to smile. I did see.

'She's wonderful.' He took out a photograph to show me.

'She's beautiful.' She was. 'I'm so glad, sweetheart.' I had been afraid he would never let himself have that, the experience of falling in love. He was so withdrawn, withholding, stiff inside himself.

'And this is serious.'

He shrugged. 'Well, yeah, serious . . .'

'But you're not ready for marriage?'

'Right.' He sipped his wine. 'We both have two more years, well, one and a half, to go. And after that, we could go anywhere. We're in the same residency program, and we could get jobs anywhere.'

'But you have something to say about where you practice.'

'Yeah,' he conceded. 'But with tropical medicine you usually take what comes up.'

'Tropical medicine! I didn't know that was your specialty! I thought you were studying internal medicine!'

'I was. I am. I'm going to do an extra year to study the infectious diseases of the Third World . . . you know, bilharziasis and malaria and yellow fever and byssinosis and parasites and things like that.'

I sat back. 'Billy!' I breathed. 'Oh, Billy!' This was no slimy creep, no calculating toad, no self-advancing cold-hearted money-mad golf-playing suburban medical predator! This was the son I'd wanted.

'What is it?'

'Nothing. I mean, I'm moved. So you'll go to Africa or Asia?'

'Or South or Central America. Wherever there's an opening.'

'I'm very proud of you, sweetheart.' I reached forward and stretched my arms out to him; he shifted his body forward and let me embrace him, embracing me in return. 'I'm really so proud,' I whispered. My throat was full.

'I'm glad, Mom, but . . . this is what I always intended. I mean, it shouldn't be a surprise.'

'I didn't know that. I don't recall hearing you say that.'

He looked annoyed. 'I told you.'

'When?'

'Years ago. You never listen when I talk.'

I didn't know what to say. Would I not have heard, remembered, such a thing? 'Sorry.'

He shrugged. 'I didn't talk about it much around Arden because I didn't want Dad to know.'

I pulled away from him. 'Because then he might not have paid for your school?'

He sat up blinking. 'What? Why? He would have paid, whatever I did. . . . You have some idea about me. You sound as if you think I'm really a creep.'

What could I say?

He glared at me. His voice sounded irritable. 'You know Dad always wanted to be a doctor himself. He was really happy about my going to med school. But, well, you know how Dad is. He'd already picked out a site where he was going to build me an office, and he was talking about all the patients he'd get me, all his friends, these middle-aged guys getting ready to croak. And I didn't want that, but I didn't want to upset him before the fact. Because I wasn't sure, you know, that I'd get through, or that I'd still want to do this when I got older. But now I am and I do. I'm positive I don't want to go out to Long Island and live in a ranch house and treat well-to-do white people who have all their lives overindulged – oh, I guess they get really sick too, I don't mean to be snarky. But I don't want that life, playing golf with the same guys once a week like Dad does, seeing the same people at the Country Club every Saturday night, all that, you know. I couldn't stand it. Livvy feels that way too. So maybe we'll be able to go out together . . .' He moved into a dreamy smile, his eyes focused on an inner sight.

I rested against the back of the sofa, comfortable, at rest, relaxed. My body felt suddenly recovered from rheumatism, arthritis, some stiffening disease.

'I didn't know your father wanted to be a doctor. I thought he wanted to be a saxophone player. But why didn't you want Arden to know?'

'Oh, it was stupid I guess. You remember how she was in those years. We didn't get along too well. I thought if she knew, she might, if she got angry with me or something, blurt it out to Dad. I know that was stupid, she never would have, no matter how angry she was at me. But I felt I had to keep my ideas to myself.'

'But Arden was gone. I mean, by the time you started medical school she was married and off on the commune and hardly ever home. You didn't want to tell *me*,' I concluded with the triumph of being right.

'I *did* tell you!'

'Billy, if you did, it was in passing, one of a number of ideas you were considering. Although I don't recall your mentioning it at all.'

His facial muscles twitched, he frowned. He got his mouth in order. 'I didn't make a point of it. You know . . . you didn't seem to like me very much. I know I wasn't too great . . . I mean, I know I was sort of angry . . . in those years, but to have your mother turn against you . . . it's . . . it's . . . And I wasn't exactly sure I was going to do this. I didn't want to come and tell you something that I knew you'd like, as if I was sucking up to you, trying to make you like me.'

'Sucking up to me! Why shouldn't you tell me something that would please me? How could you think I didn't like you!' I cried, reaching for his hand. 'Billy, I've been so hurt because I felt you turned away from me! You were never home, you were always with Daddy.'

'You *didn't* like me, Mom,' he said quietly. 'You were furious with me for spending time with Dad – even though you were the one who told me to.'

'I *was* furious, you're right,' I recalled. 'I felt you were sucking up to Daddy so . . .' I stopped in time.

'So . . . what?'

'Oh! So he'd help you, I guess,' I confessed, hot in the face.

He considered. 'You mean, pay for school. That's what you insinuated before.' He was quiet. 'It's really true, you didn't think much of me.' He started to get up. Would he leave? Oh, god! How could I keep him?

I raised my voice. 'Well, what was I supposed to think? You're home, we're close, everything's fine, then suddenly you start practically living at your father's house! What would you have thought if Arden did that? Really!'

'I might have thought she went there because she couldn't bear being around you and Toni, you know? She had quite a crush on Toni in those days.' He was in a cold rage, but he sat down again.

'I know she did.' I stopped. 'What . . . ?' I stopped again.

'You know, Toni wasn't that much older than me. It was hard to watch the two of you. I didn't like being around the house. Especially after Arden left. You two were so . . . cozy . . . I didn't want to explode at him, tell him he was a disgusting pig. I didn't want to upset you.' Now he did get up – but went only as far as the kitchen to fetch the wine bottle. He filled our glasses.

When he returned I burst out, 'I thought you loved Toni! And he wasn't a pig! Why do you say that?'

He was leaning way back in the chair with his long legs crossed up high, and his hand shielding his face so I couldn't see him. 'I did, when we were little. Something changed. I don't know, things seemed different. Maybe you were more open about . . . because we were more grown up. I know he wasn't a pig. I even sort of knew that then.'

My god.

'Why didn't you talk to me, tell me?'

He shrugged. 'I couldn't, I was too angry. Anyway, what was I going to say? Don't love your husband? I mean, he *was* your husband, even if it never felt that way. And then he was gone, and you seemed so pissed all the time, well I guess he broke your heart, it was hard to talk to you. And by then I was someplace else too.'

And now that he was in love, now that desire was part of his daily hunger and its satisfaction part of his daily bread, he understood how it had been for Toni and me, could forgive it. But why hadn't I seen? I, who pride myself on my perceptiveness, my acuity! Where in hell *was* I?

'I'm annoyed with myself. I should have realized,' I mumbled.

'I should have tried to talk to you.' Didn't because you were too busy calling him a slimy toad for sucking up to his father. No trust, Anastasia!

'Well, maybe. I'm not sure it would have helped – then. You know, sometimes you just have to wait for things to change. I see that often, in medicine. Everything we do, we think we're so smart, but whatever intervention we make, we have to wait and see how the patient himself, his body, his psyche, how he handles it, what he does with what we do.'

'Or she.'

'What?'

'Aren't some of your patients women?'

'You're right,' he laughed. 'Med school gets you like that.'

'I'm sure. So un-get like that.'

'Livvy should hear you, she'd be giving me such a look right now!' he laughed.

'Good! We'll get along!'

'Do you think so? I was wondering . . .' He eyed me. Yes, he'd been jealous of me and expected me to be jealous of him. But I wasn't. Not at all. Was I? 'Livvy's visiting her family. They live outside of Boston. But we both have three more days off, and I wondered . . .'

I considered. 'You can have my room and I'll sleep on the couch.'

'No! No, Mom! I won't do it like that. But you have a futon, don't you? We could sleep in here.'

'Done. Call her.'

He looked at his watch. 'It's too late now. I'll call her in the morning. That's great, Mom, thanks.'

'Oh, honey,' I said 'it is, truly, deeply, my pleasure.'

So he did and she came and she is wonderful and I love her, and I'm *not* jealous! Or if I am, I'm not jealous enough to cause difficulties, to me, him, or her. Franny liked her too, and when we were all home together, around the dinner table, it felt as if we were a family again. This turned out to be a wonderful Christmas. Only Arden was missing.

I have my boy back, though I'm not sure I deserve him. Maybe it won't last. It was so easy. But it was easy because of what has happened to him – our reconciliation had to wait until he fell in love. But maybe it's only temporary. That could be. Oh, let it not be!

I forgot to tell him that Toni did *not* break my heart. I don't like him thinking that. I'll have to remember to tell him next time I see him.

May 4, 1979. Mom is very bad. She was here for Easter dinner – Easter means nothing to us, we celebrate it only because of her, and she celebrates it because her mother did. I decided to have it here and ask her to make the drive because she got so angry about my messing up her oven at Christmas. I can't cook and leave a clean kitchen behind me. Neither can she, why is she so pissy?

They arrived here about two o'clock Sunday and she went immediately into my room to lie down. She got up at four, when we had drinks and appetizers. She made it through dinner, but was back in bed by eight-thirty, and didn't get up again. Was she that tired or was she just furious at having to drive in here? You can't tell. She is always so tired. I wanted to take her shopping on Monday – there's a shop here that sells fashionable clothes in large sizes and I thought maybe they might have some nice suits to fit her. That would make her happy, I thought. But she was too tired. They went home immediately after breakfast.

June 24, 1979. Clara, Franny, and I are going to take a trip together this summer, to Italy. Clara can't really afford it, but she'll get an APEX fare, and we'll all stay in one room, in cheap pensione, so she'll be able to manage. I'll pay for the car rental, it would be the same whether she was with us or not. She'll use the trip to interview European feminists, and I have an assignment to photograph Italian women in politics, mainly in Milan. We'll start at Rome and drive north. I'm sort of excited. Maybe we'll have fun.

September 15, 1979. Joy has a new man and is going to marry him. I was at Mother's Saturday and she told me about it. We were sitting in the TV room, the eleven o'clock news was over, but she didn't get up to go to bed, she was waiting for me to begin our usual evening chat. And I sat there trying to think up things to tell her, but she doesn't listen to anything I say anymore. I'll tell her an entire story about somebody – my latest news from Arden, say – and ten minutes later she asks me how Arden is. After I've exhausted all my news, I ask for hers – it's like extracting teeth. How's Elvira? And Jean? She answers briefly, disgusted with everyone. Dad was sitting beside Mother on the loveseat, his arm across the back of the chair, embracing her, protecting her, without touching her.

'How's Joy?' I ask.

'Oh. She has a boyfriend.'

'Really!'

She grimaced. 'I think she's going to marry him. Well, you know, she's like the Dabrowskis, she needs a man. She's not like us.'

Not like *us:* independent, alone. What is that man's arm doing around the back of your chair?

Still, I see her point – even though I resent her making it. There's only one person in this family who pays the price of this vaunted independence, and that's me. I'm the only one who's alone. How dare she!

But on the other hand, what is Joy doing? Now that she is finally fully independent, she's going to leash herself to someone again. Jonathan is working as an assistant coach at a small college in the Middle West; Julie's midway through her Ph.D., Jennifer is nearly finished with high school. They did it all themselves, working and getting fellowships, with just a little help from Amy. They are not a burden to Joy anymore. Why, then?

I met him Sunday – Joy had a brunch and invited the family. He seems okay. Nice, even. He's a widower, he owns the insurance agency where she's been working these past years. She seems ecstatically happy, but she defers to him all the time just the way she did to Justin.

Why?

October 19, 1979. I've broken with Clara. It was too much, it's been too much for a long time. Italy cinched it, I suppose, although because Franny was there we kept the lid on, stayed polite. Constant squabbles, it was hopeless. We had to eat in the cheapest restaurants because that was all she could afford, even though I offered to pay. And when the cheap pensione began to get to me – I longed for a comfortable room with bath, a few luxuries – she wouldn't stay at a good hotel, even though I offered to pay. She had pride, she said.

And I know we agreed that we would both work on the trip, but what that meant to her was that she would work and I would hang around. She wanted to meet with the feminist women of Milan and that was fine with me, I wanted to photograph them too. But we went to Milan partly to see La Cena before it's gone, and the Brera and the Poldi Pezzoli, go to La Scala and the Galleria. But she has as much interest in art as I have in mountain climbing! All she wants to do is sit around talking with these women – she speaks Italian, and she's fascinated by them. But I *don't* speak Italian, and I wanted to be seeing! So that's okay, I said okay, if that's what you want, we'll go to the museums without you. And then she's hurt! The same thing happened in Florence. She didn't set foot in the Uffizi! I couldn't get over it!

The thing about being involved with someone is you do nothing but compromise. And the one who compromises is always me. I always have, it's my nature, I can't hold my own when I love someone. I end up giving up myself. It's intolerable!

On top of all that, she presents an ultimatum! She has waited patiently, and now it is time: we must become lovers. How can I be a lover when desire has dried up in me, when it is hard enough for me just to spend an evening making conversation. It's a drain. Everything drains me. The trip exhausted me, I was in a fury the entire time.

It's when we are alone together, Clara and I, that the magic happens. Something . . . what is it? . . . something to do with the way she nags me, insists on my speaking what I feel, pushes me until I do, and then I feel better, I feel healed. She doesn't give a damn for my reputation, my accomplishments. There is someone inside me that she loves, someone sweet and hurt and frightened that she tries to bring out. I don't recognize that person, don't want to either. Still, I feel different after I've spent time with Clara, the way your stomach feels after you eat mashed potatoes, warm and calm and full.

But when there are other people around, I feel her pressing on me, she wants to have me to herself. Unless she is meeting an important feminist, someone she can use. She wants us to live together. How can we, when we agree on nothing? when we do not live the same way? I am too old now to change, so is she. At our age, compromise is impossible. We can no longer merge our lives.

So that's that.

Clara says I am sick, neurotically depressed. I don't know who she thinks she is, diagnosing me. What is she, living like a graduate student, insisting on being marginal but hating the marginality! Enough, I said, say I'm sick and let it go! I'm tired, I'm old, I'm nearly fifty, let me be! She says there is no room in my heart for compromise because I am in love with my own pain, committed to it, and have no energy for any other kind of love. She says my mother is enshrined in the center of my heart, and jealously refuses to let anyone else in except my children, who are also her blood. I think she is insane on the subject of mothers because she hated her own. I am *not* influenced by my mother.

Maybe I was when I was young, but I'm not now, in 1979, my god I'm going to be fifty next month. I hardly ever see Mother and I'm impatient with her when I do. My main feeling toward her is guilt. What is Clara talking about?

I am the way I am because my life has been hard and I was always too sensitive and I've been hurt too much and I'm worn out. And I don't mind being alone, I even like it. *She* may need someone but I don't. I've been alone all these years, essentially alone, even when I've been with someone. I can't change now. I don't even want to. I like being alone, doing what I want to do when I want to do it, no begging leave, no compromising.

Depressed indeed! What else could I be? who suffers the inevitable consequences of having a grandmother who died of grief and a mother who didn't. I combine them in myself, a living grief, a pillar of salt, an inconsolable, indestructible monument to sorrow, a rock like Niobe, too hard for tears.

When I rose to leave – we'd had dinner in her apartment – she cried. I could hear her all the way down the four flights of stairs.

Tues. I can't understand how she can want me, given the way I am.

Wed. It's funny how I've become used to speaking to Clara every day on the telephone. No matter how busy she was, she always took time to listen to me, to talk to me. We talked about little things, how we slept and what we ate. If we ate – Clara is so driven that sometimes she forgets. We told each other whom we talked to that day and what we worked on, and we discussed problems – I have this pain, do you think I should see a doctor about it? Franny is acting up, what do you think is bothering her? This is the third time this writer has been late with her copy, but she is good, do you think I should stop giving her assignments, or should I go on doing it and lie to her about deadlines? What do you think is the best way of dealing with this guy at Major-media? He's such a macho pig, but I don't want to lose their patronage, they give me interesting assignments. What do you think?

I say: 'I slept badly last night.' In truth I sleep badly every night, have for years, maybe always. She says, 'I'm sorry, sweets.' Her voice is a caress on my soul.

Was.

*

I called Clara last night. She said she didn't want to see me. Too painful, she said. I acted haughty and cold. She cried.

November 10, 1979. A marvelous assignment has come up and *I* got it! I am off to France for three weeks to photograph Simone de Beauvoir, Marguerite Duras, Nathalie Sarraute, women like that, for *Style* magazine – an in-depth photoessay on French woman writers. A real boon to my career! lots of prestige and *Style*, unlike *Woman*, pays top dollar. I happened to meet Maggie Dunne on the street and told her about it: she always gets the high style photographic assignments, but not this time, and my dear, her face turned quite green.

Maybe I'll buy myself a fur coat for this trip, why not, I can afford it. Paris can be raw in November. Something high style, impressive. Why not?

It will be good to get away. Franny can stay at Jillian's.

February Sanibel Recuperating – since just after Christmas. Got sick right after France. In France. Mussels, Diarrhea – dehydration, aches arms legs, high fever. Didn't go away. Could barely move. Too weak to walk. No one seemed to know what it was. Even Billy – who flew down from Boston and examined me. He spoke to Mina – she discussed all the test results with him. Everyone mystified. When the fever passed – got up and tried to function.

Couldn't. Couldn't do anything at Christmas. Mother so angry that we didn't come out there and cook that she didn't come Christmas Eve. First Christmas in my life I didn't spend with her. Didn't say she wasn't coming – just 'got sick' the last minute. But Joy and her man and the kids came – and Billy and Livvy. And *Arden* and kids. Don't know where they all stayed. All helped – tremendous help – couldn't have done it. Dizzy. Weak.

Then pneumonia. Mina sent me down here, found the name of an internist here. She said: Do nothing but sit in the sun. Wouldn't pay any attention to her but can't do anything. Can't even lift my camera.

Too tired to write more.

Feb. Think it's the third. Never know what day it is anymore.

Sitting out on the deck of this rented house looking out at the Gulf of Mexico. Blue-green and calm today sky pale blue. Nice. Been here – a month? – chilly and cloudy – everything grey – water – sky. Blessing today: sun – warmth – color.

*

Mon Feeling a little stronger today. Going to try to write a little every day.

Am I one of those women who use weakness to hold their kids. Because Arden is here – came down to nurse me – Franny wrote her before Christmas – I didn't know – I didn't plan it. I didn't know much. She came down with the children and she and Franny made the Christmas Eve feast. Where did everybody stay, I have to ask her. And then she insisted on coming with me to Florida.

It is so nice, her here, warms me.

Tues At a motel! Those poor kids had to pay to stay at a motel over Christmas. Makes me feel awful.

We have a beautiful house here facing the water, with four bedrooms – Arden and I each have one, the boys share one, and Sarah has a tiny one to herself. She's adorable. But I worry: Jeremy ought to be in school. Arden says no. She says school ruins children destroys creativity. She wants to keep him out as long as she can. But what about learning to get along with other children. He has a brother and a sister, she says. Every afternoon, while Sarah is napping, she sits with the boys in the family room or whatever they call it of this house. She's set up a blackboard and she teaches them writing and counting. They already know how to read. After their lessons, they read together, each taking turns.

It's good she came. Good for me. But good for her too. She doesn't look well, she's pale and too thin and strained three little children it's so hard she looks older than thirty-one. Maybe, if the sun will stay out for a while, she'll get some color.

Friday Missed a few days, feeling cronk again.

Letter from Franny this morning cheered me up. What a sweetheart she is. Poor baby must feel strange living with Jillian, even though the Murrays are very fond of her. She makes herself sound cheerful. Maybe she even *is* cheerful. I thought I was making myself sound cheerful but I wasn't. Angry they said, all of them. Fooled no one but myself. Thought I was Pollyanna and all the while I was Medea. Used to be Pollyanna.

Grey weather today.

Saturday Just realized I forgot Mother's birthday. Forgot my own too. Fifty. I turned fifty it came and went and I hardly knew it. Did anyone wish me a happy birthday? Was I home? Surely Franny did. Did Billy call? Too sick to know.

*

Monday Don't know how to explain it to her without telling her how sick I've been. Don't want to tell her the truth, she worries so about me, she's sick enough herself. Not today.

Tuesday She's probably feeling hurt and abandoned. She already feels no one cares. Evening I spent with them last fall, went out there after Clara and I . . . Sitting in TV room after the news, looking for conversation.

How's everyone? I ask.

Grimace, tragic face. No one comes to see me.

I know how she is to me, I know she is the same to Joy and her children, Joy has told me so. I say: 'But, Mother, when people do come to see you, you act as if you aren't interested in them. You don't listen to what they say. Maybe they don't come because you act as if you don't care about them.'

'Well, the truth is *I don't*!' she rages, flushing.

'I know,' I say, sadly, accepting her, accepting whatever she is, licensing her self-absorption.

That's how I feel too when I'm in the black hole, but look at me, all my kids came. They do love me. I'm not utterly alone, it isn't true, not true. Why do I go on feeling it then?

Wednesday But it isn't true for her either. So why does she feel it is? Why does she insist it is? Because it's her truest feeling, it's what she felt when she froze into her present shape, when I was nine years old my father died my mother never combed my hair it is her enduring truth and nothing that has happened since has touched it. Her sorrow is the one thing she trusts, her jewel, her truth; it is the pearl she has created out of her wretchedness, the one thing she owns, the one thing that is indisputably hers.

But cruel, cruel to us who love her, who have tried. And self-centered, incredibly, nothing exists but self, that feeling. Bad, selfish, cruel, yet I understand it, I am just like her, I am being transformed into her, clutching *my* pearl of inconsolability. My mother combed *my* hair: I still remember how she pulled it, tears streaming down my face. Felt like hate. Her life wasn't mine. But I drank hers in, I made it my own, trying to lift its burden from her. Didn't help her, only ruined myself. Joke my struggling all those years not to be like her not to have her life.

All my struggle just the self-deluded squirming of a trapped worm.

Thursday Well, I did it. I called her. I disgust myself. Such a coward! Telling myself not to call her because she'd be upset at hearing I am sick. Liar, dreamer. When the truth was I was afraid she'd hurt me by not caring that I was sick. 'Oh? That's too bad.' Distant, cool, uninterested. Didn't believe I was so sick I couldn't remember her birthday. How is it that I know how she feels better than I know how I feel? I can see her sitting in the rocker staring out, sorry for herself, ruminating, chewing it over and over, her grief. Her grief: my grief. She keeps choosing it. Clara said so do I. How do I unchoose?

She said they are coming to Florida, tomorrow, driving down, I invited them here.

Arden said it's Valentine's Day today.

Sat   I keep trying to fight it off – the black hole. Pierce through the self-pity to my part in things. I don't know why I choose it, but maybe I can figure out *how* I choose it. Is that enough to enable me to stop?

This afternoon I took a walk along the beach with Arden and the children. The gulls were crying in the grey sky, the children cried out at their finds, collecting shells, running far ahead of us. A photograph. Can't shoot the cries and calls though, the music of the surround, you have to hear them in the photograph. In a good photograph, you can.

Arden held my arm.

I feel like someone who has had a life-threatening illness, come partway back from death, still on the threshold, I could still fall backward. But I haven't been that sick, have I? I wake like an invalid, my head heavy, hard to raise. I look out at the day, it is far away, a retreating sky, greyness. I get up feeling aged, I totter to the bathroom. I walk out into the world and it looks unfamiliar, I have been so long away from it. I have to learn to walk again, to talk, to think. I have to get my mind out of itself. I feel trapped there, locked into my mind. Imprisoned in repetition.

Sunday   Arden is cooking chicken soup for me. She makes great pots of soup every week – chicken, turkey, oxtail when she can get them, they're hard to find down here. All they have here is WASP food, everything filleted and neat, no bone no fat no flavor, the kind of food the Carpenters ate. Another life. Last week Arden made lamb broth with barley and vegetables – that was delicious. It is like being a child again – Mother always made chicken soup, beef soup, and lamb stew when we were sick. Arden doesn't make the lamb stew, I think she's right.

*

Monday Mom and Dad are here. They drove straight here, arrived last night. Mom is still tired from the drive, she's napping now, Dad is walking along the beach with the boys and Arden, he wouldn't do that if I weren't here, someone here for her if she needs someone. Actually, she looks good, she looks terrific. Her hair is so pretty – she didn't turn white but silver, and she is still gold, the two are mixed. Short and fluffy. And her color is good, and she's pretty.

She hates the way she looks. I can understand that. It's awful to get old. Dad of course always looks wonderful with that huge shock of white hair and his young face and body. But, oh, poor Mom. Weak as I am, when I saw them drive up I ran out to help her up the stairs.

Wed Well, they're gone.

Fri Black hole the whole fucking week. Today Arden said, That's what happens everytime you see your mother.

Can that be true?

Sunday Since she has known she has emphysema, Mother has become even more intensely focused on something dark and churning inside her. As if now there is nothing worth contemplating but death. Her gaze doesn't stretch to the outside world, she looks only inward and sees only desolation. Everything outside her hurts her, like someone who has been horribly burned, whose skin is so sensitive that a touch causes agony, who can't stand even the air brushing against them.

So even the children's noises were painful to her, she kept turning off her hearing aid. She was taken with Sarah, but she didn't feel up to spending time with her, talking to her, playing with her. She likes Arden – she's always liked Arden, Arden impresses her somehow. She was impressed at her educating her own children. She even sat and watched for an hour.

She wanted me to take some trips with them. She is bored. She likes my company. She couldn't seem to take it in that I have been sick, am still not entirely recovered. Or maybe she takes it in, but is angry about it – angry with me for being sick. We drove together over to the nature reserve, enough of a trip for me. She was furious that I would not go up to Palm Beach with them even for a few days. She said she was glad I had Arden here to take care of me, and off they went. She doesn't like to be around sickness.

Hard for me to bear. But I guess I will have to learn, I, the favored child. The truth is she doesn't see me. She doesn't know who I am. And I, who love her so much, I have to accept that she does not love me. There is no room in her heart for me except when I am triumphant. She cannot tolerate me needing – anything. Probably because she cannot tolerate needing anything herself. She treats me the way she treats herself. The way her mother treated her. It is to weep.

Monday, 25/2 Clara called last night. She didn't know I was sick. She met Franny on the street yesterday, and found out. She was extremely upset. Things are going very badly with the magazine and she's broke, but she's going to fly down here to see me, tomorrow.

Tomorrow!

Thursday I can't yet drive, don't trust myself, the dizziness still overcomes me at times, so Arden drove all the long way up to Fort Myers to pick up Clara at the airport. She wasn't nice about it. But oh the sight of Clara! Same as always, those huge eyes with so much longing in them, that utterly controlled manner, a study in contradiction. Just like me, she says.

We were walking along the beach when she said this, walking with our arms around each other, I couldn't not put my arm around her, my hand on her sweet body. Still, she's wary of me, I can see it in her eyes. Why shouldn't she be? she demanded. I whispered in her ear: I love you.

But after she left this morning, I thought: suppose I let myself love her, love her fully, entirely, as she wants. And suppose she changes, the way Brad did? Or Toni? Suppose she leaves me? I couldn't bear it, how could I bear it, I couldn't stand that again. No.

Friday, February 29 a leap year! It is 1980. I just realized that. I knew there was a new year, but somehow I didn't think about it until now. It's beautiful here this afternoon. Huge white cloud puffs, sharp-edged against the deep blue of the sky, gold-edged near the sun, as if someone had run a pen around them with golden ink; large and indolent and reflective, changing shape as they move, like dandelion white opening opening blowing dispersing in wisps, easily, like lying back in a pool. No friction, no reluctance. Surrender. Abandonment to what only looks like annihilation, but is really transformation.

There is a quality of attention you can pay to yourself that makes you more sensitive to other people. Egotism, selfishness, these words should be discarded. Everything I learned when I was young was lies. Because the way Mother feels, the way I feel when I am in the black hole, is totally self-involved, yet there is no self in it, but an absence of self, an absence of love, abandonment to the ecstasy of feeling abandoned. And the absence of self is a punishment of others: I know this, I feel it.

Whereas when you start to think if you can think if you can let yourself think about how you are and how you act and what you want and what you like and don't like – suddenly other people jolt into color, pop into relief like a movie film suddenly brought into focus.

Clara made me see this. She had to go back, she could only stay a day and a half, but we sat holding hands on the big rock down the beach, and talking, and looking at each other, and I don't know how I let go of her . . .

Her voice is balm on my spirit, her eyes make me want to reach out and hold her forever. Why is it so hard for me to tell her that?

But why must I tell her that? I never told Brad, I never told Toni. They knew, they could feel it. She can't feel it. Not her fault: you cannot feel much from a dead person

Half-dead.

Arden was in a fury while Clara was here – she was the old bad Arden, the thirteen-, fourteen-year-old child. And suddenly I saw her in a new way too, saw something about her I had not realized. Why was she so angry? Because she had to share me, she was jealous of whatever was happening with Clara, she could feel it. But if she was jealous, she doesn't hate me. All the while I had been thinking she hated me, she'd actually been jealous of my attention.

For years – how many? – whenever I looked at Arden I felt a pang of what I called sorrow – but wasn't it self-pity? – at my loss, my emptiness of her, her distance from me. But my very sorrow kept her away from me, was a punishment. All of this came to me last night after Clara left. I couldn't sleep, and today I had a long talk with Arden. We went to the market en famille, I took us out to lunch, poor Arden, she's been cooking three meals a day all this while, it's too much. And I bought a pack of cigarettes, I know I shouldn't but I do love to smoke. And after we came back and Arden had finished teaching the kids, and had set them to their 'homework' (which they do religiously), she came out and sat with me awhile. She was still pissy, but I ignored that and chatted easily about the kids' lessons, the weather, the poem she's been working on. And in time, she softened and talked without an edge.

Then I said, 'It has been hard for you, taking care of the children and me, doing all that cooking, the laundry, teaching them. I want you to know I appreciate it. Very much. More than I can say.'

And my eyes filled with tears. Tears: I was so grateful. It was like getting my period for the first time – I was so old, so much older than the other girls, fourteen nearly fifteen, when the others had started some of them at nine, and I was grateful for that flow, it made me what I was supposed to be, it made me normal, human. I haven't had tears in my eyes in years.

She laughed. 'You know, there's a washing machine and a dryer here and a dishwasher. And you don't have to fill the lamps every few days, and water comes hot out of the tap. And the stores are only a couple of miles away and we have a car that starts when you start it! God, it's luxury, Mom!'

I burst out, 'Oh, Arden, it broke my heart when I was at the farm, watching you do the laundry, filling that huge tin tub on top of a wood stove, scrubbing the clothes on a washboard! Oh god, Arden!'

Mother at the washtubs, Mother at the stove, Mother running out to pull the sheets off the line when a storm threatened. Mother sewing late into the night – spring coats for us, sunsuits, clothes for a doll, my first and last.

She laughed again. 'Yes. But I didn't mind. I loved living there.'

She doesn't have my memories.

She is still laughing. 'I really did,' she concludes.

Did.

March 1 Mother is sick. Dad called last night. She felt ill a few days after they left here and insisted they drive back home. All that way for a little more than a week's stay! She has a bad flu, she thinks she caught it from me. Is that possible?

March 2 Something she makes me feel, something I let her make me feel: if Mommy doesn't love me no other love is worth anything. Christ.

Anyway she does love me. In her fashion. In the only way she knows how to love. As she was loved by her poor mother. All the generations of mothers, anxious, angry with their daughters, terrified for their survival, but knowing what their lives will be if they do survive. God.

*

March 3–4 I've been walking, even running along the beach with the kids. I carried my camera! I took pictures of them!

This afternoon they were so tired from romping on the beach that they all took naps and Arden sat with me for a while. Her hair is long and droopy, it hangs in her face. She has some color now, but she's still very thin, and she hunches over when she sits. Her clothes – long old-fashioned things, modest and drab – are all shabby, faded. It hurts me to look at her: my proud, fiery beautiful daughter looking like a bedraggled slavey. She looked too weary and weak to be attacked, but I couldn't keep quiet another day. So I did it: I asked her why she'd been estranged from me for so long.

She said, 'I just decided to protect myself.' Thin hard voice.

'From me?'

She eyed me. 'Who do you think?'

'Arden, I don't understand.'

'Oh!' She tossed her head and I had a glimmer of what she used to be. 'You are so blind! You see nothing! How you favored Billy, sweet Billy, dear Billy . . .' She turned her head sharply away from me.

'Arden, I don't believe that.'

She swung back. 'Believe it! Whatever he did was wonderful, fine; whatever I did was wrong. I was always the bad one, always the troublemaker!'

I considered. 'But you were.'

'Oh!' She tamped out her cigarette and stood up. 'There's no point in talking to you!' She headed for the sliding door that led to the living room.

'Arden, please sit down. For once in your life, see an argument through. You have been storming out of rooms as long as I can remember. Can you sit and talk and tell me more about this? Because – ' I continued as she reluctantly, resentfully sat, 'I know that there is something that Billy and I have that you and I don't have – some kind of closeness. I always felt you had it with your father . . .'

'A lot of good *that* did me!'

'You were always too angry with him. Probably because he denied that thing, that closeness.'

Her eyes filled with tears then, and I fell silent. She sat gazing over the Gulf. A few tears streamed down her cheeks. She wiped them away with her hand, like a child (twisting my heart). She blew her nose and I spoke again.

'But that's chemical, or biological, or who knows? maybe it's sexual. Maybe Freud was right. But it isn't true that I love Billy more than you. It was never true.'

She twisted her mouth.

'You made things hard. Maybe you don't remember. You were jealous of my relationship with Toni . . .' (And I thought it was Toni she was jealous of.)

'The bastard!'

'And maybe I didn't handle things as well as I could. I didn't know what to do, that's the truth. But it's broken my heart that I lost you. I never wanted that . . .'

She jumped up suddenly. 'Want some wine?'

I nodded and she went indoors. She came out with two glasses, but set hers down on the table and began to pace the deck. Staring out at the water, the woods around us, the water again. She turned around, her hands behind her leaning on the railing, and looked at me with cold eyes.

'I came down here to take care of you.'

'Arden! I know! You know how I appreciate it!'

She ignored me. 'I told Jake I had to do it, you were my mother and you needed me and all that crap. I don't know if he believed it, but he accepted it.' She licked her lips. They seemed to be dry and chapped. She reached for her wine and sipped it. 'But that's not the only reason I came. I mean, I did want to help you. But I didn't feel I owed you anything. You hardly helped me at all when the kids were born . . .'

Oh, that bitter voice. I tried not to scream. 'I tried to help! I came up when Jeremy was born. It was hard for me, Arden, to watch you trying to raise an infant without hot water, without running water for god's sake, having to go out to the outhouse in the freezing weather every time you wanted to pee – ' I sipped my wine, trying to get my voice into control, trying to keep my face calm, still she would know I was furious, she always knew how I felt. 'And you know, the meals up there, turnip, cabbage, carrots, potatoes, lentils every night, night after night . . . But even so, I would have stayed, I would have stayed as long as you wanted me if it weren't for the others, the way they treated me, the way they looked at me! It was like being white and living among black people or a Nazi living among Jews – only I wasn't, I didn't know what I'd done, but I knew I was hated!' My voice had risen by now, my face was hot, I couldn't help it.

She looked at me steadily, then dropped her eyes. 'Well, if I have another kid, you can help me without worrying about hot water.' Her voice was sarcastic. 'Jacob wants to leave the commune, he's a great big grown-up lawyer now and he wants to live in town. In fact, he wants to live in the city.'

'New York?' I couldn't help it: I was overjoyed.

She nodded. She sipped her wine again. She paced.

'But I'm not sure I'm going to go with him.'

Ah.

'But I don't know how I'll live if I don't!' Her voice was furious, her face a mask of rage. She breathed out a few times, then sat down on the bench that ran along the railing, at some distance from me. 'I can't support us selling dried flowers and writing poetry,' she said bitterly.

'Won't Jacob support his kids?'

She shrugged. 'You should know the answer to that. How much did Daddy contribute to our support? And what about that bastard Toni? Jacob's angry, he wants me with him, he doesn't understand why I don't want to go. He wants us all in a nice modern cardboard box in the city, living like all the other gentry. I don't even know him anymore. How much will he help and for how long? I don't feel sure I can depend on him anymore.'

'But what is this about, sweetheart? Is it that you want to stay on the commune? Or that you want to leave Jacob?'

Her grey gaze on me was no longer so hard, just cool. 'Yes. That's the problem: I don't know.'

I thought about her life up there. It was hard. Their only heat came from the fireplace, and that required chopped wood; the women chopped it as well as the men. The women did most of the kitchen work. Arden's hands, long and elegant once, were thick and red now, scraped. Some of the rawness had faded since we'd been in Florida. No hot water for baths, for dishes, for laundry. A vegetable diet meant hours of chopping and pounding; they made their own bread, their own cheese out of the goat's milk. She had to boil the baby's diapers in a huge heavy pot. At least she didn't have to iron – they had no such thing. One task she was spared. It was cold there in the winter, hot in the summer. But she liked living there. I had to remind myself of that.

'I believe in our life there,' she said finally. 'I believe in the principle of it: living on and by the earth, shunning the artificial, avoiding commercialism, materialism, the hot shot and the main chance and the fad . . . I want to want to stay there . . .' Her eyes filled.

I waited.

'But things have changed. The people – well, of course there's been turnover, that's inevitable on a commune. But the way it is now, I hate it!' She stood up and began to pace again, running her hand along the wooden deck railing. I wanted to say – don't do that, Arden, you'll get a splinter – but I shut my mouth and waited.

'It's so hard, and I don't know why, but the women end up doing most of the work, I mean, we help with the plowing and the sowing and the other heavy work. When we needed to repair a cabin last year, we all got up on ladders with hammers and nails. But when it comes to the kids or the laundry or the cooking or the dishwashing, the guys do fuck-all! . . . I work so hard! It was all right until the kids were born. It was still all right after Jeremy was born, there were three other women and Jacob helped then. But once he started law school, forget it. And then those women left, and the new women aren't like that . . .'

She plopped down on the railing bench, her body hunched over, her hair falling limp and greasy in her face. 'And the schools are after us now, they're going to win of course, I'll have to send the boys to school next fall. And that's a horror story – I'll have to drive them down the mountain every morning at six-thirty to the highway where the bus can pick them up – pick them up every afternoon. You know what it's like there. That will take hours out of my day, every day, and there's no one on the farm now who's willing to help me except . . .'

'Except?'

'There's this guy.' She flipped her cigarette butt, hard, into the sand. She pulled her face into a hard firm line, then turned to me. 'Philip. He's new. He's really attractive, and he . . . well, he likes me. I could stay on. With him. But he's awfully young.' She looked keenly at me. Her face was ravaged.

I gazed steadily back. She turned away.

'I don't know what to do.' She tossed this vaguely, in the direction of the wind.

'Well,' I said firmly, 'I know the first thing you should do.' Her head swung around. 'Get a haircut.'

Tuesday Ten years ago if I'd told Arden to cut her hair she would have jumped up screaming that I am always attacking her, but this time she smiled, and today we went into town and she had her hair cut short and she looks years younger, so much better! And maybe because she looked better, she felt better and when I said I'd like to buy her some Florida clothes, she didn't snap that I was trying to turn her into a bourgeoise but went quite happily into some of the nice shops in town and we got her pants and shorts and tops and a couple of skirts and some shoes – she looks wonderful! I did mind my manners, though, and did not go so far as to suggest she toss those Indian print shmattas of hers into the trash . . .

I went further. I have to test my limits. We had lunch out, at a nice little place, hanging plants and windows facing the water. And I brought up a possibly unpleasant subject.

'I've been thinking about what you said yesterday, about wanting to want to stay on the commune because you like the principle of it. And I understand that. But – well, *principles* – I find that usually the people who uphold such principles are not the people who have to do the work. I've read my share of articles deploring commercialism, consumerism, deploring people's yearning for washing machines, refrigerators – and they're always by men. I mean – it is beautiful to see women washing clothes in a river, or at a communal well – but is it beautiful to do it? If you go to Greece or Turkey or India, it's the women who do most of the work, on the farm and in the house. I'd respect these ideas more if the men who urge them did the laundry or fetched the water or walked every day to the market. It's easy to have principles when you don't do the work.'

She gazed at me. She was considering what I had said. Arden has not done that since she was eleven. Since . . . Toni . . .

We came home and she gave the boys their lessons, and came out onto the deck with me for a four o'clock glass of wine. We sat in silence for a while, watching the swollen red globe of the sun lower itself in the sky. Then she turned to face me. 'Have you loved a lot of men?'

'That depends on how you define love. I've loved a lot of men for the moment, maybe even for a month or two. But I've been able to maintain love only a few times.'

'For Daddy, Toni, and who else?'

'A man named Grant. You never met him. A reporter.'

Her eyebrows rose. 'You fooled around?'

'I did, Arden.'

She smiled. 'I'm glad.'

'I am too. I would have regretted not doing that.'

'The trouble is, it's not enough.' She didn't look at me. 'Love. I couldn't understand when you and Daddy divorced, I thought love, true love, lasted forever. By the time Toni left – well, I blamed *him* for that, not you. He was seduced by Hollywood, rotten values, money, it was disgusting . . .'

'That isn't fair. It isn't understanding. Toni did what he had to do. Or feel self-contempt. And he knew I was fooling around. To blame him for leaving me is like blaming me for Daddy's getting involved with Fern. You have everything upside down.'

'Oh, Mom, when you and Daddy divorced, I was a kid, of course I blamed you for making my father go away. And anyway, what is this wronged wife act I hear? You weren't unhappy when Daddy got involved with Fern.'

I grinned. 'You saw through me.'

'Well, so does he, for god's sake! Why do you think he goes around badmouthing you all the time? He'll never forgive you for railroading him.'

'Listen, Arden, I'll take only so much blame! I wasn't happy in that marriage and I knew if I left him he wouldn't support you kids. I just refused to become the kind of wife he wanted or thought he wanted and sat back and let things take their course. I'm not fucking omnipotent!'

She laughed. 'Okay, okay! Sorry. But you're my mother, and mothers always seem omnipotent, right?'

'And you're wrong to blame Toni too. He had to get away from us, from me. He had to grow.'

'Nonsense. He could have grown with us.'

'I don't think so. Our relation was too fixed – I was too – I'm not blaming myself, it was just what it was – dominant. There was no room for him to grow.'

She considered. 'You mean I have to revise my moral categories?'

'Maybe not your moral categories. But your judgment of people. If you're not generous to others, how can you allow yourself anything?'

She gazed out toward the water. 'When I was little, I adored you. I wanted to be just like you. And then when you and Daddy divorced, I determined I wouldn't be the kind of mother and wife you were, never wanting to cook, never wanting what Daddy wanted, always playing – that was fun when we were little, but it was scary too, as if we had a sister, not a mother. And then, when I was a teenager – I don't know – I went crazy – or the world was crazy – you seemed wrong, all the time, you felt oppressive. And I was angry with you for always being away . . .'

'I was away a week a month!' I protested. 'Except for a few long trips!'

She pondered. 'I guess that's right. It didn't feel like that.' She lighted a cigarette and turned around to face me. 'I didn't want to put anything before my children. *They* would be my life, but, oh god! . . .'

I kept absolutely still.

She turned around again. 'It's just not enough, is it,' she said in a whisper. 'Not even them.'

'Not without work,' I said quietly.

'But even work isn't enough. If you work, you want success. God, what are we, what are we! We want everything!'

You want everything, Anastasia!

'Why shouldn't we? What's the sin in wanting to experience all you can, wanting to use all of yourself?'

'It seems so . . . so selfish!' she shuddered. 'Especially when you think about all the people in the world who have nothing . . .'

'If you are prepared,' I spoke sharply, 'to spend your life helping people who have nothing, then do it. If you are not, then drop it!'

'No middle ground?'

I shrugged. 'Oh, of course. Checks sent to appropriate agencies. Avoiding waste. Eschewing complacency.'

'You're probably right,' she sighed. 'Okay, I want everything. And part of what I want is success. And I don't get it.' She bent forward as if she were in pain, and looked at the floor between her legs. 'I think I'm good. Now. I think I've learned my craft. I publish a fair amount of stuff.' She raised her head. 'What do you think?'

I nodded. 'The poems you've sent me over the past couple of years have been good . . .'

'But?' Sharp.

'Good,' I repeated, more strongly.

'What is it?'

She's so acute, I thought. Always wanting to know everything, even the worst. Like me. But Arden wasn't like me. Or maybe she was. 'They are good, Arden, Only, they come from someplace protected, safe . . . from a walled garden.'

She leaned back against the railing.

'Look, you shouldn't ask me. Lots of poets write like that – complacently. Look at late Auden. Lots of poets offer moral lessons learned from nature, instruction in harnessing passions and bending to necessity, learning to live with depression. It's perfectly acceptable. I just don't happen to like it. Or respect it very much.'

In the silence that followed, I reheard my own words. When I let go, I really let go. If I could call my words back . . .

'I think the kids are awake. I should go in.' And she did.

Damn it. And we were getting along so well.

March 6 2 a.m.: A few minutes ago Arden knocked on my bedroom door. I was writing in my journal. I closed it and slid it under my blankets, picked up a book and opened it, and called to her to come in.

She had been in bed, she was tousled and puffy-faced. Maybe she'd been crying.

'Mom?' Her voice was exactly as it had been when she was twelve or fourteen, a little girl voice, a cry. 'I know they treated you like shit, Mom. The guys at the farm. I'm sorry. Really. It had nothing to do with you, it's just the way they were . . . are.'

'They?'

'You mean I was the same way? Maybe I was. We were rotten. I don't know why. It was the times. It made sense then. But I'm sorry.'

I stretched out my arms and she came into them. She perched on the edge of my bed and we embraced each other, in silence, for long minutes.

'Now go to sleep,' I whispered, kissing her ear.

First time Arden has apologized to me since she was twelve. And after I'd offended her. Is it possible we can quarrel and make it up? then we can be real with each other.

Mar. 7 I have been walking, every morning, to the wildlife reserve. I set up a tripod and my camera and wait – for the anhingas, the alligators, the herons, the giant tortoises. This is a joy to me. It is so clean: animals live without moral searching, so, without a sense of corruption. For animals, pain is physical only. Or is that all a projection, a delusion?

March 8 I feel recovered, I feel strong. I can carry my camera bag and walk for several miles through the reserve. I think I am getting wonderful photographs. I haven't developed them yet. Maybe I am healed. To some degree, anyway. The black hole still happens to me. I fall into it some nights – or rather, I suppose, it flashes through my brain, an image of letting go, of death as rest and peace and no more pain, as *freedom* . . .

Mar. 10 Arden came into my room late last night again – carrying a tray with a bottle of brandy and two glasses.

'Up for this?'

How could I not be, no matter how I felt? And no matter that brandy upsets my stomach. It was only a little after eleven. I was sitting in bed reading. I patted the bed beside me, but she sat on the chair, pulling it forward so we could see each other clearly.

'I've been thinking,' she began. 'I think I have to leave the farm. There are only five people left there, besides Jake and me and the kids. The times, they are achangin'' she grinned. 'It's not right for me, even if I still feel it's the right way to live. It's too hard. And maybe at some point that kind of life is too isolated for the kids.

'And Philip . . . he's cute, I'm attracted to him, I wouldn't mind going to bed with him. But I can't base a life on that, not now. I did once – I went to the commune in the first place because of a guy. But now I have the kids, I have to be more responsible. And Philip is sweet now, but who knows what he'd be like once we were lovers, they're not *his* kids, after all and he's so young, only twenty-two . . .

'But I'm not sure how I feel about Jacob. Do you think it would be morally wrong for me to go with him and try it out, knowing that I don't feel the same way about him that I used to? Knowing that I probably don't love him anymore?

'I can't figure it all out . . .' Her voice petered out. She had begun so bravely, so confidently, so logically.

I leaned back against my pillows. 'Arden, I have no clear moral rules. I know only one thing: it is immoral to violate yourself. I mean – if you do something that makes you feel rotten, makes you feel corrupt, or dirty, or like a user – it is wrong. It isn't much of a guide, I think.'

She looked troubled.

'How do you feel about going to the city with Jacob?'

She lighted a cigarette. 'I don't know.' She sipped her brandy. She does know, I thought.

'I don't like Jacob anymore,' she said finally. 'I have liked him less and less since he went back to school. Law school. It did something to him.'

'How would you feel about living with him?'

She made a face.

'And the kids?'

She frowned. 'The kids love him. That's the problem.'

'And how is he to them?'

'He's good to them. When he's around. In New York – I just imagine he isn't going to be around much.'

'Does he know how you feel?'

'I don't know.' Lost faint voice.

That sounded like a finished marriage. But who knows? Some people renegotiate. It's not a talent I am familiar with. But I am doing it with my children, am I not?

'I used to think that love was cowardly if it didn't come from strength. Couples who clung together in mutual dependency seemed to me weak, contemptible. I thought truly adult love was an overflowing of energy and affection emanating from a powerful spirit in control of its own fate. And I think part of me felt that any need, any dependency, was contemptible. No compromises. No surrender to another . . .'

Arden was sitting starkly straight in her chair. No slump.

'I believed freedom was independence, needing no one, having your work and doing what you damn well wanted to do.' I sipped brandy. 'And that this was what the heroic man – or woman – did, this was how they lived. And if you ended up lonely, then you lived with that. Because being with people was a compromise, a deference, a dependency. You gave up what you wanted in order to have their company. And that was second-rate. That's what I felt. Until very recently,' my voice broke.

'But then,' I managed a choked laugh. 'I am a child of the fifties. But now . . .'

' . . . that you're old and wise,' Arden laughed, and I too.

'Yes. Now I think that no one is emotionally self-sufficient. That you can only pretend to be, and if you pretend well enough, you will get sick – in your mind or in your body.'

Arden raised her eyebrows at me. 'Is that what happened to you?'

I nodded.

'And when you need, you make compromises, you have to make compromises to get along with another person and if you need them, you will. Even though, for some of us . . . for me . . . making compromises is difficult, makes me feel . . . corrupt, somehow, weak. I'm never sure whether I'm giving up too much or not enough.'

She stared at me. 'So what should I do?'

'Oh, sweetheart,' I sighed. 'I can only tell you what I know.'

I am Arden's mother. She will remember me always the way I remember my mother. My mother is dying in such a way as to make us all feel we have failed her. She is furious with us because she is dying, because she never lived the life she wanted. This is not fair to us. I want to do better. If I can. For Arden, for Billy, for Franny, whom I love, I love, I love . . .

March 15, 1980 I've been neglecting my journal. But things have been happening. Jacob called and summoned Arden home. That did it, I'm afraid. She's going back, but with weapons drawn, and she looks like a goddess, tan and tawny-haired and strong . . . She's gained a little weight and she doesn't slump anymore. He won't recognize her.

I'm going to drive her and the children to the airport, but stay on here myself for another week or two. It will be dismal without her. I've grown used to being with my sweet girl.

March 20 Clara came down shattered: *Outsiders* is bankrupt. She is devastated. She came to me because, she said, 'When you're in agony, you go to the person you love, whether or not she loves you back.' She is so touching, she is like a child in her hurt, every time I touch her or do something kind for her, she curls up against me like a baby.

It comes to me what it is with us: we *mother* each other. I don't know if that is how all women are with each other, but we are. That's why she was always yammering at me about my mother, I guess. Telling me I could get mothering – better mothering – elsewhere if I would just look, reach out my hand.

She's too distraught right now to be sexual, so I haven't had to make any decisions about that. We are talking about possible futures. Maybe we'll start a new magazine together, one with photographs and fiction and poetry as well as analysis. Arden might like to be part of it. But I'm afraid it would take more money than I have.

Clara and I are going to stay on here for another couple of weeks and try to decide what to do.

It is April, and the city is still cold and very windy. The wind blows through the old ill-fitting windows in Clara's apartment. She has nailed plastic over the windows, but the wind is so strong it inflates the plastic, it billows out, it seems alive.

Anastasia and Clara are curled up on the sofa with blankets around them. Anastasia is upset. She is telling Clara that Arden and Jacob had a terrible fight, he stormed off and left her at the commune, 'without a car, Clara! Can you imagine being stuck up there without a car! So of course she ended up getting involved with Philip after all, well, there they were and they were attracted to each other . . . I can't fault her. I know how useless principle is against desire.'

'Oh? I thought you knew more about the uselessness of desire in the face of principle.'

Anastasia punches Clara lightly on the arm. Clara smiles then gets up and fetches the wine bottle. They are visiting at Clara's tonight because Anastasia's apartment is full of people: Arden, Jeremy, Jeffrey, Sarah, and Franny. Arden has left the commune and come to New York with the three kids and eighteen bags, bundles, and boxes containing their entire worldly possessions. She has to stay at Anastasia's, she has no place else to go.

'So what is she going to do? She can't stay with you indefinitely.'

'What can she do? They don't pay you for writing poetry. She could be a waitress. But what about the kids?'

'She can't go on staying with you in that little apartment.'

'Clara – I told Arden that I would buy a loft somewhere and we could divide it and all live together.'

"No!' Clara swings around. 'What about us, Anastasia! You promised me, you promised me you'd think about being with me! You promised! How can we be together? She doesn't like me!'

'Clara, she's my child!'

Clara pulls away from Anastasia, lights a cigarette.

'Anyway, she turned me down.'

Clara turns. 'She *did*!' Incredulous.

'She was very serious and responsible. She thanked me, she said that would be wonderful, the solution to her problems. But she said – well, she reached over and laid her hand on mine, and said, "Thanks, Mom. Really. But you know – our problems, yours and mine, yours and Billy's – mostly they arose because we were too close, too much together. I don't want to repeat that."

' "Too close?" I cried, "I thought we were too distant!"'

'She shook her head. "No, Mom. All those years. Before Toni, even after Toni . . . even when we were still living with Daddy . . . it was the three of us against everybody, the three of us together."

' "I wanted to be like that! I wanted us to have a sense of being a family!"'

' "I know. But it wasn't good. Oh, it was good in some ways. And I know you meant well. But we were too tied together, too *bound*."'

'I began to cry. Arden rolled her eyes. She patted my

shoulders, she handed me tissues, she said, "Come on, Mom."

' "I'm all right," I sniffled. Then burst out in a voice that sounded more angry than pathetic, "I just wanted to protect you! From your father's ill-temper! His anger! And from anxiety, you didn't know how poor we were, how hard things were for me! I wanted you both to feel secure, loved, close. I didn't want you to suffer the way I did as a child, from my mother's distance, her anger! . . . " I cried some more.

'Franny came in from school then. She dropped her books on a chair and ran over to me. She darted a furious look at her sister, exclaiming "Arden!" and put her arms around me.

' "What's the matter, Mommy, little Mommy? Don't cry."

'And I began to laugh, and so did Arden, and Franny, hurt and bewildered, glared at both of us, and we both reached out to hug her at the same moment. And I said to them, "See! I've unleashed a monster. I got back my feelings, and now I bawl!" '

Anastasia laughs.

Clara looks troubled. 'It pains me the way you put your children before me. When it comes to them, I'm not even second-best.'

'Oh, Clara,' Anastasia wails, 'what can I do?'

They have given up the idea of founding a magazine. It was more than they could manage, and Clara, the expert money-raiser, was not able to find a backer. She did find a job, however, scouting feminist books for a group of foreign publishers. She gets a small retainer from each of them – enough for her to live on, frugal as she is – and a percentage on the books they accept. And she gets to read everything she is interested in. She's a little depressed, but not despairing; she's even content, for the moment. Anastasia is having another show: the first was so successful that Alison Tate asked to see the pictures Anastasia has taken for herself over all these years. She has decided to do another show featuring these pictures. Anastasia is pleased, but wishes she could do something for her friend. Anastasia thinks Clara should write a book on feminist theories. Clara sighs, nods. It wouldn't make any money for her anyway, she says. Then she sighs again and says, Someday. Anastasia caresses the top of her head.

April 17, 1980. Income tax time over. Ugh. Tax on everything, goddamned tax on breathing. That's what I told Clara. Yes, I want her, I want what we have together, despite our disagreements. But what about my kids? I finally have them back, we're close again, first time in years and years, and I don't want to blow it.

But then I thought: that's blackmail. If I deny my love for Clara, if I give her up so that Arden will not get jealous – and who knows? Franny might get jealous too, they're so used to having me all to themselves . . . Yes, if I do that, then I will never again be able to be involved with anyone, it is giving in to a pressure that ought not to be brought. Because, after all, Arden has a husband of her own, and someday Franny . . .

It is like the time Brad tried to threaten me into giving up Toni.

I suppose Clara and I could be secret lovers.

No, Arden would know, she would see it the first time she saw us together.

Besides, that's cowardly.

No.

It is May, a nice month in New York. The trees have a green tinge and soft edges. Central Park looks like a pale green lake from here. People walk jauntily along the sidewalks of the West Side, their jackets unzipped, blown open. And the wind gusting in from the river along Riverside Drive has lost the sting of winter.

Anastasia has just returned from China, where she went to do a set of pictures for a publisher who's rich enough to do anything he feels like doing – and he wanted to do a book on women in China. She was away for six weeks, it was glorious, her eyes are full of rice fields and mountains, everything on earth tinted the colors of earth – gold and sepia and the palest of blues. Tiny figures carrying parasols, walking slowly through the rice fields, which they weed with their feet; ancient houses of adobe, with red-tiled roofs darkened by time into sienna, gardens filled with sunflowers, a duck pond, children leading water buffalo.

On the way back she stopped in France, where she was given an award for her photographs of French women authors, and treated as an honored guest. She enjoyed this.

She says to Clara: 'I like being old.'

'You're not old.'

'I'm old enough. I have twinges of arthritis in my thumbs, I can't carry my camera bag as far as I used to, my hearing is a little faded, and I need eyeglasses to read the telephone book. I'm twenty pounds heavier than I ought to be, and you know I'm not going to get any younger.'

Clara puts her hand on Anastasia's face and strokes it. 'You're more beautiful than when you were young. I was looking at your photograph albums while you were gone, It's true.'

'Well.' Anastasia tries to pretend she isn't pleased. 'But that's not what I mean. I mean – when I was young – all through the early years – I was walking around in terror. Not of anything in particular, just of my own ignorance. I felt I didn't understand anything, how the world worked, why people did and said the things they did and said, how I should act, what would happen if I risked or didn't risk, whether I could afford – in myself, I mean – to live out my life; or whether I could only afford to live through it.

'But now ... everything is still uncertain, always changing ... but I feel I understand why things happen, why people act as they do, up to a point. I feel I *know*. It's wonderful, it's calming. I know my expanses and my limits, and I am content with them.'

Clara raises an eyebrow: 'Have you been to see your mother lately?'

Anastasia smiles: this is a rhetorical question. Clara and Anastasia know exactly what the other does every day. No day passes that they do not speak together, if only for a few minutes. 'You know I have,' Anastasia grins. Anastasia goes to visit her mother immediately after she returns from a long trip. Always.

'I've been waiting for the reaction,' Clara says, teasingly, smiling, trying not to arouse anger.

'I came home and hit the wall forty times. Then I went about my business.'

'I don't believe it.'

'We talked. About growing old.' She turns to Clara. 'Do you see how teary I am these days? It's all your fault.'

'Better outside than inside,' Clara says shortly.

'I told her that of the two states, youth and age, I preferred age. She said, "Things are better now than in my childhood – oh, the not-knowing, so terrible!" But she didn't like age either. I said, "But here you are, loved, comfortable, you have beauty around you." And she turned away from me, her face was angry. I said, "What, Mom?"

' "Oh, Anastasia, how can you ask?"

'She was not looking at me, she was not looking at anything. Her face was tragic, all its lines sinking down, the eyes like my grandmother's eyes, clouded with sorrow. "I used to ask myself Why am I so depressed? Other women have less than I. All women's lives are miserable, I'm better off than most. But . . . " and she turned toward me then, "there's such a great void in me. The lack of accomplishment . . . "

'It broke my heart,' Anastasia says, thickly.

'She could have done something!' Clara says sharply. Clara has no tolerance for despair. 'She had years and years after you were all grown! She could have gone back to drawing, painting, something!'

Anastasia looks at Clara. Clara does not understand that fifty years of training in self-sacrifice cannot simply be thrown off like a shabby shawl. Clara has no children, will never have children. Anastasia lays her hand on Clara's. She understands that Clara's sharpness comes from pain.

They are having a drink in Anastasia's apartment. They are talking about living together. They have become lovers, but Clara wants greater intimacy. Franny is uncomfortable with the idea, and Franny still lives here. Franny has gone to bed.

Franny is going to be graduated next month, and after all the work she and her mother did last September, filling out college applications, now she says she doesn't want to go to college, she wants to stay with her mother in New York, she wants to be a photographer, and will apprentice herself to her mother.

'But I'm going to insist. She's been accepted at Oberlin, and that will be a good place for her. She can take her camera. She can study photography there. I don't want to repeat the mistake I made with the others.'

'Good!'

'But do you know? Now she's starting! She's yelling at me. Franny! She says I never wanted her, she feels like an intruder in life and it's my fault, she says I left her all through her childhood and now I owe her my presence!'

'She can never get enough of you,' Clara sighs.

'There is never enough mother.'

'I had enough of mine. Years ago!' Clara laughs.

June days in the city are golden and bright, people walk along the streets humming, carrying their jackets over their shoulders, or tied around their waists. Anastasia is busy. She is planning parties. First there will be a graduation party for Franny, to be held in the apartment. It will consist of pizzas and gelati.

And Billy is about to finish his residency and to marry Livvy. Then they will go off for a honeymoon to Somalia. Everyone laughs at that, although Somalia is no laughing matter. But they are happy about it.

There's a hum in Anastasia's head. She's thinking about how many pizzas and what to give Billy and Livvy for a wedding present, and the best way to hang the new show. She considers whether she should really fish out those old pictures of mothers and babies, as Alison Tate had asked, for a show next year. They're old, fifties photos, just right, Alison says, a comment on the period.

Anastasia thinks the fifties weren't that different from 1980. Look at poor Arden, forced to go back to Jacob because what else could she do? Feeling compromised, corrupt. He too, maybe. They're trying but they are strained with each other, the children are showing the tension, Jeffrey acting up so wildly. Can't protect them, ever.

Anastasia is thinking, I can't ask Clara to move in the minute Franny leaves for school, she'd feel usurped. Maybe I should move to a bigger apartment, but they're so expensive and now that this building is going co-op, I have a chance to buy this one so cheaply . . .

Anastasia doesn't know what she should do.

In July, Anastasia picks up her journal again. She writes:

Graduation party for Franny a huge success, and she's gone off with Jillian to wait table at a resort in Maine, anyone who can get those two gigglers to work has my respect. She's still a giggler, a baby, despite school in New York. I'm glad.

And Billy and Livvy, a beautiful wedding, her parents are not ostentatious, I was worried they might be. Such sweet kids, they both glowed. And went to Capri first, on the way to Somalia, for five days of luxury before the deprivation that awaits them, the heartbreak. But they won't be heartbroken because they will feel they are doing something, that they are not helpless.

The show a great success again, again despite the critics. They scream: why does this woman photograph only women? When for the ten years I was with *World* I photographed only men and no one complained about that. But they're lying about what upsets them, it isn't that I photograph women, it's the kind of women I shoot: Chinese women sweeping the street, women working in a corset factory in Queens, women carrying fardels in Greece, working in the fields in India, cleaning public lavatories in Penn Station. They like shows featuring women if Richard Avedon does them: images of the impossible, women who transcend body: stark black poles with a white blur of a face, frozen whipped cream caught in space, big black blurs for eyes, women who don't exist, for even the models don't look like that in life, they are made of flesh and blood and muscle and bone and when they move their blouses pull out of their skirts, and when they laugh their mascara runs, and they can't walk in those heels without falling.

Whereas my women are a little gross, not gross enough to be grotesque (that would be all right), just enough to seem real. And they probably wouldn't have minded so much if I'd concentrated only on women in Turkey or Greece or India – it's the American women they are offended by.

Still – someone must like them, my pictures, because they're selling.

An undated entry: Mother pours a glass of water and sips at it for a half-hour. Then she puts it in the refrigerator. I ask her why she does this. 'Why waste it?' she asks, surprised at my question.

Franny opens a can of soda, takes a few swigs, and leaves it on the kitchen counter. If I don't pour it out, it will remain there for days, along with all the others she will have opened in that time. I tell her she should visit Billy and Livvy in Somalia. She doesn't understand.

How can a woman with such a mother have such a daughter?

It is November, 1981. Anastasia is packing. She is going to the Middle East on an assignment for UNICEF. She is excited. She imagines sailing down the Nile, riding over bumpy sandy roads to dusty little villages in Morocco, in Egypt, in Algeria. She would like to see Isfahan, she has always wanted to see Isfahan, to stand awed at the ancient carvings, the mosaics, the towers rising miraculously in the sand in the middle of miles of barren land. But Americans cannot go to Iran now. And women cannot go unescorted to Iraq, so she will not see Baghdad either. Someday, she thinks.

Still, she will see bent brown peasants pulling carts as they have pulled them for centuries, and women walking along the roads, wraiths in purdah, yet proud, their carriage belying their status. She is going to photograph those women, to talk to them, perhaps even photograph their faces. She thinks: Faces and bodies tell everything about us. What kind of state is it that does not allow women's faces and bodies to speak? I want to let them speak.

She is hungry for it, the new, the strange, that which she must learn to see. She is happy to be on the road again, doing, riding in the wind, drying up under the desert sun, collapsing exhausted in a dusty hotel, or on a sleeping bag laid beneath palm trees, the smell of camel dung on the air, the camels' squeaks and grunts punctuating the silence of blackness, night as night never comes where she lives.

She picks up her journal, wondering whether to take it

with her. Her bags are already too heavy for comfort. She looks at her watch: it is after midnight. She is almost finished, she can do the rest tomorrow. She takes a pen from the desk and sits down on her bed. She pulls her legs up with a wince – a twinge of arthritis – and leans back. She opens the book and writes.

I am off again. A wonderful assignment! Three months in the Middle East photographing women, women and children. For UNICEF. Strange – I got the assignment largely because of my last show. With the outcry it created, I didn't expect much. Feminists, nonfeminists, antifeminists united in outrage: women are *not* like that, motherhood is *not* like that! Mothers don't hate, feel rage at tiny babies! Mothers don't feel jealous if a father pays attention to a child! Still, thousands of people came to see the show and many of them bought pictures. And this job came out of it.

My stomach is in a knot, though. Clara is angry that I am going. It *is* a long time. I said, Come with me. She says, How can I? I have to work. I said, I will support you Clara – for ever. She says she can't do that. She says she cannot tolerate all this travel. She says not to be surprised if she is not here for me when I come back.

I can't bear to think about that.

I can't not go.

Clara says my mother wins after all: I choose aloneness, as she wants me to, because then I am entirely hers. I don't know. Is that true? I went to see Mother two days ago, stayed overnight with them. She was sad, not angry this time. I took her some albums I'd made of pictures from my major projects. She was very impressed with the assignment. She doesn't understand that I am not trying to impress her, that I don't think this trip, or any trip, is *impressive* – just *fun*. The life I wanted.

She doesn't know me.

But I know her. While I am gone, she will sit in her rocking chair gazing out at the birds that populate her world – sparrows and robins, cardinals, blue jays, ducks, geese, swans, gulls. Once in a while she will take out one of the albums I took her – maybe the one dated 1958 – and open the creaky leather cover and stare at a picture encased in plastic.

The first picture is a portrait of a couple, husband and wife, in their fifties. She will study it. She will see the lines on either side of the wife's petulant mouth, and the hard emptiness of the man's eyes. She will know that the wife's blonded beehive hairdo and the man's well-cut suit go with the ornate gilt-framed mirror and the reproduction eighteenth-century console table behind them. She will understand that the prim position of the wife's legs, and the sense of disconnection of the man's head and neck from his extremely substantial body are part of the price paid for the fancy mirror, the table and the oriental vase that rests upon it – just barely perceptible; for the large pale room reflected in the mirror, and the dogwood tree she knows stands on the front lawn. She understands all this without thinking, without words. She accepts the price as worth what it bought, but sighs as she turns the page.

She'll look away from the next picture, unable to bear it. It is a portrait of her. She is sitting stiffly, legs crossed at the ankle, hair sprayed into waves, a stiff smile lipsticked onto her powdered face. What she sees when she looks at this picture is that there is no gilt-framed mirror, reproduction console table, and no lines on her face. She prefers to look out at the birds.

She understands them too, she knows at least their habits, which, she thinks, is the greatest understanding one can achieve with other animals, even humans, who like to believe that language breaks through silence. But she, locked into silence, believes that language is part of silence, and breaks it only to deceive. Whereas the way a man slurps his coffee, or a woman waves around hands adorned with long bright red fingernails does not deceive, nor does the flap of a wing on an upward draft. For her, words, smiles, manners, are part of a smoke screen hiding the self from others, hiding the self from the self – noises hiding the void, chatter hysterically vainly trying to fill the void. Aloneness is all there is. Her hearing aid is turned off.

She picks up the binoculars to watch the birds. She has never read Tennyson, nor heard literature students joke about nature red in tooth and claw. Still, she's seen the neighbor's cat with a bloody bird in its mouth, she's watched the gulls plummet down and pluck a fish from the dappled water. She doesn't much like the gulls, she hates the cat, but she accepts them. She has always believed that life is a matter of economics. Therefore her own depression, when now she has everything she ever wanted, puzzles her.

But she doesn't linger over it. Why should she not be depressed, sick and dying as she is? She prefers to watch the mother duck who promenades at a dignified pace across the lawn every day, followed by her twelve little ones. Sometimes momma-duck (as my mother calls her) has to extricate one of those little ones from the wire mesh fence around the next door property. Then she grows exercised, her feathers flap, her head pokes, jabs. And always at those times, the father duck – my mother is sure he is the father duck – squawks loudly from the lake, demanding her presence, jealous of her attention to the young ones. Maybe she confuses him with her husband, my father, whose sighs seem as loud as a squawk even to her deaf ears when she wants to sit up with her daughter and have one more cigarette, one more drink.

My father does not like the geese, who shit on his lawn. But she likes the geese. They cluster in the water just behind her house and squawk to her, asking her to feed them. She saves up bread and suet. And on nice days, she asks Ed to help her, and he holds her arm and they walk out to the water, Ed carrying the plastic bag of food. She reaches in and grabs a bit and hurls it. She hates the pushy geese who manage to get to the front. She is sure they are all male. She pities the smaller geese in back, hovering, afraid to venture forward. She is sure they are females. She hurls the bread or suet to them, throwing as hard as she can. But her arm is weak, her throw unpracticed, and most times, the forward birds catch the prizes. Disgusted, she turns on her heel and returns to the house, alone now, anger makes her strong enough to walk unassisted. That life is an economic matter does not make its budgets pleasant. She does not begrudge the robins and sparrows their worms, but she grieved over a dead monarch in her broccoli patch.

'Throw it far out! To the little ones!' she orders Ed.

She puts down the binoculars, they are too heavy to hold for long. She returns to the album in her lap, turning the pages without really looking at the pictures. She comes upon a photograph of a suburban ranch house somewhat like the one she lives in. It is a large house with neatly trimmed shrubs and lawn. It looks deserted: the shades are neatly pulled halfway down, but there is nothing in the picture except a shiny 1958 Buick parked in the driveway. She does not understand why I took that picture, why it is in the album.

But the next picture makes her exclaim aloud. It is the street in Williamsburg where she lived as a child. It is as poor and chaotic in 1958 as it was in 1914, but there is little that is famliar in it. Still, she recognizes it. Her stomach flutters. She studies the picture for a long time. Then she closes the album.

She sits back in the rocker and half-closes her eyes. She is tired. She should not sleep, she has already had a two-hour nap. She yawns. She reaches over to the little table beside her and lights the half-cigarette she cut in the morning, after breakfast. She inhales deeply, satisfied for the first time in hours. She looks out at the lake. She does not think about Williamsburg, about the past, about her life. She does not think about her husband, her children, her grandchildren, about the present. She does not think about the future, believing she does not have one. She does not let herself down into the well of black rage that lies beneath the soft folds of her face. She does not think: my mother never combed my hair.

It is I who will be thinking that, I, five thousand miles away lying under the stars that glitter through the palm fronds, smelling camel dung and desert flowers and thinking of her.

No: she thinks of Anastasia. She sees her at a great reception, meeting the shah, passing rows of men in elaborate uniform, gold braid and ribbons, boiled shirts and black suits with rosettes in their lapels, Anastasia in a flowing gown, her hair long and fair floating behind her, her body young and lithe as she strides past them. She is beautiful, as beautiful as a princess with her slender legs and hands, her shining hair, and she passes through these throngs of kings with grace and disdain. Her bearing, her slight smile, announce that she is unattainable: utterly desirable but full of scorn, independent, self-sufficient. She approaches the throne but does not kneel. The shah confers upon her the award of Greatest Photographer in the World. Belle's heart is full of pride.

When I return, she may ask me about this reception. She will not understand when I look at her bewildered. She will not understand when I say the shah is gone, dead, and that I am fifty, greying, plump, tired, back from an assignment to photograph women. She will not believe me. After all, she saw it. When she is a hundred and ten she will sketch for her great-grandchildren the picture of Anastasia in a flowing white gown, curling her lip at the heads of state of fifty nations.

The vision passes. She forgets it. It goes to join all the other visions of this sort she has had of the Anastasia she knows. Her cigarette half is down to stub. She taps it out. She sits. She thinks she should do something, but she is too tired, and besides, what is there to do? She gazes at the grass, the birds, the water with its puddles of light. She rocks a little. There is a draft somewhere, she can feel it on her neck. Where is Eddy? He must do something about this draft.

She crosses her hands precisely in her lap and smiles a stiff smile, a social smile, although she is alone. She cannot be patronizing the birds, she knows they do not see her. Maybe she is patronizing her reflection in the window. She offers herself an arranged smile. The image, she thinks, is not without dignity.

When I left her last, yesterday, I held her for a long time, I kissed her temple. She looked at me. She said: 'I will never forget how sweet you were to me.'

It is the most she has ever given me. It is the most I can expect. It has to be enough.